WOMEN AT
INDIANA UNIVERSITY

WELL HOUSE
BOOKS

WOMEN AT INDIANA UNIVERSITY

150 Years of Experiences and Contributions

—⚡—

ANDREA WALTON, editor

INDIANA UNIVERSITY PRESS

This book is a publication of

Indiana University Press
Office of Scholarly Publishing
Herman B Wells Library 350
1320 East 10th Street
Bloomington, Indiana 47405 USA

iupress.indiana.org

Manufactured in the United States of America

First printing 2022

Cataloging information is available from the Library of Congress
ISBN 978-0-253-06245-1 (hardcover)
ISBN 978-0-253-06247-5 (paperback)
ISBN 978-0-253-06246-8 (e-book)

Cover Illustrations: *Top*, Graduates cheer during the Indiana University
Bloomington Graduate Commencement at Assembly Hall on Friday,
May 3, 2019, by James Brosher, copyright Trustees of Indiana University.
Bottom row, Sarah Parke Morrison, Grace Jackson Brown, and the women
of Alpha Hall; used with kind permission of Indiana University Archives.

CONTENTS

ACKNOWLEDGMENTS

First and foremost I'd like to thank the IU women whose stories are explored here and to whom this book is dedicated. Their stories have provided us with inspiration, compelled us to reflect, and energized us throughout the project. Contributors also owe a debt of gratitude to generations of historians whose work on women in education has shaped our own.

I had mused about editing a book on women at IU for quite some time. My service as Bloomington campus historian for the IU Bicentennial nudged me to rearrange some other projects, solicit contributors, and propose the book to IU Press. I am very glad I did. Working on the project, I learned more about my home institution but also gained new perspectives on the intersecting threads of women's fight for educational opportunity and broader developments in higher education. In particular, I gained a deeper appreciation of the history of coeducation at state universities and the importance of regional culture and state history in shaping campus climate. I expect my work on this edited book is just the beginning of a new thread in my research.

I could not have produced this volume without the colleagues whose essays appear in these pages. A heartfelt thank you to them for saying yes to my invitation—for their willingness to share their research and to make room in their busy teaching and research schedules to take this journey with me. I especially appreciated their patience and understanding as we navigated completing the book during the uncertain and extraordinarily challenging days of the pandemic.

Thank you to Kelly Kish, Director, Office of the Bicentennial, and James Capshew, University Historian, for involving me in various activities related to IU's observance of its two-hundredth anniversary. They were enthusiastic about the project when I first described it, have been encouraging throughout, and have been firm believers in the value of history—wherever research leads. Similarly, Gary Dunham, Director of IU Press, lent his full support and has patiently shepherded this project, even as operations went remote. Peggy Solic, my first contact at IU Press, offered her suggestions and assisted in the project's earliest stages. I appreciate the support and insight everyone has offered to me in my work as editor and all that IU Press staff members have done to bring this book to publication. Stephen Williams and his marketing team created a book cover that captures the spirit of the stories told in these pages. Nancy Lightfoot and Carol McGillivray, project managers, worked closely with me throughout the various stages of producing the book and were a constant support. I appreciated the energy and creativity they brought to working on the project. This book has been part of my life for quite some time, from the early idea as part of the IU Bicentennial observance, through a pandemic, and, now, finally, to publication. It was a great relief to me that at the end of this long process Paula Durbin-Westby would use her skill to prepare an index to guide readers as they explore the 150 years of IU women's history discussed in this volume.

I owe a debt to the students who provided timely research assistance and helped with various other tasks related to producing the edited volume. Ree Palmer shared her knowledge of student affairs, especially the history of deans of women, and helped to compile a useful bibliography on IU history. She, with assistance from Sarah Jacobi, did a wonderful job advertising a number of brown bag discussions related to research that provided the backbone of various chapters. Pooja Saxena facilitated the logistics of organizing draft materials, finding suitable images, and securing permissions. Stephanie Nguyen wrote detailed research memos on her trips to the IU Archives, tracked down esoteric references and checked footnotes, and helped ready the manuscript for submission to IU Press.

IU has a superb library and archives system and a dedicated, knowledgeable staff who lent their expertise and support throughout the project. Dina Kellams, Director of University Archives, shared her knowledge of the collections and helped several contributors find needed resources; Kristin Browning Leaman, Bicentennial Archivist, and Barbara Truesdell, Assistant Director, Center for Documentary Research and Practice, brought a number of relevant oral histories to our attention and helped us access materials.

A number of staff in various IU Library units answered queries along the way, helped with permissions, and provided photos—Stephen Towne, Bradley

D. Cook, Erika Dowell, Matt Sieber, Rhonda L. Seward, Shawn C. Wilson, and Scott Shoger.

Claire Repsholdt did an early sweep of IUB bulletins and faculty rosters to compile an initial list of interesting historical female figures who merited further study; even after her graduation from IU she remained an enthusiastic reader of draft material.

Colleagues in the broader field of higher education also read and commented on material related to their expertise. I appreciated input from Michael Hevel, University of Arkansas; Robert Schwartz, Florida State University; and Berenice Sánchez, Idaho State University.

Finally, many thanks to my family members for sharing my enthusiasm and commitment to the project. Their generous, unwavering support made all the difference to me. They sat and talked through new ideas, provided feedback on draft material, and gave me time and space to write. I am forever grateful.

WOMEN AT
INDIANA UNIVERSITY

INTRODUCTION

The almost universal absence of women from college faculties is a grave
defect in co-educational institutions; and negatively, at least, their absence
has as injurious an influence upon young men as upon women. . . . Women
in the faculty, women on the board of visitors, women on the board of
trustees, holding these positions, not because of their family connections,
not because they are the wives or sisters of the men in the faculty and on
the boards, but because of their individual abilities, are the great present
need of co-educational colleges. Only the presence of women in these
places can relieve young men who are students in these institutions from
an arrogant sense of superiority arising from their sex, and the young
women from a corresponding sense of subordination.

—May Wright Sewall, "The Education of
Woman in the Western States," 1891

"NO FORMAL HISTORY OF THE MOVEMENT in the West on behalf of the
higher education of women has been published," observed well-known reformer and suffragist May Wright Sewall (1844–1920) at the outset of her 1891
essay for *Woman's Work in America*. Absent a standing history of her topic,
Sewall culled and interpreted details from Bureau of Education reports, correspondence, catalogues, historical monographs, sermons, newspapers, and
biographies to provide her readers with a broad snapshot of the state of women's
education.[1]

Perhaps few commentators of her day had a better vantage point and more respected public platform to discuss the state of higher learning for women in the West—and Indiana in particular—than May Wright Sewall, herself a first-generation college woman. In 1866, a year before the first woman entered Indiana University, Sewall graduated from Northwestern Female College in Illinois.[2] It was a bittersweet achievement, as she could not, on account of her sex, realize her girlhood dream of attending her father's alma mater, Yale. But Wright lost no time in utilizing her college degree by becoming a teacher. After holding positions in Michigan and Mississippi, she arrived in Franklin, Indiana, and later moved to Indianapolis. Her contributions to education in the capital city were especially notable. After teaching high school, she (together with her second husband) founded the Girls' Classical School of Indianapolis in 1882 and then went on to organize the Western Association of Collegiate Alumnae and to cochair, along with local teacher Amelia Platter, the Association of Collegiate Alumnae's (ACA) committee on extension work in Indianapolis. The group were pioneers in adult education and engaged Indiana University professors from Bloomington as lecturers—the likes of economists Jeremiah Whipple Jenks, John R. Commons, and Edward A. Ross; biologist John M. Coulter; and historian James Woodburn. The success of the ACA lecture series helped pave the way for the Indianapolis Extension center, the foundation of today's Indiana University–Purdue University Indianapolis (IU-PUI). Strikingly, then, as May Wright Sewall was drafting her essay on women's education, her own education-organizing efforts in Indianapolis were making history—broadening opportunities for Hoosier women and helping to extend the pedagogical reach of IU, then a single-campus state university based in Bloomington.[3]

Still usefully read today, Sewall's writings from the 1880s and 1890s point to an acute observation that has since been accepted as conventional wisdom but left understudied by historians of women's higher education—namely, the importance of locale in determining women's educational opportunities.[4] In the East, higher education for women had emerged first in all-female and "mixed" (coeducational) seminaries and academies and, ultimately, endowed women's colleges, but the circumstances west of the Allegheny Mountains were different. In this region of the country, coeducation was more readily adopted and quickly became the norm. "Without intention on the part of either men or women, they become used to working together in unaccustomed ways; and the idea of going to college together does not seem so unnatural as in older communities. . . . In the Western States and Territories, the higher education of women is generally identical with co-education," Sewall observed.[5]

A zealous suffragist and ardent advocate for women's education, Sewall, having surveyed dates for the chartering and opening of coeducational colleges and universities and for women's admission to established institutions in the country's western regions (from Ohio to California), saw Indiana University's all-male status until 1867 as an unfortunate blot on its early history, inconsistent with its proclaimed stature as "the *crown* of the *public school system*" and its sustenance at "public expense."[6] But Sewall's steadfast support for coeducation did not blind her to the reality that coeducation did not necessarily mean equity for women or that women's mere entrance into the university to study the liberal arts alongside men fulfilled the goal of coeducation—to provide women with opportunities in society. Indeed, she believed that women, beyond equitable access to liberal arts study with their male peers, should have the opportunity to serve based on their "individual abilities" and be present in all positions of power in the university—as professors, administrators, and trustees—to stand as role models, not only for women but also for men.[7]

Though progress came slowly and incrementally, particularly beyond women's acceptance as students, both IU and the larger society have changed considerably since Sewall's late nineteenth century observations about coeducation and women's proper place in higher education. And, despite the reality that more remains to be done to achieve much deeper gender equity on campus, the expansion of women's presence at IU during the long span of the past century and half has been significant. Women's enrollment as students grew substantially, a boon to university expansion, and by the 1920s women were nearly half the Bloomington student body and a decided presence in the liberal arts. Since 1977–78, women have consistently been half if not the majority of the university-wide student body.[8] As faculty, women, long denied opportunity by IU's hiring patterns (i.e., appointing women as fellows, tutors, and assistants rather than as professors), have slowly made inroads into every academic unit and have increased their percentage as holders of endowed chairs.[9] As administrators, women have demonstrated leadership as department chairs, deans, and upper-level academic officers. And as trustees, women, though not represented on IU's board of trustees until the end of IU's first century, have finally made significant advances into the university's governing body in recent decades. This progress has been woefully slow in coming, as women's representation on the board for decades remained exceedingly poor compared to the composition of the student body. IU elected its first female trustee, alumna Nellie Showers Teter, in 1924. Only two more women followed Teter in service on IU's board through the early 1970s—Mary Rieman Maurer (elected, 1945–62) and Harriett Simmons Inskeep (gubernatorial appointee, 1962–71)—and for nearly four decades thereafter women held only one to two seats at the same time on the nine-member board. But finally, in 2019, as IU approached its two-hundredth year, four women served together on the board.[10]

This book draws inspiration from and makes common cause with May Wright Sewall's writings of long ago—her appreciation of the perspective of history, the importance of locale, and the interconnectedness of women's and men's educational experiences in a coeducational university as well as her belief that genuine gender inclusion and equity are integral to the university's mission in a democratic society. It is the goal of this book to offer, through a selective collection of scholarly snapshots, an overview of women's experiences at and contributions to IU, starting with women's admission in the 1860s to recent decades. Albeit limited in scope (by necessity and compared to the possibilities awaiting future researchers), this volume speaks to an important institutional and scholarly need. It strives to be a preliminary attempt at incorporating women's stories into IU's history and, in doing so, help situate IU's history in the larger narrative of US higher education.

While reasons to study IU women are clear and compelling, writing about the history of women at IU poses at least two challenges worth noting. First, the standing histories of IU—works by Theophilus A. Wylie (1890), James Woodburn and David Banta (1940), Ivy Chamness and Burton Myers (1952), and, most recently, Thomas D. Clark (1970–77), for instance—all describe IU's early adoption of coeducation, in the later part of the 1860s, in a positive light but contain only sparse coverage of IU women's subsequent experience and contributions.[11] Unfortunately, too, IU did not garner much attention as scholars interested in academic women, inspired by the rising women's movement and new social history approaches, began in the 1970s to produce new, more inclusive campus and disciplinary histories. Indeed we had no book-length study or extensive scholarly portrait of IU women to serve as a point of departure, a springboard, for this volume.[12] Given the state of the secondary literature on IU's history, this edited volume, then, is less concerned with challenging well-established interpretations of IU's history than with providing an exploratory investigation and documentation of how women experienced and contributed to the university.

Second, the contributors of these essays encountered difficulties with the scope, nature, and availability of source material. Working with a university archive that until recently tended to privilege administrative, especially presidential (male) records, we often, frustratingly, came up short in our search for women's voices and evidence of their varied experiences. In the case of women's records, we could learn a lot more about the decision-making or priorities of deans than the views of other women on campus. For certain time periods, reporting of the numbers of men and women was not systematic, and data about the number of Black students had to be mined from correspondence. Further, only since the mid-1970s has enrollment data been broken down by gender, race, and ethnicity.[13]

Disappointingly, stories of certain notable IU figures, events, or achievements proved difficult to reconstruct—and, in some cases, unfortunately seem destined to remain elusive. Just to illustrate, consider two nationally known figures on IU's faculty: Ingeborg Schmidt and Martha E. Dawson. Both women were on the Bloomington campus in fairly recent decades (post-World War II), but we have few archival materials and other primary sources to document their IU years. Schmidt, a noted color theorist and expert in visual testing, emigrated from Germany to the United States and was affiliated first with the University of Texas (1946–52) and then Columbia University (1952–53) before spending the final two decades of her career at IU (1954–70). Dawson, an innovative thinker in multicultural education and holder of two graduate degrees from IU (MS, 1954; EdD, 1956), was recruited from her position as chair of the Department of Elementary Education at Hampton University (Virginia) back to IU in 1970, to join the faculty as a tenured full professor. The first African American female scholar at IU to hold this rank, she was one of the few African American faculty on the Bloomington campus during the 1970s. Dawson later returned to Hampton in 1977, as vice president of academic affairs.[14] Fortunately, Dawson did pen one short autobiographical essay that, together with her published writings, serves as an entry to the biographical portrait presented in chapter 12. One hopes, though, that future years will bring greater access to relevant source material to tell more fully the stories of scholars like Schmidt, Dawson, and a host of others whose distinctive contributions have been identified through IU Bicentennial research efforts.

We had hoped to complement our portraits of scholarly women with insight into women trustees, figures whose contributions are missing from writing on women in higher education but whose importance was recognized by leaders of the ACA/AAUW and the leaders of the modern women's movement.[15] Unfortunately, little source material is available to scholars hoping to study women's representation on IU's board of trustees, especially the notable 1924 election and influence of Nellie Showers Teter, the university's first woman trustee. Teter was an IU alumna (class of 1893), an active member of the Association of Collegiate Alumnae (ACA), and a well-connected member of the prominent Bloomington's Showers furniture manufacturing family. One wishes we had more extensive records to understand the circumstances leading up to her election (advocated by members of the Bloomington and Indianapolis AAUW chapters), the perspectives on coeducation and women's education she brought to IU board discussions, and her connection to the wide community of IU women.[16]

As frustrating as the gaps in university records related to women's power in administrative or governing roles are, more considerable is the challenge of gaining a broad, diverse perspective on student life. IU, like many universities, has far more extensive and detailed records that shed light on the thoughts and actions of administrators and faculty (albeit mostly men) than capture the ideas, sentiments, and voices of a wide range of students and, in particular, alumnae—and most especially women of more recent generations, different IU campuses, first-generation women, and women of color. And we lack access to the mix of official and private correspondence that would allow us to better understand and document the vision of women donors who across the years gave to IU, in many cases to honor a male relative, and often anonymously.[17]

Admittedly, the task of the contributors to this volume, with chapters finalized in 2020, was not as challenging as May Wright Sewall's in the 1890s. Unlike Sewall, we have had the benefit of library collections, the internet, and electronic databases. Contributors made use of this wide variety of materials. We have tapped earlier histories of IU departments and schools, source materials held by the IU Archives (increasingly available in digitized form), and a host of student history blogs and other class projects related to the IU Bicentennial. The records of the IU Office of Dean of Women; presidential reports; university bulletins; the *Alumni* [sic] *Quarterly* (especially class notes and reminiscences); the *Arbutus* yearbook; the *Indiana Daily Student* (*IDS*, IU's student newspaper) and local and state newspapers; ephemera clipping folders; the list of honorary doctorates (including the six women honored in 1967, the centennial of coeducation at IU); an extensive collection of photos (some included here); and memoirs and transcripts of oral histories have informed our portrayal of women's experiences and contributions to Indiana University. Fortunately, too, in some instances, contributors have been able to conduct oral history interviews and hear firsthand the recollections of women who participated in—or led—events we describe in this volume. In some instances, these original interviews have been central to the chapters, making it possible for this volume to include the experiences and voices of diverse women and IU women of more recent generations.

It has been an exhilarating yet, in some respects, daunting task to produce what is the first book of its type about women at IU. How could we best portray the history of women at IU, through snapshots, even as we kept in mind that no single edited collection of essays could ever capture fully the wide-ranging stories of women who have been associated, in various capacities, with Indiana University over the span of nearly a century and half? Such is especially the case when one considers large-scale transformations in the academy and the disciplines, changes in women's status in society, and more fluid gender norms.

The essays in this volume focus largely on women's experiences as students and faculty as well as deans, administrative staff, and donors, documenting their contributions to IU's academic culture and their reaction to and efforts to influence campus climate. Following chronology, our focus has been on the founding campus in Bloomington and on developments in Indianapolis, first the medicine school and then the rise of an added core campus, Indiana University–Purdue University Indianapolis (IUPUI). Thus, the stories told in the various chapters of this book do not provide a comprehensive history of IU, nor are they necessarily representative of all IU women over the decades. Rather, these snapshots together lay some necessary initial groundwork for seeing the larger picture of women at IU. While some chapters focus on what might be seen as traditional, predictable choices—e.g., stories of pioneers, luminaries, well-known scholars, and firsts in IU's history—a number of chapters, by design, cast a wider net, looking at the gender-related challenges and the agency of particular groups of women during certain periods or in academic fields or units with distinct gender norms and professional cultures. Still other chapters use oral histories and student newspapers to adopt a more grassroots or social history approach, focusing on a small number of female students, perhaps just a few individuals, to illustrate a story of larger significance. These chapters capture voices that are often unheard and offer a different angle of vision on the history of women at IU than the story of better known academic women, who perhaps had greater institutional power or prominence.

In writing about women at IU, the contributors to the volume are mindful of the now familiar fractures in women's history and differences in the backgrounds and experiences of individuals we discuss. For example, between an IU professor's or trustee's daughter who grew up familiar with college life and the young woman, likely an aspiring teacher, who left her family's farm, came to Bloomington, and lived in a modest boardinghouse room during her IU student years. Between the white, middle-class woman who felt the weight of being female in a male-dominated university and the Black coed who remained excluded from women's housing, even as deans of women spoke of advancing opportunities for IU women. Or the experience of the Latina or Asian

American woman who felt the weight of being female in a male-dominated university but also felt marginalized in other respects and for whom cultural programing and culturally supportive spaces became crucial.

IU included no gender or racial exclusion in its charter and yet remained a small, homogeneous, all-male institution for most of its first half century. It was not until 1867 that the first woman, Sarah Parke Morrison (1833–1919), hailing from a white Hoosier family with progressive views on women's rights and well-established ties to IU, was admitted to the liberal arts course. Decades passed before female enrollments were substantial, and it was not until the end of the nineteenth century that women of color enrolled—and even then their numbers were sparse. When speaking of IU women, it is important to underscore that Carrie Parker, the first African American woman known to enroll at IU (1898), and Frances Marshall, the first African American woman to graduate from IU (1919), studied on the Bloomington campus decades after Sarah Parke Morrison's admission marked the advent of undergraduate coeducation. Their experiences and those of later generations of IU women were profoundly shaped by the interplay of gender, race, and class and by the larger context of women in US society.

Many of us at the beginning stages of research for our chapters, given our own intellectual standpoints, lived realities, and perspectives on gender's interplay with other markers of difference, expected, and perhaps even wanted, to find stories of self-conscious feminist challenges to the status quo in the lives we studied—such as we did find in the career of Dean Agnes E. Wells, a champion of women's housing and self-government and a national figure in the American Association of University Women and the National Women's Party.[18]

But not all the women described in the chapters that follow would identify themselves as feminist or activist or, even while keenly aware of the sexism they encountered directly, would put women's social condition front and center. In some cases, the subjects of our research forced us to think more deeply, as a number of other historians have done recently, about the varied modes of challenge to barriers and bias women have marshalled and the sometimes "quiet" nature of activism.[19] Moreover, we became increasingly aware of the importance of understanding context—understanding women at IU meant understanding the mission and character of a public university and being attentive to the importance of region and locale. Accordingly, the various chapters reveal ways in which the story of women at Indiana University was profoundly shaped by the circumstances of a specific campus or professional school, the university's proximity to the South, and the broader midwestern setting.

By design, the volume has brought together and been enriched by the insights of a group of contributors who are diverse in many senses—in terms of demographics, a mix of IU alums and affiliates and outside scholars, and individuals at different stages of their careers including senior scholars, emerging scholars, graduate students, and history-minded administrators and staff. As is the case in any collective writing project such as this, what could be achieved in this volume was shaped not only by the nature, scope, and accessibility of sources but also, inevitably, by the availability and intellectual orientation of contributors. Each chapter draws on the contributor's expertise and seeks to add a snapshot, a glimpse, of a larger understanding of women's experience as a distinctive part of IU history. It does so, for example, by conveying the essence of a pivotal moment on campus or of a cultural era, by studying a particular female personality, or by examining women's contributions to a particular discipline or field of inquiry, department, or school.

Together, the chapters, roughly organized chronologically and thematically, locate the story of women at IU in the examination of lives, anchored in the context of local and national circumstances. The volume is divided into two parts: part one focuses on the experience and perspectives of students while part two focuses on faculty, staff, and supporters. Admittedly, in some cases the assignment of a chapter to a particular part was a bit arbitrary given that the story of women's lives rarely falls into such neat compartments. Some women assumed various roles at IU. For example, Martha Dawson was an IU student and then an IU faculty member, yet her story appears in part two, along with stories of other faculty.

Reading across the chapters, we see aspects of change within IU's history and the larger narrative of higher education in the United States. For example, compare and contrast the deans of women's expectations for IU coeds and their concerted push for all-female housing in the early 1900s with the rise of student preference for coeducational living in the 1960s and 1970s. Consider the deans of women's vision of an all-female residential environment as central to coeducation that dominated campus life in the first two decades of the twentieth century and the later experience of urban commuters attending classes on a new consolidated urban campus, IUPUI. Examine the impulse driving Edna Henry's efforts to professionalize the field of social work at the turn of the century and by contrast Nobel Laureate Elinor Ostrom's rejection of the compartmentalization of departments and disciplines in favor of an interdisciplinary approach to both personal and professional life that created a highly productive synergy with colleagues across fields and institutions. And finally, recognize the leadership of the students who carved identity-affirming physical and cultural spaces on campus and the intellectual influence of both early pioneers in academic fields and later generations of women scholars and their supporters who, drawing inspiration from the women's movement, challenged the canon and old paradigms and sought to reconstruct academic life—promoting new ways of seeing, including new voices, and advocating equity for all.

This book is dedicated to the generations of IU women who went before us. While engaging the past, the volume inevitably also looks to the future. We began work on this project before the pivotal events of 2020 that posed such profound issues and challenges for US colleges and universities, including our own, and indeed for the country and, beyond that, all corners of the world. We were enthused by the opportunity to work together on this women's history project and committed to making women's history part of IU's Bicentennial observance. It has been a rewarding experience for all of us. In some ways, though, the project is even more relevant and meaningful for us now, as we conclude our work, than when we began. In the months since we began our research, much has happened in the world around us—most recently, historic events from the pandemic, to protests for racial justice, to the renaming of buildings and the removal of statues as higher education leaders reexamine the views and values of historical figures honored on their campuses. Such events have brought a new appreciation of the power and importance of history and history writing. Simply put, history matters. We hope readers will find in this volume an invitation to pick up where we have left off—to document new stories, identify and draw on new sources, and capture and preserve oral histories from an ever broader range of women, all with the goal of producing new works that extend, complement, refine, and provide alternative, more inclusive, and more accurate ways of seeing the past. As both the search for IU women's history and recent world events remind us, all history, including campus history, must always be open to reconsideration, revision, and reimagining. Only with the spirit of intellectual questioning and openness can IU, now two hundred years old, live up to being a "people's university" in the truest sense.

NOTES

The epigraph is from May Wright Sewall, "The Education of Woman in the Western States," in *Woman's Work in America*, ed. Annie Nathan Meyer (New York: Henry Holt, 1891), 54–89, quote at 87.

1. Sewall, "The Education of Woman," 54. At the time, the term "West" referred to the region of the country beyond the Allegheny Mountains.

2. The short-lived Northwestern Female College opened in 1855. It was located nearby but was not affiliated with all-male Northwestern. Rechartered as Evanston

College for Ladies in 1871, with Frances Willard as its president, the institution became the Women's College of Northwestern University in 1873 (with Willard as dean of women).

3. Ralph D. Gray, *IUPUI—The Making of an Urban University* (Bloomington: Indiana University Press, 2003), especially page 6. Sewall was a central figure in the Indianapolis Woman's Club, the Indianapolis Propylaeum, the Art Association of Indianapolis (later known as the Indianapolis Museum of Art), the Contemporary Club of Indianapolis, and the John Herron Art Institute, which became the Herron School of Art and Design at Indiana University–Purdue University Indianapolis (IUPUI). See Jane Stephens, "May Wright Sewall: An Indiana Reformer," *Indiana Magazine of History* 78, no. 4 (December 1982): 273–95 and Ray E. Boomhower, *Fighting for Equality: A Life of May Wright Sewall* (Indianapolis: Indiana Historical Society Press, 2007). Recognition of Sewall's role in the women's educational organizations and in organizing extension classes (staffed by professors from IU, Butler University, and other institutions) is found in a memorial tribute appearing in the *Journal of the Association of Collegiate Alumnae* 13, no. 7 (July 1920): 8–13.

4. Andrea G. Radke-Moss focuses on the opportunities for women at land-grant institutions in the nineteenth century in *Bright Epoch: Women and Coeducation in the American West* (Lincoln: University of Nebraska Press, 2008).

5. Sewall, "The Education of Woman," 71, 65. Claudia Goldin and Lawrence F. Katz, "Putting the 'Co' in Education: Timing, Reasons, and Consequences of College Coeducation from 1835 to the Present," *Journal of Human Capital* 5, no. 4 (winter 2011): 377–417.

6. May Wright Sewall, *A Report on the Position of Women in Industry and Education in the State of Indiana* (n.p.: Carlon & Hollenbeck, Printers, 1885), 14–15.

7. Sewall, "The Education of Woman," 87.

8. Women remained the majority of students across the IU system after 1977–78. Nationally, women became the majority of undergraduate students in 1979–80. Female enrollment reached 50 percent of the total Bloomington campus enrollment by 1981–82 and surpassed men from 1984–85. Since 2014–15, IUB enrollments have been roughly fifty-fifty for men and women. Student data for Indiana University are found in "Indiana Enrollment and Attendance (1824 to date)" and *IU Fact Book* for 1977–78 and 1984–85, Reference File, Indiana University Libraries Archives, Bloomington, Indiana. For national data, see National Center for Education Statistics, *120 Years of American Education: A Statistical Portrait* (Washington, DC, 2003), Table 23, 75.

9. The year 1922 saw the first two IU alumnae, Juliette Maxwell, '83, and Lillian Gay Berry, '99, rise through the university's ranks to be promoted—on the same day, June 6—to full-time full professorships.

10. The first woman of color to serve as an IU trustee was alumna Cora Smith Breckenridge (bachelor's 1959; master's 1963), who was elected in 1997 and served three terms on the board. See https://honorsandawards.iu.edu/awards/honoree

/5743.html (accessed October 31, 2021). Another milestone occurred while this book was in production. Pamela Whitten became the nineteenth president of Indiana University on July 1, 2021. She is the first woman to hold this position in IU's history.

11. Theophilus A. Wylie, *Indiana University: Its History from 1820, When Founded, to 1890: With Biographical Sketches of its Presidents, Professors and Graduates: And a List of its Students from 1820 to 1887* (Indianapolis: Wm. B. Burford, 1890); James Albert Woodburn and David D. Banta, *History of Indiana University*, Vol. 1: 1820–1902 (Bloomington: Indiana University Press, 1940), 287–88; Burton Dorr Myers, *History of Indiana University*, Vol. 2: 1902–1937, ed. Ivy Chamness and Burton Durr Myers (Bloomington: Indiana University, 1952); and Thomas D. Clark, *Indiana University, Midwestern Pioneer*, 4 volumes (Bloomington: Indiana University Press, 1970–77).

12. Wylie, *Indiana University*. Correspondence recently found in the IU Libraries Archives suggests that perhaps a volume about IU women was in fact planned to mark the university's 150th anniversary in 1970, but this project apparently never came to fruition, and no manuscript materials have been located. Examples of early women-centered histories are Dorothy McGuigan, *A Dangerous Experiment: 100 Years of Women at the University of Michigan* (Benton Harbor: R. W. Patterson Printing Company, 1970); Charlotte Williams Conable, *Women at Cornell: The Myth of Equality* (Ithaca: Cornell University Press, 1977); and Marian Swoboda's edited volumes on women at the University of Wisconsin (see University of Wisconsin–Madison Archives, "The History of Women at University of Wisconsin," https://search.library.wisc.edu/digital/AUWWomen. Examples of later volumes include Polly Welts Kaufmann, ed., *The Search for Equity: Women at Brown University, 1891–1991* (Hanover, NH: Brown University Press, 1991); Ruth Bordin, *Women at Michigan: The "Dangerous Experiment," 1870s to the Present*, foreword by Martha Vicinus/introduction by Kathryn Kish Sklar and Lynn Y. Weiner (Ann Arbor: University of Michigan Press, 2001); Laurel Thatcher Ulrich, *Yards and Gates: Gender in Harvard and Radcliffe History* (New York: Palgrave, 2004); and Rosalind Rosenberg, *Changing the Subject: How Women of Columbia University Shaped the Way We Think about Sex and Politics* (New York: Columbia University Press, 2006).

13. Frank O. Beck discusses the hindrance posed by the lack of data in *Some Aspects of Race Relations at Indiana University, My Alma Mater* (Bloomington: privately printed, 1959), 8–9.

14. Dawson's career merits further study by scholars of higher education. Neither IU nor Virginia State University has archival records related to Dawson's career, and her administrative papers at Hampton University remain unprocessed. Andrea Walton draws on Dawson's 1997 autobiographical essay and published material to situate Dawson's IU years within the context of a lengthy career marked by outstanding achievements at several institutions. See "Martha E. Dawson:

Forty Years of Leadership in Multicultural Education and Teaching for Understanding and Excellence" (chap. 12 in this volume).

15. Mariam K. Chamberlain, "Women as Trustees," in *Women in Academe: Progress and Prospects*, ed. Mariam K. Chamberlain (New York: Russell Sage Foundation, 1988), 333–56.

16. In 1921, the ACA was reorganized as the American Association of University Women (AAUW). For family background, see Carol Ann Krause, *Showers Brothers Furniture Company: The Shared Fortunes of a Family, a City, and a University* (Bloomington, IN: Quarry Books, 2012), 223–24.

17. IU publications editor Ivy Chamness's records of gifts merit further investigation. See Box 2 of Indiana University Publications Editor's records, 1905–72, bulk 1935–55, Indiana University Archives.

18. Wells held a PhD in astronomy and was a member of the Indiana Academy of Science, organizer of a Million Dollar Fellowship fund for the American Association of University Women, and chair of the National Woman's Party in 1949. See "Retired I.U. Teacher Dies," *Indianapolis Star*, July 29, 1946, 9.

19. Linda Eisenmann, "A Time of Quiet Activism: Research, Practice, and Policy in American Women's Higher Education, 1945–1965," *History of Education Quarterly* 45, no. 1 (2005): 1–17. Linda M. Perkins, "Is She a Feminist and Do I Like Her? Dilemmas of a Feminist Biographer," *Vitae Scholasticae* 31, no. 2 (2014): 64–76.

PART 1

STUDENTS

ONE

—ᴍ—

FROM WHETHER AND HOW TO COEDUCATE WOMEN TO EDUCATING ALL STUDENTS EQUITABLY AT INDIANA UNIVERSITY

ANDREA WALTON

Andrea Walton offers an overview of the 150 years of women at IU through the lens of coeducation. Walton emphasizes the importance of IU's midwestern setting but notes its connectedness to larger currents in women's and US history.

> How does it happen there are no women on your board? Do you not consider them of the alumni?
>
> —Sarah Parke Morrison to IU's Committee
> on the Alumni Building in 1911

SARAH PARKE MORRISON (1833–1919) was a firm and fierce advocate for women in education. The first woman to attend, graduate, and teach at Indiana University, she stood ready to challenge any factor that excluded or marginalized women, from the use of gendered Latin terms to the nomination process for campus-related boards and committees. When asked to cast her vote on an all-male slate of candidates, she often dissented by simply writing "for some woman."[1] Years after her 1869 IU graduation, Morrison's memories of her campus days remained vivid and affirming, but as her 1911 letter to leaders of the IU Committee on the Alumni Building illustrates, she felt compelled to raise issues of gender equity in hopes of pricking the conscience of the men who administered her alma mater. To her mind, women's representation at a state university such as IU was a right, and achieving coeducation in its fullest sense meant nothing less than seeing women advance, equitably, into every part of university life.

Sadly, Morrison did not live to see alumna Nellie Showers Teter (class of 1893) become the first woman elected to IU's Board of Trustees in 1924. Like Morrison, Teter was an advocate for IU women. In particular, she saw campus housing for women as integral to improving the quality of women's under-graduate education and elevating IU's stature as a coeducational university. In 1925, Teter took great satisfaction in dedicating IU's first on-campus women's dormitory. IU women's supporters had long advocated for a women's hall—an all-female living environment guided by the ideals of self-government and best practices in student services. Members of the Women's League, the Associa-tion of Collegiate Alumnae, and, later, the American Association of Univer-sity Women had all expressed the need for women's housing to IU university administrators. And housing for women had been the dream of successive IU deans of women, from Mary Bidwell Breed—the first dean, appointed in 1901—to Agnes E. Wells, appointed in 1918, who raised IU's early female cam-pus housing efforts to national prominence in the eyes of student affairs profes-sionals.[2] In 1925, at long last, a women's dormitory became a reality, paid for by the Memorial Fund Campaign, in which women's leadership and philanthropy figured prominently.

Nearly two decades later, in 1942, Teter and a committee of university women were searching for a suitable way to commemorate the seventy-fifth anniversary of IU coeducation and settled on honoring one of the campus's female pioneers and attaching her name to a women's residence hall. Thanks to their efforts, Beech Hall, located in Women's Quad, was renamed Morrison Hall after the woman who wrote the petition for coeducation, became the first female student, and was appointed as the first woman faculty member at Indiana University. The *Indiana Alumni* [sic] *Quarterly* coverage of the nam-ing ceremony included a photograph of trustee Nellie Teter standing proudly alongside an undergraduate dressed in period costume to portray Sarah Parke Morrison, IU's first coed. The point was clear: there were ties between IU women, past and present.

Figures like Sarah Parke Morrison and Nellie Teter kept alive the spirit of the formative decades of coeducation at IU by using the avenues available to them—the pen and a seat in the board room, respectively—to advocate for women's interests on the coeducational campus. Later generations of IU women, though beneficiaries of these earlier efforts, often had little awareness of early campus history or the experiences of their female predecessors. When

the Office of Women's Affairs opened in 1972, their efforts were preoccupied not
with the past but with women's contemporary status on the male-dominated
coeducational campus. They had little sense of what earlier deans of women
or women faculty had experienced or achieved in the formative decades of
coeducation. Part of the challenge of their own historic moment in the 1970s,
with the rising women's movement, would be to recover women's history and
scrutinize the ideas, beliefs, and power structures undergirding early academic
life and the establishment of a coeducational campus—access to which had
been a goal of their foremothers and foresisters.

Imagine for a moment the year 1972—the year of Title IX, the opening of
many women's centers and advocacy offices on US campuses, and baseline
efforts to document the status of women across the disciplines. Consider an
academic woman at IU reaching to the library shelf for books that might give
her historical perspective on her own situation. What would she have found?
Likely little to guide her. Even IU's own institutional histories told little of IU
women, beyond their admission as students in 1867. And until that point, scholars studying women in education had tended to focus on the endowed liberal
arts colleges for women in the East, especially the Seven Sisters.

In the early 1970s, though, a group of scholars—many of them academic
women who saw history as personal and political—were setting about to write
books about women for those library shelves. These historians identified new
sources, looked anew at well-known records, and worked to recover the neglected stories of women on campuses; indeed, they were just embarking on
the task of bringing the perspectives of women's history to a reimagining of the
standard narrative of US higher education. The first substantial attempt would
be Barbara Miller Solomon's *In the Company of Educated Women*, appearing
in 1985.[3]

The revisionist spirit in writing academic women's history that began in
the 1970s has borne fruit, but work remains. Although we have a voluminous
literature on the history of higher education, the field awaits more inclusive
narratives and new syntheses. Still widely read, classic surveys of the history of
the American university—one thinks of works by Frederick Rudolph or Lawrence Veysey, for instance—either included scant information on women or
framed discussions of women narrowly, touting admission at men's institutions
as equality achieved.[4] Moreover Barbara Solomon's still influential narrative,
which by centering women was nothing less than pathbreaking in 1985, appears
less satisfactory and outdated to many contemporary readers, especially those
who do not see their experiences reflected. Bounded by their era's mindsets,

surveys such as Rudolph's or Solomon's, even while aiming for a comprehensive view, were perhaps inevitably partial, emphasizing certain stories, voices, and institutions over others.

Consider now what an IU woman of today, 2021, might find on the library shelf. No doubt she would find a far wider range of engaging books about women—examples of the efflorescence in scholarship about women and gender since Solomon wrote—but she would still find little about her own campus.[5] My recognition that the story of women at IU, though dating back to 1867, remained to be told, and that doing so could contribute to ongoing efforts to revise our narratives of women in higher education, informs this essay. Although the history of women at midwestern state universities did attract interest among historians in the 1970s (especially scholars focused on the politics of access), these institutions and the diverse experiences of women on their campuses merit renewed attention today. The Midwest is associated with openness to educating college men and women together, but there is no single story of collegiate coeducation. Some institutions adopted coeducation incrementally while others, as in the case of IU, admitted women on an equal basis—with all applicants meeting the same admissions criteria and having access to the same programs of study. We have some sense of the history of coeducational public higher education in the Midwest—from now classic early studies of women at Michigan and Wisconsin, for instance—but overall the scholarly portrayal of the state university is rather homogenized. Emphasis is on the institutional type, funded by and for a state's citizens. More works are needed to capture the distinctive character and particularities of individual campuses, illuminate their geographical circumstances, or touch on issues of gender, race, and class.[6]

In the eyes of many observers at home and abroad, coeducation became a distinguishing feature of US higher education, and the Midwest played a central role in popularizing coeducation and experimenting with its execution.[7] Claudia Goldin and Lawrence F. Katz note that by 1897 over half of all US undergraduates were studying in coeducational institutions, but striking variations were seen by region. Being coeducated "was the case for 29 percent of undergraduates in the Northeast and 40 percent in the South," but in the Midwest and West the figure rose dramatically to "around 86 percent."[8] Indiana University did not have a gender exclusion in its charter, but due to cultural practices and the realities of schooling in the state, the institution remained all-male from the first classes in 1825 until 1867. Despite this lag, IU was among the earliest state universities to admit women and to do so on the same terms as men. Women would comprise most of IU's student body by the end of the 1970s, in line with national trends.[9]

—w—

This essay uses the lens of coeducation—the policy and practice of educating men and women together—to gain insight into women's relationships to Indiana University over nearly 150 years from the admission of Sarah Parke Morrison in 1867 to recent times. By examining women's aspirations and the opportunities they found, forged, or were denied at IU, we may better understand how women fared at the state university—an institution that by virtue of its public nature was meant to be democratic in both values and practice.

This essay explores three sweeping, overlapping but distinctive periods in the history of women at IU: First, the "Prelude and Beginnings of IU Coeducation (1833–1901)" highlights events and social movements shaping US women's education in the East and Midwest that provided a context for understanding women's eventual entrance at IU in 1867 and early coeducation at the university. Second, "The Rise and Leadership of the Dean of Women (1901–1946)" explores the establishment of this new administrative position—a woman educator overseeing women students—and how successive deans advocated for the needs of IU women students up through 1946, when IU eliminated the gender-specific position. Third and last, "The Epic Struggle for Civil Rights" looks at the postwar ferment that inspired a new generation of women and various social groups to raise their voices in an effort to make the university more inclusive and responsive to the rights and needs of diverse individuals. In terms of coeducation, the period saw women seeking equity in all spheres of academic life and greater recognition of the diversity of women. But, importantly, a confluence of forces had begun to broaden what coeducation meant. In the nineteenth century, the term referred to educating men and women together, and for many, it was associated with women's educational rights. One might look at recent history and argue that IU and other universities are in the process of conceptualizing the term anew, embracing the more pluralistic concerns of identity and a rethinking of the gender binary.

PRELUDE AND BEGINNINGS OF IU COEDUCATION (1833–1901)

The nineteenth century saw women's entry into higher education and the formative decades of IU coeducation. The broader context of this period encompasses developments from the rise of women's higher learning in academies and seminaries in the East to the founding of the paradigm-setting coeducational Oberlin in 1833, the admission of women at young midwestern state universities like IU shortly after the Civil War, and finally IU's decision to appoint a dean of women.

Although the first woman student, Sarah Parke Morrison, entered IU in 1867, the rise of coeducation at IU had earlier roots. Indeed, the trajectory of coeducation west of the Alleghenies reflected the combined influences of regional circumstances and educational models, ideas, and debates about women's educational rights seen in the East, where the earliest colleges had been founded exclusively for men. Most of these institutions resisted coeducation well into the nineteenth century—in fact some—notably most of the Ivy league institutions—did not admit women until the 1960s and 1970s. As agitation for women's educational rights stirred, education, and particularly coeducation, was increasingly viewed as integral to women's improved status in society. Early interest in educating the sexes together was quickened in large part by the reform ethos that led, eventually, to the Seneca Falls Declaration in 1848. Signers of this historic document—sixty-eight women and thirty-two men—argued that by their refusal to admit female students, colleges "denied" women "the facilities for obtaining a thorough education."[10]

Certainly not all women who pursued advanced education did so with women's rights on their mind, but the spirit of Seneca Falls was evident in many of the public debates about female intellect and the improvement of female education.[11] Whereas many female students secured higher learning in the seminaries and academies that dotted the landscape, women increasingly set their sights on access to collegiate liberal arts study. Arguments about the nexus between women's education and women's status and opportunities in society resulted in newsworthy fundraising campaigns and gifts to support female students and highly publicized petitions for women's admission at men's colleges. Such initiatives, together with the nationwide expansion of schooling, drove increasing support for coeducation in higher education that predated and, in figurative terms, paved the way for Sarah Parke Morrison's entrance to IU in 1867.

But no woman had yet been admitted to college or had even attended a coeducational public high school when the state of Indiana and its seminary were founded. After Indiana's rise from the Old Northwest Territory to statehood in 1816, significant time was needed for the lofty educational aspirations expressed in the new state constitution to become a reality. Without sufficient levels of preparatory schooling and public funding, the young state university encountered difficulty attracting students, paying its bills, and fulfilling its intended role as the "crown" of public education in Indiana, from the common school to the university.[12]

Though modeled on the eastern classical college, IU's founding was tied to realities of daily life in the young state. President James Madison designated the site for the seminary township in 1816 on what were indigenous lands of the Miami, Delaware, Potawatomi, and Shawnee peoples.[13] In 1820, seminary builders embarked on their ambitious enterprise with lofty educational ideals but with uncertainty about the number of prospective applicants nearby or the means to attract and transport students from farther distances. The population of Indiana was growing rapidly, from 24,520 in 1810 (before statehood) to 147,178 in 1820 and 343,031 in 1830. Yet in 1828 the population of Monroe County was still, according to David Banta's estimate, only "about 4,600 and of Bloomington, 600."[14]

In the decades before the Civil War, the seminary, though legally recognized as a university in 1838, remained a modest and traditional academic enterprise: enrollments were low, curriculum was classical, and finances were tenuous. Although the university's charter did not bar women's admission, the question of coeducation at IU would not be raised for forty years. Yet women who migrated to Indiana from eastern states carried with them a respect for women's education and helped to found and staff schools, libraries, clubs, and seminaries. Women students had access to Indiana's statewide system of academies, many of them coeducational. In 1833, the same year as the founding of the country's first coeducational college at Oberlin, the Monroe Female Seminary was established in Bloomington and provided for female education before the public high school in Bloomington and before the opening of Terre Haute Normal (today's Indiana State University) in 1870.[15]

In 1851, Indiana passed a new constitution that clarified and strengthened the state's commitment to education. In turn, Indiana University began a noteworthy but brief experiment with a model school and normal department, open to both male and female students.[16] In the nineteenth century, teacher preparation courses often became an "entering wedge" by which women advanced into formerly all-male colleges and universities.[17] In the case of IU, it was the need for teachers and the university's effort to serve the state of Indiana and its schools, rather than a push by women for university entrance per se, that in the early 1850s presented a synergistic opportunity for the university and female students. Yet, uncertain finances and the departure of Professor Daniel Read, the force behind the initiative and a supporter of women's education, led to the effort's discontinuance.[18] In retrospect, the brief experiment in pedagogy was a false dawn of coeducation.

Instead, women's admission to IU for liberal arts study on the same basis as men (to the classical and scientific courses) came after the Civil War. Though institutional records related to women's admission are sparse, there seems to have been no public campaign or large-scale initiative for women's admission presented to the IU trustees. Rather, the question was taken up by one woman, Sarah Parke Morrison, the daughter of IU trustee and Hoosier political leader John Morrison, who, together with his wife, owned the well-respected Salem Female Collegiate Institute. According to IU trustee Isaac Jenkinson, himself a proponent of coeducation, Morrison, who attended her parents' institute before pursuing higher studies back East, had a long-standing interest in seeing women enrolled at Indiana's state university and "for several years had been agitating the question among her friends."[19] Sarah Parke Morrison's now historic 1867 letter to the board of trustees, deliberated by them at their end of year meeting, hinged on a question of policy: Were the doors of the state university open to women? Finding the university's charter did not bar women, the trustees voted 4–3 to announce that admission to Indiana University was open to female applicants. And when no woman stood ready to enter IU, Morrison, encouraged by an IU faculty member to "fill the breach," decided to enroll.[20] At thirty-four years old, she had already attended Mt. Holyoke, Vassar, and Williams in the East but felt compelled to take this step on behalf of women. It is worth underscoring that college attendance was still a rarity, regardless of a student's gender. In 1869–70, only about 1 percent of the eighteen- to twenty-four-year-old white population in the United States (62,839 students) was enrolled at one of the nation's 563 colleges. Collegiate enrollment in the state of Indiana totaled 3,367 students.[21]

Morrison's admission and attendance in 1867 and her designation as a sophomore by the winter of 1868, opened the era of coeducation at IU. But the women who soon followed her—twelve appear on the "freshman roster" (a gender-biased term then in use) for 1867–68—perhaps played a more instrumental role in shaping the character of early coeducation at IU, negotiating gender expectations, and organizing daily life around women's needs on the formerly all-male campus.[22] Most hailed from local Protestant families, and several were daughters of IU families. Many became teachers. As white women, these early coeds might apply their education in common schools, academies, and seminaries across Indiana and nearby states.

The first African American woman to attend IU, Carrie Parker, enrolled in 1898, thirty years after the first cohort of female IU students. Her story before arriving at IU speaks to the barriers black students were forced to overcome in their pursuit of further education. A bright student, Parker was flunked three times by her middle school principal, who intended to prevent her from going on to high school (where she would later graduate at the top of her class). Beyond sexism, then, IU's black coeds also endured the much larger burdens of racism and segregation. As much as IU's midwestern setting meant an openness to educating men and women together, the racial attitudes and norms that dominated the region constrained the possibilities of true coeducation of the sexes and races.[23]

Eventually, residential life would become central to the gender dynamics of IU coeducation. Like most midwestern state universities, IU was reluctant to invest its limited resources into campus housing in the nineteenth century. Instead, students—women and men alike—lived with relatives or in local boardinghouses. Organizing social life outside the lecture hall, where women and men sat together, assumed great importance in university coeducation.

Early IU women, though excluded by male classmates from a few student groups, found ample opportunities for leadership and peer-to-peer exchanges in both coeducational and single-sex activities and organizations.[24] Sorority life provided space for women to be leaders with control over an all-female counterpart to IU's fraternity men. In 1886, women organized the Indiana University chapter of the Young Women's Christian Association (YWCA). By 1891, women were one-third of the twenty-seven-member Philomathean Society, founded in 1885 by "Barbs" (non-fraternity men) on campus.[25] In 1893, Arda Knox, a member of Kappa Alpha Theta, was elected senior class president. In 1897, Florence Reid Myrick was named editor in chief of the *Student* (later the *Indiana Daily Student*), and a few years later, in 1900, Marie Louise Boisen, granddaughter of faculty member Theophilus Wylie and daughter of IU alumna Louisa Wylie, served as the first woman editor in chief of the *Arbutus* yearbook. These were substantial achievements for women on a campus that had not yet marked its fortieth anniversary of coeducation.

IU women also achieved early distinction in academic life. Enrolling together with her husband to study with ichthyologist David Starr Jordan, Meadie Hawkins Evermann became IU's first married female graduate in 1887.[26] As IU grew in intellectual substance and adopted the title of university in 1838, women's presence on campus was inextricably woven into larger institutional developments. By the end of the nineteenth century, demand for collegiate-level coursework delivered by IU faculty was evident in parts of the state beyond Bloomington. Notably, the first IU extension course, offered in Indianapolis beginning in 1891, was the fruit, at least in part, of organizing by suffragist May Wright Sewall and members of the Association of Collegiate Alumnae (ACA).[27] The enterprise in Indianapolis that laid the foundation of what in the late 1960s would become Indiana University–Purdue University Indianapolis (IUPUI), would soon be followed by other extension centers.

Women also entered IU's professional schools of law and medicine. In 1892, Tamar Althouse became the first woman to graduate from IU's School of Law, founded in 1842 in Bloomington, and soon, at age twenty-one, she became the first woman admitted to the Indiana Bar Association.[28] The history of women at the IU School of Medicine points to a harsher climate for women in that male-dominated professional world. Edna Henry skillfully negotiated the gender politics of professionalizing the feminized field of social work as founding director of IU's Social Service Department, but credit for that initiative has focused largely on the efforts of IU School of Medicine dean Charles P. Emerson.[29] Lillian B. Mueller (1885–1961), the only woman in her freshman medical class in Bloomington, became the first woman to graduate from IU's newly consolidated medical school in Indianapolis in 1909 but faced difficulty securing an internship. Undeterred, Mueller built her career at Methodist Hospital, where she was the first female physician.[30]

As was the case at many other coeducation institutions, women gained more opportunities at IU as students than as faculty, administrators, or trustees. Early academic positions for women were generally at the level of instructor or assistant and were often secured by insiders. Sarah Parke Morrison earned her IU master's degree in 1872, became a tutor in 1873, and the next year was appointed as an adjunct professor of English literature, becoming the university's first woman faculty member. Another early female instructor was Anna Ballantine (daughter of IU professor Elisha Ballantine), who attended the Monroe County Female Seminary, earned her AB from the Ohio Female College at Glendale in 1861, and then returned to Bloomington as a Latin instructor in IU's preparatory department. IU alumna Margaret Hemphill McCalla, a former head of Monroe Female Seminary who helped found Bloomington High School, was appointed as an assistant in IU's preparatory department in 1873 and in 1874 was elected superintendent of Bloomington Schools—the first woman to hold this position. She was joined in the preparatory department by at least one other female assistant: Suda May, a local woman who was also a private tutor and active in the Women's Foreign Missionary Society of the Methodist Episcopal Church. Maria Brace, a Vassar College faculty member with family ties to the Midwest, offered specially arranged classes in elocution at IU in 1882–83 (leading to a brief appointment as professor of elocution), and Katherine Merrill Graydon, a.k.a. Katharine, a member of Indiana's prominent Merrill and Ketchum families, was briefly an assistant professor of Greek in 1883–84, before accusations of a romantic entanglement with IU President Lemuel Moss led to his abrupt departure and her resignation. She subsequently rebuilt her career at Butler University in Indianapolis.

THE RISE AND LEADERSHIP OF THE
DEAN OF WOMEN (1901–1946)

The years between 1901 and 1946 saw rising female enrollment at IU. This change in campus demographics led to the solidification and maturing of coeducation under the leadership of successive deans of women. Whereas educators in the East had pioneered women's higher education and provided evidence of its merits—in seminaries, academies, single-sex colleges, and the region's few coeducational universities— educators in the Midwest pioneered and popularized the role of the female dean.[31] The dean of women envisioned a particular type of education for women within the gender-segregated structure of university coeducation; she connected her home campus to networks of women educators and brought these insights and practices—elements of what would become known as student affairs—to her oversight of residential life for women.[32]

During the first several decades of coeducation at IU, female enrollment grew from a small cluster of women to 40 percent of the student body, but only limited, ad hoc arrangements existed for addressing the needs of women students on the formerly all-male campus.[33] Female instructors, faculty wives, and collegiate alumnae living in Bloomington served as informal advisors and women's advocates. This community of women founded a chapter of the Women's League in 1895, pushed for a dean of women, pursued ACA accreditation, and argued the need for gymnasium facilities and a dormitory for women.[34] Especially prominent among these advocates was Frances Morgan Swain, an IU alumna, an equality-minded Quaker, and, not insignificantly, the wife of university president Joseph Swain.[35] Himself a supporter of women's educational rights (in addition to being married to the woman spearheading this campus initiative), President Swain secured trustee approval to hire a dean and then canvassed midwestern coeducational and eastern women's colleges in search of a suitable candidate. In 1901, Mary Bidwell Breed joined the faculty as the first dean of women and an assistant professor in the chemistry department. A born and bred easterner, Breed was a graduate of M. Carey Thomas's Bryn Mawr, known for its scholastic excellence and for cultivating student leadership. Breed was influenced by the ideas of women's self-government promoted at her alma mater and other women's colleges and affirmed the social and intellectual importance of women's access to liberal arts study.

Breed began her deanship at IU at a point when educating men and women together was no longer an oddity. In fact, even if there were pockets of challenge and even hostility, coeducation was becoming mainstream. In 1900, 71.6

percent of US colleges were coeducational, and women represented 24 percent of enrollment.[36] In the last decades of the nineteenth century, coeducation had been adopted at a few eastern universities (e.g., Boston, Syracuse, and Cornell) and two endowed coeducational universities opened in more western regions (Chicago and Stanford).

In the context of this new gender-specific administrative position and growing female enrollment, the issue of women's housing at IU assumed great importance. It would take two decades of advocacy, but IU's female deans and their allies finally saw their dreams of residential facilities for women materialize in the 1920s. From their perspective, university-sponsored housing was politically important, symbolic, and integral to three interconnected goals: accommodating rising female enrollments at IU, regulating student behavior (both women's conduct and social interactions between the sexes), and advancing a particular design for women's education within the gender-segregated structure of coeducational campus life. Lecture halls, laboratories, and libraries were open to all, but gender segregation prevailed in spiritual and moral life, hygiene courses, physical education and gymnasium facilities, and living accommodations. Developing a system of self-government for female students and connecting IU educators and staff to women's professional networks and decanal associations, IU's women deans answered the question of how to coeducate women and, significantly, in the process contributed to the development of the area of student affairs.[37]

In the 1910s and 1920s, women's enrollment grew, the university expanded, and academic units became more specialized. In some noteworthy instances, sharper gender and racial boundaries were drawn. Founded in 1909, the Indiana Union, open only to men until 1952, occupied the east wing of the new Student Building while women's activities were housed in the west wing. In 1913, a Women's Athletic Association and a department of home economics were established. As part of the curriculum, the department opened its first "practice house" (complete with a live-in baby) to teach home management in 1920. But the facility would be open only to white students.[38] In 1919, the position of dean of men—a male counterpart to the dean of women—would be created. In 1921, the Board of Aeons, a student advisory to the university president, was formed, but its membership was restricted to men and would remain male-only until the 1970s.

The affluence of the 1920s solidified women's place on US campuses as national female collegiate participation peaked. But the early decades of the twentieth century also brought some resistance or even backlash in relation to coeducation. Some administrators, faculty, and male students began to voice concerns about feminization in certain fields or university units, especially women's disproportionate enrollment in liberal arts courses. In several high-profile instances, new policies were implemented to stem the tide of women's advances. At Chicago, the growing number of women gaining Phi Beta Kappa honors prompted some calls for separating the sexes during the early college years. Wisconsin considered a measure of sex segregation. Stanford implemented a quota on women students, and Wesleyan returned to its all-male status.[39]

Even President William Lowe Bryan, who, through his office and in tandem with his wife, Charlotte Lowe Bryan, did much to support women on campus, worried collegiate studies must be made more appealing to IU men.[40] Bryan saw gender as relevant to his plans for professional schools at IU and to ongoing efforts to build a strong, well-regarded university:

> Indiana University is a co-educational institution. We rejoice to have equal number of girls as well as of boys. It appears that in practically all of the Colleges of Liberal Arts the number of women grows increasingly greater than the number of men. It has therefore been a matter of major interest with me throughout my administration to develop courses, departments, and schools which should appeal especially to men students. This was a principal motive in establishing the School of Medicine, the Department of Journalism, the School of Commerce etc. I submit figures showing a number of departments and schools in which the number of men greatly exceeds the number of women.[41]

The 1920s opened up a new era in coeducation at IU. In some respects, as mentioned, gender boundaries became more clearly drawn, but new areas for women's influence also opened. IU elected its first female trustee, alumna Nellie Teter, in 1924 and, the following year, finally opened on-campus housing. Both female board representation and a dormitory system were long sought-after goals of successive deans of women, members of the local AAUW, and others who advocated for women on campus.

The first residence hall opened in 1925, with the Women's Quadrangle completed by the 1940s. As the dormitory system expanded, housing policy and regulations allowed the university through the dean of women's office to exercise control over student living and conduct. Visitation hours, etiquette, dining options, overnight stays, dancing, riding in cars, and many other aspects of daily life (even marriage announcements) were carefully regulated, with the rules for IU "coeds" taking into account both Bloomington campus needs and practices at other institutions. But there were also opportunities for women's leadership and for student voices to be heard through the Association of Women Students, to which all female students were eligible to belong.

The deans of women, guided by a particular view of how best to educate college women, advocated for women students and negotiated male-female boundaries, but they left racial boundaries unquestioned. Though the numbers of African American women enrolled at and graduating from IU increased, Black women were excluded from the on-campus residence halls.[42] IU's Black coeds were required to live off-campus in private facilities rented out by Samuel Dargan, the first Black graduate of the Indiana School of Law and a longtime university employee. Desegregation of IU's residence halls would not occur until after World War II.

By the late 1930s, civil rights sentiment and activity in Indiana gained momentum. Lawmakers and university administrators were urged to remedy any disconnect between the espoused democratic values of a state university and the discrimination and prejudice students faced on campus and in the surrounding town. The combined efforts of the NAACP, social justice–minded faculty and students, and sympathetic and politically skillful President Herman B Wells achieved the dismantling of racial campus restrictions in dining halls, the Indiana Memorial Union, and athletics. Work to integrate service at local restaurants and other businesses continued but with slower results. President Wells was both empathetic to the cause and keenly aware of the significance of the 1938 Gaines decision in Missouri—which eroded *Plessy v. Ferguson*'s principle of "separate but equal" (1896)—for all public institutions, even at ostensibly racially tolerant institutions like IU, where Black students were already enrolled. Wells had the prospect of litigation on his radar and was sensitive to mounting pressures from the NAACP and other civil rights advocates as he spearheaded the final push to desegregate campus life, including IU's residence halls.[43]

In retrospect, efforts to address racial exclusion in the late 1930s and the new demands and pressures that followed World War II played a pivotal role in reshaping the contours of coeducation in terms of gender and race. Precipitously declining male enrollments during wartime as men left for military service brought unexpected gains for women—greater visibility and leadership roles in newspaper, band, and other campus activities, for instance. But this ground was quickly lost when returning students and GI Bill matriculants flooded the campus. At IU, reflecting a trend seen at campuses nationwide, the position of dean of women was eliminated as gender-specific deanships were consolidated into one position, the dean of students. At IU, both Kate Mueller (dean of women) and Robert Bates (dean of men) were passed over for this new office in favor of Col. Raymond Shoemaker, who, as professor of military science and tactics (PMST) had overseen IU's ROTC.

More than a few university administrators at IU and elsewhere welcomed the post–WWII consolidation and restructuring of student personnel services. From their perspective, the prior system of two gender-specific decanal offices was outdated and unsustainable. It seemed logical to apply the wartime lessons of efficiency and scale to the complexities of the dramatically expanding post–WWII university. By contrast, women's groups, most notably deans of women and members of the AAUW, found this new structure worrisome and demoralizing. To them, consolidation was a form of backlash against women's leadership on campus—the loss of women's hard-fought-for ground in the administrative structure.[44]

THE EPIC STRUGGLE FOR CIVIL RIGHTS

The third period, sweeping from 1946 to the present, has been defined mostly by an epic struggle for civil rights. This push has taken on different foci and highlighted particular concerns at different junctures, but overall various groups have sought to bring the reality of experience on campus in line with the rhetoric of democracy and inclusion. Most relevant here, the post–WWII decades have brought a reenvisioning of coeducation.

The initial reenvisioning came in relation to housing policy for Black women, who bore the burdens of both gender and race. In the 1930s, debates, sermons, protests, town hall meetings, and communication between NAACP leaders and President Wells had helped to raise awareness of the discrimination Black students faced, including their exclusion from campus residence halls. On the heels of WWII, IU trustees moved swiftly to desegregate men's housing. The housing emergency created by returning GIs and building moral pressures drove the decision. Shouldn't universities, especially a public university, uphold the same democratic principles for which a world war had been fought? critics asked. Board members agreed that opening dorms to all men was the best course of action.

By contrast, the desegregation of women's housing was more contested and took three years longer to achieve, coming in 1949. At the time IU's Board of Trustees finally desegregated women's housing, Black enrollments were still quite small. IU's student body of 8,151 included only 155 Black men and 71 Black women. Forty-seven Black male undergraduates were already living on campus.[45] But social attitudes about race relations prevailed, and students were asked to identify their race on the rooming application.

At IU, as at many campuses, civil rights agitation and other student protests of the 1960s provided a larger context for rethinking nearly every aspect of university life. In this social and political environment, questions arose related to gender and college admission policies. National news coverage in relation to changing women's status on US campuses in the 1960s tended to focus on the Northeast. In this older region, whose selective, better endowed colleges and universities were still steeped in the single-sex tradition, change was now underway. A combination of financial considerations, the preference for coeducation among applicants in an increasingly competitive student market, and pressure from women's groups was ushering in a second wave of coeducation— finally dismantling all-male admission policies at selective eastern liberal arts colleges and the prestigious Ivy League.[46] But the headlines about Princeton, Yale, and Columbia eclipsed another newsworthy story—that a coeducation revolution, so to speak, was also occurring in the Midwest. Indeed, student-led calls for change were heard at large public institutions like IU that had already been educating men and women together for nearly a century.

In retrospect, the challenge to the status quo at IU and coeducational campuses in similar circumstances emerged from the era's larger, sweeping concerns about power, representation, and inequalities in US society. Student groups had led protests against ties between universities and the federal government, the Vietnam War, and racial injustice.

Many student leaders rejected single-sex residential halls and parietals as archaic, paternalistic, and undemocratic—a violation of student rights. Protests against the social strictures of coeducation represented a push for personal freedom and recognition of student sexuality and an assertion of student rights in a supposedly democratic university. The goal of the major student group organized to address campus issues, the Progressive Reform Party (PRP), was to "re-integrate the academic community with the outside world," and, as historian Mary Ann Wynkoop noted, "part of that process was to give all women at IU the freedom to control their own lives, their own time, and their own behavior—sexual and otherwise."[47]

Leaders of the agitation focused on creating a better approach to coeducational living for women and men and hoped to engage students who had become complacent. The student activists aspired "to help in building . . . a dynamic community profoundly committed to maximum educational opportunity for every student." Perhaps most important is how student protesters (re) defined democracy: "The heart of a democracy is in the rights of the minority rather than the rule of the majority. . . . If one woman does not want them, she should be free to decide for herself."[48] Further support for dismantling the double standard for men and women, long institutionalized in IU housing policy, came in the fall of 1967, when the student senate underscored unequivocally that undergraduate men and women shared equal freedoms and rights as students, declaring that "women's regulations, from whatever the source derived, violate Article VII of the Student Bill of Rights."[49]

By the end of the 1960s and early 1970s, the landmark Civil Rights Act of 1964 had provided both inspiration and leverage for student groups, women faculty, and other groups on campus to fight for equality. This new era, preoccupied with equality of opportunity and rights, brought a reconsideration of coeducation and the assumption that access—women's admission and physical presence on campus—ensured fairness, inclusion, and equality.[50] Evidence contradictory to familiar academic rhetoric—heralding the university in genderless terms as the house of intellect or a community of scholars—was readily captured by a 1970 survey of salaries and patterns of tenure and promotion. The report was the work of an IU campus AAUP committee chaired by Margaret Jean Intons-Peterson, a well-known cognitive psychologist. The results pointed to the glaring underrepresentation and lower salaries of women on the Bloomington faculty. Of the university's 1,300 faculty members, only 138 were women. Moreover, women were overrepresented in the lower ranks—26.9 percent of all the instructors and only 5.2 percent of full professors.[51]

Whereas for students the issue was residential life, the issue for women faculty and staff was the need to address inequalities in university policy, disparities embedded in tradition and routine practice, and bias—various elements of what researchers Kathleen Hall and Bernice Sandler would later describe as the "chilly climate."[52] The attention of women faculty and staff focused on childcare, personal safety, prevention of harassment, professional development and mentoring, tenure and promotion, and, increasingly, challenges associated not only with gender but also with race.

Established in 1972, IU's Office of Women's Affairs—a woman-directed and -centered administrative unit—stood alongside the advocacy centers established in response to demands by diverse student populations. This included IU's new Black Culture Center (founded in 1972, now renamed the Neal-Marshall Center to recognize IU's first male and female black graduates) and the Latino Cultural Center (La Casa, founded in 1973). Affirming the diversity among IU women, this cluster of advocacy centers provided multiple avenues for IU women—diverse in their affinities and social identities, backgrounds, and concerns—to connect to communities of support they found most meaningful and to join others in addressing campus issues they deemed most important.

Conceptualized by many nineteenth-century women's rights advocates as levers of equality, coeducation and the liberal arts curriculum were now scrutinized for biases. Scholars unmasked what feminist Florence Howe described bluntly as the "myths of coeducation," providing evidence that merely being admitted and educated alongside men was not inherently equitable and liberating.[53] IU scholars tapped into women's political groups, women's liberation and radical feminism, and the national currents of feminist scholarship that challenged old research paradigms, decentered the male experience as the norm, and sought to recover and elevate voices that were eclipsed from the liberal arts curriculum.[54] Jean Robinson, an IU faculty member in political science and dean of women's affairs from 1998 to 2003, later reflected, "When Women's Studies was born in the mid-1970s, politics was its midwife."[55]

The trajectory of women's studies at IU was shaped by the local campus context, but scholars frequently collaborated across the regional campuses and met once a year as the University Women's Studies Co-ordinating Council. In Bloomington, three literary scholars—Martha Vicinus, Susan Gubar, and Sandra Gilbert, the English department's only female professors—helped to establish IUB's early prominence as a center of women's studies research and teaching. In South Bend, Gloria Kaufman, a professor of English since 1967, started the speakers series that evolved into that campus's women's studies program, created a women's resource center, and served as IU South Bend's first affirmative action officer. And at IUPUI, scholars "changed minds" and gained traction for the idea of what became their women's studies program (known today as WOST) by simple but effective measures—faculty pitch-ins, posters about significant themes in women's history, and birthday parties to commemorate important women figures.[56]

With these pioneering efforts as a springboard, scholarship and teaching in women's studies at IU have matured into a full-scale academic department and evolved in tandem with theorizing and intellectual developments in the field. In Bloomington, for example, women's studies was founded in 1973, with its first faculty lines twenty years later, in 1992. In 1997, the program's name changed to gender studies, and in 2006 IU offered the first PhD in gender studies in the country.[57] Over these years, scholarly discussions of various feminisms, reflecting the discourse among scholars internationally and the activism of IU students, have brought into the curriculum and campus programing a more probing exploration of the lived realities of minoritized women and the various intersections of gender, class, ethnic, racial, and sexual identities and other social categories.[58] Proponents of coeducation in Sarah Parke Morrison's day had often seen the goals of coeducation as a question of access and women's advancement within the university.

In addition to the OWA efforts and curricular reform, the early 1970s, like the 1880s, saw a number of firsts for women at IU, reflecting the role of affirmative action and an emergent consciousness that brought long-delayed recognition of women's potential and achievements as faculty and administrators and, further, of the diversity among women. By way of example, in 1970, pioneer multicultural educator Martha E. Dawson returned to IU, her doctoral alma mater, as the first African American woman to hold the rank of tenured, full professor on the Bloomington faculty.[59] In 1974, Iris Rosa, an alumna and the first Latina to hold a faculty appointment at IU, was named the founding director of the African American Dance Company, a position she held for forty-three years. Slowly women began to be more visible in upper-level administrative roles. In 1972, Sylvia Bowman, chair of arts and sciences at Fort Wayne, was named chancellor of the IU Regional Campus Administration, becoming the first female chancellor at a Big Ten university. At the beginning of the next decade, 1980, Elaine Sloan was appointed the first female dean of libraries.

And, finally, women also made some inroads into all-male or nearly all-male advisory and governance structures within the coeducational university. In 1971, the Board of Aeons inducted its first female members. In 1971–72, Mary Scifres was elected the first female president of the Indiana University Student Association (IUSA). In 1978–79, women for the first time represented half of the university's student body and have done so up to the present. Since 1980 women have had greater representation on the board of trustees, including as student trustee, and in 1997 alumna Cora Smith Breckenridge (BA, 1959; MA,1963), who had served as secretary of her senior class in 1959, became IU's first African American female trustee.[60]

The last twenty-five years have seen yet another new chapter in coeducation. By the 1990s, the concept of woman—around which the early female deans and, later, members of women's liberation had galvanized—has seemed less inclusive. As minority student enrollments at IU grew, concerns about the campus climate were voiced. Students of color and their allies organized to demand curricular reform and the hiring of faculty of color and advocacy deans. The diverse needs and leadership of IU women became more apparent in this new era in which student activism centered on confronting bias and affirming diverse cultural and ethnic identities on the predominantly white campus. Latinas founded their own sorority, Gamma Phi Omega, in 1991 and rose as vocal advocates for racial sensitivity and justice on campus. Simultaneously, Asian and

Asian American women were able to build a powerful coalition across various student groups to help pave the way for an Asian culture center in 1998.[61] Most recently, in 2007, the opening of the First Nations Educational and Culture Center has provided a culturally supportive space for indigenous students.

In both symbolic and tangible ways, we are today the beneficiaries of the progress made by earlier generations of women in advancing women in education at IU. We are also beneficiaries of the post–World War II activists who championed their rights within the university and enlarged upon the gender-specific concern of whether and how to educate women to ask how we might best educate all students. In the spirit of the epic civil rights struggle, reformers of the 1960s sought to reenvision democracy—not simply to focus on the wants and needs of the majority but to elevate the welfare of the minority. Within this context, the conceptual underpinning of the coeducational university has evolved.

At its founding in 1820, IU was a single campus and exclusively male in the composition of its students, faculty, and trustees, but for most of its history IU has in fact identified as a coeducational university. As such, it has conceptualized its pedagogical task as educating men and women together—that is, its policies and practices related to coeducation have been based on a male and female binary and heterosexual norms. Influenced by the gay rights movement and responding to the destructiveness of homophobia, several student government organizations in the 1980s passed resolutions affirming that students identifying as lesbian, gay, and bisexual are an "integral part of the Campus" community.[62] In 1989, the Board of Aeons called for a campus center for gay, lesbian, and bisexual "advocacy, awareness, and support." Founded in 1994, the center, reflecting greater inclusiveness, added "transsexual" to its name in 1997 and eventually became the LGBTQ+ Center.

Reflecting the contemporary rights movement associated with evolving understandings of gender, the Bloomington administration, in its policy orientation, has moved to make the campus a more welcoming and inclusive place for members of the LGBTQIA+ community, transgender and gender nonconforming students, and others whose identities have been marginalized. Today, activists call attention to the persistent gender-related inequalities women faculty and students experience while at the same time being open to the fluidity of gender and connecting university policy to discussions of gender identity. The IUB campus is improving the availability of gender-neutral bathrooms, allows the use of preferred names on university identity cards, has seen the first transgender sorority sister speak publicly about "expanding Greek sisterhood," and sponsors a thematic residence hall community for students of all gender and sexual identities: Spectrum, in Teter Quad.[63]

This new era in coeducation, still a work in progress, seeks to build a university that is more inclusive—one that champions and sustains an educational environment that is coeducational in the broadest and deepest of senses, acknowledges gender identities and upholds the rights of all, and, by striving to provide all students with equitable opportunities, furthers IU's mission as a public university to serve democratic society well.

NOTES

The epigraph is from Sarah Parke Morrison to Alumni Building Committee, Correspondence, 1897–1913, Box 1, Indiana University Archives, Bloomington, Indiana. Morrison (1833–1919) enrolled in 1867, graduated in 1869, and earned her master's degree in 1872. She was appointed at IU as a tutor in 1873 and the next year was appointed as an adjunct professor of English.

1. Morrison's handwritten note about the all-male slate of candidates, June 3, 1906, and her note casting a vote for "some woman," March 5, 1910, are in Box 1, Librarian Folder, Morrison Papers, Indiana University Archives. Sarah Parke Morrison, "Some Sidelights of Fifty Years Ago," *Indiana University Alumni Quarterly* 6, no. 3 (October 1919): 530–35. A longer handwritten essay with similar content is Sarah Parke Morrison, "My Experience at State University," 1911, Series: Writings, 1911–1912, Box 1, Indiana University Archives. The author wishes to thank Ree Palmer, Pooja Saxena, and Stephanie T. X. Nguyen for research assistance in the preparation of this essay, which draws from a larger project.

2. Agnes Wells oversaw the daily lives of IU women in IU housing and cocurricular activities. Alice McDonald Nelson (University of Chicago, 1920) oversaw the construction, physical maintenance, and administration of IU housing, which during her forty-five-year IU career was one of the country's largest residential hall systems. See Alexandria Ruschman's profile of Nelson at https://blogs.iu.edu/bicentennialblogs/2020/05/21/ius-landlady-alice-mcdonald-nelson-and-the-evolution-of-ius-residence-halls/ (accessed January 3, 2021).

3. See Barbara Miller Solomon, *In the Company of Educated Women: A History of Women and Higher Education in America* (New Haven: Yale University Press, 1985). Examples of early women-centered histories are Dorothy McGuigan, *A Dangerous Experiment: 100 Years of Women at the University of Michigan* (Benton Harbor: R. W. Patterson Printing Company, 1970); Charlotte Williams Conable, *Women at Cornell: The Myth of Equality* (Ithaca: Cornell University Press, 1977); and Marian Swoboda's edited volumes on women at the University of Wisconsin (see University of Wisconsin-Madison Archives, "The History of Women at Uni-

versity of Wisconsin," https://search.library.wisc.edu/digital
/AUWWomen). Examples of later volumes include Polly Welts Kaufmann, ed.,
The Search for Equity: Women at Brown University, 1891–1991 (Hanover, NH: Brown
University Press, 1991); Ruth Bordin, *Women at Michigan: The "Dangerous Experiment," 1870s to the Present* (Ann Arbor, MI: University of Michigan Press, 2001);
Laurel Thatcher Ulrich, *Yards and Gates: Gender in Harvard and Radcliffe History*
(New York: Palgrave, 2004); and Rosalind Rosenberg, *Changing the Subject: How
Women of Columbia University Shaped the Way We Think about Sex and Politics*
(New York: Columbia University Press, 2006).

4. Frederick Rudolph, *The American College and University: A History* (New
York: Alfred A. Knopf, 1962), especially chapter 10; Laurence R. Veysey, *Emergence
of the American University* (Chicago: University of Chicago Press, 1965).

5. See, for example, Margaret A. Nash, ed., *Historical Studies in Education Series*
(New York: Palgrave Macmillan, 2017).

6. Helen Olin, *Women at the State University* (New York: G. P. Putnam Sons,
1909).

7. See Anna Tolman Smith, "Coeducation in the Schools and Colleges of the
United States," in *Report of the Commissioner of Education*, vol 1, 1903 (Washington,
DC: Government Printing Office, 1905), 1047. See May Wright Sewall, "The Education of Woman in the Western States," in *Woman's Work in America*, edited by Annie Nathan Meyer; with an introduction by Julia Ward Howe (New York: H. Holt
& Co., 1891), 71–77.

8. See Claudia Goldin and Lawrence F. Katz, "Putting the 'Co' in Education:
Timing, Reasons, and Consequences of College Coeducation from 1835–Present,"
Journal of Human Capital 5, no. 4 (winter 2011): 379; Christine D. Myers, *University
Coeducation in the Victorian Era: Inclusion in the United States and the United Kingdom* (New York: Palgrave Macmillan, 2010); and Doris Malkmus, "Origins of Coeducation in Antebellum Iowa," *Annals of Iowa* 58 (Spring 1999): 162–196, https://
doi.org/10.17077/0003-4827.10237.

9. Women remained the majority of students across the IU system after
1977–78. (Nationally, women became the majority of undergraduate students in
1979–80.) Female enrollment reached 50 percent of the total Bloomington campus enrollment by 1981–82 and surpassed men from 1984–85. Since 2014–15, IUB
enrollments have been roughly fifty-fifty for men and women. Student data for Indiana University are found in "Indiana Enrollment and Attendance (1824 to date)"
and IU Fact Book for 1977–78 and 1984–85, Reference File, Indiana University
Archives. For national data, see National Center for Education Statistics, *120 Years
of American Education: A Statistical Portrait* (Washington, DC, 2003), Table 23, 75.

10. The "Declaration of Sentiments" (signed in 1848 at Seneca Falls, New York),
reprinted in *The Essential Feminist Reader*, edited by Estelle B. Freedman (New
York: Modern Library, 2007), 57.

11. My reference to Seneca Falls is meant to emphasize the attention the convention attendees gave to education. The convention must be viewed within a history of activism for women's rights that is long and complicated by issues of race, class, ethnicity, and other markers of difference. See Lisa Tetrault, *The Myth of Seneca Falls: Memory and the Women's Suffrage Movement, 1848–1898* (Chapel Hill: University of North Carolina Press, 2014).

12. Sewall, "The Education of Woman in the Western States," 87.

13. For the First Nation's Land Acknowledgment, see https://firstnations .indiana.edu/land-acknowledgement/index.html.

14. For a vivid account of the challenging physical and political circumstances encountered by settlers and early college leaders, see David Demaree Banta, "History of Indiana University," in *Indiana University, 1820–1937*, ed. James A. Woodburn (Bloomington: Indiana University, 1940), 9–113; Samuel Bannister Harding, ed., *Indiana University, 1820–1904: Historical Sketch, Development of the Course of Instruction Bibliography* (Indianapolis: Wm. B. Burford, 1904); James Albert Woodburn, *Higher Education in Indiana* (Washington, DC: Government Printing Office, 1891), 84; Robert Carlton (Baynard Rush Hall), *The New Purchase: Or, Seven and a Half Years in the Far West* (Princeton: Princeton University Press, 1916).

15. Lee Ehman, "Monroe County Female Seminary," accessed June 22, 2020, https://monroehistory.org/wp-content/uploads/2019/12/Newsletter-Oct-Nov -2017.pdf.

16. Drawing from the French teacher training model of an "école normale," normal schools or normal departments at colleges and universities prepared high school graduates to enter the teaching profession. The normal program of study blended coursework (pedagogy, curriculum, and methods of instruction) and practice teaching in a graded "model" public school classroom.

17. For the concept of an "entering" or "opening" wedge see, May Wright Sewall, "The Education of Woman in the Western States," in *Woman's Work in America*, ed. Annie Nathan Meyer (New York: Henry Holt, 1891), 87. Later historians have used this concept to discuss women's education; see Margaret W. Rossiter, "Doctorates for American Women, 1868–1907," *History of Education Quarterly* 22, no. 2 (Summer 1982): 168. For information on the normal school, see Minutes of the Indiana University Board of Trustees, April 11, 1852; April 15, 1852; and August 4, 1853.

18. Discontinued in 1870, the Normal Department was reinstated in 1886 as the Department of Pedagogy, later renamed the Department of Education.

19. Sewall, "Education of Woman," 72. Jenkinson was an IU trustee from 1866 to 1870 and 1875 to 1906 and served as president from 1889 to 1906.

20. Quoted in Morrison, "Some Sidelights," 531. We have few original records related to Morrison's petition, but her memories in "Some Sidelights" are useful and a fuller discussion is found in Sarah Parke Morrison, "My Experience at State

University," June 8, 1911, Sarah Parke Morrison Papers, 1855–1913, C54, Box 1, Folder Writings, 1911–12, Indiana University Archives.

21. US Department of Health, Education, and Welfare, National Center for Education Statistics, *120 Years of American Education: A Statistical Portrait* (Washington, DC: Government Printing Office, 1973), 75, Table 23; 76, Table 24; 78, Table 25.

22. This count is based on names. Theophilus A. Wylie's history also notes that twelve women followed Morrison; see *Indiana University: Its History from 1820, When Founded, to 1890: With Biographical Sketches of Its Presidents, Professors and Graduates: And a List of its Students from 1820 to 1887* (Indianapolis: Wm. B. Burford, 1890), 75.

23. Dina Kellams, "An Update on Miss Carrie," *Blogging Hoosier History*, last modified September 1, 2015, https://blogs.libraries.indiana.edu/iubarchives/tag /carrie-parker/; and Dina M. Kellams, "Pioneering Students of Color: Carrie Parker and Frances Marshall" (chap. 3 in this volume). For a discussion of racism in Indiana history, see James H. Madison, *A Lynching in the Heartland: Race and Memory in America* (New York: Palgrave, 2001). For one IU administrator's awareness of IU's proximity to the Jim Crow South, see Alice Nelson to P. J. Hill, August 25, 1948, Integration of Housing, C178.B7, Housing Inquiries for Negro Students 1947–48, Indiana University Archives.

24. For alumna Kate Milner Rabb's memories of being one of four women in a class of twenty, see "Reminiscences of '86," *Indiana Alumni Quarterly* 13, no. 1 (January 1926): 3–8.

25. "Indiana University Philomathean Society Records, 1836–1891," C221, Indiana University Archives, http://webapp1.dlib.indiana.edu/findingaids/view?doc .view=entire_text&docId=InU-Ar-VAA2756.

26. Sarah J. Reynolds, "Early Scientific Women of Indiana University and Their Impact" (chap. 4 in this volume). Jordan was IU president from 1885 until 1891, when he left to become Stanford's founding president.

27. Sewall was well-known in Indiana for her leadership in promoting women's rights, education, and civic improvement. She was known internationally for her suffragist activities. Chair of the executive committee of the National Woman Suffrage Association from 1882 to 1890, Wright joined Frances Willard in planning the national meeting to mark the fortieth anniversary of the Seneca Falls Convention.

28. Colleen K. Pauwels, "Tamar Althouse Scholz, First Woman Law Graduate," *Indiana University Law Update* 10, no. 2 (Summer 1992): 10, https://www .repository.law.indiana.edu/facpub/959.

29. Katherine Badertscher, "'The Sharp Sword of the New Alliance,' Edna Henry and the IU School of Social Work" (chap. 10 in this volume).

30. Angela Bowen Potter, "Learning Human Anatomy: Women and the Changing Student Body at the Indiana University School of Medicine, 1907–2007" (chap. 8 in this volume).

31. See Jana Nidiffer, *Pioneering Deans of Women: More than Wise and Pious Matrons* (New York: Teachers College Press, 2000); Jana Nidiffer and Carolyn Bashaw, eds., *Women Administrators in Higher Education: Historical and Contemporary Perspectives* (Albany: State University of New York Press, 2001).

32. Lois Kimball Mathews, *The Dean of Women* (Boston: Houghton Mifflin Company, 1915); Katherine Rothenberger, "An Historical Study of the Position of Dean of Women at Indiana University" (master's thesis, Indiana University, 1942). For the role of early deans of women in developing student affairs, see Nidiffer, *Pioneering Deans of Women*; and Kelly Sartorius, "A Coeducational Pathway to Political and Economic Citizenship: Women's Student Government and a Philosophy and Practice of Women's U.S. Higher Coeducation between 1890 and 1945," in *Women's Higher Education in the United States: New Historical Perspectives*, edited by Margaret A. Nash (New York: Palgrave Macmillan, 2017), 164–84.

33. As of 1873, only three of the country's seven coeducational state universities had yet to enroll 100 students or more. Women's enrollment was comparatively small: Indiana University had 174 men and 16 women; Iowa State University had 146 men and 31 women; and University of Michigan had 396 men and 28 women. See Commissioner of Education Report, vol. 1, 1903, 1065. By the end of the century, IU women's enrollment had grown significantly: the June 1899 enrollment included 318 women and 732 men. See President's Report June 8, 1899, C654 B1, Presidents' Reports to the Indiana University Board of Trustees, 1881–1947, Indiana University Libraries Archives.

34. The Women's League—an antecedent to the Women's Self Government Association (1920; WSGA) and later the Association of Women Students (1927; AWS)—aimed to help students adjust to university life. It sought to "promote a wholesome and democratic social life" and to strengthen social connections among women across various parts, units, and campus affiliations—students, faculty, wives, and staff. See Whitney Olthoff, "The Association of Women Students: Advocating for Women," *Blogging Hoosier History*, last modified July 9, 2012, https://blogs.libraries.indiana.edu/iubarchives/2012/07/09/association-of-women -students. See also President's Report to the Trustees, June 10, 1896, Indiana University Libraries Archives.

35. Frances Morgan Swain was already married when she began her studies in 1887. She completed her AB in mathematics in 1893 at Stanford, where her husband, Joseph Swain, had accepted a faculty position.

36. *Commissioner of Education Report*, 1903, Vol. 1 (Washington, DC: Government Printing Office, 1905), 1064.

37. Historians have pointed to the widening influence of Bryn Mawr College's distinctive system of women's self-government as Bryn Mawr alumnae assumed deanships in colleges and universities across the country. Bryn Mawr graduate Anna Crosby, who became dean of women at Wisconsin in 1897, founded the first

women's self-government association at a public university when she arrived in Madison. See Lois Kimball Mathews, *The Dean of Women* (Boston: Houghton Mifflin Company, 1915), 127–149, esp. 127. Many thanks to reference librarian Rebecca Payne and archivist Kayci Harris at the University of Wisconsin–Madison Libraries for information related to Dean Crosby.

38. Edna Munro, *History of the Department of Physical Education for Women at Indiana University* (Bloomington.: Indiana University, 1971).

39. Charles R. Van Hise, "Educational Tendencies at State Universities," *Educational Review* 34 (December 1907): 504–20; *Report of the Commissioner of Education* (Washington, DC: Government Printing Office, 1909), Vol 1., 178–186.

40. Lowe was born in 1867, the same year coeducation was introduced to IU. She graduated from IU with an AB in Greek in 1888 and received her master of arts in 1889. Soon after, she married IU alum William J. Bryan (AB 1884; master's degree, 1886). Symbolizing their equitable union, she took his last name, and he adopted her surname as his middle name.

41. Though IU's enrollment by gender was not actually fifty-fifty, women's enrollments were substantial. Enrollment data for this period are not available by gender and field of study. President's Reports and Reports to the Legislative Visiting Committee, October 24, 1921, 93, C654, Presidents' Reports to the Indiana University Board of Trustees, 1881–1947, Box 9, IU Libraries University Archives, Bloomington, Indiana.

42. Carla Yanni, *Living on Campus: An Architectural History of the American Dormitory* (Minneapolis: University of Minnesota Press, 2019).

43. Frank O. Beck, *Some Aspects of Race Relations at Indiana University, My Alma Mater* (Bloomington: privately printed, 1959); James H. Capshew, *Herman B Wells: The Promise of the American University* (Bloomington and Indianapolis: Indiana University Press and Indiana Historical Society Press, 2012).

44. Margaret W. Rossiter, *Women Scientists in America: Before Affirmative Action, 1940–1972* (Baltimore, MD: Johns Hopkins University Press, 1998), 34–35; Kathryn Tuttle, "What Became of the Dean of Women? Changing Roles for Women Administrators in American Higher Education, 1940–1980" (PhD diss., University of Kansas, 1996); Kelly C. Sartorius, "Kate Hevner Mueller: Women's Influence and Marginalization at Indiana University," chap. 11 in this volume.

45. In 1948–49, the IU student body of 8,151 included 155 Black men and 71 Black women. Theodore B. Cooper, "Adjustment Problems of Undergraduate Negroes Enrolled at Indiana University," (PhD diss., Indiana University, 1952), 183. See also Dormitory Committee Minutes on Integration, June 1947, C310, Indiana University Halls of Residence Committee minutes, 1939–71, Box 1, Folder September 1946–June 1947; Alice Nelson, Margaret Wilson, and R. L. Shoemaker (Residential Halls Committee) to H. W. Jordan, April 13, 1948; Jordan to J. H. Franklin, April 16, 1948, Indiana University Archives.

46. Andrea Walton, "The Dynamics of Mission and Market in the Coeducation Debates at Columbia University in 1889 and 1983," *History of Education* 31, no. 6 (November 2002): 589–610.

47. Mary Ann Wynkoop, *Dissent in the Heartland: The Sixties at Indiana University* (Bloomington: Indiana University Press, 2002), 138.

48. Quoted in Wynkoop, *Dissent in the Heartland*, 142. For general background on the "awakening of activism" at IU in the mid-1960s, see Wynkoop, *Dissent in the Heartland*, 22–48.

49. Student Senate R-17, September 28, 1967. Barbara Mary Varchol, "Study of Student Concerns at Indiana University and Purdue University from 1961–1969," (PhD diss., Indiana University, 1971), 32–33.

50. Wynkoop, *Dissent in the Heartland*, 135–52.

51. "Study of the Status of Women Faculty at Indiana University, Bloomington Campus," American Association of University Professors Committee on the Status of Women, January 1971, accession number 0556, Women's Status, Dean of Faculties, President Joseph Lee Sutton papers, Indiana University Archives; Mary Ann Wynkoop, "The Women's Movement: An Idea Whose Time Had Come," in *Dissent in the Heartland*, 135–52, esp. 150. Although gender was the focus of the report, one could add there was a lack of racial diversity on campus.

52. Herman C. Hudson, "The Black Faculty at Indiana University, Bloomington 1970–1993," Reference Files, African American Affairs, Indiana University Archives; Roberta M. Hall and Bernice R. Sandler, "The Classroom Climate: A Chilly One for Women?" (Washington, DC: Association of American Colleges, 1982).

53. Florence Howe, *Myths of Coeducation: Selected Essays, 1964–1983* (Bloomington: Indiana University Press, 1984); Rosalind Rosenberg, "The Limits of Access: The History of Coeducation in America" in *Women and Higher Education in American History: Essays from the Mount Holyoke Sesquicentennial Symposia*, ed. John Mack Faragher and Florence Howe (New York: Norton, 1988), 107–29; Linda Eisenmann, "Reconsidering a Classic: Assessing the History of Women's Higher Education a Dozen Years after Barbara Solomon," *Harvard Educational Review* 67, no. 4 (Winter 1997): 689–717; and Andrea Walton, "The Dynamics of Mission and Market: Debates over Coeducation at Columbia University in 1889 and 1983," *History of Education* 31, 6 (November 2002): 589–610, especially the section "Beyond Access" at 591–93.

54. Elizabeth Minnich, Jean F. O'Barr, and Rachel Rosenfeld, *Reconstructing the Academy: Women's Education and Women's Studies* (Chicago: University of Chicago Press, 1988); Ellen Carol DuBois, Gail Paradise Kelly, Elizabeth Lapovsky Kennedy, Carolyn W. Korsmeyer, and Lillian S. Robinson, *Feminist Scholarship: Kindling in the Groves of Academe* (Urbana: University of Illinois, 1985); and Elizabeth Minnich, *Transforming Knowledge* (Philadelphia: Temple University Press, 1990).

55. Jean Robinson, "From Politics to Professionalism: Cultural Change in Women's Studies," in *Women's Studies on Its Own: A Next Wave Reader in Institutional Change*, ed. Robyn Wiegman (Durham, NC: Duke University Press, 2002), 202–11, quote at 202.

56. Oral history, Martha Vicinus, March 23, 1977, #77–008, interview by Katherine R. Martin. Women's History, 1977–80, Project No. ohrc106; Indiana University Center for Documentary Research and Practice, Bloomington, Indiana. See Catherine A. Dobris, Rachel Jean Turner, and Lorée B. Wilcox, "We Changed Minds": *A History of the Women's Studies Program at IUPUI* (chap. 14 in this volume).

57. For a brief history, see https://genderstudies.indiana.edu/about/history .html.

58. Stephanie Thanh Xuan Nguyen, "'Little Steps of Courage Forward': How Asian American Women Leaders Fought for Culturally Supportive Spaces at Indiana University Bloomington" and Ebelia Hernández and Merylou Rodriguez, "The History of the First Latina Sorority at IU Established during an Era of Student Activism" (chaps. 6 and 7 in this volume).

59. Richard Davis Johnson, IU class of 1950, was IU's first Black faculty member. He became an instructor of percussion in 1951 and remained at the university for thirty-two years. See Robert Bruce Slater, "The First Black Faculty Members at the Nation's 50 Flagship State Universities," *The Journal of Blacks in Higher Education* no. 39 (Spring 2003): 122.

60. Cora Smith Breckenridge, oral history interview with Barbara Truesdall, June 19, 2009, https://iu.aviaryplatform.com/collections/123/collection_resources /10111?embed=true.

61. See chapters 6 and 7 (note 56).

62. Quoted in Board of Aeons, Proposal for a University Funded Center for Gay, Lesbian and Bisexual Advocacy, Awareness and Support (April 1989), Box One, Indiana University LGBTQ+ Culture Center records, 1970–2018, C435, Indiana University Archives.

63. Giselle Krachenfels, "Expanding Greek Sisterhood," accessed December 1, 2017, https://studybreaks.com/students/greek-life-transgender.

MAKINGS OF MORRISON

The Legend and Legacy of Indiana University's First Female Student

TANNER N. TERRELL

A native of Salem, Indiana, Tanner N. Terrell grew up often hearing about a well-known hometown daughter and iconic figure in IU history—Sarah Parke Morrison (1833–1919), the first woman to be admitted to the college, to earn a bachelor's degree, and, later, to join the faculty. Terrell began this research for a doctoral seminar paper, intrigued by the often-recounted story of the five dollars Sarah received from her father, an IU trustee, as encouragement to write the now historic petition for women's admission to IU. Moving beyond lore, Terrell explores family and local history records to provide a portrait of Morrison's upbringing in southern Indiana and the factors that shaped her aspirations. Grounded in her Quaker roots and her family's commitment to female education, Morrison advocated for women in higher education for years after she departed from IU and retired from academic life. This research inspired Terrell to submit a nomination (recently approved) for an Indiana State Historical Marker to honor Morrison in her hometown of Salem, Indiana.

> What if no young woman should step forward to enter those hitherto unnecessarily closed doors? Wouldn't people think and say, "They don't want (to vote!) to enter."
>
> —Sarah Parke Morrison

SARAH PARKE MORRISON WAS INVIGORATED by the crisp fall air as she stepped onto the dusty footpaths of the Seminary Square campus and walked to the classroom where she would attend her first IU lecture. Years later, she could still recall vividly that momentous day in 1867. It was the beginning of a new term at the state university in Bloomington and her first day of college. But in truth, this was not actually Morrison's *first* day of college. Thirty-four years old when she entered IU, Morrison had already studied at two of the country's finest institutions of higher learning for women: she had graduated from Mount Holyoke Seminary a full decade earlier and then attended Vassar College and Williams College briefly.[1]

Though one of IU's new matriculants, Morrison was quite familiar with the Seminary Square campus—her family had long-standing ties to the university and had once resided in Bloomington. Sarah's father, John Morrison, was one of Indiana University's early faculty members and had served on the board of trustees as both a member and its president.[2] One can only imagine the upwelling of mixed emotions—part pride, part reluctance, and perhaps even a measure of indignation—that swept over Morrison as she traversed the familiar campus footpath that particular morning with a new sense of purpose. Simply put, she viewed her physical presence on IU's all-male campus that historic day, and in the months (and years) ahead, as a form of activism. Earlier, in the spring of 1867, she had successfully petitioned the IU trustees to admit women, inspired to champion the cause on behalf of her sex. Now, entering the classroom, she gained the further distinction of becoming Indiana University's first female undergraduate. In doing so, she also became one of the earliest women in the country to be admitted to college on equal terms as men.

Histories of IU and timelines of women in higher education make note of Morrison's historic importance as the first woman student, graduate, and faculty member at IU, but we have few glimpses into the woman behind those noteworthy public actions. What shaped her path to her 1867 admission to the university? What motivated her to be a pioneer in collegiate coeducation? Is there a deeper story than the widely told but overly simplistic anecdote of IU trustee John Morrison giving an incentive of five dollars to his daughter, in hopes she would draft the petition to bring coeducation to the state university? What prompted her, already a graduate of Mt. Holyoke, to pen the petition for women's admission at IU—and then to enroll? This biographical sketch looks beyond the notion of famous first to explore Sarah Parke Morrison's life and education in richer detail.

A FAMILY TRADITION: PIONEERS AND ACTIVISTS

When IU was founded in 1820 and held its first classes a few years later, higher education was just taking root in the new state of Indiana, organized from the former Northwest Territory. No college in the United States had yet to admit women. Indeed, questions of women's intellectual power and right to higher education were still widely debated throughout the country when Sarah Parke Morrison was born on September 7, 1833, in the small southern Indiana town of Salem (Washington County).[3] It was her good fortune to be the daughter of well-educated parents who believed unabashedly in the power of the female intellect and, therefore, supported providing women with access to high-quality learning. The first of eight children born to Catherine (Morris) Morrison and John I. Morrison, Sarah spent her formative years in southern Indiana, experiencing girlhood in two quite different but similarly prominent hubs of advanced learning—Salem and Bloomington. Her birthplace, Salem, was known as the Athens of the West for its unusually wide array of schools and institutes that attracted pupils (male and female alike) from across Indiana and nearby states. When she was eight years old, her family left Salem and took up residence in Bloomington, approximately forty-five miles northwest of Salem. Bloomington was the seat of Indiana University, the state's institution of higher learning. The young Morrison would reside there while her father held a professorship in languages at IU.[4] In retrospect, the synergistic combination of parental encouragement of a young daughter's curiosity and the stimulating nature of daily life in these two distinctive southern Indiana settings shaped the contours of Sarah's early education. Indeed, one could hardly imagine a more powerful environment for a young woman's intellectual aspirations to grow and quicken.

Catherine and John Morrison were both well-educated and progressive in their social and educational views. Neither had been born in Indiana. Both hailed from families that had helped to settle the new state. John I. Morrison (1806–82) had immigrated to Indiana at age eighteen from Pennsylvania and graduated from Miami University in Oxford, Ohio, in 1828—four years after the institution enrolled its first students.[5] Degree in hand, he returned to Salem and taught at several schools before becoming headmaster of the Washington County Seminary. His reputation as a stern, skillful educator earned him the sobriquet "the Master."[6] Shortly after his appointment as headmaster, John asked Catherine Morris (a former student) for her hand in marriage. The couple wed on September 11, 1832, before a justice of the peace. It was a simple civil ceremony as neither John's Presbyterian nor Catherine's Quaker religious traditions permitted nuptials between individuals of different faiths to be performed within their houses of worship.[7]

Sarah Parke Morrison's mother, Catherine Morris, had been born near Albemarle Sound, North Carolina, in 1812 to a Quaker family that was increasingly uneasy with the prevalence of slavery in their region.[8] Catherine was just four years old when the Morris family joined the wave of southern Friends who migrated northward, to free states like Indiana, to escape the immorality of living in a slave-dependent economy.

The Morris family settled just east of Salem, Indiana, in 1816—the year of Indiana's statehood. As a teenager, Catherine traveled alone back East to enroll at the prestigious Westtown School, a Quaker boarding school near Philadelphia, Pennsylvania. As Sarah Parke Morrison recalled in her three-volume family history *Among Ourselves* (vol. 2 details her mother's life and heritage), the Morris family made their daughter Catherine's advanced education a priority, even though she had a number of brothers and the cost was significant. As Sarah explained, her grandparents lent their financial and emotional support because Catherine's "capabilities deserved it."[9] At Westtown, Catherine applied herself to her daily lessons and had ample opportunity to develop the talent her parents discerned in her. She followed what might be considered a progressive curriculum for a young woman at the time—philosophy, geography, astronomy, botany, and algebra.[10]

Upon completing her studies at Westtown, Catherine returned to Salem, married John in 1832, and, not long after, worked alongside her husband in opening the Salem Female Collegiate Institute. This was an ambitious, collaborative enterprise. The classroom building was considerably larger than the Washington County Seminary, where John had been headmaster—three stories and a basement—and the Morrisons staffed the institute with female teachers hired from the East. These young women teachers would ensure the rigor of the education offered at the young institute and provided models of educated womanhood to their female students. In 1841, at the start of the ninth session of the institute, John Morrison made clear the value both he and Catherine placed on high-quality teachers: "It is believed that the day has passed, when individuals, who have been unsuccessful in other pursuits for the want of mad character, suitable literary attainments, and skill in their profession, will be employed to mold the character and sustain the literature of the present and future generations."[11]

AT HOME IN EDUCATION

To say that Sarah Parke Morrison was born into the world of higher education would be only slight creative hyperbole. While not Sarah's actual birthplace, the Salem Female Collegiate Institute was central in her early life—her childhood home and the setting for her most powerful early learning experiences. The Morrison family moved into quarters on the third floor of the institute when Sarah was still a young child. As such, Sarah grew up surrounded by students and teachers, in a physical and family environment that was defined by education. "As the home life was in the Institute, and the Institute invaded the home life, it has seemed impossible to separate them," Morrison wrote in her published reflections on her childhood.[12]

Some of Sarah's earliest memories of her childhood in the institute quarters are of being surrounded by the "big girls," as she called the institute students.[13] These young women had come from various parts of Indiana and even traveled to Salem from other states to attend the highly regarded school.[14] These girls, along with the female teachers also employed there, filled Morrison's childhood with inspiring examples of women applying their intellect in two different but interconnected roles: pupil and teacher. These memories, coupled with the sights and sounds of her mother and father collaborating to operate the institute, instilled in Sarah an appreciation of women's intellectual and organizational abilities and a philosophy of women in education that was progressive for her day.

One might say, then, given Sarah's early years at the institute, that her own education never so much began as it merely became increasingly structured with the passing years. Her mother's Quaker faith was an early influence, imbuing the young girl with the discipline and interest that would propel her academically and professionally. Sarah later recalled, "At Sabbath School I did manage to learn verses, hundreds of them, and began to be very fond of verse, rhyme, and things bettered in some respects as I learned better how to take care of myself."[15]

By 1840, the reputations of the Washington County Seminary and the Salem Female Collegiate Institute as model institutions providing exceptional instruction captured the attention of President Andrew Wylie at the fledgling state university in Bloomington. Wylie himself traveled to Salem to offer John Morrison the position of chair of the Ancient Languages Department.[16] At the time, the state institution, founded in 1820, was still quite small, with only around sixty-four students.[17] By comparison, the Morrison family's private Female Institute enrolled approximately two hundred students.[18] It would take time and talent to build IU's intellectual foundation. Answering Wylie's call to join the early IU faculty, John Morrison moved his family to Bloomington.[19] Sarah was then eight years old.

In Bloomington, John Morrison served Indiana University as a professor and department chair for three years. Whatever its intellectual rewards, the position did not bring financial security. The fledgling institution, lacking an endowment, struggled to balance its books and often paid professors *in scrip*.[20] But young Sarah, as a child far removed from campus-related challenges, was swept up in the excitement of Bloomington. The college town was a community where educators, like her father, were held in high esteem and weekends promised faculty dinners and parties.[21] However, the Morrison family returned to Salem in 1844, after only a few years in Bloomington. According to the account Morrison provides in her family history, *Among Ourselves*, the family moved in part because of the young college's tenuous finances. Once settled back in Salem, Morrison resumed her studies at her parents' institute, and life continued much as it had prior to the time spent in Bloomington.

By her teenage years, though, Morrison had matured intellectually and took more delight in her studies. "I read papers and learned to devour stories. I do not remember of much active pleasure, though I had playing; running in the air; going to Grandpa's; to Sunday—'Sabbath School;' out to Friends' and Quaker Meeting."[22] The blossoming interest in education Morrison described was no doubt influenced by the values exemplified by her parents. In Catherine and John, Sarah Morrison had two well-educated parents who were themselves passionate not just about schooling but also about ensuring these opportunities regardless of sex. In the 1830s, promoting this inclusive, equitable view of education was nothing short of social activism. Moreover, Morrison's parents functioned as partners to manage and educate at their Male Seminary and Female Institute. While there is no doubt that her father's educational accomplishments had their impact, Sarah's mother—guided by Quaker values and unhesitant to buck gender norms—surely emboldened her daughter to continue the family tradition.

AN EDUCATION IN THE EAST

Sarah Parke Morrison remained in Salem until completing her education at the Institute in 1853. Then, as her mother, Catherine, had done years before, Sarah left behind the comforts of family and home in Indiana and traveled alone to the East to take advantage of the educational opportunities there. She enrolled at Mary Lyon's Mount Holyoke Seminary (now College) in 1854.[23] Morrison graduated with a bachelor of arts degree in 1857 and served as a faculty member at Glendale Female College in Ohio for one year. She then returned home to Indiana to teach for a time before traveling back east to Williams College, in Massachusetts, to complete postgraduate work. When Vassar College opened to students in 1865, Morrison moved to New York to serve as a pupil teacher. "This was my first experience of a real college," she wrote of her time at Vassar, "and the difference between it and the female seminaries and colleges, so-called, I had attended was very marked and delightful, though we had it in the others, especially Mt. Holyoke, the benefit of lectures and professors and presidents even of the New England college, who gave us the same courses they gave in their respective seats."[24] During these years, Morrison discovered the intellectual importance higher education served in her own development. Her reflective quote accentuates the degree to which she valued the opportunity to learn from the most talented scholars.

By the time Sarah Parke Morrison returned to Indiana from Vassar, the Morrison family was spending most of its time in Indianapolis and Bloomington. Her father was serving as Indiana state treasurer while others in the Salem community managed the seminary and institute.[25] For her part, Sarah, having just spent ten years furthering her education, was ready to begin a teaching career and eager to devote her time and energies to serving the community and various social causes and interests. She did not yet know that one cause would soon have her back in the classroom—a student once again.

PETITION, DECISION, AND MATRICULATION

In the aftermath of the Civil War, many academic institutions, especially in the country's midwestern and western regions, began to adopt coeducation. In some cases, the decision was a matter of financial expediency. In others, there was an orchestrated campaign among supporters of women's educational rights. In Indiana, coeducation could be found in many of the state's county seminaries as well as in more than a few of the private church-related institutions. There was even a brief experiment with coeducational teacher training that involved IU and Bloomington's Monroe Female Seminary. But with IU's half-century mark just a few years off, Hoosier women had yet to enroll in baccalaureate studies at the state university.[26]

During an 1866–67 academic year meeting of the Indiana University Board of Trustees, trustee Isaac Jenkinson, of Allen County, Indiana, offered a resolution to admit female students to the same studies and standing as males.[27] Jenkinson was a known proponent of coeducation and had been instrumental in opening Fort Wayne Female College (now Taylor University) to both sexes.[28] Other members of the board were less enthusiastic; the resolution failed, with Jenkinson casting the only vote in favor of the measure. Perhaps his petition failed because the request was hypothetical—Jenkinson was not advocating on behalf of any particular female aspirant. Regardless, change was not far off. Less than one year after Jenkinson's defeat, Sarah Parke Morrison would be admitted and enroll as an Indiana University student, pursuing a baccalaureate degree with her all-male cohort.

Unfortunately, original records related to Sarah Parke Morrison's petition and the subsequent beginnings of coeducation at IU are sparse. Much of what we do know about the petition has been told to us by Sarah. Morrison's lengthy handwritten manuscript dating from 1911, "My Experience at State University," became the basis for a profile in the *Indianapolis Star* and an essay, "Some Sidelights of Fifty Years Ago," published in the October 1919 issue of the *Indiana University Alumni Quarterly*. In all versions of the petition story, Morrison describes an exchange with her father, John Morrison, a former university trustee then serving as Indiana's state treasurer, as he prepared to travel to Bloomington for the university graduation ceremony: "One day father, who was President of the Board, and soon to go to Bloomington to Commencement, said to me that he thought the time was about ripe for the admission of women; and that if I would prepare an appeal to that effect he would present it, and to show his interest would give me five dollars. So I prepared it and offered to read it to him, but he said No, that he would hear it there and took it, and I the bill."[29]

Over the years, newspaper accounts and popular writings about Sarah Parke Morrison have amusingly highlighted this vignette—the five-dollar transaction between father and daughter—with such headlines as "IU's First Female Student Admitted after Fatherly 'Bribe.'"[30] But the notion of a bribe trivializes Sarah's motivation, the commitment to women's educational rights father and daughter shared, and Sarah's place in IU history. Any suggestion that Sarah acted upon a financial incentive fails to capture her personal commitment to the cause of coeducation and gender equity overall—a cause to which she would devote her life. Perhaps rather than a bribe, her father's five dollars can be better seen as a payment—a contract for work—or as a token of recognition of his daughter's professional writing skills. No doubt John Morrison, an experienced trustee, knew an official appeal to the state university needed to be well-conceived and well-written to receive full, earnest consideration from the board. He even, in anticipation of board deliberations, asked Sarah to accompany him to Bloomington on the chance that the board of trustees might request to speak with the appeal's author. This was far more than a whimsical fatherly bribe or a daughter's impulsive action.

As it turned out, Sarah was never asked to address to the IU board, but her petition did receive their full attention. On Commencement Day 1867, family friend Richard Owen (a doctor and Indiana University professor) rushed to the Wylie home, where Sarah Parke Morrison was staying, and delivered the exciting news: "The law had been examined, and finding no impediment, the

Board had declared the doors of the University open to young women upon the same terms as to young men."[31] But the measure passed by the narrowest of margins—a vote of 4–3.[32]

As Morrison attended commencement festivities with her father, she likely felt a sense of accomplishment. She had used her preferred weapon of choice, the pen, to deliver a mortal blow to women's exclusion from the state university, but the appeal was made on principle, not for her personal benefit. She had been educated at some of the finest institutions for women in the East *after* receiving significant instruction at the school for women founded and run by her own parents in Salem. As Morrison relates in her accounts, she soon came to realize that her engagement in the issue of women at IU was not over. Latin Professor Cyrus M. Dodd's observation that further action might be needed broke the celebratory mood and came as "a cloud on the sunny horizon." Morrison had written the successful petition but, as Dodd urged, might also "have to come and fill the breach" and enroll as the institution's first female student should no others apply.[33]

Thus began a summer of anxiety for Sarah Parke Morrison as she considered the public ramifications of seeing no woman immediately step forward to avail herself of the hard-won opportunity. When Morrison returned to the topic of becoming IU's first female student in a 1911 letter, she recalled her personal torment as she weighed the situation and the difficult decision of whether to enroll: "What if no young woman should step forward to enter those hitherto unnecessarily closed doors? Wouldn't people think and say, 'They don't want (to vote!) to enter. All that discussion and fuss and appeal even were foolish, as they have proved futile. They, the young women after all know as their parents know, what is best for them. Let them continue to go to their "Female Colleges" and avoid the terrible risks of such association as they would have in classes with young men. Let us continue to save professors and communities from embarrassment—yea scandal.'"[34]

Though Morrison delayed acting as long as she could, as fall approached she grew increasingly worried the possibility of historic change was slipping away. "No woman, after men had declared the door open?" she ruminated.[35] Morrison's convictions compelled her to ensure that at least one woman enrolled during the institution's first coeducational baccalaureate session. The decision to enroll was not taken lightly. She had been out of school for some time, and requirements like Greek presented a particular challenge. She felt the pressure not simply to pass the course but to excel. Morrison knew that she would inevitably be the standard-bearer for her sex. "And if one could slip along, it must not be the elective woman, who must show for the credit of her sex that her brain was fully as capable as that of the male. That woman must come up to the mark. Must be careful to establish no precedent injurious to her interests."[36]

Morrison also received some cautionary words, perhaps even opposition, from concerned family members. While confident of her intellectual abilities, they encouraged her to disregard any pressure to "fill the breach." Some felt Sarah, a well-educated woman now in her thirties, had no obligation to go "if no one was grateful or appreciated the privilege."[37] Sarah's mother expressed concern for her daughter's well-being—a concern echoed by Morrison herself, who recognized she "was never in robust health."[38] One can imagine that together these concerns and the financial expense of being a college student might have dissuaded Morrison from acting on any sense of personal responsibility to ensure women's presence at the university. But Morrison, who grew up with the example of her own parents' commitment to gender equality in education, saw no other option: "I simply had to go."[39]

THE LIFE OF AN IU COED

IU, like most cash-strapped midwestern state universities, had no dormitories in the late 1860s. Students were expected to make their own arrangements with relatives or one of Bloomington's many private boardinghouses. Morrison arranged to stay in the home of family friends Professor Theophilus and Rebecca Wylie, doing light housework to offset the cost of her room and board. The Wylie and Morrison families remained close from John's first stint as a professor of ancient languages at IU, with the Morrisons even naming one of Sarah's brothers after Theophilus. The boarding arrangement gave Sarah a safe environment while undertaking her studies but was less than fully satisfactory, at least for her hosts. Letters preserved at the Wylie House written by Theophilus Wylie's wife, Rebecca Wylie, and daughter Louisa Boisen Wylie reveal that the Wylie women found "Sallie," as they cryptically referred to Sarah, to be "selfish" and her presence in the household a frustration.[40] For her part, Sarah wrote publicly of the generous housing arrangement provided by the Wylie family, "But I went to B[loomington] to prepare and paid my way by light work for Mrs. Wylie, who didn't have me pay for my salt hardly."[41] Whatever aggravations existed, the strong bond that endured over decades between the two families overshadowed them.

The morning of Tuesday, September 17, 1867, must have felt typical in so many ways and exceptional in so many others. The routine of preparing for the first day of classes at a new institution was an experience that Morrison knew well—certainly much better than most of the young women who enrolled the next term. To be pursuing another baccalaureate degree, this time in her early thirties, surely gave her the sensation of déjà vu. The setting was also familiar. Bloomington, the university campus, and its employees were all part of her childhood. But the circumstances were historic—and she knew it. On this Tuesday, Sarah Parke Morrison would take her place alongside 132 men as Indiana University's first female undergraduate student.[42]

Years later, recalling that first day on campus, Morrison described her self-consciousness of being the first female student in the otherwise all-male academic setting:

> It was the fashion then to wear large sun hats, tied with a rather broad ribbon going over the crown and tied under the chin. The young men were not dangerous to me nor I to them, but I was thankful for the protection that hat afforded me from six hundred eyes presumably furtively "casting a sly glance at me." No one could have been in more favorable circumstances. Bloomington was an old home. Everyone treated me with profound respect, i.e. who had occasion to notice me at all and after a little while I suppose the hat was laid aside, possibly never worn in recitation except for the first day or two.[43]

Because of her previous schooling at Mt. Holyoke, Vassar, and Williams, Morrison began her Indiana University career as a sophomore studying English literature. Throughout her life, she found great satisfaction in both reading and writing. She spent her Saturdays completing literary exercises in the works of Dickens, Longfellow, and Hawthorne, among others. Gender expectations entered not so much as questions of whether Morrison could do the same work as her male counterparts but as how she might demonstrate her learning and understanding. It was customary in many courses for examinations to take the form of oration or declamation, which required students to discuss the given content and respond to questions posed by the examining faculty member. Faculty assumed that she would choose the less intimidating option of an essay to avoid direct debate with a male member of the university faculty. "*Why?* became my one and only, but effective ammunition upon all occasions when approach to the 'Woman question,' was bold enough to lift its head."[44] Debating courses provided another opportunity for Sarah Parke Morrison to display women's scholarly abilities on the public stage. "Again: when under Dr. Owen, and our exercise was Debate, a student said to me, 'we know of course, Miss Morrison you can declaim and so forth, but I never heard of a lady debating!' 'Why?' said I. So the boys and I had our two formulas."[45]

While perhaps not as immediate as she would have preferred, Sarah Parke Morrison's petition to the board of trustees and subsequent enrollment certainly had an effect on other women. In the second term of the 1867–68 academic year, twelve other female students joined Sarah at Indiana University. That number increased again to nineteen by the end of the academic year.[46] By the end of the nineteenth century, roughly 30 percent of students enrolled at Indiana University were women.[47]

Academic credit from her previous schooling and an accelerated course load allowed Sarah Parke Morrison to graduate in only two years. As commencement approached, the men of the university provided her one final opportunity to brandish her armament against their gendered assumptions. "'You will have an essay at commencement I suppose, Miss Morrison, I never heard of a lady having an Oration.' 'Why?' I said."[48] Though she committed herself to representing her graduating class with zeal, significant weight accompanied the decision. "I could not come down to their notions, could I lift them up to mine?"[49] Morrison sought advice from her elocution professor, Dr. Kidd, and spent hours walking the countryside and standing in empty barns, reciting her oration. She chose her topic strategically. "The choice of a subject must be popular. It was not so far from the Civil War that its echoes did not thrill in our veins. I believed then in defensive war. My subject was *Nam pariter pax bello*— 'from war, peace,' as translated in our program."[50]

After considerable preparation, Morrison stood on the rostrum on Commencement Day, 1869, two years after learning of the board's decision to admit women, and gave her patriotic oration. "I came off with my Oration with such éclat the band struck up *Yankee Doodle* and Dr. McPheeters wrote me a nice letter praising Father and Mother for what I had been enabled to do."[51] Indeed, her family had made her the woman she became. From her early childhood days spent on the fourth floor of a women's institute cofounded by her parents, Morrison had honed the skill of asking, "Why?"

The noteworthiness of Morrison's achievements at IU assumes even greater clarity when seen in the larger context of mid-nineteenth century higher education. During the years Sarah Parke Morrison studied at IU, college attendance was still rare. In 1869–70, only 1 percent, or 62,839, of the total US population of eighteen- to twenty-four-year-olds were enrolled. And women attending college was an even rarer occurrence. Thus, when Sarah Parke Morrison earned her bachelor's degree from IU in 1869–70, she accomplished a monumental achievement that was granted, and available, only to a small percent of the American population.[52] In 1871, only two years after Morrison's accelerated graduation, six women received their baccalaureate degrees during commencement.

AFTER GRADUATION WHAT? A LIFETIME OF SERVICE AND ACTIVISM

Baccalaureate graduation in 1869 was not the end of Sarah Parke Morrison's historic relationship with Indiana University. Three years later, in 1872, Morrison earned her AM in English. In 1873, she was appointed as a tutor, thus becoming the institution's first female faculty member. And the next year, she received the title of adjunct professor of English literature.[53] She also served as tutoress and governess of the young ladies, a title and advising responsibility that was a precursor to the position of dean of women.

Unlike her time as an IU student, historical materials do give us insight into Morrison's time on the faculty and the hostility she incurred from IU's predominantly male student population. In 1875, *The Dagger*, a newsletter published by Indiana University's Beta Theta Pi fraternity, provided a mocking and demeaning review of Morrison's courses:

> Never before in all of the history of the institution, has there been so gross an imposition upon the taxpayers of Indiana . . . and there is not a single finger among faculty or students that can point to any benificial [*sic*] results achieved at her hands. . . . Classes have sensibly refused to recite to her and stated their valuable objections in her face. Petitions for her removal have been thrust in the faces of both her and her father. . . . The majority of the senior class hereby give due notice that in twenty four hours after receiving their diplomas the mark of her impudent fingers shall be as quickly erased as the footprint of an uneducated ape.[54]

The same edition of *The Dagger* included appraisals of five faculty men—all positive. The sharp contrast between the student evaluations of their male instructors and the dehumanizing reviews of Morrison's teaching highlight some of the targeted gender discrimination she faced.[55] In this respect, Morrison's brief faculty days resonate with the experience of isolation and hostility endured by many of the early women faculty at coeducational universities. Nevertheless, Morrison persisted. She continued as an adjunct professor of English literature at Indiana University until the end of the 1874–75 academic year at age forty-two.[56] Sarah Parke Morrison remained dedicated to education for the rest of her life. As an advocate for women at the university, she wrote repeatedly to the Indiana University Board of Trustees, encouraging greater representation of women throughout the campus structure. "Pardon me but why have ladies not been placed upon the Board of Visitors? To think that ever since 68 you have declared the half of the kingdom theirs, and yet they have not even a name among you as co-lookers," wrote Morrison pointedly in a letter to the board in 1906.[57]

As a lifelong learner, Morrison went on to complete a certificate from Indiana Commercial College in 1882. Later, at age sixty-five, she took up the study of Hebrew through correspondence courses offered by the University of Chicago.[58]

As an educator, Sarah taught at Glendale College in Cincinnati, Ohio; Western Seminary in Oxford, Ohio; and State Normal School (now Indiana State University) in Terre Haute, Indiana.[59] She also used her English and Hebrew language skills to tutor many Indianapolis students who were preparing for college admission.[60]

Morrison devoted herself to writing and speaking on suffrage and temperance.[61] She used her pen to write poetry that examined issues of equity with humor and reverence. As an homage to her mother and her deep influence in Morrison's own life, Morrison authored a three-volume biography of Catherine and the Morris family lineage, *Among Ourselves: To a Mother's Memory*, and *A Monody: To a Father's Memory*. Never marrying, Sarah Parke Morrison chose to live with close family in either Knightstown or Indianapolis, Indiana. Her life was devoted not to conventions of domesticity but to her sincerest intellectual interests and reform activities. She remained firm in these commitments and passion up until her death on July 9, 1919.

CONCLUSION

This biographical sketch of Sarah Parke Morrison has aimed to look beyond the moniker of famous *first* and the often-repeated anecdote of a young woman who wrote a petition for coeducation based on a five-dollar incentive. Though one wishes we knew more about the details of Morrison's life and IU days, what we can see clearly is that her decision to write the petition, and then to enroll, must be viewed within the larger context of her biography and times. No doubt hers was a path of privilege, made easier by the model and support of two highly educated parents—an independent-minded mother and a liberal, well-connected father. No doubt her family's Quaker heritage shaped her unwavering belief in women's intellect and educational rights. And, though little is known about her personal assets, Morrison's volunteerism and activism hint at a life of at least modest financial security. This distinctive combination of social and political capital and material comfort enabled her to champion ideals in which she believed and made her public achievements possible.

As this essay has considered, the influence of the Morrison family and the range of Sarah's educative experiences were integral to her life's path—from the girl born in the rural southern Indiana town of Salem in 1833 to becoming the adult Sarah Parke Morrison who, as a thirty-four-year-old woman, penned the historic petition for women's admission to Indiana University. These life experiences help us to understand her motivations and aspirations—the traits that made John Morrison realize his daughter was indeed the perfect person to ask IU trustees whether the state university's doors were open to women.

In the end, it is important to underscore the purposefulness that guided Morrison's life. Sarah Parke Morrison did not have to write the petition. A woman in her thirties with an exceptional level of schooling, Morrison could have understandably declined the challenge and accepted that high-quality institutions like Mt. Holyoke and Vassar existed for the education of women. When Indiana University decided to open to female students, Morrison certainly did not have to enroll. She had multiple degrees from esteemed institutions and had no vocational use for another baccalaureate degree. Once enrolled, nothing required her to finish the degree. She stepped in to fill the breach, and once other female students enrolled a term later, Morrison could have celebrated by stepping away and returning to a life more comfortable than that of a college student. Morrison's journey at the university would have been simpler had she chosen not to participate in orations during courses and at her commencement, if she had not continued on to earn a master's degree and not subjected herself to the disparaging comments of male students she later encountered as Indiana University's first female faculty member. Certainly, Morrison could have occupied her time with something other than a decades-long writing campaign with the board of trustees regarding female representation throughout the campus population. Morrison's actions throughout her life make it clear that she had strong convictions and felt a calling to use her position to enact significant change.

She was relentless until her death, in the summer of 1919, about improving female representation throughout Indiana University. Because of Morrison's letters, we know about her calls for the IU Board of Trustees and various committees to be concerned with female participation. We also know that her criticism of the status of women at the university was balanced with deep respect and enduring ties to her alma mater. This sentiment was perhaps most poignantly captured in her support of the university after a fire. Hers was a timely donation of five dollars—the exact amount she had received years earlier from her father for crafting the petition. The Indiana University Board of Trustees meeting minutes from July 24, 1883, contained this note, cementing in official memory the tie between Sarah Parke Morrison and Indiana University: "And Sarah Morrison, Knightstown, Indiana, the first lady student of this University, kindly enclosed five dollars as an expression of her kind regard for the University, and which contribution it was resolved should be appropriated to the purchasing of a Record and Minute Book for the Trustees of the University, the Minute Book having been destroyed by fire."[62]

NOTES

The epigraph is from Sarah Parke Morrison, "My Experience at State University: 2d Instalment," June 9, 1911, A [6], Sarah Parke Morrison Papers, 1855–1913, C54, Box 1, Folder Writings, 1911–12, IU Libraries University Archives, Bloomington, Indiana.

1. Mount Holyoke College, "Alumnae Association Form," Mount Holyoke College Alumnae Association, February 17, 1915, Mount Holyoke College Archives, South Hadley, Massachusetts.

2. Thomas D. Clark, *Indiana University: Midwestern Pioneer*, Vol. 1, *The Early Years* (Bloomington: Indiana University Press, 1970).

3. See Barbara Miller Solomon, *In the Company of Educated Women: A History of Women and Higher Education in America* (New Haven, CT: Yale University Press, 1985).

4. James May, *First Educational Report of Washington County, Indiana* (Richmond, IN: Nicholson Printing and Mfg., 1915), 11. One sibling did not reach adulthood. Sarah Parke Morrison, *Among Ourselves: Catherine and Her Household*, Vol. 3 (Plainfield, IN: Publishing Association of Friends, 1904).

5. IU held its first classes in 1825, one year after Miami University. Annie Morrison Coffin, "John Irwin Morrison and the Washington County Seminary," *Indiana Magazine of History* 22, no. 2 (June 1926): 183–93.

6. Sarah Parke Morrison, *Among Ourselves: Catherine and Her Surroundings*, Vol. 2. (Plainfield, IN: Publishing Association of Friends, 1902), 20.

7. Morrison, *Among Ourselves: Catherine and Her Surroundings*, Vol. 2., 28–29.

8. Sarah Parke Morrison, *Among Ourselves: Out of North Carolina*, Vol. 1. (Plainfield, IN: Publishing Association of Friends, 1901), 79.

9. Morrison, *Among Ourselves: Catherine and Her Surroundings*, Vol. 2., 51.

10. Morrison, 151–52.

11. H. E. Baker, "John I. Morrison," n.d., n.p., John Hay Center, Washington County (IN) Historical Society.

12. Morrison, *Among Ourselves: Catherine and Her Household*, Vol. 3, 112.

13. Morrison, 90.

14. May, *First Educational Report of Washington County, Indiana*, 12.

15. May, 177.

16. Morrison, *Among Ourselves: Catherine and Her Household*, Vol. 3.

17. Indiana University Archives, "Student and Faculty Population," IU Libraries University Archives Exhibits, n.d., http://collections.libraries.indiana.edu /iubarchives/exhibits/show/student-life-and-culture/student-and-faculty -population.

18. Baker, "John I. Morrison."

19. Morrison, *Among Ourselves: Catherine and Her Household*, Vol. 3.

20. Morrison.

21. Morrison, *Among Ourselves: Catherine and Her Household*. Vol. 3., 134, 140.

22. Morrison, 246.

23. Mount Holyoke College, "Alumnae Association Form."

24. Sarah Parke Morrison, "My Experience at State University," June 8, 1911, 4, Sarah Parke Morrison Papers, 1855–1913, C54, Box 1, Folder Writings, 1911–12, IU Libraries University Archives, Bloomington, Indiana.

25. Burton Dorr Myers, *Trustees and Officers of Indiana University, 1820–1950*. Greenfield, IN: Wm. Mitchell Printing Company, 1951.

26. James Albert Woodburn, *Higher Education in Indiana* (Washington: US Government Printing Office, 1891).

27. Theophilus Adam Wylie, *Indiana University: Its History from 1820, When Founded, to 1890* (Indianapolis, IN: Wm. B. Burford, 1890), 74.

28. Wylie, 74.

29. Morrison, "My Experience at State University," 4–5; and Sarah Parke Morrison, "Some Sidelights of Fifty Years Ago," 6, no 3, *Indiana University Alumni Quarterly* (October 1919): 530–35. John Morrison served as a trustee of Indiana University during several periods, including 1847–55 and 1873–78, and as president of the board during 1854–55 and 1874–75. See Annie Morrison Coffin, "John Irwin Morrison and the Washington County Seminary," *Indiana Magazine of History*, 22, no. 2 (June 1926): 183–93, esp. 183.

30. R. McIlveen, "IU's First Female Student Admitted after Fatherly 'Bribe,'" *Herald-Times*, January 9, 1982.

31. Morrison, "My Experience at State University," 5.

32. Wylie, *Indiana University*, 75.

33. Morrison, "My Experience at State University," 5.

34. Morrison, "My Experience at State University: 2d Instalment."

35. Morrison, "My Experience at State University," A [6].

36. Morrison, B [7].

37. Morrison, C [8].

38. Morrison, C [8].

39. Morrison, C [8].

40. Rebecca Wylie, Correspondence to Louisa Wylie Boisen, July 25, 1867, Theophilus Adam Wylie Family Correspondence, Folder July 1867, Wylie House Museum, IU Libraries Indiana University Archives, Bloomington, Indiana.

41. Morrison, "My Experience at State University: 2d Instalment," C [8].

42. Board of Trustees, *Annual Report of Indiana University, Including the Catalogue for the Academical Year 1867–1868* (Bloomington: Indiana University, 1868), IU Libraries University Archives, Bloomington, Indiana.

43. Morrison, "My Experience at State University: 2d Instalment," D [9].

44. Sarah Parke Morrison, "3d Instalment of My Experience at State University," June 9, 1911, 1–2 [11–12], Sarah Parke Morrison Papers, 1855–1913, C54, Box 1, Folder Writings, 1911–12, IU Libraries University Archives, Bloomington, Indiana.

45. Morrison, 2 [12].

46. Board of Trustees, *Annual Report of Indiana University, Including the Catalogue for the Academical Year 1867–1868.*

47. Board of Trustees, *Indiana University Academic Bulletin, 1898–1899* (Bloomington: Indiana University, 1899), IU Libraries University Archives, Bloomington, Indiana; Morrison, "3d Instalment of My Experience at State University," 2 [12].

48. Morrison, "3d Instalment of My Experience at State University," 2 [12].

49. Morrison, 4 [14].

50. Morrison, 4 [14].

51. Morrison, 5 [15].

52. For national data, see National Center for Education Statistics, *120 Years of American Education: A Statistical Portrait* (Washington, DC: US Department of Education, 2003), Table 23, 75.

53. Board of Trustees, *Annual Report of Indiana University, Including the Catalogue for the Academical Year, 1873–1974* (Bloomington: Indiana University, 1874), IU Libraries University Archives, Bloomington, Indiana.

54. "The Faculty Reviewed: Sarah P. Morrison," *The Dagger* 1, no.1, June 1873, 1, *The Dagger*, 1875–1880 C591, Box OS3, Folder *The Dagger*, June 1875, IU Libraries University Archives, Bloomington, Indiana.

55. See Geraldine Jonçich Clifford, *Lone Voyagers: Academic Women in Coeducational Universities, 1870–1937* (New York: Feminist Press at the City University of New York, 1989).

56. Wylie, *Indiana University: Its History,* 146.

57. Sarah Parke Morrison, Letter to Isaac Jenkinson and Board of Trustees, January 19, 1906, 1, Sarah Parke Morrison Papers, 1855–1913, C54, Box 1, Folder Correspondence, 1897–1913, Board of Trustees, IU Libraries University Archives, Bloomington, Indiana.

58. Mount Holyoke College, "Alumnae Association Form."

59. "Archival Notes: Morrison, Sarah Parke," n.d., Sarah Parke Morrison Papers, 1855–1913, C54, IU Libraries University Archives, Bloomington, Indiana.

60. A. Garber, "They Told Her Poppa to Air His Views with Action–Lo! He Did–with Her Action," *The Indiana Daily Student*, March 12, 1948.

61. "News of the University," *The Indiana University Alumni Quarterly* 3, no. 1 (January 1916): 75–76.

62. "News of the University," *The Indiana University Alumni Quarterly* 3, no. 1 (January 1916): 76, IU Libraries University Archives, Bloomington, Indiana.

THREE

PIONEERING STUDENTS OF COLOR

Carrie Parker and Frances Marshall

DINA M. KELLAMS

Dina M. Kellams, Director of IU Archives, writes about Carrie Parker and Frances Marshall—the earliest Black female student and the earliest Black female graduate at IU. Together, their stories shed light on gender and race in the Indiana University experience as well as the factors shaping institutional memory. Drawing upon her original research, Kellams describes how she serendipitously found a brief mention of Carrie Parker's IU attendance in a newspaper clipping. Her chance discovery led to months of detective work and, eventually, to connecting with the Parker family and rediscovering Parker's interviews and writings (which speak to her consciousness of racism). Finally, Kellams describes recent institutional efforts honoring Parker's place in IU history. Kellams's discussion illustrates the spirit of discovery guiding the chapters in this volume—namely, that our understanding of Indiana University's past is always subject to revision and reconceptualizing as we find new sources, probe unconsidered dimensions of familiar materials, and bring new questions and sensibilities to the historian's task.

CARRIE PARKER HAD ALWAYS been fearless. She and her family navigated racial isolation as one of the few Black families living in Vermillion County on the western border of Indiana, between Illinois and the mighty Wabash River. At the county school, she and her siblings physically confronted their classmates who hurled racial slurs. In the classroom, she achieved two important distinctions—head of her class and the first Black graduate of the county—despite her teachers' and principal's repeated and blatant attempts to deny her, on the basis of her skin color, advanced secondary education. Her fearlessness, put to the test daily in the predominantly white county where she lived, in the schoolyard, and in the classroom, propelled her to become the first Black woman to enroll at IU in 1898.

Carrie Parker's status as *the first Black woman* forever cements her and Frances Marshall—IU's first Black woman graduate—into IU's history. Because of a mix of historical, social, and archival factors, Carrie, however, became lost to IU's institutional memory. Fortunately, the university community came to rediscover Carrie Parker more than a century later thanks to a combination of technological advances, luck, and intellectual curiosity.

The extensive planning and project work to commemorate IU's Bicentennial in 2020 presented a welcome opportunity for the university to reflect on its past and to consider how IU history has been preserved and recounted. The moment has inspired us to undertake the research and deliberations needed to supplement the existing record as well as to rethink past, perhaps poor, decisions and correct errors and omissions. Largely supported by the Office of the Bicentennial, IU community members—sharing new perspectives on IU in lectures, blogs, intern projects, publications, artwork, naming honors, and library exhibitions—have pushed to highlight figures who may have been forgotten, overlooked, or unknown but whose stories are integral to IU's story. As part of this initiative we have been able to acknowledge or bestow new honors on IU's pioneers such as Carrie Parker.

During our work on the Bicentennial projects, world events made even more salient the importance of history and historical decision-making to the campus community. The growing national (and even global) attention for racial equity has also spurred IU—as well as universities and colleges nationwide—to critically examine some of our own darkest moments in institutional history. In 2019, IU chose to remove the name of late IU trustee Ora Wildermuth from the recreational fieldhouse after critically reexamining a 1940 letter in which Wildermuth wrote openly racist comments to a fellow board member. In June 2020, IU renamed the fieldhouse after William (Bill) Garrett, the first Black basketball player at IU from 1948 to 1951.[1]

FORGOTTEN STORIES

A serendipitous stumble upon a story in a historical newspaper database in 2015 provided the first clue to Carrie Parker's role at IU. The January 1898 headline read, "First Negro Girl in Indiana University." The short paragraph recognized Miss Parker from Clinton, Indiana, as the "first colored girl" to enter the institution.[2] Further research revealed a compelling story of triumph and disappointments. But, frustratingly, there was no institutional awareness of Parker's time on campus. Campus archivists and historians were unfamiliar with her name and role, finding no mention of her in any lists of firsts or among their files on early African Americans affiliated with IU. Other institutions have experience similar rediscoveries of their history. Quite recently, in April 2020, Purdue University archivists announced the rediscovery of Purdue's own first Black female student, a woman whose name had been long forgotten and never noted as a first within their records.[3]

It is a curious but instructive exercise to consider why these stories and voices were lost for so long. Literature that explores silences and exclusions in the archival record proffers that the primary reason for these omissions is quite straightforward: the stories of people of color, the stories of women, the stories of those on the fringe of society just did not capture the attention of society's documenters—archivists. For centuries, archivists instead focused on the lives of leaders and prominent figures, believing—not mistakenly, unfortunately— that those were the stories that would matter to society and future historians. With the catalyst of the Civil Rights Movement in the 1960s and historians' call for new, more inclusive approaches to studying the past, archivists be- gan to "slowly and cautiously respond," wrote Randall C. Jimerson in *Archives Power*, "resulting in demands for archival sources for underrepresented social groups." As Jimerson related, "This new cohort of young historians committed themselves 'to listen to the voices that had been silenced by elite indifference' and to create 'powerful identities for those people on the bottom who had so long been ignored.'"[4] Historians wanted to discover and explore the stories of those who had been forgotten or ignored due to one or more "isms," including racism, elitism, and sexism.

In 1971, activist historian Howard Zinn told those in attendance at the Soci- ety of American Archivists annual meeting that "the existence, preservation, and availability of archives, documents, [and] records in our society are very much determined by the distribution of wealth and power" and that archival collections are "biased towards the important and powerful people of the soci- ety, tending to ignore the impotent and obscure."[5] At the same meeting, urban historian Sam Bass Warner echoed those thoughts and challenged archivists to aggressively collect current and past materials to remedy this imbalance and to seek materials that would reflect the experiences of those outside that circle in order to more accurately depict the human experience. Jimerson notes that these "radical historians thus challenged archivists to re-examine their as- sumptions and policies . . . and to engage actively in balancing the documentary record with the voices of marginalized groups."[6]

The top-down approach that focused on collecting records from upper-level administration was indeed the case at IU, made very clear by the purposeful inclusion of the five-story President's File Room in the 1936 Administration Building, known today as William Lowe Bryan Hall. That room served as the institutional archives until 2008, the floors packed with file cabinets holding presidential records dating to the 1820s.

These two reinforcing factors—the hierarchical nature of IU's environment and the practices and priorities then embraced by the archival community—help explain why Carrie Parker's IU connection was lost or forgotten for so many years. Later research revealed that a prominent Indiana University folklorist met Carrie quite by chance in the 1950s as he conducted field research on African American folktales. She told him of her connection to IU, which he included as a passing reference in his 1956 book.[7] But this moment of possibility, when Carrie's story might have become part of IU's understanding of its own history, was missed. Her story, for whatever reason—whether overlooked or ignored—remained hidden to history.

By the time Carrie Parker's role at Indiana University was rediscovered in 2015, archivists and historians had already spent decades turning their professional eye to documenting and uncovering the stories of society's forgotten peoples. Still, finding institutional firsts in academic archives remains challenging. Across the United States, universities and colleges did not, as a rule, systematically collect information on race until the 1970s. As a result, identifying firsts is difficult or impossible unless a contemporary source highlighted the achievement. In the case of Carrie, as with Purdue University's recent rediscovery of Rhoygnette Webb, its first known Black female student, technological advances—i.e., digitization of historical resources and full text search capabilities—made these firsts, long lost to institutional memory, now discoverable.

AFRICAN AMERICANS AT INDIANA UNIVERSITY

It is necessary to consider Carrie Parker's milestone against the African American student presence at Indiana University, which largely began in 1882. That year, Indianapolis native Harvey Young became the first known African American to enroll at Indiana University when he entered as a freshman. A Bloomington newspaper bid him welcome and hoped that "his fellow white students show him the highest respect."[8] Research has revealed that Young may not have been the only student of color on campus that year, however. Two Black students from Bloomington's public schools, Maggie McCaw and Samuel Tucker, are listed in the 1882 IU catalogue as juniors in the university's Preparatory

Department. The Prep Department was outside the collegiate program of the university and helped students complete courses necessary for entrance to the university proper or for individuals not yet at the minimum age for enrollment. Going forward, we know other African American students—all men—came and went, but the first Black student to graduate was Marcellus Neal, who earned a bachelor of arts in mathematics in 1895.

ENTER CARRIE PARKER

More than fifty years after her time at Indiana University, Carrie Parker Taylor Eaton told IU folklorist Richard Dorson, "I was the first colored graduate from Vermillion County in Indiana, and was the head of the class, and was treated like a dog—never invited to their parties, had no class picture taken. And I was the first colored girl to go to Indiana University in 1898. Almost killed myself trying to work my way through, for a year." [9]

In 2015, while conducting research in Indiana newspaper archives for an unrelated project, my eye caught the headline "First Negro Girl in Indiana University." The January 8, 1898, article that followed—only five short sentences—noted that nineteen-year-old Carrie Parker of Clinton, Indiana, had become the first "colored girl to enter Indiana University in its history." The story stated that Parker intended to "take a complete course" (i.e., earn her degree), and in order to pay her school fees she would live with a professor's family, presumably where she would do light housework in exchange for room and board.[10] Parker's name was wholly unknown to the staff of the University Archives, and further research was necessary to confirm her place in IU's history and to learn the details of her life.

Carrie's story begins in North Carolina, where her father, Richard, was born enslaved in 1834. After Emancipation, he settled in Enfield, North Carolina, with his new wife, Martha. They had six living children together; Carrie was the youngest, born on December 9, 1878. While Carrie's father was illiterate, her mother could read, and it was at Martha's urging that the family decided to move north, where she believed her children would have better educational opportunities. The Parkers made Indiana their destination and began the journey when Carrie was just over a year old, settling in the small town of Clinton in January 1880. Sadly, tragedy struck just two months later, when Martha died in childbirth.

Devastated and likely overwhelmed in his new environs without his partner at his side, Richard wanted to return to North Carolina. Martha's mother, Penny, who had moved with the family, persuaded him to stay in Indiana, as had been her daughter's wish. While Richard found employment as a laborer, Carrie's grandmother helped with the home and children, ranging in age from one to thirteen years old, until her death when Carrie was around eight years old.

It is not known why the family chose to settle in Vermillion County, Indiana. Perhaps acquaintances or other family members from North Carolina had settled there in recent years. Or, maybe it was far enough north in Indiana that they were able to avoid some of the Confederate sympathies that may have still lingered in the southern portion of the state. But it had to be quite an isolating experience, as according to the 1880 US Census, there was an extremely small African American community in the county. That year, Vermillion County had a recorded population of 12,025; only 74 of these inhabitants were African American.[11] Even neighboring Parke and Vigo Counties boasted Black populations of 1.5 percent and 3.4 percent, respectively.[12] Whatever the reason, the family ultimately made a home in their adopted state in a small house on the Wabash River.

Growing up in this predominantly white community in Central Indiana, Carrie and her siblings first met with prejudice in the place she least expected it—her church. While she and her sisters had been put into a Sunday school class of all African American children, this did not bother her. But at Christmastime, they were thrilled to attend a Sunday school party at the home of the richest man in the congregation, only to learn they would not be allowed to stay because of the color of their skin. "Even now I can see us three little girls stumbling home through the darkness and cold, with tears streaming down our faces because we could not understand why our color banned us from the party," Parker later wrote. "That was my first wound from race prejudice and it took years to heal."[13]

The Parker children attended the county schools, from which Carrie successfully graduated in 1897, but there, too, she faced significant discrimination from adults and children alike. With the children, the Parker brothers and sisters banded together in physical confrontations against those who hurled racial slurs in their direction, and before long their white classmates learned to leave them be. The teachers required a different tact. According to Parker, some of the educators felt there was no reason for African American students to progress beyond the eighth grade and devised ways to flunk or frustrate the students until they simply dropped out. A strong student, Carrie was distraught when her eighth grade teacher chose to fail her after an extended illness, claiming he feared she would be unable to manage high school work due to lingering effects of her illness. Determined, Carrie repeated eighth grade, and when it came time for final exams and she took first place in the county examinations, she was elated—until the teacher sought to discipline her for an unnamed offense. When she refused to accept the corporal punishment, the teacher failed her once again. Her father appeared before the school board to plead Carrie's case but was told they could not rule for a Black child against a white teacher. "I gritted my teeth and blinked away my tears and said, 'They have bluffed [flunked] every colored child out of this school but they are not going to bluff me. I'm going through this school or die trying.'"[14]

In her short unpublished memoir, "Race Prejudice and Me," Parker wrote, "What I said, I meant. The next year found me back again [in] the 8th grade. By that time I had the grade by heart." Yes, Carrie was going to attempt to get passed into high school a third time. By year's end, she once again tested at the top of her class. This time, however, even the white citizens of the town told the school they needed to pass Parker on to the ninth grade. "That night I felt bigger than I did three years later when I graduated from the high school, for I had fought a good fight and won!"[15]

Carrie wrote that her high school years were uneventful and that she received fair treatment from the teachers throughout; in fact, one of Parker's classmates claimed she was the teacher's pet. Sadly, at least some resentment and prejudice simmered under the surface. Come graduation celebrations, Carrie was excluded from the class farewell party, and the students elected to forgo a class picture so that they would not be in a photograph with an African American. The day before commencement, Carrie learned that a classmate she had tutored—and really did her classwork for her—had said she would not sit next to Parker during the ceremony. Parker remembered that despite being deeply hurt by this treatment, she continued with the ceremony. As required of all the students, she delivered her original oration, "Home and Its Influences," and received a standing ovation when she finished. News of Carrie's graduation as the first African American from a Vermillion County school spread, and the story of her triumph was shared in Indiana newspapers as far north as Logansport and as far south as Bedford. The Indianapolis-based African American newspaper The Freeman reported, "When it came her time to speak she stepped to the front, cool and unembarrassed. She handled her subject with the skill and judgment of a professional lecturer, and it was the wonder of the audience how so young a girl could have learned so much of the practical affairs of life. Her speech was plain, common sense, clothed in beautiful language; her voice was good and her enunciation perfect. She easily carried off the honors of her class, and the applause was hearty."[16] Carrie later remembered that so many flowers showed up at her house that she could not keep them all, and she received congratulatory letters from all over the country. Newspapers across the state reported that she intended to enter Indiana University, earn her degree, and then serve as a missionary to Africa.

While still in high school, Carrie had already begun to set her sights on college. After the indignities she suffered in junior high school, she found an ally in Oscar B. Zell, Indiana University alumnus (1894) and superintendent of schools in Cayuga, Indiana. In January 1897, he wrote to IU president Joseph Swain on Carrie's behalf, cataloging the tremendous amount of work she did both in and outside of school to further her studies. Parker, Zell wrote, would like to attend the university, but her financial situation could possibly keep her from enrolling. Working as her advocate, Zell contacted IU professor Carl Eigenmann, who offered to provide Carrie with room and board in exchange for a part-time position at his house, a not-unusual arrangement for students with limited financial means.[17] Swain responded the next day: "We shall be glad to have the colored girl of which you speak here. I will turn her credentials over to the dean for classification."[18]

Not much is known about Carrie's time as an Indiana University student. She said she had not "been made to feel her color much" but also recounted the heaping amounts of work the faculty family she lived with—not the Eigenmanns, as originally planned—thrust upon her.[19] Newspapers of the period tell us that while a student, Carrie found a home with Bloomington's Bethel AME Church and in November 1898 was elected president of the Christian Endeavor Society. In January 1899, a year after Carrie entered IU, the prominent African American newspaper the *Indianapolis Recorder* reported she was ill; by the next month, they reported she had to discontinue her studies due to "nervous trouble" but that she hoped to continue her studies the next term. In fact, Parker's doctor had told her she could not continue to work and go to school as it was detrimental to her health. Still desiring her college degree, Parker decided to teach for a few years to save money and then return to Indiana University.[20]

The *Recorder* seemed very keen on Parker and her life, as the next month they reported another update in "A Quiet Wedding." Indeed, Carrie had married John G. Taylor in a small house ceremony. According to the *Recorder*, the marriage was "quite a surprise to their many friends."[21] Later in life, Carrie would report that she had married only because Taylor promised he would pay for her to continue her studies.[22] Even though they waited several years before starting a family, she never did return to school. Carrie told IU's Richard Dorson, "Both my husbands lied to get to me. . . . Every year I'd cry to go back."[23]

After marriage, the couple settled north in Lafayette, Indiana, where they lived for eighteen years. There, Carrie said, she found racial prejudice in full blast. She recalled, "The colored children went to school in a building that was condemned. They had a principle [sic] who was inefficient in every way. I doubt if he even had an 8th grade education. The colored people were almost all raised in the south and were afraid to stand up for their rights. At last some of us got together and under my leadership we put up such a strong fight that the school board had to build a new building and furnish competent teachers." Unfortunately, Carrie's own children did not benefit from these educational gains, as the family moved to Chicago.[24]

In addition to raising six children, Carrie was an involved member of her community, with a focus on her church and work on behalf of African Americans. In the early 1900s, newspapers reveal, she served as superintendent of the Indianapolis District Sunday School Convention for Bethel AME. In this role, Carrie traveled throughout the area, where she was able to use the speaking skills for which she had been so greatly praised in high school. In 1915, she could be found speaking at a three-day meeting of the Pilgrim Knights of the World, a fraternal organization founded in Fort Wayne in 1911. The group's motto was "The Negro for the Negro, first, last and all the time," and their call for members proclaimed they sought individuals who believed in "Race Pride, Race Patriotism, Race Advancement, Race Protection and Race Unity."[25] She also wrote poetry throughout her lifetime. The family holds most of the unpublished work in their private archives, but in 1915 "A Negro's Challenge," a poem penned during her involvement with the Pilgrim Knights of the World, reached a broader audience through publication in African American newspapers such as *The Tulsa Star* (Oklahoma) and *The Chicago Defender* (Illinois).

These strong passions and interests reflect what Indiana University folklorist Richard Dorson recorded of Carrie in the 1950s. Yes, by coincidence, in conducting fieldwork for his 1956 *Negro Folktales in Michigan*, Dorson traveled to Calvin, Michigan, in pursuit of stories from African Americans living in what was called the New Black Belt of the north. Carrie had moved to the predominantly African American southern Michigan community in 1932. On page two of his final work, Dorson wrote, "Learning about the strong new Adventist group in the township, I found my way on Saturday to their trim white meetinghouse, and on Sunday drove through mud to the century-old Chain Lake Baptist Church. Right after the Adventist service a stiff, pear-cheeked lady rushed up to meet me, thrust some religious literature into my hands, and began speaking volubly. She was Carrie Taylor Eaton, daughter of a slave, the first Negro girl to graduate from the Indiana high schools and enter Indiana University, known as a local poetess, fluent, sharp, shrill, race-bitter."[26] Dorson collected stories from Carrie and her sister Lulu as well as several of Carrie's neighbors. Indiana University's Lilly Library holds his fieldwork from the book.

Carrie's husband John died in 1933, and in 1937 Carrie married Richard Eaton. In 1958, she died a widow in Cassopolis, Michigan, survived by four of her children. While there is much more to learn about Carrie's life, so much is known because she was so very active and involved in her community; she left a record. What's more, her descendants, thrilled about the recognition of Carrie's role at IU, have been generous with their family archives and stories.

Now that Carrie's story has been rediscovered by Indiana University, her status as an IU pioneer has been marked in a number of ways. There are now two commissioned portraits of Carrie on the Bloomington campus: one has a place in the campus art collection, and when it was unveiled it spent nearly a year in a place of prominence as part of the "Women of Indiana University" exhibit in the Indiana Memorial Union; the other was commissioned by and hangs in the Neal-Marshall Black Culture Center. Even more far-reaching is the Carrie Parker Taylor Scholarship established by James Wimbush, Indiana University vice president for Diversity, Equity, and Multicultural Affairs (DEMA). The scholarship, designed to assist a participant in one of DEMA's support programs with priority funding going to first-generation college students, was awarded to four students in its inaugural year, 2017.

The fresh recognition of Carrie's connection to Indiana University has also had an impact on her family. Within two months of first learning that an IU archivist had stumbled upon Carrie's name, her family, including her then-ninety-nine-year-old son, Leon "Parker" Taylor, traveled to Bloomington to share her story and have done so several more times since. In the fall of 2015, nearly one hundred family members celebrated IU's homecoming weekend with the Neal-Marshall Alumni Association, Mr. Taylor participated in the Homecoming parade, and the Alumni Association named Carrie an honorary alumna. Representatives of Indiana University were guests of honor at Mr. Taylor's one-hundredth birthday that following spring. Sadly, Mr. Taylor passed away in 2019, but he repeated numerous times that this reconnection of his mother to IU had been one of the greatest things to happen in his long life. Mr. Taylor was thrilled his mother has received this recognition, albeit so many years later.

NEXT MILESTONE: FRANCES MARSHALL

Archival records on the race of attendees at Indiana University are spotty until the 1970s, but the IU Archives does hold random lists or counts for earlier periods that, while less than comprehensive and systematic (having been gathered for various reasons), provide historians some insight into the earlier student body makeup. Early African American attendance is also confirmed through available housing information. Because IU did not have university-owned student housing until the 1920s, students secured their own housing in rooming houses or with local families, both of which had to receive approval from university administrators. Among the early records that document student housing are approved rooms for "colored" men and women, making clear that these students were in attendance. Still, the university's inconsistent documentation of race leaves the identification of many of its African American students incomplete. However, we do know that in 1919 Indiana University marked a new milestone with its first female African American graduate, Frances Marshall.

Frances was born on July 17, 1898 in Elizabethtown, Kentucky, but moved to Rushville, Indiana, where she attended the local schools. For at least some of Marshall's childhood, her family was economically comfortable, with her father working as a brick mason and her mother a homemaker. The death of her father while Frances was still in school, however, changed their financial situation significantly. To help the household, Frances worked as a domestic with a local family to bring in a small income. According to Frances's daughter Rosalind, Frances's mother told her, "We cannot afford to send you to college, but we will not stand in your way if you find a way."[27]

And that was Frances's intent. Shortly after graduation, she wrote to Indiana University inquiring of employment opportunities that would help pay for school. In reply, William Rawles, assistant dean in the then–College of Liberal Arts, sent Frances a catalog and a short letter telling her, "Concerning the matter of self support [sic] I beg to say that a good many of our students do make a part or all of their expenses while attending the University. It is more difficult for a girl to do this than it is for a boy. There are more opportunities for work open to the boys."[28] Rawles then suggested Frances contact the dean of women for additional information on potential positions. Frances did so, explaining to Dean of Women Ruby Mason that she needed to make her way through school and that it would be particularly beneficial if she could secure a position before classes began: "I would love to have a place where I could make my board if possible. I am a colored girl 17 years of age can do most any thing [sic] and can give good references. I would like a place in a nice family and I like small children."[29]

Marshall came to Bloomington and first stayed with a Black family in town, the Evans family, but went on to work as a domestic in the home of local limestone executive Hiram P. Radley in exchange for room and board for the remainder of her time at IU. Outside of work and classes, she frequented the west side of town, where most of Bloomington's African American families lived. In 1982, Frances told IU's student newspaper, the *Indiana Daily Student*, that her years at IU were uneventful. "I never worried about being a woman going to school. I never worried about being Black going to school. I just went on with what I had to do. I got my lessons, did my work, and went home." She followed, however, that Blacks and whites did not intermingle: "You went your way, and they went theirs. They were pleasant, and that was all."[30]

Knowing her financial situation, Marshall's home community supported her after she entered IU. In December 1916, Rushville's *Daily Republican* reported that the parent-teacher association for the African American school in town had given a benefit concert on Marshall's behalf. The group was able to send $50 to Frances—no small sum when a semester's fees came in at just under $10. "The Parent Teachers association wishes to thank their white friends, members of the Methodist and Baptists churches and the Eastern Stars for giving so generously. The Eastern Stars gave $7.12 collected from individuals; white friends gave $6.70; the general collection was $6.20 and the State Federation of Women's clubs donated $35."[31]

When Frances graduated from IU with her bachelor's in English in 1919, she made the front page of the *Bloomington Evening World*, which called her an "exceptional woman." The article noted her wish to teach and that she had already received several "flattering offers." It went on to reprint a letter Marshall had shared with them from the president of West Baden's (Indiana) Community Service League, which opened with, "I am quite sure that you do not know me but we have watched your career anxiously, hopefully, for four years and now that you have reached your goal we want again to show our appreciation of the first race girl who has had the courage to push, and the faith to fight it out to the finish." The president closed her letter to Frances with an invitation come to West Baden "as one of the family" after commencement.[32]

As an IU student, Frances met Wilson Vashon Eagleson, a chemistry major and son of Preston Eagleson who, in 1896, had become the second Black man to graduate from IU. Frances and Wilson became a couple and married directly after Frances's graduation. Frances began her career as a teacher and in 1921 settled at what is now North Carolina Central University but what was then a private high school for African Americans called the National Training School. There, Frances taught English but also did whatever else was needed, from assisting with costumes in the theater department to cosigning loans for students. After Wilson graduated from IU in 1922, he joined Frances and their two children in North Carolina as the school's football coach and chemistry teacher.

It was not long after her appointment at NCCU that Frances moved into an administrative role as the institution's registrar and admissions officer. The Eaglesons both continued their studies; Frances focused on educational administration at the University of Chicago and the Teachers College, Columbia University, as time allowed while Wilson pursued his doctorate in chemistry at Cornell University. The children stayed with Frances's mother, who was then living in Bloomington in a house Frances purchased for her. In 1933, a week before the conferral of his degree, Wilson died in an automobile accident. Now a widow with two young children, Frances moved to North Carolina, where she enrolled her children in boarding school so she could continue to work. Her daughter Rosalind remembered that she would work in the office all day as the registrar and teach extension classes for the university at night. "That was how she earned additional money to be able to send us to college. It never crossed her mind that Vash and I were not going to college."[33] Rosalind went on to become a mathematics professor, and Vash (i.e., Wilson Vashon Jr.) was a highly decorated member of the elite all-Black Army Air Force squadron the Tuskegee Airmen. After forty-three years of service to NCCU, Frances retired in 1964 but was soon lured to St. Augustine, Florida, to serve as the registrar for Florida Memorial College. She worked for FMC for four years and then tried to retire again but was recruited by Spelman College, which was in need of a registrar. Frances served the prestigious HBCU institution from 1968 to 1972 before retiring for good. She went on to live to with her daughter until her death in 1987.

Like Carrie, Frances has been memorialized at the institutions she touched. At Indiana University, the newly constructed Neal-Marshall Black Culture Center was dedicated in 2002, honoring the legacies of both Frances and Marcellus Neal, the first African American to graduate from IU in 1895. The center features her portrait so that students and faculty can see her and remember those who came before them; a reproduction is on regular display in the "Women of Indiana University" exhibit in the Indiana Memorial Union, where thousands of people can see it and read about Marshall's legacy on a daily basis. IU is also home to the Neal-Marshall Alumni Club for African American alums to connect and network and in 2021, the city of Bloomington announced that Jordan Avenue, upon which the Neal-Marshall Center sits, will be renamed for the Eagleson family. This decision came after an extensive review of former IU president David Starr Jordan's scholarship revealed that he was not only a proponent of but was in fact a leader in the eugenics movement. In North Carolina, in 1969 NCCU dedicated and named a new dormitory in Frances's honor, and in 1979 they unveiled a portrait of her that has found its home in Eagleson Hall.

CONCLUSION

These two women, highlighted because of their status as firsts, are undeniably important in IU's history. As fearless as she seemed, it is difficult to believe that Carrie did not feel at least a small amount of apprehension at being the first Black woman in a place she had never visited. She did it, though, because she had a desire and determination for education—and someone had to be the first. Between Carrie and Frances there were certainly others whose stories are worthy of telling. What brought them to Indiana University but prevented them from finishing their collegiate work? Family? Society? Money?

Indiana University's Bicentennial presented an impetus and resources for researchers to scour collections at the University Archives to reevaluate, acknowledge, and update our histories. We have made substantial progress toward achieving a more inclusive history, and there will be so many more stories to be acknowledged as the institution advances into its third century. Such an examination has been needed. Too often, at least until fairly recently, the energies of historians and archivists, not only at IU but across academic institutions, have focused on the actions and voices of campus-related figures who were unquestionably important but with whom many in society find too few commonalities. The stories of men and women who walked the same paths— sometimes literally—can serve as powerful sources of inspiration, especially for students who do not see a terrific amount of similitude in the sea of faces in their midst. Archival collections hold thousands of stories waiting to be explored and shared so that history can be reflective of the people, not just the powerful.

"The Negro's Challenge"
By Carrie Parker Taylor
Originally appeared in *The Tulsa Star* on October 8, 1915

You complain, my brother, my lily white brother,
Of our poor race now and then,
Yet you never have said what we should do
To prove to you that we're men.
We've done everything so far that you've done,
Except sit in the president's chair,
And the only reason we haven't done that
Is because you won't let us sit there.
In every walk of life that you've been,
There's at least one of us there,
And you cannot deny but that we do
Our work just as good and as fair.
Among the more common crafts of men,
Such as carpenters, masons and painters,
We have quite a number, and plasterers, too,
And many stock raisers and planters.
We have lawyers and doctors, and bankers a few,

And teachers we have by the score,
Undertakers and merchants and manufacturers
And preachers, we have them galore.
We have sculptors, architects, artists and inventors,
And poets and statesmen of fame,
Actors, orators and authors, and goodness knows what,
For everything we do I can't name.
We print our own papers, publish our books,
We sing and we play same as you,
And in some cases we have been known
To compose some good music, too.
In fact, I don't know anything that you've done,
When you've given us a chance and we've tried,
That we haven't done as well as you could,
And sometimes better besides.
We've even gone farther in some things than you,
And now we need not despair,
For, if we don't like our heads like sheep's wool,
Why, we can straighten our hair.
You say that at least we can't change our skins?
Well, we've knocked that in a hat,
For, by the aid of your sensual men,
Many of us have even done that.
You say we have vices? We got them from you,
You're all the pattern we've had,
So don't charge the race up with the misfits you see,
Since our patterns so often were bad.
So, what more, my brother, my lily white brother,
Must we do to prove that we're men?
If 'tis aught you can do and you'll give us a chance
We'll do it as good as you can.[34]

NOTES

1. "Intramural Center Renamed for Trailblazing Basketball Star Bill Garrett," accessed October 27, 2021, https://wayback.archive-it.org/219/20200713210616 /https://news.iu.edu/stories/2020/06/iu/releases/12-intramural-center-renamed -for-basketball-star-bill-garrett.html.

2. "First Negro Girl in Indiana University," *Logansport Pharos Tribune,* January 8, 1898.

3. "The Search for Miss Webb," *Memoirs & Memories*, last modified April 23, 2020, http://blogs.lib.purdue.edu/asc/2020/04/23/the-search-for-miss-webb.

4. Randall C. Jimerson, *Archives Power: Memory, Accountability, and Social Justice* (Chicago, IL: Soc. of American Archivists, 2021), 169. Kindle.

5. Jimerson, 170.

6. Jimerson, 170–71.

7. Richard M. Dorson, *Negro Folktales in Michigan* (Cambridge: Harvard University Press, 1956).

8. "Doings of a Week," *Bloomington Telephone*, September 16, 1882.

9. "Memories (Carrie Eaton)" in "Michigan (Calvin and Benton Harbor), 1952–1953. Black Folklore," Dorson Mss., Box 53, Folder 7, Lilly Library, Indiana University, Bloomington, Indiana.

10. "First Negro Girl in Indiana University," *Logansport Pharos Tribune*, January 8, 1898.

11. United States Census Bureau, 1880 Census, "Population of Each State and Territory, by Counties, in the Aggregate, at All Censuses," census.gov, 59, last modified December 3, 2018, https://www2.census.gov/library/publications /decennial/1880/vol-01-population/1880_v1-08.pdf.

12. United States Census Bureau, 1880 Census, "Population, by Race, Sex, and Nativity," census.gov, 389, last modified December 3, 2018, https://www2.census .gov/library/publications/decennial/1880/vol-01-population/1880_v1-13.pdf.

13. Carrie Parker Taylor Eaton, "Race Prejudice and Me," unpublished memoir (unpaginated), circa 1940s, "Carrie Parker" clippings file, IU Libraries University Archives, Bloomington, Indiana.

14. Eaton.

15. Eaton.

16. "Triumph of a Colored Girl," *The Freeman* (Indianapolis, IN), June 5, 1897.

17. Oscar B. Zell to Joseph Swain, January 19, 1897, Indiana University President's Office records, "Pard-Parks" file, Collection C174 Box 33, Indiana University Archives, Bloomington, Indiana.

18. Joseph Swain to Oscar B. Zell, January 19, 1897, Letterpress book September 15, 1896–March 23, 1897, Indiana University President's Office records, Collection C174 Box 49, IU Libraries University Archives, Bloomington, Indiana.

19. Eaton, "Race Prejudice and Me."

20. Eaton.

21. "A Quiet Wedding," *Indianapolis Recorder*, March 25, 1899.

22. Eaton, "Race Prejudice and Me."

23. "Memories," Dorson mss., 3–4.

24. Eaton, "Race Prejudice and Me."

25. "New Order Founded," *Indianapolis Recorder*, December 23, 1911.

26. Dorson, *Negro Folktales in Michigan*, 2.

27. Quoted in Jennifer Bailey Woodard, "A Phenomenal Woman," *Indiana Alumni Magazine*, January/February 1999, 26.

28. W. A. Rawles to FM, July 28, 1915, "Marshall, Frances" file, Indiana University President's Office correspondence, Collection C286 Box 168, IU Libraries University Archives, Bloomington, Indiana.

29. FM to Ruby Mason, August 24, 1915, "M-1915–1917" file, Dean of Women's records, Collection C165 Box 2, IU Libraries University Archives, Bloomington, Indiana.

30. Carmen Lee, "First IU Black Woman Graduate Recalls Her Struggles, Rewards," *Indiana Daily Student*, February 23, 1982.

31. "Benefit Realizes $50," *The Daily Republican* (Rushville, IN), December 11, 1916. The "State Federation of Women's clubs" was the Indiana State Federation of Colored Women's Clubs, organized in Indianapolis in 1904.

32. "Colored Woman Receives Degree From Old I.U.," *Bloomington Evening World*, June 3, 1919.

33. Woodard, "A Phenomenal Woman," 29.

34. C. Parker Taylor, "The Negro's Challenge," *The Tulsa Star*, October 8, 1915.

FOUR

EARLY SCIENTIFIC WOMEN OF
INDIANA UNIVERSITY
AND THEIR IMPACT

SARAH J. REYNOLDS

Sarah J. Reynolds, a historian of science, weaves together biographical details and insights into the world of nineteenth century science education and university-led expeditions. She discusses both the intellectual engagement and barriers faced by early scientific women of Indiana University. As Reynolds notes, women were an important part of the development of the sciences at IU, but their significant contributions were often unrecognized because of gender norms and roles or because of competing demands between family and intellectual career. These tensions are most poignantly illustrated in the case of Rosa Smith Eigenmann, the first female ichthyologist in the United States. Her scientific work fell to the wayside with her growing responsibilities as a wife and mother of five. By contrast, her husband and colleague, Carl, focused on continuing their research and went on to assume the IU professorship vacated by their mentor, David Starr Jordan. Other examples highlight how women applied their scientific training to opportunities, interests, and concerns that differed from those of their male counterparts, forging an impact of their own.

INTRODUCTION: A "NEW SPECIES"

"The atmosphere was, if you please, very scientific," the author of the 1899 *Arbutus* yearbook section on Indiana University's summertime biological field school at Turkey Lake assures us. "Pretty young ladies cut up snakes and rabbits in the most bloodthirsty manner to find out whether the interior anatomy of these creatures looked anything like the pictures in books."[1] Jocular as the account may be, the scene it describes was a regular occurrence at IU's summer field station, where young women became skilled collectors and dissectors of various specimens as they studied—and even taught—alongside their male colleagues. Another *Arbutus* account parodied the surprised comments of others as these enthusiastic investigators of nature searched the shorelines for fish: "'Them gurls cannot be college gurls; why they wade in the water three hours at a time and don't take cold.' They must be a new species."[2] Regardless of any such doubts, women were actively engaged, capable students of science at Indiana University since the earliest days of their admittance in 1867.

As this chapter will explore, the early scientific women of Indiana University made substantial and sometimes surprising impacts through their lives and their studies. While the history of women in science is often evaluated solely in terms of individuals' impact on scientific knowledge itself, that tendency risks missing out on a richer history of people's interactions with, contributions to, and uses of science. As higher education opened to women in the nineteenth century, science was still undergoing the process of professionalization that would even make *scientist* a separate career option. American colleges and universities sought to establish themselves as critical to the scientific development and technological success of the nation, but they did so primarily by emphasizing the development of a more broadly capable, scientifically minded citizen. This larger vision of scientific citizenship looked different for male versus female graduates, despite its advance of educational opportunities for both. Consequently, the choices women made on how to use and apply their scientific training and abilities were shaped by a separate set of motivations, options, and perceived responsibilities. Recognizing the diversity of these choices uncovers the importance of women's experiences in learning science at Indiana University, the ways that women influenced IU's emerging scientific community, and how women carried their scientific education forward into lives beyond the university itself.

SCIENCE, EDUCATION, AND OPPORTUNITY FOR WOMEN

For women, connections between scientific pursuits, educational opportunities, and occupational paths developed along a different historical trajectory than for their male counterparts. A new ideal of highly literate and well-informed women had emerged during the Renaissance and continued through the Enlightenment, even as the doors of higher education remained largely closed to them. As historian Londa Schiebinger has pointed out, the new scientific developments of that period were not firmly encapsulated within the universities either, and many women of the upper classes were enthusiastic consumers—and occasionally well-known producers—of scientific lectures, literature, exhibitions, and collections.[3] By the nineteenth century, science was often associated with the same reforms that provided greater educational opportunities for women, though the purposes underlying women's education were still often starkly separated from their male counterparts and frequently defined in terms of their benefit to *men*. In the young United States, both education and science were seen as essential to the development of an informed, capable, and *moral* citizenry, with knowledge of the natural world and the skill to intelligently explore it being viewed as essential for all. Particularly in the heavily religious tones of education in antebellum America, study of the natural world was thought to provide new insight into a divine plan and moral order, making it an important pursuit for both men and women.[4] Although the practical benefits of women of scientific insight running the home were often touted, the moral and educational role that women played in childrearing was considered even more important as a reason for women to be well-educated.[5] Women were involved in many of the popular lyceums and natural history museums that were established around the country, and prominent female educational reformers such as Emma Willard at the Troy Female Seminary and Mary Lyon at Mt. Holyoke strongly emphasized science as an essential part of improving education for women.[6]

This progressive connection between science education and women's education also held true at Indiana University. In 1852, the board of trustees reviewed several proposals from the faculty regarding measures to make the university better connected to public interests and "into more general connection with the great educational wants and interests of the State."[7] These proposals included new courses in agricultural chemistry and civil engineering, the elevation of the "scientific course" of study to an actual degree option, and the establishment of a normal school (a training school for teachers) for both male and female students. The latter was cited as one of the most important routes to better connecting the university with education across the state, with women already playing a major role in precollegiate education. Although the resulting normal school, which divided the students into separate male and female departments, lasted only a few years, the fifteen female students in its initial class were the first to be formally associated with IU.[8] The normal school is thus an important but little known part of the larger history of women at IU and reflected IU's critical interest in the quality of women's education around the state—especially since women teachers were educating many of their enrollees—and that they would make educational opportunities and resources such as attendance at the college's science lectures available to women even if not allowing full enrollment at that time.[9] Fifteen years later, IU science professors such as Theophilus Wylie and Richard Dale Owen supported Sarah Parke Morrison as she petitioned the university for the full and equal admission of women in 1867. Morrison reported that she waited in the Wylies' house for word of the board of trustees' decision on admitting women and that the positive news was brought to her by Owen, a professor of natural science and chemistry whose brother Robert Dale Owen had championed women's rights in the Indiana legislature in the early 1850s.[10] When Wylie later wrote up the history of the university, completed in 1890, he proudly and prominently highlighted the university's admission of women and highlighted their accomplishments as graduates alongside the young men's.

Morrison and the first class of female students entered a university that was largely undifferentiated in its curriculum, with no majors and few options for student concentration in one area versus another. Although there were two official courses of study, the "classical" versus the "scientific," these initially differed primarily in the amount of emphasis placed on ancient languages and literature versus modern. Many of the earliest female graduates at IU earned the BS degree not because of any substantially greater scientific interest or training on their part but because that was the curricular track that offered study in French or German rather than Greek. Even as elective concentrations and student majors developed over the next couple decades, science remained a regular part of the curriculum for all students, with women studying chemistry, natural philosophy (physics, in today's terms), geology, astronomy, and other sciences alongside their peers.

Newly emerging educational ideals brought to IU by science faculty such as Thomas Van Nuys (professor of chemistry, hired 1874) and David Starr Jordan (professor of biology, hired 1879) had an impact on both how science was taught and the development of the larger university. Science, in this new view, was an active pursuit that could truly be learned only in the same way it was to be conducted: outdoors in the field or indoors in a laboratory. Students were to be directly engaged in the processes of scientific inquiry instead of learning primarily through lectures, books, and recitation sections, no matter how well these were illustrated with demonstrative experiments or geological collections. First as professor and then as university president from 1885 to 1891, Jordan in particular focused on developing active research opportunities for students, believing that "the highest function of the real university is that of instruction by investigation."[11] While at some universities this emphasis on research served to limit or exclude women, IU's history of admitting women on equal terms and Jordan's own commitment to coeducation helped establish

women's inclusion within IU's early scientific community and provide opportunities for women both at and beyond IU.

Jordan came to IU having already learned and worked with many well-
educated women. Near his hometown in western New York state, he had actually done part of his college preparatory work by attending classes at the local
female seminary, taught by two alumnae from Mary Lyon's Mount Holyoke.[12]
Although the newly opened Cornell University admitted only men when Jordan attended there, his sister Mary was one of three women allowed to attend
classes and work in laboratories in the fall of 1871, paving the way for the full
admission of women a few years later.[13] However, Jordan's experience in Louis
Agassiz's summer school on Penikese Island in 1873, just after his first year of
teaching post-graduation, was probably the strongest influence on Jordan's
encouragement of women in science, as well as on his general philosophy of
education. This summer school was a profoundly transformative educational
opportunity for Jordan and many of the other attendees, all of whom had been
selected by Agassiz—the preeminent natural scientist in the United States at
the time—as promising candidates to revolutionize both the teaching and
study of the natural sciences. The Anderson School for Natural History, as
the summer program was formally called, promoted the natural world as its
own university, in which students learned through the direct exploration and
investigation of nature. In his opening speech on the island, which was reported
by newspapers across the country, Agassiz explained, "Our object is to study
nature. I hope to teach you to read [it] for yourselves. You must not begin by
using any report of others, but we will try to begin by making nature around
us our text-book. I will try to make you the investigator."[14]

The coeducational nature of the summer school at Penikese, with about one-
third of the first summer's students being female, was itself a substantial advancement for American women in science, particularly when graduate study
was still almost entirely closed to women and Agassiz's reputation was such
that the opportunity to study with him was coveted by anyone eager to advance
in their field. Historian of education Joan Burstyn has noted that Agassiz's
summer school also had a significant impact as a model that established other
summer training schools, providing a means of educational advancement for
working female schoolteachers as well as research and employment opportunities for science students and faculty.[15] However, Agassiz's explicit decision to
make the summer school coeducational was not without objections. Some of
the young men attending the summer school even protested the inclusion of the
women with a prank, tossing a fake pillow "baby" into the women's quarters at

night to alarm them. Agassiz, firm and unamused, dismissed the men involved from the island and school the following morning, impressing upon Jordan and other participants that women were colleagues deserving of respect.[16] Rosa Smith Eigenmann, whose early career in ichthyology was aided by Jordan and several Penikese alumnae, credited Agassiz and his wife, Elizabeth Cary Agassiz—an active participant and co-organizer—for having essentially opened the field of zoology to American women through the summer school's establishment.[17] Regarding the inclusion of women in Agassiz's educational vision, Jordan concluded that "the results justified the innovation" and brought the Penikese model to IU, taking his students, both men and women, out into nature to study it directly whenever possible.[18]

In Jordan's view of coeducation, students benefited from the interaction of the sexes because of their supposedly inherent differences, "men growing more refined and sensitive, women more sane and self-contained."[19] Although Jordan "made no special claims for women," according to one newspaper article on the matter, he argued that improving the education of women was critical to the advancement of society.[20] Such views dovetailed with Jordan's more problematic eugenicist work but served in this case to motivate the development of an inclusive collegiality among male and female students as they explored and studied nature together. The power of these experiences is evident in reunion reflections of IU's class of 1883, written over thirty years after they had all joined Jordan on a two-week "tramp" around the Cumberland Gap:

> To the members of the class, bred mostly among the level cornfields and sluggish creeks of Indiana, this trip had come as the opening of a new world. The sight of the forest-clad mountains of the Cumberland range, ... of mountain streams dancing their way down pebbly beds, of foaming rapids and forest aisles bordered by the mountain laurel with its white and crimson blooms, was all that such things could be to those who looked on them for the first time with the glad eyes of youth. Dr. Jordan took the class afoot through the country, fifty miles from a railroad, across bridgeless streams where the boys rolled up their trousers and carried the girls across. They stopped at night with quaint and hospitable mountaineers and feudists, the girls occupying the bedrooms at night while the men lay on "shake-downs" in the main sitting-room. They sang class songs, ... studied geology and botany, and fished and seined the creeks, one or two new specimens of fish being discovered.[21]

Learning directly from nature, as practiced by Jordan and by his trainees and successors at IU, was an opportunity for men and women to flourish together.

MIXED VISIBILITY: SUCCESSES AND
STRUGGLES OF IU WOMEN IN SCIENCE

One of the women Jordan had met at Penikese was Susan Bowen, a recent graduate of Mount Holyoke Seminary who was teaching science there under the
mentorship of the seminary's longtime botany teacher Lydia Shattuck. After
spending the summer learning, discussing, and conducting studies in natural
science on Penikese, Bowen worked on establishing Mount Holyoke's own
natural history collection.[22] In the summer of 1874, she returned to Penikese
along with Cornelia Clapp, a fellow Mt. Holyoke teacher who later became a
prominent marine biologist. Susan Bowen, on the other hand, married Jordan
the following year, leaving her own collecting and teaching days behind to
accompany and support her husband instead. In his autobiography, Jordan
noted that she traveled with him and his pupil Charles H. Gilbert in the summer of 1876 as they studied the fish of northern Georgia, but his publication of
the trip's results did not mention Susan's participation. The couple's first child
was born in February 1877, and Susan seems to have traveled little more with
Jordan on his trips in the years following. When she died from pneumonia ten
years after her marriage, the papers noted her personal virtues, her literary accomplishments, and her charity work but made little to no mention of her prior
work in science. Despite Jordan's support, encouragement, and advancement of
women's involvement in science, his own wife was one of the many women of
this era whose scientific interests and pursuits faded from view upon their marriage, yet who served to bolster their husbands' scientific careers. Such women
formed an important, though often little recognized today, complement to the
early scientific community and faculty at IU, as well as aiding other female
scientists from behind the scenes.

Meadie Hawkins Evermann's passion for natural science brought both her
and her husband, Barton Warren Evermann (born Everman), to IU. Married in 1875, the couple spent several years teaching together as principal and
schoolteacher in Camden, Indiana. While spending the summer of 1877 in
Indianapolis, Meadie first met David Starr Jordan and the small community of
naturalists he had formed about him during his pre-IU positions teaching high
school and at Butler University. At the time, this group, which included Susan
Bowen Jordan; Dr. Alembert W. Brayton and his wife, Julia Dewey Brayton;
and Charles Henry Gilbert, had been collecting bird specimens, leading to
Brayton's publication of the first systematic catalogue of birds in Indiana.[23]
Meadie quickly learned the skill of preparing taxidermy bird "study skins"
well enough to assist the group's efforts as well as start her own collection. She

passed her enthusiasm for studying nature on to her husband, and the couple turned their teaching and study interests to botany, ornithology, and zoology. In the summer of 1878, the two joined Jordan, Gilbert, Brayton, Jordan's Penikese colleague Cornelia Clapp, and a collection of others in a summer "tramp" from Kentucky to Georgia.[24] The Evermanns continued to travel and study with Jordan on trips over the next few years before following him to IU to become students. Years later, the *Indiana University Alumni Quarterly* reported that the Evermanns reasoned that going through college together, despite the demands of raising two young children as they did so, was the best way to grow together while maintaining the equality of "education . . . social equipment and standing" that they had possessed when they married.[25] In 1887, Meadie became the first married woman to graduate from IU. Because her class was the first to graduate with formal majors, reflecting the move toward specialized study under Jordan's presidency, Meadie was also the first woman to officially graduate with a science major—namely, biology. After his own graduation, her husband Barton's scientific career continued to progress, and he eventually became director of the Natural History Museum of the California Academy of Sciences. Meadie reportedly remained enthusiastic about science throughout her life but focused her own efforts on supporting Barton's career, raising a family, and advocating for women's education through a variety of clubs and social organizations.

The most scientifically prominent of the early women who studied with Jordan at IU was Rosa Smith Eigenmann, widely recognized as the first female ichthyologist in the United States. Rosa Smith met Jordan in January of 1880 when he arrived in California to lead a Pacific Coast survey for the US Fish Commission, having only barely started as professor at IU the year before. Smith, then twenty-one, was an avid member of the San Diego Society of Natural History (SDSNH), whose meetings and scientific activities she both dutifully recorded for the society and reported on for the *San Diego Union*.[26] Recruiting help from the SDSNH in collecting information about local fish and fishing activity, Jordan found Smith an eager student and capable worker. By February, Jordan was answering her letters with advice on how best to identify, preserve, and ship the fish specimens she was collecting for him. In March, he wrote back to Smith regarding an unusual specimen of fish she had found by noting the opportunity she might have before her to establish her own name in the field, "Better send it to me at Monterey by mail, unless you wish to describe it yourself and this have the honor of being the first woman who has entered descriptive ichthyology. In that case, send me the fish with your description."[27] Finding her description "very satisfactory," Jordan helped Smith with navigating the delicate waters of publishing about what may or may not be a distinct, new species.[28] He wrote to her, "When your paper is published you will have the honor of being the first woman who has described and named a fish. I hope your first one will not be the last one."[29] It would not be; Smith went on to publish descriptions of many new fish specimens in the following decades, carefully documenting their appearance, their anatomy, and whatever details were known about their natural environs, development, and common habits.

Jordan invited Smith to join his traveling survey team that summer, noting, "Prof. Evermann and his wife, ornithologists, will join us the first of June, and the presence of another lady would make our camp less disagreeable to you. I can get you half-fare tickets and reduced rates of board, if you should think it proper to meet us anywhere, and your parents should think it wise. . . . If you wish to be an ichthyologist however, you ought to do this—or else go to Bloomington next winter."[30] Smith wrote back enthusiastically, "Your proposition for me to join your party during some of the summer months and get instruction about fishes is exactly what would suit me to do, and it may be that I can."[31] Jordan and Smith's communication shows some of the challenges that faced young women interested in science, as Smith's involvement in the trip and her later study at IU depended on her father's approval and willingness to help fund her interests. To navigate the social demands of the time period, each woman's individual pursuit of science was influenced by the interest and engagement of other women. Meadie Hawkins Evermann's participation in the scientific survey alongside her husband meant better opportunity for Smith to go.[32] Since Jordan was traveling without his wife, he also had to be cognizant of such social rules: requesting a letter of introduction in order to meet Smith's scientist friend Kate Sessions, he wrote, "I don't think I should have the cheek to call upon her unless I was armed with something of that kind."[33]

Smith continued her scientific studies initially by correspondence when Jordan returned to Bloomington that August, writing up a descriptive list of San Diego fishes for publication by the end of the year. In the early months of 1881, Smith made the expensive and difficult trip east to begin studying at Indiana University, where she took French with the freshman class but studied botany with the junior and senior classes and studied ichthyology privately with Jordan and his assistant Gilbert.[34] Smith was thrilled to receive permission and funding from her parents to join in on Jordan's 1881 summertime expedition to Europe. Listing her in the trip roster as "Rosa Smith, San Diego, Cal., naturalist," Jordan presented Smith to his European scientific connections as a young colleague. On one occasion he took her with him to meet with ichthyologist and herpetologist Dr. Albert Günther, the head of zoology at the British Museum.[35]

While waiting for their meeting, Smith studied the collected fish and other specimens in the room they were in, noting that a good number of the fish were ones she had assisted with from Jordan's California expedition.[36] Günther complimented Smith on her published list of fishes of the San Diego area and offered her opportunity both to study there at the museum and to correspond with him further about her research.

When Smith returned to Bloomington, her time as a student at IU was limited. She was one of few students at the time to attend the university from so far away, and the separation from her family and expense of travel was difficult for her.[37] Returning home to California in the summer of 1882, she was unable to return in the fall, instead resuming her position as an active member in San Diego's growing scientific community and forming new scientific connections up and down the West Coast. Although Smith had not finished her degree at IU, Jordan seems to have recognized her training as largely complete, since in late 1882 he was supporting Smith in applying for teaching and research positions on the West Coast.[38] By March of 1883, Smith was publishing new fish descriptions, reporting back to Jordan on her latest explorations, and suggesting she was ready for some larger engagements: "Don't you think I deserve to be sent somewhere where I shall see a few species that are not common in San Diego waters? I had hoped to get *Cremnobates* in tide pools but the Todos Santos rock pools are even more destitute of species than our own."[39]

In the next few years, Smith did some science teaching, curated fishes for the California Academy of Sciences, and also collected specimens for the Smithsonian Institution. When IU lost much of its scientific collection in the fire of 1883, Smith was one of many who helped rebuild it, donating part of her own collection and then collecting further specimens for it at Jordan's request. When Jordan suggested Smith come back to Bloomington and then go on to Washington, DC for further study and publications, she wrote to her mother eagerly about the possibility, but with the awareness that it might be a hardship to the family:

> You know I do not want to go and spend so much money if it is not best. Still it would give me the chance to do a little more scientific work, which I enjoy, and on many accounts, I could be better spared now than when I went before. If you and father should be very ill you would telegraph and I would come right home. . . . Of course, I enjoy my home and can study here somewhat, but I know I do better to be pushed, as one is where a school full of students are studying together.[40]

Unfortunately, family obligations or disapproval kept Smith in California at the time.

In 1887, Rosa Smith married Carl Eigenmann, another of Jordan's students, who had recently graduated Indiana University and who shared her passion for the study of fish. As enraptured with each other as with the fish they studied, the young married couple set off to work together on studying Louis Agassiz's largely neglected collection of South American fish specimens at Harvard University.[41] In Massachusetts, Rosa found a variety of new opportunities available to her. She studied lichens in W. G. Farlow's laboratory and took botany courses at the Harvard Summer School that had been established by Asa Gray. She was given a worktable at the US Fish Commission's station at Woods Holl (now known as Woods Hole), which was a scholarly honor. She and Carl worked fervently together on producing a comprehensive catalogue and coherent taxonomy of the known freshwater fish of South America, part of what would become an extensive set of publications as the well-known team Eigenmann & Eigenmann. Both Eigenmanns wrote to Rosa's parents bragging about the other's latest work, with Carl noting that Rosa was finding "ever so many nice things."[42] Rosa, however, seems to have found new standards to hold her own work to in the more exacting and often elitist New England scientific community. As a former science reporter for the *San Diego Union*, she had gladly published her latest journeys and discoveries in that paper throughout the years, but she turned down such an opportunity now, writing to her mother that she felt it would be inappropriate and might look bad to potential employers as the couple sought a more permanent position.[43] Rosa gave examples of the other women she knew in the scientific community there who were quietly and diligently working as hard as or even harder than she felt she was, with less recognition.

In 1899, with a child on the way, Carl and Rosa returned to California to continue their fish studies in a familiar locale. The birth of their first daughter, however, added new pressures to Rosa's life, and she began to worry that she could not pull her weight as a scientist or as a full colleague to her husband. Although she had worked diligently up to and shortly after childbirth, by the following year Rosa was writing despondently in her diary that she felt not just unproductive herself but like an actual impediment to their scientific work together, claiming, "I help Carl less than ever and can see that I hinder him a great deal."[44] Such concerns continued to haunt Rosa as their family continued to grow and as the Eigenmanns returned to Indiana University in 1891 for Carl to take over the professorship that Jordan was vacating. With five children, one that was mentally disabled and another that was sickly, as well as occasional struggles with her own mental and physical health, Rosa's ability to participate in IU's intellectual life even as a faculty wife was severely limited. In an 1899 article "Some American Women in Science," the author reported that Rosa had "done but little scientific work" since the family's move to Bloomington, explaining, "As the mother of four little children her time is occupied with their training, that being to her of more importance than any amount of scientific work."[45] Whereas Carl was known and admired for his intensity and absolute dedication to his scientific work, Rosa's mental focus was necessarily caught up in the demands of children and household by which she as a wife and mother would ultimately be judged, as well as helping her husband with editing and correspondence. Consequently, Rosa's ability and activity in science faded in and out of view in the following decades, even as Carl and his fellow professors incorporated new generations of young women into their labs and fieldwork at IU. Despite these limitations, she was the first female member (1905) and later the first female president (1914–15) of IU's chapter of Sigma Xi, a scientific honorary society.[46] She helped Carl found IU's own coeducational summer scientific school by establishing the biological field station at Turkey Lake (later relocated to Winona Lake). Rosa and the children spent at least part of most summers at the field station with Carl and his students, where she helped with instruction and management.

Rosa Smith Eigenmann's career shows how the love of science could place challenging and sometimes conflicting burdens on its female devotees. Rosa addressed these in her 1895 speech on the topic "Women in Science," delivered as president of the National Science Club for Women, where she claimed that women had made many indirect contributions as supporters of science but few praiseworthy advances in scientific knowledge itself. She emphasized that women ought to be held to the same standards as their male counterparts in that regard, stating, "Her work must not be simply well done for a woman."[47] Yet she also argued that women rarely had circumstances akin to those of a man, particularly the discretion to fully devote their time and focus to scientific pursuits: "Science is exacting, requiring the devotion of months and even of years to the completion of a series of observations which frequently must be carried on with little or no interruptions. Women are seldom in a position to do work in this way."[48] While Rosa went on to discuss examples of the important contributions American women had made, her speech offered no true resolution to the tension between the many demands and obligations a woman faced and her ability to truly contribute to the advance of scientific knowledge. Unable to find any way to successfully reconcile these in her own life, Rosa resigned herself to a supporting role in science, enabling her beloved husband's scientific career as best she could.

For other women, the "textbook of nature" that they had learned to read at IU led them to well-recognized careers sharing this revelation with others. Jennie Foster and her future husband, classmate David A. Curry, had fallen in love with the great outdoors as well as one another on the 1883 IU graduating class expedition with Jordan. After marriage and starting school teaching jobs in Utah, they began organizing and leading summer treks through Yellowstone National Park for fellow educators.[49] Moving to California a few years later, the couple found that the cost to visit Yosemite National Park was prohibitively high for many researchers and would-be explorers, who could not afford to stay in Yosemite's high-priced tourist hotels, especially for any extended scientific study. The summer campground they founded as a small collection of tents and one hired cook quickly grew into a full-time occupation, with David becoming well-known for his booming voice, larger-than-life personality, and enthusiastic welcome to guests. Jennie played a quieter role for many years, managing the camp from behind the scenes and making sure that the rapidly growing number of guests (over one thousand each summer by 1905) were properly housed and fed. Her gentle-but-firm management and care for others earned her the title Mother Curry from the camp's numerous summer employees, often young men and women from local colleges and universities. Yosemite historian Shirley Sargent recounts: "While David Curry was busy in the office or meeting guests, 'Mother' Curry was everywhere in the camp. Although her work was mainly supervisorial, she admitted 'I did a little of everything, one time or another. I have made soap and put up tents. I've been baker and headwaitress, postmistress and pantry woman.'"[50]

Camp Curry became a major Yosemite institution over the years, regularly frequented by naturalists, educators, researchers, and artists as well as by numerous vacationing families. When David died in 1917, Jennie continued to run the successful and seemingly ever-expanding campground with her children. In 1933, she was honored by IU at her fifty-year class reunion for her work as one of the "pioneers in the movement which opened up this [Yosemite Valley] region."[51] She and her family were known for their love of Yosemite and the High Sierras, a passion they shared and inspired in many of their camp's visitors through educational tours, programs, and their sheer enjoyment of nature. While Jennie Foster Curry's life's work may not seem like a scientific contribution as we normally understand it, the substantial reputation she earned in supporting American naturalists grew out of her science education at IU. Furthermore, her example serves to illustrate how the differing context of the death of her husband and a business vocation that could outlast his personal reputation allowed her to gain widespread recognition for the same sort of household and managerial work that other scientific women did without acclaim.

Another IU graduate, Rousseau McClellan, became an influential and much-admired science educator in the Indianapolis public schools, credited with developing an especially strong program in the biological sciences and inspiring a number of students to successful scientific careers.[52] Even before her graduation from IU in 1898, McClellan was one of the early instructors at the summer biological station the Eigenmanns had opened, where she led courses on "nature study," an approach that promoted nature-centered educational ideals at the lower grade levels.[53] McClellan's teaching engaged students in ways that cultivated a love of nature while also deepening their scientific understanding of it. As instructor of botany and nature studies at Shortridge High School in Indianapolis, McClellan led her students in such activities as exploratory nature walks, dissections of sheep's hearts, and hatching tadpoles from frogs' eggs.[54] In 1909, students dedicated their yearbook to her, with the declaration, "To Rousseau McClellan, who has opened unto us the door of the true fairyland of nature, and while guiding us along those unaccustomed paths, has given each one the priceless treasure of a wholesome influence."[55] Beyond her own classroom, McClellan gave popular lectures on scientific topics to local clubs, coordinated grade-school campaigns against destructive caterpillars, and planned material for local celebrations of Arbor Day.[56] As World War I created concerns about farm labor shortages affecting the produce supply, McClellan organized a massive school garden project in the Indianapolis schools, engaging nearly twenty thousand students.[57] At the time of her death in 1939, forty years' worth of students, including a number who had become scientists, paid tribute to the impact that she'd had on them. When Indianapolis Public School 91 was renamed a couple years afterward in her honor, the *Indianapolis Star* reported, "Through the personal ties established with her students, she was able to inculcate in them some of her own love of the outdoors.... Many today are thankful for the insight into nature and its creatures which they gained under her capable supervision."[58]

SCIENTIFIC CITIZENSHIP AND LEADERSHIP AMONG WOMEN OF IU

Even at proudly coeducational institutions such as Indiana University, the university's impact tended to be presented in terms of male students' potential as leaders in innovation and social progress, yet it is clear that women took higher education's call to lives of meaningful contribution to society just as seriously. Many university women were active in larger issues of improving women's general welfare, rights, and education, which were themselves compelling issues for the scientifically trained woman to tackle in an era during which better scientific understanding was expected to bring about a more just and ethical society.[59] Effa Funk Muhse, the first woman to earn a PhD at IU, was one such graduate, traveling widely as a speaker on both women's suffrage and matters of science and public health. Starting as a student at IU in 1900 alongside her husband, Muhse had filled her lab notebooks with series of microscope observations and detailed sketches of animal dissections that she had performed.[60] She helped with summer instruction at the Winona Lake biological field station in 1902 while still an undergraduate. Although she also studied at Cornell, Muhse earned her AB (1903), AM (1906), and PhD (1908) from IU, culminating in her published dissertation on *The Cutaneous Glands of the Common Toads*.[61] Moving to Washington, DC, she became involved in the early days of the movement toward a constitutional amendment for women's suffrage and was one of the national organizers sent out across the country by the National Woman's Party to gain support for this cause.[62] She also frequently lectured on matters of genetics, heredity, and eugenics, of which she thought there was a critical need for better scientific understanding.[63] For Muhse, these two causes were connected, with one newspaper reporting that Muhse found it "sufficient reason" for women's suffrage that "scientific knowledge proves that men and women inherit equally from their ancestors and that in the United States it is a matter of pure justice that women should vote on the same terms as men, since we live in a so-called democracy."[64] Using her scientific training to advance the position of women and to evaluate critical issues facing women of her day, Muhse fulfilled the ideals of scientific citizenship but did so in a way specific to her interests as a woman. She went on to teach biology to young women at Chevy Chase Junior College for nearly twenty years.

Focusing on issues of particular interest to women proved a mix of opportunity and impediment in the university, particularly as standards for faculty research achievement in the sciences continued to grow. Jordan himself had set a precedent in resisting hiring a female professor in 1887, writing to the trustees that he doubted they could hire any of the "very rare" women suitable for a full faculty position, as a woman "could not succeed as the occupant of a chair in the university" unless her "special scholarship" fully equaled that of her male colleagues.[65] While such a statement may seem equitable on the surface, it was part of a fundamental inequity in which universities hired "promising" young men more easily than well-qualified women, reflecting an irony noted by historian of science Margaret W. Rossiter: "American society, and especially its university faculties, became far more willing to educate women in science than to employ them."[66] Consequently, women's occupancy of more than minor or temporary faculty positions was limited at IU until the population of female students was large enough that the university had to intentionally incorporate women into leadership roles. Chemist Mary Bidwell Breed became IU's first female member of the regular science faculty when she was recruited and hired in 1901 as both dean of women and assistant professor of chemistry. Breed had earned a PhD from Bryn Mawr with her meticulous synthesis and investigation of the polybasic acids of mesitylene, at the same time developing an interest in academic governance and administration.[67] Although she had studied overseas in the prestigious laboratory of chemist Victor Meyer at the University of Heidelberg and taught science at the Pennsylvania College for Women (now Chatham University), Breed did little scientific work after coming to IU. Her efforts focused primarily on addressing issues facing IU's female students, which indeed were the main purpose behind her hire.[68] As the first dean of women at IU, she took responsibility for establishing new social standards for coeducation, but her emphasis on etiquette and propriety aggravated many around campus, especially among male students and faculty who viewed such matters as trivial. At the end of her first year, the *Arbutus* mockingly labeled her "Miss Breed: Dean of Conventionality" and portrayed her as an incompetent teacher of chemistry and math.[69] While she eventually earned a measure of respect for her work with the university's young women before moving on to become a successful administrator elsewhere, Breed made little impact on or contribution to the scientific community at IU, and her teaching responsibilities in chemistry slowly diminished.[70]

Breed's time at IU also marked a shift in the way women were treated and viewed within the university. IU historian Thomas D. Clark credits her with breaking "the traditions of informality in the university and the community by reordering relationships between the sexes," but this development at IU reflects a more widespread shift in the view of women's education and scholarship with the growth and promotion of what historian of education Andrea Turpin has described as "gendered moral visions."[71] At IU, much like other public universities in the Midwest and West, the coeducation that had developed had been permissive and unstructured, with matters like housing and socialization largely unregulated other than through the social norms of what constituted "good behavior" and by disciplinary action when it was clearly warranted. But where in 1890 there had been 10 women students in IU's graduating class of '65, by 1900 there were 35 women in a class of 105, and by 1910, 85 women in a class of

360.[72] Such rapidly growing enrollments raised new concerns about the university's ability to appropriately manage and mentor young women, especially as students of both sexes began to compete for resources in the university. While the moral formation of young men was already considered to be well within the domain of the university's mostly male faculty and administration, the moral formation and supervision of women students became a task relegated to the dean of women and to organizations such as the Women's League, founded by IU "First Lady" Frances Morgan Swain in 1895.[73] This new attention to the distinctly female portion of the student body again had benefits and drawbacks, recognizing women's interests while at the same time circumscribing them.

Although women's education had long been influenced by views of the two sexes' "separate spheres of influence," Turpin argues that as the turn of the century approached and the number of women entering universities grew, the vision of the ideal college graduate became more explicitly defined, and hence divided, according to gender.[74] Rossiter claims that much of the movement toward the professionalization of science during this time period similarly served to define and defend "masculine" science against a growing influx of women.[75] At the same time, the increase of college-educated women and their professional influence in fields such as education and social work was leading to discussions, among both men and women, of whether there were certain contributions to science and society that women might be uniquely suited to making. Although science faculty such as Jordan and Eigenmann believed in distinct gender traits, they had generally recognized fields of study like ichthyology as neither masculine or feminine in nature, meaning Rosa or Carl could discover and define a new species of fish equally well according to their talent. By contrast, by the turn of the century, the new field of home economics was a science promoted primarily by and to women. IU's Department of Home Economics began with an experimental course in 1911 testing the appeal of the new "domestic science" to women in the college and the surrounding community.[76] The coursework focused substantially on practical training for female students in subjects such as cooking and sewing, but such topics were approached in a scientific manner, with emphasis on aspects like minimizing costs of production, analyzing nutritional value regarding health and well-being, experimental analysis of foods, etc. In 1914, the *Indiana Daily Student* reported, "The third floor of Wylie Hall has been transformed. Instead of a sleepy class assembled to hear a lecture, fifty girls are found at work in large well-equipped laboratories for cooking and making chemical tests of foods."[77]

The head of the department at IU was chemist Mabel Thacher Wellman, an 1895 graduate of Wellesley College who had become an early part of the home economics movement, teaching summer courses alongside the field's founding leaders, women such as Alice Peloubet Norton and Ellen Swallow Richards. Wellman's textbook on "food study" presented basic cooking recipes as the start of laboratory experiments to be done to build an understanding of bacteriology, nutritional chemistry, digestion and metabolism, the chemical properties of water, etc.[78] She argued that instruction in cooking could balance the inductive approach essential to the sciences with the benefit of accumulated knowledge and inspire students to further experimentation, writing, "Here, as in other sciences, sufficient discovery to arouse interest, to enable the pupil to question understandingly, and to give control of the situation, is of undoubted benefit and leads on naturally to research."[79] Despite Wellman's understanding of the science underlying home economics, such aspects of the field were frequently subsumed by larger social goals for women or missed altogether by those who saw it as purely practical vocational training for domestic work in the home.[80] A 1917 account of the value of studying home economics at IU reported that this would help young women "grow into womanhood equipped to meet home and social problems in an intelligent and practical manner," cultivating a variety of personal virtues as well as helping her "concentrate" her household work in order to spend more time pursuing projects of value to the larger community.[81] While the all-female faculty complement of the rapidly growing Department of Home Economics added to the representation of early scientific women at IU and provided valuable opportunities for women as scientists and scholars, the heavily gendered context in which the department's contributions were viewed simultaneously distanced their work from the main scientific community.

CONCLUSION

While this chapter cannot possibly cover all of the women involved with science in the first fifty years after their admission to IU, those featured here demonstrate that women were an essential part of the early scientific community at the university and a substantial part of its legacy as alumnae. Although differing social responsibilities and professional opportunities frequently constrained women's ability to pursue a full, independent scientific career, women's chance to pursue their interests throughout their studies at the university was less restricted, particularly in the biological sciences that dominated scientific activity at IU for several decades leading up to the turn of the century. While a number of East Coast universities focused their efforts on scientifically training young men whom they saw as being the best future leaders of science and industry, Indiana University reflected the trend toward broader and more permissive coeducation in the public universities of the Midwest and West, where better science education was expected to benefit both sexes. The inclusion of women at IU was promoted by the development of a sense of coeducational camaraderie and shared enthusiasm for scientific study, especially in outdoor fieldwork. However, IU faculty's encouragement of women as students, junior colleagues, educated companions, and scientific citizens did not clearly extend to full confidence in women's abilities to become equal leaders in the academic and scientific community, unless that leadership was somehow targeted toward women or to specific feminized domains. Despite this, even with limited professional paths and well before women gained voting rights, the scientific women of IU found a variety of ways to make meaningful contributions after graduation, shaping education or contributing to science through patronage or support of others' scientific careers.

NOTES

1. *Arbutus '99* (Chicago: A. L. Swift & Co. College Publications, 1899), 185, HathiTrust, https://hdl.handle.net/2027/umn.31951002210080h.

2. *Arbutus '96* (Chicago: A. L. Swift & Co. College Publications, 1896), 150, HathiTrust, https://hdl.handle.net/2027/umn.319510022100776.

3. Londa Schiebinger, *The Mind Has No Sex?: Women in the Origins of Modern Science* (Cambridge, MA: Harvard University Press, 1989), 30–44.

4. The natural theology that connected the purposes of science, education, and moral society was deeply woven into American education well into the late nineteenth century. For a discussion of this religious aspect of American higher education, particularly in the natural sciences, and how it changed, see John H. Roberts and James Turner, *The Sacred and the Secular University* (Princeton, NJ: Princeton University Press, 2000).

5. Linda K. Kerber, *Women of the Republic: Intellect and Ideology in Revolutionary America* (Chapel Hill: University of North Carolina Press, 1980), 228–31.

6. Margaret W. Rossiter, *Women Scientists in America: Struggles and Strategies to 1940* (Baltimore, MD: The Johns Hopkins University Press, 1982), 3–8.

7. Indiana University Board of Trustees, Minutes, April 10, 1852–April 15, 1852, digitization by Indiana University Libraries Digital Collections Services, Indiana University Archives, and the Board of Trustees Office, http://purl.dlib.indiana.edu/iudl/archives/iubot/1852-04-10.

8. Theophilus A. Wylie, *Indiana University, Its History from 1820, When Founded, to 1890* (Indianapolis, IN: Wm. B. Burford, 1890), 60–61, https://books.google.com/books?id=tL4oAAAAYAAJ.

9. Indiana University Board of Trustees, Minutes, July 30, 1853–August 4, 1853, http://purl.dlib.indiana.edu/iudl/archives/iubot/1853-07-30; for more on both the Monroe County Female Seminary and women's involvement in local preparatory education, see *History of Lawrence and Monroe Counties, Indiana: Their People, Industries, and Institutions* (Indianapolis, IN: B. F. Bowen & Co., Inc., 1914), 261–67, https://books.google.com/books?id=cxwVAAAAYAAJ.

10. Sarah Parke Morrison, "Some Sidelights of Fifty Years Ago," *Indiana University Alumni Quarterly* 6, no.4 (October 1919): 529–31, HathiTrust, https://hdl .handle.net/2027/uc1.b2872365.

11. William A. Rawles, "Historical Sketch," in *Indiana University, 1820–1904*, ed. Samuel Bannister Harding (Bloomington: Indiana University [Burford], 1904), 21.

12. David Starr Jordan, *The Days of a Man: Being Memories of a Naturalist, Teacher, and Minor Prophet of Democracy*, Vol. 1, 1855–99 (Yonkers-on-Hudson, NY: World Book Company, 1922), 35–36, https://books.google.com/books?id =na4aAAAAYAAJ.

13. Jordan, *Days of a Man*, Vol. 1: 67; Morris Bishop, *A History of Cornell* (Ithaca, New York: Cornell University Press. 1962), 145.

14. "Penikese. Students of Natural History at the Island," *Boston Globe*, July 9, 1873, 1.

15. Joan Burstyn, "Early Women in Education: The Role of the Anderson School of Natural History," *Journal of Education* 59, no. 3 (August 1977): 50–64.

16. Burt G. Wilder, "Agassiz at Penikese," *The American Naturalist* 32, no. 375 (March 1898): 193, https://www.jstor.org/stable/2452464; Jordan, *Days of a Man*, Vol. 1: 111; Rosa Smith Eigenmann, "Women in Science" [speech given January 3, 1895, at the first annual meeting of the National Science Club for Women in Washington, DC], in *Proceedings of the National Science Club for Women* (Washington, DC: Judd & Detwiler, 1895), 14, HathiTrust, https://hdl.handle.net/2027/mdp .39015011940858.

17. Eigenmann, "Women in Science," 14.

18. Jordan, *Days of a Man*, Vol. 1: 108.

19. Jordan, 82

20. Excerpt from *Indianapolis Times, Bloomington Telephone* (Bloomington, IN), January 7, 1882; David Starr Jordan, *"The Ethics of the Dust": Commencement Address Delivered Before The Graduating Class, June 7, 1888* (Richmond, IN: Daily Palladium Book & Job Printing House, 1888), 12–13, in Indiana University President's Office Records, 1884–91 C77, Box 2, Folder Writings and Addresses, 1886–88, Undated, IU Libraries University Archives, Bloomington, Indiana, http://purl.dlib .indiana.edu/iudl/findingaids/archives/InU-Ar-VAA2632.

21. "Reunion of the Class of '83 in the Yosemite Valley," *Indiana University Alumni Quarterly* 2, no. 1 (January 1915): 473–74, HathiTrust, https://hdl.handle .net/2027/uc1.b2872361.

22. Miriam R. Levin, *Defining Women's Scientific Enterprise: Mount Holyoke Faculty and the Rise of American Science* (Hanover, NH: University Press of New England, 2005), 68–74.

23. "Alumni Notes by Classes: 1887," *Indiana University Alumni Quarterly* 16, no. 1 (January 1929): 288, HathiTrust, https://hdl.handle.net/2027/uc1.b2872375; Alembert W. Brayton, "A Catalogue of the Birds of Indiana, with Keys and Descriptions of the Groups of Greatest Interest to the Horticulturist," *Transactions of the Indiana Horticultural Society for 1879* (Indianapolis: Douglas & Carlon, 1879), 87–165, HathiTrust, https://hdl.handle.net/2027/mdp.39015067200371.

24. "Letter from the Butler University Tramps," *Indianapolis Journal*, June 28, 1878.

25. "Alumni Notes: 1887," *Indiana University Alumni Quarterly* 16, no.1 (January 1929): 288.

26. Bridgette Anne Byrd, "Rosa Smith Eigenmann: American Ichthyologist, 1858–1947" (master's thesis, University of San Diego, 1999), 18; Anne Dobson Bullard, "The San Diego Society of Natural History, 1874–1912" (master's thesis, University of San Diego, 1994), 37–39.

27. David S. Jordan to Rosa Smith, March 22, 1880, Rosa Smith Eigenmann Papers (1880–1927) C59, Box 1, IU Libraries University Archives, Bloomington, Indiana (hereafter cited as Rosa Smith Eigenmann Papers, IU Archives).

28. David S. Jordan to Rosa Smith, April 2, 1880, Rosa Smith Eigenmann Papers, Box 1, IU Archives.

29. David S. Jordan to Rosa Smith, April 23, 1880, Rosa Smith Eigenmann Papers, Box 1, IU Archives.

30. David S. Jordan to Rosa Smith, April 15, 1880, Rosa Smith Eigenmann Papers, Box 1, IU Archives.

31. Rosa Smith to David S. Jordan, undated handwritten copy, Rosa Smith Eigenmann Papers, Box 1, IU Archives.

32. This was true in making arrangements and persuading her parents even though the Evermanns' travel with the group ended up being delayed; Rosa boarded privately with a family in the area when she traveled with Jordan and Gilbert alone. Letter from Rosa Smith to Father and Mother (C. K. and Lucretia Smith), June 26, 1880, Box 1, Eigenmann mss., 1851–1971, Collection LMC 2212, Lilly Library, Indiana University, Bloomington, Indiana (hereafter cited as Eigenmann mss., Lilly Library, IU).

33. David S. Jordan to Rosa Smith, March 4, 1880, Rosa Smith Eigenmann Papers, Box 1, IU Archives.

34. Rosa Smith to Father and Mother (C. K. and Lucretia Smith), May 1, 1881, Box 1, Eigenmann mss., Lilly Library, IU.

35. "The Indiana University Summer Tramp," *Annual Report of the Indiana University Including the Catalogue for the Academical Year, 1881–1882* (Indianapolis: Wm.

B. Burford, 1882), 48, HathiTrust, https://hdl.handle.net/2027/uiug
.30112111985443.

36. Excerpts of Smith's letters and diary are published in "I.U. 'Tramps' toured
Europe in 1881 with Dr. David Starr Jordan as Leader," *Indianapolis Star,* January 15,
1928; originals in Box 1, Eigenmann mss., Lilly Library, IU.

37. Such comments appear throughout her correspondence. One example is
Rosa Smith to Sister, Mrs. J. R. (Mary) Berry, August 13, 1881, Box 1, Eigenmann
mss., Lilly Library, IU.

38. David S. Jordan to Rosa Smith, July 29, 1882, Rosa Smith Eigenmann Papers,
Box 1, IU Archives.

39. Rosa Smith to David S. Jordan, March 17, 1883, Rosa Smith Eigenmann Papers, Box 1, IU Archives.

40. Rosa Smith to Mother (Lucretia Smith), October 10, 1886, Box 1, Eigenmann
mss., Lilly Library, IU.

41. Mary P. Winsor, *Reading the Shape of Nature: Comparative Zoology at the
Agassiz Museum* (Chicago: University of Chicago Press, 1991), 182, 216–19.

42. Carl Eigenmann to Mother (Lucretia Smith), November 11, 1887, Box 1, Eigenmann mss., Lilly Library, IU.

43. Rosa Smith Eigenmann to Mother (Lucretia Smith), June 15, 1888, Box 1, Eigenmann mss., Lilly Library, IU.

44. Rosa Smith Eigenmann, diary entry of April 17, 1890, in Diary 1887–1902,
Box 3, Eigenmann mss., Lilly Library, IU.

45. Mrs. M. Burton Williamson, "Some American Women in Science [Part II],"
The Chatauquan 28, no. 4 (January 1899): 365, https://books.google.com/books
?id=oxTZAAAAMAAJ.

46. "History of the Indiana University Chapter: The Society of Sigma Xi, 1904–
1974," typewritten document, Sigma Xi, Indiana University Chapter Records C186,
1906–74, Box 2, Folder Administrative Records, 1906–74, IU Libraries University
Archives, Bloomington, Indiana, http://purl.dlib.indiana.edu/iudl/findingaids
/archives/InU-Ar-VAA2735.

47. Eigenmann, "Women in Science," 13.

48. Eigenmann, 16.

49. Lee H. Whittlesey, *Storytelling in Yellowstone: Horse & Buggy Tour Guides*
(Albuquerque: University of New Mexico Press, 2007), 66; Shirley Sargent, *Yosemite and Its Innkeepers: The Story of a Great Park and Its Chief Concessionaires* (Yosemite, CA: Flying Spur Press, 1975), 21.

50. Sargent, *Yosemite and Its Innkeepers,* 34–35.

51. "Commencement, 1933," *Indiana University Alumni Quarterly* 20, no. 1 (January 1933): 280–81, HathiTrust, https://hdl.handle.net/2027/uc1.b2872379.

52. "A Notable Teacher," *Indianapolis News,* July 4, 1939; "Veteran Teacher Here
Succumbs," *Indianapolis Star,* July 3, 1939.

53. Sally Gregory Kohlstedt, *Teaching Children Science: Hands-on Nature Study in North America, 1890–1930* (Chicago: University of Chicago Press, 2010).

54. "Official Notices," *Shortridge Daily Echo* [Indianapolis, IN], April 18, 1912.

55. "School Annual to Appear Tuesday," *Indianapolis [Sunday] Star*, May 30, 1909.

56. "War on Caterpillars," *Shortridge Daily Echo* [Indianapolis, IN], October 4, 1907; "Plans Arbor Day Program: Miss Rousseau McClellan Offers Suggestions for Exercises," *Indianapolis Star*, April 26, 1911.

57. "School Children Respond to Appeal for Gardens," *Indianapolis Star*, June 3, 1919.

58. "As the Day Begins," *Indianapolis Star*, February 13, 1941.

59. Andrew Jewett has characterized the common view of this era as "scientific democracy," in which science was valued and promoted not just for advancing general knowledge or improving technology but as a transformative social agent that would result in a more advanced culture altogether. Andrew Jewett, *Science, Democracy, and the American University: From the Civil War to the Cold War* (New York: Cambridge University Press, 2012).

60. Effa Funk Muhse Papers (1895–1915) C593, IU Libraries University Archives, Bloomington, Indiana.

61. Effa Funk Muhse, "The Cutaneous Glands of the Common Toads," *American Journal of Anatomy* 9, no. 1 (1909), https://doi.org/10.1002/aja.1000090111.

62. "Pushes Suffrage Fight," *The Buffalo Times* [Buffalo, New York], Women's Section, August 6, 1916.

63. As a eugenics subcommittee chair for the Association of Collegiate Alumnae (predecessor to the American Association of University Women), Muhse called in 1915 for all local chapters to devote at least two meetings to the study and discussion of such topics. Effa Funk Muhse, "Heredity and Problems in Eugenics: A Report of the Subcommittee on Eugenics," *Journal of the Association of Collegiate Alumnae* 8, no. 2 (March 1915): 49–72, HathiTrust, https://hdl.handle.net/2027/coo.31924065974812.

64. "Pushes Suffrage Fight," *Buffalo Times* [Buffalo, NY], Women's Section, August 6, 1916.

65. David Starr Jordan, Report to Board of Trustees, June 1887, Presidents' Reports to the Indiana University Board of Trustees, 1881–1947, C654, Box 1, Folder President's Reports and Reports to the Legislative Visiting Committee, 1881–91, IU Libraries University Archives, Bloomington, Indiana, https://webapp1.dlib .indiana.edu/findingaids/view?docId=InU-Ar-VAD8759.xml&doc.view=items; Thomas J. Clark, *Indiana University: Midwestern Pioneer*, Vol. 1, *The Early Years* (Bloomington: Indiana University Press, 1970), 217–18.

66. Rossiter, *Women Scientists in America*, xvi.

67. Mary Bidwell Breed, *The Polybasic Acids of Mesitylene*, Bryn Mawr College Monographs, Vol. 1, no. 1 (Baltimore, MD: Lord Baltimore Press, Friedenwald Co., 1901), https://books.google.com/books?id=zOsMAAAAYAAJ; M. T. Bogert, "The Polybasic Acids of Mesitylene [Review]," *Review of American Chemical Research* 8, no. 1(1902): 354–56, HathiTrust, https://hdl.handle.net/2027/nyp .33433090824990.

68. Clark, *Indiana University*, Vol. 1: 319–20.

69. *Arbutus 1902* (Bloomington: Indiana University, 1902), 267, 212, 236, HathiTrust, https://hdl.handle.net/2027/umn.31951002210083b.

70. Harry G. Day, *The Development of Chemistry at Indiana University: 1829–1991* (Bloomington: H. G. Day and Indiana University Chemistry Department, 1992), 103–4.

71. Clark, *Indiana University*, Vol. 1: 320; Andrea L. Turpin, *A New Moral Vision: Gender, Religion, and the Changing Purposes of American Higher Education, 1837–1917* (Ithaca, NY: Cornell University Press, 2016).

72. "Register of Graduates," *Indiana University Bulletin* 15, no. 12 (December 1917): 53, 88, 154.

73. Clark discusses these concerns in the IU context while Turpin examines them more broadly and through her related case study at the University of Michigan. Clark, *Indiana University*, Vol. 1: 319–20; Turpin, *New Moral Vision*, 196–99.

74. Roger L. Geiger, *The History of American Higher Education: Learning and Culture from the Founding to World War II* (Princeton, NJ: Princeton University Press, 2015), 206–14; Turpin, *New Moral Vision*, 4.

75. Rossiter, *Women Scientists in America: Strategies and Struggles*, xvii, 73–99.

76. "Domestic Science Course Will Start Next Week," *Indiana Daily Student* [Bloomington, IN], October 4, 1911; "Co-Eds Instructed in the Art of Breadmaking," *Indiana Daily Student* [Bloomington, IN], October 14, 1911.

77. "Domestic Scene: Home Economics Department Offers Field for Women," *Indiana Daily Student* [Bloomington, IN], February 20, 1914.

78. Mable Thacher Wellman, *Food Study: A Textbook in Home Economics for High Schools* (Boston: Little, Brown & Co., 1917), HathiTrust, https://hdl.handle .net/2027/loc.ark:/13960/t08w42mon.

79. Wellman, *Food Study*, vii–viii.

80. Rima D. Apple, "Liberal Arts or Vocational Training? Home Economics Education for Girls," in *Rethinking Home Economics: Women and the History of a Profession*, ed. Sarah Stage and Virginia B. Vincenti (New York: Cornell University Press, 1997), 85.

81. "Instructor Gives Value of Study of Home Economics," *Indiana Daily Student* [Bloomington, IN], September 28, 1917.

RESILIENT BEAUTY

The Story of Nancy Streets, 1959 Miss Indiana University

ANGEL CASSANDRA NATHAN

Angel Cassandra Nathan, who holds a PhD from IUB's Higher Education program, draws on her oral history interview with graduate Nancy Streets-Lyons to tell the story of the first Black woman to be crowned Miss Indiana University and serve as an ambassador for the institution. As Nathan relates, Streets's pageant win in 1959 was a personal achievement for the nineteen-year-old South Bend native, but it also highlighted the intersecting dynamics of race and gender that have been woven into IU's history and campus culture.

> We want somebody to be recognized. We want to be acknowledged as a
> part of this university community.
>
> Nancy Streets-Lyons

"NANCY, THEY JUST CALLED YOUR NAME!" a nearby pageant organizer whispered, reaching out to nineteen-year-old Nancy Streets, who remained motionless, stunned that she had just won the title of Miss Indiana University (Miss IU).[1] The date, May 13, 1959, was a milestone in the young South Bend native's life. Indeed, the title brought a wave of publicity for the Indiana University undergraduate student, including an iconic *Jet* magazine cover, modeling opportunities, and the satisfaction of proudly representing the Tau chapter of Alpha Kappa Alpha. However, in addition to being a compelling story of personal achievement, Nancy Streets's pageant win was a milestone for Indiana

University, as she became the first Black woman to be crowned Miss IU. Her story provides a lens for understanding how gender and race have influenced campus culture at IU, reflecting in microcosm the politics of access and equity in US higher education more generally during the mid-twentieth century.

Looking back, we can discern three histories coming together and melding to shape that historic moment on the IU pageant stage in 1959. First is the personal story of Nancy Streets's upbringing in her close-knit South Bend family and how these formative experiences contributed to Nancy's strong sense of self. Second is Nancy's IU campus experience and social awareness as a Black college woman coming of age at this juncture in US history—a time of racial unrest and of the growing Civil Rights Movement's push to secure equal opportunity for Blacks in all aspects of American life, including higher education. And third is IU's own history as a predominantly white institution that, compared to its peers, had a distinctive level of multicultural enrollment (small but growing) but upheld certain exclusionary racial norms that prevailed in southern Indiana, a region with a legacy of racial tension. In 1959, Nancy found herself in a position she perhaps had never foreseen—history maker. As the newly crowned Miss IU, she, a young Black Hoosier woman, stood in the national spotlight as a symbol of female beauty and as a representative of a predominantly white institution in a midwestern state with a complicated history in matters of race.

THE FOUNDATION OF BEAUTY

Nancy Streets was born in South Bend, Indiana, on December 19, 1939, the third of the four children of Dr. Bernard and Odie Mae (Johnson) Streets. Both parents had been raised in South Bend but were not natives of the city nor Hoosiers by birth. Their respective parents had relocated to Indiana in search of a better place to raise and educate a family. Dr. Bernard Streets's parents, Rachel and Taylor Streets, had come from the South; having left Keyser, West Virginia, they had found their new home in Logansport, Indiana.[2] Their son Bernard graduated from the local high school in 1925 and then attended Indiana Dental College (known today as the IU School of Dentistry), graduating in 1929.[3] Odie Mae Johnson's parents, Odie Wingo and John Wells Johnson, had moved from Chicago, Illinois, to South Bend, Indiana, about one hundred miles to the east (on the St. Joseph river, near Lake Michigan), where Blacks had settled as early as the 1830s. Soon after her high school graduation, their daughter Odie had met her future husband, Dr. Streets. Odie and Bernard married in 1931 and made South Bend their home.[4]

Together Odie and Bernard Streets, described by their daughter Nancy as "very independent people," raised their four children—Bernard Jr., Donald, Nancy, and Sandra—in a "progressive household" where education, civic duty, and equality were important tenets. Leading by example, the Streets taught their children the values of service and giving back. Bernard and Odie both became respected, influential members of the South Bend community. A man who "didn't subscribe to the hierarchy of status," Bernard Streets routinely opened the family's home to guests from across South Bend's different cultural and ethnic communities.[5] Although the city's Black residents generally found daily life in South Bend easier to navigate than in southern towns, they did confront racial inequities, especially in social services. For this reason, Dr. Streets worked together with other Black health professionals in South Bend organizing a Negro Health Week, which aimed to improve the health status of local Black families by providing education and preventive care.[6] Similarly, Odie Mae used her talents for betterment within the community. Although she began her own collegiate studies later in life (after seeing her children graduate from college), Odie, a busy wife, mother, and educator at heart, was active in various international education and literacy programs, notably South Bend's Head Start Program, El Migrant Center, and the YMCA.[7] Mrs. Streets's longstanding interest in international education motivated her to follow her children's collegiate path, choosing to pursue a bachelor's degree in Spanish at IU.[8]

Nancy graduated from South Bend High School a year early, in 1958, and enrolled at IU that summer. There were other colleges and universities in Indiana, even closer to home, where she might have gained admission and studied—for instance, both Butler, in Indianapolis, and DePauw, in Greencastle, enrolled Black students—but attending the state university in Bloomington seemed a logical, accessible choice. Moreover, the Streets family already had strong ties to Indiana University. Several members of her immediate family had attended and earned degrees from IU prior to Nancy's matriculation. Her father graduated in 1929 from what is now the IU School of Dentistry, paving the way and inspiring her two brothers to pursue IU degrees: Bernard Jr. in 1954 and Donald in 1956.[9] The experiences she heard about from her father, her siblings, and a wider circle of Black IU alums among members of her extended family and close friends meant that Nancy was familiar with IU before she arrived on the Bloomington campus in the summer of 1958. [10] But this knowledge did not prepare Nancy fully for the experience. The first-year student was still overwhelmed by the size of the campus and by the differences she, a young Black woman away from her family, felt between the university culture she encountered and that of her hometown South Bend community.

THE INDIANA CONTEXT

The Bloomington campus of Indiana University that Nancy found upon her arrival in the late 1950s was remarkably different from the campus she would have encountered just ten years earlier. Post–WWII expansion was evident, as was the influence of the growing Civil Rights Movement and student-led efforts to confront racial prejudice and discrimination at the predominantly white university and in the surrounding small southern Indiana town.[11] While historians of race in higher education might look back to 1959 and interpret Nancy's participation and title win in the Miss Indiana University beauty pageant as a measure of progress—a push in the late 1950s toward a more inclusive future for the Bloomington campus—for Nancy, her sorority supporters, and members of the public that moment on the pageant stage was more complicated, even symbolic: it fused past, present, and future and captured the complex intersection of race and gender. This historic moment crystallized attitudes about race and beauty and evoked the history of racism in Indiana and lessons embedded in the Black experience in the Hoosier state.

Indiana's geographical setting—across the river from Kentucky—mattered greatly in determining race relations in the state and inevitably shaped the history of race at the state university. Part of the Ohio frontier under the 1787 Northwest Ordinance, Indiana gained statehood in 1816 and stood as the northern free state closest to the southern slave states.[12] This proximity attracted northward Black migration and resulted in a number of Black settlements in Indiana before the Civil War. As southern Blacks moved into Indiana, seeking opportunity and an escape from physical and social bondage, Hoosier lawmakers sought to curtail the growing Black presence in the young state. The tensions and contradictions surrounding race in the era were embedded in both custom and law. Notably, in 1851, amendments to Indiana's state constitution called for a uniform system of common schools for all Hoosier students while also prohibiting new Black settlers from entering Indiana.[13]

In the aftermath of the Civil War, Black migration to the Hoosier state increased, and Black communities coalesced in various parts of Indiana—in Evansville in the south and in Fort Wayne, Gary, Indianapolis, and South Bend in the north. Sadly, though, Black parents saw the dream of equality of educational opportunity for their children thwarted by legislative action and local custom. In 1869, the state of Indiana mandated separate common schools for Black and white pupils. The growth of schooling in the state meant more Hoosier children, Black and white, attended schools for longer periods of time, but segregated schooling reflected and perpetuated society's racial divides. By 1875, about 68 percent of school-age Black children were enrolled in public schools in Indiana, but some localities encountered difficulties providing for Black schools. In 1877, lawmakers clarified that Black students could attend with local white students if a separate, racially segregated school could not be maintained. But this legal provision, on the surface perhaps suggesting a nod toward fairness or racial tolerance, was far too often hollow and, as historian Emma Lou Thornborough noted, too easily ignored. In reality, Black students had far less opportunity than their white counterparts. In all, the Black educational experience in Indiana was shaped by an intriguing mix of a few piecemeal efforts that extended legal access to education for Black students—rights that were not afforded to them in most other parts of the nation—and yet periods of retrenchment and a culture of widespread prejudice and racism that undercut legal rights and profoundly constrained educational opportunities for Blacks.[14] Only in 1949 would Indiana state law call for the desegregation of public schools.[15]

Because a history of the collegiate experience of Black students at IU (and elsewhere throughout the state of Indiana) has yet to be written, some extensive background is needed here. The brief discussion that follows is meant to shed light on the racial history and social dynamics that influenced daily Hoosier life and the context for higher education in Indiana from the Civil War to the aftermath of the *Brown v. Board of Education* decision. These circumstances shaped both student aspirations and the campus environment and climate in terms of race and gender at IU in the late 1950s, when Nancy Streets and her generation of young Black men and women at IU began their college studies.

Black students and women were not represented in the IU student body until after the Civil War even though the school's charter included no gender or racial exclusions. As the earliest women or Black students enrolled, IU did not experience the type of heated public controversy many state universities confronted, in part because campus demographics remained male-dominated and nearly all-white in the nineteenth century. Even as IU grew, and as coeducation developed, the number of Black students remained sparse. In particular, Black women's enrollment lagged behind that of white women. While Sarah Parke Morrison, the first white degree-seeking woman, entered in 1867, more than three decades passed before the first Black woman, Carrie Parker, attended IU, in 1898.[16] It took another twenty years for Frances Marshall to become the first Black woman to receive an IU bachelor's degree, in 1919. And forty years after this milestone, Nancy Streets would make history on the pageant stage.

In the decades between Frances Marshall's graduation and Nancy Streets's pageant crowning, the Black student population at IU grew—a mix of Hoosiers and recruits from the Jim Crow South—but still fell far short of numbers that would help make Black students visible, equitable participants in daily IU campus life.[17] In 1920–21, only 19 Black students were enrolled at IU (including the Bloomington and Indianapolis campuses) among a student body of 4,218.[18] This exceedingly small Black enrollment did not reflect the state's demographics: whereas Black residents were roughly 2.7 percent of Indiana's population, Black students were only 0.45 percent of the state university's total enrollment.[19] Black student enrollment did increase as IU enjoyed a period of growth between 1921 and 1945. Although the 137 Black students studying at IU in 1945 still represented only 0.73 percent of the university's student body, IU's rapid growth in the early post–World War II years would bring discussions about how to provide appropriate auxiliary services for the rising diversity in the IU student population.[20]

THE DOUBLE-EDGED SWORD: RACIAL SEGREGATION IN IU CAMPUS HOUSING

In the immediate post–World War II years, IU's growing student body came to include more women and Black students. Women's enrollment at IUB increased to over 3,000 by 1950.[21] Black student enrollment climbed steadily as well, nearing 200 students, over half of them women.[22] Additionally, the GI Bill brought an influx of veterans, increasing enrollment on all campuses to almost double, from 9,666 to 18,688 in the 1946–47 school years.[23] The urgent need to provide space for the rapidly increasing student population may have played a part in the desegregation of IU housing, first for men and then by 1949 for women.[24]

Up until that point, IU had admitted students regardless of race, as mentioned, but allowed the imprint of racial bias and a degree of segregation to touch most aspects of daily life. The first all-male and first all-female on-campus residential halls opened in 1924 and 1925, respectively, but these facilities were for white students only. Before that time, all students—men and women, white and Black—lived off-campus in boardinghouses or with families.[25] Now the opening of on-campus housing reinforced through university policy the racial divide established earlier by rental practices. Excluded from IU's early residential halls on campus, Black students continued to live in a cluster of private houses on the east and west sides of Bloomington.[26] Several of the houses where Black female students boarded were owned by Samuel S. Dargan, the first Black graduate of the Indiana School of Law (1909), who later, as a law librarian at IU, also became an informal advisor and aid to IU's Black students. Because

Black students were excluded from basic auxiliary services on the IU campus, students not only rented rooms in Mr. Dargan's houses but also paid for space to host social gatherings and established their own dining services.[27] Only through this creative combination of student initiative and Dargan's entrepreneurial spirt did IU's Black students gain access to the supportive, community-oriented spaces they needed to succeed in their studies and that were available through the university to their white peers.

As time passed, though, the deteriorating quality and inadequate quantity of these racially separate facilities drew increased scrutiny. Letters to the university from concerned parents of Black female students voiced their growing dismay with the facilities, the room capacity, and staffing support in the Dargan house.[28] Kate Hevner Mueller, who became IU's new dean of women in 1938, regarded oversight of women's housing as a major responsibility of her office. She kept both Dargan and President Wells apprised of the complaints she received, the results of her own inspection of facilities, and recommended improvements.[29] Black women had first entered IU in the late 1890s, just before the creation of the Office of the Dean of Women. Mueller was the first dean to question the appropriateness of accommodations for IU's Black women.[30]

Appointed to succeed retiring dean Agnes Wells in 1938, Mueller assumed her administrative position during a period in which the Office of the Dean of Women was well-established at IU and student-university relationships in the US still embodied the principle of in loco parentis. This sense of broad institutional responsibility for students led university officials to regard housing rules and regulations as a means of guarding the integrity of female students.[31] Eventually, this traditional concern compelled the university to look closely at the status of Black women. In January 1942, Mueller wrote to Wells sharing her frustrations that the Dargan property did not measure up to what she believed constituted proper living space for IU women. Mueller commented on the lack of cleanliness and supervision given to the students housed in the Dargan house. She voiced her concern to Wells: "We may let them live in whichever house they choose and simply close our eyes to the hazards. In other words, we will we approve for their residence a house which we would not under any circumstances approve for white girls."[32] Mueller's question directly addressed the inequality of accommodations between races and almost challenged President Wells to acknowledge the disparity.

In Mueller's eyes, the housing situation for Black women at IU was problematic—good for neither students nor her office. In correspondence to President Wells, Dean Mueller stated that the small group of poor Black students drained her staff's services because of the additional challenge of overseeing two types of residential spaces—on and off campus, separated by race—and because working with Samuel Dargan and Mrs. Gray, the Black female chaperone, constituted a "mockery of all our efforts."[33] Mueller proposed moving the women then living in the Dargan house to an on-campus facility but cautioned President Wells that this move might have unintended consequences, writing: "1) The girls would probably patronize the union building much more than formerly; 2) It would be an opening wedge into the campus which it would be difficult to dislodge, and 3) It might eventually attract even more colored students to our campus."[34]

Dean Mueller's comments highlight the double-edged sword purportedly progressive white campus leaders at IU and other predominantly white institutions perceived in efforts to provide Black students with access to higher education. As IU grew, disparities in living arrangements for IU's Black female undergraduates, who were still barred from living along with white women in IU campus housing, could no longer be ignored. But Mueller's caution regarding unintended changes in Black student enrollment or greater use of campus facilities by Black students suggested limits to her notion of equality and that her vision of access for Black students had clear boundaries. On one hand, as a student affairs professional and dean, she was an advocate of ensuring equality in the university's student support services, but on the other hand, her concerns voiced to President Wells reflected old, paternalistic attitudes and racial biases and a resistance to full and equal access for all students in all dimensions of collegiate life.

Mueller's apprehensions were not unique to her or new in the discourse surrounding racial equity in US higher education. Individuals across IU and at other midwestern institutions voiced similar concern with the growing Black student population on their campuses.[35] Writing to President Wells in the summer of 1945, Wendell Wright, dean of the School of Education, echoed Mueller's concern about Black student housing at IU. Wright's letter contained news that the Indianapolis chapter of the NAACP had contacted the governor of Indiana, Robert Gates, in July of 1945 regarding access for Black students at IU to university facilities and the unjust treatment of Black university students in the local community.[36] In August of 1945, the organization reached out to President Wells to underscore the urgent need to improve housing for Black students at IU and to make President Wells aware of their correspondence with Governor Gates.[37] As concern and discontent about the status of Black students at IU grew among certain members of the campus community and outside observers, university officials also voiced concerns about the living conditions provided to students. But some, like Wright, repeated Mueller's concerns that increased access for Black students at IU would lead to increased expectations for an integrated student experience.

CREATING A SPACE FOR COMMUNITY AND NURTURING A STUDENT-LED CULTURE OF CHANGE

Although the institution's total enrollment swelled to over twenty thousand students in 1958, the Black student population at IU remained low.[38] While IU dealt with the structural and social challenges of a growing diverse student population, Black students—a small circle from all walks of life—responded to their isolation by creating their own warm, familial environment and forging networks of support within the larger university community. Student organizations, along with a downtown lounge called the Hole, provided safe havens for Black students and town residents.[39] There, Black students "could be open" and not have "to worry about who was looking at you, what you were doing, what you were saying."[40] These spaces were imperative because the surrounding Bloomington community was at times challenging for Black students.

Other outlets for social life and service opportunities were to be found in the Black Greek Letter Organizations (BGLO) that had begun at IU with the 1903 founding of Alpha Kappa Nu Greek Society.[41] This men's organization was spearheaded by Elder Diggs and Bryon Kenneth Armstrong, transfer students to IU from Howard University, one of the country's earliest and most influential historically Black institutions, founded in Washington, DC, in 1867.[42] In the eyes of Diggs, Armstrong, and other early members, the fraternity was a student-driven response to the isolation and discrimination IU's Black students experienced on campus and in Bloomington; it was a vehicle for strengthening the Black voice on campus, providing community, and championing Black representation at IU.[43] In 1911, the organization finalized its name as Kappa Alpha Psi Fraternity, and it remained the only BGLO at IU until the Tau chapter of the first Black female sorority, Alpha Kappa Alpha, was chartered in 1922.[44] Other BGLOs chartered chapters on IU's campus in the 1940s and 1950s. Together, the organizations hosted socials and programs that provided on-campus support for Black students who felt unwelcome using university facilities and services.

Despite Indiana's history of efforts, albeit uneven, toward racial inclusion in education, exclusionary practices preceding the Civil Rights Movement existed in Bloomington as they did around the nation. Quoted in a 1938 article appearing in the *Indiana Student Daily* newspaper, Alfred Lindesmith, a faculty member in the Sociology Department, lamented that Black students were excluded from patronizing many downtown Bloomington shops and restaurants. It was not uncommon to see a local business hang a sign boldly declaring their Jim Crow politics: "We cater to white trade only."[45]

Such attitudes sparked action on the part of IU students. The Inter-Racial Commission was formed in 1935 by both white and Black students at Indiana University in an effort to document and share some of the racial injustices prevalent on IU's campus and in the community.[46] University officials, NAACP members, and Bloomington leaders met several times in an attempt to avoid racial conflict around the university. A Race Relation Institute held by the Inter-Racial Commission in the spring of 1947 identified several restaurants and services as racially biased. Attention focused on barbershops on campus that closed their businesses to Black students.[47] University administrators worked behind the scenes to resolve issues. On campus, an out-of-town white man willing to cut Black students' hair was hired.

Bloomington restaurants proved to be a bigger issue. The tension surrounding dining facilities came to a head in March of 1950, spearheaded by the Indiana University chapter of the NAACP, which began a campaign after the 1947 Race Relations Institute exposed racial inequality in the business practices of Bloomington restaurants. President Wells wrote directly to individual restaurant owners in an attempt to quietly resolve the issue between March and October of 1947.[48] The Board of Aeons, the student organization that served as advisors to the president, was instrumental in identifying which Bloomington restaurants were unwilling to wait for President Wells's cautious negotiations, a method he utilized throughout his presidency. Unwilling to wait any longer for Bloomington restaurants to provide equal access, fifty Black and white students broke into groups of eight and, for three days in March of 1950, entered restaurants to be served.[49] Restaurant workers served the students but promptly closed for the rest of the dinner hour after the students finished their meals and did not reopen until the next business day.[50] After the third evening, the restaurant owners called for a truce. Students and restaurant owners sat down to reach an acceptable resolution.[51] The demonstrations, which occurred without violence or incident, showed the dedication of the student activists to confronting inequity on campus and in the town of Bloomington and to pushing for immediate, demonstrable change in the treatment of Black members of the IU student body.

BEAUTY'S BOUNDARIES

By the 1950s, the combined pressures of increased Black student enrollment and agitation by the NAACP, together with institutional efforts to promote inclusion (a goal that was not fully achieved), had broadened Black students' access to IU campus life, housing, and auxiliary services. Still, inequalities related to local norms remained. In 1958, when Nancy Streets applied for university housing, policy still dictated that Black students check a box identifying them as a "Negro" and include with their application a card with their photo and basic information for housing assignments.[52] The continued separation of Black and white women within the university reflected and supported historic ideologies that demanded the purity of white women be protected from what was regarded as the detrimental influence of other racial communities in American society.[53]

To Nancy's surprise, she ended up being placed in a dormitory where only white female residents were housed. Nancy brought the error to the attention of her roommate, who indicated she was not concerned with Nancy's race.[54] However, in the small, tight-knit Black community on IU's campus, news of Nancy's housing placement spread quickly. Rumors that Nancy was attempting to pass as white at college soon reached her mother in South Bend. For the proud Streets family, being accused of "passing" was an insult. Odie Mae Streets contacted Nancy immediately to address the accusations.[55]

The phenomenon of "passing" for white has a long and contentious history. The belief in the superiority of whiteness that prevailed after slavery was reflected in and perpetuated by scholarship in the rising field of psychology. Pseudoscientific theorizing of biological and psychological differences between the races led to a false belief in the inferiority of Black people.[56] This ideology led some African Americans who were light-skinned enough to pass to do so—to assimilate into white culture and be afforded the advantages of whiteness in US society. While some lighter-hued Black people embraced the ability to pass as a point of pride, others resented the association their skin color gave them with white society. Nancy's reaction to allegations she had tried to "pass" at IU was clear-minded and strong. "That's the furthest . . . that was far from the truth. I never did, I never even thought about passing. I was proud of who I was, and here's the thing . . . when they looked at the picture on the application, because my skin was a little lighter, they just assumed."[57] Nancy requested to be moved into Smithwood, the Black female housing on campus, and was moved shortly after her request. The Smithwood Center had opened in 1955 to house the growing Black female student population (and would be renamed Daniel Read Residence Center in 1960).[58]

The housing episode—including Nancy's swiftness in challenging the misconceptions of peers and reassuring her family—provides an instructive window into the interplay of gender and race that shaped the daily experience of Black women at IU. In a similar vein, the circumstances surrounding the pageant remind us that student activities are invested with cultural and political significance. From her side, Nancy viewed participating in the pageant as a way to affirm Black beauty and ensure Black representation on IU's campus. But her title win was anathema to critics who refused to accept a Black woman as the university's representative and a symbol of feminine beauty.

Both these episodes in Nancy Streets's undergraduate experience speak to realities that IU's Black coeds navigated. As Black women, they were aware of the complicated social implications of skin color, the impact of colorism within the Black community, and the values and assumptions embedded in notions of beauty. An ideology, found worldwide, that privileges lighter over darker skin, colorism in the United States "is rooted in the social, political, and economic conditions that existed during the centuries of slavery."[59] Skin color became a social marker indicating a person's role within the social order and shaping beauty standards for Black women. This historically constructed, narrow beauty standard "valued white/light-colored skin; straight, preferably blond hair; and thinness" and associated darker, more curvaceous women with service roles.[60] As a result, Black individuals whose attributes aligned more with physical and behavioral markers of whiteness were granted social integration into the white community.[61] Additionally, describing Black beauty only through its proximity to whiteness created a dichotomy where Black women "could not be considered beautiful . . . [given their] African features of dark skin, broad noses, full lips, and kinky hair."[62]

Following Nancy's crowning, a reporter with *Jet* magazine asked why she insisted on identifying as Negro when she could pass for white. Nancy snapped, "Well I am!"[63] Nancy's unwavering dedication to her Blackness, despite her ability to pass for white, was part of her identity and shaped her perception of beauty. She proudly claimed her Blackness as a central part of her beauty, rejecting both the dominant monolithic notion of beauty based on whiteness and also elevating the kaleidoscopic beauty she observed among Black women. Nancy Streets-Lyons underscored the point in an interview conducted decades after her pageant win: society tends to define beauty in narrow, restrictive ways, but "women of color, we come in all sizes, all shapes, all colors, and it's a beautiful thing."[64] She took her understanding of the broadness of beauty into her participation in the Miss IU pageant, choosing to highlight her heritage as a Black woman.

BEAUTY IN RELATION TO SPACE, TIME, AND RACE

Currently, the Miss Indiana University Pageant is a university-sponsored event that evaluates participants in terms of intellect, talent, grace, and beauty. The winner is the campus representative for the Miss Indiana pageant. There is no documented history of the Miss IU Pageant, so its inception on campus is unclear. However, college and university beauty pageants or campus queens began in conjunction with coeducation of the sexes on college and university campuses in the United States. In the 1920s, the crowning of female collegians as queens for May Day, homecoming, prom, and academic department representatives appeared as prominent aspects of US campus life.[65] The goal of these competitions was to combat the popular claim that women who engaged in intellectual activity would suffer from a physical weakening of their bodies, reducing their willingness to get married and bear children.[66] Additionally, beauty contests were one of the few opportunities for early coeds to gain prestige within and beyond the campus by becoming visible representatives of their institutions.

The study of collegiate beauty contests (and similar activities) is germane to both historical and contemporary discussions of women's higher education as a measure of the social norms and values embedded in university environments. Karen Tice, a leading historian of pageantry, argues that such contests are "barometers for generational differences in the affirmation, destabilization, and remaking of race, class, and gender norms in campus cultures."[67] In particular, in their elevation of certain ideals of beauty, pageants, a well-established cocurricular tradition in the United States, reflect racial boundaries and the meaning of racial identities, both of which are continually reconstituted in response to changing social structures and the political climate.[68]

The sixty years that have passed since Nancy Streets's title win have brought some changes in how society thinks about beauty. Although contemporary campaigns promote the beauty of diverse sizes, shapes, and tones, the core definition of beauty still resides in Eurocentric values that embrace whiteness as the standard blueprint for presenting what is acceptable in society.[69] Therefore, the long history of the stigmatization of Black women's bodies makes an investigation into Black women's participation in pageantry important when considering the "cultural victory experienced when dominant meaning is subverted and what was formerly ridiculed is finally celebrated."[70] Nancy Streets's experiences as the first Black woman crowned as Miss IU offers a deeper look into implications of pageantry to the social and political aspects of beauty.

THE BEASTLY PART OF BEAUTY

Fifty women applied to participate in the Miss Indiana University contest in 1959.[71] Nancy was one of fifteen finalists after the one-on-one interviews.[72] Nancy credits the members of the Alpha Kappa Alpha sorority with the vision and plan that led to her entering the competition and winning the title. From their side, though the sorority members were thrilled by Nancy's title win, their motivation for encouraging her to participate was less focused on her placement in the competition than with representing the growing Black community at IU.[73] The organization "wanted to make a statement on campus that we're here, we're human beings, we need to be recognized."[74] The organization felt the Miss IU Pageant offered a positive point of exposure for Black women on campus and an opportunity to celebrate their beauty. Members of the organization coached Nancy on stage presence, paid her fees for the competition, helped her practice strategies for answering questions from the judges, and provided Nancy with her attire for the pageant.[75] The women of Alpha Kappa Alpha saw the importance—to the benefit of the entire university community—of having positive Black representation at IU during this pivotal time in matters of race on campus and throughout the country.

The 1959 Miss IU Pageant consisted of an opening ceremony, a talent portion, a swimsuit and formal wear portion, and an interview question and answer period. In a personal interview, Nancy shared that all of the contestants were supportive of one another, and members of the sorority cheered her on during the competition.[76] For the talent portion, Nancy performed a modern dance to the jazz classic "Harlem Nocturne." Sticking with her musical inspiration, Nancy's comments during the interview focused on the timelessness of good music.[77] As much as Nancy enjoyed the experience, she still had no idea she would win the competition.[78] When Nancy's name was announced as Miss IU, one the facilitators of the event had to nudge her in order for Nancy to realize that she was to be crowned.[79] Nancy's title garnered news coverage not only in the United States but also all over the world. She received invitations from modeling agencies, television programs, and the movie industry as news of her crowning spread around the country. However, not all responses to Nancy's accomplishment were positive. Several members of the IU community and the public contacted the IU administration with concerns.

Reactions to Nancy's crowning ranged from joy to hate. She was featured in the IU campus newspaper, but unlike previous Miss IUs Nancy's photo honoring her crowning was omitted from the *Arbutus* yearbook.[80] One of her professors acknowledged her win in class, but IU alumni and university affiliates wrote letters to voice their deep distaste for a 'Negro' (denoting the language used to identify Black citizens in the 1950s) woman being selected as a campus beauty queen, and hence a representative of IU women and of the institution more generally. Many of the letters communicated the betrayal some individuals felt in light of Nancy's crowning. One writer called it an abnormality to compare a Black woman to white beauty, stating, "You must undoubtedly have a might sorry looking batch of white girls over there (which I doubt, personally), forasmuch as it would not be possible for a thicklipped, flat-nosed (I saw the girl's picture in a Negro paper here in Raleigh) negress to be given acclamation. In the first place, it, sir, is not normal for white people to look upon Negros as objects of beauty, insomuch as the herd instinct in nature is in the opposition to such a thing."[81] Although Nancy was a Black woman, she did not have many of the characteristics listed in the letter to President Wells. The writer chose to call upon some of the prescribed negative stereotypes of Blackness in an effort to disassociate Black and beautiful. Another blamed the institution for allowing Nancy to win the pageant:

Dr. Wells,

Dear Sir—You may not be directly responsible for choosing a negro to represent Miss Indiana. But why, oh why did this have to happen. Makes me ashamed we sent our daughter to Indiana. They, I agree, should have rights—but not equal social rights.

The Lord didn't intend it to be that way as he placed them in a place of their own.

Why do we have to bend backward to the negro race? I can't understand. Politics mostly—along with my own Presbyterian church. How sorry we may all be some day.

Sincerely,

A mother and home owner [sic] from Indianapolis.[82]

Additional letters expressed their disgust with a Black woman being the representation of beauty for the institution. They cautioned that she could never be a representative of the state of Indiana:

Dear Mr. Wells,

Saturday, May 16 1959, I picked up my copy of the *Indianapolis Star* and to say I was mad, hurt, ashamed . . . no, I was downright angry at what I saw before me. So, the Campus Queen is a colored Girl! Well, the Indiana voting stand must be real proud of themselves. . . . I'm not, however. If Indiana University wasn't to represent themselves with a colored girl as their queen, that is their business now, but to allow this girl to represent them in the Miss Indiana contest is a downright crime. Miss Indiana and then later Miss America is to be a girl typical of the state and later the country. Now, I ask you, is a colored girl typical of the girls in the state of Indiana? I certainly should hope not . . . at least I don't want to be classified in that category, even though I may not be a girl any more. . . . I do not mean for this letter to offend or [I suspect this could be what the handwriting states] cause any hard feelings, but I just want you to know the feelings of a red headed redhead formely [*sic*] once a student at the University. THIS INCIDENT DOES NOT MAKE INDIANA BIGGER!

Very truly yours, Mrs. J. R. Boese[83]

All the letters asserted the superiority of whiteness and warned of the dangers of positioning a Black woman's beauty as equal to or above the beauty of white women. President Herman B Wells, IU's president during Nancy's crowning, and concerned community members exchanged twenty-eight letters. President Wells responded to each with a handwritten explanation of the pageant's procedure, downplaying the institution's connection to the pageant but not dismissing Nancy's accomplishment.

Dear Mrs. Sullivan,

I have your letter of May 24 and appreciate your writing expressing your views. We deeply and sincerely regret your sentiments of disappointment and are sorry that an event at Indiana University has failed to please you. This contest was not an official undertaking of the University but was staged under the sponsorship of Phi Delta Theta, which you will recognize as one of the oldest fraternities connected with the University. I feel you should have these facts which, of course, have no bearing on whether the girl in question should have been chosen. I hope you will always write to me when you learn of events and situations which displease or please you at Indiana University.

Sincerely yours, Herman B Wells (President)[84]

Letters such as those excerpted above remain, in their tone and argument, important artifacts of the ideas and attitudes about race that more than a few white Hoosiers held in the late 1950s and that, in turn, shaped their expectations for campus life and traditions at the state university. Because critics tended to see Blackness and beauty as incongruous, they resented and derided the judges' decision to confer the crown and title of Miss Indiana University on a Black woman. The reaction further highlights why Alpha Kappa Alpha saw Nancy's participation in the competition as important; the IU community needed to see the presence of Black students in the total institutional landscape, and Black students needed to see themselves as valued members of the institution. What Melissa Harris-Perry describes as the "crooked room" view Black women have of themselves in American society sheds some explanatory light on why Nancy Streets's pageant participation and crowning captured such attention and carried such meaning in 1959—and, further, why her story merits study today as an important chapter in the history of women at IU.[85] As Perry notes, Black women, because of the social definition of Blackness, have viewed themselves through a lens that distorts the essential understanding of beauty, reinforces potent stereotypes, and reinforces ideologically imposed separations between Blackness, femininity, and beauty. Crowning a Black woman for her beauty and poise defied the historic parameters that defined beauty in the terms of whiteness.

BEAUTY BEYOND PAGEANTRY

After winning the Miss IU title, Nancy went on to compete for Miss Indiana. Although she was honored to represent the institution on a larger stage, she has no fond memories of the experience in Michigan City. Before the actual pageant, she was placed on a segregated float during the annual pageant parade. The overall experience was uncomfortable for Nancy. She did not feel safe or welcome during the competition.[86] Following the Miss Indiana contest, Nancy traveled on the *Ebony* Fashion Tour. The experience opened her eyes to social realities and personal possibilities beyond the familiar world of home and IU.

In Atlanta, Georgia, she mingled in Black high society and saw some of the most beautiful Black communities in the nation. She was introduced to Black movie stars, notably Sidney Portier, and influential activists, including Dr. Martin Luther King Jr. However, during her trip she also saw the vast poverty of Black citizens in the Deep South. "To see that sharp contrast, and I think that was good to see. It was good to—it was an eye-opener, and at the same time, to understand that everyone should have the opportunity to a good life."[87] The *Ebony* Fashion Tour was a life-changing experience for Nancy. It broadened her understanding of the differences and similarities in America for Black citizens. She saw that wealth increased access to education and offered professional opportunity to some Black Americans while extreme poverty driven by systematic racism denied basic needs to others.

Although she had opportunities to explore an acting career, she decided to return to IU after the tour concluded. Back in Bloomington, while finishing her coursework, she became involved in student activism. After hearing that Black students were barred from a local skating rink, she joined a group of student activists who attempted entry. The protest resulted in a legal case against Bloomington skating rink owner Robert Jones, who claimed his rink to be a private club in 1962.[88] The newly formed Civil Rights Commission in Monroe County ruled the rink owner was in violation of the state's Public Accommodations law, but the commission had no power to charge Jones with a crime.

Nancy finished her degree in the summer of 1962 and married shortly after graduation. She became Mrs. Streets-Lyons, who spent her life in Indianapolis with her husband and children.[89] She still resides in Indianapolis and returns to IU when invited to share her experiences and recollections with campus audiences. Her comments underscore the importance of community, forgiveness, and love of success in her life as a student and in her life afterward.

CONCLUSION

Three histories intersected to shape the historic moment of Nancy Streets's crowning on the IU stage in 1959. First, the central importance of the Black family. The Streets family's foundation of self-love and resilience shaped Nancy's perceptions, allowing her to counteract negative reactions to her crowning with graceful defiance. Second, the campus experiences and social awareness of Black college women entering adulthood during a time of racial tension in US history. Nancy and the sorority that sponsored her involvement in the Miss IU Pageant acknowledged the importance of Black representation on IU's predominantly white campus. IU's Black population exists and is an important part of the university's narrative as an institution of higher education. These Black women understood the importance of their moment in the university's history. Last is IU's history as a predominantly white institution with multiethnic enrollment in southern Indiana, a region with a legacy of racial tension. On a national stage in a midwestern state struggling to balance its history of racial inclusion and racial unrest, Nancy, as Miss IU, stood as a symbol of female beauty as well as the representative of a predominantly white institution.

Nancy Streets-Lyons's experiences at Indiana University exemplify the real-life occurrences that shape the reality of Black female students in higher education. Works on Black student life and women in higher education often neglect the intersection of race and gender in the history of women in higher education. Nancy's story highlights the need to consider both. Although legal practices to segregate campuses no longer exist, there are still long strides that need to be made before all students feel welcome in higher education.

The story of Nancy Streets should not be considered a rule or even an exceptional example of Black student life at a predominantly white institution. Instead, her story shows the ways in which racial and gender prejudices affect student experiences beyond blocked admittance into higher education or persistence to a degree. A combination of national, local, and campus societal norms contributed to the climate Nancy Streets encountered at IU and shaped her experience as a student representative. Despite barriers on and off campus, Black students made a space for themselves in IU's history through strategic planning, social action, and community support.

In 2013, Indiana University publicly acknowledged Mrs. Nancy Streets-Lyons for being Miss IU in 1959.[90] The institution saw the need to revisit Nancy's story and highlight the significance of her crowning in IU's history. Mrs. Streets-Lyons had a community to support her success at IU. The wisdom shared with her from her parents, older brothers, and classmates was essential as she navigated the social, political, and racial challenges she, a young Black woman, confronted as a symbol of beauty on a predominantly white campus. By becoming Miss Indiana University, she challenged historic standards of beauty, race, and womanhood.

NOTES

The epigraph is from Nancy Streets-Lyons, interviewed by Angel Cassandra Nathan, February 26, 2018 (transcript in author's possession). Ms. Streets-Lyons is referred to by her given name, Nancy, throughout the chapter to denote the young woman she was at the time she was crowned Miss Indiana University.
A special note of thanks to Ms. Nancy Streets-Lyons. Thank you for sharing with me a part of your story and entrusting me with sharing it with the world.

1. Streets-Lyons, interview, 2018.

2. "Dr. Bernard William Streets. Sr., Funeral Program, 2000," *Streets Family Collection of the Civil Rights Heritage Center,* Indiana University South Bend Archives, South Bend, Indiana.

3. "Summary Information, n.d.," *Streets Family Collection of the Civil Rights Heritage Center,* Indiana University South Bend Archives, https://library.iusb.edu /search-find/archives/crhc/StreetsFamily.html.

4. "Odie Mae Streets, Funeral Program and Estate Auction Listing, 2006," *Streets Family Collection of the Civil Rights Heritage Center*, Indiana University South Bend Archives.

5. Streets-Lyons, interview.

6. "Summary Information, n.d.," *Streets Family Collection of the Civil Rights Heritage Center.*

7. "Odie Mae Streets, Funeral Program and Estate Auction Listing, 2006."

8. "Odie Mae Streets, Funeral Program and Estate Auction Listing, 2006."

9. Bernard Streets Jr. and Sandy Streets, "Oral History, Bernard Streets Jr. and Sandra Streets," August 26, 2010, *Streets Family Collection of the Civil Rights Heritage Center,* Indiana University South Bend Archives, podcast, https://archive.org /details/OH-Streets-BernardJrSandra-2010-04-26.

10. Streets-Lyons, interview.

11. Cally Waite and Margaret Crocco, "Fighting Injustice through Education," *History of Education*, 33, no. 5 (September 2004): 573–83, https://doi.org/10.1080 /0046760042000254541.

12. Indiana Historical Bureau, "Black Settlers in Indiana," *The Indiana Junior Historian*, 1993, accessed October 30, 2017, https://www.in.gov/history/files/7015 .pdf.

13. Charles Kettleborough, *Constitution Making in Indiana: A Source Book of Constitutional Documents with Historical Introduction and Critical Notes*, ed. John Bremer, 4th ed. (Indianapolis: Indiana Historical Bureau, 1971).

14. Leslie Schwalm, *Emancipation's Diaspora: Race and Reconstruction in the Upper Midwest* (Chapel Hill: University of North Carolina Press, 2009).

15. John Taylor, "African American Education in Indiana," 2014, https://www .in.gov/history/files/African-American_Education_in_Indiana.pdf; Emma Lou Thornborough, *The Negro in Indiana Before 1900: A Study of a Minority* (Indianapolis 1959; reprinted Bloomington 1993), 325, 329.

16. Dina Kellams, "An Update on 'Miss Carrie,'" *Blogging Hoosier History*, last modified September 1, 2015, https://blogs.libraries.indiana.edu/iubarchives/tag /carrie-parker.

17. Waite and Crocco, "Fighting Injustice through Education." IU supported recruitment efforts in the South similar to those of the University of Chicago and Columbia University (especially Teachers College).

18. Indiana University did not keep systematic publicly accessible enrollment data by race during the 1920s. Information for this note pulled from presidential records noting Black student enrollment and compared that to the historic enrollment available in IU's Office of Institutional research. Indiana University, Inter-Departmental Communication, Indiana University President's Office Records, 1947, Box 414, Folder Negro Files, Negro Situation, IU Libraries University Archives, Bloomington, Indiana; University Institutional Research and Reporting,

"Historic Enrollment: Fall 1880–2017," https://uirr.iu.edu/facts-figures /enrollment/historical/index.html.

19. Indiana University did not keep systematic publicly accessible enrollment data by race during the 1920s. Information for this note pulled from presidential records noting Black student enrollment and compared that to the historic enrollment available in IU's Office of Institutional research. The 2.7 percent black population in 1920 was the author's calculations from "Series A 195–209: Population of States, by Sex, Race, Urban-Rural Residence, and Age: 1790–1970: Indiana," in *Historical Statistics of the United States, Colonial Times to 1970*, Bicentennial Edition, Part 1, Washington, DC, 1975, 27, https://www.census.gov/history/pdf/histstats -colonial-1970.pdf; correspondence from H. B Wells to C. Walter McCarty, August 7, 1945.

20. Indiana University did not keep systematic publicly accessible enrollment data by race during the 1920s. Information for this note pulled from presidential records noting Black student enrollment and compared that to the historic enrollment available in IU's Office of Institutional research. Indiana University, Inter-Departmental Communication, Indiana University President's Office Records, 1947, Box 414, Folder Negro Files, Negro Situation, IU Libraries University Archives, Bloomington, Indiana; University Institutional Research and Reporting, "Historic Enrollment: Fall 1880–2017," https://uirr.iu.edu/facts-figures /enrollment/historical/index.html.

21. "Women at IU," IU Libraries University Archives, accessed September 5, 2019, http://collections.libraries.indiana.edu/iubarchives/exhibits/show/student -life-and-culture/women-at-iu.

22. Correspondence from H. B Wells to C. Walter McCarty, August 7, 1945.

23. Indiana University did not keep systematic publicly accessible enrollment data by race during the 1920s. Information for this note pulled from presidential records noting Black student enrollment and compared that to the historic enrollment available in IU's Office of Institutional research. Colored Student Enrollment—Indiana University, Indiana University President's Office Records, 1937–1962, Box 414, Folder Negro Files, Colored Student Enrollment, IU Libraries University Archives, Bloomington, Indiana; Indiana University, Inter-Departmental Communication, Indiana University President's Office Records, 1947, Box 414, Folder Negro Files, Negro Situation, IU Libraries University Archives, Bloomington, Indiana; University Institutional Research and Reporting, "Historic Enrollment: Fall 1880–2017," https://uirr.iu.edu/facts-figures/enrollment/historical /index.html.

24. The board of trustees approved the desegregation of IU women's housing on July 20, 1948, and black women students started living on campus starting in the fall of 1949; "Minutes of the Board of Trustees of Indiana University, 30 July 1948- 01 August 1948," digitization by Indiana University Libraries Digital Collections

Services, Indiana University Archives, and the Board of Trustees Office, accessed January 20, 2017, http://purl.dlib.indiana.edu/iudl/archives/iubot/1948-07-30; "IU Chronology," IU Libraries University Archives, accessed January 20, 2017, https://libraries.indiana.edu/iu-chronology.

25. "IU Chronology," IU Libraries University Archives.

26. The City of Bloomington, "A Walk through Bloomington's African American History," *Historic Tour Guide* no. 14 (May 2017), accessed September 5, 2019, https://bloomington.in.gov/sites/default/files/2017-05/african_american _walking_tour.pdf.

27. The note pulled from Indiana University dean of woman records during the 1930s. Correspondence from Kate Mueller to Samuel Dargan, November 1, 1941, C165, Box 15, Folder Negro, Kate Mueller correspondence, IU Libraries University Archives, Bloomington, Indiana. Correspondence from Kate Mueller to Samuel Dargan, November 1, 1941, C165, Box 16, Folder Dargan House, Kate Mueller correspondence, IU Libraries University Archives, Bloomington, Indiana.

28. Correspondence from P. J. Hill to Kate Hevner Mueller, January 28, 1940, C165, Dean of Women's Office Records, 1876–1945, Box 12, Folder Dargan House Complaints and Suggestions, 1941–42, IU Libraries University Archives, Bloomington, Indiana.

29. Correspondence from Kate Hevner Mueller to Herman B Wells, April 13, 1938, C165, Dean of Women's Office Records, 1876–1945, Box 12, Folder Dargan House Complaints and Suggestions, 1938–39, IU Libraries University Archives, Bloomington, Indiana; correspondence from Kate Hevner Mueller to Samuel Dargan, September 16, 1940 and October 11, 1940, C165, Dean of Women's Office Records, 1876–1945, Box 12, Folder Halls of Residences General Correspondences 1939–40, IU Libraries University Archives, Bloomington, Indiana.

30. "Dean of Women's Office records, 1876–1951, bulk 1917–1945," IU Libraries University Archives, Bloomington, Indiana, accessed January 20, 2017, http://webapp1.dlib.indiana.edu/findingaids/view?doc.view=entire_text&docId=InU -Ar-VAB7475.

31. James Capshew, *Herman B Wells: The Promise of the American University* (Bloomington: Indiana University Press, 2012), 165–78.

32. Correspondence from Kate Hevner Mueller to Herman B Wells, January 26, 1942, C165, Dean of Women's Office Records, 1876–1945, Box 13, Folder President Herman B Wells, 1940–41, IU Libraries University Archives, Bloomington, Indiana.

33. Correspondence from Kate Hevner Mueller to Herman B Wells, January 26, 1942, 2.

34. Correspondence from Kate Hevner Mueller to Herman B Wells, January 26, 1942.

35. Correspondence from Kate Hevner Mueller to Herman B Wells, January 26, 1942.

36. Correspondence from Wendell W. Wright to President Herman B Wells, July 27, 1945, C213, Indiana University President's Office Records, Box 414, Folder Negro 1945–46, IU Libraries University Archives, Bloomington, Indiana.

37. Correspondence from Robert W. Starms, field secretary of the Indianapolis branch of the NAACP, to Governor Robert Gates, August 3, 1945, Indiana University President's Office records, 1937–62, Box 414, Folder Negro 1945–46, IU Libraries University Archives, Bloomington, Indiana.

38. Correspondence from H. B Wells to C. Walter McCarty, president and general manager, Indianapolis News, August 7, 1945, C213, Indiana University President's Office Records, Box 414, Folder Negro 1945–46, IU Libraries University Archives, Bloomington, Indiana.

39. Douglas Wissing, "Remembering the Hole," *Bloom Magazine*, February 2018, 123–29, http://www.magbloom.com/2018/02/remembering-the-hole.

40. Streets-Lyons, interview, 2018.

41. Photograph of the Alpha Kappa Nu Greek Society, 1903, Image Number P0041921, Indiana University Archives Photograph Collection, IU Libraries University Archives, Bloomington, Indiana.

42. Elder Diggs was born in Hopkinsville, Kentucky, on December 23, 1883. He earned a degree from Indiana State Normal in Terre Haute, Indiana, in 1908. After attending Howard University for one year, he transferred to IU. See his biographical profile on the Kentucky Commission on Human Rights website: https://kchr.ky.gov/Hall-of-Fame/Pages/Elder-Watson-Diggs.aspx.

43. Photograph of the Alpha Kappa Nu Greek Society, 1903; "Kappa Alpha Nu Is the Latest Fraternity," *Daily Student*, April 5, 1911; William L. Crump, *The Story of Kappa Alpha Psi: A History of the Beginning and Development of a College Greek Letter Organization, 1911–1991*, 4th edition (Philadelphia: Kappa Alpha Psi Fraternity, 1991); Ralph J. Bryson, *The Story of Kappa Alpha Psi: A History of the Beginning and Development of A College Greek Letter Organization 1911–1999* (Philadelphia: Kappa Alpha Psi Fraternity, Inc., 2003).

44. Tau Chapter of Alpha Kappa Alpha Sorority, Inc., "History of Tau Chapter," accessed August 16, 2016, http://www.tauchapter1922.org/tau-chapter.html.

45. Alfred R. Lindesmith, "One Prof Says," *Indiana Student Daily*, 1938, newspaper clipping, Reference Files, Folder African-Americans—Enrollment, IU Libraries University Archives, Bloomington, Indiana.

46. "Final Draft of the Inter-race Worksheet," ca. 1943, attached to correspondence from Herman B Wells to Robert E. Appleby, April 5, 1943, C213, Indiana University President's Office Records, 1937–62, Box 414, Folder Negro 1942–43, IU Libraries University Archives, Bloomington, Indiana; "Racial Equality Drive Planned," *Indiana Daily Student*, January 20, 1944, newspaper clipping attached to correspondence from Alfred Evens to Ward Biddle, January 22, 1944, C213, Indiana University President's Office Records, 1937–62, Box 414, Folder Negro 1943–44, IU Libraries University Archives, Bloomington, Indiana.

47. Correspondence from L. C. Smith to H. W. Jordan and J. A. Franklin, June 5, 1947, C213, Indiana University President's Office Records, Box 414, Folder "Negro Situation on Campus—Mr. Franklin's Files, 1946–1947," IU Libraries University Archives, Bloomington, Indiana.

48. Correspondence from E. Ross Bartley to Herman B Wells, Dean H. I. Shoemaker, and J. A. Franklin, May 28, 1947, C213, Indiana University President's Office Records, 1937–62, Box 414, Folder "Negro Situation on Campus—Mr. Franklin's Files, 1946–1947," IU Libraries University Archives, Bloomington, Indiana.

49. "I.U. Students Stage Drive on Jim Crow Eating Houses," *Indianapolis Recorder*, March 25, 1950, newspaper clipping attached to correspondence from E. Ross Bartley to H. B Wells and R. L. Shoemaker, April 14, 1950, C213, Indiana University President's Office Records, Box 414, Folder "Negro 1949–1950," IU Libraries University Archives, Bloomington, Indiana.

50. "I.U. Students Stage Drive on Jim Crow Eating Houses," *Indianapolis Recorder*.

51. Capshew, *Herman B Wells: The Promise of the American University*, 165–78.

52. Jeanita Richardson and J. John Harris, "Brown and Historically Black Colleges and Universities (HBCUs): A Paradox of Desegregation Policy," *Journal of Negro Education* 73, no. 3 (Summer 2004): 365–78.

53. Discussion of the illusion of the purity of women, Daisey Hernandez, *Colonize This!" Young Women of Color on Today's Feminism*, ed. Bushra Rehman (New York: Seal Press, 2002); Patricia Hill Collins, *Black Feminist Thought: Knowledge, Consciousness, and the Politics of Empowerment* (New York: Routledge, 2009); bell hooks, *Ain't I a Woman?: Black Women and Feminism* (Boston: South End Press, 1981); Audre Lorde, "Age, Race, Class, and Sex: Women Redefining Difference," in *Dangerous Liaisons: Gender, Nation, and Postcolonial Perspectives*, ed. Anne McClintock, Aamir Mufti, and Ella Shohat (Minneapolis: University of Minnesota Press, 1997), 374–80.

54. Streets-Lyons, interview.

55. Streets-Lyons.

56. Margo Okazawa-Rey, Tracy Robinson, and Janie Ward, "Black Women and the Politics of Skin Color and Hair," *Women's Studies Quarterly* 14, no. 1 (June 1986): 13.

57. Streets-Lyons, interview.

58. "Administrative History," C319, Indiana University Daniel Read Residence Center Community Council Minutes and Other Material, 1975–2002, IU Libraries University Archives, Bloomington, Indiana, http://purl.dlib.indiana.edu/iudl /findingaids/archives/InU-Ar-VAC1143.

59. Okazawa-Rey, Robinson, and Ward, "Black Women and the Politics of Skin Color and Hair," 13.

60. Carolyn West, "Mammy, Jezebel, Sapphire, and their Homegirls: Developing an 'Oppositional Gaze' toward the Images of Black Women," in *Lectures on the*

Psychology of Women, ed. Joan Chrisler, Carla Golden, and Patricia Rozee, 4th ed. (New York: McGraw Hill, 2008), 286–99, https://www.researchgate.net /publication/264707613_Mammy_Jezebel_Sapphire_and_their_homegirls _Developing_an_oppositional_gaze_toward_the_images_of_Black_women.

61. Okazawa-Rey, Robinson, and Ward, "Black Women and the Politics of Skin Color and Hair," 13.

62. Patricia Hill Collins, *Black Sexual Politics: African Americans, Gender, and the New Racism* (New York: Routledge, 2004), 85.

63. "Big Break for Indiana Beauty Queen," *Jet*, October 27, 1960, http://www .coverbrowser.com/covers/jet/6n.

64. Streets-Lyons, interview.

65. Karen Tice, *Queens of Academe: Beauty Pageantry, Student Bodies, and College Life* (New York : Oxford University Press, 2012).

66. Tice, *Queens of Academe.*

67. Tice, 5.

68. Maxine Leeds Craig, *Ain't I a Beauty Queen?: Black Women, Beauty, and the Politics of Race* (Oxford: New York : Oxford University Press, 2002).

69. Craig

70. Craig, 14.

71. Streets-Lyons, interview.

72. Streets-Lyons.

73. Streets-Lyons.

74. Streets-Lyons.

75. Streets-Lyons.

76. Streets-Lyons.

77. Streets-Lyons.

78. Streets-Lyons.

79. Streets-Lyons.

80. Charles Scudder, "A Queen Comes Home: 54 Years after Being Crowned Miss I.U., One Woman Returns to the Campus That Ignored Her Place in History," *Indiana Student Daily*, February 28, 2013, accessed August 16, 2016, http:// www.idsnews.com/article/2013/02/a-queen-comes-home?id=91521.

81. Correspondence from Sterling R. Booth Jr. to President Wells, May 20, 1959, C213, Indiana University President's Office Records, 1937–62, Box 414, Folder "Negro Beauty Queen, 1959," IU Libraries University Archives, Bloomington, Indiana.

82. Correspondence from a mother and homeowner from Indianapolis to President H. B Wells, C213, University President's Office Records 1937–62, May 26, 1959, Box 414, Folder "Negro Beauty Queen, 1959," IU Libraries University Archives, Bloomington, Indiana.

83. Correspondence from J. R. Boese to President H. B Wells, C213, Indiana University President's Office Records 1937–62, May 21, 1959, Box 414, Folder "Negro Beauty Queen, 1959," IU Libraries University Archives, Bloomington, Indiana.

84. Correspondence from President H. B Wells to Iva Etta Sullivan, C213, Indiana University President's Office Records 1937–62, June 5, 1959, Box 414, Folder "Negro Beauty Queen, 1959," IU Libraries University Archives, Bloomington, Indiana.

85. Melissa Harris-Perry, *Sister Citizen: Shame, Stereotypes, and Black Women in America* (New Haven: Yale University Press, 2011).

86. Streets-Lyons, interview.

87. Streets-Lyons.

88. Capshew, *Herman B Wells.*

89. Streets-Lyons, interview.

90. Scudder, "A Queen Comes Home."

SIX

—⚉—

"LITTLE STEPS OF COURAGE FORWARD"

How Asian American Women Leaders Fought for Culturally Supportive Spaces at Indiana University Bloomington

STEPHANIE THANH XUAN NGUYEN

Stephanie T. X. Nguyen shares insights from her forthcoming dissertation to high-light the grassroots activism of Asian American women student leaders on IU's Bloomington campus in the late 1990s. Drawing on oral histories and archival records, Nguyen explores how their activism, though incremental, helped create cultur-ally supportive spaces—student organizations, cultural programming, and a long sought-after culture center. She describes these women as "mobilizers," resourceful leaders, and determined collaborators. Their contributions celebrated the presence of Asian students at IU, helped make the campus a more inclusive environment, and diversified women's perspectives at IU.

We created something that will stand in the history of time and has given back to IU in a way we couldn't have imagined.

> —Eloiza Domingo-Snyder, IUB alumna '01 and mem-ber of the faculty-student committee to create Indiana University Bloomington's Asian Culture Center.

"I DIDN'T STRIVE TO BE A LEADER," Indiana University Bloomington (IUB) alumna Khai Truong (married name Yang), BA'97, told a campus au-dience as she recalled her experiences advocating for the university's Asian Culture Center (ACC) in the 1990s. "But I found out that I have to be a leader because that's how things can be changed." In her talk, titled "Amp It Up:

Making a Difference in the Workplace and the Community by Being You," Truong reflected on her personal journey from her childhood as a Vietnamese refugee growing up in a small, predominantly white Indiana town to her collegiate experience at IUB and, most relevant here, her role in helping to establish the ACC in 1998.[1]

The occasion for Truong's talk was the AAC's twentieth anniversary celebration, held in the fall of 2018 (October 11–13). At the ACC's invitation, Truong and a handful of former IUB women student activists joined in a weekend of festivities that included sharing memories of their student days and perspectives on IU Bloomington campus history. For these women, it was a chance to recall how they had helped to start what would be a decade-long movement to establish an Asian culture center on the Bloomington campus. Their efforts, part of a larger but as yet little studied history of Asian student activism at IUB, carried forth a vision created earlier, in 1988, by a small group of Asian American students who dreamed of a physical space on campus much like the Neal-Marshall Black Culture Center and La Casa (the Latino culture center).

This chapter, blending biography, oral history, and archival research, centers the voices and contributions of Asian American women as student activists at IUB. More specifically, it focuses on four activist-minded Asian American women who, like Truong, helped to pave the way to the ACC. Known and admired on the Bloomington campus during their student days in the pivotal 1990s, these figures are less familiar to the IU community today. Like many student leaders, especially the women, their stories and recognition of their efforts in making IU more welcoming having receded from view and in campus memory as time passed.[2] This essay helps to recover their stories as part of the history of women at IU. It describes how these women arrived at the university and embraced activism following different paths. Some, like Truong, grew up in small Indiana towns and expressed the difficulties of being the only Asians in their neighborhood and schools. Others grew up in urban cities like Chicago or Indianapolis with growing ethnic Asian communities. They attended IU during the 1990s as undergraduates on a predominantly white campus who were proud of their heritage and eager to share their talents. They joined student organizations where they found a supportive community of Asian Americans.

As this chapter elaborates, the stories of these four IUB women are interconnected on two counts that add an important dimension to this volume's examination of IU women's history: the change-oriented activities they led as students were both impactful on the Bloomington campus and meaningful in their lives. Bolstered by a sense of belonging, they rose to leadership positions in these student organizations hoping to make IU more welcoming to the increasing number of Asian Americans on the IUB campus. As leaders, many experienced what they described as a personal "awakening," which enabled them to resist Asian American and female stereotypes that women were to remain quiet about individual as well as group needs. The experience of becoming leaders helped them strengthen their abilities to advocate for themselves and for Asian American resources on campus. Their increased advocacy inspired these women leaders to tackle two major needs for the Asian American community. First, they imagined and implemented campus-wide cultural programming that reflected the perspectives of Asian Americans. Second, they mobilized the Asian American community to advocate for a culture center dedicated to promoting an awareness and understanding of Asian, Asian American, and Pacific Islander culture, history, and issues at IU and in the Bloomington community.[3]

A few more words about the aims of this chapter are in order. Although many hands over many years contributed to the eventual establishment of the IU Bloomington campus's ACC, I focus on Asian American women because their experiences are often undocumented, silenced, or excluded in existing histories—IU history, Asian American history, and women's history. Too often the university's recounting of its past, like campus history and writing on higher education in general, highlights men's accomplishments more so than those of women. For example, the *Indiana Daily Student* did publish a few news stories about the ACC's founding, but these tended to be male-centered, eclipsing the contributions of female students to the movement.[4] Similarly, histories of women leaders and the feminist movement have most extensively depicted white, middle class women's experiences, leaving the story of Asian American women's organizing in the 1960s underrepresented. Because of this double marginalization, I include Asian American women's voices in an effort to compose a more complete portrait of IUB campus history.[5]

Finally, I focus on Asian American women students as important actors in IU history because their contributions demonstrated the power of grassroots student leadership in which change occurs from the bottom up. They unified the Asian American community through interpersonal organizing—befriending people from various backgrounds and finding commonality among IUB's eighteen different Asian and Asian American student groups. Through friendship and collaboration, these women instilled a pan-ethnic confidence that together they could advocate for a culture center. Their stories exemplify how much student leadership matters to make IU more inclusive for an increasingly diverse student body. In his keynote speech for the ACC's twentieth anniversary, fellow activist and IU alumnus Joon Park, BA '98, known for his role in writing the proposal for the AAC, remarked that these women's achievements symbolized "little steps of courage" toward establishing the long sought-after culture center in 1998.[6]

ASIAN AMERICAN WOMEN'S ENROLLMENT AND ACTIVISM INCREASES IN THE 1980S AND 1990S

The national Civil Rights and Third World Strike movements of the 1960s and 1970s provided the platform and momentum for the campus advocacy of Asian American women during the 1990s. Inspired by the surge of social protest against inequities of all forms, student activists demanded their universities and colleges address systemic discrimination on campus by offering a range of culturally supportive resources—defined as spaces, student support services, programming, and courses that responded to the needs and reflected the perspectives of those who had been marginalized, notably women and minority students.[7] At IUB, Black and Latinx students were the earliest groups to advocate for such resources on campus. Starting in the 1960s, Black student activists pressured IUB administrators to create and fund resources aimed at boosting the representation of Black students and improving support services—specifically the Groups Scholars Program that was founded in 1968 to increase college enrollment for first-generation underrepresented students; the Office of Afro-American Affairs with an advocacy dean; and the Afro-American Studies Program.[8] By the 1970s, Latinx student activists, with support from campus administrators, helped expand the culturally supportive resources at IUB by increasing Latinx student recruitment into the Groups Scholars Program, establishing the Office of Latino Affairs with an advocacy dean, and launching the Latino culture center.[9]

As Black and Latinx activism at IUB forged the path for Asian American advocacy in the 1990s, so did the national enrollment of Asian American college students. In just over a decade, from 1976 to 1988, the national enrollment for Asian American students jumped from 2 percent to 4 percent of the total college-going population. This increase came largely as an outcome of the 1965 Immigration and Naturalization Act that lifted the anti-Asian exclusion laws enacted in the early twentieth century.[10] At IUB, Asian American college enrollment paralleled this national uptick, surging from 0.5 percent in 1975–76 to 3 percent of the total student population in 1995–96.[11]

Strikingly, the overall expansion in Asian American enrollment also brought a substantial rise in the number of Asian American women on campuses nationwide. In fact, beginning in 1978, Asian American women began outnumbering men in college enrollment; by 1990, women comprised 50.5 percent of the national Asian American student population.[12] Mirroring national trends, from 1975–76 to 1990–91, IUB enrollment of Asian American women increased from 48 percent to 54 percent of the university's total Asian American student population.[13]

The new critical mass of Asian American women on campus stoked their political activism in the 1990s. Indeed, as more Asian American women enrolled at IUB, some felt isolated and distanced from the university. From their perspective, many of the available Asian area studies, Afro-American, and Latinx courses, cultural programming, library holdings, and culture centers did not address their racial needs.[14] This discontent led to action. Starting in the late 1980s and through the 1990s, women helped establish and promote a number of student organizations, such as the Asian American Association (AAA) and the Korean American Student Association, to provide a space— physical and cultural—to meet other Americans with Asian ancestry. Within these student organizations, women helped plan and oversee social programming—potlucks, sports tournaments, and dances—to ease their feelings of racial isolation.[15] Women helped pivot these student organizations from social programming to political advocacy, efforts focused on increasing pan-ethnic awareness among the university's Asian American community and resolving on-campus racial discrimination.[16] Through their distinct contributions, Asian American women leaders collectively strengthened their community's pan-ethnic collaboration and political voice—steps that were central to their goal of establishing the ACC.

MONA WU, FOUNDATIONAL MOBILIZER, INITIATES ASIAN AMERICAN ADVOCACY, 1990–91

As 1990 drew to a close, IU junior Mona Wu felt she needed to do more for the Asian American community. For ten months, she and members of AAA had lobbied the IUB administration and the IU Police Department (IUPD) to apologize for a racial profiling incident that occurred on February 14, 1990. IUPD officers allegedly violated the civil rights of Asian male students after a white woman was reportedly assaulted by an Asian male in the laundry room of the Redbud Hill Graduate Student Family Housing.[17]

Then, a second incident occurred on July 25, 1990. Two local white teenagers pushed David Jung, a Bloomington resident and IUB student, off his bike, called him a "chink," and began hitting him.[18] Jung went to the Racial Incidents Team in the Dean of Students Office, but he felt that having an Asian American advocacy dean would have eased his situation.[19] Wu recognized that these separate, publicized racial incidents underscored a growing concern within the Asian American community: Asian Americans students often reported feeling isolated and misunderstood on campus.[20] She wanted to address these two glaring needs for her community: a culture center that would serve as a safe space for Asian American students and an Asian American advocacy dean who could help them navigate through these types of racial incidents.

When she became president of AAA in fall 1990, Wu formed a small team with two AAA members to undertake the necessary background research and write a proposal for an Asian American advocacy dean and a culture center.[21] Wu and her team first allied with the IU Student Association (IUSA)—elected by the student body—to garner political clout. Sponsored by two IUSA senators and David Jung, the victim of the July 1990 hate crime, Wu wrote a February 1991 student government resolution demanding more Asian American campus resources. "The University offers few Asian American cultural programs and no Asian American academic programs; thereby providing no opportunities for Asian American students to gain self-discovery and pride in their heritage," Wu asserted.[22] The absence of much-needed culturally supportive resources rendered the "Asian American population feeling neglected and excluded."[23] Wu concluded that IUB should appoint an Asian American advocacy dean and establish an Asian culture center "for the betterment of the entire IU-Bloomington community."[24]

Although IUSA's deliberations surrounding the resolution are unknown, the student senate did endorse the resolution on February 19, 1991. IUSA's endorsement marked a significant milestone for Wu and the Asian American community: gaining a crucial ally who recognized Asian American students' feelings of isolation. The endorsement gave Wu and her team the leverage to approach the appropriate decision-making bodies that had fiscal authority to consider their demands.

As undergraduates with little knowledge of the complex and decentralized decision-making structure at IUB, Wu and her team brought their cause to a number of IUB administrators—Chancellor Kenneth Gros Louis, Afro-American Affairs Dean Herman Hudson, and Latino Affairs Dean Alberto Torchinsky.[25] In April 1991, Wu and her team reached the Affirmative Action Committee, a minority affairs subcommittee that screened the feasibility of campus requests before presenting them to the Bloomington Faculty Council (BFC).[26] In front of the ten-person committee, Wu and her team described how they and other Asian American students had self-navigated campus racial incidents for years. Wu and her team then argued for increased university attention to Asian American student concerns. Although meeting details and member reactions are unknown, the committee recommended that Wu and her team write a proposal outlining the concerns of the Asian American student community and forward them to the appropriate administrators.[27]

Wu's team submitted a formal proposal for an advocacy dean and a culture center to several BFC subcommittees, who ultimately recommended not to move forward with Wu's request.[28] The recommendation was based on financial factors that Wu, her team, and even university administrators could not control. Due to decreased state funding in 1991, administrators claimed that IUB faced a "significant budgetary problem" and were reluctant to invest in new facilities, such as a culture center.[29] University administrators also hesitated to invest diminishing campus funds into hiring an Asian American advocacy dean because of a decade-long debate about the operational efficacy of the separate Afro-American and Latinx advocacy offices.[30]

In addition to financial factors, Wu and her team ended their pursuit for an advocacy dean and culture center because they were unable to successfully mobilize the Asian American community. "There was no formal proposal to the Bloomington Faculty Council," Wu explained in a 1994 Kiosk article. "The reason is that I did not feel the rest of the Asian-American population were going to support us."[31] Wu speculated that Asian ethnic differences discouraged Asian American students from supporting her proposal. "I am Chinese American.... Perhaps (Asian American students) felt I'm just out for a Chinese-American advocacy dean," she said.[32] Wu admitted that she failed to reach out and communicate with the other seventeen Asian ethnic student organizations why a culture center and an advocacy dean would benefit the Asian American community, instead of a single ethnic group.[33]

Although they did not achieve their goal, Wu and her team accomplished much in their yearlong advocacy. She gained IUSA's endorsement, deciphered IUB's decentralized decision-making chain, and wrote preliminary proposals. Her contributions built the foundation of long-term Asian American activism to establish culturally supportive spaces at IUB. Her advocacy taught a fundamental lesson that Asian American women leaders embraced two years later—the need to mobilize the Asian American community.

RESOURCEFUL LEADERS ESTABLISH THE FIRST ASIAN AMERICAN PACIFIC ISLANDER HERITAGE MONTH, 1992–94

Despite Wu's stifled political movement, the 1992–94 AAA executive boards wanted to continue her legacy with "a bigger view of what AAA could be."[34] Recognizing that the time was not right to advocate for a culture center, they pivoted toward cultural programming that aimed to "bring people together" around food and family.[35] Most important, they wanted to educate the IUB and Bloomington communities about the diversity between Asian ethnic groups while countering stereotypes like the "model minority myth."[36] Together, they created the 1994 Asian American Pacific Islander (AAPI) Heritage Month, considered the first completely student-run, large-scale event dedicated to Asian American culture, history, and issues.[37]

AAA—in collaboration with ten student groups—conceived, fundraised, and hosted six major events from January 15 through February 10, 1994: a performance by the Los Angeles-based Here and Now Asian American Theatre Company; the Taste of Asia food festival; "Finding a Voice" faculty-student discussion panel about campus racial issues; an Asian Cultural Show featuring several student organizations performing musical, dance, and theatrical acts; and an academic lecture about being a minority in the workforce.[38]

Taking almost two years to plan, Asian American women advanced their early idea of a campus-level celebration to a full-fledged and, equally important, fully funded program. Their first priority was to find cosponsors for the AAPI Heritage Month they envisioned. Because of its size and scope, the AAPI Heritage Month would be a high-risk financial endeavor. AAA, for example, needed $4,300 to cover the transportation costs of flying the fourteen-member cast of the Los-Angeles-based Here and Now Theatre Company to Bloomington.[39] Before approaching Indiana University Student Association (IUSA) and the Union Board for funding, women needed to demonstrate that multiple student groups and the IUB community—rather than a single organization—would benefit from the AAPI Heritage Month.[40]

Women leaders, over several months, convinced IUSA and the Union Board to fund the AAPI Heritage Month. Khai Truong, then a freshman and AAA's cultural programming chair, remembered in her oral history interview that AAA officers recruited community volunteers through "grassroots friendships," by leveraging their personal networks.[41] AAA officers Truong, Sue (Leung) Lin, Caroline Lu, Christine Hsu, Ellen Wu, and Candy Truong proactively approached their friends in other student groups—such as the Indonesian Student Association, the Korean Student Association, and Latinos Unidos of IU—to volunteer their time and talents for the month-long event.[42]

In IUSA funding requests, the first AAPI Heritage Month coordinators argued that the campus-wide celebration would fill a void in university programming. "Our goal is to set a precedent of celebrating the Asian American Heritage Month [at] IU," Swan Song, Aimee Maandig, and Lubna Khan wrote in a March 9, 1993 funding request. "By celebrating through planned events, it will set an example for future observance for this month."[43] They also reiterated how multiple student groups would benefit from the AAPI Heritage Month. "Because Asian heritages are vast, we would like to bring unity among Asian Americans by emphasizing one thing that we have in common; our experience of growing up in America and the obstacles that we face now, as minorities, and the obstacles that we have to face in the future."[44] In the end, IUSA and the Union Board agreed to fund the AAPI Heritage Month thanks to the women's abilities to acquire multiple co-sponsorships.[45]

In addition to securing funding, the women leaders brought "fresh ideas" to pack the month with academic and cultural programming.[46] Drawing on her personal background, Christine Hsu, then a sophomore, created the Taste of Asia food festival because her family ran a number of successful Chinese restaurants in Indianapolis.[47] Hsu designed the food festival to be an immersive learning experience where people could sample homemade dishes while wandering through cultural displays of different Asian ethnic groups. Hsu and members from eight Asian student organizations spent two days preparing homemade dishes from family recipes, such as Korean-style sushi rolls *kimbap*, Japanese pork soup, and Singaporean radish cake. Historically, international and domestic Asians had organized separately on campus (for example, IUB hosted both a Korean Student Association and a Korean American Student Association) and held separate club events because of language and cultural barriers. Now these two communities collaborated to present unified ethnic tables with traditional garments and cultural artifacts.[48]

On January 22, 1994, the Taste of Asia's attendance records shattered AAA's expectations. Organizers had anticipated 800 attendees, but nearly 1,200 people lined up in the bitter cold outside the Mathers Museum.[49] Food quickly ran out, but in the eyes of its organizers, the Taste of Asia achieved its goal of educating the larger community. Sue (Leung) Lin, BA '95, then a junior and AAA's secretary, recalled in her oral history interview the strong community support for the Taste of Asia. "It was also very nice because the community turned out.... It wasn't just students; it was faculty and even community people that came."[50]

The Taste of Asia set the precedent for the rest of the month's events. Attendance ranged from fifty for the "Finding a Voice" discussion panel to four hundred people for the Here and Now performance.[51] The turnout for the AAPI Heritage Month inspired the organizers to make it an annual tradition. "It was such a huge success that we started planning for the next year and figuring out how do we do it better," Truong said in her oral history interview, adding that she actively organized the second, third, and fourth annual AAPI Heritage Months until her graduation in 1997.[52]

Aside from recalling how these events shattered attendance records, the Asian American women fondly remembered the "bonding experience" when planning and coordinating events for the first AAPI Heritage Month.[53] By working—and having fun together—toward a common goal of hosting this campus-wide celebration, women embraced the collaborative effort of progressing toward social change. "I think the social aspect of it is really important because that's how you can also mobilize people for a bigger agenda," Ellen Wu, BS/BA '96, said in her oral history interview. "And so, it seemed, at the time, anything that you could do might go towards something long-term. It's the little incremental things."[54] These pan-ethnic efforts provided the momentum for the Asian American community to mobilize for larger group goals such as hosting the Midwest Asian American Student Union Conference at IUB.

POLITICAL ORGANIZERS BRING REGIONAL EXPOSURE TO IUB THROUGH THE MIDWEST ASIAN AMERICAN STUDENT UNION CONFERENCE, 1995–96

Riding on the success of the 1994 AAPI Heritage Month observance, Asian American women aimed to draw regional exposure to IUB's Asian American issues. From April 4–7, 1996, eight IUB Asian student groups collaborated to host the Midwest Asian American Student Union (MAASU), a four-day Asian American regional conference.[55] At the helm of this massive endeavor was Nicole Lee, BS '96, a Chicago Chinatown native and then a junior when the MAASU board elected her to be 1995–96 executive committee chair of the regional conference. Under her leadership, the collaborating student groups won the bid to host the conference at IUB. Hosting MAASU would draw campus attention to the Asian American community's goal to obtain a culture center with an advocacy dean.

Lee committed to this yearlong leadership position after attending a march with hundreds of other Asian American students from the Midwest during the MAASU conference at the University of Illinois Urbana Champaign (UIUC) from March 23–26, 1995.[56] "That was the first time I had ever marched in anything like that," Lee recalled in her oral history.[57] She remembered the overwhelming sense of power marching alongside other Asian American students. To her, the march symbolized the collective voice of Asian Americans and the hope that change was possible. The effect was so powerful that Lee wanted to intimately be a part of MAASU. "I was just so inspired [that] when it came time for open elections, I went just to see," Lee continued. "I went in with the mentality that I'd like to contribute in some way. . . . I want to be involved with this."[58] On a whim, she decided to run for chair of MAASU's Executive Board, and an hour later she cinched the election and determined to bring MAASU to IUB next year.

During the spring and summer of 1995, Lee and several Asian American women, notably Khai Truong and Fidelia Park, drafted IUB's bid proposal to host MAASU.[59] Lee and her local coordinating team won the conference bid because they convinced the MAASU executive board about "the expected gain for the campus."[60] In a welcome letter in the 1996 conference booklet, Truong and Park revealed their intentions to bring MAASU to IUB. "In hosting this conference, dedicated students at IU are making a statement that Asians and Asian Americans are a unified community," they wrote. "We are working to make positive changes such as establishing an Asian culture center and an Asian American studies program."[61] The conference, they argued, would educate the IUB community about the value of Asian American resources on campus.

As MAASU chair, Lee led her local coordinating team to fundraise for the conference. Lee requested grant funding from IUSA as well as from IUB academic units and programs such as the American Studies, East Asian Studies, Latino Affairs, and International Programs.[62] Lee and her coordinating committee also solicited donors through their community networks. They received financial support from several Asian American health, political, legal, and educational nonprofit organizations located in Indiana and Illinois. In addition, donations came from individuals and local businesses like Mr. and Mrs. Yang H. Kim of Kim's Grocery in Indianapolis. Because of her ingenuity, Lee covered most of the $33,000 operations cost through private donations while cutting registration fees for students to attend the conference.[63] "This kind of private fundraising ought to be commended. It shows that when credible organizations hold quality events contributors will be available," the *Indiana Daily Student* Editorial Board expressed in an April 10, 1996 opinion piece. "Further, it demonstrates that hard work from students such as Lee will pay big dividends with events such as MAASU."[64] Because of Lee's leadership, IUB's Asian American community, indeed, received direct and indirect dividends.

The immediate effect was greater publicity for their cause—their ongoing effort to establish the ACC. Local media such as the *Indianapolis Star* praised the IUB Asian American community for its collective organization and educational programming.[65] MAASU also drew university attention to the IUB Asian American student population. "We had the opportunity to really make a statement to the university to say that we're [Asian Americans] here," Lee revealed in her oral history interview. "It really was to change the way that

Asian American students were viewed," she said, adding that MAASU helped flip campus perceptions of Asian Americans from quiet, studious stereotypes to proactive, confident advocates for culturally supportive resources on campus.[66]

Hosting MAASU also indirectly affected the Asian American community by increasing pan-ethnic interaction. "Motivated individuals, MAASU staff members, and over seven different student groups at IU have come together to work as a team. Through countless hours of hard work, we are closer to achieving our goals and have come to depend on each other for support," Truong and Park wrote in their MAASU welcome letter. "We have found inspiration in each other's commitment and enthusiasm and have realized that everyone's help is needed."[67] This yearlong pan-ethnic teamwork injected the IUB Asian American community with the momentum for long-term activism.

MAASU transformed the IUB Asian American community from a social network to a politically active one. "There was an awakening, and it was a real acknowledgement to what it took to bring us there," Lee recalled about the pan-ethnic work to organize the MAASU conference. "Because it did take everybody coming together at IU to take on this challenge, which no one had ever done before."[68] After MAASU, the Asian American community recognized the shared responsibility to advocate for a culture center. The Asian American community could now take the next step of advocating collectively for the ACC.

DETERMINED COLLABORATORS UNIFY THE ASIAN AMERICAN POLITICAL VOICE THROUGH THE ASIAN STUDENT UNION, 1995–97

The 1994 AAPI Heritage Month and the 1996 MAASU conference spurred community interest to "collaborate and achieve something greater than anyone could achieve on their own."[69] Activist-minded students like Khai Truong and Christine Hsu grasped the need for a formal structure to unify the Asian American political platform.[70] To present a "clear, strong voice" to IUB administration for an Asian American advocacy dean and a culture center, they established the Asian Student Union (ASU).[71]

Several women, including Hsu and Truong, cofounded ASU in October 1995 to serve as an umbrella organization, facilitating joint social activities for IUB's eighteen different Asian and Asian American student groups.[72] "We have seen in the past, our collaborative efforts have drawn very positive responses from the IU community; during Asian American Heritage Month, for example, the event that is most well attended is the one in which all the groups have worked together," Hsu noted in a November 1995 IUSA funding request to host a Friendship Dinner. "We want to continue to contribute to the IU community as a group."[73] Inspired by the AAPI Heritage Month, ASU symbolized a formal coalition while building credibility to advance community issues.[74]

To encourage various Asian ethnic groups to socialize and collaborate, Hsu and Truong arranged pan-ethnic activities such as the October 1995 Asian Unity Night, a cultural showcase with interactive skits, dances, entertainment, and team-building exercises. "We organized the program because we wanted to show that each of the student groups sometimes face the same kinds of problems and can work together for a solution," Truong said in a September 1996 *Indiana Daily Student* article. "We also hope to get every Asian student group on campus to participate in ASU," Truong continued, anticipating that Asian Unity Night would encourage student organizations to embrace pan-ethnic advocacy.[75]

Within a year of the coalition's founding, Hsu and Truong recruited nearly twelve out of eighteen Asian student groups to join. When planning ASU's structure and voting procedures, Hsu and Truong wanted to respect the individual affinity of each Asian ethnic organization while ensuring "a collaboration of all Asian student voices on campus."[76] They formed ASU as a unicameral structure, with a chairperson guiding a legislative body and with two voting representatives from each student group. ASU's decision-making process was a "groundbreaking step towards understanding and cooperation" because the seventeen Asian ethnic groups could now make joint decisions to benefit the entire Asian American community.[77] Hsu and Truong co-led ASU in its first year in 1996–97, and with consensus from all representatives, they directed ASU's political agenda toward advocating for the ACC and an Asian American advocacy dean.[78]

CARRYING FORWARD THE LESSONS FROM ASIAN AMERICAN WOMEN LEADERS

Almost three weeks after IUB hosted MAASU, on April 26, 1996, ASU chairs Christine Hsu and Khai Truong presented the Asian American community's demands for an advocacy dean and culture center to twenty press members attending a media conference at the Black Culture Center organized by the Student Coalition, a multicultural student advocacy group.[79] In January 1997, ASU, the Student Coalition, and several other student groups convinced administrators to grant $50,000 to create the ACC.[80] Although they graduated before the ACC's grand opening on October 3, 1998, these women imprinted their legacy on the Asian American community.

Today's readers can learn three lessons from the stories of these IUB women leaders. Asian American women repeatedly mentioned their "awakening" as they assumed leadership positions on campus. They found a political voice that helped them advocate for Asian American resources on campus. As leaders, women resisted the Asian American stereotype of "heads down, work hard" while "not making waves," a term that Nicole Lee described in her oral history interview as not vocalizing individual needs to stay out of trouble.[81] Yet, women realized the value of self-advocacy to get these Asian American resources on campus. "We started to really create a distinct period of time where we wanted a seat at the table, and they [university administration] were open about that," Lee remarked. "We weren't waiting for an invitation. We were initiating the conversation.... We were making waves."[82]

When they recognized self-advocacy, women discovered the power of collaboration in creating these culturally supportive resources. "One of the things I've learned through my experience at IU is that you can't do it alone," Truong noted in an interview for an IU Bicentennial podcast on the founding of the ACC. "You have to come up with the idea but then figure out how to work with others to really bring their skills and their values and inspire them to act." Finding common ground, like similar passions and ambitions, helped Truong connect with other communities to create culturally supportive resources on campus.[83] Lee echoed the importance of pan-ethnic and racial collaboration. "Collectively, you're bringing more to the table together," Lee reminisced in her oral history interview about organizing MAASU and leading several diversity initiatives while residing in the Foster International Living Learning Community.[84]

Finally, women imparted the importance of understanding the ACC's history to appreciate how advocates, for over a decade, built and sustained Asian American resources on campus. "I think it's important to understand the struggle because once you understand the struggle and the history, there's an appreciation for taking advantage of those resources," Truong expressed in her oral history interview.[85] Knowing the ACC's history helps people move toward self-affirmation and toward the ability to "leave a legacy" for their community.[86] Lee, Truong, and Sue (Leung) Lin shared how their leadership experiences helped them find a deeper sense of purpose beyond themselves. Even more, making a lasting impact does not entail large steps. For Truong, she started by talking to her friends late at night at the library and brainstorming ideas for things to try while at college.[87] For Lin, she started by finding a core group of friends and becoming involved in student groups, mainly AAA.[88] Lee started during her sophomore year when she witnessed an adopted Asian and his group of white friends bully an Indonesian international student outside of Foster residence hall, motivating her to apply to be a diversity advocate for the Living Learning Center and lead antiracism initiatives on campus.[89] These women demonstrated that all it takes is little steps of courage forward.

NOTES

Kathryn de la Rosa, "Founding the Asian Culture Center Podcast," posted on February 21, 2018, Voices from the IU Bicentennial, Bloomington, Indiana, podcast, 9:29, http://blogs.iu.edu/bicentennialblogs/2018/02/21/founding-the-asian -culture-center.

1. Khai (Truong) Yang, "Amp It Up: Making a Difference in the Workplace and the Community by Being You," Asian Culture Center Anniversary Symposium lecture, October 12, 2018, Bloomington, Indiana (field notes in author's possession). Thanks to the IU's Bicentennial celebrations that brought graduates back to campus, I had the opportunity to meet and conduct oral history interviews with Truong and several other Asian American IU alumnae.

2. For more on the historical establishment of the Asian Culture Center, see Adrianne D. Sarreal, "The Formation of the Asian Culture Center at Indiana University," 20th Anniversary ACC History Archive, accessed March 10, 2020, https:// asianresource.indiana.edu/anniversary/archive/sarreal.php; Daisy Rodriguez Pitel, "Change Does Not Occur Overnight," 20th Anniversary ACC History Archive, accessed March 10, 2020, https://asianresource.indiana.edu/anniversary /archive/rodriguez.php.

3. David Chih, interview by Stephanie T. X. Nguyen, August 3, 2018, digital recording, in Bloomington, Indiana (copy in author's possession); "About the ACC," Asian Culture Center, accessed May 22, 2020, https://asianresource.indiana.edu /about/index.html.

4. *Indiana Daily Student* articles like Paul Gillespie's October 5, 1998, work, "Asian Center Opens Its Doors," (pp. 1, 8) most often named Joon Park (BA '98), an Asian American male, as the lead figure who wrote the proposal to establish the ACC.

5. Esther Ngan-Ling Chow, "The Feminist Movement: Where Are All the Asian American Women?" *U.S.-Japan Women's Journal*, English Supplement, no. 2 (1992): 96.

6. Joon Park, keynote speech for the twentieth anniversary of the Asian Culture Center, October 12, 2018, digital recording, Bloomington, Indiana (copy in author's possession).

7. Robert A. Rhoads, "Student Activism, Diversity, and the Struggle for a Just Society," *Journal of Diversity in Higher Education* 9, no. 3 (2016): 189–202; William Ming Liu, Michael J. Cuyjet, and Sunny Lee, "Asian American Student Involvement in Asian American Culture Centers," in *Culture Centers in Higher Education: Perspectives on Identity, Theory, and Practice*, ed. Lori D. Patton (Sterling, VA: Stylus Publishing, 2011), 26.

8. Advocacy deans and their offices represented their respective constituents to the IUB administration for services that were "perceived to be unique" to racial and gender-based campus groups; Charlie Nelms and others, "20/20: A Vision for Achieving Equity and Excellence at IU-Bloomington," Bloomington Faculty Council Minutes Digital Archives, accessed December 1, 2016, https://institutional memory.iu.edu/aim/handle/10333/1234, 3; Mary Ann Wynkoop, *Dissent in the Heartland: The Sixties at Indiana University* (Bloomington: Indiana University Press, 2002), 116–34; Shanalee S. Gallimore, "Setting the Stage for Change: The Groups Scholars Program at Indiana University," *Journal of the Student Personnel Association at Indiana University 2017–2018* (2018): 105–09.

9. Berenice Sánchez, "'Tambien Nosotros Podemos Aprender': The Struggle for Latinx Student Support Services at Indiana University in the 1970s," *Journal of the Student Personnel Association at Indiana University 2017–2018* (2018): 116–29.

10. For more on how the 1965 Immigration and Naturalization Act changed the national Asian American demographics, see Erika Lee, *The Making of Asian America: A History* (New York: Simon and Schuster, 2015), 59–173, 283–313; Eugenia Escueta and Eileen O'Brien, "Asian Americans in Higher Education: Trends and Issues," *Research Briefs* 2, no. 4 (Washington, DC: American Council on Education, 1991), 3.

11. Author calculated the percentage of IUB Asian American student population using student enrollment data by race in the 1975–76 and 1995–96 *IU Factbooks*. In 1975–76, the Office of the Registrar reported 161 Asian Americans on campus out of 32,651 total students, graduate and undergraduates combined. By 1995–96, Asian Americans constituted 1,053 out of 35,063 total students. University records, like the *IU Catalogue* and enrollment reports from the Office of the Registrar, do not consistently report enrollment by race until the 1975–76 *IU Factbook*. Office of the University Registrar and Director of Admissions, "Total Student Headcount by Campus, Ethnic Group, and Sex First Semester, 1975–76," *Indiana University Factbook*, December 1975, Reference Files, Folder "Enrollment: 1975," 5, Indiana University Archives, Bloomington, Indiana; University Budget Office, "Total Student Headcount Enrollment by Campus, Ethnic Group and Sex: Fall Semester, 1995–96," *Indiana University Factbook 1995–96*, November 1995, Reference Files, Folder "Fact Books 1995–96," 29, Indiana University Archives, Bloomington, Indiana (hereafter *IU Factbook*).

12. Higher Education Research Institute, "Beyond Myths: The Growth and Diversity of Asian American College Freshmen: 1971–2005," University of California

Los Angeles, last modified October 2007, https://www.heri.ucla.edu/PDFs/pubs /briefs/AsianTrendsResearchBrief.pdf.

13. Author calculated the percentage of Asian American women enrollment using the 1975–76 and 1990–91 *IU Factbook*. In 1975–76, the Office of the Registrar reported 161 (84 men and 77 women) Asian American students on campus. By 1990–91, Asian Americans totaled 800 (373 men and 428 women) on campus. "1975–76 *IU Factbook*," 5; "1990–91 *IU Factbook*," 29.

14. Since the 1920s, IUB had Asian international student resources, such as the Cosmopolitan Club and the Leo R. Dowling International Center. In the 1960s, IUB established Asian area studies resources, like the Department of East Asian Languages and Cultures, that focused on US/Third World political, economic, and language relations. Kate Ball, "Cosmopolitan Club Records, 1916–1970, Bulk 1922–1958," Indiana University Archives Online, accessed March 18, 2020, http:// purl.dlib.indiana.edu/iudl/findingaids/archives/InU-Ar-VAA2766; Daniel J. Idziak, "50 Years of East Asian Languages and Cultures at Indiana University," Spring 2013, IU Archives, Reference Files, Folder "East Asian Languages and Cultures"; "International Center History," Office of Overseas Study, accessed March 18, 2020, https://overseas.iu.edu/about/ic-history.html.

15. In 1988, IU undergraduate David Chih began voicing the needs for an advocacy dean and culture center through Indiana University Student Association (IUSA) when he served as the director of minority affairs. Through IUSA, he hosted the first meetings for the Asian American Student Association (AASA), which was later renamed the Asian American Association. IUSA and AASA representatives met with several administrators (dean of students, culture center directors, advocacy deans, and the chair of the Department of East Asian Languages and Cultures) about Asian Americans needs that laid the groundwork for the activism in the 1990s. David Chih, interview by Stephanie T. X. Nguyen, August 3, 2018, digital recording, in Bloomington, Indiana (copy in author's possession); Gillian Gaynair, "IU's Korean Students Try to Bridge Cultural Gaps," *Indiana Daily Student*, October 3, 1989, 3, Microfilms Collection, Reel #297399, IU Libraries, Bloomington, Indiana.

16. Mona Wu and Joe Chen, Asian Rights Discussion Panel, March 8, 1990, Indiana University Student Association (1953–2010), Collection 234, Box 16, Folder "Asian Rights, 1990," Indiana University Archives, Bloomington, Indiana.

17. Elissa Milenky, "IUPD Apologizes for Insensitivity in 'Redbud Incident,'" *Indiana Daily Student*, December 3, 1990, 1, Microfilms Collection, Reel #297403, IU Libraries, Bloomington, Indiana.

18. Michael Kelsey, "What Price Hatred," *Bloomington Monthly Magazine*, September 1990, 15, magazine clipping, Ellen Wu personal collection.

19. Kelsey, 17–18; Elissa Milenky, "Asian Americans Asking IU for Dean," *Indiana Daily Student*, February 22, 1991, 3, Microfilms Collection, Reel #197101, IU Libraries, Bloomington, Indiana.

20. Indiana University Student Association [IUSA], SEA 1426 (91-2-8) Resolution to Endorse the Proposal for an Asian American Advocate Dean at IU-Bloomington, February 5, 1991, Indiana University Student Association (1953–2010), Collection 234, Box 8, Folder "1990–1991," 1, Indiana University Archives, Bloomington, Indiana.

21. Jules Lin, interview by Stephanie T. X. Nguyen, October 26, 2018, digital recording, in Bloomington, Indiana (copy in author's possession).

22. IUSA, "SEA 1426 (91-2-8)," 1.

23. IUSA, 1.

24. IUSA, 1.

25. Linda Yung, "The Incredible Invisible Minorities: Asian-American Students as (Not) Seen by IU Administration," *Kiosk*, December 1994, 29, Ellen Wu personal collection.

26. The Bloomington Faculty Council (BFC) is a consultative faculty body that advised IUB's chancellor on financial and curriculum decisions. See Bloomington Faculty Council, "About," accessed March 11, 2020, https://bfc.indiana.edu/about/index.html.

27. BFC, "Affirmative Action Committee Annual Report," Bloomington Faculty Council Minutes Digital Archive, accessed November 7, 2018, http://webapp1.dlib.indiana.edu/bfc/view?docId=B30-1991.xml&doc.view=print&toc.depth=1&toc.id=0&brand=bfc.

28. Ellen Wu, email correspondence to Chancellor Kenneth Gros Louis, November 30, 1994, Ellen Wu personal collection.

29. Wu, email correspondence.

30. In fall 1980, Afro-American Advocacy Dean Herman Hudson (1980–99) proposed to consolidate the women, Latino, and Afro-American Advocacy offices to streamline support services for all of its constituents. IUSA as well as the Latinx and Black student communities protested the merger, believing it would neglect the needs of specific populations. In 1981, an ad hoc faculty committee decided to keep the advocacy offices independent; but throughout the 1980s and 1990s, IUB administrators continued efforts to consolidate. Alberto Torchinsky, "Indiana University Office of Latino Affairs History," accessed October 25, 2021, https://institutionalmemory.iu.edu/aim/handle/10333/6302,11–12, 20–21.

31. Mona Wu as quoted in Yung, "Invisible Minorities," 29.

32. Mona Wu as quoted in Milenky, "Asking IU for Dean," 3.

33. Yung, "Invisible Minorities," 29.

34. J. Lin, interview.

35. J. Lin, interview; Jules Lin, keynote speech for the Asian Culture Center Twentieth Anniversary, October 12, 2018, digital recording, in Bloomington, Indiana (copy in author's possession).

36. J. Lin, interview; Jules Lin as quoted in Michelle Magat and Yvette Kolb, "Asian Food Tasting Draws Massive Turnout," *Indiana Daily Student*, January 24,

1994, 3, Microfilms Collection, Reel #295538, IU Libraries, Bloomington, Indiana; Jennifer C. Ng, Sharon S. Lee, and Yoon K. Pak, "Chapter 4: Contesting the Model Minority and Perpetual Foreigner Stereotypes: A Critical Review of Literature on Asian Americans in Education," *Review of Research in Education* 31, no. 1 (March 2007): 95–130.

37. Traditionally, Black and Latinx student groups collaborated with their respective culture centers to host the Black History Month and Latino Cultural Months. Elissa Milenky, "Black Women Focus of History Month," *Indiana Daily Student*, February 1, 1991, 3, Microfilms Collection, Reel #197101, IU Libraries, Bloomington, Indiana.

38. For the 1994 AAPI Heritage Month, ten student organizations collaborated with the Asian American Association: the Friendship Association of Chinese Students and Scholars, Indian Students Association, Indonesian Student Association, Korean Student Association, Korean American Student Association, Japanese Student Association, Latinos Unidos of Indiana University, Mongolian Society, Singapore Students Association, and Vietnamese Student Association. Michelle Magat, "Performances at Talent Night Showcase Asian Culture," *Indiana Daily Student*, February 7, 1994, 14, Microfilms Collection, Reel #295538, IU Libraries, Bloomington, Indiana; Yvette Kolb, "Heritage Month Diversifies," *Indiana Daily Student*, January 13, 1994, 2, Microfilms Collection, Reel #295538, IU Libraries, Bloomington, Indiana.

39. AAA, Here and Now Theatre Company: Indiana University Student Association Grass Roots Initiatives Fund Grant Application, February 14, 1993, Indiana University Student Association records (1953–2010), Collection C234, Box 56, folder "Asian American Association," 4, Indiana University Archives, Bloomington, Indiana.

40. Sue Lin, interview by Stephanie T. X. Nguyen, October 22, 2018, digital recording, in Bloomington, Indiana (copy in author's possession).

41. Khai (Truong) Yang, interview by Stephanie T. X. Nguyen, October 19, 2018, digital recording, in Bloomington, Indiana (copy in author's possession).

42. As a note, Jules and Sue Lin are married. S. Lin, interview; J. Lin, interview.

43. AAA, Asian-American Heritage Month: Indiana University Student Association Grass Roots Initiatives Fund Grant Application, March 9, 1993, Indiana University Student Association records (1953–2010), Collection C234, Box 56, Folder "Asian American Association," 3, Indiana University Archives, Bloomington, Indiana.

44. AAA, Asian-American Heritage Month: Indiana University Student Association Grass Roots Initiatives Fund Grant Application, 3.

45. Kolb, "Heritage Month Diversifies," 2.

46. AAA, Here and Now Theatre Company: Indiana University Student Association Grass Roots Initiatives Fund Grant Application, February 14, 1993, Indiana University Student Association records (1953–2010), Collection C234, Box 56,

Folder "Asian American Association," 2, Indiana University Archives, Blooming-ton, Indiana.

47. There is no relation between Mona Wu and Ellen Wu. Ellen Wu, interview by Stephanie T. X. Nguyen, March 7, 2017, digital recording, in Bloomington, Indiana (copy in author's possession).

48. Magat and Kolb, "Tasting Draws Massive Turnout," 3.

49. Yang, interview.

50. S. Lin, interview.

51. Michelle Magat, "IU Asian Americans Speak Out," *Indiana Daily Student*, January 31, 1994, 2, Microfilms Collection, Reel #295538, IU Libraries, Blooming-ton, Indiana; Michelle Magat, "Acting Troupe Explores Asian-American Issues," *Indiana Daily Student*, January 18, 1994, 8, Microfilms Collection, Reel #295538, IU Libraries, Bloomington, Indiana.

52. Yang, interview.

53. Yang, interview; S. Lin, interview.

54. Wu, interview.

55. In 1989, Asian American college students founded MAASU to create po-litical unity across twenty Midwest universities. "Our Mission," Midwest Asian American Students Union, accessed February 29, 2020, https://maasu.org /mission. Also see "Our Hxstory" for a time line on MAASU's creation and de-velopment, https://maasu.org/history. Midwest Asian American Students Union Spring Conference Program, April 4–7, 1996, 18, Ellen Wu personal collection; hereafter "MAASU 1996 Program."

56. Nicole Lee, interview by Stephanie T. X. Nguyen, November 9, 2018, digital recording, in Bloomington, Indiana (copy in author's possession).

57. Jeremy Bautista, Sameeta Sheth, and Jigar Shah, MAASU-UIUC Confer-ence Co-coordinators Letter in the Midwest Asian American Students Union Spring Conference Program, March 23, 1995, 4, Ellen Wu personal collection.

58. Lee, interview.

59. Editorial, "Tip of the Cap to MAASU," *Indiana Daily Student*, April 10, 1996, 7, Microfilms Collection, Reel #297150, IU Libraries, Bloomington, Indiana.

60. Editorial, "Tip of the Cap," 7.

61. Khai Truong and Fidelia Park, "Co-chairs' Letter" in the Midwest Asian American Students Union Spring Conference Program, April 4, 1996, 2, Ellen Wu personal collection.

62. "MAASU 1996 Program," 19–25.

63. Lee, interview; "MAASU 1996 Program," 19–25.

64. Editorial, "Tip of the Cap," 7.

65. Editorial, "Tip of the Cap," 7.

66. Lee, interview.

67. The eight IUB Asian student groups that helped host MAASU included the Asian American Association, Asian Student Union, Commission on Multicultural

Understanding, Filipino Student Association, Kappa Gamma Delta Asian American sorority, Korean American Student Association, Japanese Student Association, and Vietnamese Student Association. Truong and Park, "Co-chairs' Letter," 2.

68. Lee, interview.

69. Kenneth Rogers, dean of International Services and ASU's faculty advisor, as quoted in Liseanne V. Carothers, "Asian Union Brings Groups Together," *Indiana Daily Student*, September 26, 1996, 14, Microfilms Collection, Reel #297152, IU Libraries, Bloomington, Indiana.

70. Asian Student Union [ASU], Friendship Dinner: Indiana University Student Association Grass Roots Initiatives Fund Grant Application, November 8, 1995, Indiana University Student Association records (1953–2010), Collection C234, Box 61, Folder "Asian Student Union," 2, Indiana University Archives, Bloomington, Indiana.

71. Amy Young, "ASU Strives to Unify IU's Asian Students," *Indiana Daily Student*, September 19, 1997, 1, Microfilms Collection, Reel #501221, IU Libraries, Bloomington, Indiana.

72. ASU was founded approximately in 1995, but the organization was not officially recognized by Indiana University Student Association until 1997; ASU, "Friendship Dinner," 2; Young, "ASU Strives to Unify," 1.

73. ASU, "Friendship Dinner," 3.

74. Yang, interview.

75. Carothers, "Union Brings Groups Together," 14.

76. Carothers, "Union Brings Groups Together," 14; Yang, interview.

77. ASU consisted of seventeen student organizations: the Asian American Association; Chinese Student Association, Taiwan; Filipino Student Association; Friendship Association of Chinese Students and Scholars; Hong Kong Student Association; Indian Student Association; Indonesian Student Association (Permias); International Friendship Association; Japanese Student Association; Kappa Gamma Delta Sorority; Korean Student Association; Korean American Student Association; Korean Undergraduate Student Association; Malaysian Student Association; Pakistan Student Association; Thai Student Association; and Vietnamese Student Association. ASU, "Our Participating Organizations," May 10, 1999, web page clipping, Records of the Asian Culture Center, Collection C691, Box 1, folder "Asian Student Groups"; Carothers, "Union Brings Groups Together," 1.

78. ASU, "Friendship Dinner," 2.

79. Ronnetta S. Slaughter, "Asian-American Students Desire Center," *Indiana Daily Student*, April 25, 1996, 1, Microfilms Collection, Reel #297150, IU Libraries, Bloomington, Indiana.

80. Jennifer Emily, "Student Coalition's Demands Met," *Indiana Daily Student*, January 22, 1997, 1, Microfilms Collection, Reel #501218, IU Libraries, Bloomington, Indiana. The chancellor and the BFC did not fund the Asian American advocacy dean position because IUB was merging the independent advocacy dean

offices into the current-day Office of the Vice President for Diversity, Equity, and Multicultural Affairs. Administrators instead granted a hiring line for a permanent director. Randy Fabi, "Students Push for Dean," *Indiana Daily Student,* January 15, 1998, 1, Microfilms Collection, Reel #501224, IU Libraries, Bloomington, Indiana.

   81. Lee, interview.

   82. Lee, interview.

   83. Khai (Truong) Yang on Kathyrn de la Rosa, " Founding the Asian Culture Center Podcast," posted on February 21, 2018, Voices from the IU Bicentennial, Bloomington, Indiana, podcast, 9:29, http://blogs.iu.edu/bicentennialblogs/2018 /02/21/founding-the-asian-culture-center/.

   84. Lee, interview.

   85. Yang, interview.

   86. Yang, interview; Lee, interview.

   87. Khai (Truong) Yang on Kathyrn de la Rosa, " Founding the Asian Culture Center Podcast," posted on February 21, 2018, Voices from the IU Bicentennial, Bloomington, Indiana, podcast, 9:29, http://blogs.iu.edu/bicentennialblogs/2018 /02/21/founding-the-asian-culture-center/.

   88. S. Lin, interview.

   89. Lee, interview.

SEVEN

—ɯ—

THE HISTORY OF THE FIRST LATINA SORORITY AT IU ESTABLISHED DURING AN ERA OF STUDENT ACTIVISM

EBELIA HERNÁNDEZ AND MERYLOU RODRIGUEZ

Ebelia Hernández and Merylou Rodriguez describe the founding of IU's first Latina sorority, Gamma Phi Omega, in 1991 as a student-driven response to build a sense of sisterhood on the predominantly white campus. In the absence of archival records, the authors draw on student newspaper coverage to capture the voices and perspectives of the sorority leaders while shedding light on the evolving political leadership of what had originated as a social group. The sorority leaders emerged as vocal advocates for IU's Latinx community after four white IU student senators made racially inflammatory comments in light of a budget request for a student organization's annual Parents Weekend. The story of Gamma Phi Omega highlights the diversity among IU women and the role of women of color's activism in discussions of campus climate.

> A lot of Hispanics where I'm from, a lot don't think of college or a university. . . . I guess they need somebody to look up to.
>
> Cristina Rodela, founding member of Gamma Phi Omega

ON OCTOBER 19, 1993, MONICA GUZMÁN, president of Gamma Phi Omega, IU's Latina sorority, sent a sharply worded letter of criticism to Jay Fultz, president of Indiana University's student government (IUSA), in which she denounced IU's elected student leaders for their racially insensitive conduct during a recent public exchange with members of Latinos Unidos of Indiana University (LUIU). The incident—referred to in this essay as the Taco Bell incident—had occurred two weeks earlier, on October 7, when members of LUIU attended a meeting with Fultz and IUSA senators to request cultural event funding.[1] The power dynamics of the meeting rested with the senators—nearly all of them white; only two were students of color—who controlled and distributed the programming funds on which all campus student groups (diverse in their membership and orientation) relied.

Guzmán's letter to Fultz conveyed her sorority's outrage at the hostile, culturally insensitive treatment LUIU members received before the student senators and demanded a firm, just response from IUSA and the university: [2]

> As a student leader here at Indiana University, I am appalled by this incident. I cannot understand how an elected president of the student body, who ran and won on minority issues, could not comprehend the seriousness of such remarks. . . . I have reviewed your proposed solutions [to address the incident] which contain four steps of action. I find these solutions not only offensive but ignorant. Your senators need to understand that racial discrimination cannot and will not be tolerated by the Latino community at Indiana University. I would also like to add that no human being should ever be put through an incident of this kind, especially one lasting 45 minutes, while administrators and student leaders sit back and do nothing . . . . Gamma Phi Omega is also asking the resignation of [IUSA advisor] Jim Gibson who should not over see [sic] any student activities if he cannot comprehend when a racial incident is taking place.[3]

Guzmán's bold stance in her letter of protest belied that she was a relative newcomer to IU campus politics, leading one of the university's youngest student organizations. Founded just a few years earlier, in 1991, Gamma Phi Omega had never been politically active on campus; the sorority had been organized by Guzmán and five other Latinas primarily as a culturally affirming space to serve the social needs of its all-female membership and help build the bonds of sisterhood. But from Guzmán's vantage point, the Taco Bell incident and IUSA president Fultz's woefully inadequate response compelled swift, clear-headed action. Her letter to the IUSA president (now widely regarded as an essential document in the history of student activism at IU) propelled Guzmán into a critical role among campus student activists in denouncing the Taco Bell incident, a role she had not anticipated but to which she rose. As Gamma Phi Omega president, she was the only female leader and, further, the sole representative of an all-women's organization in a coalition of Bloomington campus Latinx organizations whose leadership united in protest against the incident. Beyond the matter of gender, though, Guzmán distinguished herself

among her campus peers for being the most adamant and outspoken of the protesters. Together, Guzmán, as president of Gamma Phi Omega, and Georgina
Burgueño, the sorority's campus advisor, voiced the strongest criticism of the
situation surrounding the Taco Bell incident and demanded the most severe
consequences for the student senators and their university advisor, Jim Gibson.

The Taco Bell Incident occurred on October 7, 1993, during what should
have been a routine business meeting of IUSA and a routine matter—the senate's allocation of funds to student organizations. Following IUSA guidelines,
LUIU leaders appeared before the senators to request hospitality funds to help
cover expenses for the group's upcoming annual Parents Weekend, an event
for Latinx students and their families to connect on campus with culturally
inclusive activities.[4] But the meeting took an unexpected and controversial
turn. Instead of receiving a respectful hearing from senators, the LUIU representatives and their group's plans for Parents Weekend were ridiculed and
subjected to racially and culturally insensitive questions from members of the
elected student government, Guzmán vociferously complained in her letter to
IUSA president Fultz.

In this essay, we share a brief history of a young IU Latina organization that
stood up in response to this bias incident and, at other moments, to advocate
for their community. This history is about the women of Gamma Phi Omega—
Monica, Georgina, and many others—who not only took on the members of
IUSA as a result of the Taco Bell Incident but also dealt with the day-to-day
realities of being Latinas on a predominantly white campus in the Midwest.
This is a story of the sorority's founding during a time of racial tensions at IU
in the 1990s and their struggles and triumphs in creating a family of sisters that
ultimately grew to become one of the largest Latina sororities in the Midwest.

LATINA/O COLLEGE STUDENTS—A HISTORY
OF INVISIBILITY AND RACISM

The story of Gamma Phi Omega and its leadership responding to the Taco
Bell incident provides a much-needed window into the experience of women
of color at IU as part of the university's history, the larger history of Latinxs
in US higher education, and the role fraternities and sororities have played for
these students.

Unfortunately, there is little recorded history or scholarship about Latinas/
os in the United States who attended college before the Civil Rights Movement and few archival materials related to the Latinx experience at IU. Names
appearing on the roster of IU degree recipients are some of the only indicators

that Latinas attended the university in the late nineteenth or early twentieth century. Linda Henrietta José completed a degree in biology in 1897, and Maria Mercedes Manosalva earned a degree in education in 1919.[5] Like many other institutions that did not begin to record Latinx students as their own distinct racial/ethnic group until the 1970s, IU did not track the number of Latinxs who attended since its founding in 1820 up to the 1970s. The earliest recorded figures for Latinx student enrollment at IU revealed that only 150 out of more than 30,000 students were Latinx in the 1970s, which equaled 0.05 percent of the total student enrollment.[6] Latinxs could have walked across the Bloomington campus and attended class all day and not seen another Latinx person because so few were on campus. Albert Torchinsky, dean of Latino Affairs, described the problem to a local *Herald-Times* reporter in August 1992: "It is a very shocking experience when you go to a place where you just don't see anyone who is like you."[7] He noted that the cultural isolation was further exacerbated because many Latinx students, many of whom were first in their families to go to college, did not know how to seek out campus support or where to find other Latinxs for friendship and community.[8]

To make matters worse, Latinx students often faced bias, discrimination, and, in some instances, violence on campus and in the small southern Indiana town of Bloomington. IU's Racial Incidents Team (RIT) recorded and tracked these cases of violence and harassment. In the 1990–91 school year, sixty-three incidents were reported to the Racial Incidents Team; in the 1991–92 school year, the number increased to seventy.[9] These tallies are believed to be lower than the actual number, as many incidents went unreported. Bill Shipton, cochair of the RIT and director of diversity education in the Residence Life department, stated to the *Herald-Times* that many incidents go unreported because Latinxs and other minority students believe that harassment is just "something they have to endure" and that "part of being a (minority) student on campus is you have to put up with these things." Shipton further explained that some students did not know about RIT, were skeptical about anything being done, or were afraid of retaliation.[10]

Lillian Casillas, a graduate student in the early 1990s who later became the director of La Casa, reported an incident that occurred over Homecoming weekend in the fall of 1992, describing how three white youths threw bottles and yelled derogatory names at her and her friends.[11] Georgina Burgueño, the coordinator for Latino Services in the Office of Latino Affairs and later Gamma Phi Omega's first advisor, shared a story of a Latina woman from Texas who suffered from several incidents of racial discrimination in her English class and ultimately chose to leave IU. Such incidents, Burgueño noted, "evoke feelings of fear and isolation and cause many minority students to leave school," which, unfortunately, was not rare for her to see.[12]

In addition to feeling the weight of being a person of color on a predominantly white campus, Latina women struggled with gendered issues that distinguished them from their Latinx counterparts. An October 1990 article in the IDS focused on the family expectations that Latinas at IU faced as daughters in traditional Hispanic households. One Latina commented that "for the daughter, she is often encouraged to go to community college to stay close to home.... Parents wonder if they are safe and healthy more so than the sons." Another Latina commented that as a first-generation college student, she found it hard to get through college and could not talk to her parents about her daily struggles because they would most likely want her to leave IU and come home. She shared, "My dad wanted me to stay home and commute to school."[13]

CREATING THEIR OWN FAMILY—THE FOUNDING OF LATINX FRATERNITIES AND SORORITIES

In founding a sorority, as a student-driven response to the interconnected challenges of gender and ethnicity they faced on the predominantly white Bloomington campus, Guzmán and her sisters were embracing a path earlier generations of Latinx college students had followed as a way to deal with cultural isolation. Indeed, Latinx college students in the US began to create their own organizations as soon as their numbers were sufficient on a given campus. These organizations provided much-needed opportunities to develop valued friendships with other Latinxs who shared the same cultural values and desire to become leaders at school and beyond. The first Latino fraternity was founded in 1931 at Rensselaer Polytechnic Institute, one of the oldest technical institutions in the United States, located in upstate New York.[14] Phi Iota Alpha was founded with the mission to empower the Latinx community and to preserve and uplift Latin American culture.[15] In 1975, the first Latina sorority, Lambda Theta Alpha, was founded at New Jersey's Kean University (formerly the New Jersey State Teachers College) by a group of women "who were eager to be at the forefront of an era of a new educational, political and social consciousness."[16] These organizations functioned as familial support systems and provided a way for Latina women to advocate for the Latinx community to university administration in one united voice.[17] This consciousness and orientation toward advocacy generally set them apart from traditionally white fraternities and sororities. As one member of Lambda Upsilon Lambda fraternity shared, he wanted to create an organization whose members would "become the leaders of our people, that will make great sacrifices for the benefit of our people, that stand for and live up the best of the Latino culture."[18] In other words, Latinx fraternity and sorority members embraced a commitment to integrate service to their communities into their fraternal functions and to use their organizations as platforms for leadership in their communities, both on and off campus.

The 1980s was a significant time of growth for Latinx fraternities and sororities on US campuses. This decade was named *Fuerza* (Force) by Susana Muñoz and Juan Guardia in their review of the history of Latinx fraternities and sororities to denote the relatively quick expansion of these organizations from their origins in the East to universities in the West and Midwest.[19] Several national organizations were established during this time, but each had a small membership due to the small numbers of Latinxs attending college. In 1988, only 6 percent of American college students were Hispanic, compared to 78 percent white, 9 percent Black, and 4 percent Asian students.[20] The number of Latinxs in college in the Midwest was even smaller; the majority were enrolled at institutions on the East or West Coast. The number of Latinxs at IU continued to be quite small, increasing to only 1.5 percent of the student body by the late 1980s.[21] Despite these small numbers, a chapter of Sigma Lambda Beta, a Latino-oriented fraternity, was established at Indiana University in 1989. The start of a chapter in Bloomington—Sigma Lambda Beta's eighth chapter nationwide, only three years after the fraternity's founding in 1986 at the University of Iowa—was confirmation that Latinxs were increasing in numbers in the Midwest and were seeking out ways to forge strong connections with each other and to reap the benefits of Greek life.[22]

The establishment of a Latino fraternity at IU seemed quite a feat, as there were only about 450 Latinxs enrolled at the university in the 1980s, half of them men.[23] However, the presence of a Latino fraternity on the Bloomington campus was long overdue, considering the significant role that Greek life had played since the university's early days. In the early 1990s, Indiana University had the largest fraternity and sorority membership in the country, numbering more than 5,500 members, with almost 1 in 4 undergraduates "going Greek."[24] There were twenty-eight historically white fraternities and four historically Black fraternities, and finally, there was an option for Latino men to join an organization of their own. The Greek community at IU was growing, much like the Greek communities across the country, due to students shifting from antiestablishment attitudes of the 1960s and 1970s to what could be described as a less political or more conservative orientation, one that aligned well with the ethos of most fraternities and sororities. As IU Panhellenic advisor Jane Campaigne observed, fraternities and sororities were "basically conservative groups." She continued, "Even though they're all different, they're all kind of the same.... When you come to a large university such as [IU] you have to have some sort of a niche you can fit into, a way to meet people who have similar beliefs to yours."[25]

Latinxs at IU, like their white peers, wanted to find their niche, an avenue by which to "fit into" the large campus. They were inspired by the success of Latinx-oriented fraternities and sororities that were rapidly being established at universities across the country and were motivated to establish their own organizations on the Bloomington campus that allowed them to combine their cultural values with the camaraderie fraternities provided. Sigma Lambda Beta was a clear signal to the fraternity community at IU that Latinss wanted to participate in Greek life, but in their own way and with their own organizations.

THE FOUNDING OF THE FIRST LATINA
SORORITY AT INDIANA UNIVERSITY

The journey to founding Gamma Phi Omega, the first Latina sorority on the IU campus, began in the fall of 1989, around the same time that Sigma Lambda Beta, an all-male fraternity, was officially recognized on campus. Veronica Montemayor, after considering the options available for her on campus, realized that none of IU's twenty-one historically white sororities or the four historically Black sororities were able to meet her unique needs as a Latina on campus. Veronica, joined by two other students—Monica Guzmán and Cristina Rodela—embarked on a nation-wide search for a sorority that would fit well with students' needs on the Bloomington campus and that they could establish at IU. The original group of three expanded to a group of six the following year to include Margaret Escabalzeta, Laura Garcia, and Barbara Graves.[26] With the guidance of Georgina Burgueño, they began to create the foundation for their own organization comprised of women who could relate to their culture, family dynamics, and academic struggles as Latinas on a predominantly white campus.[27]

These six women—five in-state students from the northern Indiana cities of East Chicago, Portage, and South Bend and one international student from Spain—began to function as an organization by holding meetings to manage their activities. As detailed in their meeting notes on March 27, 1991, they aimed to create a prominent presence on campus and to become leaders of the Latinx community at IU. They started to work on activities that exemplified the kind of sorority they aspired to be based on sisterhood, commitment to their campus community, academic excellence, and an embrace of diversity and inclusivity for all women regardless of race, ethnicity, sexual identity, or abilities. Their agenda items included participating in Latino Day, setting up study tables, and cosponsoring social events with Sigma Lambda Beta.[28]

Equally important during this time were their final attempts to secure the interest of a sorority that held the national status necessary to expand on IU's Bloomington Campus. Indiana University's policy on establishing a new chapter on campus required the host fraternity or sorority to be a national organization. The rationale was that the involvement of a national organization not only would provide the level of support, guidance, and structure needed to establish the new chapter on campus but could help ensure its success and longevity. The IU women sent letters and made phone calls to chapter presidents of national organizations as well as local Latina and multicultural sororities to learn as much as they could about these organizations. Unfortunately, many of these efforts went unanswered due to unresponsiveness, disinterest in expansion, or out-of-date contact information. Recall also that during the early 1990s, the internet was in its infancy; fraternities and sororities had yet to use social media or create websites to promote their organizations, so familiarity with organizations was generally limited to whom they knew or saw at parties and social gatherings.

In retrospect, the inability to locate an organization interested in expanding to IU served as a blessing in disguise. On the one hand, the sorority founders had to endure an intricate process of establishing an organization from scratch within the constraints of the Greek system that existed at IU. Their tasks included gaining the support of the existing Greek organizations and university administrators by demonstrating a need for a new sorority and their ability to sustain it and formally presenting their proposal to the Expansion Committee for approval. On the other hand, they had the opportunity to create an organization that centered their experiences and identities as Latina women in the Midwest. The desire to create an organization that reflected one's regional culture and community was common among other newly created Latina organizations during the 1990s. For example, the founders of Sigma Delta Lambda, a Latina-based sorority founded at Texas State University, San Marcos, created an organization focused on their particular region's Latino culture, stating that they "were very proud Tejanas (Texans) and . . . wanted a sorority that was Texas based."[29] Latino identities can vary from one region to the other and are primarily influenced by the community's histories of immigration, political realities, racial and ethnic diversity, and social norms. Latinas at IU were unique from their counterparts in the West Coast, for example, because they often experienced cultural isolation in schools and their communities since few Latina/os lived in the Midwest compared to the West.

On April 17, 1991, Gamma Phi Omega was founded. With the strong support of the IU administration as they worked toward creating their own organization, the sisters had accomplished their goal. They declared their new name and founding date in the minutes of their meeting on April 28, 1991. The many tasks outlined for this key meeting included the sorority's identity branding (for example, choosing the swan as their mascot and maroon and navy as their official colors), processes and procedures, community involvement initiatives, and the task to "call the [Panhellenic] office and find out the deadline dates for the rush book," which suggested their eagerness to start recruiting more women to join their new organization as soon as possible.[30] Indeed, this was important as they intended to create a national organization from the very beginning.[31] The university officially recognized the organization on January 22, 1992. On reflecting on this achievement, founder Rodela commented, "It's been like 2½ years that we've been working on it and finally got it established. . . . Where it is now, I don't want to say it's like a dream, but it's a lot of hard work and dedication."[32]

Three key people were invested in supporting the sorority from the start.[33] Georgina Burgueño, whom Gamma Phi Omega's founders affectionately nicknamed Muffy, was their first sorority advisor. She helped them understand the ways the university worked and whom to go for support. Alberto Torchinsky, the dean of Latino Affairs, and Richard McKaig, the dean of Student Affairs, also provided their support and influence to help these women go through the required vetting process and secure final approval as a recognized organization. All three university administrators were present for Gamma Phi Omega's first Public Initiation, held on March 5, 1992, at Beck Chapel; Burgueño was made an honorary member right before the ceremony.[34] This ceremony officially presented the new sisters to the campus community and became a tradition that was repeated for each new member class thereafter.

While fraternities and sororities are oftentimes competitive with each other—seeking prestige and recruits—Latinx Greeks have a strong history of supporting each other. Gamma Phi Omega's early history clearly demonstrated how the support from their fellow IU Latinx Greek organization, Sigma Lambda Beta, helped the women establish their own sorority from conceptualization to expansion. Though these organizations were not officially affiliated with each other, the support the fraternity provided reflected a trend in Latinx Greek-Letter Organization (LGLO) history where oftentimes, a Latino fraternity would be the first organization to be established on campus, followed by the establishment of a Latina sorority. The degree of support that Sigma Lambda Beta showed Gamma Phi Omega was substantial, demonstrating a strong friendship between these organizations dating back to 1989, when the initial group of three women began to explore the idea of establishing a Latina sorority at IU. The women saw for themselves the role that Latinx Greeks could play on campus and the benefits of Greek life, such as the strong familial bond, elite social status, and other joys of being Greek. Sigma Lambda Beta cosponsored many social and cultural events and shared their knowledge on how to run a fraternal organization, including the process and procedures to expand to more campuses. This friendship extended beyond the IU chapters: a group of women at the University of Illinois–Chicago wrote a letter to Gamma Phi Omega stating their interest in establishing a chapter at their campus and said that "by our side is a national organization by the men of Sigma Lambda Beta."[35]

At the heart of all their work and efforts was the goal to create a new family that women could join to help them get through college. They hoped to form bonds that were stronger than friendships, which many felt was needed to cope with being at IU. The founding sisters were also committed to working to increase the number of Latinas going to IU. Rodela, who was from South Bend, Indiana, and majored in criminal justice and Spanish, hoped to serve as a role model for Latina high school students and to provide them with scholarships to pay for books. The sorority ultimately developed four goals to guide their sorority's purpose: academic excellence, community service, cultural awareness, and sisterhood.[36]

Gamma Phi Omega started with high hopes and big plans. The local Bloomington paper featured the organization with an attention-grabbing headline— "IU Gets First Hispanic Sorority: Students Hope to Attract More Minorities, Dispel Stereotypes"—a few weeks after the university officially recognized the sorority in January 1992.[37] The article not only described the founders' aspirations for their organization but also spoke to the broader issues that university administrators wished to address with the sorority's leadership. First, university administrators noted they had difficulty in minority recruitment and concluded that the sorority could be a "good recruiting tool" to show prospective students that there was an active social community in which incoming Latinas/os could get involved and find friendship.[38] Second, cultural isolation was a significant issue, so the new sorority was eager to create campus programs to raise awareness about Latinx culture in the greater IU community "to make others aware we [Latinos] do exist" as well as dispel negative stereotypes their peers might have about them, such as the misguided belief that all Latinos are illegal aliens."[39] The sorority began to regularly appear as sponsors for cultural programs in major Latinx events hosted by La Casa, they collaborated with other Latino organizations, and they also created their own programs. Most often, these were cultural events that allowed fellow Latinx students to enjoy sharing their culture with each other and with the broader IU community, such as food fundraisers, salsa lessons, and socials.

The new leaders of Gamma Phi Omega were soon invited to departmental banquets and university-wide events where Latinx leadership and accomplishments were recognized. They, like the leaders of the other Latinx student organizations, also served as institutional representations of diversity and an indicator of a vibrant Latinx student community. These invitations provided exposure to their sorority and also validated them as being part of an elite group of Latinx leaders on campus.

DEMANDING IU TO WORK FOR OUR PEOPLE—
ACTIVISM DURING THE TACO BELL INCIDENT

During the first few years of existence, Gamma Phi Omega enjoyed rapid growth and support from the university administration. The sisters worked hard to create cultural programming and social activities to build a more inclusive campus for Latinx students, became prominent student leaders on campus, and were well on their way to expanding their sorority to other universities in the Midwest. Then the Taco Bell incident occurred on October 7, 1993. This incident mobilized the community of color at IU, who began to question how much IU was doing for Latinxs. How much did the university work to ensure their safety and make the campus welcoming for them?

The campus newspaper, the *Indiana Daily Student* (*IDS*), provided extensive coverage of the Taco Bell incident and the protracted campus debate that ensued. According to one *IDS* account, a number of the IU senators disparaged LUIU's request for funds to help defray the catering bill from a local Mexican establishment, La Charreada, by mockingly calling the restaurant "La Cucaracha." One senator, knowing all meeting attendees were aware IUSA funds could be applied only to hosted meals having a culturally significant component, asked if Taco Bell might suffice as a culturally appropriate option.[40] Chris Hamm, another senator, vehemently opposed funding the dinner altogether, declaring that IUSA was not a "[expletive] bank" from which LUIU could take money whenever it wanted.[41] In a letter to the editor published in the *IDS* on November 8, Hamm continued to disparage LUIU's Parents' Weekend proposal. "The dinner was merely an opportunity for Latino students to take their parents out on IUSA's tab, which the students pick up," he asserted. "This past parents' weekend, I did not ask students to pay for me to take my parents out, and I was not going to give student money to anyone who intended to do so."[42]

IU's Latinx community, members of the broader community of color at IU, and their allies were outraged by widespread accounts of the disrespectful behavior of the white student senators. Students were upset by the senators' mocking tones and cultural insensitivity during the proposal presentation, but further, many saw this incident as a symptom of a more significant problem on campus that existed along racial lines. Indeed, the 1990s were a time of racial tension on campuses across the country, and Indiana University was no exception.[43]

Several Latinx student organizations voiced their concerns and demands that university administration take action against the senators who made the racially insensitive comments. Gamma Phi Omega was one of five organizations (including Latinos Unidos of Indiana University, Puerto Rican Student Association, Sigma Lambda Beta, and Latino Law Student Association) who took part in several protest activities that included press releases, press conferences, and letters of demand. The sorority was the only exclusively women's organization, and Monica Guzmán was the only president in the coalition who was female. A relative newcomer to Bloomington campus student leadership, she was the singular female voice in the top leadership group heading the campaign protesting the Taco Bell incident.

In her October 19, 1993 letter of protest to Jay Fultz (described at the opening of this essay), Guzmán went beyond a general expression of outrage at the Taco Bell incident to list the following demands:

1. The resignation of senators implicated in the grievance.
2. Public apologies from each of the IUSA senators to be printed in the student newspaper.
3. Revision to the procedures of money allocation by IUSA.
4. Resignation of the IUSA advisor, Jim Gibson, who did nothing to stop the student senators from speaking in an offensive way to the members of LUIU, nor did he voice any concerns about the comments made during the meeting.

Unlike the other Latinx organizations that sent demand letters of their own, Gamma Phi Omega was the only organization to call for Gibson's resignation. They concluded that Gibson "should not oversee any student activities if he cannot comprehend when a racial incident is taking place."[44]

On October 27, the Latinx student coalition presented a list of demands to the campus community in a full-page advertisement in the *Indiana Daily Student*, which included the demand for all four of the implicated senators to resign, all IUSA officials to attend mandatory race sensitivity workshops, and a public apology.[45] The Racial Incidents Team, which was comprised of a small group of university administrators, including Burgueño, initiated an investigation. Students mobilized by attending student government meetings en masse, voicing their grievances in the student paper, and other activities to publicize their concerns to the campus community.

On November 11, approximately a month after the Taco Bell incident, the Racial Incidents Team publicly announced their conclusions via a press release. The report concluded that the actions by the senators in question were racially motivated but stopped short of calling the actions or the students racist. The report stated that "whereas the reasons for not wanting the funding to be approved may not have been linked to racism, the method used to discourage approval of the funding was directly determined by the racial identity of the LUIU president."[46] The Racial Incidents Team—whose purpose was to investigate incidents of racial bias, report their findings, and propose recommendations to improve race relations—did not have the power to sanction the implicated senators. The Latinx community was incensed because they hoped that the IUSA senators would be held accountable by the university administration. But the policies that existed in student government did not provide procedures to remove senators from office or any sanctions for acts of racism or misconduct.

Burgueño continued to publicly share her disdain over Jim Gibson's inaction during the IUSA meeting. "As an administrator, why did he sit back and not take action? . . . He is there for all students, not just as an advisor," she asserted.[47] Burgueño also challenged the student government leaders, such as IUSA president Fultz, who promised during their campaigns to increase the diversity of the student government and to take action and commit to creating a more hospitable environment in student government for students of color. She commented, "This is a very serious offense to all of our Latino students. . . . They will not let this rest until they get some closure and feel it is a safe place for them to be on this campus. . . . Fultz ran on the stance that he wanted to get more minority students involved, this is not the way to do it by calling them names."[48]

Some student government leaders did take action in an effort to improve race relations on campus, specifically within student government. These students (who, incidentally, were not the implicated senators from the Taco Bell incident) signed an open letter to the IU community, which was published in the *Indiana Daily Student* the day after the Racial Incidents Team's report.[49] Their letter explained the university policies and the student government constitution's policies that did not allow them to remove students from office or be found in violation of the Student Code of Conduct. They apologized for the incident, and they expressed their hopes to organize a meeting with Latinx student leaders in the near future.

The efforts made were not enough to quell the racial tensions on campus, which continued throughout that fall semester. Several of the implicated senators continued vehemently and publicly to defend themselves as non-racists. Other students wrote opinion letters published in the student paper, the *IDS*, challenging the Racial Incidents Team's conclusions that the senators' actions were racially motived; some insisted that it was time to move on, as the student government had more important things on which to focus. The students of color continued to be frustrated with what they perceived as student government leaders getting away with racism. Many of them participated in protests at IUSA meetings, including Dara Neeley, who publicly shared her concerns about being a minority in student government and her beliefs that she was discriminated against due to her race. She stated, "We are here to tell you our belief is that it will not blow over! How can you talk about recruiting more minorities into IUSA when you don't even know how to treat the ones you have?"[50]

On December 1, Kenneth Gros Louis, vice president of Indiana University and chancellor of the Bloomington campus, and Richard McKaig, dean of students, published an open letter in yet another effort to smooth over the campus tensions and to ask that the campus community come together. They first endorsed the findings and recommendations of the Racial Incidents Team and then stopped short of supporting LUIU's demands for justice by diverting the focus away from sanctions and accountability and toward engaging in dialogue as a campus community:

> While we support [RIT's] recommendations, what is important about them is not that one side has been proved more righteous than the other, or that blame can now be neatly assigned. . . .

> What is important instead is that the Team's support of LUIU's claims, based as it is on an objective appraisal of both the incident itself and our campus' expectation of sensitivity, offers a place from which to begin a sincere dialogue. That dialogue should take place not only between IUSA and our minority student organizations, but among the rest of us as well.

Gros Louis and McKaig concluded their letter to the community by offering their vision of how these dialogues could be approached by the senators accused of racism and LUIU:

> It is our hope that those accused of offense will lay aside defensiveness and posturing for the sake of real understanding; that those who feel victimized will reach out to their offenders; and that all of us will recognize that naïve insensitivity toward issues of diversity causes harm, much of the same as blatant bigotry, racism, and hatred do. Unless we begin to comprehend that reality, incidents such as this one will only be repeated.[51]

McKaig and Gros Louis's directive for students who were the victims of racism—the Latinx students involved in the Taco Bell incident—to "reach out to their offenders" continued to burden the offended to take actions to make it right. They suggested those accused—the white student senators who were found to be guilty of making comments in a racially charged way—should lay aside their defensiveness and be open to understanding, which was woefully short of a more active role in accepting responsibility and taking on the heavy work needed to improve the campus climate.

Missing from the Racial Incidents Team report and the open letter was some acknowledgment of how the university's administration and policies and the overall campus climate might have played a role in creating these racial tensions. Both of these documents centered their focus on students—their past behaviors and what they should do—to address the deep-rooted racism on campus that has unfortunately been a part of Indiana University's history for decades. The open letter did not hint of any plans for a university-wide initiative to address inequities, sensitivity training for staff who work directly with students, or any personal actions that Gros Louis or McKaig would do as institutional leaders to influence change.

The Taco Bell incident highlighted the expectations that the university had for Latinx students to provide their own care: create their own cultural programming, assist the university in recruiting students of color, and hold people accountable in instances of discrimination and racism. Latinx students often had to fight for their own resources, such as the appointment of their own dean of Latino affairs (IU had a Dean of Afro-Americans and a dean of women to support the needs and interests of particular minority groups on campus); the establishment of La Casa, the Latino cultural center; and the hiring of Latinx faculty and staff.[52] The Latina women of Gamma Phi Omega continued this tradition of activism by voicing their demands for the university to provide the Latinx community access to campus resources (such as programming funds from IUSA) without fear of being belittled or treated like second-class citizens asking for handouts.

THE IMPACT OF LATINA/O GREEKS IN CAMPUS POLITICS

The women of Gamma Phi Omega played key roles in the Taco Bell incident, as they were the few women who were leaders in the movement. However, Gamma Phi Omega was not founded on a strong political agenda. Latinx fraternities and sororities, which were often created by students who needed a support system to deal with an inhospitable campus climate for minority students, vary in their political engagement, from no engagement in activism to making political statements in support of or in protest to current issues affecting Latinx communities, such as immigration rights. Their existence clearly acknowledged the lack of inclusivity in mainstream organizations, and many worked hard to overcome the shortcomings of the university in providing appropriate support and access for Latinx students, but many fraternities and sororities stopped short of considering themselves politically oriented. It was one thing to understand and deal with the racial realities of campus, and it was another to become activists with a clear political agenda.

The Latinx Greek community made significant contributions to IU by raising awareness in the campus community about the racial realities of Latinx students. In addition to participating in the protests associated with the Taco Bell incident, Sigma Lambda Gamma organized a panel of Latino men in March 1993 to discuss discrimination and racism at IU, where they shared their own experiences with negative stereotypes and unsupportive faculty.[53] Their discussion brought to light for the campus community the ways they had been targets of racism and raised awareness about the negative campus climate, but this event did not promote a political agenda or critique of particular university policies. Certainly, the discussion could have motivated people to act in political ways, but that was not Sigma Lambda Gamma's ultimate goal in sponsoring these kinds of programs.

Gamma Phi Omega had the strong support of key university administrators in its early years to help create their organization and appeared to prosper with that support. Yet, considering the obstacles they faced as the first Latina sorority at an institution that had a history of blatant discrimination and difficulty diversifying its student body, their presence was revolutionary. Instead of assimilating into mainstream organizations, the Latina women created an organization for themselves that was relevant to their own needs and also the needs of their community. They became politically savvy in learning how to work with university administrators to earn their support and financial assistance, and they also learned about the relevant university policies to navigate the complicated process of becoming a new sorority on campus. Like their fellow Latina/o-based fraternities and sororities, Gamma Phi Omega did not seek just to be included in the Greek system but to create an organization that would be more inclusive and welcoming for a group of students who had been historically left out.

CONCLUSION

This chapter reviews the history of the establishment of the first Latina sorority at Indiana University during a time of racial tensions and activism. The stories of the founding members who rose to the occasion by taking on leadership roles during an era of student protest are remarkable. Many reasons could have led a small organization of women of color, many of whom were first-generation college students, to fail. The telling of this history recognizes the contributions of Latina leaders who created their own family of sisters and fought with their community, alongside other students of color, to demand respect and equity from their white peers.

Gamma Phi Omega continues to play a special role for IU women today. It is unique in providing for women who identify as Latina as well as women of other races and ethnicities leadership opportunities where they can embrace both their cultural values and identities. Members learn how to become leaders in the sorority, which then gives them the experience and knowledge to take their leadership skills to the greater campus community and beyond. Its founding paved the way for women to establish their own culturally based sororities on campus, including other Latina sororities, multicultural sororities, an Asian-interest sorority, a South Asian sorority, and a faith-based sorority.

Today, Gamma Phi Omega is a member of IU's Multi-Cultural Greek Council, which is the umbrella organization for thirteen multicultural fraternities and sororities.[54] Gamma Phi Omega is considered one of the most well-established Latina sororities in the Midwest. It has grown from a group of six founders at IU's Alpha Chapter to twenty-two undergraduate chapters located in Indiana, Illinois, and Texas and five alumnae chapters—totaling more than one thousand members today.[55] Their story is uplifting as it reveals the power that a small group of IU Latinas possessed when they banded together, from bravely challenging the "big dogs" on campus (IUSA) to creating a family for hundreds of Latinas in the Midwest who live out their motto: "Unity and Sisterhood, Now and Forever, One and Inseparable."

NOTES

Epigraph is from Teri Klassen, "IU Gets First Hispanic Sorority: Students Hope to Attract More Minorities, Dispel Stereotypes," *Herald-Times* (Bloomington, IN), February 5, 1992.

1. Matthew S. Bajko, "IUSA Reacts to Minority Charges of Inaction," *Indiana Daily Student*, November 22, 1993, 1, 6.

2. Latinos Unidos is the largest Latina/o student organization at IU. It was established in 1979 "to promote the identity and unity of the Latino students through intellectual, cultural and social growth and to increase their visibility and involvement in campus and community activities." http://www.indiana.edu/~luiu/ (accessed July 23, 2020).

3. Monica Guzman to Jay Fultz, October 19, 1993, Indiana University Latino Cultural Center Records C245, Box 3, Folder Subject Files: Racial Incidents Report 1993, IU Libraries University Archives, Bloomington, Indiana.

4. Matthew S. Bajko, "IUSA Remarks Deemed Racist," *Indiana Daily Student*, November 15, 1993, 1, 10.

5. For Jose's listing, see p. 67 of *Indiana University Bulletin*, "Registrar of the Graduates of Indiana University, 1911," https://books.google.com/books?id=3C7 tAAAAMAAJ&pg=PA67&lpg=PA67&dq=linda+henrietta+jose+IU&source=bl &ots=9A_jCC_5Po&sig=J64yEapM_nM2Ca8KJwqA_nHBUg4&hl=en. Manosalva was one of three students from South America who received scholarships to attend IU in 1919; see https://www.google.com/books/edition/Hispania/J4dJAA AAYAAJ?hl=en&gbpv=1&dq=Mercedes+Manoslava&pg=PA316&printsec=front cover (accessed July 23, 2020). See also, Trustees of Indiana University, "1910–1930: Latino Timeline: About: La Casa, Latino Cultural Center: Indiana University," 2018, https://lacasa.indiana.edu/old-site/latinotime/1910-1930.shtml (accessed July 23, 2020).

6. Correspondence from Concerned Latino Students of Indiana University to President J. W. Ryan, September 17, 1974, Indiana University President's Office Records C459, Box 169, Folder Latino Affairs 1974–75, IU Libraries University Archives, Bloomington, Indiana.

7. Lewis Jones, "Minorities Find Ways to Cope," *Herald-Times* (Bloomington, Indiana), August 29, 1992, http://ww.heraldtimesonline.com/stories/1992/08/29 /archive.19920829.121fbae.sto (accessed April 17, 2018).

8. Jones, "Minorities Find Ways to Cope."

9. Jones.

10. Jones.

11. Robin Holtzman, "Latino Students Subject to Abuse," *Indiana Daily Student*, October 21, 1992, 1.

12. Holtzman, "Latino Students."

13. Elissa Milenky, "Traditional Hispanic Families Find College Decision Difficult," *Indiana Daily Student*, October 8, 1990, 3.

14. There is disagreement about which is the first Latino fraternity, as there is a difference in opinion in defining what *Latino* means. Founded in 1931, Phi Iota Alpha's membership included many men from Latin America who returned to their home countries after completing their university studies. Established in 1975, Lambda Theta Phi stakes its claim to be considered the first Latino fraternity as their focus is on addressing the needs of Latino men in the United States and their local Latino communities (see their website at https://thelambdas.org/our-history/; accessed July 23, 2020).

15. Phi Iota Alpha Fraternity, Inc., "General Information," accessed July 23, 2020, https://www.phiota.org/fact-sheet.

16. Lambda Theta Alpha Latin Sorority, Inc., "Explore Our History," accessed July 23, 2020, http://lambdalady.org/about-us/history.

17. Susana M. Muñoz and J. R. Guardia, "Nuestra Historia y Futuro (Our History and Future): Latino/a Fraternities and Sororities," in *Brothers and Sisters: Diversity in College Fraternities and Sororities*, ed. Craig L. Torbenson and Gregory S. Parks (Teaneck, NJ: Fairleigh Dickinson University Press, 2009), 104–32.

18. La Unidad Latina, "The Story of LUL," accessed February 20, 2019, http://www.launidadlatina.org/story.htm.

19. Muñoz and Guardia, "Nuestra Historia y Futuro (Our History and Future)."

20. US Census Bureau, "College Enrollment, by Selected Characteristics: 1980–1996," in *Statistical Abstract of the United States: 1999*, 119th ed. (December 9, 1999), Section 4: Education, Table No. 309, 193, accessed July 23, 2020, https://www.census.gov/library/publications/1999/compendia/statab/119ed.html.

21. Teri Klassen, "IU Gets First Hispanic Sorority: Students Hope to Attract More Minorities, Dispel Stereotypes," *Herald-Times* (Bloomington, Indiana), February 5, 1992, http://ww.heraldtimesonline.com/stories/1992/02/05/archive.19920205.c2f53b9.sto (accessed April 16, 2018).

22. Sigma Lambda Beta Fraternity, Inc., "Our Story," accessed July 23, 2020, https://www.sigmalambdabeta.com/history.

23. Report by Aida Martinez and Joseph Villanueva, "The Office of Latino Affairs—January 1973–June 1999", n.d., Indiana University Latino Cultural Center Records C245, Box 3, Folder "Subject Files—Office of Latino Affairs 1981," IU Libraries University Archives, Bloomington, Indiana.

24. Teri Klassen, "Sororities Plan More Expansion on IU Campus," *Herald-Times* (Bloomington, IN), February 19, 1990, http://ww.heraldtimesonline.com/stories/1990/02/19/archive.19900219.25acc64.sto (retrieved April 17, 2018).

25. Klassen, "Sororities Plan More Expansion."

26. Gamma Phi Omega, "History," accessed July 23, 2020, http://gammaphiomega.org/about/our-history/.

27. Gamma Phi Omega International Sorority, Inc., "Our History," accessed September 2, 2018, http://gammaphiomega.org/about/our-history.

28. "Gamma Phi Omega Sorority Meeting Minutes," March 27, 1991, Gamma Phi Omega Records C253, Box 1, Folder "Alpha Chapter—Administrative Files Meeting Minutes 1991–1998," IU Libraries University Archives, Bloomington, Indiana.

29. Muñoz and Guardia, "Nuestra Historia y Futuro," 114.

30. "Gamma Phi Omega Sorority Meeting Minutes," April 28, 1991, Gamma Phi Omega Records C253, Box 1, Folder "Alpha Chapter—Administrative Files Meeting Minutes 1991–1998," IU Libraries University Archives, Bloomington, Indiana.

31. Correspondence from Richard McKaig to Margaret Escabalzeta, January 20, 1992, Gamma Phi Omega Records C253, Box 1, Folder "General Correspondence, 1990–1993," IU Libraries University Archives, Bloomington, Indiana.

32. Klassen, "IU Gets First Hispanic Sorority."

33. Gamma Phi Omega International Sorority, Inc., "Our History."

34. "Gamma Phi Omega Organizational Timeline 1991–1998," 1998, Gamma Phi Omega Records C253, Box 2, Folder "Subject Files—Timeline," IU Libraries University Archives, Bloomington, Indiana.

35. National Board of Directors—Beta Chapter, University of Illinois—Chicago, 1992–1998, October 1992, Gamma Phi Omega Records C253, Box 1 Folder "National Board of Directors—Beta Chapter, University of Illinois—Chicago, 1992–1998," IU Libraries University Archives, Bloomington, Indiana.

36. Gamma Phi Omega International Sorority, Inc., "Sorority Facts," accessed March 29, 2019, http://gammaphiomega.org/about/sorority-facts.

37. Klassen, "IU Gets First Hispanic Sorority."

38. Klassen, "IU Gets First Hispanic Sorority.".

39. Klassen, "IU Gets First Hispanic Sorority.".

40. Joe Nickell, "Taco Bell, Cockroach, You Know What I Mean," *Bloomington Voice* (Bloomington, Indiana), October 27, 1993, 8.

41. Andrew Welsh-Higgins, "Remarks Termed Racist," *Herald-Times* (Bloomington, Indiana), October 28, 1993, A1, A9.

42. Christopher Lane Hamm, "Letter to the Editor," *Indiana Daily Student*, November 8, 1993. Indiana University Latino Cultural Center Records C245, Box 3, Folder "Subject Files: Racial Incidents Report 1993," IU Libraries University Archives, Bloomington, Indiana.

43. Sylvia Hurtado, "The Campus Racial Climate: Contexts of Conflict," *Journal of Higher Education* vol. 63, no. 5, Racial Harassment on Campus (September–October 1992): 539–69.

44. Monica Guzman to Jay Fultz, October 19, 1993, Indiana University Latino Cultural Center Records C245, Box 3, Folder "Subject Files: Racial Incidents Report 1993," IU Libraries University Archives, Bloomington, Indiana.

45. Correspondence from IU Latino Organizations to IUSA, October 27, 1993, Indiana University Latino Cultural Center Records C245, Box 3, Folder "Subject Files—Racial Incident Report 1993," IU Libraries University Archives, Bloomington, Indiana.

46. Racial Incident Team Judgment Report—Indiana University—Bloomington, November 23, 1993, Indiana University Latino Cultural Center Records C245, Box 3, Folder "Subject Files—Racial Incident Report 1993," IU Libraries University Archives, Bloomington, Indiana.

47. Matthew S. Bajko, "IUSA Comments Lead to Racism Charges," *Indiana Daily Student*, October 21, 1993, 1, 8.

48. Bajko, "IUSA Comments."

49. Jay Fultz et al., "An Open Letter to the Indiana University Latino Community," *Indiana Daily Student*, November 12, 1993. Indiana University Latino Cultural Center Records C245, Box 3, Folder "Subject Files: Racial Incidents Report 1993," IU Libraries University Archives, Bloomington, Indiana.

50. Matthew S. Bajko. "Minority Students Protest at IUSA meeting," *Indiana Daily Student*, November 19, 1993, 1, 6.

51. Kenneth R. R. Gros Louis and Richard N. McKaig to the *IDS* Opinion Page, December 1, 1993, Indiana University Latino Cultural Center Records C245, Box 3, IU Libraries University Archives, Bloomington, Indiana.

52. Ebelia Hernández "Demanding Social Change at Indiana University: Latino Student Activism in the Mid-1970s," *Journal of the Indiana University Student Personnel Association* 2007 Edition (2007): 9–21, https://scholarworks.iu.edu/journals/index.php/jiuspa/article/view/4647.

53. Chad Hesting, "Latino Students Discuss Racism," *Indiana Daily Student*, March 31, 1992, p. 3.

54. Indiana University Multi-cultural Greek Council, "Organizations," accessed June 24, 2020, https://www.mcgciub.com/organizations.

55. Gamma Phi Omega International Sorority, Inc., "Undergraduate" and "Alumnae," accessed June 24, 2020, http://gammaphiomega.org/chapters/undergraduate.

EIGHT

LEARNING HUMAN ANATOMY

Women and the Changing Student Body at the Indiana University School of Medicine, 1907–2007

ANGELA BOWEN POTTER

Angela Bowen Potter provides a poignant view of the experience of women students and faculty at one of IU's earliest professional schools—the Indiana University School of Medicine (IUSM), located in Indianapolis. Weaving her discussion around the multiple meanings of the concept of "student body," Potter discusses the gendered aspects of medical school enrollments and pedagogy. Using enrollment data, photographs, and oral histories, Potter documents patterns of discrimination and women's perspectives—including recollections years later—on both the culture they encountered and the one they built together through their affiliation with IUSM.

ANATOMY PROFESSOR EDWIN KIME (1891–1968) famously belittled all the students at Indiana University School of Medicine (IUSM)—but saved the worst of his ire for female medical students, remarking that there was "no place here for panty-waists!"[1] More than fifty years later, IUSM alum Elsie Flint Meyers (1922–2019) remembered sitting in the lecture hall with her fellow first-year medical students, dreading Professor Kime's rapid-fire questions. Meyers recalled a particularly important lecture where Kime posed a question that stumped all the male students he called on. Meyers correctly answered the question. Kime then patronized her: "Now, men, you have let little Miss Flint get ahead of you. How is it that she got the answer and you stupid men did not?" He returned to her:

> "And now, Miss Flint," he leered in his most awful voice, "What went wrong distally?"
> "I'm sorry, Dr. Kime. I couldn't figure that out."

Well, Dr. Kime spent the last half hour raking me over the coals in front of the class. I was the lowest form of low life, an idiot who just memorized stuff and didn't know or understand anything.[2]

Later that day, Meyers took a chance and went to Kime's office, despite the potential of serious consequences for challenging faculty authority. She recalled:

Dr. Kime answered my knock at his door. "Oh, Miss. Flint, do come in! And please sit down!" He motioned grandly to a chair. I sat on the edge.

"Dr. Kime, I think there are a few things that you and I need to get straightened out! I'm sorry that I missed the second half of the question. It was news to me that blood from a hemorrhage could travel so far along the nerve! But you didn't need to castigate me in front of the whole class for thirty minutes!"

"Oh, it was nothing personal, Miss Flint."

"I took it very personally!"

"Oh, no, I was just teaching the fellows. Believe me, it was nothing personal."

I said that it was hard not to take it personally.[3]

Kime taught a "body of knowledge," a corpus written on paper and flesh, where anatomy dissections, laboratory diagnostic tests, and clinical encounters prepared Hoosier students for their future as physicians. In medical education the "student body" is both the subject and location of education. In Kime's class, students learned that women's bodies violated normative human anatomy—as subjects and students. In the late nineteenth century, a new paradigm of experimental science altered this relationship by privileging laboratory research over clinical observation. Supporters of the new laboratory science touted it as more rational, detached, and objective. Historian Wendy Kline explains how medical education was embodied knowledge, inseparably linked with changes in the "historical relationship between scientific knowledge, women's bodies, and medical practice." Reducing the history of women in medical education to discussions of pioneering women and demographic changes reinscribes biological readings of gender that form the bedrock of scientific discourses and evidence-based medicine.[4]

Meyers felt that her treatment was *personal*, that his questioning of her place at IUSM was part of larger social and political discrimination against women in medicine. Kime was just the most recent in a series of male physicians that placed obstacles in her path to becoming a physician. He embodied the hypermasculine climate of the "Golden Age of Medicine," which elevated physicians to gods and dehumanized patients in the name of science. He was a product of this system of education, graduating from medical school in 1915 and then joining the faculty. His response that he was "just teaching the fellows" evidences the challenges for women in medical education, both in Indiana and across the country. Many of the faculty members continued to conceptualize the student body as male and referred to coed groups of students as "you men" or "you boys," even when women were a sizeable minority of each new cohort.[5]

Outside the Ruth Lilly Medical Library on the IUSM campus, photographs of each graduating class offer a snapshot of the history of the student body at IUSM to patients, faculty, and students as they rush by. At first glance, the most notable feature is the steady growth of the number of earnest-faced medical students in each image, from a few dozen in 1907 to over three hundred fifty a century later—one of the largest medical student bodies in the nation. Elsie Flint Meyers earned her place on this wall, alongside the more than four thousand women who graduated from IUSM in its first century. Meyers's voice joins with those of other female physicians who have recorded their personal stories. Women have always been, and are still, in the minority at IUSM, but they played critical roles as students and faculty. The intersection of gender, race, class, and social and medical values and expectations had unique and powerful implications for each of these students' experiences at IUSM. Merely counting the number of women in each image misses the embodied personal experiences of these intelligent, sleep-deprived, pregnant, harassed, in love, and courageous women that fought for their place in the student body.[6]

THE MEDICAL STUDENT BODY

Looking at the image of the IUSM graduating class of 1924, the forty-six men and women formed the *student body* of the IU School of Medicine on metaphorical, institutional, and corporal levels. With the students lined up on the steps of Emerson Hall on the Indianapolis campus, the graduation photo was an annual ritual that marked the end of their collective identity as medical students and a new individual identity as a physician. The phrase *student body* provides a lens for exploring the historical experience of medical education for women. Now a cultural shorthand for the total enrollment in a school, the phrase first emerged in the 1880s as universities grew and all the students no longer knew each other.[7]

From its beginning in 1903, IUSM had its own unique student body. In terms of *demography*, the composition at the IUSM student body changed more slowly than the rest of the university and most notably grew to one of the largest in the nation. In the 1924 class photo, the three white female students stand at the margins of the image, drawing attention due to their individuality in contrast to the male homogeneity. On closer look, two black male students stand at the center of the image, almost blending into the male student body. For more than three decades, longtime faculty member and dean Burton Myers (1870–1951) was responsible for admissions decisions, which assured steady admittance patterns seen in 1924. Beginning after World War II, the actual bodies of individual students slowly became more diverse, in terms of race, gender, class, and religion. The percentage of female students remained relatively static until the 1960s, but even this increase was largely due to the overall expansion in the size of the medical school.[8]

As a *metaphor*, the student body reflected the university's gender, educational, and scientific ideals. As seen in the photo, the women were present but did not challenge the predominant image of the class as male. In the classroom, the transformation of the cultural values associated with becoming a physician, with a focus on the science over the art of healing, served to marginalize women and minorities. Even when the female students were begrudgingly admitted into the classroom, they were not included in extracurricular activities preserved in the yearbooks. The medical students had the reputation for working and playing hard, with violent football matches, elaborate pranks, and ribald humor. The IUSM students were part of the IU student body but also reveled in their separate identity. The perennial split between the Bloomington and Indianapolis campus identities was only part of the larger cultural split between students and student-doctors. Lessons were not just academic but could have life and death consequences in the clinical setting.[9]

At the *corporal* level, the medical student body was the site and subject of lessons about human anatomy. The faculty consistently required complete devotion of both mind and body for future physicians. Students' bodies took on a didactic role, with frequent use as anatomical models for peer demonstration. Kime and Meyers likely had received similar instruction in human anatomy, connecting textbook images and physical dissection. Due to the small size of the faculty, a few misogynist faculty members set the tone for instruction. Not surprisingly, some of the female students could not tolerate the combined burdens of sexual harassment and academic pressure, and as many as a quarter dropped out over the course of the first year.[10]

CREATING THE MEDICAL STUDENT BODY: 1903–40

In March 1903, Indiana University president William Lowe Bryan (1860–1995) proposed establishing a medical department as part of his broader vision of

transforming IU into a modern research university. Dean Burton Myers developed the medical department to combine classroom instruction on the
Bloomington campus and a clinical component at proprietary schools in Indianapolis. From 1905 to 1908, IU and Purdue University both worked to connect
their embryonic medical schools with existing proprietary medical schools
while seeking to undermine political support for each other. In May 1907, IU
graduated its first class of twenty-seven physicians, but the future of the two
medical schools in the state was still uncertain. The conflict ended when Purdue president Winthrop Stone (1862–1921) agreed to stop operating a medical
department in April 1908, allowing the consolidation of several departments
and private schools into the new IU School of Medicine.[11]

Indiana's competition over the future of medical education corresponded
with national medical education reforms. Medical reformer Abraham Flexner
visited the school, and IU President Bryan strove to model his fledgling school
along his recommendations. The Carnegie Foundation for the Advancement
of Teaching–funded report, *Medical Education in the United States and Canada* (1910), commonly known the Flexner Report, called for new minimum
entrance requirements, longer courses of study, laboratory training, and diverse clinical experience. Nationally, the admission and curriculum reforms
resulted in far fewer, less socially and economically diverse, if better trained,
physicians. Historian Thomas P. Duffy reflects, "American medicine profited
immeasurably from the scientific advances that this system allowed, but the
hyper-rational system of German science created an imbalance in the art and
science of medicine." The "feminine" virtues of healing and care were now to
be taught only in the newly professionalized nursing program. In 1915, female
physicians organized to form the American Medical Women's Association but
struggled to grow in size and influence, as women made up less than 6 percent
of practicing physicians.[12]

As a result of the reforms and consolidations, IUSM admitted fewer female applicants than the earlier proprietary schools. In 1909, Lillian B. Mueller
(1885–1961), an Indianapolis native, was the first woman to graduate from the
consolidated school. She was inspired to pursue a career in medicine by her
physician, Amelia Keller (1871–1943), who was one of the first female physicians
in Indianapolis. Keller taught as a professor of children's diseases from 1908
to 1919, was IUSM's first female faculty member, and served as a leader in the
women's movement in Indianapolis. Prior to the formation of IUSM, Keller was
a member of the Department of Pediatrics on the Central College faculty but
was not included in the original list of active faculty members for the new medical school. She wrote to President Bryant, querying if they had excluded her

because she was a woman: "Is it possible there is not a man on that committee big or broad enough to permit a woman to be the head of a department, however small that department might be? Alternatively, is it just 'friends' that were retained?"[13]When Mueller enrolled in Bloomington in 1905, she was the only woman in the freshman medical class. Though she received the same training as her male classmates, Mueller struggled to find an internship following medical school. She stayed in Indianapolis and served as the first female physician at Methodist Hospital and supported other female physicians.[14]

While in the masculine classroom, male teachers and students could allow women to participate without challenging their hegemonic position. As described by Meyers, both male and female students spent much of their time in classrooms in Bloomington and Indianapolis learning basic science and anatomy. Edith Schuman (1907–2007) remembered, "There was no relaxation. There was no play. Every minute went into memorizing what you had to know. And of course, in those days we had to learn Gray's Anatomy, that great big book, almost by heart." One of the most memorable clinical rotations for female students was outdoor obstetrics, or community-based obstetrics. Making house calls, particularly for childbirths, would be a mainstay of many of the future physicians' medical practices. Childbirth did not conform to the schedules and strictures of hospital life and meant going into unfamiliar homes and bedrooms. Many men recalled the struggle in their first few deliveries to reconcile their classroom learning with clinical realities. In this realm, many female students recalled that they were seen as having more expertise than the male students, even if they actually did not. Naomi Dalton (1914–2000) recalled being paired with a male junior during her senior outdoor obstetrics course: "I had a junior man who was very upset because he was junior to a woman. And at first he just didn't like it." For Dalton and many other female students, a growing understanding of their own bodies and the ability to teach others became a form of empowerment.[15]

In the early decades of the medical school, women were frequently targeted for physical pranks, and university officials found their presence on campus an irritating anomaly but hardly a threat to the overwhelming white, male Hoosier student body. Frank M. Ramsey (1902–93) recalled that many male medical students thought their fellow female classmates were "old hens," and they "didn't see how they'd ever become doctors." Conversely, Frank P. Albertson, who matriculated in 1930, stated of his fellow female medical students, "Oh, we treated them well. I more or less felt like they were my sisters." Schuman's recollections were similar: "We weren't, I wasn't aware, honest to goodness, I wasn't aware of being treated in any special way, except in the way Dr. [Burton] Myers picked on me," most likely because her Latin was so much better than her fellow students'. Margaret (Yoke) Newhouse (1905–99) reported a story of being the first to finish a blue book exam, where she earned an A. Her professor's response was, "That's the reason we have [to] let women in medical school." Alone, it would be easy to dismiss Newhouse's story, but together with Schuman's and Meyers's stories, it illustrates how each female student was held to a separate standard than the rest of the (male) student body.[16] The few female physicians in Indiana built informal networks and a medical sorority. Some notable examples were Sarah Stockton (1842–1924), a pioneer in psychiatry, and Ada E. Schweitzer (1872–1951), a leader in the public health movement at the state and national levels. Early female obstetricians, psychiatrists, and anesthesiologists nurtured the next generation of female physicians.[17]

Even comparing the advances of women at IUSM in the 1930s and 1940s to those earlier in the twentieth century, the small number of females continued to face great pressure from male students and faculty to prove their worth to be doctors. Byron Kilgore Jr. (1911–2000) graduated in 1939 and recalled that two of the four women in his class dropped out in the first year, and only one "durable" woman survived. By the late 1930s, medical licensure increasingly required an internship or residency, which added another barrier to entering practice. Increasing standards for medical licensure reduced diversity in the profession and in the case of internships compounded gender discrimination in admission with the less regulated environment of the hospitals. Female graduates were having such trouble finding internships that by 1935 the IUSM Medical Council recommended an increase in the admission standards for women, thereby reducing the number of female graduates that needed to be matched into internships.[18]

The experiences of Mary Keller Ade (1908–2008) offer a portrait of the struggles of the second generation of women coming through the medical school. Ade grew up in a farming community in northern Indiana and graduated with a BS degree in 1930 and an MD in 1932, both from Indiana University. During her time at IUSM, she recalled, "The girls were harassed some. Mostly being made fun of or they [male students] tried to make us feel that we could [not] take it . . . particularly in anatomy class. They got a bit rough sometimes. . . . They were just teasing us that we might faint or that we might [drop out]." As Ade worked closely with some of the male students, she found some who "were very kind and helpful and considerate and never condescending in any way." Ade's career showed her dedication to both the art and science of medicine, where she focused not only on women's physical health but also on mental health and social justice. After graduation, Ade worked with other women doctors until she was ready to open her own practice. She first worked at the Fletcher Sanatorium, under the direction of Sarah Stockton, which resulted in her lifetime advocacy for the humane care for the mentally ill. In 1939, she built a family practice in Lafayette with her husband, C. H. Ade. Before her retirement in 1987, she delivered more than three thousand babies, including about two hundred second-generation babies, and at least one third-generation baby. She was a leader not only in medicine but also in the broader Lafayette community. Her public service included the YWCA, philanthropic societies, and Grace United Methodist Church, where she taught Sunday school for over thirty years. As a mother, she balanced her work and service commitments with raising her two daughters and eight grandchildren until she died just shy of her one-hundredth birthday.[19]

A SEXED MEDICAL STUDENT BODY: 1941–63

The 1940s to 1960s represented a period of unprecedented prestige and social standing of doctors based on new "wonder" drugs and lifesaving surgeries. For example, within this span of a single generation the dominant experience of childbirth changed from home deliveries to hospital births. Between 1941 and 1963, IUSM trained the increased number of doctors needed to meet this new demand as well as a growing number of nurses and other allied health professionals. This was done without a faculty or facilities large enough for either classroom or clinical teaching. The public and state legislature hoped to train Indiana's brightest male students and keep the newly minted physicians in the state. The *Indianapolis News* took frequent interest in the new research and treatments at the school but took a lighthearted tone when it came to female students at IUSM. The 1956 article "4 IU Girls Don't Mind 38 to 1 Odds" focused not on the excellent academic records of the women but instead on their favorable odds of landing an eligible husband. Elsie Meyers defied expectations, and her exceptional experience stands for more than one hundred and fifty women who studied medicine during this period.[20]

Medicine was rigidly segregated by gender; doctors were sexed male and nurses sexed female. Men comprised 90 percent of medical school graduates in the 1940s. The gender gap and general misogyny of many of the IUSM faculty undergirded discrimination for allied health and nursing students, in addition to the female medical students. The IUSM program in nursing began in 1914, to serve the joint role of providing staff to care for patients within the medical center and train future nurse-educators and leaders in the field. As the discipline became more professionalized, particularly during World War II, the demand for nurses increased. In the area of allied health and medical social work, Edna Henry (1874–1942) led the development of IU's professional training for medical and social workers, one of the first in country.[21]

The experience of Elsie Meyers, discussed above, shares much with the experiences of Ade and other pioneering female physicians. Meyers grew up in rural northeastern Indiana and graduated from Wollcottville High School in 1940. She hoped to have a career in nursing, which was in demand due to the impending war. To gain experience and raise tuition money, she took a job in a busy medical practice. She was drawn to the work because she felt that "doctors could be trusted with one's very life, sort of like a minister could be trusted with one's soul." The physicians asked her to sign a pledge to work for them for three years as an "office girl, sort of a 'Jack of all trades'": part receptionist, medical tester, and assistant on medical procedures. Meyers's skill and judgment led to the physicians trusting her with more clinical responsibilities, particularly on child deliveries. She even administered ether to a few women during complex labors, which presaged her later career as an anesthesiologist.[22]

Meyers respected the physicians and felt that they were on a "higher plane than regular people"; however, Dr. C (the pseudonym for her employer) proved untrustworthy. Medically, he asked her to do serious clinical procedures well outside and beyond her level of training. Most egregiously, Dr. C raped Meyers in the clinic. Late one night he forced her into a treatment room and violently sexually assaulted her:

> It happened in the small room at the end of the hall where we did diathermy treatments. It was late at night, after Dr. A and all the patients had left. He weighed about 200 pounds, and was much stronger than I. I was shocked when he unzipped his pants. I cried out, "No, no, let me be. Please let me be. I don't want a baby!" The pain of penetration was intense. I screamed, "No, no, let me be! Stop, stop!" And then it was over. He withdrew before ejaculation and spilled his semen all over my abdomen. I was shattered. And I bled for a couple of weeks. The next day, I brought up the subject of what he had done to me. He replied, "That's not true. You wanted it." "You know I didn't want it. I told you!" . . .
>
>   After Dr. C raped me, I had nowhere to turn. Nobody would believe me, should I make a fuss. I knew that. He was an influential, respected doctor, an elected official. I was nobody. And besides, I had signed a paper stating that I would work there three years, and I didn't have enough money for college yet. I had nowhere to turn, no place to go. I went to bed at night in my little room and cried myself to sleep. . . . Dr. C had sex with me other times after

> that and I ceased to resist. But I felt awful, betrayed, guilty, dirty, a sinner of
> the worst order. I began to realize that he was having sex with other girls in
> the office also. I decided that I would be better off dead.

Meyers resisted her suicidal feelings and resolved to work out her contract in
the "den of sin." She shifted her ambitions from becoming a nurse to becoming
a physician.[23]

Meyers defied the odds against her and graduated with a bachelor's degree
from IU in 1947, with her sights set on medical school admission. Even for an
IU graduate, competition was stiff to gain admission to IUSM. World War II
brought a surge in applicants for medical school and accelerated overall matriculation rates. The government even urged medical schools to appoint women as
interns and residents to release men for military service. In 1947, medical school
applications swelled due to the GI Bill, and there were thirteen applicants for
each open spot. Aside from her gender, Meyers shared much in common with
the other students in her cohort. The student body demographics remained
unchanged until the expansion of the medical school in 1969, and the number
of women remained well below the national average.[24]

While at IUSM, Meyers faced skepticism and hostility from not only physicians but also interns and fellow students. Her memoir mentions several faculty
members who were supportive but no female faculty. Her earlier clinical experiences soon placed her ahead of her male peers during her clinical rotations,
particularly in her time at Riley Children's Hospital and outdoor obstetrics
rotations. Female students generally suffered in silence, as seen in the opening
story, and many male students claimed to be unaware of the struggles of their
female colleagues. The women tended to cluster together for mutual protection
and support. Meyers and another female student lived in a small "room over the
garbage heap," to save money. The structural and informal discrimination took
a physical toll on her body. At the end of the first term of her freshman year,
Meyers caught infectious mononucleosis with pneumonia—"I had contracted
the kissing disease without a single kiss!"—and would struggle to regain her
strength as she attempted to keep up with classes. Meyers gives an example
of how medical students used their own "student bodies" for medical experiments and as part of their education. Meyers and other students sometimes
volunteered for "lucrative offers" for medical studies to earn money. Meyers
recounted participating in an Eli Lilly test of the experimental drug Demerol
where she initially "felt fine and had fun lounging about and visiting," but afterward she came home and vomited for thirty-six hours. Years later, as a physician, she had a visceral reaction when she noticed that the Demerol drug insert

mentioned "occasional, minimal nausea and vomiting." Meyers reflected that this experience ended her willingness to be a "human guinea pig" and taught her "to take what drug companies had to say with a grain of salt."[25]

IUSM had a small number of female faculty who were critical mentors for female students. Many women pointed to Doris Merritt, assistant dean, who was responsible for grants and contracts, as a mentor and inspiration. Merritt graduated from George Washington University School of Medicine in 1952, one of three women in a class of eighty. She completed her pediatrics residency at Duke and took the unusual step of beginning her career at the National Institutes of Health's Division of Research Grants. She followed her husband to IUSM in 1961, just as the school was ramping up its research efforts. Between 1961 and 1978, Merritt oversaw more than $55 million in successful external grant funding for the growing campus. She was the youngest in the office and the first with the specific responsibility for coordinating grant activity at the medical school.[26]

Reflecting on graduation, Meyers wrote, "I had done it: I had reached my goal of being a doctor. But little did I realize that my medical education had just begun." Meyers left Indiana because she "needed to venture forth from my comfortable school and surroundings and widen my vistas." The era of the country doctor, as Meyers had worked with before medical school, was rapidly ending. The growth in knowledge, techniques, tools, and therapies required specialization to provide the best diagnosis and treatment for each disease. She was selected for an internship in anesthesiology at the prestigious University of Pennsylvania. Like Meyers, the physicians that studied in the post–World War II era would find the medical field in which they had learned profoundly changed due to new treatments and pharmaceuticals. The clinical advancements and specialization added two or more years of residency. This often forced women to delay marriage and childbirth, or risk, in Meyers's words, becoming an "old maid doctor." She married psychiatrist Robert Meyers in 1962 and balanced her roles as a wife, mother of three children, and owner of a successful anesthesiology practice. Upon her retirement, she set out to craft a portrait of her experiences in medicine as a patient, medical assistant, and physician. The next generation of female physicians would find more female students in each class and more female faculty, but the misogynist culture would continue—and even get worse. A small number of women filed formal complaints of discrimination and harassment with the university, but most women remained silent. The investigations of allegations are sealed in the archives to protect privacy. Meyers never spoke about her rape with her colleagues or even her family. In her 2008 memoir, she chose to "tell it like it was" so that her story might educate others.[27]

CHANGING STUDENT BODIES: 1964–2007

In the 1960s, the Golden Age of Medicine and the cultural power of physicians came under attack as an increasing number of Americans began to question the rapid expansion of medicine in their lives. Physician and hospital visits were on the rise due to new treatments for communicable diseases such as syphilis and tuberculosis and endemic conditions such as diabetes and cancer. Many of these changes related to pharmaceuticals and the burgeoning market in consumer health products. The American Medical Association, and many Indiana physicians, fought the expansion of national health insurance, Medicare, and Medicaid. This changed the economics of the provision of care, particularly at academic medical centers. Nationally, the growth of medical schools in the 1960s resulted in an increase in the overall admissions, with many of the new positions going to women. When women attended IUSM in small numbers, they never challenged the gendered nature of the student body. Over this same period, IUSM gave birth to the largest medical school student body—in numbers and size. The school became one of the largest in enrollments in the United States but also geographically among the nine regional medical education centers spread across more than three hundred miles.[28]

The career of IU clinical psychiatrist Clare M. Assue (1922–90) illustrates the intersection of cultural changes in race and gender roles, student admissions, and the healthcare landscape coming together in the experiences of female students and faculty at IUSM.[29] Assue defied the gender and racial expectations at IUSM not only for herself but also for her students and patients. Assue was born in New York City in 1922, a world away from the Hoosier cornfields. Later, when at IUSM, she regaled her students with stories from her upbringing; she had even worked as a real Rosie the Riveter in the Brooklyn Naval Yard during World War II. She did her medical training at Howard University (1954) and her internship at Beth-El Hospital in Brooklyn when it was exceedingly difficult for both African Americans and women to find internship positions. She spent a brief time at IUSM as a resident in 1955, then went to St. Elizabeth's Hospital in Washington, DC, one of the largest and most innovative psychiatric hospitals in the nation. She returned to IUSM in 1958 as a staff psychiatrist at LaRue Carter Memorial (Carter) Hospital and a clinical instructor in the Department of Psychiatry. Hugh Hendrie, chairman of the Psychiatry Department and the

Affirmative Action Task Force, helped to recruit Assue, as well as other female faculty. Assue moved up the academic ranks and took on administrative duties such as director of medical education and, later, coordinator of undergraduate curriculum for the Department of Psychiatry. From 1981 to 1989, she served as superintendent of Carter Hospital—the first African American, male or female, to hold this position in the United States. She led the hospital through the difficult period of political and racial challenges that came with deinstitutionalization. In this position, she was able to expand her advocacy for patients and staff who were subject to unfair working and living conditions as well as provide meaningful clinical experiences for students. Additionally, Assue worked with local schools and churches and the Indianapolis Juvenile Justice Commission.[30]

Assue's recruitment was part of a broader effort by IUSM dean John D. Van-Nuys (1907–64) to bring new, talented outside faculty to Indiana as part of his campaign to expand the medical school. After years of planning and debate, the Indiana state legislature adopted a new Statewide Medical Education System in 1971. The IUSM statewide system was a new form of distributed medical education—the first of its kind in the nation. The plan began with the creation of nine regional medical education centers that would offer the first year of coursework and gradually increase their offerings. This required establishing medical instruction at eight new sites, with the promise that each would be equal to what existed at the fully functioning and recently consolidated medical school in Indianapolis.[31]

IUSM began to use its regional campus plan as a blueprint for conceptualizing a new student body. This meant significant growth in the number of students as fears of a national oversupply of physicians conflicted with political demands in Indiana to increase students. The plan assured that IUSM would remain the sole provider of medical education in Indiana for the near future and would shape the healthcare landscape in Indiana. IUSM was again present at the IU—Bloomington campus, along with the campuses of former rivals such as Purdue, Ball State, and Notre Dame universities. It would take twelve years before each campus taught the first two years of medical school curriculum. After 1976, each of the nine regional centers admitted a class of 20 students and then steadily began to grow. IUSM began admitting roughly half of its students (140) at the regional centers and an equal number at Indianapolis, with all 280 finishing their third and fourth years at Indianapolis.. Spread across nine campuses, the students no longer had the shared experience of all learning from the same faculty, as in the case of anatomy with Kime. The increase in attention to sexual harassment opened new avenues for female students to file complaints, but the medical school culture discouraged students from reporting violations of university polices. The archival sexual harassment and assault investigations are closed for privacy concerns; this policy prevents historians from learning more about these students' experiences.[32]

While the dramatic increase in size and the statewide medical education system attracted the most attention nationally, changes in the number of women presented the greatest challenge on this new type of campus. Female admissions and graduations at IUSM grew steadily through the 1970s and 1980s, remaining slightly above the national average. During the 1970s, IUSM saw an increase in the number and percentage of women students along with growth of the overall class size. IUSM increased female admissions from 19.1 percent in 1974 to 35 percent a decade later, reaching a high of 41 percent in 1993. Female applicants' GPA and MCAT scores did not vary greatly from the school average. The only constant was the extremely high percentage of students admitted from in-state, which remained well above 90 percent each year.[33]

This increase in female admissions was part of broader national trends that helped to break down the tradition of perceived social cohesion in medical training. There were several factors leading to the rise in female medical school graduates. Increasing the number of female physicians and ending the misogynist and hypersexualized medical school environment was high on the list for many second wave feminists, though the women's health movement was less active in conservative Indiana. Most important demographically, a rise in the female undergraduate population and the implementation of federal educational affirmative action policies, coupled with specific forces within the field of medicine, created an increase in available medical school positions and a decline in male applicants.[34]

In 1972, IUSM created an Affirmative Action Standing Committee and the position of associate dean for student affairs to meet new accreditation requirements, national minority admissions and hiring targets, and Title IX Affirmative Action requirements. IUSM appointed top faculty to the committee, such as Assue's champion, Hugh Hendrie. The committee reported that to meet their modest goals, the university would need to review and raise faculty salaries for both men and women, as both were in the lowest quartile in faculty compensation nationally. IUSM implemented some of the committee's recommendations but did not significantly increase the number of women in leadership roles and in the tenured faculty, as some of the new positions were limited appointments and did not address the overall higher turnover rate for female faculty. With such low pay, it was difficult to recruit top female and minority talent so far from the urban centers on the East and West coasts. After the new 1975 policies went into effect, the total number of female student admissions increased to 10 percent over target, but the total overall increase in admissions meant that male admissions grew as well. It was not until the next decade that female students represented 25 percent of total of admissions and not until the 1990s when a third of the class was female.[35]

The demographic expansion did not mean a decrease in discrimination or a hostile educational climate for these women. IUSM yearbooks provide a ribald window into the growing hostility toward female medical students and the hypersexualized atmosphere of gender relations at the medical school. Somewhere between an official university publication and personal correspondence, each volume illustrates the struggles of medical school in the students' own words, addressed to the student body that shared this life-defining experience. In the 1960s and 1970s, the rising numbers of female students led to increased male hostility and sexual intimidation, as individual women went from "not male" to being women. In the 1979 *Retrospectoscope*, the editors mocked women's claims of ill treatment and accused the university of reverse discrimination. They couched their complaints about gender expectations in an advice column:

> Dear Ann Slanders, I am a medical student who has the terrible misfortune of being in a minority group in my class. I am a female. Now, most people would assume that this is an enviable position since the ratio is in my favor, but let me tell you what it is really like. Imagine the cold, stiff, dismembered hand of a cadaver slinking up your thigh as you are industriously dissecting [an] eyeball. Or picture yourself being blamed by your resident for the spontaneous erection your comatose patient has during morning rounds. Or what do you say when your Psych resident is more interested in his students than in his patient's sexual history? Or your surgery staff who feels that your grade is better correlated with your ability to flirt and bake cakes than with your suturing skills? Ann, how can I respond to these sexist pigs? Signed . . . Used and Abused in Indianapolis

Ann Slanders responded, "Dear Used: The only women who attract pigs are the ones who cry, 'Sooeee!' Read on as the pigs respond. (Oink, oink.)" The second letter read:

> Dear Ann Slanders, I am a serious, hard-working, dedicated medical student with a problem—female medical students. I am sick and tired of spending 18 hours each day in the hospital providing superior care for my patients and barely getting a passing grade while my female colleague spends one night 'on call' so to speak with the resident and receives

'honors.' I considered imitating my competition's strategy, but let's face it—I would look ridiculous in a short skirt and a tight white coat. Besides, Home Ec was not one of my Pre-Med courses and I had the embarrassing experience of having the one cake I baked refused by even the patients at the VA Hospital. The only one who gave me 'Honors' in a course was my Psych resident—and he was gay! How does one survive this reverse discrimination? Signed . . . Dedicated and Disgruntled

Ann Slander's response: "Dear Dedicated: Won't you also be a resident some day? Then maybe some disadvantages will become advantages."[36]

As IUSM celebrated their centennial, the medical student body had fundamentally changed. By the 1990s, changes in the university culture and broader national trends had led to the disbanding—or renaming—of the Affirmative Action Committee. With increases in the number of female student admissions and faculty and a limited number of women in key leadership positions, IUSM could justifiably point to increased opportunities for women. While the gender gap in medical school graduation had narrowed, it lagged more than a decade behind in medical school faculty. Women's slow integration into academic medicine resulted in a struggle for them to see many key cultural issues at the forefront. Informal supports from female faculty were critical for female physicians at the beginning of their careers, and the regional system further reduced the availability of female mentorship at each campus. Even with these barriers to the success of female students and physicians, the campus had several female faculty leaders during this period of transition. Elizabeth Buchanan Solow, professor of neurosurgery from 1962 to 1985, worked through programs and committees such as the Women's Faculty Club to support students. Moving beyond inclusions, student reform efforts focused on broader issues such as access to childcare, gender issues, pay disparities, and sexual assault.[37]

CONCLUSION

Today, we can still look into the faces of Lillian Mueller, Mary Keller Ade, Elsie Flint Meyers, and nearly four thousand other women of the IUSM student body. Their lives offer dramatic and emotional portraits of the experience of medical education that was, and continues to be, different in many traditions from the broader university. What set them apart as physicians—namely, their medical education—brought them together as women across racial, cultural, and social boundaries. These decades of growth in size, in both matriculation and geography, have fundamentally challenged the concept of a "student body"

and even the concept of a medical school. Due to this growth, somewhat ironically, no available space exists outside the Ruth Lilly Medical Library to hang
the annual student body portrait. The university still hangs the portraits, but
they are no longer together but scattered across the many new buildings on
the Indianapolis and Statewide Medical Education Centers. The first class in
1907 boasted twenty-seven physicians; the 2017–18 class image will include 363
students—209 males (58 percent) and 154 females (42 percent). This does not
include the 1,176 residents, 44 percent of which are female[38]

The extreme growth of IUSM challenged the basic idea of a medical school,
as place, university, or program no longer bound it together. During the 1994
self-study for Liaison Committee for Medical Education (LCME) accreditation, the university had to defend the implementation of the statewide medical
campus and prove that it provided the same education to all students. The 902
full-time faculty members taught 1,072 medical students, plus an additional 287
in ten MA and PhD basic sciences programs. This was in addition to training
694 residents and fellows in twenty-two specialties and subspecialties. The
faculty worked in twenty-four departments on nine medical education campus
sites around Indiana. The clinical departments of the school provided care for
tens of thousands of patients each year in their practices (earning $138 million
in revenue) while staffing four hospitals plus two specialty hospitals for children and psychiatric patients. The overall revenue of the school in fiscal year
1993 was over $295 million, more than a 280 percent increase in the revenue
(adjusted for inflation) from a decade earlier. The LCME had been critical in
previous visits over the implementation of the statewide plan, but this accreditation visit marked the end of serious questioning over the model and size of
the school. Several other universities had adopted the statewide campus model,
and more would follow.[39]

NOTES

1. This chapter is part of a larger project on the history of the Indiana University School of Medicine. See William H. Schneider, *The Indiana University School of
Medicine: A History* (Bloomington: Indiana University Press, 2021). This research
was supported by the Indiana University Bicentennial. The author thanks William Schneider, Kelly Gasgoine, and Kevin Grau, who assisted with research on
this chapter and other related history projects. Elsie F. Meyers, "Doing the 'Not
Possible': The Memoirs of Elsie F. Meyers, M.D.," *Indiana Magazine of History* 104,
no. 4 (December 2008): 353. For context on Meyers, see Alexandra Minna Stern,
"Against the Odds: Becoming a Female Physician in Midcentury Indiana," *Indiana*

Magazine of History 104, no. 4 (December 2008): 323–28. For Kime, see Edwin Kime Obituary, *Indianapolis Star*, May 27, 1968; Anatomy Departmental Histories, Indiana University School of Medicine Records, 1848–2005, Ruth Lilly Special Collections and Archives, University Library, Indiana University–Purdue University Indianapolis (IUPUI).

2. Meyers, "Memoirs of Elsie F. Meyers, M.D.," 353.

3. Meyers, 354.

4. Wendy Kline, *Bodies of Knowledge: Sexuality, Reproduction, and Women's Health in the Second Wave* (Chicago: University of Chicago Press, 2010), 1.

5. Meyers, "Memoirs of Elsie F. Meyers, M.D.," 349. For broader literature on the role of the body in medical education, see, for example, Frank Huisman and John Harley Warner, *Locating Medical History: The Stories and Their Meanings* (Baltimore: Johns Hopkins University Press, 2006); John Harley Warner and James M. Edmonson, *Dissection: Photographs of a Rite of Passage in American Medicine, 1880–1930* (New York: Blast Books, 2009).

6. This estimate is based on graduation statistics. The reporting of admissions, matriculation, and graduation numbers fluctuates over the years, making exact comparisons difficult. This chapter draws on a rich body of scholarship on female physicians; see Thomas Bonner, *To the Ends of the Earth: Women's Search for Education in Medicine* (Cambridge, MA: Harvard University Press, 1995); Regina Morantz-Sanchez, *Sympathy and Science: Women Physicians in American Medicine* (Chapel Hill: University of North Carolina Press, 2000); Ellen S. More, ed., *Women Physicians and the Cultures of Medicine* (Baltimore, MD: Johns Hopkins University Press, 2008); Stern, "Against the Odds"; Ellen S. More, *Restoring the Balance: Women Physicians and the Profession of Medicine, 1850–1995* (Cambridge, MA: Harvard University Press, 2009).

7. Barbara Miller Solomon, *In the Company of Educated Women: A History of Women and Higher Education in America* (New Haven, CT: Yale University Press, 1985); Walter P. May, "The History of Student Governance in Higher Education," *College Student Affairs Journal* 28, no. 2 (March 2010): 207–20.

8. There are several ways of measuring the size of the student body, such as the inclusion of residents and other post-doctoral programs. The University of Illinois and IUSM have competed for the "top" honors for nearly 50 years. Walter Daly, "Essay on Medical Education: Historical Perspective," October 2010, 5, unprocessed papers, Indiana University School of Medicine Records UA 073, 1848–2005, Ruth Lilly Special Collections and Archives, University Library, IUPUIA, Indianapolis, Indiana.

9. Race and religion played critical roles in the formation of the IUSM student body, which I have not explored in this essay. Overall, IUSM had an unwritten quota system for a limited number of African American and Jewish students that lasted well over fifty years. Daly, "Essay on Medical Education." For the national

context, see Kenneth M. Ludmerer, *Time to Heal: American Medical Education from the Turn of the Century to the Era of Managed Care* (New York: Oxford University Press, 1999). Copies of the IUSM yearbooks are held at IUPUIA, Indianapolis, Indiana.

10. Daly, "Essay on Medical Education."

11. IU worked with the Medical College of Indiana and the College of Physicians and Surgeons, both of which operated in Indianapolis. This is a quick summary of a complex story. For more details, see Walter Daly, "The Origins of President Bryan's Medical School," *Indiana Magazine of History* 97, no. 4 (December 2002): 266–84.

12. Thomas P. Duffy, "The Flexner Report—100 Years Later," *The Yale Journal of Biology and Medicine* 84, no. 3 (September 2011): 269–76. The increased educational requirements also decreased the number of African American physicians of either gender; Ann Steinecke and Charles Terrell, "Progress for Whose Future? The Impact of the Flexner Report on Medical Education for Racial and Ethnic Minority Physicians in the United States," *Academic Medicine* 85, no. 2 (February 2010): 236–45.

13. Amelia R. Keller to Bryan, August 19, 1910, Folder 34, Box 1, E126, Indiana University Archives.

14. Jacob Piatt Dunn and General William Harrison Kemer, *Indiana and Indianans: A History of Aboriginal and Territorial Indiana and the Century of Statehood. Index* (New York: American Historical Society, 1919), 816. For the rich history of the nursing program, see Leslie Flowers, *A Legacy of Leadership: Indiana University School of Nursing, 1914–2014* (Indianapolis: Indiana University Press, 2014).

15. Edith Schuman, interview by Steven Stowe, May 25, 1993, transcript, 4; Naomi Dalton, interview by Steven Stowe, March 25, 1993, transcript, 4–16; Indiana Medicine 1993 Oral History Project, Center for Documentary Research and Practice, Indiana University, Bloomington (IU-CDRP). The unsettling experience of Outdoor Obstetrics was frequently mentioned in the oral history interviews. See, for example, Frank P. Albertson, interview by Patrick Ettinger, October 29, 1993. Albertson's experience is particularly interesting given the role he later played in the debates over homebirth and the formation of the specialty of family medicine. For the national context, see Jacqueline H. Wolf, *Deliver Me from Pain: Anesthesia and Birth in America* (Baltimore: Johns Hopkins University Press, 2009), 83–85.

16. Frank Ramsey, interview by Patrick Ettinger, February 5, 1993, transcript, 6; Albertson, interview by Ettinger, 17, Schuman, interview by Stowe, transcript 6; Margaret Newhouse, interview by Patrick Ettinger, August 3, 1994, transcript, 13, IU-CDRP.

17. Sarah Stockton Obituary, *Indianapolis Star*, March 14, 1924; Philip M. Coons and Elizabeth S. Bowman, *Psychiatry in Indiana: The First 175 Years* (New York:

iUniverse, 2010); Alexandra Minna Stern, "Making Better Babies: Public Health and Race Betterment in Indiana, 1920–1935," *American Journal of Public Health* 92, no. 5 (May 2002): 742–52. For the trend of specialization and residencies, see George Weisz, *Divide and Conquer: A Comparative History of Medical Specialization* (New York: Oxford University Press, 2005).

18. While the dropout rate could be higher for women, the small number of women in the program makes it difficult to determine underlying reasons for the decline. Byron Kilgore, interview by Patrick Ettinger, March 17, 1994, transcript, 10, 13. Thus, discrimination in medical school admissions increased during the inter-war period, against not only women but also African Americans and other minorities. Minutes, June 1, 1935, Medical Council of the IU School of Medicine, for the direction of the Committee on Admissions, Box 52, Indiana University School of Medicine Records UA 073, 1848–2005, Ruth Lilly Special Collections and Archives, University Library, IUPUIA, Indianapolis, Indiana; "At the Medical Center," *Indiana University Alumni Quarterly* 23, no. 3 (Summer 1936): 318–19.

19. Mary Keller Ade, interview by Chad Berry, March 18, 1993, transcript, 2, IU-CDRP, 7; "Mary Keller Ade, Obituary," *Journal and Courier*, January 3 and 4, 2008; David J. Bodenhamer, Robert Graham Barrows, and David Gordon Vanderstel, eds., *The Encyclopedia of Indianapolis* (Indianapolis: Indiana University Press, 1994), 580.

20. "4 IU Girls Don't Mind 38 to 1 Odds," *Indianapolis News*, April 20, 1956. The history of the various health-related schools is critical to understanding the development of IUPUI but beyond the scope of this chapter; see Ralph D. Gray, *IUPUI—the Making of an Urban University* (Bloomington: Indiana University Press, 2003).

21. Flowers, *A Legacy of Leadership*; Burton D. Myers, ed., *The History of Medical Education in Indiana* (Bloomington: Indiana University Press, 1956), 164; Bodenhamer, Barrows, and Vanderstel, eds., *The Encyclopedia of Indianapolis*, 506–507. For more on Edna Henry, see chapter 10, Katherine Badertscher, "The Sharp Sword of the New Alliance": Edna Henry and the IU School of Social Work.

22. Meyers, "Memoirs of Elsie F. Meyers, M.D.," 330–35.

23. Meyers, 342; 343; 344–45.

24. A 1963 report to the Indiana state legislature indicated that the most recent class was only 5 percent women and a total 4 percent African Americans. This was progress over past ratios and better than the national percentage of Black medical students enrolled at predominantly white medical schools, which remained steadily around 2 percent. Meyers, "Memoirs of Elsie F. Meyers, M.D.," 345–50; Liaison Committee on Medical Education, "Report on the Survey of the University of Indiana School of Medicine," December 9–12, 1963, 15–17, Box 234, Indiana University School of Medicine Records UA 073, 1848–2005, Ruth Lilly Special Collections and Archives, University Library, IUPUIA, Indianapolis, Indiana;

Andrew A. Sorensen, "Black Americans and the Medical Profession, 1930–1970," *Journal of Negro Education*, 41, no. 4 (Autumn 1972): 337–42; "Bigger 'n Better 'n Ever: Medical School Enrolls 214 First-Year Students; Largest Freshman Class in School's History," *Quarterly Bulletins-Indiana University Medical Center* 25, no. 3 (fall 1963): 39, Box 31, Indiana University School of Medicine Records UA 073, 1848–2005, Ruth Lilly Special Collections and Archives, University Library, IUPUIA, Indianapolis, Indiana.

25. Meyers, "Memoirs of Elsie F. Meyers, M.D.," 352, 355, 356–62.

26. Mary Owen, Doris H. Merritt Oral History Interview, July 17, 2007, IUPUI Oral Histories, IUPUIA, Indianapolis, Indiana.

27. Meyers, "Memoirs of Elsie F. Meyers, M.D.," 365, 366, 345. For her later life, see "Robert Meyers, Obituary," *St. Louis Post-Dispatch*, January 24, 2014; Stern, "Against the Odds," 328. For anesthesiology at IUSM, see Vergil K. Stoelting, *History of the Department of Anesthesiology at Indiana University School of Medicine: The First 30 Years* (Indianapolis: Indiana University Press, 1977).

28. For the changing national context, see Paul Starr, *The Social Transformation of American Medicine* (New York: Basic Books, 1982); Rosemary Stevens, *In Sickness and in Wealth: American Hospitals in the Twentieth Century* (Baltimore, MD: Johns Hopkins University Press, 1999); Nancy Tomes, *Remaking the American Patient: How Madison Avenue and Modern Medicine Turned Patients into Consumers*, Studies in Social Medicine (Chapel Hill: University of North Carolina Press, 2016).

29. For the national context, see Morantz-Sanchez, *Sympathy and Science*; Wendy Kline, *Bodies of Knowledge: Sexuality, Reproduction, and Women's Health in the Second Wave* (Chicago: University of Chicago Press, 2010); Ludmerer, *Time to Heal*.

30. She retired in 1989 and died the next year from lung cancer. Assue's profiles are silent on her husband, Frank Meuler Brown, whom she married on August 24, 1956, in Arlington, Virginia. Coons and Bowman, *Psychiatry in Indiana*, 289; Jeanne Spurlock, *Black Psychiatrists and American Psychiatry* (Washington, DC, American Psychiatric Association, 1999), 14.

31. VanNuys was dean from 1947 to 1964, during a critical period of the growth for the school that would have far-reaching implications across the university. G. T. Lukemeyer and G. W. Irwin, "Statewide Medical Education in Indiana," *Indiana Medicine: The Journal of the Indiana State Medical Association* 89, no. 3 (June 1996): 264–70.William T. Mallon, ed., *Mini-Med: The Role of Regional Campuses in U.S. Medical Education* (Washington, DC: Association of American Medical Colleges, 2003). On national notoriety, see "Medical School Expands off Campus," *American Medical News*, October 1, 1973, clipping in Indiana Statewide Medical Education, Box 47, UA 073.

32. Lukemeyer and Irwin, "Statewide Medical Education in Indiana." Because the emphasis on more diverse admissions coincided with the emergence of the re-

gional campus system, this cohort of medical school students was followed closely, even as their performance and specialties developed over the long term. See, for example, James J. Brokaw et al., "The Influence of Regional Basic Science Campuses on Medical Students' Choice of Specialty and Practice Location: A Historical Cohort Study," *BMC Medical Education* 9, no. 29 (June 6, 2009): 29.

33. "Affirmative Action Office & Committee, 1974," Box 51, IUSM Annual Reports, 1974–95, Box 202, Indiana University School of Medicine Records UA 073, 1848–2005, Ruth Lilly Special Collections and Archives, University Library, IUPUIA, Indianapolis, Indiana; Philip Scarpino, oral history with Walter Daly, May 10, 2017, IUSM Oral History Collection, IUPUIA, Indianapolis, Indiana. For analysis of the national trends, see Ludmerer, *Time to Heal*, 209–215; William G. Rothstein, *American Medical Schools and the Practice of Medicine: A History* (New York: Oxford University Press, 1987), 283–86.

34. Ludmerer, *Time to Heal*, 250–53.

35. "Affirmative Action," Box 9, "Affirmative Action Advisory Council, 1974– 1982," Box 5, IUPUI Records UA 083, Ruth Lilly Special Collections and Archives, University Library, IUPUIA, Indianapolis, Indiana.

36. "Ann Slanders: Sexism In Medicine," in *Retrospectoscope* [Indiana University School of Medicine yearbook] (Indianapolis: Indiana University, School of Medicine, 1979), 44.

37. "Faculty Women's Club of IU School of Medicine, Misc., 1973–1979," Box 91, Indiana University School of Medicine Records UA 073, 1848–2005, Ruth Lilly Special Collections and Archives, University Library, IUPUIA, Indianapolis, Indiana; Indiana University School of Medicine, *The Indiana Initiative: Physicians for the 21st Century: Final Report* (1996); "Affirmative Action, 1988–1995," Box 51, "Merritt, Doris, 1987–2001," Box 130, Office of the Chancellor Records, 1914–2006, UA 041, IUPUIA, Indianapolis, Indiana; Association of American Medical Colleges, *Assessment of Minority and Nonminority U.S. Medical School Graduates' Premedical and Medical School Specialty Selection, and Success in Obtaining Choice of Residency Training: Final Report*, ed. Charles D. Killian and Wendy L. Colquitt (Washington, DC: AAMC, 1991).

38. Association of American Medical Colleges maintains a national database on medical school graduates and residency placements annually at https://www.aamc .org/data/facts.

39. AAMC, *Assessment of Minority and Nonminority U.S. Medical School Graduates*.

MOVING ON TOGETHER

Women Students during the Early Years of IUPUI

NANCY VAN NOTE CHISM, MARY GIORGIO, AND KATHLEEN SURINA GROVE

Nancy Van Note Chism, Mary Gorgio, and Kathleen Surina Grove—all of whom have been faculty or staff at Indiana University–Purdue University Indianapolis (IUPUI)—base their essay on original oral history interviews with a group of women who were enrolled at IUPUI during the campus's formative years. Opened in 1969, IUPUI was a new urban collaboration between the state's two major public universities—Indiana University and Purdue University—as they consolidated their once separate extension programs in Indianapolis. This chapter captures the women's personal backgrounds, their aspirations and challenges in pursuing their studies, and their recollections of what it felt like to be an IUPUI student during those early years. The voices of the interviewees as they describe their educational aspirations and IUPUI experiences provide a glimpse into more recent IU history and the demographic broadening of women's higher education enrollments at both IU and campuses nationwide.

> I got to be a student in the '70s, early '70s, it was like paradise when you look back on it. . . . I just think, oh my God, what a fun life that was. Even though it was hard work, it was so incredibly fun.
>
> —Dorothy

THEY WERE WOMEN IN TRANSITION: moving on from high school to college, from homemaking to paid career, and from marriage to divorce. Some focused on career preparation; others wanted to continue their schooling simply because they loved learning. Some were actively embracing the major societal

changes of the time; others were more conservative. All were fiercely independent, appreciative of their opportunity to attend college, and ready to deal with
the challenges that came their way.

These women were also immersed in profound transitions beyond their
personal lives. They were students during a period of major, pivotal social and
institutional changes in the United States—among them, prominently, the
Women's Movement and its challenge to old gender norms; national changes
in student demographics and in the mission of higher education; and, locally,
the consolidation of educational programs in Indianapolis that led, in 1969, to
the founding of IUPUI—a new core campus for IU. The practicality, commitment, and energy of the women who attended IUPUI during its early years set
an example for the many women students who have followed. As such, their
stories add a distinctive dimension to our evolving understanding of women's
contributions and experiences at IU during different moments in time and
across the university's campuses. This essay, anchored in original oral history
interviews, offers a glimpse into the experiences of a number of these early
IUPUI women, using their own words and voices. Their stories and perspectives shed light on a recent, still understudied chapter in IU history and evoke
what it was like to be a woman student during the formative years of IUPUI.[1]

Founded in 1969, IUPUI emerged during a very turbulent period in the history of US higher education. Colleges and universities were still reeling from
the sit-ins, student protests, and demonstrations that rocked campuses in the
1960s while institutions struggled to adapt to new ideas on race, gender, class,
and social justice. College administrators were forced to rethink policies on
admissions, student life, and academics. Scholars were challenging the tenets
of the Western canon as the basis for the curriculum; revisionist historians were
questioning narratives that were inattentive to the experiences and contributions of various social groups; and scientists, artists, and professional researchers were embracing new foundational philosophies and approaches.[2]

Perhaps because community attention in Indianapolis was focused so in-
tently on the social upheaval and changes seen locally and across the country,
government officials who wanted to establish a great public university in Indiana's capital city were able complete their task without much fanfare by negotiating the consolidation of the Indianapolis extension programs of Indiana and
Purdue Universities in 1969. Indianapolis and state officials had wanted a new,
independent university in the capital city, but administrators at Indiana University and Purdue University—the state's public university (est. 1820) and land
grant university (est. 1869)—did not want to give up the ground established
with their respective extension programs in the urban capital. Although these

two state universities eventually reached a compromise through much public debate, over several years the resulting decision was implemented quietly and steadily as administrative structures were set up, buildings were erected, and personnel were transferred or recruited.[3]

The consolidated campus in Indianapolis, commonly known today as IUPUI, was a new venture for both Indiana and Purdue Universities and the only such experiment in interuniversity collaboration in the country.[4] Nine components were involved in the merger: the IU Schools of Medicine, Nursing, Dentistry, Law, and Social Work; the National College of the American Gymnastics Union; the Herron School of Art; the Purdue Extension Division at 38th Street; and the Downtown Campus of Indiana University.[5]

The Downtown Campus, soon a vital part of the educational landscape for Indianapolis women, had its origins in the late nineteenth century, when educational trends aimed to make collegiate-level education more widely available to the average American. In Indianapolis, these efforts were led initially by the local chapter of the Association of Collegiate Alumnae (ACA), an organization of women college graduates. May Wright Sewall, prominent educator and women's rights activist, along with Amelia Platter, an Indianapolis High School teacher, were among the most prominent advocates.[6]

In 1891, the ACA invited Jeremiah Jenks, a professor from Indiana University Bloomington, to present a series of lectures on economics in Indianapolis. Over the ensuing decades, public lectures and extension courses were offered regularly in Indianapolis. Most of these opportunities were organized by community groups and were taught by professors from a variety of nearby universities.[7]

In 1912, Indiana University established its Extension Division and brought a formalized public collegiate program to Indianapolis. The division offered both noncredit enrichment programs and credit courses. In the early years, Extension Division courses were held across the city, often in high school classrooms or at the Indianapolis Chamber of Commerce offices. In 1928, the division purchased a downtown building to serve as both headquarters and classroom space.[8]

From the earliest years, both men and women made use of extension services. A small number of women were even employed as instructors. Notably, Mary Orvis, originally employed by the administrative office, began teaching English and journalism courses in 1920.[9]

Following World War II, the demand for commuter courses increased drastically in Indianapolis. Men returning from World War II sought to study under the GI Bill. Many adults desired to earn a college degree while retaining their employment and raising families in the city.[10] Indiana University's extension division, along with Purdue University's Indianapolis campus (which had opened in 1939), filled this need. For the first few years after Purdue came to Indianapolis, its offerings were limited to a series of technical courses aimed at industrial employees. In 1943, the Division of Technical Studies opened a branch in Indianapolis and began offering degree programs in technology. Science degrees soon followed. By the end of World War II, Purdue was offering basic undergraduate courses in Indianapolis as well.[11]

While administering their respective undergraduate extension programs had already given IU and Purdue experience with offering degrees at a distance from their main campuses (in Bloomington and West Lafayette, respectively), the focus of the extension centers had been on instruction. Neither university had yet encountered the need to establish for students attending classes in Indianapolis much in the area of support services, such as housing, counseling, or extracurricular activities. This situation would change as IUPUI came into being and matured.

In addition to addressing this broader range of student needs, leaders administering the new collaboration also had to deal with change in campus size and demographic composition, following both programmatic shifts and the dynamics of the times. Students at the undergraduate programs of the two extension divisions, the units most affected by the consolidation, numbered over eight thousand in 1969. Over the next decade, enrollment more than doubled on the IUPUI campus, and the percentage of women enrolled increased from 41 to 58.8.[12] These trends reflected the national statistics for the late 1960s and 1970s, which showed a dramatic increase in the total higher education population and an increase in the percentage of women, who went from 41 percent to 51 percent of total enrollment.[13]

Archival sources document the ways in which IUPUI leaders were conscious of and responded to the growing presence of women on campus. IUPUI policy discussions and initiatives related to gender equity reflected the types of inquiry and reviews seen on many campuses in the early 1970s. For example, an IUPUI Commission on Women, announced in May 1972 and chaired by professor of English Frances Dodson Rhome, focused on the status of women faculty while the Office of Affirmative Action, announced in November 1972, was established to look at legal issues.[14] In 1975, the campus opened the IUPUI Continuing Education Center for Women to offer services such as counseling, job search assistance, workshops, and continuing education classes on personal and career development.[15] For many years, however, the center operated from within the Continuing Education Division before being combined with the resources of the Women's Studies Program to become the Office of Women's

Research and Resources in 1987. In 1996, upon the recommendation of another Task Force on the Status of Women, convened in 1994, the Office for Women officially opened.[16]

WITH A FEMALE STUDENT'S EYE

To explore the early days of IUPUI through the eyes of students who experienced the transition, this study focuses specifically on women undergraduates, a segment of the student population that was likely to be affected by important societal changes. The study relies on oral histories of ten students who attended IUPUI from just before its official establishment in 1969 through its first decade. In addition to attending an institution in transition, these women were seeking education during a time when the Women's Movement was challenging old barriers and spurring new opportunities for women in higher education. All-male institutions were opening up to women, and women who had previously felt restrained by marriage and childrearing from attending college could now envision new options and professional goals. Women could now entertain moving from homemaking to careers outside the home and from a limited choice of traditionally feminized majors, such as teaching or nursing, to other majors and career paths—for example, business, computer science, mathematics, social science, and medicine.[17] The stories of the women in this study illustrate the ways in which these trends were manifest at IUPUI.

THE PARTICIPANTS

The women who are the focus of this essay were all studying for a baccalaureate degree during the late 1960s and early 1970s. Their majors varied—three (Dorothy, Donna, and Miriam) were in liberal arts, five (Barbara, Eleanor, Margaret, Molly, and Meredith) in professional degree programs, and two (Abby and Lavinia) in the sciences.[18] The group of women reflected the composition of the IUPUI population of the time, composed of both traditional age students who enrolled immediately after high school and completed their degrees in four years and others who attended as returning students or who spread their studies out over a number of years.[19] They came to IUPUI from various educational entry points. Six began immediately after graduating from local Indianapolis high schools; an additional two had started straight from high school at the Indiana University Bloomington campus and transferred after one and three years, respectively. Both transfers were motivated, in part, by the desire to be close to a partner and the availability of part-time work in Indianapolis. The remaining two women participants in the study entered IUPUI later in life, having married and stayed at home with children for several years before completing college. One of the six who had started immediately after high school interrupted her studies for several years to marry, have children, and work full-time before finishing her degree.

The women were enrolled at a time when the population of the IUPUI student body more than doubled, going from 10,731 in 1970 to 22,797 in the fall of 1980.[20] The composition of the student body changed as well. Women students became the new majority. Additionally, the population increased in age, with those 25 and older increasing from 28.4 percent in 1971 to 47.4 percent in 1981, caused in part by the percentage of graduate students on campus, which increased from 3.3 percent to 14.1 percent during this period.[21]

REASONS FOR ATTENDING

Several participants said that they began college studies because it seemed to be the natural next step in their education: others in their families had gone to college, their high school classmates were going, or their parents urged college attendance. Dorothy voiced what others in this group indicated, saying that she went to college "because that's what one did" after high school.

By contrast, a few encountered opposition to the idea of furthering their education. Abby reported that growing up in Canada, she heard that "boys are important. They're going to be people like doctors and engineers.... They make jokes about dumb women and that's just the way the society was. And it just never occurred to me that I could actually get an education." Molly said that high school girls were not urged to prepare for college: "Back then ... they thought, 'Oh well, girls don't need to go to college. Or, they're only going to college to find a husband.'"

Some of these students had career goals in mind; four of them envisioned they would teach. Margaret observed, "It seems funny in this day and age, but when I went to school, women were teachers or nurses.... I couldn't even think of other options." Some, however, did envision other possibilities. Miriam thought an undergraduate degree would prepare her for law school: "My friends and I were going to get a job, get a degree in academia.... I was very keen about the job thing. That's one reason why I fixed on being an attorney. Because I knew that there would be a job out there, and I could probably make a good living and it would be really fun to be an advocate."[22]

Others were motivated more by a love of learning than a specific career goal. Abby said, "I think learning was always important to me. It just always was.

I like to know about things. And it just answered a need in me at that time." Donna said, "I took classes because I loved school. I loved my friends. I loved my teachers. I loved the whole environment. I wasn't there particularly to get a degree."

For the two nontraditional students, attending college was a way to develop a new identity. For years, Abby had helped her husband, a scientist, while raising children. She performed routine calculations and conducted background research until she finally realized that she could be a scientific professional herself if she went to college. She also feared that her marriage was crumbling, and she anticipated needing to have a career to support her children. Without the stimulation of intellectual work, she said, "Before I actually started back at school, I felt like I was drowning." Eleanor had been maintaining a home day care center along with raising her own children but aspired to obtain a doctorate in psychology, which she had never been encouraged to pursue. Her marriage, too, was in trouble. Both women saw going to college as a way of surviving divorce and serving as role models for their children.

This mix of motivations—from the sheer love of learning to the development of a new identity to the pursuit of a career—often changed over the course of the participants' studies. As they encountered new ideas and people, matured, and experienced different life circumstances, their ideas about why they were in college took different forms and often became a combination of motivations.

THE PRACTICAL ALTERNATIVE

For the women we interviewed, IUPUI was the practical alternative. It was inexpensive and enabled them to continue living at home. They would be able to find or continue to hold part-time jobs because their studies would be in a city with needs for labor. Several had taken courses at the Indiana University and Purdue University extension programs before the consolidation, so these centers were familiar to them as the "commuter college" option. Choosing between the extension programs was often dictated by one's major field or more practical reasons, such as those expressed by Lavinia, who said, "Purdue had a fifty-dollar admissions fee, and IU's was ten dollars. . . . I could start at either, and depending on what kind of a degree I wanted, and I thought, well, I'm not paying Purdue fifty dollars. . . . And [the IU Extension] was closer. It was handier." The women were representative of those IUPUI students surveyed for the campus's accreditation self-study in 1971, 36.3 percent of whom indicated they chose IUPUI because it was "close to home" and 20.3 percent of whom said that "low cost" was the reason.[23]

For some participants, limiting their choice of college to the Indiana or Purdue University systems and to commuting was initially a disappointment. They had hoped to go to other colleges or universities away from home but faced parental opposition or financial obstacles. For example, Lavinia and Barbara had both wanted to go to Butler University—Lavinia to study music and Barbara to study dance. Miriam was crestfallen when her parents refused to allow her to go to the University of Chicago. All three of these women, however, decided in retrospect that IUPUI was right for them. Looking back, Miriam said, "I sort of gave up going to the University of Chicago as an undergraduate because I saw this real vital community that was just humming. It was a real wonderful group of people who were just brilliant and they were living these real rich, full lives on very little money. All of us."

BEING A COLLEGE STUDENT

The women in this study described their states of mind as they entered college in positive terms. For those who began through a summer session directly after high school, life continued uninterrupted as they lived at home and, in several cases, continued holding the part-time jobs they'd had in high school. A few students stated that they were unfamiliar with the area where classes were located and had some anxiety about navigating parts of the city they had not encountered before. Molly revealed the lack of experience she had with being on the west side of Indianapolis before attending IUPUI: "I drove right by IUPUI because I couldn't find it because I didn't know what I was looking for." Some were relieved to be attending smaller classes because they came from large Indianapolis high school settings. As a group, the students were confident that they belonged in college and were eager to continue their studies. Dorothy captured the positive mood of the group in saying that she was excited but anxious at the same time.

Abby and Eleanor, the two nontraditional students who were married with children, expressed having more initial unease than the traditional students. Eleanor said, "I had anxiety about speaking in public and being a part of a class and having to ask questions and that sort of thing. Generally, there were a lot of younger kids just out of high school." Abby echoed this sentiment: "In the beginning I was so scared that I even signed up for how to learn in college. I was just terrified. I had no confidence in my abilities to do this, but I felt like I had to. . . . I felt embarrassed and inferior and I couldn't believe it when I got a good grade on some of my classes." Abby was grateful for an exceptionally helpful advisor who helped her find her major and chart out a path for her studies.

The stress of a new lifestyle varied across the students. Since IUPUI and its former extension sites had no housing or extensive study spaces available, students had to find alternatives on their own. Those who were living at home had the comfort of having meals, laundry, and other accommodations arranged; a few were taken to and from classes by their parents. But living at home was sometimes problematic. Barbara found that as a first-generation college student, her family did not anticipate her needs. She shared a room with her sister, who was not in college and did not understand the need for a quiet study environment, but "the biggest problem with living at home and going to college was convincing my parents that when I said I had to study, I had to study. No, I couldn't fix dinner, or I couldn't do the laundry that day. I had to study." Similarly, Abby, Molly, and Eleanor had to juggle the needs of their families in order to find time to study and get to class.

The three students who were living in apartments, rather than with their families, felt liberated and sophisticated but at the same time had some anxieties about their newfound independence. They faced locating a safe place to live and living on very little money, yet they remembered being happy with a simple existence. Dorothy said that she lived with three other students and drove an old car. "Our idea of a good time was to sit around a coffee crate in the evening and talk. We would go to plays and things at the art museum or Butler for students that were free. And, I really had no idea or no desire to spend a lot of money on anything." Donna recalled a similar feeling of contentment: "I didn't have a sense of, 'Oh, poor me, I'm doing this thing instead of something else I would really like to do.'" Reflecting instead on one of the low points of this independent living, Miriam said, "I remember when I was around a senior, I was living on North Meridian, and a friend of mine came to visit me, and I just started to cry because life was so hard. I had to plan every penny, how I was going to spend it, so I would have bus money and all the rest of that. But for the most part, I actually would just plow on ahead."

Except for one full-time homemaker, all the students in the study were in paid employment during the course of their studies. Off-campus positions included typing at a car dealership, doing clerical work at the public library, working in retail, and operating a home day care center. Five students found employment on campus—one with the dean of students, two with the registrar, one with a campus journal, and one with laboratories in the medical school. These campus jobs not only paid better and were more convenient than off-campus jobs, they came with mentoring benefits. The students' employers helped them to navigate the college system and offered flexibility in arranging schedules around class times and student responsibilities. For three students, this on-campus employment led to full-time positions on campus after they graduated. Students working off campus also found for the most part that their employers understood their needs as students and worked with them on schedules.

As these women commuted to the multiple locations of their classes, work, and, in some cases, other responsibilities such as student teaching sites, they employed their own cars, rides from others, buses, and walking. According to Margaret, bus travel was much more prevalent during that period than it is today. It was not necessarily easy, however, judging from Miriam's testimony: "In my first year, I had to walk a mile to highway 67 and get a Trailways bus in order to get into town. And of course, there weren't buses at night, so it was really difficult, and I ended up not getting very good grades the second term mainly because I couldn't get there. Or I'd get there and then I had to try to get people to take me out of their way to take me home."

The women with families had an equally complicated routine. Eleanor, who operated a home day care along with caring for own children, described her situation:

> I had the children during the day, and when they napped in the afternoon, I studied. . . . You know, it was the children leaving from the day care and me hurrying to get ready and get in the car, drive to either downtown or the campus, and going to the class, and then rushing back home. There wasn't a lot of time for socialization. There wasn't a lot of time for involvement in anything that was going on campus. It was pretty busy. During that time, we divorced. Then I moved into the city and so for the last two years of the degree, I lived in the city and that was a whole different kind of challenge.

THE PHYSICAL CAMPUS

One of the complications students in the 1970s faced as they moved around the city were the several physical locations of their classes. As Ralph Gray's history of IUPUI details, prior to the establishment of the IUPUI campus, students studied at the Purdue Extension on Thirty-Eighth Street across from the Indiana Fairgrounds and in several locations in downtown buildings.[24] The construction of the first three IUPUI campus buildings—Cavanaugh Hall, Lecture Hall, and the library (now Taylor Hall)—took place in 1971.[25] Other buildings, such as Education/Social Work, Business/SPEA, and the science and engineering buildings came later in the 1980s, meaning that students often needed to attend classes both in the new location and in several city locations as the new physical campus was coming together. Some were at remote locations—for example, Meredith, who studied physical education, had most of her classes at what was called Leonhart Center on Sixty-Fourth Street. She described this unique option as being in "our own little world."

Students' memories of the older extension buildings were both positive and negative. While some students liked the older buildings, others complained of their condition and environment for learning. Lavinia remarked, "I looked around, and my first thought was, this is a college campus? Those buildings were in terrible shape, especially S building. I came from Tech, which is 76 acres. I came from a college campus. This is not a college campus. I'm just taking classes here." Students remembered the Thirty-Eighth Street location, where some took science classes, as a building that straddled a Burger Chef, a source of convenient food but also of fumes that pervaded their classes. They also recalled parking problems when there were offerings at the state fairgrounds competing for space.

Those who attended classes in the downtown IU buildings had many stories to tell about their condition and the urban environment. Lavinia observed, "The S building was at 122 E. Michigan, and around the corner at 518 N. Delaware there was A building. Those two should have been torn down years before they were . . . because in that A building, you'd be in the library and you could feel it swaying in the wind." Meredith recalled noisy classroom conditions in the C building: "It was one of those hot, steamy rooms with the steam heat and so we'd have the windows open and kids would be out in the alley playing football. We'd hear that and then there was a pop machine right outside the door." Miriam experienced a suicide as a person jumped from an adjoining building while she was in class: "So, it was this real dense urban environment. You saw everything there was to see in an urban environment there."

Safety issues were a concern to the women navigating the downtown buildings, particularly with the M building on Meridian Street, situated next to a bar called the Duck In, which separated the class building from the student parking lot. Barbara observed, "The Murat, the M Building, was the one that nobody wanted to walk by themselves from the building past the Duck In bar, and there was another alley to get to the parking lot. But we just learned, you walk in a group." Lavinia recalled an assault on her mother, who had parked outside the M building to pick her up from class: "A gang had come over and started rocking the car, and they ended up throwing a rock through the side window and she ended up with a bloody leg. And I almost quit." Some women perceived safety issues at the Thirty-Eighth Street location as well. Abby recalled, "Back then Thirty-Eighth Street was actually becoming not always the safest place, and I remember being pretty nervous when I went down there." Lavinia said that physical safety within the aging downtown buildings was also a concern: "In the S building, if you had a class on the second or third floor, as I did, you walked up those narrow, steep steps, rather than take the elevator. It was old. Nobody would take a chance on riding the elevator."

Despite the shortcomings of the older buildings, students experienced the new consolidated campus buildings with some nostalgia for the older ones. Eleanor commented, "I missed Delaware Street. It was such a nice, close, old kind of place, and I missed that when we went to the new space, which was colder." Some criticized the angular architecture of the new buildings as ugly. Dorothy contrasted the campus with her previous experience at Indiana University Bloomington:

> I thought this was not very pretty. . . . I obviously understood I was in a city rather than in a little college town. And I had a real sense of it being this hunk of junk in the middle of downtown and that's where I was going to school. And so, in a lot of ways it didn't seem pleasant to me, and that's a big deal for me. Inside of Cavanaugh Hall, which is where I spent most of my time, the lobby of Cavanaugh Hall was just so grotesque. . . . Bloomington was beautiful, and this wasn't.[26]

Although the new campus's architecture did not appeal to the students we interviewed, increased safety was an asset. Molly observed, "I could say that back in the '70s, if you were over in the library and you were studying and you left your stuff at your seat and went to the bathroom, you'd come back, and it would be there. So, we didn't have to worry." However, at the time, the campus newspaper, *The Sagamore*, discussed the problems of continuing safety issues for women on campus.[27]

As it developed, the IUPUI campus, situated in a former African American neighborhood, brought some feelings of remorse to students who were conscious of the plight of the former residents. Lavinia recalled, "You could go up to the fourth or fifth floor of Cavanaugh Hall and look out and see the neighborhood. You could see the houses. And then little by little, they were torn down, and I still feel bad about that. Those were people's homes." As homes were demolished, the students, said Molly, "just felt like you were out in the wilderness almost, because there was nothing around you. Just those few buildings." Abby commented on the temporary buildings that were being constructed: "They kind of looked like huts they put up during the war. It reminds me of some of the things, some of the buildings in the POW camp in England. You know, the very modest little things." During the first decade of IUPUI, then, the physical campus was not a selling point to students.

BECOMING IUPUI

In his history of IUPUI, Ralph Gray discusses the communication issues that arose as the IU and Purdue Extensions were being integrated into the new university.[28] Faculty were often unaware of changes; the general public was confused, too. Since new buildings were not available for the first two years of the consolidation, students continued to attend classes at the various extensions, and this pattern continued to a lesser degree for certain courses even after the first three academic buildings were in place on the new campus. All but one student in our study attended IUPUI during this transition. These students did not report experiencing significant changes as the merger progressed. Miriam called the change "a middle of the night kind of thing, similar to the way the City of Indianapolis acquired the Colts." She said, "When that happened, it changed things a little bit," mainly changes in locales of classes. Barbara remembered one of the quirky bureaucratic changes: "I have vivid memories of them closing restrooms at times because they had to change the toilet paper because it had to be the same toilet paper as IU used."

The liberal arts students noticed a shift from older female faculty to younger male faculty as new hires were made. Indeed, the faculty composition was changing as more programs were added, particularly graduate programs that required faculty members with doctorates. A 1972–73 campus survey of faculty showed that male faculty holding doctorates outnumbered female faculty holding doctorates, 76.4 percent to 29.2 percent.[29] But for the most part, student life went uninterrupted while the transition occurred.

The increased availability of daytime classes during the 1970s was changing the demographic from students who worked full-time and attended night classes to students who worked part-time and attended both day and night classes. Miriam observed, "With my generation came a lot of people who started attending the college full-time during the daytime. When we moved out to Cavanaugh Hall, a lot of that changed. There were classes all during the day, and it was possible to work and go to school at the same time."

THE LEARNING ENVIRONMENT

Overall, the students in this study were highly positive about the education they received at IUPUI. Dorothy looked back from her graduate studies to assess the quality of her IUPUI education: "It became a kind of standard of comparison for me, and it really kind of stood pretty well. . . . It led me to graduate school; it kind of stood as a measure of judging what good teaching and learning could be." Barbara found that in her career as a teacher, teachers coming from other schools did not have the preparation and theoretical background that was provided to students at IUPUI.

Students described most classes as somewhat formal and recalled being addressed by their titles and last names, although there were some exceptions. For the most part, they remembered the classes as being at an appropriate level of difficulty and delivered in a conventional teaching style. As they took their required classes, some of the women were intrigued by subjects that they had not expected to like; several cited geology, taught by Arthur Mirsky, who elicited much interest in the field.

In trying to capture the uniqueness of IUPUI as a learning environment, Barbara observed, "One of the greatest things about IUPUI was the acceptance; all kind of students were valued and that was a hallmark of IUPUI, the acceptance of every student for who they were. . . . The extreme flexibility was very unique as well. Larger, more established colleges were pretty set in their ways, but at IUPUI, the faculty were willing to make adjustments. The classes were small, and students had actual faculty, not teaching assistants, so it was really hands-on. Students could become close with them." Margaret echoed the acceptance theme: "I liked the diversity of the students. They weren't all young people. There were older people and younger people, married, unmarried—you know, all kinds. Working. I really think it gave me a good, broad introduction to the world, meeting all these people."

Across the students, relationships with their peers were experienced differently according to major and life situation. At the remote physical education setting, Meredith described a small, close-knit group of students: "We were kind of in our own little world. We were forced to. You were taking the same classes over and over. . . . The thing that helped me get where I wanted to be was that sort of cohort experience where you had everybody moving along the same sort of program. A familiarity. You built a community. We felt responsible for one another. . . . I appreciated that a lot of the students brought their life experience with them and had a lot to overcome . . . but you pulled together."

Students in the liberal arts seemed especially able to form bonds, yet all three liberal arts students in our study were traditional-age students living independently from their families, which likely enabled more peer social interaction. The specific case of the English Department was described by three students who were closely mentored and inspired by two female faculty members, Rebecca Pitts and Alegar Stewart, who exposed the students to literature, met with them outside class, and organized the English Club. Dorothy described the lifelong friendships that formed through these experiences: "We had English Club once a month, and we would read a book and we would come and talk about it and have coffee. . . . It was enormously important to me and to other people. That's how I made friends." The students also participated in the production of a literary journal.

Aside from these instances, most of the students described themselves as very task-oriented, focusing on getting to class, studying, and working to support their studies, feeling that they had no time for engagement on campus, faculty interaction, or friendships. Barbara said, "There was no camaraderie beyond just class time. Everybody went to their jobs. . . . There was also a difference in that it wasn't residential. When you live on campus you have a different mindset. You are more inclined to play rather than just get down to studying and getting done what you came to do." Lavinia explained, "Basically, I went to school and studied, came home and studied."

Although a few extracurricular activities were established as IUPUI came together—a campus newspaper, athletic teams, a literary magazine, and a dance club—the students' busy lifestyle and their focus on studies and completion made extracurricular activities unappealing.[30] Abby captured the sentiments of most of the students about participation in extracurricular activities: "It never would have occurred to me. . . . No, I was just so goal oriented. And I wouldn't have wanted to be distracted by anything else. I didn't have time for that." Only two students, in addition to the three participating in English Club, joined a campus group. Lavinia cited "the fractured campus" physical environment as a possible reason for low student engagement as well.

Similarly, only a few students engaged actively in the dramatic social movements of the 1970s. All were aware of the press for racial, gender, and economic equality; a few expressed conservative opinions about these, but most sympathized with the underlying premises. Eleanor described the limited involvement that she was able to afford: "I had my little patch on my coat sewn on that said, 'War is not healthy for children and other living things,' and the Women's Movement—philosophically I was involved in it, but actively, I don't think I was. I remember my son as a teenager saying, 'Why didn't you go to Woodstock?' and I was saying, 'Well, I was changing your diapers.' There was too much going on personally to get super involved, although I did go to some events and protests and things." Margaret, too, had an antiwar necklace but said that she did not get involved: "Maybe I was just focused more on what I could do. I could study, I could go to classes. Keep my head down and work."

The three liberal arts majors reported avidly reading feminist literature and literary works outside the usual Western canon. They described intense discussions in their classes, but only Miriam talked about participating actively by going to antiwar rallies, consciousness-raising sessions, sit-ins, and voter registration drives and starting a group called Students for Peace, an arm of Hoosiers for Peace. Meredith participated in an equal rights rally and an Earth Day celebration. On the whole, though, academics and work crowded out the impulse to become politically active. None spoke of the activities of the Black Student Union on the IUPUI campus in the early 1970s and campus protests that occurred while they were studying.[31]

SUPPORTS AND CONSTRAINTS

All the women in the study completed their degrees, although two interrupted their pathways by several years, both to marry and start a family. When asked about the factors that helped them achieve their goal, most study participants answered that they simply had a strong internal drive to complete what they started. They were not easily defeated by fatigue, financial setbacks, or tension in their personal lives. This inner source of support was buttressed by several external supports, such as encouragement from family, friends, and employers. Most of the students had supportive parents. Those living at home cited room, board, and the use of a car as major advantages.

For a few, their families had to be convinced that a college degree was appropriate for a woman or that the struggle was worthwhile. Barbara describes how a faculty member helped with such an issue when she was assigned a student teaching locale that her husband and parents deemed unsafe: "He had mentored several of the students. I went over to his house, and he just talked me through the whole thing. Basically, he just listened and let me talk. And he said well, bottom line of what you're telling me is, how much do you want to teach? And that's how much I wanted to teach. From that point on, my parents and my now ex-husband were supportive."

A few students recalled how support staff, as well as faculty, helped them. Meredith gave an example: "The school's secretary, Helen Straub, she was 'Mother Straub,' she was the one who would take you under her wing and make sure that you were getting nurtured. And I'm pretty sure that especially students who didn't live at home who had come from afar that she probably really kept an eye on them." Support also came from employers, particularly those on campus, who counseled students on their goals, gave them the opportunity to learn new skills, and urged them to complete their degrees. Two students were able to use a 50 percent tuition benefit available to those working full-time in a campus office.

Unfortunately, none of the women in this study had any recollection of the IUPUI Continuing Education Center for Women or any other initiatives concerning women. A possible explanation is that these services were just beginning, and some were not in operation until six of the students in this study had graduated. Except for one student who used health services, these students did not report the use of any campus services. When asked what might have made their journey easier, the students mentioned such things as day care, better counseling, and food outlets.

The main constraints to student success were the occasional naysayer, stresses such as divorce, lack of time, and money. Although several students recalled that tuition at IUPUI was extremely inexpensive, most struggled to finance their education. Institutional financial aid was not a fixture in their lives. Reflecting the situation for many women in the 1970s, Donna said, "It would have never occurred to me to borrow money. In the first place, women at that time couldn't even get a credit card." The students found that financial aid awards at the time excluded those from middle class families, even single-income families with many children. Decisions were based on the expectation that the parents would be supporting the students, which in some cases, like Miriam's, was not true:

> My parents also wouldn't sign any financial aid forms. My father was from the old country, and he said it wasn't any of the government's business how much money he made. And so I went to the first year there, and it was really difficult. My parents wouldn't let me have access to my money, which was in a savings account, which had started out in their names and my name both. . . . And so I took a year out of school and just left my parents' house, established financial independence, worked at a minimum wage job, saved up enough money to go back to school in the fall of the following year.

Her on-campus employers helped her to get an affidavit of nonsupport so that she could obtain some financial aid. All the same, Miriam reported, "And so I was pretty much able to stay in school, but I usually had to work a number of jobs. I usually worked at least two jobs every term. And sometimes three, which was difficult, but all my friends and I were pretty poor, so you managed." A few of the students had small grants, awards, and scholarships that eased the financial burden, but their paid work was the main source of support, a factor that again underlines their resilience and self-reliance.

LIFE EFFECTS

How did going to IUPUI affect the subsequent lives of women students who attended in the 1970s? First, all were either employed or went on to further schooling after graduation. Interestingly, several took positions outside their field of study. Only one of the four education students, Barbara, became a teacher; Margaret and Meredith studied for master's degrees in library science and became librarians; and Molly, who worked for the IUPUI registrar while completing her degree, continued to work in this campus unit. After beginning a career in her degree area of cytotechnology, Abby obtained a degree in library science and became a librarian as well. Eleanor, who studied psychology, studied for a master's degree in social work before getting a degree in library science and working as a librarian. Miriam and Dorothy, history and English majors, pursued additional degrees and careers in college teaching. Donna, an English major, had a long career with the US Postal Service. Lavinia, whose undergraduate and master's degrees were in chemistry, is the second student who translated her part-time work with the IUPUI registrar into a long career with that office. For Lavinia, the degree was a pathway to work: "I knew that even if I never used my degree in chemistry, I had a degree. And had good grades. And any time I would apply for a job, even if it was outside the chemistry area, I could say, yes, I have a bachelor's degree. And then later, I have a master's degree. So that's something I've never regretted."

The women in our study detailed not only the expected career outcomes associated with college attendance but some major life changes. Abby, who had put aside her interest in science for a life as a homemaker, cited the profound effect that achieving her degree had for her: "It was an absolutely marvelous experience for me. Being no job, no education, and no driver's license when I arrived here, to when I actually got to the point where I got my degree, it was wonderful. . . . IUPUI was probably my first experience of being equal." Eleanor, also coming from a homemaker role, echoed this observation of a major life change: "It probably helped the adjustment to the divorce. . . . In some ways that school experience opened my world up again; I loved it and I took full advantage of it." Following their studies, nine of the ten women chose to blend marriage and career.

For Barbara, a shift in attitude toward service and the urban experience was characteristic of IUPUI students, and this internalized ethos affected her life and career. She observed the differences between teacher applicants who had been prepared at IUPUI and those from other colleges: "IUPUI candidates were saying to them [recruiters], 'What can I give you?' not 'What are you going to give me?' And I think a lot of that has to do with how hard we were all working to get through. We were all surviving. And we dealt a lot with the inner city."

Several women cited effects on intellectual growth. Dorothy said, "I saw my model at IUPUI for people who were doing intellectual work, and I figured out that's what I wanted to do. I think at IUPUI, there was no explicit talk that I remember about 'we're going to give you a foundation for going to graduate school' or something—but in fact, it did."

Miriam, Margaret, and Meredith talked about character development: leadership skills, increased comfort with and knowledge about diverse populations, and social awareness. The women participating in this study expressed gratitude and satisfaction with IUPUI and were able to identify ways in which their experiences during the 1970s had lasting, positive effects on their lives afterward.

"A MORE INNOCENT TIME"

The women in this study contrasted their experiences with those of current female students. Bonnie said, "In many ways, it was a more innocent time than it is now." Dorothy explained, "I didn't have the care of anybody else, and I think that a lot of women students now do have children—they might be single mothers, they might have the care of other family members besides children. . . . A lot of women students now are leading lives that I would call almost impossible to do." Participants also talked about the escalating cost of college that causes more students to scramble for funds or take on significant debt, yet they also pointed out that students in the 1970s led lifestyles that were more spartan than most current students are willing to maintain.

The women in this study also identified advantages that current women students have. Eleanor said, "I think it's very, very different now. I think there's a lot more opportunities for women, and I think that women are being listened to a lot more . . . and women are standing up and saying, these are things we need. These are things we want. And getting them more." Referring to her Midwest colleagues, she added, "We didn't do that." Meredith observed that current women students are more likely to be thought of as serious students, saying that the message women received as they went to college in the 1970s "was pretty much a given thing that you're really just going to find a husband. And I don't think that's the case [that women are told that] anymore." Participants also identified several campus resources that current women students have today, such as on-campus childcare and rooms for nursing infants, gym facilities, women's centers, a wide array of campus activities, more financial aid, and advising.

CONCLUSION

A key theme describing the pioneering women students at IUPUI is their determination. For the participants in this study, quitting was not an option. Whether they were experiencing supportive or oppositional forces, they carried on, drawing on inner strength to do so. As they pursued their degrees, they gained confidence and developed plans for the future—a future that in many cases they had not been able to envision when they began their studies.

The experiences of these women also illustrate the societal tensions of the time within the context of Indiana. Focusing on their studies, most of the women were not especially tuned into broader social conversations about the role of women. When asked, they could not recall instances of discrimination on campus by either faculty or male students. Several expressed conservative attitudes about feminism while only a few were more open to changes in thinking. By their actions, however, they modeled independence, perseverance, the capacity to juggle multiple roles, and the inner strength needed to attain their goals. They were not protesters, but they did not let relationships with men, family cautions about women's roles, or other potential roadblocks get in their way.

As a new institution, IUPUI was engaged in several types of activities—construction of facilities and displacement of a neighborhood; development of policies and new relationships with Indiana and Purdue Universities, community figures, and government actors; and expansion of the student body with the consequent need for new faculty, new programs, and organizational structures. Attention to women students was slow in coming, growing steadily over the first decade in the shape of programs such as a women's center and the Center for Continuing Education for Women. Against this backdrop, these women students in the late 1960s and early 1970s worked with the conditions available to them to lay the groundwork for the success of their successors. Soon, the campus population would become majority female; professional schools would enroll high percentages of women; support services for women would increase; and significant progress toward the goal of gender equality would be achieved.

NOTES

1. We focused on women undergraduates who attended IUPUI during the transition period from 1968 through the decade of the 1970s. We selected former students for participation through solicitations made by mailing lists of alumnae as well as referrals by the first participants (Michael Q. Patton, *Qualitative Research*

& Evaluation Methods, 4th ed. [Thousand Oaks, CA: Sage, 2014]). We attempted to select women from a range of undergraduate majors, but no other sampling criterion was used. We interviewed each participant using a standard open-ended interview protocol; three were interviewed by telephone and seven in person. Responses were tape-recorded and transcribed. Each woman was given a pseudonym, although all waived confidentiality and gave permission for their interview content to be used for the study and nine gave permission for their interviews to be publicly archived. We then wrote case descriptions of each participant and conducted cross-case analysis by theme (C. E. Moustakas, *Phenomenological Research Methods* [Thousand Oaks, CA: Sage, 1994]), with the results reported thematically and reviewed by each team member for reliability. Participants' quotations have been minimally edited to exclude repeated words and filler words.

2. Stacey Jones, "Dynamic Social Norms and the Unexpected Transformation of Women's Higher Education, 1965–1975," *Social Science History* 33, no. 3 (fall 2009): 247–91, http://www.jstor.org/stable/40268002; John R. Thelin, *A History of American Higher Education,* 2nd ed. (Baltimore: Johns Hopkins University Press, 2011): 260–316, 317–62.

3. Ralph D. Gray, *IUPUI—the Making of an Urban University* (Bloomington: Indiana University Press, 2003): 79–106.

4. Gray, 81.

5. Gray, 81.

6. Gray, 6.

7. Cedric Cummings, "The Extension Division," in Burton Myers, *History of Indiana University,* Vol. 2 (Bloomington: Indiana University, 1952): 658–82; for a discussion of early extension activity in Indianapolis, see also Robert E. Cavanaugh, *Indiana University Extension: Its Origin, Progress, Pitfalls and Personalities* (Bloomington: Indiana University Extension, 1961).

8. Cummings, "The Extension Division," 665–66.

9. Mary Orvis Faculty Biographical File, Indiana University Archives, Bloomington, Indiana. See also https://ofw.iupui.edu/Leadership/Online-Archive -Women-Creating-Excellence-at-IUPUI/Women-Creating-Excellence/mary -orvis.

10. Gray, *IUPUI,* 36.

11. Gray, 30–31.

12. Gray, 97.

13. National Center for Education Statistics, *120 Years of American Education, A Statistical Portrait,* ed. Thomas M. Snyder (Washington, DC: U.S. Department of Education, 1993): 64–66.

14. Green Sheet, vol. 2, no. 20, May 14, 1972, https://archives.iupui.edu /bitstream/handle/2450/7411/1972-05-14.pdf?sequence=21&isAllowed=y, IUPUI University Library Special Collections and Archives, Indianapolis, Indiana; Green

Sheet, vol. 2, no. 46, November 12, 1972, https://archives.iupui.edu/bitstream /handle/2450/7411/1972-11-12.pdf?sequence=48&isAllowed=y, IUPUI University Library Special Collections and Archives, Indianapolis, Indiana.

15. Green Sheet, vol. 5, no. 36, September 14, 1975, https://archives.iupui.edu /bitstream/handle/2450/7409/1975-09-14.pdf?sequence=38&isAllowed=y , IUPUI University Library Special Collections and Archives, Indianapolis, Indiana.

16. Kathleen S. Grove, "Milestones in the History of Women at IUPUI since 1969," *IUPUI Office for Women*, https://ofw.iupui.edu/OFWContent/Html/Media /OFWContent/Resources/OFW724641.pdf; Gerald R. Bepko, "Remarks on the Inaugural Meeting Commission on Women," IUPUI Office for Women, last modified January 29, 1997, https://ofw.iupui.edu/OFWContent/Html/Media /OFWContent/Resources/OFW741658.pdf; Caroline Lamkin, "Twenty Years of the Office for Women at IUPUI," *News at IUPUI*, May 2, 2017, https://news.iu.edu /stories/2017/05/iupui/inside/02-office-for-women-20-years.html.

17. Stacey Jones, "Dynamic Social Norms and the Unexpected Transformation of Women's Higher Education, 1965–1975," *Social Science History* 33, no. 3 (2009): 247–91.

18. See note 1 for details about the study and interviewees.

19. *IUPUI 1982 Institutional Self-Study for North Central Association Review*, 23, IUPUI University Library Special Collection and Archives, Indianapolis, Indiana.

20. *Indiana University Fact Book* (Bloomington: University Budget Office, 1975), 1; *Indiana University Fact Book* (Bloomington: University Budget Office, 1980), 26.

21. *IUPUI 1982 Institutional Self-Study*, 23.

22. Miriam ultimately became a community college faculty member.

23. *IUPUI 1982 Institutional Self-Study*.

24. Gray, *IUPUI*, 9–10.

25. "About IUPUI, History—IUPUI Timeline," https://www.iupui.edu/about /history.html.

26. For a discussion of the shortcomings of the first three buildings at IUPUI, see Gray, *IUPUI*, 123–24.

27. "For the Women at IUPUI—Is IUPUI Safe?" *Sagamore*, February 10, 1975, 1.

28. Gray, *IUPUI*, 107–31.

29. "Sexual Status at IUPUI Analyzed," Green Sheet, vol. 5, no. 6, February 16, 1975, 1, IUPUI University Library Special Collections and Archives, Indianapolis, Indiana, https://archives.iupui.edu/bitstream/handle/2450/7409/1975-02-16.pdf ?sequence=8&isAllowed=y.

30. Gray, *IUPUI*, 131; see also Gray, 197–222 for a discussion of student life.

31. Gray, 115–30.

Fig. 1. Frances Morgan Swain (*center,* looking straight into camera) and the League of Women. An advocate for women's rights, Swain was an IU alumna, an equality-minded Quaker, and the wife of university president Joseph Swain. *Courtesy Indiana University Archives (P0088014).*

Fig. 2. Agnes E. Wells (*center*) at a reception. Wells, appointed dean in 1918, shepherded IU's early female campus housing efforts to national prominence. *Courtesy Indiana University Archives (P0024330).*

Fig. 3. Nellie Showers Teter (*far right*), the first woman elected to the IU Board of Trustees in 1924, at a trustees meeting. *Courtesy Indiana University Archives (P0025726).*

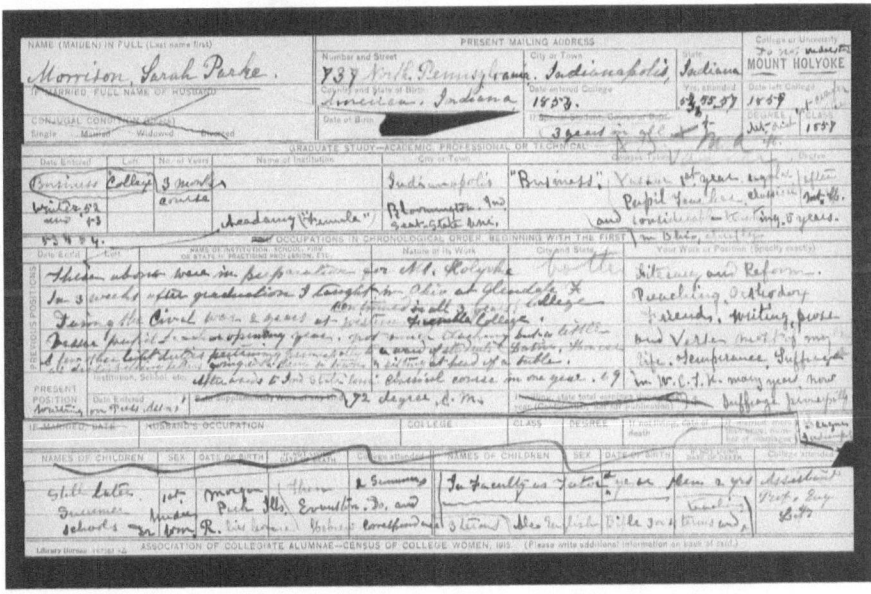

Fig. 4. The Mount Holyoke student card of Sarah Morrison, the first female student at Indiana University. *Courtesy Archives and Special Collections, Mount Holyoke College.*

Fig. 5. Nancy Streets-Lyons, the first Black women to be crowned as Miss Indiana University in 1959. *Courtesy Indiana University Archives (P0043484).*

Fig. 6. The 1924 IUSM student body class in front of Emerson Hall. *Courtesy IUPUI Image Collection (UA024I item IDUA24-000271).*

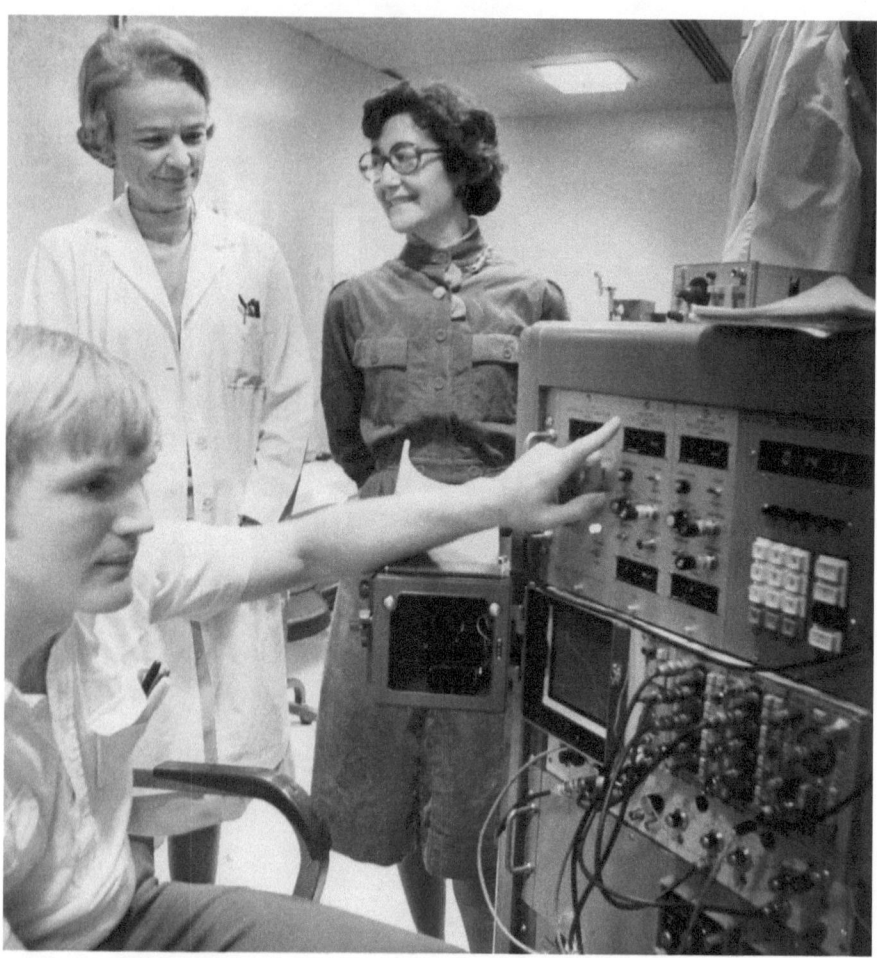

Fig. 7. Dr. Doris Merritt, IUPUI Assistant Dean of Sponsored Programs (*left*) and Dr. Suzanne Knoebel, Assistant Dean for Medical Research. Between 1961 and 1978, Merritt oversaw more than $55 million in successful external grant funding for IUSM. *Courtesy IUPUI Image Collection (UA024 Item IDUA24-000362).*

Fig. 8. Dean Kate Hevner Mueller (*center*) with two students. Mueller was the last dean of women at Indiana University (1938–46). *Courtesy Indiana University Archives (P0031237).*

Fig. 9. Martha E. Dawson, who in 1970 became the first African American woman to hold the rank of tenured full professor on the Bloomington faculty. *Courtesy Indiana University Archives (P0026433).*

Fig. 10. Lin Ostrom and Vincent Ostrom, 1968. Lin Ostrom went on to be awarded the Nobel Prize in Economics in 2009. *Courtesy Lilly Library, Indiana University.*

Fig. 11. Elaine Sloan was appointed the first female dean of libraries in 1980. *Courtesy Indiana University Archives (P0052863).*

Fig. 12. In 1948, Barbara Shalucha cofounded the Hilltop Garden and Nature Center, a program designed to promote community gardening at Indiana University. She served as the director until her retirement in 1986. *Courtesy Indiana University Archives (P0052530).*

Fig. 13. *Left to right:* Jean Brown, Dorothy Collins, Cornelia Christenson, and Paul Gebhard working on the index for Alfred C. Kinsey's *Sexual Behavior in the Human Female* (1953). *Courtesy Kinsey Institute, Indiana University.*

Fig. 14. IU alumna, noted choreographer, and the first-tenure track Latina at IU, Iris Rosa (*standing*) retired in 2017 after forty-three years as the founding director of the African American Dance Company. *Courtesy African American Arts Institute, Indiana University.*

Fig. 15. Making her debut in 1946 as the first female African American singer to have a contract with the New York City Opera, Camilla Williams traveled extensively and achieved international renown as a concert singer and recording artist. In 1977, she became the first African American professor of voice at Indiana University. She retired from teaching in 1997 and in 2009 received the Indiana University President's Medal for Excellence. *Courtesy Indiana University Archives (P0064533).*

PART 2

FACULTY, ADMINISTRATIVE STAFF, AND SUPPORTERS

TEN

—ɯ—

"THE SHARP SWORD OF THE NEW ALLIANCE"

Edna Henry and the IU School of Social Work

KATHERINE BADERTSCHER

Katherine Badertscher, a scholar of philanthropy, situates the career of faculty member Edna Henry in the broader history of social welfare and the early years of Indiana University's Social Service Department. Mindful of the politics of gender that shape academic and professional fields, Badertscher traces the roots of Henry's intellectual orientation in both biography and the history of charity work in Indiana. She explores why Henry's pioneering contributions as a professor and director of IU's Social Service Department—a subdepartment of the Bloomington Depart-ment of Sociology at the Medical Center in Indianapolis—have been overshadowed in histories of social work's rise and IU's own account of its place in this history.

LISTEN TO *THE INDIANAPOLIS STAR* from February 19, 1924: "Fund Picks Woman as 'Best Citizen.'" Edna G. Henry had received honorary (as a woman) fund membership for her "outstanding and unselfish service for the public welfare" at the Indianapolis Community Fund's annual dinner.[1] Sources do not tell us Henry's response to this honor as she had been a wheelchair user for three years and did not attend the dinner. In 1925, she received honorary membership in the American Association of Hospital Social Workers, prompt-ing the *Indianapolis News* story "Unusual Honor for Miss Edna G. Henry." The association had awarded only one other honorary membership (to a man) in its six-year history. Miss Henry, the paper noted, was "one of the most interesting women in the city."[2]

By the time Henry was honored as Indianapolis's "best citizen," she had earned a doctorate, achieved associate professor rank at Indiana University,

233

published her dissertation in book form, and established and directed the university's Social Service Department—today the IU School of Social Work. The Community Fund's silver cup inscribed her title as "Miss"—not "Professor" or "Doctor"—underplaying her accomplishments. Henry's legacy as the founding director of IU's Social Service Department remains relatively obscured in broader accounts of the university she served from 1911 to 1926 and, similarly (perhaps partly because of her eclipse in IU campus histories), her career and contributions have been understudied by scholars in a number of relevant areas—the history of academic specialization, the field of social work, studies of the career trajectory and contributions of university women, and Indiana women's history, among them.[3]

INTRODUCTION

This chapter, making common cause with efforts to better document both gender barriers and women's intellectual and administrative leadership at IU, explores Indiana University's Dr. Edna Gertrude Henry (1874–1942) in the context of what historian Thomas D. Clark dubbed the university's "Long Step into Professionalization."[4] As Clark described, state officials at the turn of the century called for reform, pressuring IU to "break out of the shell of the past and the restrictive old line liberal arts college."[5] When Henry joined IU in 1911, William Lowe Bryan, who by his retirement in 1937 had served thirty-five years, had enjoyed the longest presidential tenure in IU's history to date and was in the process of implementing a number of reforms to augment graduate and professional education.[6] These efforts, reflecting broader trends in US higher education, would help facilitate IU's crucial transition from university in name to university in substance.

An important but understudied part of IU's transformation during Bryan's tenure was the rise of female enrollments. Coeducational since the 1860s, the university, then still a single campus in Bloomington with a student body of approximately 30 percent female students, hired its first dean of women in 1901. But even as student demographics changed and helped account for growth, the university remained male-dominated: consistent with both norms in higher education and gender roles at the time, IU's faculty ranks included very few female instructors, with most women holding teaching-oriented appointments or positions in what were regarded as "feminine" fields, such as language.

Finally, Bryan's university-building efforts coincided with changes in the nature of medical education in the US. Medical instruction had migrated gradually away from individual apprenticeships toward full-time academics so that institutions of higher education assumed the full burden of physicians' training by around 1900.[7] The question remained of whether and how IU might by incorporating medical training bolster its profile in the state and beyond. In 1903, just a year into his presidency, Bryan successfully proposed the opening of a Department of Medicine in Bloomington and then considered the possibilities of establishing IU-sponsored medical training in the state capital, Indianapolis.

Edna Henry witnessed and navigated these changes firsthand—as a woman, a scholar, and a practitioner—and her career was affected by them. So, too, is our historical knowledge of Henry's contributions to the field and the university. Scholars of multiple arenas (including religion, education, social services, health, and the arts) have charted a gendered, hierarchical pattern over time, with a male elite holding power and female staff and volunteers doing the day-to-day work.[8] During Henry's lifetime, women who served in mixed-gender organizations or ran all-female auxiliaries related to men's associations wielded less power than their male counterparts.[9] Women developed creative and productive outlets in what historian Kathleen McCarthy calls "parallel power structures" that did not threaten prevailing gender boundaries.[10] As a female scholar in a new field, Henry's achievements accordingly appeared limited during her lifetime as they were at times muted amid power struggles and budget restrictions. Looking back, however, we now understand how successfully Henry built her field's legitimacy despite uneven support from male authorities, and we gain insight into how the politics of history have undervalued Henry's achievements.

Strikingly, the career of Dr. Charles P. Emerson, dean of the Indiana School of Medicine, has long overshadowed Henry's contributions in various accounts of IU's history. While it is certainly true that Emerson hired Henry, she was the individual who conceived, created, and ran the social service practice. She earned her master's (1914) and doctorate (1917) degrees from Indiana University while building, staffing, and operating her department. In her capacity as Social Service Department director, moreover, Henry remained embedded in the inner workings of the important Indianapolis charities, in particular the Indianapolis Charity Organization Society (today's Families First), the city's largest and most comprehensive social welfare agency of the time.[11] She recognized and supported the newly developing and crucial pedagogical element that contemporary social work education in all practice settings involved significant clinical experience. Her career demonstrated skillfulness in connecting the worlds of higher education, medicine, various social networks, and social welfare philanthropy. As such, through an exploration of Edna Henry's legacy, we recover an often overlooked figure in IU's history whose biography reflects the opportunities and constraints of her generation of academic women at IU. Henry's story holds relevance both within and beyond her home institution and invites reconsideration of intellectual leadership and innovation in her field of expertise. Here was a woman whose career in social welfare was anchored not in Baltimore or Chicago—the backdrop for the pioneering work of Mary Richmond and Jane Addams—but in the Hoosier state and its history.

BACKGROUND: INFORMAL POOR RELIEF AND SCIENTIFIC PHILANTHROPY, WITH A VIEW OF INDIANA

If you turn to any number of entry-level social work textbooks, they will locate social work's foundations in late nineteenth-century charity organization societies and settlement houses. Two women in particular—Mary Richmond and Jane Addams—are discussed to evoke the ideologies and practices of these interrelated social movements. The Baltimore Charity Organization Society's (COS) Mary Richmond, the most influential social work practitioner, writer, and teacher of her time, published texts that remain the basis for social work curricula today.[12] Jane Addams, the most famous settlement house leader, cofounded Hull House in Chicago (1889) and became widely recognized for her expertise in and influence on social issues.[13] These two responses in the long-term trajectory of poverty relief allow us to appreciate how institution building and specialization had an impact on community members who needed assistance, which in turn led to the formation of the IU Social Service Department. A close look at the small community of Indianapolis, though, reveals that the social work field dates back much further. Exploring this deeper but less studied history—namely, the rise of social welfare in Indiana—helps us better understand the importance of time and place in Henry's story. In tracing state and local welfare history, we better understand the milieu in which her ideas matured and, eventually, her IU career developed.

When it formed in 1835, the Indianapolis Benevolent Society (IBS) exemplified nineteenth-century neighborhood benevolence and a sense of optimism for what was then the tiny town of Indianapolis. City fathers formed the IBS "to relieve the necessities of the poor of the city of Indianapolis . . . by means of voluntary contributions."[14] Members of the IBS comprised, donated to, and operated the all-volunteer charitable society. They came from economically secure families and served as donors, fundraisers, caseworkers, and aid distributors. The IBS's traditional, door-to-door approach to caring for the poor suited Indianapolis while the population remained small and relatively homogeneous, most people knew one another, and the outer points of the city could be reached on foot or horseback. As village turned to city, however, both the IBS and public welfare had to adapt along with it. The Civil War, industrialization, immigration, and urbanization exposed increasing numbers of families to the harsh realities of urban life: orphans, single women, low wages, economic uncertainty, factory accidents, women and children working in sweatshops, life in tenements and slums, lack of sanitation, crime, and disease.

With industrialization, the menacing symbol of the dependent pauper emerged as the person unwilling to work, but who chose to live on either government poor relief or charity—or both.[15] US civic and charitable leaders grew to believe that the existing kaleidoscope of churches, benevolent associations, asylums, and poorhouses could not keep pace with the rapidly changing industrial economy and related societal problems—especially urban poverty. New charities proliferated but did not coordinate relief or fundraising efforts, much less address all the need that existed. New York City's Charles Loring Brace bemoaned in 1872, "This city is full of multiplied charities, which are constantly encroaching on each other's field; and yet there are masses of evil and calamity here which they scarcely touch."[16] He presciently recommended "all the offices of the great charities in one building . . . or a 'Bureau of Charities.'"[17] Brace and other social welfare leaders called for efficiency, prevention of the causes of poverty, more strategic charitable giving, and an end to the dependence on charity that the proliferation of agencies had unwittingly enabled. The able-bodied who depended on assistance, beyond the traditional orphans, widows, elderly, ill, and disabled, became increasingly stigmatized and something to be identified and driven away, not nurtured.

Taken together, these changes provided the setting for the late nineteenth-century scientific philanthropy movement that swept into Indianapolis, its charities and hospitals, and the new Indiana University School of Medicine when it formed in 1907. Scientific philanthropy rested on several fundamental concepts: use of businesslike processes to tackle societal problems, emphasis on data and root cause analysis, and strategies of prevention rather than relief. Organizers attempted to purge charity of its sentimentality and provide relief via a comprehensive system.[18] The broader movement was signaled more by philosophy than structure and encompassed a range of orderly or systematic approaches to giving; it included charity organization societies, and, after 1900, federated giving, community foundations, and the early modern foundations of Carnegie, Rockefeller, and Sage. The movement's methods melded voluntarism, noblesse oblige, religion, social Darwinism, and simultaneous benefit to donor, recipient, and community.[19]

Why did scientific philanthropy take root in Indianapolis? Growth and in-dustrialization created both social problems and opportunity for philanthropy. The city's population increased approximately 40 percent in one decade, from 75,000 in 1880 to 105,000 in 1890. The 1880s "gas boom" (the discovery of natural gas in east-central Indiana) contributed to general prosperity and an increase in manufacturing in the area. Between 1880 and 1900, the number of manu-facturers in the city nearly tripled, from 688 to 1,910.[20] Marion County, where Indianapolis is located, produced more manufactured goods (in terms of dollar value) than any other county in Indiana, a status it would hold until 1919.[21] Em-ployment in manufacturing and transportation grew as the number of agricul-tural workers began a long, slow decline. Men, and women and children to a far lesser degree, increasingly worked as skilled and unskilled laborers. Common laborers ever so gradually joined the ill, infirm, aged, orphaned, widowed, and transient who depended on government relief or charity. When prominent men and women learned of the budding scientific philanthropy movement, they applied its precepts to the problems they perceived in their own backyards.

A CLOSER LOOK: ORGANIZED CHARITY IN INDIANAPOLIS

Charity Organization Societies (COSs), the institutional embodiment of sci-entific philanthropy, promised efficient, rational, and scientific solutions to the intractable social and economic problem of poverty. The COS of Indianapolis subsumed the Indianapolis Benevolent Society (IBS) in 1879. The IBS had maintained its traditional elements of neighborhood charity: cooperation with churches, other charities, and the township trustee; neighborhood districts; volunteer members; involvement of prominent men and women; and home visitation to investigate families and give advice. It also incorporated tenets of scientific philanthropy that would become hallmarks of the COS movement: centralization, the prevention of begging and pauperism, paid staff, and the sharing of the results of investigation among potential donors and city offi-cials.[22] Shortly after it formed in 1879, the Indianapolis COS wielded virtual control over poor relief, making it one of the most progressive, powerful, and successful charity organizations in the country.[23]

The COS immediately established the Confidential Exchange, at times known as the charity clearing house or the central registry. Offices on Monu-ment Circle remained open twenty-four hours a day.[24] Prospective clients of-ten applied in person to the IBS or COS, so a steady stream of needy people filed in each day. Whether applicants self-reported or were referred by others, interviews occurred in the offices, applicants' homes, and chance meetings

on the street. COS staff and volunteers—acting as both caseworkers and de-
tectives—consulted with applicants' neighbors, landlords, clergy, doctors,
teachers, policemen, and patrons who referred the applicants, to round out
application data. The registrar combed local newspapers for stories about applicants—such as arrests or deaths of family members—or cases of need and
pasted clippings into the permanent record. This nature of data gathered in the
1880s adumbrates the fundamentals of social work practice today: interview-
ing, intervention, and connecting people to resources.[25] Indianapolis COS
records reflected each of these three key elements a full twenty years before
they appeared in handbooks or textbooks that received national attention.[26]
When Edna Henry arrived in Indianapolis, therefore, she stepped into a well-
established social welfare setting.

HENRY'S EARLY YEARS

This fascinating milieu provides the setting for us to appreciate Edna Henry's
early years. She was born in 1874 to Charles Lewis and Eva N. Henry in the
small town of Anderson, Indiana.[27] During her childhood, the natural gas
discovery, the so-called "gas boom," caused Anderson and neighboring towns
to double in size by 1900, which presented an auspicious opportunity for the
Henry family. Charles Henry, already a successful graduate of Indiana University Bloomington's law school, practicing attorney, and state senator, built
eleven miles of electric railway track between Anderson and Alexandria, Indiana in 1897. He connected the track and a city car and dubbed the system
an "interurban line," basing the idea on a Chicago World's Fair exhibit of a
small "intermural" electric line. The wildly successful, albeit short-lived, Indianapolis and Cincinnati Traction Company was launched, the first regional
electric railway in the country. The lines eventually connected the gas belt cities
with Indianapolis and Cincinnati, making Henry's invention a national model.
Henry moved his family, law practice, and railroad acumen to Indianapolis in
1904, where he founded Indianapolis's Union Traction Company.[28]

Charles Henry believed in community service alongside his business and
professional lives. Henry served as an Indiana University trustee from 1894 to
1903, just as William Lowe Bryan began his thirty-five-year tenure as university
president. Shortly before moving to Indianapolis, at the peak of the interurban
business in Anderson, the Henry family convened a small group of "church and
charitable-minded people" at their home to form a charity organization society
known as Associated Charities.[29] Edna Henry was the agency's first secretary.
By this time, she had graduated from May Wright Sewall's Girls' Classical

School in Indianapolis and with a BA degree from Indiana University Bloomington. She was already "well known in the development of the better things" in town and put her energy into the new agency, organized to provide for basic needs of children and their families.[30] Her education, practical experience in charity, and family's social standing created a solid foundation for her future work. By the time Indiana University considered a Social Service Department, President Bryan had known the Henry family for at least fifteen years.

Edna Henry's social connections and her career both took off when the family moved to Indianapolis in 1904; the personal and professional reinforced each other. She first worked as an assistant in Indianapolis Public School's Social Service Department. No doubt with her father's introduction, she spoke as a panelist in 1906 with Indiana University President Bryan.[31] The combination of her social service experience with her father's connections made her a visible, knowledgeable resource for the Indianapolis community. Within a few short years, Henry was a sought-after guest speaker around the city on topics including social (friendly) visiting and child welfare. Her social circle brought her speaking opportunities. She joined the Fortnightly Literary Club, for example, one of the elite women's clubs that met at the fashionable Propylaeum. As a program committee member, she invited the club's founder, Cornelia Fairbanks (wife of Charles Fairbanks), to open the club's 1908 season.[32] It is plausible to assume that the Fortnightly was a deliberate choice on Henry's part, as its members paid close attention to both literature and matters of social welfare.[33]

THE FRIENDLY VISITOR

Edna Henry moved to Indianapolis when the COS's friendly visitor program was at a crossroads. In the 1880s the Indianapolis COS stated its primary object as the "social and moral elevation of the poor," which it would achieve "by bringing the richer and poorer classes into closer relations with each other by means of a thorough system of house-to-house visitation."[34] The door-to-door IBS volunteer member thus evolved into the role of the COS volunteer friendly visitor. The organization hoped one-on-one counseling along with data gathering and analysis would completely obviate the need for material relief.

Friendly visiting, often described as an extension of feminine *noblesse oblige*, would bring women's value as households' moral guardians into their communities. But because visitors were merely well-intended amateurs, their function easily gave way to trained charity workers.[35] On the surface, these traditional interpretations appear consistent with the COS's gender stratification of male trustees and female volunteers. This division of labor and subordination of men over women, however, does not mesh with the crucial nature imputed to visitation work. We should use caution, moreover, when we apply the stereotypical images of powerful, professional, businesslike men and gentle, empathetic, caregiving women to the Indianapolis COS. In May 1880, six months after the COS apparatus was in place, active recruitment of visitors began with this announcement: "We can not [sic] relieve the great need by gifts of money. Money touches but the surface needs of life. There can be no permanent helping of the poor until we give ourselves. . . . We wish now to develop this personal work, to have visitors who shall go among the poor as friends go, with delicate consideration, kindness, courtesy. We need *hundreds* of such visitors. . . . Will you unite with us in this work?"[36]

The COS never came close to marshalling hundreds of volunteers and chronically struggled to attract and retain friendly visitors. Visiting was a topic at virtually every annual meeting and throughout board minutes between 1879 and 1910. Visitation experts constantly reminded COSs of the purposes, benefits, and ideal qualities of reliable visitors, but recruitment proved to be easier said than done. The pampered, callous friendly visitor began to appear in benevolence literature across the United States, an image that the COS surely hoped to dispel in Indianapolis. Visitors became known as "Lady Bountiful," who often came across as well-intended but patronizing, sanctimonious, and out of touch with the realities of poverty. In the satirical 1898 short story "Company Manners," for example, rich and poor women met during a friendly visit that highlighted what had become stereotypes. The visitor, moved to volunteer by a vague sense of duty, viewed her "case" with indifference, boredom, and condescension. She spoke mainly in platitudes, using the royal "we." The client spoke in educated dialect and could recite the visitor's robotic questions by rote: "Ain't it 'most time for you to say now, 'I will make out an order for a few groceries'?"[37] While the plot resolved when the women recognized a common human experience, COS leaders took exception to the story as an unfair portrayal of organized charity methods.[38]

The corps of Indianapolis friendly visitors appears to have peaked at seventy-five in 1894. The COS told the public that those visitors were its agents who delivered "sympathy, encouragement, and hopefulness," more important than any material wants.[39] The COS promised that volunteers would conduct their home visits and investigations "with the utmost kindness and delicacy."[40] Yet the language of the appeal for visitors belied the very delicacy the COS promised by describing the poor as inmates in their own homes: visitors entered "these humble dwellings in no patronizing way, but recognizing ... the brother-hood and sisterhood of every inmate."[41] The COS targeted women from the most prominent neighborhoods, "up and down Meridian and Pennsylvania and Illinois Streets," who would come "out of their homes that are luxurious and beautiful ... and become the voluntary servants of the poor and needy."[42] Records do not indicate that peer relationships among visitor and client ever developed. The few resulting sustained relationships reflected mentor to men-tee, or "special guardian-mother" to child, much as "Company Manners" sati-rized.[43] Much of the rhetoric surrounding friendly visitor qualifications made the job seem challenging but feasible for people of the proper temperament. *Friendly Visiting among the Poor* (1899) described visiting as neither a pleasant diversion nor an exacting profession but "intimate and continuous knowledge with a poor family's joys, sorrows, opinions, feelings, and entire outlook upon life."[44] An article in *Charities* similarly stated that "friendliness is the most natural thing in the world" and that visitors need only be truly friendly and patient enough to wait for results.[45]

Indianapolis no doubt had friendly and patient citizens, but most did not embrace friendly visiting. By the end of 1896, only thirty visitors volunteered for the COS. In two more years, the number had dropped to twenty. COS General Secretary Charles Grout spent much of his time in 1895 and 1896 personally soliciting ministers' support and courting current and prospective friendly visitors.[46] Grout compiled church membership rosters and met with ladies aid societies and other charitable groups to drum up support. Visitors expressed hopelessness with their clients and were discouraged that their clients had deceived them or would not heed advice. Ladies usually pledged their com-mitment to the work, but their enthusiasm more often failed to materialize.[47]

By the end of 1899, the COS bemoaned that friendly visiting was "practically at a standstill."[48] The Society of Friendly Visitors minutes from 1896 to 1901 pro-vide insight as to why this initiative had stalled. Eight women resurrected the dormant society with the object of "holding regular meetings in which there may be a free interchange of thought as to the best methods of doing friendly visiting."[49] The secretary's deliberate use of the word *free* indicated a previous environment not conducive to information exchange. Sources do not allow us to know, however, who squelched the conversation, or at least gave the ladies the impression of limiting conversation.

The newly established visitors' society met monthly and discussed approxi-mately ten cases. Brief commentary recorded whether children attended school and whether adults were working, in jail, or in the hospital. Early meetings reflected enthusiasm, as visitors perceived improvements in their clients' situations. On one pleasant day, the women felt engaged and interested and metaphorically "left loaded with roses." Optimism gave way to frustration, and reports began to be "somewhat discouraging in regard to most of the families."[50] The Society of Friendly Visitors sputtered and expired by 1901 as it had done in the 1880s. As friendly visitors retreated around 1900, the COS began to lobby for trained workers, opening the door for someone with interest and expertise: Edna Henry.

HENRY'S INFLUENCE IN SOCIAL WELFARE

Henry began training COS visitors in 1907, two years after moving to Indianapolis. Her integral role in social welfare from then on helps us understand the evolution of social casework in the city. Many social welfare studies allude to or explicitly address the professionalization of social work, often concluding that paid, trained, professional social workers gradually replaced COSs' volunteer friendly visitors. A close examination of Indianapolis demonstrates the nuances of this trend and Indiana University's demand for a social work school. Henry's name first appears in Charity Organization Society of Indianapolis minutes in 1908. The annual report notes that friendly visiting had "always been one of the most difficult to develop, and yet it is one of the greatest value. A class of volunteer students have been working the past year under the able guidance of Miss Edna G. Henry, her visitors being persons interested in the unfortunate. Here is a great and useful field for the volunteer college worker."[51] The COS had been training young people for "charity work" for a few years but noted that it could not meet the demand for "efficient service" even after it had trained nine young people for social service employment in recent months. Its new lecture series, taught in part by Indiana University's U. G. Weatherly, was an important aspect of the training program.[52] In 1909 Henry presented her paper "Friendly Visiting" at the annual meeting of COS of Indianapolis, after it had practiced friendly visiting for decades. The Indianapolis Star reported that "she showed what had been done in the line" and that "friendly visitors visit dwellings and see the actual conditions that exist to really appreciate the opportunities" to assist the poor.[53]

Henry embedded her expertise deeply into the organized charity network, which had been growing in tandem with the Indianapolis economy and population. She held leadership in three influential, interrelated social welfare agencies: the Children's Aid Association (CAA), Mothers' Aid Society (MAS), and the COS of Indianapolis. Her casework expertise is imprinted in each agency's theory and practice and clearly prepared her to lead IU's Social Service Department.

One of the most successful child welfare agencies in Indianapolis, the Children's Aid Association (CAA), incorporated in 1905 "to aid and protect children" with "its membership comprised of all probation officers of the Marion County Juvenile Court." Born out of several related child-welfare initiatives, the CAA emerged from the Board of Children's Guardians, the juvenile court, and the Volunteer Probation Officers Association.[54] The juvenile court judge's experience led him to believe a "specific volunteer organization" would best coordinate children's services in the city. Henry's name first appears in 1907 as a director of the Employment Committee, the team responsible for managing probation officers and "preventing as well as curing delinquency" by placing children into urban homes, on farms, or into age-appropriate, wholesome employment positions.[55] The CAA, like the COS, made many of the same promises to their constituencies in classic scientific philanthropy fashion: coordination, cooperation, investigation, efficiency, modern business methods, personal service, and relief only through human friendliness.[56]

Investigation required training and experience, as no one could by chance discover the significant facts of a case when the facts hung "in the air."[57] In its first five years of operation, the CAA claimed effectiveness and penetration deep into poor or troubled families. Volunteer probation officers used statistical blanks virtually identical to COS application forms.[58] Like COS friendly visitors, volunteer probation officers received an instructional pamphlet to guide them on befriending children and becoming a positive influence in their lives (see table 10.1). Guidance to probation officers was strikingly similar to the COS's instructions to friendly visitors.[59]

As mothers' and children's welfare are naturally interdependent, women also volunteered in large numbers for the Mothers' Aid Society (MAS), founded in 1907. Henry was one of ten founding executive committee members of the agency, which sought to "offer any and every sort of permanent assistance to any widow or deserted woman, with young children, who requires it." Without the burden of rent, the MAS wrote, mothers could be "free and able to meet all other needs of their families."[60] The MAS never drifted from its original conception as an "organization of women, managed by women, for women."[61] In 1915, approximately sixty volunteer visitors, largely comprised of MAS member/donors, made weekly calls on widows and families either to determine necessary aid or to provide advice.[62] Visitors sometimes remained advisors to their clients long after direct assistance was no longer necessary.[63]

Table 10.1. Guidance to probation officers

CAA Volunteer Probation Officers Guidance on Working with Delinquent Children	COS Friendly Visitors Guidance on Working with Poor Families
Gain confidence of child	Get acquainted with family
You are to be a friend	Establish a friendly relationship
Never let him deceive you	Be very guarded
Study home conditions	Study home and neighborhood, suggest changes
Study habits and interests	Learn outside influences
Visit school and teacher	Get children into kindergarten or Sunday school
Visit employer (if applicable) and understand labor conditions	Give advice or assistance regarding employment
Encourage savings	Create the habits of saving and thrift
Encourage relationship with church	Encourage church attendance
Encourage reading and library use	Take books and read stories to children
Do not discipline	No advice unless asked
Report regularly to court	Report regularly to COS
Chief probation officer supervises volunteer	Society of Friendly Visitors supervises volunteers
Do not become discouraged	Do not feel discouragement or failure

In addition to serving in CAA and MAS leadership roles, Henry became a COS leader in short order. Front-line COS employees and volunteers assessed families' needs, determined the extent of existing available resources, and recommended action. A district committee wielded the COS's power as it diagnosed applicants' domestic problems and set the course for possible government or private response. As districts expanded, a central council formed to preside weekly over *all* district committees to establish referrals to related agencies or set conditions for assistance. By 1910, Henry served on the central council as part of the leadership team that included the senior staff and visitors. This role provided her a holistic view of clients' circumstances and the network of agencies that could aid them.[64]

Through the 1910s, the COS emphasized friendly visiting less and professional casework more, consistent with national trends.[65] Popular and professional opinions increasingly regarded "Lady Bountiful" as outmoded, presumptuous, and cocooned in her socioeconomic class.[66] Taken to the extreme, as in Konrad Bercovici's *Crimes of Charity* (1917), she was a villain in a criminal system that ruined the lives of the poor.[67] Staffing decisions in Indianapolis gradually supported the Boston COS founder's observation that "philanthropy is becoming a business and a profession."[68] By 1915, the COS employed three full-time fundraisers and ten full-time caseworkers; it added four additional caseworkers by 1921.[69] Staff worked hard for relatively low salary, causing burnout and illness, and therefore turnover.[70] During the 1910s COSs used volunteers to supplement staff depending on workforce strength at a particular time.[71] The Indianapolis COS accordingly did not abandon friendly visiting, even as paid staff gradually assumed the majority of casework responsibility. It resurrected its dormant Society of Friendly Visitors in 1914; the society's president, Julia Jameson, hoped to "give joy to others" and "asked that a new era might be started" for visitors.[72] She noted within a few months that "by giving themselves [in volunteer service] the Friendly Visitors are doing real constructive social work."[73] This group of women, however, experienced the same pattern of highs and lows as the previous society women had: initial enthusiasm, an ephemeral feeling of making a difference, then disappointment when clients' living conditions did not substantially change.[74]

HIGHER EDUCATION AND INSTITUTION BUILDING

While the pendulum swung between friendly visitor and caseworker within social welfare agencies, Indiana University looked toward expanding its educational offerings. The meaning of casework, as well as who conducted it, evolved with the organized charity movement. Individual investigations for decades had aimed at the material, moral, and spiritual elevation of the poor with nominal concern for economic structures or the environment in which individuals lived. Casework after 1911 produced not only a decision on aid based on putative worthiness but a "social diagnosis." Likening social work to medicine, the first social work textbook defined social diagnosis as "the attempt to arrive at as exact a definition as possible of the social situation and personality of a given client."[75] By 1920, the Indianapolis COS defined case treatment as the process that "seeks out the causes of distress and poverty. [Casework] seeks out the resources of the family, and the community for combating these causes, and it makes the connection to get this curative treatment in motion."[76] Historian Robert Wiebe further clarified how science undergirded social work, calling casework "the scientific analysis of a life in process."[77] Investigation, social research, and scientific method intertwined to lead caseworkers to a diagnosis.

In Indianapolis, formal and extensive training began in 1890—earlier than in most cities, although many historians credit the New York COS's practitioner training, its Summer School of Applied Philanthropy (1898), as forming first. The Indianapolis COS created a formal lecture series in practical sociology when Alexander Johnson, newly arrived in Indiana from Chicago's COS, taught the first ten-part "Study Class in Social Science in the Department of Charity" at Plymouth Church.[78] He began by clearing away "the hazy and inaccurate ideas [about] whether there is a science of charities."[79] Johnson took students to the field to study "charity in a practical manner" at the County Asylum.[80] Training expanded with Butler College and Indiana University professors conducting lectures and discussions for staff and volunteers. An internal sketch of the COS called Johnson's class the first planned social work course and claimed that his class influenced the organization of Indiana University's Social Service Department.[81]

Social work today encompasses many practice settings.[82] Functional specialization began early in the twentieth century; hospital, or medical, social work and family social work initially dominated the field.[83] Medical social work developed early because COSs' three decades worth of data had demonstrated *convincingly* that illness led to unemployment and poverty.[84] With the concomitant rise of scientific medicine, hospitals emerged from asylums and poorhouses into legitimate institutions in which people of all classes sought medical treatment. Dispensaries and hospitals accordingly faced increasing demand for services without the ability to assist clients with long-term recovery after medical treatment was completed.

The first formal *medical* social service department began in 1905 at Boston's Massachusetts General Hospital, ushering in a national movement.[85] Indianapolis was not far behind, but to form a school of medical social work the city required a hospital or dispensary—and a champion. U. G. Weatherly had been teaching what he called "practical sociology" in cooperation with the COS for several years and had come to view social work through the lens of sociology. He believed the principles of social action could be found through the study of groups, not isolated individuals, so a research facility that collected data on a group of patients could illuminate the causes of social problems.[86]

HENRY ORGANIZES THE SOCIAL SERVICE DEPARTMENT

The Indianapolis medical landscape included the public hospital (City Hospital), the City Dispensary, and three denominational hospitals when the Indiana University School of Medicine (IUSM) formed in 1907. Until then, twenty-four proprietary medical colleges had existed in the state at some point during the nineteenth century. Without regulatory oversight, schools did not have to be well capitalized, academically rigorous, or scientifically legitimate in order to enroll students and award degrees.[87] After IU president William Bryan surveyed the medical education landscape, he reported to his board of trustees in March 1903 that the trend in medical education was moving away from proprietary schools toward endowed universities. He recommended that Indiana University "establish the medical department at once."[88] The trustees agreed, but rivalry between Indiana and Purdue University for dominion over the state's medical education system culminated in competing bills in the 1907 Indiana General Assembly. Edna Henry's father, Charles Henry, argued the case on behalf of Indiana University. Purdue withdrew, leaving Indiana with exclusive rights to medical education in the state.[89]

Weatherly chose to form the Social Service Department close to IUSM, the City Dispensary, and the plethora of social service agencies in Indianapolis. In 1911, Indiana University established the Social Service Department, a sub-department of Economics and Social Science, housed with the IUSM and the dispensary.[90] A 1911 bequest from Dr. Robert W. and Clara J. Long endowed the Robert W. Long Hospital of Indiana University to serve the State of Indiana's rural poor.[91] Once the 138-bed hospital opened in 1914, the Social Service Department moved its main operations there.[92]

The new Social Service Department served two masters: Charles P. Emerson, IUSM's dean, and U. G. Weatherly, chair of economics and social science. Emerson had seen hospital social work develop when Johns Hopkins University medical students in 1902 formed an auxiliary board of the Baltimore COS to visit poor families in their homes. Students learned the intimate relationship between the home environment and physical illness.[93] Emerson therefore supported Weatherly and the Social Service Department at Indiana University as he believed social work added to medical students' appreciation of a patient as a whole person, not just an aggregation of organs.[94]

Emerson and Weatherly appointed Edna Henry to organize the department; records do not indicate that they considered any other candidate for the position. Henry's active participation in social networks and social welfare agencies prepared her well, and she embraced the job wholeheartedly. Henry built the Social Service Department on organized charity principles: prevention of future illness through patient education, research and data collection to end illness and poverty, and the education of doctors, social work professionals, and "all persons interested in social conditions."[95] Like the COS, the department recorded extensive demographic patient data and its own version of a circle of charities, claiming forty-four agencies and nineteen churches with which it cooperated to serve its patients. It reported a team of two hundred volunteers to multiply the paid workforce and to "come into closer relations with the patient, and a more kindly humane one, than can any member of the department."[96] It is not clear whether Henry truly managed two hundred volunteers. Two hundred may have been an exaggeration, but even a fraction of that number was many times more than the city's charities ever rallied.

Early on, physicians were reluctant to refer patients to the department as they did not expect it to survive, but the Social Service Department assisted over 3,200 patients in its first five years.[97] Even by its fifth year, the department saw a small fraction of dispensary patients, who poured in at a rate of over one hundred people per day.[98] Henry was undaunted by physicians' slow acceptance of social work. As she built the department on COS theory and practice, she validated many of its findings about the causes of poverty and possible solutions.[99] The 1915 Indiana University newsletter described the department as a "sociological laboratory" that showed sickness to be the leading cause of dependency and asserted that doctors, social workers, universities, relief agencies, and the public should all join forces to save ill patients—and therefore the entire city. The department pledged to act as the "sharp sword of the new alliance" to bridge theory and practice.[100]

Henry embodied the bridge between theory and practice, as she earned her master's and doctorate degrees while building, staffing, and operating her department.[101] Social work training connected Indiana University, the COS, and the CAA. Weatherly led weekly lectures at the COS, promoted as valuable to both "the Church and Social Worker," which Henry attended as her schedule permitted.[102] Henry coordinated weekly talks for her students on medical and social issues, delivered by herself, Weatherly, IU doctors, and COS and CAA executives.[103] She collected both theoretical and practical textbooks for the department's library and established the school's curriculum to include research methods, sociology, and practical training.[104]

The Social Service Department stated three missions of equal weight from its inception: teaching, prevention, and research.[105] The department had to define its missions with clarity and regularity. Its leaders believed social workers had to acquire scientific knowledge of the relationship between disease and social conditions, thus they had to understand people and their neighborhoods, schools, and industries. As such their work was not purely clinical; it was a humanitarian endeavor.[106] Social work, however, was *not* charity. It was clear in Edna Henry's mind that social workers could facilitate recovery from illness through patient education and connection to resources while the COS and other charities relieved the immediate conditions of poverty.[107] She had difficulty convincing the general populace of this distinction. Seeking publicity advice in 1919, she bemoaned that "the majority of the people in Indianapolis and Indiana still think that we are some sort of branch of the COS or . . . the Red Cross or the jail."[108] To increase awareness, provide oversight, and raise funds for the school, Henry created a female advisory committee of prominent women who were active volunteers in social welfare agencies.[109] The women understood that medical social work among the sick poor had proven to be vital. They raised funds for two full-time staff members through donations and a special knitting fund and followed individual cases with particular interest.[110]

SOCIAL WORK MERGES PRACTICE, THEORY, AND EDUCATION

Henry filled a unique and vital role within Indiana University during the 1910s as the Social Service Department director. She had to navigate, and often succeeded in linking, multiple domains: male and female, volunteer and professional, social agency and higher education, the worlds of wealth and privilege and poverty and illness, and local and national communities. Henry remained embedded in the inner workings of Indianapolis charities, the COS in particular. Henry at times mediated her students' relationships with the COS, which influenced her own status with the agency. Social work students and graduates moved to and from the COS and other agencies with fluidity. Current and prospective students confided in Henry about either their satisfaction or displeasure with working at the COS. Crystal Benton Fall, for example, graduated from the Social Service Department, volunteered as a COS friendly visitor, and later joined the COS staff as a paid caseworker. Henry held Crystal Fall in high regard and supported her when she abruptly left the COS in 1915.[111] Six months later, Charles Grout retired from the COS, and rumors flew through the social service community about his successor. Although the COS never offered her a position, Henry believed she was a potential candidate. Weatherly advised her to stay out of the "COS muddle" and not to abandon the social work school for the "stormy times" that were surely ahead if she were to leave. Henry concurred, adding that she sympathized with whoever joined the COS.[112] Neither the school nor the COS, however, could deny the other's role in serving the sick poor of Indianapolis, so cross-training continued despite the tension.

The COS had preached that "any woman with a kindly heart, common sense, faith, and a sense of responsibility" could be an excellent volunteer but acknowledged the "usefulness" of an even rarer commodity: the professional social worker. Training made for better staff members, but volunteers' intimate knowledge of the conditions of the poor benefited everyone: the poor, the volunteer, the social worker, and the community.[113] The new Indianapolis COS general secretary, Eugene Foster, began to hire either graduates of social work schools or caseworkers with prior experience.[114] He wrote that with appropriate staffing and direction, the COS would enter "upon a new era in Indianapolis Social Work."[115] Foster optimistically envisioned some elusive ideal blend of love, religion, and science: "As true scientists, we long for the ability to combine with delicacy and precision, the elements necessary to produce the desired results. . . . We shall have to release in proportionate parts, all that we have of heart, brain and energy."[116]

Over time, the CAA aligned closely with professional social work. Its 1916 *Our Children* included a scathing story about "My Lady Bountiful" and surrounded it with photos of smiling, prize-winning babies. "My Lady Bountiful" captured every negative stereotype in a mere ten inches of type. She went "slumming," patronized "the poor things," promised "abundantly" but delivered only a modicum of assistance.[117] The 1917 *Our Children* described social work at length as "a task of education" and equated good casework with a medical diagnosis.[118] The CAA recognized the balance of character and education: "Social workers should be people of upright character and natural aptitude . . . [and] as well trained and qualified for his task as the school teacher or the health officer." It continued, "She must have a course of practical work, combined with certain prescribed reading and instruction and study," adding that the local college's training, presumably IU's Social Service Department, was second to none.[119]

Henry's quest for a blend of character and education remained equally elusive. After years of practice and teaching, she ultimately believed she understood who made an ideal social worker: "No amount of training will make a good social worker out of a person without good health, imagination, or the wrong temperament, or character, or personal appearance. Any successful social worker must be a teacher, and the best teaching is by example."[120] The social worker-teacher, she continued, must be able to work effectively with patients, doctors, students, and volunteers. Finally, this rare individual must "have a true knowledge of the texture of normal society, of modern social problems, of the interrelation of dependence and disease."[121] By the end of her tenure as director, Henry's realization that teaching and communication skills outweighed casework skills appears to have been painful for her to admit. Her conclusion that this work relied more on innate talents than education placed her at odds with the emerging social work pedagogy that emphasized casework skills, sound reasoning, clear thinking, and advanced standards.[122]

HENRY'S LATER YEARS

As social welfare agencies vacillated between volunteer and professional, and social case workers struggled for status and legitimacy, Edna Henry ultimately faced an enemy she could not defeat: illness. Henry suffered an undiagnosed medical event in March 1918 at the age of forty-four. Later that year she battled influenza. By May 1919, she despaired to President Bryan of the "trying situation" of her "long illness, the influenza epidemic, the war, consequent restlessness, the changing conditions of women everywhere."[123] The energy and drive in her previous correspondence began to dissipate, replaced by fatigue and frustration. Late in 1920 Henry wrote that her physician insisted "that I stay in my room," the terrifying fate that Charlotte Perkins Gilman hauntingly portrayed in *The Yellow Wallpaper*.[124] She resigned as Social Service Department director in 1921 but taught classes in her home until 1926 while confined to a wheelchair.

By the early 1920s, Dr. Edna Henry's contributions had left their indelible mark on her students, on Indiana University's Social Service Department, on the social welfare agencies she had served, and among her male colleagues. Social work had become a way of life and established a new field that allowed women to fuse both traditional and emerging spheres into a single profession: traditional domesticity, benevolence, women and children's issues, civic engagement, the scientific method, medical education, and social science. As such, social workers advocated for systemic solutions to poverty, much as the wider social welfare field had come to understand.[125] Historian Mary Ritter Beard remarked, for example, that more social workers agreed on the wisdom of mothers' pensions than any other single piece of social welfare legislation.[126] Nationally, the Russell Sage Foundation (1907) devoted itself to modernizing social work, advancing women's and children's welfare, and shaping reform in housing, city planning, industrial relations, and social research.[127] Dr. Edna Henry positioned Indiana University's Social Service Department as a national leader in medical social work with a rare understanding of the connections between wide cultural influences and the most intimate details of family life. Whether installed at a university, hospital, charitable agency, or foundation, the professional social worker had arrived.

NOTES

1. "Fund Picks Woman as 'Best Citizen,'" *Indianapolis Star*, February 19, 1924, Indiana State Library Clipping File, Biography: Henry, Indiana State Library, Indianapolis, Indiana.

2. "Unusual Honor for Miss Edna G. Henry," *Indianapolis News*, October 16, 1925, Indiana State Library Clipping File, Biography: Henry, Indiana State Library, Indianapolis, Indiana.

3. This chapter will refer to the school as the Social Service Department for consistency. Debra Mesch, Una Osili, Jacqueline Ackerman, and Elizabeth Dale, *How and Why Women Give: Current and Future Directions for Research on Women's Philanthropy* (Indianapolis, IN: IUPUI Women's Philanthropy Institute, May 2015), 8.

4. Thomas D. Clark, *Indiana University: Midwestern Pioneer*, Vol. 2 (Bloomington: Indiana University Press, 1973), 65.

5. Thomas D. Clark, *Indiana University: Midwestern Pioneer*, Vol. 1. (Bloomington: Indiana University Press, 1970), 297.

6. William Lowe Bryan (1860–1955), born on a farm near Bloomington, Indiana, earned his PhD in psychology from Clark University (1892) and held various positions at Indiana University: professor of philosophy 1885–1902, vice president 1893–1902, and tenth president 1902–37. IU evolved from a small liberal arts college into a modern research university during Bryan's tenure (see https://president .iu.edu/about/past-presidents/bryan-william.html). See also William Lowe Bryan, "Economy in University Administration," *Science* 36, no. 915 (July 12, 1912): 41–45.

7. Abraham Flexner, *Medical Education in the United States and Canada* (New York: Carnegie Foundation for the Advancement of Teaching, 1910), 20; Kenneth Ludmerer, *Learning to Heal: The Development of American Medical Education* (New York: Basic Books, 1985), 6; and Joe Robertson Jr., "Indiana Frontiers in Medical Education," *Journal of the Indiana State Medical Association* 66, no. 10 (October 1973): 943–52.

8. Ronnie J. Steinberg and Jerry A. Jacobs, "Pay Equity in Nonprofit Organizations: Making Women's Work Visible," in *Women and Power in the Nonprofit Sector*, ed. Teresa Odendahl and Michael O'Neill (San Francisco: Jossey-Bass, 1994), 94.

9. Suzanne Lebsock, *The Free Women of Petersburg: Status and Culture in a Southern Town, 1784–1860* (New York: W. W. Norton & Co., 1984), 198, 229–30.

10. Kathleen D. McCarthy, "Parallel Power Structures: Women and the Voluntary Sphere," in *Lady Bountiful Revisited: Women, Philanthropy, and Power*, ed. Kathleen D. McCarthy (New Brunswick, NJ: Rutgers University Press, 1990), 1.

11. Katherine E. Badertscher, "Organized Charity and the Civic Ideal in Indianapolis, 1879–1922" (PhD diss., Indiana University, 2015), 4.

12. Mary Richmond (1861–1928) delivered a historic speech in 1897 at the National Conference of Charities and Correction, calling for a professional school in "applied" philanthropy to train social workers. She published the first comprehensive presentation of practical suggestions, *Friendly Visiting among the Poor: A Handbook for Charity Workers* (New York: Macmillan, 1899). Richmond also served as

general secretary of the Philadelphia Society for Organizing Charity and director of the Russell Sage Foundation's Charity Organization Department. Her *Social Diagnosis* (New York: Russell Sage Foundation, 1917) formalized the concept of social work as a democratic process in which the caseworker and client could cooperate for mutual advantage; it was widely hailed as the first formulation of theory and method in identifying the problems of clients.

13. For a biographical sketch of Jane Addams (1860–1935), see Kathi C. Badertscher, "Addams, Jane," *1914–1918 Online: International Encyclopedia of the First World War*, last modified October 8, 2014, https://encyclopedia.1914–1918-online. net/article/addams_jane.

14. The Indianapolis population was 1,900 in 1830 and only 2,700 by 1840. "Indianapolis Benevolent Society," *Indianapolis Journal*, December 17, 1872, 4.

15. Nancy Fraser and Linda Gordon, "A Genealogy of Dependency: Tracing a Keyword of the U.S. Welfare State," *Signs* 19, no. 2 (winter 1994): 316.

16. Charles Loring Brace, *The Dangerous Classes of New York, & Twenty Years' Work Among Them* (New York: Wynkoop & Hallenbeck, 1872), 383–84.

17. Brace, *The Dangerous Classes of New York*, 386.

18. Robert H. Bremner, *American Philanthropy*, 2nd ed. (Chicago: University of Chicago Press, 1988), 87.

19. Bremner, *American Philanthropy*, 85–99; Peter Dobkin Hall, "The Community Foundation in America, 1914–1987," in *Philanthropic Giving: Studies in Varieties and Goals*, ed. Richard Magat (New York: Oxford University Press, 1989), 183; Judith Sealander, "Curing Evils at Their Source: The Arrival of Scientific Giving," in *Charity, Philanthropy, and Civility in American History*, ed. Lawrence Friedman and Mark McGarvie (New York: Cambridge University Press, 2003), 218.

20. George W. Geib, *Indianapolis: Hoosiers' Circle City* (Tulsa, OK: Continental Heritage Press, 1981), 48.

21. Clifton J. Phillips, *Indiana in Transition: The Emergence of an Industrial Commonwealth, 1880–1920* (Indianapolis: Indiana Historical Bureau and Indiana Historical Society, 1968), 276.

22. "Benevolence," *Indianapolis Journal*, January 17, 1879, 8; COS Historical Sketch, ca. 1910, Box 3, Folder 5, The Family Service Association of Indianapolis Records, 1879–1971, Collection #M0102, Indiana Historical Society, Indianapolis, Indiana (hereafter: FSA Records).

23. Ruth Crocker, "Making Charity Modern: Business and the Reform of Charities in Indianapolis, 1879–1930," *Business and Economic History*, 2nd series, 12 (1983): 161; Stephen Ray Hall, "Oscar McCulloch and Indiana Eugenics" (PhD diss., Virginia Commonwealth University, 1993), 100, 133–34, 140; Michael B. Katz, *In the Shadow of the Poorhouse: A Social History of Welfare in America*, rev. ed. (New York: Basic Books, 1996), 85.

24. Oscar C. McCulloch, "Fifty Years' Work of the Indianapolis Benevolent So-ciety," *Year-Book of Charities: 1885–86*, Indiana Historical Society Pamphlet Collec-tion, 18.

25. Mary Ann Suppes and Carolyn Cressy Wells, *The Social Work Experience: An Introduction to Social Work and Social Welfare*, 3rd ed. (Boston: McGraw Hill, 2000), 6–12.

26. Mary Richmond codified these principles in *Friendly Visiting among the Poor* (1899) and her National Conference of Charities and Correction speech "Chari-table Cooperation" (1901), for which she received national recognition.

27. Anderson's population in 1890 was 10,719 and in 1900 was 20,178. See US Census Bureau, "Population of Cities, Towns Villages and Boroughs," in *Eleventh Census (Part I & Part II) Report on Population of the United States*, Vol. 1 (October 24, 1884), Table No. 8, 378, https://www.census.gov/library/publications/1895/dec/volume-1.html; and US Census Bureau, "Population of Indiana by Minor Civil Divisions, 1880–1990," in Census Bulletin of the Twelfth Census of the United States: Indiana (December 18, 1900), no. 22, Table 4, 9, https://www.census.gov/library/publications/1900/dec/bulletins.Demographics.html (accessed July 23, 2020).

28. "Funeral of Traction Head to be Thursday," *Indianapolis News*, May 3, 1927; "An Interurban City," *Forward! The Magazine for Indianapolis*, February 1911; Jerry Marlette, "Interurbans," in *The Encyclopedia of Indianapolis*, ed. David J. Boden-hamer and Robert G. Barrows (Bloomington: Indiana University Press, 1994), 824–27.

29. "Scrapbook Shows Size of Anderson's 'Heart,'" *Anderson Herald Bulletin*, April 12, 1962, 7.

30. "Family Service Marks 70th Year," *Anderson Sunday Herald*, May 6, 1973.

31. The panel addressed alumni as the rivalry between Indiana and Purdue for dominion over the state's medical education system had heated to a fever pitch. Walter J. Daly, "The Origins of President Bryan's Medical School," *Indiana Maga-zine of History* 98, no. 4 (December 2002): 279.

32. Attorney Charles Warren Fairbanks (R) served as US senator (1897–1905) and US vice president (1905–09). "Social Side of City," *Indianapolis Star*, October 7, 1908.

33. Fortnightly Literary Club members regularly presented papers on charity, philanthropy, and social science during the 1890s and 1900s.

34. March 12, 1880 report of the Committee on District Work, BV 1170, FSA Records.

35. Dorothy G. Becker, "Exit Lady Bountiful: The Volunteer and the Profes-sional Social Worker," *Social Service Review* 38, no. 1 (March 1964): 57–72; Kenneth L. Kusmer, "The Functions of Organized Charity in the Progressive Era: Chicago

as a Case Study," *Journal of American History* 60, no. 3 (December 1973): 657–58; Roy Lubove, *The Professional Altruist: The Emergence of Social Work as a Career, 1880–1930* (New York: Atheneum, 1983); Kathleen D. McCarthy, *Noblesse Oblige: Charity & Cultural Philanthropy in Chicago, 1849–1929* (Chicago: University of Chicago Press, 1982); Edward N. Saveth, "Patrician Philanthropy in America: The Late Nineteenth and Early Twentieth Centuries," *Social Service Review* 54, no. 1 (March 1980): 76–91.

36. 1880 Pamphlet "The Need and Work of Visitors," BV 1170, FSA Records.

37. Florence Converse, "Company Manners," *Atlantic Monthly* 81, no. 483 (January 1898): 133.

38. Richmond, *Friendly Visiting among the Poor*, 195.

39. 1894 Annual Report, Box 4, Folder 7, FSA Records.

40. 1896 Annual Report, Box 4, Folder 8, FSA Records.

41. 1895 Annual Report, Box 4, Folder 7, FSA Records.

42. 1896 Annual Report.

43. 1896 Annual Report.

44. Richmond, *Friendly Visiting among the Poor*, 180.

45. "The Friendly Visitor of the Charitable Society," *Charities* 10, no. 14 (April 1903): 325.

46. Charles Spaulding Grout (1858–1944) graduated from Black River Academy in Vermont and worked for Atlas Engine Works for eleven years before joining the COS. Grout replaced James Smith, who had served as COS executive secretary since 1889. His wife, Emma Doran Grout, participated in several COS committees. They belonged to University Park Christian Church. "Charles S. Grout," Biography Series Vol. 28, 1, Indiana State Library (ISL).

47. Journal 1895–1896, BV 1173, FSA Records.

48. 1899 Annual Report, Box 4, Folder 8, FSA Records.

49. Society of Friendly Visitors Secretary's Book, 1896–1901, BV 1182, FSA Records.

50. Society of Friendly Visitors Secretary's Book, 1896–1901.

51. Annual Report 1908–9, Box 5, Folder 1, FSA Records.

52. Ulysses Grant Weatherly (1865–1940), professor of economics and social science; president, American Sociology Society; president, Indiana Conference of Charities and Correction. Weatherly lectured in 1908 for the COS on the physical basis of society, the family as a social unit, social aspects of youth, the parasitic classes, social progress and the industrial order, and social solidarity. Delbert C. Miller, *One Hundred Years: The History of Sociology at Indiana University, 1885–1985* (Bloomington: Indiana University, 1985), 11–23. Weatherly gave six lectures in 1908: Historical Evolution of the Family; The Man of the Family; Female Workers, Married and Unmarried; Economic Aspects of Childhood; Housing and Home Life; and Social Ethics of the Family and Divorce. Annual Report 1908–9, Box 5, Folder 1, FSA Records.

53. "Points Out Some Evils That May Destroy Many Homes," *Indianapolis Star*, December 7, 1909, 3.

54. The CAA was first titled the Children's Aid Society; it changed its name to Children's Aid Association to avoid confusion with the Indianapolis Free Kindergarten and Children's Aid Society. Children's Aid Association, Articles of Incorporation, Box 1, Folder 8, FSA Records.

55. Children's Aid Association, *The First Report of the Children's Aid Association of Indianapolis, February 11, 1905 to October 31, 1908* (Indianapolis: Children's Aid Association, 1908), 16–18.

56. Children's Aid Association, *The First Report*, 8.

57. Frank D. Loomis, "The Children's Aid Association of Indianapolis," *The Indiana Bulletin: Proceedings of the Annual State Conference of Charities and Correction* (ISL Clipping File: Indianapolis—Charities, 1930–1939): 418. Date of article estimated at 1909.

58. Probation forms for children's case histories requested name, address, age, sex, legitimacy, race, school, grade, mental ability, birthplace, physical condition, arrest record, home conditions, habits, siblings, and associates. The forms requested the same information for the child's parents, plus nationality, religion, education, occupations, income, and mental condition. "The New Juvenile Court Forms," *The Indiana Bulletin: Proceedings of the Annual State Conference of Charities and Correction* (June 1907): 9; Harald Salomon, *The Juvenile Court: Indianapolis* (Indianapolis: Juvenile Court of Indianapolis, 1910), 18.

59. Badertscher, "Organized Charity and the Civic Ideal," 295, 302–3.

60. First Annual Report of Mothers' Aid Society, 1908, Box 5, Folder 13, FSA Records.

61. Mothers' Aid Society, "For Our Friendly Visitor," 1915, Indiana Department of Public Welfare Manuscript Collection, Collection #L196, ISL.

62. 1917 Auditor's Report for Mothers' Aid Society, Box 1, Folder 12, FSA Records.

63. Mothers' Aid Society Minutes November 8, 1916, COS Minutes 1916–1920, BV 1171, FSA Records.

64. The Indianapolis COS began operations under the assumption that one district committee, essentially encompassing the Mile Square, could manage all relief applications. As the organization matured and the city's population climbed, the COS expanded to three district committees in tandem with police precincts. COS Council Meeting Minutes 1910–1911, Box 1, Folder 3, FSA Records; Mothers' Aid Society Annual Reports, 1908, 1909, 1910, and 1911, Box 5, Folder 13, FSA Records; Lois Ann Piepho, "The History of the Social Service Department of the Indiana University Medical Center, 1911–1932" (master's thesis, Indiana University, 1950).

65. Becker, "Exit Lady Bountiful," 57–72; Edward T. Devine, *The Practice of Charity: Individual, Associated and Organized* (New York: Lentilhon & Company, 1901), 104–20; Katz, *In the Shadow of the Poorhouse*, 168–77; Lubove, *The Profes-*

sional Altruist, 49–52; McCarthy, *Noblesse Oblige*, 136–38; Walter I. Trattner, *From Poor Law to Welfare State*, 6th ed. (New York: Free Press, 1999), 233–52; Frank Dekker Watson, *The Charity Organization Movement in the United States: A Study in American Philanthropy* (New York: Macmillan Company, 1922), 422–24, 440–41.

66. Dawn Marie Greeley, "Beyond Benevolence: Gender, Class and the Development of Scientific Charity in New York City, 1882–1935" (PhD diss., State University of New York at Stony Brook, 1995), 241–45; Norman Hapgood, "Modern Charity," *Harper's Weekly* 60, no. 3038 (March 20, 1915): 268.

67. Konrad Bercovici, *Crimes of Charity* (New York: Alfred A. Knopf, 1917).

68. Lubove, *The Professional Altruist*, 49.

69. COS Account Book 1905–1915, BV 1188, FSA Records; 1922 Audit by George S. Olive, CPA, Box 1, Folder 2, FSA Records.

70. COS Minutes 1916–1920, BV 1171, FSA Records.

71. "A Year of Social Service," 1910–11 Annual Report, Box 5, Folder 1, FSA Records; Francis H. McLean, *The Formation of Charity Organization Societies in Smaller Cities* (New York: Russell Sage Foundation, 1910), 25.

72. January 8, 1914 Society of Friendly Visitors Secretary's Book, BV 1183, FSA Records.

73. July 8, 1914 Society of Friendly Visitors Secretary's Book, BV 1183, FSA Records.

74. Meeting attendance varied between twenty-nine and forty-nine women. Fifteen meeting entries between 1914 to 1916, Society of Friendly Visitors Secretary's Book, BV 1183, FSA Records.

75. Richmond, *Social Diagnosis*, 51.

76. 1920 Six Months Report, BV 1171, FSA Records.

77. Robert H. Wiebe, *The Search for Order, 1870–1920* (New York: Hill and Wang, 1967), 150.

78. Alexander Johnson (1847–1941), superintendent, Indiana School for the Feeble Minded (Fort Wayne); secretary, Indiana Board of State Charities; and secretary, NCCC. Plymouth Church housed the COS's offices at this time. Indianapolis Benevolent Society, *Year-Book of Charities: Work of 1889–90* (Indianapolis: Baker Randolph Co., 1893), 32–39.

79. "Benevolent Society's Work," *Indianapolis News*, November 3, 1890, BV 1191, FSA Records.

80. "Over the Hill," *Indianapolis Sentinel*, January 25, 1891, BV 1191, FSA Records.

81. Untitled COS Overview, ca. 1950, Box 3, Folder 5, FSA Records.

82. Practice settings include family and children's services, mental health, the workplace, developmental disability, addiction prevention and treatment, the elderly, and medicine. Suppes and Wells, *The Social Work Experience*, vii–viii.

83. Lubove, *The Professional Altruist*, 22, 32–35.

84. The Indianapolis COS recorded applicants' illness throughout its entire existence. From 1879 to 1896, illness was a class worthy of relief, from 1897 to 1911

a condition of application, and after 1911 a reason for application. Visitors often mentioned illness (tuberculosis, smallpox, diphtheria, scarlet fever) in narratives, usually related to the breadwinner's inability to work and need for medical treatment. Cases of illness peaked in 1918 during the influenza epidemic. Illness and unemployment were consistently the two highest causes of need, but it is not possible to determine how an individual case of illness and unemployment was categorized. BV 1170; BV 1171; Box 1, Folder 4; Box 4, Folder 8; FSA Records. The Board of State Charities similarly reported in 1916 that illness was the leading cause of seeking trustees' assistance. Frances Doan Streightoff and Frank Hatch Streightoff, *Indiana: A Social and Economic Survey* (Indianapolis: W. K. Stewart, 1916), 185.

85. Richmond, *Social Diagnosis*, 35; Watson, *The Charity Organization Movement*, 366.

86. Edna G. Henry, *The Theory and Practice of Medical Social Work* (Ann Arbor: Edwards Brothers, 1924), 20; Helen Cintilda Rogers, *Seventy Years of Social Work Education at Indiana University* (Indianapolis: Indiana University, 1983), 11–12.

87. Burton D. Myers, *The History of Medical Education in Indiana* (Bloomington: Indiana University Press, 1956), 2–17, 80, 90–91.

88. Myers, *The History of Medical Education in Indiana*, 123.

89. Clark, *Indiana University*, Vol. 2, 82; Daly, "The Origins of President Bryan's Medical School," 279; Myers, *The History of Medical Education in Indiana*, 142.

90. Report of the Social Service Department of the Indiana University, September 20, 1911–June 15, 1913, Box 26, Indiana University School of Social Work Records, Ruth Lilly Special Collections and Archives, University Library, Indiana University–Purdue University Indianapolis (hereafter: IUSSW Records).

91. Clark, *Indiana University*, Vol. 2, 98; Katherine Mandusic McDonell, "Hospitals," in *The Encyclopedia of Indianapolis*, 712.

92. The department supervised the social workers working with dispensary patients from its new hospital offices. In 1918, the Social Service Department added operations at City Hospital. Report of the Social Service Department of the Indiana University, June 15, 1913–September 30, 1915, Box 26, IUSSW Records; Alice Shaffer, Mary Wysor Keefer, and Sophonisba P. Breckenridge, *The Indiana Poor Law, Its Development and Administration with Special Reference to the Provision of State Care for the Sick Poor* (Chicago: University of Chicago Press, 1936), 155–57.

93. Charles Phillips Emerson (1872–1938) trained under Dr. William Osler and received his medical degree from Johns Hopkins University School of Medicine. He was resident physician at Johns Hopkins and assistant professor of medicine at Cornell University. Emerson served as dean of IUSM from 1911 to 1932. Ida M. Cannon, *Social Work in Hospitals: A Contribution to Progressive Medicine* (New York: Russell Sage Foundation, 1923), 12–13, 211–12.

94. Report of the Social Service Department, 1911–1913, Box 26, IUSSW Records.

95. Report of the Social Service Department, 1911–1913.

96. Report of the Social Service Department, 1911–1913.

97. Report of the Social Service Department, 1913, 1915, Box 26, IUSSW Records.

98. Piepho, "The History of the Social Service Department," 13, 29–30.

99. Report of the Social Service Department, 1911–1913, Box 26, IUSSW Records.

100. "The Social Service Department," Indiana University Newsletter 3, no. 8 (August 1915), Box 31, IUSSW Records.

101. Henry earned her master of arts in economics and social science (1914) and PhD in sociology (1917) from Indiana University. She published her doctoral dissertation, *The Theory and Practice of Medical Social Work* (1924). Piepho, "The History of the Social Service Department," 14.

102. "Sociological Discussions 3:30 Mon Afternoons at the COS," Box 1, Folder 1, FSA Records.

103. Edna Henry to William Lowe Bryan, May 17, 1917, Box 1, Folder 2, IUSSW Records; Edna Henry to U. G. Weatherly, August 11, 1917, Box 2, Folder 3, IUSSW Records; "Social Workers' School Opens with 30 Enrolled," *Indianapolis Star*, March 5, 1912, 4.

104. Representative titles included NYCOS's Devine, *Principles of Relief*; Dugdale, *The Jukes*; and Warner, *American Charities*. Edna Henry to U. G. Weatherly, May 3, 1913, Box 2, Folder 2, IUSSW Records.

105. Report of the Social Service Department, 1911–1913, Box 26, IUSSW Records.

106. Edna Henry to William Lowe Bryan, October 21, 1914, Box 1, Folder 1, IUSSW Records; Edna G. Henry, "The Sick," *Annals of the American Academy of Political and Social Science* 77, no. 1 (May 1918): 48.

107. Henry, "The Sick," 55; Report of the Social Service Department, 1911–1913, Box 26, IUSSW Records.

108. Edna Henry to Dorothy Buschman, New Haven Hospital Social Service Department, December 23, 1919, Box 1, Folder 6, IUSSW Records. Henry expressed resentment at the conflation of social work and charity in her letter to U. G. Weatherly, February 20, 1920, Box 2, Folder 4, IUSSW Records.

109. Mrs. Allerdice, Emerson, Holliday, Hornbrook, Lilly, MacDonald, Nicholson, and White were either Indiana Free Kindergarten (IFK) or MAS members when they joined the twenty-seven-member Social Service Department Advisory Committee. Members of the three societies found in *Indianapolis Free Kindergarten Society, 1882–1942* (Indianapolis: Indianapolis Free Kindergarten and Children's Aid Society, 1942), 28–29; Mothers' Aid Society letterhead, Box 1, Folder 12, FSA Records; Report of the Social Service Department, 1917, Box 1, Folder 5, IUSSW Records.

110. Dispensary Advisory Committee Minutes, Box 1, Folder 6, IUSSW Records; Report of the Social Service Department, 1917, Box 1, Folder 5, IUSSW Records.

111. Crystal Benton Fall rejoined the COS after Eugene Foster became general secretary. COS Minutes 1916–1920, BV 1171, FSA Records.

112. Edna Henry and U. G. Weatherly letters between July 1915 and December 1917, Box 2, Folder 3, IUSSW Records.

113. "Volunteer Visitors," *The Helping Hand* 1, no. 2 (January 1911): 23.

114. Eugene Cary Foster (1880–1948) served as COS general secretary from 1916 to 1922 and as the Indianapolis Foundation staff director from 1924 to 1948. Foster was active in the Church Federation, Indiana Probation Board, Emergency Work Committee (1929–33), Christamore House, American Red Cross, Wheeler City Rescue Mission, Flower Mission, and American Association of Social Workers. COS letter November 16, 1916, ISL Pamphlet Collection.

115. Report of General Secretary, August 15, 1918, COS Minutes 1916–1920, BV 1171, FSA Records.

116. "Scientific Charity—What Is It?" Semi-Annual Report April 22, 1919, COS Minutes 1916–1920, BV 1171, FSA Records.

117. "My Lady Bountiful," *Our Children* 3, no. 3 (November 1916): 911.

118. "Social Work Is Educational," *Our Children* 4, no. 2 (April 1917): 11.

119. "When Is a Social Worker 'Trained'?" *Our Children* 4, no. 3 (September 1917): 17–18.

120. Edna Henry letter to Delia A. Vochem, June 28, 1919, Box 2, Folder 1, IUSSW Records.

121. Henry, "The Sick," 58.

122. Edna Henry letter to U. G. Weatherly, December 5, 1917, Box 2, Folder 3, IUSSW Records; Henry, *The Theory and Practice of Medical Social Work*, 47–48; Richmond, *Social Diagnosis*, 99.

123. Edna Henry letter to William Lowe Bryan, May 8, 1919, Box 1, Folder 3, IUSSW Records.

124. Edna Henry letter to William Lowe Bryan, October 1, 1920, Box 1, Folder 4, IUSSW Records.

125. Lubove, *The Professional Altruist*, Chapter 5.

126. Mary Ritter Beard, *Woman's Work in Municipalities* (New York: D. Appleton and Company, 1915), 251.

127. Major works on the Russell Sage Foundation include Ruth Crocker, *Mrs. Russell Sage: Women's Activism and Philanthropy in Gilded Age and Progressive Era America* (Bloomington: Indiana University Press, 2006); David C. Hammack and Stanton Wheeler, *Social Science in the Making: Essays on the Russell Sage Foundation, 1907–1972* (New York: Russell Sage Foundation, 1994); Barry D. Karl and Stanley N. Katz, "Foundations and Ruling Class Elites," *Daedalus* 116, no. 1 (winter 1987): 1–40. Locally, Edna Henry cited support of Prohibition, more institutions for the dependent, disease prevention, and public health initiatives as medical-social solutions to community problems. Henry, "The Sick," 57.

ELEVEN

—ɯ—

KATE HEVNER MUELLER

Women's Influence and Marginalization
at Indiana University

KELLY C. SARTORIUS

Kelly C. Sartorius, PhD, highlights the career of Kate Hevner Mueller, IU's last dean of women (1938–46), pointing to Mueller's decanal career accomplishments at both the local and national level. She underscores how Mueller struggled with IU's 1946 proposal to merge the Dean of Women's and Dean of Men's Offices into a unified student service structure. This consolidation reflected a time when IU's male reformers valued structural efficiency that dismantled four decades of support services for women students at IU.

IN 1947, KATE HEVNER MUELLER opened a letter from Syracuse University dean of women Eunice Hilton, who was working to stop the dissolution of dean of women's offices on US university campuses. "I realize I am asking a lot, and if you don't want to commit yourself in writing a letter marked 'confidential,' I will understand. If you feel that you can give me this matter, I'll use it and destroy it. We women have a big nut here to crack and I'd like to help a little if I can."[1] Mueller, responding by hand so as not to involve a secretary, wrote eleven pages regarding the elimination of her office as dean of women at Indiana University (IU). "To understand our situation here, you have to understand a number of things," penned Mueller, noting that IU president Herman Wells's decision to reorganize student affairs under a male dean of students occurred partly due to Wells's background in business.[2] She also believed the death and illness of her two closest administrative allies—the vice president/treasurer and the educational vice president—strongly contributed to the loss of her office. Without these male advocates, Mueller believed, the other administrators lacked understanding about how her office's infrastructure supported women students for autonomous adulthood.[3] When IU reassigned Mueller from dean of women to assistant dean of students, she lost her platform for activism. Since the position's national inception in 1892, deans of women oversaw women's higher coeducation and reported directly to university presidents—which ensured that the chief executive learned directly about women students' needs from a woman and also guaranteed women a voice on the campus's major decision-making committees.[4]

Despite World War II (WWII) opening some higher paying jobs to women, IU and the nation's universities still segregated students by sex and mirrored society's expectations that middle- and upper-class white women—even those with college educations—would marry and stay home as mothers.[5] Across the United States, the dean of women's position and the universities and colleges that employed them reflected the societal norms of rigid gender roles and heterosexual normativity in a nation that privileged white male students as future household breadwinners. However, sex segregation, while marginalizing women and their student life, also created a space that deans of women leveraged to conduct "quiet activism" on behalf of women students.[6] Rather than running disciplinary offices (as was common for deans of men), deans of women administered a well-developed infrastructure focused on citizenship development that prepared female undergraduates for autonomous political and economic participation.

It was this infrastructure that Hilton and Mueller feared losing—the gender-focused career services, women's student government that honed students' leadership skills, extracurricular activities, and residential life.[7] In a national environment where campus-wide career services employed a Strong Interest Inventory that was printed on blue and pink paper to align men and women into gender-appropriate employment futures, deans of women worried that folding women students into a consolidated student affairs model meant that women students would lose the support for them to enter nontraditional leadership or career roles.[8] When Hilton wrote Mueller, she was not simply concerned about female deans losing their stature as the highest-ranking women on campus. Instead, the two worried that the loss of the nation's dean of women's offices would result in losing the infrastructure of quiet activism they—and fifty years of their dean of women predecessors—built to educate college women for citizenship.[9]

Mueller was not the first dean of women to lose her high-ranking position to a "neutral" (male) dean of students, nor would she be the last. However, she was one of the most influential as recognized by IU chancellor's professor

emeritus George Kuh and his student affairs contemporaries.[10] By 1946, Mueller had emerged as a nationally prominent dean of women and was establishing
herself as a "highly productive female scholar-practitioner" along with Esther
Lloyd Jones (Columbia Teachers College [CTC], 1928–66), Ruth Strang (CTC,
1929–60), and Melvene D. Hardee (Florida State University, 1948–90), all of
whom shaped the student affairs profession. Nationally, she served on the 1946
National Association of Deans of Women (NADW) Executive Committee as
university section head, and she also edited the American Council on Education's (ACE) student mental health statement, chaired the American Association of University Women's (AAUW) National Committee on Education,
and served on of the American Psychological Association National Executive
Council.[11]

Despite Mueller's accomplishments, IU subordinated her as an assistant
dean reporting to the new dean of students, Raymond L. Shoemaker, a military
man with no student affairs or counseling training.[12] While this reorganization
eliminated redundancies caused by serving male and female students separately, the NADW and the AAUW both saw the IU reorganization as a demotion for Mueller. Historians have agreed with this interpretation and credited
it to the period's sexism.[13] Mueller's loss of stature was closely watched by her
contemporaries, a fact that historians of gender see as a significant indicator
of women's declining influence on campuses before Title IX of the Education
Amendment of 1972. On many campuses, as at IU, the male administrators
thought of student affairs as a project for ensuring appropriate student conduct.
As such, these men overlooked the women's citizenship preparation programming that consolidation would remove.[14] While Mueller, Hilton, the NADW,
and the AAUW all tried to stem the tide of the "disappearing deans" of women,
the preference for consolidation of student counseling, career services, and
extracurricular activities meant that the women's campus "sphere" would be
absorbed into a system that served male students and reflected gender role
conformity.[15]

KATE HEVNER MUELLER: A BRIEF BIOGRAPHY

Mueller was one of the most influential thinkers in student affairs as it professionalized in the mid-twentieth century. The National Association of Student
Personnel Administrators (NASPA) awarded her the Outstanding Contribution to Research and Literature Award, and the NADW successor organization, the National Association for Women Deans, Administrators, and
Counselors (NAWDAC), awarded her its highest honor, the Distinguished

Service Award.[16] Mueller "introduced a higher level of scholarship to the field than most people could muster," noted IU's Robert Shaffer, dean of students from 1955 to 1969.[17] She edited the NAWDAC journal for most of the 1960s, making her a primary purveyor of ideas and field development during one of the most tumultuous times for student affairs due to student protests, civil rights advocacy, and the emergence of the "second wave" of the women's movement as it intensified across the United States.[18] The field recognizes her textbook *Student Personnel Work in Higher Education* (1961) as one of the first scholarly approaches to student affairs, and deans of women often used her book *Educating Women for a Changing World* (1954) as the philosophical underpinning for their practice.[19] Her stature was significant—a 1959 Women's News Service Poll listed Mueller as one of seventy women qualified for the US vice presidency.[20] Ironically, IU's elimination of the dean of women's office provided Mueller time to publish on student affairs regarding topics such as dual career marriage, continuing education, and sexual education for women.[21]

Born Kate Lucile Hevner on November 1, 1898, in Pennsylvania, she was raised by a Presbyterian minister father and schoolteacher mother. She majored in English at Wilson College, an all-female Presbyterian institution in her home state. Like many women's colleges, Wilson based student life upon women's student government, which introduced Mueller to one of the key elements of deaning.[22] For Mueller—as with many deans of women before her—self-governance undergirded her vision for educating women to become engaged citizens.[23]

After college, Mueller's graduate work occurred at two of the most influential locations for the development of women's deaning—Columbia University and the University of Chicago. Mueller moved to New York to earn her master's degree in psychology at Columbia in 1923 after teaching high school mathematics for two years. At Columbia, Mueller interacted with educators at Teachers College, where many early deans of women studied. She returned to Wilson College to teach psychology and mathematics before beginning her PhD in 1926 at the University of Chicago with influential psychologist L. L. Thurstone.[24] While at Chicago, Mueller lived in Green Hall, a women's dormitory largely housing female graduate students that was supervised by Sophonisba Breckinridge, who helped define the practice of deaning.[25] There, Mueller experienced campus life without differential rules over her conduct—autonomy that she enjoyed.

Hired by the University of Minnesota as a psychology faculty member in 1929, Mueller taught and researched as an assistant professor. Her research introduced her to her husband, John H. Mueller, a sociologist. Married in 1935, the two moved to Bloomington when IU offered John a faculty position in the sociology department.[26] Thus, she arrived in Indiana as a trailing spouse, a highly educated psychologist, an experienced instructor, and familiar with both early student affairs operations and women's self-governance. Being a dean of women, however, had never crossed her mind.[27]

THE DEVELOPMENT OF DEANING AT IU AND NATIONALLY

When Mueller took the position of dean of women at IU in 1937, she stepped into an office with almost four decades of institutional history fashioned from the best practices of women's higher coeducation. Coeducational institutions first hired deans of women in the late 1800s to chaperone women so they could attend classes with men.[28] College experiences were formally separated by sex, and male administrators and faculty routinely thought of the dean of women as a disciplinarian—a panopticon—monitoring women students, who followed different behavioral rules than did male students. This practice marginalized female students into a limited sphere. However, these deans of women were free to organize their space in the margin and borrowed the practice of women's self-government from women's colleges.[29] They used student government as the mechanism to coordinate campus residences and to teach citizenship to the women governing their own halls or sororities, who were learning the machinery of democracy, voting, coalition building, and leadership.[30]

By the early 1900s, female enrollments at coeducational state schools like IU approached 50 percent of the student body.[31] By necessity, deans of women developed a philosophy and practice beyond simple discipline to oversee the growing number of female students. Most early deans of women were PhD-educated scholars who actively participated in the AAUW predecessor, the Association of Collegiate Alumnae (ACA), and coordinated their campuses' self-governments through the Intercollegiate Association of Women Students (IAWS), a group they developed to nationally link the Associated Women Students (AWS) government leaders from various universities and colleges.[32] IU followed suit, hiring three significant deans of women—Mary Bidwell Breed (1901–06), Agnes E. Wells (1919–38), and Kate Hevner Mueller (1938–46). Breed, a chemist, tied IU into the early network of pioneer deans of women such as the University of Chicago's Marion Talbot and Sophonisba Breckinridge.[33] Breed chaired the second major meeting of deans of women in 1905, leading the consideration of college women's opportunities for economic citizenship through paid work.

At IU, the lack of any residence halls meant Breed had to rely on sororities and boardinghouses to implement women's student government.[34] This significantly constrained her operation of women's government, which functioned out of the living units, and pushed her to accept employment at the University of Missouri.[35] When Agnes Wells, an astronomer and suffragist, took over the IU role in 1919, she established women's residence halls, agreeing with most deans of women that dormitories anchored women's student affairs practice. She noted, "I look upon the college house as a laboratory for work as well as a social center for the development of the all-around girl."[36] Wells implemented expanded women's self-government across all female IU undergraduates and coordinated all women's activities and residential arrangements through it. Her success and national influence were clear as NADW elected her the 1923–25 president. Wells's office cooperated with the physical education and health services departments to manage women's health needs and provided $39,000 in women's scholarship dollars. In addition, her AWS student governance structure taught citizenship and political skills by involving women in voting to set their own study hours and curfews.[37]

Under Wells's leadership, the dean of women's office thrived. There was a "never-ending flow of individual students who came for appointments" along with "student officers, committee chairmen, wrongdoers, complainers and the casual out-of-town visitors, to say nothing of the telephone calls and the mail."[38] Wells's program reflected the best of deaning practices, which was just becoming known as the field of "student personnel" in the late 1930s. Wells told Mueller, "My idea of the office of the dean of women is to plan for the development of the women on the campus through good housing, good management of the housing, good social conditions, good direction of social conditions, the development of the care of any discipline in each house through the Association of Women Students [student governance], and the development of that organization so that it would have a comprehensive outlook and work in a cooperative way with all organizations whose membership includes women."[39] Deaning at IU, as at most coeducational public institutions, was a large, comprehensive project where one dean and several staffers oversaw the extracurricular agenda for the female student body in concert with academic counseling.[40] In this arrangement, deans of women oversaw policies and programs that promoted leadership, citizenship, career preparation, graduate school application, sex education/marriage preparation, and the development of the whole individual. While the actual number of deans of women increased during the 1930s, the rumors of "disappearing deans of women" grew as the emerging offices of deans of men became more active and advocated to become their campuses' deans of students to oversee both male and female undergraduates. University leaders clearly saw deans of women as specialists trained to work with women—and considered deans of students (who would be almost universally men) as able to serve both sexes.[41]

MUELLER AS IU DEAN OF WOMEN

In 1936–37, Agnes Wells announced her retirement and recommended to IU's new president, Herman B Wells (no relation), that he hire Mueller as dean of women. Wells thought that Mueller's academic training in psychology was strong preparation for the role since the emerging student personnel field preferred it.[42] In hiring her, President Wells matched Mueller's Minnesota professor's salary and gave her a nine-month appointment along with two twelve-month staffers: Lottie Kirby, who handled the sororities, and Fanny Weatherwax, who managed loans and scholarship funding for female undergraduates.[43]

When Mueller took over for Agnes Wells in 1937–38, she "knew very little about the functions of a Dean of Women" though she was well acquainted with the University of Minnesota's dean, Anne Blitz, through her social connections while on the faculty there.[44] After accepting the role, she spent the 1937 summer researching deaning practices and meeting with deans of women or counselors of women at the universities of Minnesota, Chicago, and Northwestern. She learned about the "shift away from the older paternal or maternal attitudes, and toward the mental health and counseling points of view."[45] Like IU's Agnes Wells, the deans whom Mueller met relied upon women's student government to socialize behavioral expectations so that only problematic discipline cases in which students acted far outside the dictates of current social mores rose to the dean's involvement. Thus, as Mueller practiced deaning, discipline was considered a small part of the program she oversaw—though male administrators, including IU president Herman Wells, still thought of it as a primary function of the dean of women. Mueller recalled that President Wells called her and the dean of men his "disciplinary deans."[46]

At IU, as at most large public institutions, Mueller's office oversaw women's residential and extracurricular arrangements for women's development.[47] Mueller's overall infrastructure included counseling for each female student's educational, financial, and therapeutic needs; advising for groups ranging from women's student organizations to the YWCA to a first-year student orientation; financial aid for women; and provision and coordination of student housing including residence halls and sororities. She supervised all social activities and provided the "social education" that accompanied it, handled discipline, and coordinated with faculty and offices across campus regarding women's needs such as sex education.[48]

Mueller met her new position with academic rigor. She researched approaches and implemented the practices that she felt supported women's advancement through a liberal education. As she would later write, "Only a liberal education, a truly liberating experience in their education, can set them [women] free."[49] She saw women's college education as the force that would free women from their second-class status and gender discrimination. Former Forest Hall head resident and student of Mueller's, University of Kansas (KU) dean of women Emily Taylor, noted that the staff spent hours with Mueller discussing the nature of women's education and women's preparation for citizenship.[50] Mueller believed that "good citizenship would recognize no sex differences," and higher education would teach young women the self-discipline and self-reliance necessary for adult autonomy.[51]

With these goals in mind, Mueller expanded her professional staff. In addition to the two original employees, she employed a residence hall coordinator, Margaret Wilson, to whom all the head residents reported, and Catherine Evans, who led career counseling. While Agnes Wells had employed housemothers in the residence halls, Mueller replaced these with counselors trained in student personnel work.[52] For these head residents, she sought women from the top master's programs such as the ones at Syracuse University and Teachers College to supervise the halls, counsel the women residents, and advise the halls' student government.[53] "Our theory about Hall discipline was that the freshmen should feel that the Head Resident was always on her side, and it was just that awful presence in the Dean's office that was arbitrary and threatening. Therefore the ultimate punishment for an offender was an interview with the Dean!"[54] In addition, Mueller shifted the IU AWS away from a disciplinary point of view, changing the Disciplinary Committee of faculty members to the Board of Standards, which she reworked to consist of a group of female students selected by the AWS. This allowed students to self-govern their own disciplinary concerns. "We promoted the idea of good will in personal relations in contrast to the multitudinous petty rules that the student officers (and faculty such as the law school [dean]) loved."[55] While student behavior that could cause significant safety or university public relations problems still rose to the dean's level, the student government dealt with the majority of disciplinary infractions under the advice of the dean's office. When problems arose with campus policies or the administration, Mueller searched for solutions by having the AWS leaders gather data about the true nature of the issue. She helped them craft surveys to determine what the women students wanted and thought of the various administrative policy requests—from dance rules to noise complaints.[56] This allowed her to base her decisions on the opinions of the students and made it difficult for male administrators to argue with her requests. This also taught AWS leaders decision-making and surveying skills.

She also offered vocational guidance, career placement services, a university part-time employment office, and women's health counseling. For career programming, Mueller employed AWS leaders in organizing a career conference to provide "a realistic picture of the employment scene," hosting keynote speakers such as Mary Beard, Eve Curie, Jan Struthers, and Margaret Bourke-White.[57] In conjunction with the career efforts, Mueller also ran a women's week in which the female students took over the student newspaper and focused on women's issues.

For women's health, Mueller helped launch one of the nation's most influential sex education and sex research projects. In her first year, Mueller worked with the AWS to develop what would become Alfred Kinsey's famous human sexuality course. She approached Kinsey about the effort because the AWS had requested further education on sex and how to navigate dating.[58] Often called "marriage courses," they were regularly incorporated by deans of women through their offices or through YWCA chapters. At IU, after small "trials" in the summer of 1938, Kinsey offered his first "marriage course" to over three hundred students that fall. Committed to providing college women with information about their bodies and sexuality, Mueller bought books on sex education and put them on the shelves in all the residence halls. "Of course they circulated surreptitiously but widely, and we always lost most of them by the end of the year, but we cheerfully bought new ones and made sure that they were at least available."[59]

The overlap between sex education and women's behavioral rules was significant. Mueller called for the AWS to develop "appropriate standards" for women's heterosexual dating, calling for older students to guide younger, more immature ones in making good decisions regarding sexuality. She advocated AWS rules and their changes should be geared toward "short, compromising" steps to move forward, which also provided time to bring the women's student body into compliance with the new rules.[60]

It was an infrastructure with a breadth and depth of programming, and by 1942, Mueller noted that her most time-consuming projects had been developing a women's career booklet, bringing online new residence halls, creating a "Junior Division" that included a counseling system for first-year students, and developing a "women's committee" that "visited colleges all over the country . . . to report on what is going on in Women's Education."[61] For that, Mueller traveled to Reed College, Scripps, Oberlin, Antioch, and Ohio State, among other institutions, to identify best practices for women's education. In addition, she taught graduate courses in order to better prepare the women who counseled her students.[62] This began Mueller's practice of providing a two-year internship that competed with Syracuse and Columbia's Teachers College and also provided one of the kernels for the growing IU student affairs administration PhD program, which awarded its first student personnel master's degree in 1951 and doctorate in 1959.[63]

By the middle of WWII, Mueller's program had matured and portrayed the model for women's education that she would later present in *Educating Women for a Changing World*. Her approach centered on using student government to facilitate women's adoption of full citizenship—both economic and political—so that women could choose marriage or career, and possibly combine both. Later, Mueller admitted that she could have been better at long-term vision and in administration of day-to-day details. These, it turned out, were extremely important to President Wells—who found annoying the complaints that sometimes arrived in his office from students and parents about women's housing. All in all, though, Mueller felt positive about her programming, telling longtime friend Margaret Disert, "The war gets me down, but we *are* making progress in Women's Education at Indiana."[64] The war's end, however, would bring significant change to the nation's higher education, to IU, and to Mueller's efforts.

THE EFFECTS OF THE WAR AND
CONSOLIDATION OF STUDENT AFFAIRS

With the end of World War II, male student enrollments exploded at campuses across the United States as soldiers matriculated through the Serviceman's Readjustment Act of 1944. Demand was so intense that 87 percent of large public and prestigious private institutions lacked needed housing for the returning GIs.[65] These mass enrollments strained institutional capacities. As campuses scrambled to accommodate the increasing numbers, some presidents turned to military men to coordinate the veterans flooding their campuses. At the universities of Missouri, Kentucky, Florida, and Michigan, an ROTC commandant led student affairs. The same forces pushed IU to reorganize student personnel and appoint Raymond Shoemaker, IU's previous ROTC leader.[66] By default, and to the detriment of deans of women and their female students, IU's case illustrates how veterans' enrollments on some campuses stretched to the breaking point the five-decade tacit agreement within coeducational practice that women's marginalized and sex-segregated space would be controlled and managed by women for women.

The seeds for reorganizing student affairs under a single dean of students were laid in the 1930s when the Great Depression forced campuses to look for efficiencies to reduce costs. ACE published *The Student Personnel Point of View* (1937), which ushered into larger practice women's focus on counseling the whole student, but it also confirmed the assumption that student affairs was a "service-based" practice—an approach that male administrators preferred given that much of male student academic advising happened with faculty members.[67] Women, however, were often academically advised through the dean of women's counselors because the predominantly male faculty were less likely to mentor the women students toward careers or leadership roles due to the hegemonic culture. As such, higher education and deans of men were increasingly considering student affairs as a service-driven enterprise of managing student bodies.[68]

By the time deans of men established offices, deans of women already had developed a nationally coordinated women's self-government alongside a national career services operation for women, both of which IU was significantly involved in.[69] Deans of men lagged behind women deans' achievements and did not have the infrastructure developed at the level women did. For instance, the student government linchpin upon which women's deaning rested did not exist at the same level for male students—a full two-thirds of colleges had no men's student government in the 1930s.[70] IU's student government for men did not begin until 1947. IU reflected national trends, hiring its first dean of women in 1901, almost two decades before it decided to create the dean of men position in 1919.[71] However, once deans of men established offices and began to organize nationally through the National Association of Deans of Men (NADM), they borrowed heavily from the women's established practices of deaning. Then, they recommended rearranging and professionalizing deaning into a streamlined model under a (male) dean of students.[72] In fact, by 1939, only twelve campuses had centralized under a single dean of students, but the deans of women had begun to worry about the stability of their institutional positions—and they were correct in their concern. By 1948, thirty-four campuses had consolidated under a dean of students, and another twelve had begun the process.[73] As they did so, they chipped away at the influence women had built within the margins of the academy.

After WWII, the loss of women's student affairs administrative leadership would be swift and substantial. Male veterans engulfed campuses, outnumbering female students. While undergraduate enrollments in large public universities were 50 percent women since the early 1900s, the end of WWII saw institutions curtail women's matriculation in favor of men's—with twenty-six campuses even placing quotas on women's enrollment.[74] The mass male enrollments so overwhelmed university administrative capacity that campuses began to use military efficiency processes to handle veterans' matriculation. In addition, advising so many first-year students tested the limits of the interpersonal one-to-one counseling method deans of women preferred. This prompted the use of psychological testing to determine students' courses of study just as the military had done to slot soldiers into defense functions. By 1948, the National Association of Deans and Advisers of Men (NADAM) embraced the efficiency of military procedure. As that year's conference keynote speaker D. H. Gardner, of the University of Akron, advocated, "The war taught us much about chain of command and this same theory of administration should be adopted by our institutions of higher education in the personnel field."[75]

At the same time, ACE began to revise the *Student Personnel Point of View* and by 1948 strongly recommended that universities centralize their student affairs under one office—a dean of students, who was most often the promoted dean of men.[76] The blatant sexism of the student personnel approach was clear. For instance, C. Gilbert Wrenn, professor of education involved in Minnesota's influential consolidated program, noted that deans of women "might just as well face the fact now as ever that higher education is masculine-dominated, as is the world."[77] Likewise, the American Council of Guidance and Personnel Associations president David Feder was quoted as saying, "Women played a secondary role in culture, and therefore, they should be willing to do so in personnel."[78] Some deans of students (men) spoke directly against women becoming equal counterparts in student affairs. For instance, University of Texas dean of student life Arno Norwotny noted his reticence toward admitting women into the male student affairs association, saying, "I am always going to belong to NADAM no matter what you call it, and if some gal is smart enough to get elected Dean of Students in some institution and merit that title, I may let the old gal in. I don't know."[79] The comment received laughter from the male audience. Clearly, most men did not envision consolidation on campuses to include equity for the deans of women.

By 1948, over 40 percent of deans of men had been appointed to the dean of students position, which increased their responsibilities, salary, and prestige.

These former deans of men brought to their new leadership positions a revised version of deaning practice. "Many of the deans [of men] were tolerant but not eager to address the issues of women students and the resentments were often expressed in sarcasm or humor toward women and especially, the NADAW [National Association of Deans of Women]."[80] This realignment often eliminated deans of women's direct report to presidents and their seats on the decision-making committees, curtailing their influence substantially.[81]

Minnesota's dean of students E. G. Williamson led the ACE committee that updated the *Student Personnel Point of View* in 1948 to support this perspective.[82] Williamson's committee of twelve included three women, none of whom were known for operating the traditional dean of women's program. Williamson, a former student of Mueller's from her days as a professor at Minnesota, rose to his deanship at a young age and was known for emphasizing guidance tests rather than interpersonal one-on-one advising. He also popularized the in loco parentis disciplinary approach of the university acting in place of a student's parents:[83] "He held the opinion that the responsibility for the behavior of underage students living away from home was transferred from the parents to the University. He was also deeply concerned with damage to the University's public image due to student misbehavior. [At Minnesota] Williamson's paternalistic style brought him into frequent conflict with student organizations. Fraternities were a special concern and one of Williamson's campaigns was to control drinking by underage students."[84] As a result, Williamson's national leadership on consolidation ingrained a disciplinary perspective that privileged competency testing over personal interviews into the version of student personnel that the powerful ACE endorsed. In addition, the assumption of male superiority evidenced by Wrenn, Feder, and Norwotny was a part of Williamson's worldview. This obviously grated on the women who worked with him. In private correspondence, Mueller noted that Minnesota dean of women Anne Dudley Blitz referred to Williamson as "God" and his close colleague John Darley as "Deputy God," phrasing that illustrated the women's frustration with the paternalistic approach these men took.[85]

As the consolidation efforts gained ground, the NADW leadership politely responded to the creation of a dean of students position, saying, "Those who understand her functions feel that 'a separate women's program is indispensable [sic] and that it is important that a women [sic] dean head up that program."[86] The comment implied men did not see the full purpose of the women's programming, which supported nontraditional careers, a full liberal arts education, citizenship training, and graduate school preparation. Ultimately, WWII's conclusion ended coeducational higher education's mandate that a sphere for women and its quietly activist infrastructure would be overseen by a female scholar. The new consolidated approach would marginalize women once again while simultaneously removing their access to administrative levers of influence. [87] As the deans of women feared, the number of male administrators who did not "understand her functions" would prove too difficult to overcome—and some of those leaders were IU's top brass.

THE IU REORGANIZATION

In Bloomington, even before veteran enrollments almost doubled the student body to 9,500 students, a reorganization of student affairs already percolated— though conversations around it did not always include Mueller.[88] Wells considered consolidation of the men's and women's student personnel offices thanks to a late 1930s committee recommendation calling for the change. By early 1942, an assistant dean of men, Robert Bates, floated a consolidation proposal to upper administration because IU's long-serving dean of men, Clarence Edmondson, had announced retirement. Bates, advocating one staff serve both men and women's needs, also promoted himself as the new dean of students.[89]

No record exists of Wells asking for Mueller's opinion on this early proposal. The vice president and dean of the faculties Herman T. Briscoe indicated full support for the reorganization but noted to Wells that "shifts of personnel in these offices [is] way too difficult to make at this time." [90] According to Bates, difficulties with personalities had surfaced between housing, the dean of men's office, and the dean of women's office. Bates may have been referring to the frequent disagreements between Mueller and Alice Nelson, director of the residence halls. Emily Taylor, a close confidant of Mueller and IU's Forest Hall head resident in the early 1940s, recalled that Nelson and Mueller often butted heads. Nelson, responsible for hall functions, pushed for her operational view of residential management while Mueller saw the halls as a classroom for women's development and education and offered her self-government program through the counselors there.

The fact that Edmondson had announced his retirement in 1942 and then forewent it indicates that the conflicts were not easily solved with the existing personnel. [91] Wells was reluctant to replace him.[92] When Edmonson died in 1944, Bob Bates became dean of men and was left to manage the flood of veterans with only one secretary since "the anticipated reorganization of the student personnel agencies" made it "desirable to delay making additional appointments until this reorganization was effected."[93] The largest issue was housing—and Bates found "inadequate" the coordination between him and

Nelson's office of residence halls, directed by Nelson. The two tried locating a "temporary Secretary of Men's Housing" who handled off-campus housing requests while Nelson's office handled on-campus requests. Rather than fixing the problem, the two offices provided incoming students conflicting information.[94]

Bates was not considered ready for the dean of students role, and no one considered Mueller. Instead, Colonel Shoemaker was Wells's choice for the upcoming dean of students position. Shoemaker impressed Wells during the war by leading IU's Army Specialized Training Program. Although Shoemaker had no training in psychology, counseling, or student affairs, Wells thought of the student personnel field as conduct and student discipline related, making a retired colonel seem perfect for the position as veterans poured onto the campus. In July 1944, Wells personally recruited Shoemaker: "I further stated that the Survey Committee Report called for a Division of Student Personnel, to be headed by a Director or Dean of Students, and that we hoped to begin this program immediately upon the conclusion of the war. I stated to him that at that time I would like to discuss with him the possibility of his heading the Division, if his plans call for retirement at the conclusion of the war and if he would be interested in such discussion. He stated that he most assuredly would be interested, and would be honored to be considered."[95] The relationship between the two men was collegial; Shoemaker invited Wells to his home for the weekend, noting that the two would enjoy drinking together.[96]

Sublimating the deans of men and women's offices under the dean of students realigned all academic counseling to the faculty, leaving Mueller unable to provide women with academic support for career-related options. In addition, the proposal addressed the tension between Mueller and Nelson by removing all control over residence halls and the head residents.[97] For this proposal, Briscoe collected feedback to present to Wells. Bates responded that he "enthusiastically supported" the reorganization, noting that "it is strongly recommended that the new division be developed on a functional basis rather than on a basis of sex as is now the case in many areas," with "present responsibilities" "distributed among new offices established on a functional pattern."[98] Bates thought consolidation would result in little interruption to either the men's or women's offices. Consolidation "has the additional important advantage of disrupting existing offices to a lesser extent than other possibilities," he noted, indicating that there were "no major omissions" in the plan.[99] The fact that Bates could not see the significant dissolution of the women's programming that would occur in the dean of women's office illustrates how little he understood Mueller's infrastructure and programming. That no one corrected him indicated the other men did not understand it either.

The September 1945 proposal review is the first formal request for Mueller to weigh in—over a year after Wells had recruited Shoemaker as dean of students. Mueller wrote extensively to Wells, carbon copying Briscoe, about the loss of women's programming. She was quite concerned over losing control of the head residents as that gutted the programming Agnes Wells initiated to use the halls as living laboratories for women's education and student government. She agreed that the current operations did not work smoothly but suggested the problems could "be solved in terms of a strong and well-trained counselor of men."[100] Rather than dissolving her office, she thought in terms of extending her programming into the dean of men's office for the benefit of male students—and her comment indicates she felt Bates was not qualified for the job.[101]

Despite her extended response, Briscoe noted to Wells only that Mueller's feedback amounted to "two pages of comments and suggestions, mostly about the needs of women and for *well trained* staff members."[102] The consolidation of comments from the various heads of the areas did note that Mueller objected to dividing "academic and personal counseling" and that she "feels that resident counselors should still be responsible to Dean of Women."[103] At this point, the president's office was not yet ready to eliminate the gender-based structure, as the final draft of the proposal crossed out the reference to complete consolidation and elimination of the dean of men and dean of women, and then it was signed "respectfully submitted" to Wells.[104] Since Wells asked Briscoe's opinion on all of these documents, it was likely Briscoe who crossed out the full removal of sex segregation.

Still, Wells was ready for the change, as two weeks after Mueller submitted her comments, Wells asked Briscoe to prepare an announcement of the new dean of students structure, not incorporating any of Mueller's feedback. However, that announcement did not go out in October of 1945—and there is no record of why in the president's papers.[105] During this time period, Briscoe was sick, and someone was discussing proposals with Briscoe and returning the information to Wells, making it possible that Mueller was correct that his illness influenced his ability to advocate for her. Even before they asked Mueller's opinion on the proposal in September 1945, though, Briscoe was already trying to find a place for Mueller outside of student affairs—potentially in a new aesthetics department chaired by her husband.[106] This makes it unlikely Briscoe advocated for the women's program and illustrates that the decision to move Mueller was under consideration in Wells's office long before 1946.

The ramifications of these upcoming changes were not fully shared with Mueller, but they happened swiftly in early 1946. On April 1, Shoemaker submitted an organizational chart for approval to Briscoe in which both Bates and

Mueller retained their titles as dean of men and dean of women, respectively. However, residence hall counselors no longer fell under either Bates or Mueller, and Bates received supervision over "all student organizations to include fraternities and sororities."[107] Thus, by April 1946, her role had been reduced to one-to-one counseling of women and women's discipline as Shoemaker no longer included any student organizations or staff reporting to her and she was given "general counselling [sic] and advising of women students" as her purview.[108] Mueller recalls learning of the appointment of Shoemaker in March. In April, Briscoe announced to Mueller and Bates that all requests to him or Wells should be submitted through Shoemaker.[109] In addition, the coordination between Shoemaker and Mueller was sparse from Mueller's point of view: "We always expected that when the rush of the end of the year was over, he would consult with us about our functions, but in this we were very sadly mistaken," Mueller wrote to Hilton.[110]

In May, Wells and Briscoe decided to withhold Mueller's change in title from her and instead send only her salary information to her.[111] Also, Shoemaker quickly reworked the finances to eliminate Mueller's office as well as the budgetary supports for the citizenship, leadership, and career preparation infrastructure for female students. In fact, two weeks after Wells and Briscoe withheld Mueller's title change, Shoemaker submitted a budget overhaul that removed the two budget lines titled "Dean of Students—Dean of Women" to fund Mueller's office and "Dean of Students and Association of Women Students" to fund the women's student government organization.[112] This change eliminated the earmarks for women's programming, removing the $19,130 allotted to the dean of women and the $1,260 to support what had been the anchor for women's programming for almost five decades—women's student government.

In their place, Shoemaker asked for four subcategories under "Dean of Students" that included a "counseling office" where he assigned Mueller, a central housing office (where Nelson would continue to lead residential operations), scholarships and loans (combining men and women's financial aid), and student activities.[113] Then, three days after Wells approved the budget reappropriation, he informed Mueller in a letter that her title would be assistant dean of students.[114] Since Mueller was rarely on campus in the summer, it is unclear if she received the communication. She reported to friends that she learned about her reassignment and new title in the newspaper.[115] Her staff who once reported to her directly were also reassigned to positions with the same title of assistant dean of students. While Briscoe approved this title change immediately and Wells approved it a week later, the trustees deferred the decision until September because two of them—including the one female trustee, Mary Rieman Maurer—were absent from the July meeting.[116]

On a nine-month appointment, Mueller returned from her summer to find all of the budgetary and office changes complete and most of her responsibilities reassigned to others. She was placed under the supervision of future IU dean of students, Assistant Dean of Students Robert Shaffer, who was then in his thirties and a newly minted New York University PhD with little student affairs experience.[117] Shaffer reported feeling mortified that he was assigned to tell Mueller about her new title and duties.[118] She later said she felt "misled" by Shoemaker, who often told her "I admire your work," or "Everybody knows that the Dean of Women's office does fine work, and that the Dean of Men's does not."[119] Mueller recalled Shoemaker not understanding how deans of women operated their programs and him telling her, "After all you have been lucky in this job. No woman at Minnesota has so much authority"—showing that he felt her programs overreached her proper sphere of influence.[120] While the final organization set out that the residence halls would be run by the dean of students, Shoemaker assigned that role to Nelson, which permanently removed Mueller's influence with resident assistants and the women's programming carried out there.[121]

The women's programming began to atrophy under the new approach. Within the first year, Mueller described, the residence hall and student organizations declined, and the fundraising of the YWCA dramatically failed under the men's leadership. She lauded her former staffers' work, noting, "The women counselors kept the work of Mortar Board, AWS, WAA, YWCA up to very high standards. There were not the paid and trained workers to do the same for the men, and of course men students don't accept that kind of leadership as readily as women students. Men, at least so far this year, are not giving the attention to student groups that is needed."[122] As for women's vocational counseling, Shoemaker eliminated the large-scale women's career conferences. Mueller noted that this expansive effort required a university administrator's commitment due to both cost and planning needs, neither of which Shoemaker provided. Perhaps most devastating, Mueller was removed from all the university-wide committees where she represented the needs of women students.

Mueller talked to President Wells once, noting her displeasure with her assignment and that she was "distressed over the trend to eliminate the AWS and to merge women's interests with men's," and Wells told her to address her concerns with Shoemaker.[123] When she did, "the Colonel laughed heartily and said, 'Every day I have to do things I don't want to do.'" Shoemaker clearly saw Mueller as concerned with her loss of stature. His lack of counseling training

and the sexism of the time meant he did not see the consequence of the dissolution of women's programming. Instead, he saw a simple shift in residence
hall management. While Mueller was extremely embarrassed by the demotion,
she was most devastated by the losses she perceived her students took under
Shoemaker's leadership.[124]

In IU's reorganization, neither Wells nor Briscoe understood the educational outcomes embedded in her infrastructure. Nor did they recognize that
the conflict between Mueller and Nelson was a disagreement over how student affairs should be offered—and that Mueller's entire operation was conducted within the residence halls through her staff of head residents. Since the
decision-makers overlooked her infrastructure, the majority of the change discussion occurred without asking Mueller about her opinion. When she was
asked for her input in 1945, she was too late to change the thinking of the men
who had already agreed to the fundamental new structure. And none of them
viewed the reorganization as Mueller did; she thought it had the result of "chop-
ping up" students into "little pieces" with multiple staff members advising one
student in separate offices rather than offering each student wholistic advising
by one counselor.[125] While the NADW and the AAUW refuted consolidation
at IU and at other campuses, such efforts, recalled Shaffer, angered President
Wells, who found the outside organizations' reactions to be interference.[126]

WOMEN'S RESPONSE

IU's reorganization of student affairs was a harbinger of coeducational higher
education's future. NADW and many deans of women recognized the permanent disappearance of their positions—and their activist infrastructure—on
the horizon. After Shoemaker's appointment, Mueller immersed herself in
studying women's education, becoming a part of AAUW's efforts as well as
ACE's Rye Conference in the 1950s, where women educators created the model
for a new philosophy and practice of women's liberal arts education, specifically
resisting the hegemonic push for college women to focus on a home economics
education.[127] Many deans of women saw IU's change as a sign that they, too,
could be removed unless they maintained a particularly strong, well-informed
relationship with their president.[128]

In an effort to stem the tide of disappearing deans and their programming,
the two groups began working closely. The AAUW, which accredited schools
for providing an equitable education for women, designed a questionnaire that
asked two questions: "1, the status of Deans of Women in educational institutions, and 2, whether the position of Dean of Women was being abolished, [and]

the place of women in academic, administrative, and counseling procedures in the institutions."[129] With 165 coeducational campuses returning the survey, the results showed that 96 campuses retained a dean of women while 69 reported having no female administrator "of importance." In the fall of 1946, Louisville dean of women and NADW president Hilda Threlkeld asked the executive committee to consider adding to their national conference agenda a program on "the replacement of the dean of women by the dean of students." Although the board decided such a topic should not be legitimized by discussing it at the national convention, they decided that sessions on "what the administration expects of a dean of women" and how to "resolve conflicting ideologies" would be useful to deans working to preserve their influence on behalf of women students.[130] These strategies would have likely helped in the IU case—both would have informed Wells and Briscoe that there were competing ideologies and that those different views were causing conflict in the student affairs arena.

In addition, Threlkeld appointed Hilton to chair a special committee on consolidation in 1945–46, for which she wrote Mueller the letter requesting the confidential information. Afraid of losing the infrastructure at more institutions, the NADW worked on the disappearing deans by creating a coordinating committee with AAUW. The group included some of the most powerful deans of women—Hilton, Alice Lloyd, Dorothy Stratton, and Lloyd-Jones. It would be Lloyd-Jones, however, who would advocate for the consolidation position, sure that women's stature would not be diminished. Later, in the 1960s, Lloyd-Jones apologized to the NADW for not foreseeing that the sexism of the academy would eliminate the quietly activist infrastructure deans of women had created.[131] Despite their national network and their partnership with AAUW, when male presidents and the male-led student personnel profession decided women would no longer preside over women students' concerns, they could only slow—not stop—the demise of women's programming. Kate Hevner Mueller's case made this inevitability clear as neither her national reputation at NADW, her stature at AAUW, nor her influence at ACE deterred Wells from making the change.

CONCLUSION

Mueller's career both defined the development of student affairs at IU and its top-ranked higher education administration program and also, simultaneously, reflected how, in the middle of the twentieth century, men appropriated and redefined the student affairs practice from the deans of women who invented it. While Mueller later established herself as a leading student affairs academic and psychologist, her widespread recognition outside of circles of women leaders would not arise until the 1970s and 1980s, when the women's movement helped to reestablish women's administrative foothold in higher education. Mueller, who in 1946–47 suddenly had enormous amounts of time, poured herself into her academic work, publishing on student affairs and the psychology of music. She used the data from her campus visits across the nation and authored *Educating Women for a Changing World*. Today, in some ways, the book reads as a treatise on what was lost when deans of women no longer administered a women's sphere in coeducational higher education. Mueller was concerned that female students attend a college that would teach them to understand and practice citizenship and to prepare them for a future of paid work—even foreseeing dual-career parents. Adopted by quietly activist deans who still retained their positions in the 1950s and 1960s, Mueller's book was a manual on the special needs of women students in a world that systematically discriminated against women.[132]

IU's reassignment of Mueller not only illustrates the sexism of the time; it also portrays how little male administrators understood the full operation of women's philosophy and practice in deaning. When Wells closed the dean of women's office in order to serve all students together, women lost their political and economic citizenship training, career counseling, and leadership development programs. The activist infrastructure withered in postwar IU without an influential dean of women to oversee it.

Mueller's experience at IU is a microcosm of how the dissolution of deans of women's offices proceeded across the nation. Within three years, Shoemaker had largely disassembled the operation Mueller and her predecessors had spent almost five decades building. Mueller, relegated to a counseling role, had a husband who did not want to leave IU. As a result, she felt resigned to accept the situation. Seeing the trend of consolidation negatively, she remarked privately, "The new theory . . . that the problems of men and women are the same [and] that women do not have any special problems . . . and therefore all counselors and deans will treat men and women together [is problematic]. Men will always resist any other theory because it keeps the women where they want them! It prevents women from organizing themselves for concerted action. That is what we have lost on this campus. Formerly we were a force to be reckoned with."[133]

NOTES

1. M. Eunice Hilton, Letter to Mueller, January 6, 1947, in Kate Hevner Mueller papers, 1909–81 (C170), Box 2, Folder: Dean of Women 1938–1948, IU Libraries, University Archives (IULUA), Bloomington, Indiana.

2. Mueller, Letter to Hilton, January 14, 1947, C170, Box 2, Folder: Dean of Women 1938–1948.

3. Mueller, Letter to Hilton, January 14, 1947.

4. Jana Nidiffer, "More Than 'a Wise and Pious Matron': The Professionalization of the Position of Dean of Women, 1901–1918" (EdD diss., Harvard University, 1994); Jana Nidiffer, "From Matron to Maven: A New Role and New Professional Identity for Deans of Women, 1892 to 1916," *Mid-Western Educational Researcher* 8, 4 (1995): 17–24; Jana Nidiffer, "Deans of Women," in *Historical Dictionary of Women's Education in the United States*, ed. Linda Eisenmann (Westport, CT: Greenwood Press, 1998), 121–24; Jana Nidiffer, *Pioneering Deans of Women: More Than Wise and Pious Matrons* (New York: Teachers College Press, 2000); Jana Nidiffer, "The First Deans of Women: What We Can Learn from Them," *About Campus* 6 (2002): 10–16. Marion Talbot, "The Education of Women" (Chicago, IL: The University of Chicago Press, 1910), http://pi.lib.uchicago.edu/1001/dig/pres/2005-182; Marion Talbot and Lois Kimball Mathews Rosenberry, *The History of the American Association of University Women, 1881–1931* (Boston: Houghton Mifflin, 1931); Marion Talbot, *More Than Lore: Reminiscences of Marion Talbot, Dean of Women, the University of Chicago, 1892–1925* (Chicago: The University of Chicago Press, 1936).

5. Post–WWII US gender roles: Elaine Tyler May, *Homeward Bound: American Families in the Cold War Era* (New York: Basic Books, 1988). Social attitudes: Lynn White Jr., *Educating Our Daughters: A Challenge to the Colleges* (New York: Harper & Brothers, 1950). Women's employment: Alice Kessler-Harris, *In Pursuit of Equity: Women, Men and Quest for Economic Citizenship in the 20th-Century America* (New York: Oxford University Press, 2001); Dorothy Sue Cobble, *The Other Women's Movement: Workplace Justice and Social Rights in Modern America* (Princeton, NJ: Princeton University Press, 2004).

6. Linda Eisenmann, "A Time of Quiet Activism: Research, Practice, and Policy in American Women's Higher Education, 1945–1965," *History of Education Quarterly* 45, 1, (Spring 2005): 1–17; Eisenmann, *Higher Education for Women in Postwar America, 1945–1965* (Baltimore, MD.: Johns Hopkins University Press, 2006).

7. For examples: Lois Kimball Mathews, *The Dean of Women* (Boston: Houghton Mifflin Company, 1915); Kate Hevner Mueller, *Educating Women for a Changing World* (Minneapolis: University of Minnesota Press, 1954). On citizenship training: chapters 1 and 2 in Kelly C. Sartorius, *Deans of Women and the Feminist Movement: Emily Taylor's Activism* (New York: Palgrave Macmillan, 2014); Kelly C. Sartorius, "A Coeducational Pathway to Political and Economic Citizenship:

Women's Student Government and a Philosophy and Practice of Women's U.S. Higher Coeducation between 1890 and 1945," in *Women's Higher Education in the United States: New Historical Perspectives*, ed. Margaret A. Nash, *Historical Studies in Education Series* (New York: Palgrave Macmillan, 2017), 161–84; Kelly C. Sartorius, "Counseling Women for Economic Citizenship: Deans of Women and the Beginnings of Vocational Guidance," *Paedagogica Historica: International Journal of the History of Education* 56, no. 6 (December 2020): 831-46.

8. Nancy K. Schlossberg identified discriminatory campus-wide career services models. Nancy K. Schlossberg, Clemmont E. Vontress, and Daniel Sinick, "Dynamics of Client-Counselor Differences," *Vocational Guidance Quarterly* 23, 1, (1974): 28–33; Nancy K. Schlossberg and John J. Pietrofesa, "Perspectives on Counseling Bias: Implications for Counselor Education," *The Counseling Psychologist* 4, 1 (1973): 44–54; John J. Pietrofesa and Nancy K. Schlossberg, "Counselor Bias and the Female Occupational Role," in *Sex Bias in the Schools*, ed. J. Pottker and A. Fishel (Teaneck, NJ: Fairleigh Dickinson University Press, 1977): 221–29.

9. Eisenmann, "A Time of Quiet Activism," 1–17; Eisenmann, *Higher Education for Women*; Sartorius, *Deans of Women*; Sartorius, "A Coeducational Pathway," 161–84; Kelly C. Sartorius, "Hidden Behind 'Vocation': The Missing History of Women's Role in Developing Career Services in Higher Education" (paper presented at the History of Education Society Annual Meeting, Albuquerque, NM, November 1, 2018).

10. Michael D. Coomes, Elizabeth J. Whitt, George D. Kuh, "Kate Hevner Mueller: Woman for a Changing World," *Journal of Counseling and Development* 65, 8, (1987): 407–15.

11. Kate Hevner Mueller, "Memoirs," 1971, C170, Box 2, Subseries: Memoirs, 1969–1970s, IULUA.

12. Kathryn Nemeth Tuttle, "What Became of the Dean of Women: Changing Roles for Women Administrators in American Higher Education, 1940–1980" (PhD diss., University of Kansas, 1996), 189.

13. Margaret W. Rossiter, *Women Scientists in America: Before Affirmative Action, 1940–1972* (Baltimore, MD: Johns Hopkins University Press, 1998), 33–35; Tuttle, "What Became of the Dean of Women," 33–35, 167–213; Harold S. Wechsler, Lester F. Goodchild, and Linda Eisenmann, eds., *The History of Higher Education* (Pearson Custom, 2007), 741–42, 747; Eisenmann, *Higher Education for Women*, 132–33; M. S. Hevel, "Toward a History of Student Affairs: A Synthesis of Research, 1996–2015," *Journal of College Student Development* 57, 7 (2016): 844–62; Sartorius, *Deans of Women*; Jennifer Buckley, "Kate Hevner Mueller: A Retrospective Analysis of a Dean of Women and Exploration of White Women's Gender Identity in the Interwar and World War II Generations," *Journal of the Indiana University Student Personnel Association* (2004): 26–40.

14. Mueller, "Memoirs," 1971.

15. The term *disappearing deans* was coined to reflect the movement of deans of men to the new position of dean of students. In reality, deans of women were the ones vanishing. Robert Schwartz, "The Disappearing Deans of Men: Where They Went and Why: A Historical Perspective" (paper presented at the American Educational Research Association Conference, Seattle, WA, April 10–14, 2001). The phrase was first coined in W. H. Cowley, "The Disappearing Dean of Men," *Occupations* 16, no. 2 (1937): 147–54.

16. Coomes, Whitt, and Kuh, "Kate Hevner Mueller," 407–15.

17. Coomes, Whitt, and Kuh, 407.

18. The phrase *second wave* has been questioned because it implies a lack of activism between suffrage and the late 1960s. Linda Nicholson, "Feminism in 'Waves': Useful Metaphor or Not?" *New Politics* 12, no. 4 (Winter 2010), 34–39; Kessler-Harris, *In Pursuit of Equity*; Cobble, *The Other Women's Movement*.

19. Sartorius, *Deans of Women*.

20. Coomes, Whitt, and Kuh, "Kate Hevner Mueller," 407–15.

21. Kate Hevner Mueller, "The Role of the Counselor in Sex Behavior and Standards," *Journal of the National Association of Women Deans and Counselors* 26, 2 (January 1963): 3–5; Kate Hevner Mueller, "My Notes from Rye Conference on Employment of Women," 1957, C170, Box 8, Folder: Speech Notes—Women Education ca. 1950s, IULUA; Mueller, *Educating Women for a Changing World*; Kate Hevner Mueller, "Others: Counseling for Mental Health," (ACE, Washington DC).

22. For the word *deaning*, Ruth A. Merrill and Helen Bragdon, *The Vocation of Dean* (Cambridge, MA: Harvard Graduate School of Education, 1926).

23. Judith Evans Longacre, *The History of Wilson College, 1868 to 1970* (Lewiston, NY: Edwin Mellen Press, 1997), 88; Sartorius, *Deans of Women*, 51–52.

24. Kate Hevner Mueller, Letter to Marion Park, March 21, 1928, C170, Box 3, Folder: Job Inquiries, notices 1926–1937, IULUA.

25. Sartorius, *Deans of Women*; Sartorius, "Hidden Behind 'Vocation'; Sartorius, "Counseling Women for Economic Citizenship."

26. Coomes, Whitt, and Kuh, "Kate Hevner Mueller," 407–15.

27. Kate Hevner Mueller, "Memoirs," 1971, in C170, Box 2, Subseries: Memoirs, 1969–1970s, IU Libraries, University Archives, Bloomington, Indiana.

28. Mueller, "Memoirs." Commonly, the dean of women cooperated "very closely with the physical education department and the health service department" as at IU. Agnes E. Wells, Letter to Mueller, June 27, 1938, C170, Box 2, Folder: Dean of Women 1938–1948, IULUA.

29. Nidiffer, *Pioneering Deans*, 98–99. Sartorius, *Deans of Women*; Sartorius, "A Coeducational Pathway," 161–84. On women's college student self-governance: Helen Lefkowitz Horowitz, *The Power and Passion of M. Carey Thomas* (New York: Alfred A. Knopf, 1994), 246.

30. Sartorius, "A Coeducational Pathway," 161–84.

31. On enrollments: Barbara Miller Solomon, *In the Company of Educated Women: A History of Women and Higher Education in America* (New Haven: Yale University Press, 1985), 58–61.

32. On deans and women's student government: Sartorius, *Deans of Women,* 45–51; Sartorius, "A Coeducational Pathway," 161–84; Janice J. Gerda, "A History of the Conferences of Deans of Women, 1903–1922," (PhD diss., Bowling Green State University, 2004).

33. On Talbot and Breckinridge: Nidiffer, *Pioneering Deans*; Tuttle, "What Became of the Dean of Women," 18–40; Sartorius, "A Coeducational Pathway," 161–84; Sartorius, "Hidden Behind 'Vocation'"; Sartorius, "Counseling Women for Economic Citizenship. On early deans meetings: Gerda, "A History of the Conferences."

34. Nidiffer, *Pioneering Deans,* 55, 74. IU deans of women succession: finding aid for C165 in IULUA.

35. On self-government in coeducational institutions: Sartorius, "A Coeducational Pathway," 161–84.

36. Agnes Wells, Letter to Mueller, June 27, 1938, C170, Office of the Dean of Women, 1938–48, IULUA.

37. Wells, Letter to Mueller, June 27, 1938. On Mueller's residence hall assistants: C165, Box 12, file: "Staff in Dormitories and Salaries, 1937–1938"; Box 13, "Halls of Residents (Appointments), 1939–1940"; Box 14, "Halls of Residence (Staff), 1940–1941"; Box 15, "Halls of Residence (Staff), 1941–42"; Box 18, "Halls of Residence, Resident Counselor Appointments, 1943–1944," IULUA.

38. Mueller, "Memoirs," 1971.

39. Wells, Letter to Mueller, June 27, 1938.

40. Wells.

41. NADW Executive Committee, "Appendix A," 1945, MS218, Box 4, Folder: Executive Board Minutes, September 1944–April 1948, Bowling Green State University (BGSU), CACNSAA, Bowling Green, Ohio; Tuttle, "What Became of the Dean of Women," 213. Indiana University President's Office records (C213), Box 522, Folder: Division of Student Affairs, especially Raymond Shoemaker, Letter to H. T. Briscoe, April 1, 1946; and "Functions of the Office of Student Personnel," n.d., both Box 522, Folder: Division of Student Personnel, IULUA.

42. ACE, *The Student Personnel Point of View: A Report of a Conference on the Philosophy and Development of Student Personnel Work in Colleges and Universities* (Washington, DC: ACE, 1937).

43. Mueller, Letter to Margaret C. Disert, August 6, 1942, Dean of Women's Office records (C165), Box 16, Folder: Mueller (Personal), 1942–1943, IULUA.

44. Mueller, Letter to Disert, August 6, 1942, 2.

45. Mueller.

46. Mueller, "Memoirs," 1971.

47. Mueller, Letter to Disert, August 6, 1942.

48. Mueller, "Memoirs," 1971.

49. Mueller, *Educating Women for a Changing World*, 254.

50. Emily Taylor, interview by author, December 13–14. 2003, author's records (Lawrence, Kansas).

51. Mueller, *Educating Women for a Changing World*, 147.

52. Mueller's hall counselors: Box 14, Folder: Halls of Residence (Staff) 1940–41; Box 15, Folder: Halls of Residence (Staff) 1941–42; Box 18, Folder: Halls of Residence, Resident Counselor Appointments, 1943–44 and Folder: Appointments (Halls of Residence titles, salary, etc.), 1944–1945; all in C165, IULUA. Mueller's commentary in: Office of the President, n.d., C213, Box 522, Folder: Division of Student Personnel, IULUA.

53. Emily Taylor, interview by author, April 7, 1997, author's records (Lawrence, Kansas).

54. Mueller, "Memoirs," 1971.

55. Mueller.

56. Mueller, 37–49.

57. Mueller.

58. Mueller and protégé Emily Taylor, among other deans, implemented sex education. Sartorius, *Deans of Women*, chapter 4.

59. Mueller, "Memoirs," 1971.

60. Sartorius, *Deans of Women*.

61. Mueller, Letter to Disert, August 6, 1942.

62. NADW Executive Committee, "Report of Standards Committee," 1946, MS218, Box 4, Folder: Executive Board Minutes, September 1944–April 1948, BGSU, CACNSAA.

63. Sydney Freeman, Linda Serrra Hagedorn, Lester Goodchild, Dianne Wright, *Advancing Higher Education as a Field of Study: In Quest of Doctoral Degree Guidelines—Commemorating 120 Years of Excellence* (Herndon, VA: Stylus Publishing, LLC, 2013), 35; Taylor, interviews by author.

64. Mueller, Letter to Disert, August 6, 1942.

65. Tuttle, "What Became of the Dean of Women," 168–69.

66. Tuttle, 167–213; Robert Schwartz, *Deans of Men and the Shaping of Modern College Culture* (New York: Palgrave Macmillan, 2010), 196; Eisenmann, *Higher Education for Women*, 28–29, 44, 47–49, 54–55, 132.

67. Efficiency emphasis increased in 1947 onward. ACE, *The Student Personnel Point of View*, 1947; Edmund Griffith Williamson, *The Student Personnel Point of View* (Washington, DC: 1949); Dennis C. Roberts, "The Student Personnel Point of View as a Catalyst of Dialogue: 75 Years and Beyond," *Journal of College Student Development* 53, no. 1, (January/February 2012): 2–18. On IU: Robert E. Bates,

"Dean of Men's Office Annual Report 1945–46," November 8, 1946, C213, Box 159, Folder: Dean of Men's Office Annual Report 1945–46, IULUA.

68. Richard B. Caple, *To Mark the Beginning: A Social History of College Student Affairs* (Lanham, MD: University Press of America, 1998), 44–45.

69. Sartorius, *Deans of Women*; Sartorius, "A Coeducational Pathway," 161–84; Sartorius, "Counseling Women for Economic Citizenship."

70. Eunice Mae Acheson, *The Effective Dean of Women: A Study of the Personal and Professional Characteristics of a Selected Group of Deans of Women* (Chicago, IL: University of Chicago Press, 1932), 51, 76.

71. Schwartz, "How Deans of Women Became Men," *Review of Higher Education* 20, no. 4 (Summer 1997): 419–36; Schwartz, "Reconceptualizing the Leadership Roles of Women in Higher Education: A Brief History on the Importance of Deans of Women," *Journal of Higher Education* 68, 5 (1997): 502–22; Schwartz, *Deans of Men*. For how men ousted deans of women: Schwartz, "The Disappearing Deans of Men." On dissolution of role: NAWE Executive Board, "Board Minutes, Columbus, Ohio," November 9–10, 1946, MS218, Box 4, Folder: Executive Board Minutes, September 1944–April 1948, BGSU, CACNSAA. IU followed the pattern. IU lost its first woman dean in 1906, and the first dean of men, Clarence Edmondson, was not appointed until 1919. Discipline for male students was handled by IU's university president and academic deans until Edmondson. Jason Gerdom, "Indiana University Dean of Students records, 1941–2000: A Guide to the Records at the Indiana University Archives," http://webapp1.dlib.indiana.edu/findingaids/view?doc.view=entire_text&docId=InU-Ar-VAA2639.

72. Schwartz, *Deans of Men*; Schwartz, "How Deans of Women Became Men," 419–36.

73. National Association of Deans and Advisers of Men, "Proceedings," (1921–1951, 1948), 57–68.

74. Tuttle, "What Became of the Dean of Women," 169.

75. D. H. Gardner as quoted in Tuttle, 211.

76. Tuttle, 168–71, 209; Sartorius, "A Coeducational Pathway," 161–84; Sartorius, *Deans of Women*.

77. As quoted in Tuttle, "What Became of the Dean of Women," 203.

78. As quoted in Tuttle, 200.

79. As quoted in Schwartz, *Deans of Men*, 181.

80. Schwartz, 193.

81. Tuttle, "What Became of the Dean of Women," 209–10. Some schools created a dean of students but retained the dean of women's direct report to the president as at KU.

82. New version: ACE, *The Student Personnel Point of View* (Washington, DC: American Council of Education, 1949).

83. Tuttle, "What Became of the Dean of Women," 199; Mueller, Letter to Disert, August 6, 1942.

84. Penelope Krosch, "Finding Aid Historical Note," 2018, Office of the Dean of Students papers, University of Minneapolis Archives and Special Collections, Minneapolis, Minnesota, https://snaccooperative.org/view/6770795.

85. Mueller, Letter to Disert, August 6, 1942.

86. As quoted from Catherine J. Robbins, dean of women, Pasadena Junior College, Pasadena, CA: Committee, 1946, NAWE MS218, Box 4, Folder: Executive Board Minutes, September 1944–April 1948, BGSU, CACNSAA.

87. Mildred Sayre, "The Illusion of Dichotomy: Personnel, as a Profession," 1948, NAWE, in Box 12, Committee Files, CACNSAA. Sartorius; "A Coeducational Pathway," 161–84. Sartorius, *Deans of Women*.

88. Tuttle, "What Became of the Dean of Women," 168.

89. For Bates's proposal, E. E. Edwards, Letter to H. B Wells, March 11, 1942, C213, Box 522, Folder: Division of Student Personnel, IULUA.

90. Briscoe's support of consolidation, E. E. Edwards, Letter to H. B Wells, March 11, 1942. Wells appointed Briscoe director of student guidance and dean of the faculties (1939) and then vice president and dean of the faculties (1940). Kristina Gray and Amanda Hunt Perez, "Indiana University Vice President and Dean of the Faculties Records, 1940–1959: A Guide to the Records at the Indiana University Archives," http://webapp1.dlib.indiana.edu/findingaids/view?doc.view=entire_text&docId=InU-Ar-VAC0759.

91. Edwards, Letter to Wells, March 11, 1942.

92. Edwards.

93. Bates, November 8, 1946, C213, Box 159, Folder: Dean of Men's Office Annual Report 1945–46, IULUA.

94. Bates, November 8, 1946.

95. Wells, Memorandum of conversation with Colonel R. L. Shoemaker, July 22, 1944, C213, Box 500, Folder: Shoemaker, Raymond, IULUA.

96. Shoemaker, Letter to Wells, July 20, 1945, C213, Box 500, Folder: Shoemaker, Raymond L., IULUA.

97. Office of the President, n.d., C213, Box 522, Folder: Division of Student Personnel, IULUA.

98. Bates, November 8, 1946.

99. Bates, Letter to Wells, September 18, 1945, C213, Box 522, Folder: Division of Student Personnel, IULUA.

100. Mueller, Letter to President Wells, September 19, 1945, C213, Box 522, Folder: Division of Student Personnel, IULUA.

101. Mueller, Letter to President Wells, September 19, 1945.

102. Mueller.

103. Office of the President, n.d., C213, Box 522, Folder: Division of Student Personnel, IULUA.

104. Support for the dean of women's office possibly came from Briscoe as he reviewed and initialed all reorganization proposals before Wells decided them.

105. Wells, Letter to Briscoe, October 2, 1945, C213, Box 522, Folder: Division of Student Personnel, IULUA.

106. Unknown author (noted as Briscoe in file under Briscoe's wife's name), Letter to Wells, September 5, 1945, Herman B Wells Papers (C75), Box 1, Folder: Correspondence, Briscoe, Orah, IULUA.

107. Shoemaker, Letter to Briscoe, April 1, 1946.

108. Shoemaker.

109. Briscoe, Letter to Dean Bates, Dean Mueller, Dean Shoemaker, April 10, 1946, C213, Box 500, Folder: Shoemaker, Raymond L., IULUA.

110. Mueller, Letter to Hilton, January 14, 1947.

111. Wells, Letter to Mueller, May 29, 1946, C213, Box 401, Folder: Mueller, Dean Kate H 1946–47, IULUA.

112. Shoemaker, Letter to Wells, June 15, 1946, C213, Box 500, Folder: Shoemaker Raymond L. 1946–47, IULUA.

113. Mueller seems to have incorrectly assumed that Vice President and Treasurer W. G. Biddle was her advocate as he quickly approved the budget change. She may, though, have been correct that the illness was influencing communication as the Indiana University Board of Trustees final approval was written by a deputy in Biddle's office. Shoemaker, Letter to Wells, June 15, 1946.

114. Wells, Letter to Mueller, June 18, 1946, C213, Box 401, Folder: Mueller, Dean Kate H., IULUA.

115. Tuttle, "What Became of the Dean of Women," 183–84.

116. Wells, Letter to Shoemaker, July 13, 1946, C213, Box 401, Folder: Mueller, Dean Kate H. 1946–47, IULUA; Shoemaker, Letter to Briscoe, July 3, 1946, C213, Box 401, Folder: Mueller, Kate Hevner 1946–47, IULUA. Wells's interdepartmental communications date the demotion decision as a presidential one that preceded trustee approval.

117. Mueller, Letter to Hilton, January 14, 1947.

118. Tuttle, "What Became of the Dean of Women," 183, noting Shaffer believed Mueller was inflexible, Wells wanted to solve difficulties with Nelson, and Mueller's administrative skills were weak and her staff were pleased by the change. Emily Taylor, KU dean of women who worked closely with Mueller as a 1940s residence hall counselor, refuted this, noting the demotion was pure sexism. Sartorius, Deans of Women, chapter 2.

119. Mueller, Letter to Hilton, January 14, 1947.

120. Mueller.

121. Mueller.

122. Mueller.

123. Mueller, "Memoirs," 1971.

124. Mueller.

125. Mueller, Letter to Wells, September 19, 1945.

126. Robert Shaffer, quoted by Tuttle, "What Became of the Dean of Women," 204.

127. Rye conference on continuing education, Eisenmann, *Higher Education for Women*, 100–05.

128. Committee, 1945, NAWE Records, MS218, Box 4, Folder: Executive Board Minutes, September 1944–April 1948, BGSU, CACNSAA.

129. Committee, 1945.

130. Board, November 9–10, 1946, MS218, Box 4, Folder: Executive Board Minutes, September 1944–April 1948, BGSU, CACNSAA.

131. Tuttle, "What Became of the Dean of Women," 207–08.

132. KU's Taylor required her staff read Mueller's book. Donna Shavlik, telephone interview by author, May 31, 2014, author's records.

133. Mueller, Letter to Mrs. Balz, June 5, 1948, C170, Box 8, Folder: Women, IULUA.

MARTHA E. DAWSON

Forty Years of Leadership in Multicultural Education and Teaching for Understanding and Excellence

ANDREA WALTON

Andrea Walton first learned about Martha Dawson's contributions in multicultural education and university administration a few years ago, when a student recommended Dawson's essay "Climbing the Administrative Ladder in the Academy: An Experiential Case History." Walton, herself a former high school teacher, a historian of academic women, and a faculty member at the Indiana University School of Education, immediately gravitated toward studying Dawson. Aware of her own positionality as a white woman, Walton in this sketch aims to highlight the influences of both race and gender in Dawson's career trajectory and her intellectual contributions to multicultural education.

IN A SHORT AUTOBIOGRAPHICAL ESSAY, published in 1997, IU alumna and former faculty member Martha E. Dawson, a pioneer in multicultural education, reflected on the contours of her four-decades-long journey as a Black woman in the academy. Sharing memories and advice about "climbing the administrative ladder," Dawson, who was born in segregated Richmond, Virginia, in 1924, commented on how she had navigated the snares of racism and sexism to build a productive faculty career—one that was both intellectually innovative and socially engaged, and that prepared her for later responsibilities in upper-level university administration.[1] This brief but revealing self-narrative was one of the few instances when Dawson wrote about her journey as an educator. One can imagine, though, that she, a thinker who often wove historical perspective into her writings on multiculturalism, viewed "Climbing the Administrative Ladder in the Academy" as a personal contribution to highlighting the legacy of academic women—and most especially the achievements of women of color as intellectuals and leaders.

Unfortunately, this 1997 essay is one of the few direct windows we have into Dawson's views on the interplay of gender and race that shaped her life, professional advancement, and scholarly contributions. Personal records related to Dawson's career are sparse. There is no archival record of her time at Virginia State or Indiana University. Moreover, professional papers related to Dawson's senior administrative roles at Hampton are still unprocessed. The limited availability of primary sources leaves Dawson's biographers the formidable challenge of weaving a true-to-life portrait from the published, visible threads of an academic career spanning more than four decades and three campuses: her undergraduate alma mater, Virginia State University; her doctoral institution and later faculty home, Indiana University; and the institution she served longest, in her faculty career and later as a senior administrator, Hampton University.

This biographical sketch foregrounds the IU chapters of Martha Dawson's career—from her doctoral student days in the 1950s, to her design of an innovative urban education program as a senior School of Education faculty member in the 1970s, and to her recognition as IU Distinguished Alumna in 1980. To understand Dawson's contributions to IU, though, means casting one's net widely, looking at her biographical details in light of larger social, intellectual, and institutional dynamics, and, importantly, considering her time at IU within the context of her entire career. Indeed, no single chapter in Dawson's career can be understood fully either in isolation or apart from the much larger backdrop to her personal life and professional endeavors—the struggle for civil rights and the search for equity in society. Her contributions and achievements—at various junctures in life, at different types of campuses, at several levels of professional responsibility, and at crucial moments in national debates within the field of education—were, as she put it, part of "climbing the administrative ladder." But each step of the ascent was shaped by and, in turn, further shaped the arc of a forty-plus-year academic career wedded to the pursuit of equity and excellence in education.[2]

Dawson pursued these values, which are core to democratic education, in her writing and workshops on multicultural education and embraced and furthered them by choices she made in her life and career. Earning her IU doctorate in 1956, she returned to the South to build her career, navigating the path from teacher, to district teacher supervisor, to teacher educator before the end of the decade. Doing so was not easy, especially for a married woman with a young family. One needed both talent and tenacity to forge a path to achievement and advancement as an academic, given the stark reality that institutions of higher education hired relatively few women faculty and administrators (especially women with young children) and even fewer women of color.

Dawson had both talent and tenacity. These career-enhancing attributes were shaped by the contours of her life. The encouragement of family and mentors and her growing social consciousness as a Black woman in America steeled her passion for books and reading about new ideas, strengthened her commitment to an academic career, and sharpened her insights into how teachers might invigorate democracy by providing all students innovative, diverse, and equitable learning experiences. She achieved early recognition as a skillful teacher and innovative educator (as an expert in nongraded classrooms and multicultural education), and soon took on various administrative roles. Whether chairing a department or committee, spearheading an accreditation team, or designing a new program, Dawson enthusiastically accepted the challenges of leadership and crafted a distinguished career that included appointments of increasing responsibility and visibility at both major predominantly white and Historically Black institutions.

As this biographical sketch will highlight, her career was marked by great purposefulness and coherence; valuing friendships and the power of professional networks, she stayed in touch with former professors, mentors, colleagues, and students. Her ties to institutions where she had studied or worked were enduring. Always ready to embrace the next challenge, she was called upon and answered the call to return to all three institutions that had been formative in her early career: Virginia State, Indiana, and Hampton. Throughout her forty-year academic career, in all the roles she fulfilled with distinction—researcher, teacher educator, and university administrator—she displayed steady leadership, high standards, and deep respect for the power of teaching. Her educational ideals, professional ethics, and personal faith enabled her to envision and commit herself to working toward a better future—for Black, Brown, and white children as well as students of different economic backgrounds. To her mind, a multicultural approach in the curriculum and culturally diverse approaches to teacher preparation were integral to promoting greater social understanding and more democratic public education.

SARAH'S DAUGHTER: GROWING UP IN THE JIM CROW SOUTH

Born Martha Elizabeth Eaton on January 21, 1924, in Richmond, Virginia, Dawson was the eldest of four children. Her mother, Sarah, a domestic worker, and her father, John, a Baptist preacher, instilled in their children the dignity of a life well lived, a respect for education, and the values of family and faith.

Dawson's mother provided her a female model of strength, heart, and intellect. "My mother was a big, hefty lady. You didn't play with Sarah; she meant business. But she was kind and gentle," Dawson recalled in a 1991 interview.[3] Her memories of childhood pointed to lessons learned from each of her parents and to the affirming nature of daily life in the Eaton household. Notably, her mother had the "farsightedness" to buy beautiful dolls and have them painted brown for her young daughter. Her father taught her at an early age to read the Bible, shared his love of Shakespeare and poetry, and guarded his daughter's time to delve into books.[4]

The blend of heart and mind embraced in the Eaton household shaped how the children engaged the world around them. "In spite of the problems of the times, we lived in a mixed neighborhood. We were never taught to hate people but to love people and to judge people by the way they responded to you. That was just instilled in us," Dawson recalled. Proud of her heritage, Dawson, the great-granddaughter of a houseslave, attributed her self-confidence and a sense of self-worth while growing up in Jim Crow Richmond to her parents' childrearing: "My family had overprepared and insulated me for the black 'inferiority game'"[5]

Dawson attended segregated schools in Virginia from the primary grades through her undergraduate years. She would translate her personal experience into a lifelong professional commitment to improving education, to encouraging students, and to upholding excellence, as her family and teachers had done for her. Refusing to accept the inequality of Richmond's segregated and poorly funded public schools, the Eatons decided to send their daughter to Van de Vyver Catholic Institute, a well-known private Black school, founded in 1887 in Richmond's Jackson Ward. This section of the capital city was then, in the words of architectural historian Robert P. Winthrop, "the center of Negro religious life and education . . . indeed, the social, economic and political hub of central Virginia's Black population."[6]

Dawson looked back on her attendance at Van de Vyver as pivotal in building her self-confidence and in shaping her aspirations to become a teacher. Even years later she carried one of her mother's dollar-a-week tuition receipts in her pocket as a reminder of this life-changing opportunity in girlhood and of her family's sacrifices for her education.[7] She was even known to wave the receipt proudly in the air when speaking to audiences of school personnel and teacher educators about the need to continue the push for equality of educational opportunity.

In telling her story, Dawson, a woman of deep faith, focused on both the role of providence and the power of mentors in helping her to develop and grow through her educational experiences and successive professional responsibilities.[8] In many respects, Dawson's career exemplified the combined power of agency and enabling community ties that historian Stephanie Shaw, in her study of Black middle-class women professionals, identified as "responsible individualism."[9]

Because education was generally valued as the key to a Black woman's upward mobility—that is, to open new opportunities outside domestic service or unskilled labor—families often made sacrifices for daughters to pursue a college degree.[10] As a young Black southern woman, Dawson's aspirations to become a teacher reflected her early passion for reading and learning (a zeal encouraged by her father) but were also shaped by gendered career possibilities and further limited by the constraints of Virginia's system of segregated higher education. Indeed, it is worth noting that less than a decade had passed since Richmond native Alice Jackson's application for fall 1935 graduate admission to the University of Virginia was denied on account of her race. Aware that other controversial admission cases and NAACP litigation were likely, state lawmakers developed a two-prong strategy of resistance to stave off further desegregation efforts: plans were made to introduce limited graduate studies at Virginia State University, a Black land-grant, and funding was allocated for Black students to go out of state (under the Dovell Act, House Bill 470, passed in 1936). [11] In Virginia and elsewhere in the South state education policy thus circumscribed opportunity for Blacks students seeking graduate and professional education and became an influential factor in increasing enrollment diversity at northern campuses—notably at urban privately-endowed institutions close to centers of Black intellectual and cultural life, such as Columbia Teachers College (NYC) and University of Chicago, but also at midwestern state universities such as Ohio, Michigan, Iowa, Illinois, and Indiana. Historians Cally L. Waite and Margaret Smith Crocco point to the scope of this policy and its impact on both students and institutions: "Between 1942 and 1955, over US $900,000 was paid to universities outside Virginia so that more than 3,400 qualified Black graduates could study in those institutions as opposed to integrating the University of Virginia."[12]

When Dawson was fifteen, her father passed away. Although family circumstances had changed, Sarah Eaton remained deeply committed to her daughter's further education and supported her plans to become a teacher, as a great-aunt in the family had done. With Mrs. Eaton's encouragement—and in fact advocacy on her daughter's behalf with administrators at Virginia State College—Dawson secured a job in the campus dining hall and worked her way through college. She earned her bachelor's of science in elementary education in 1943.[13]

Black teachers of Dawson's generation had far narrower employment options than their white counterparts, but they were able to carve out within the disparities and injustices of segregated schooling paths to civic leadership, professional accomplishment, and influence as role models in the classroom and school administration.[14] Beginning what would become a distinctive pattern of her career—that is, finding advancement and new professional opportunities through established ties with former teachers, colleagues, and academic employers—the Virginia State graduate found herself returning to Van de Vyver Institute as a lay teacher, recruited by one of her elementary school teachers, Sister Pancraus. This was a pivotal moment in Dawson's young adulthood; she began her teaching career, married, and in 1943 gave birth to the couple's first of three children. A particularly abled early career teacher, she was soon tapped for a position in the public school system, at Richmond's Baker Street School. The culture among Baker Street's teachers sparked Dawson's interest in the professional development needed to maintain her teaching certificate and eventually led her back to Virginia State for graduate education. There she came to regard Professor W. Bruce Welch, an educational psychologist, as a mentor. He encouraged her to explore intellectual and social opportunities beyond the familiar world she knew until that point in life—and more specifically to consider pursuing a doctorate at Indiana University.[15] It was through Welch, an IU alum (EdD 1951), that Dawson was introduced to Indiana University educator Merrill Eaton.[16]

Each spring, Professor Eaton made an outreach trip to the South on behalf of Indiana University's School of Education in order to connect with Black IU alums, hoping through their professional and social networks to meet prospective graduate students. He was particularly interested in reaching out to Black teachers who might enroll in summer session classes at the Bloomington campus. Welch made sure Eaton's recruitment trip included speaking with Martha Dawson. As Welch explained to Dawson, studying at a major university outside the segregated South would be an invaluable educational venture, one that would be career enhancing and bring a new dimension to Dawson's experience and thinking as an educator. But, Welch was also well aware that there would be challenges ahead.

In 1950–51, the year he received his IU doctorate, the university still had only 349 Black students enrolled out of a total student body of 10,715. Even though IU's Black enrollment was growing in the postwar years, Dawson would find herself in an environment quite different from VSU's campus.[17] Most of IU's Black student population came to Bloomington from various corners of Indiana, choosing to remain close to family and home by studying at the state university. But each entering class also included a number of students who, like Dawson, traveled from the Jim Crow South. Even though some racial exclusions and barriers in southern higher education were beginning to fall as the civil right movement gained momentum—one recalls, for example, that George Swanson had been admitted to the University of Virginia's law school in 1950—Black students still faced overt hostility, violence, and unequal access to advanced education. Many Black southerners were compelled to look for advanced educational opportunity elsewhere. Leaving home and family, they took the long train ride or bus trip to northern cities, where they enrolled in private universities with established student networks and opportunities for paid work or traveled to the closer small, predominantly white midwestern towns, like Bloomington, that were home to large state universities, where tuition and living costs were lower. After graduation, their career paths were shaped by the interplay of race and gender, reflected in the meeting point of their aspirations and educational background and prevalent attitudes and hiring practices in different areas of the country. In the early 1950s, Martha Dawson was faced with a decision not unlike that of a young Talladega graduate named Jane McAllister, who nearly three decades earlier had left Mississippi to study at Teachers College, Columbia University, and in 1929 she became the first Black woman in the United States to earn a PhD in education. McAllister went on to teach for twenty years at Miner Teachers College (Washington, DC), taught and consulted at Southern University, and served as head of the normal department at Fisk University, before ending her distinguished career at Jackson State College. Dawson was among a generation of talented Black women educators who followed in McAllister's footsteps—aspiring teachers, student affairs professionals, and administrators—who left the South for graduate studies in the North. And, like most of these women, Dawson would spend at least part of her professional career at a Black institution in the South.[18]

Dawson valued the chance to earn her degree from a nationally regarded curriculum and instruction department, and her decision to attend graduate school at IU was pivotal in shaping the trajectory of her career, but it came at personal sacrifice. The Dawsons had planned to move together to Indiana while Martha attended IU, but her husband, James, a craftsman, could not find employment, given the racial exclusion of Blacks from Indiana's trade unions. The couple endured distance and separation; James remained in Virginia while Martha studied in Bloomington.

Unfortunately, we have no direct knowledge of Dawson's daily life during her IU graduate student days. There are no archival or personal records available related to this period, and her biographical essay, "Climbing Ladders," speaks only to the intellectual rather than the social aspects of this period. Whether this omission had meaning remains unclear, but one can turn to the oral histories and memories of other Black IU alums—men and women who were roughly Dawson's contemporaries—to gain some sense of the racial climate on the IU campus and in the surrounding town during the era.[19]

In the context of the 1950s, IU had a reputation and sense of itself as a racially tolerant northern institution. It had never excluded students based on race and by most accounts enrolled more Black students than any institution in the Hoosier state. And yet, admission did not mean full access to campus life. Notably, the Bloomington campus Dawson would have encountered in the mid-1950s had desegregated residential living just a few years earlier, and then only amid substantial activist pressures by students and the NAACP, and, ultimately, by the state of Indiana's 1949 law against segregation in public education.

Dawson would have found herself among a small but growing number of Black students at IU—among them Hoosiers and Southerners such as herself—who were attracted by the university's academic strengths and reputation as the alma mater of many Black college presidents, administrators, and faculty. Such recognized achievement in graduating Black leaders, however, did not mean IU's campus environment was unblemished by racism. In the 1940s, IU sociologists studying attitudes and experiences among IU's Black undergraduates had pointed to the mix of experiences—satisfying friendships and opportunities offset by instances of bias and marginalization—their survey respondents reported. Most students described being engaged by their courses and degree programs, but some had negative feelings toward their college experience overall. Arriving at IU with high hopes, they felt the sting of being made to feel unwelcome by some of their classmates and professors and encountered levels of segregation in campus facilities, student activities, and daily life in the small southern Indiana town of Bloomington. In the years immediately following World War II, Black students would have seen the fruits of earlier civil rights activism on IU's campus and the influences of broader changes in society, but substantial progress was still needed. In retrospect, a host of inequalities remained, festering—and would only be elevated to public scrutiny by Black student activists and their demands for change in the late 1960s.

Importantly, there was no single Black experience at IU. Years later, some Black IU alums who attended in the 1950s or early 1960s, roughly the same period as Dawson's student days, still held very fond, positive memories of their interactions with white classmates and faculty, while for others the experience was far from Edenic.[20] Even as Black students perceived attending IU as a chance for mobility, they had to navigate the challenges of racism on and off campus. James Comer, who earned an outstanding scholastic record at his East Chicago, Indiana, high school, did well academically at IU, graduating in 1956, but felt "defeated by the social situation." Interviewed about his collegiate experience some thirty years later, Comer, by then a noted professor of psychiatry and authority on Black child development, spoke vividly of his lack of comfort on the Bloomington campus. "All of a sudden I was a Black, poor kid. . . . I had to deal with racial antagonisms. My confidence was shot. I was petrified."[21] Acting on these feelings, Comer decided against attending IU's medical school in Indianapolis and instead enrolled at Howard University in Washington, DC. Among the nation's oldest HBCUs, Howard had a distinguished Black faculty and Black president (its first), Mordecai Johnson.

Gloria Randle (later Scott), a young Black IU undergraduate from Texas, recalled being ostracized by some white classmates and excluded from seminar gatherings at the home of her professor in zoology. Still, she engaged in and emerged as a leader in campus life, serving as president of her residence hall and her sorority and as an officer of the IU Foundation Student Committee. She found a more welcoming environment later as a graduate student at IU's School of Education—studying with nationally known student affairs practitioner-scholars Kate Mueller and Bob Shaffer. Named the Outstanding Black Student in the State of Indiana in 1964, she earned her PhD in higher education in 1965.[22] Scott would later head the Girl Scouts USA, from 1975 to 1978, and would serve as president of Bennett College, one of the country's few all-female HBCUs, from 1987 to 2001.

Cora Smith (later Breckenridge) took IU classes through the extension program at the Calumet Center in East Chicago (antecedent of IU Northwest) before transferring to IUB and earning her bachelor's and master's degrees in speech and hearing therapy in 1959 and 1963, respectively. She was elected secretary of the senior class and vice president of the Pleiades Honorary Society and was a member of Mortar Board, Alpha Kappa Alpha (AKA) Sorority, and the IU Student Foundation. Breckenridge maintained ties with IU over the years and in 1997 made history as the first Black elected as IU trustee. She went on to gain prominence for her service on the National Board of Directors of the NAACP (2000–12).[23]

The profiles of this small group of IU's Black collegians offer poignant, varied memories of the Bloomington campus experience during the 1950s and early 1960s—of both racism encountered and opportunities for participation and leadership in majority white student activities. No doubt, Dawson would have similarly felt a mix of sentiments, ranging from affirmation to frustration. Most relevant here, like all three of these individuals, Dawson's time at IU contributed to her educational ideas and her identity as an educator. And for her, student days began what would be a lifelong association with IU.

For Dawson, graduate studies at IU soon proved to be the type of career-enhancing experience her Virginia State mentor W. Bruce Welch had described. Entering as a master's student, Dawson was mentored by Leo Fay, an international authority on reading, and was among the graduate assistants recognized by the School of Education award for teaching excellence. Earning her IU master's degree in reading in 1954, she continued to an EdD in elementary education. With Fay's guidance, Dawson followed an efficient timeline toward completing her degree; she returned to Richmond to collect data at Baker School and traveled back to Bloomington the next summer to write up her results and defend her dissertation. Her research, pointing to the influence social and economic factors have on learning, focused on the size of a student's vocabulary in relation to the home environment and documented lower social economic status.[24]

Dawson's newly minted EdD placed her among the nation's small number of Black individuals—and, fewer still, Black women—to earn a doctorate before 1960. But for those women who did pursue doctoral studies, education held strikingly greater opportunity than other fields. As Horace Mann Bond highlighted in his now classic *Black American Scholars*, between 1928 and 1955, about 60 percent of doctorates in the field of education went to men and 40 percent to women. Other fields were decidedly less open; between 1896 and 1960 only about 16 percent of doctoral degrees across all disciplines were awarded to Black women. To put Dawson's graduation, her return to the South, and her new position as a consultant in Richmond public schools in much larger national context, recall just two major news headlines from 1956. Indeed, 1956 was the year in which Autherine Lucy enrolled at the University of Alabama, after successfully suing the state for admission, and a group of white southern senators defiantly signed the "Southern Manifesto" in opposition to the *Brown v. Board of Education* decision and racial integration.[25]

At the time of her graduation in the mid-1950s, but even more so from the vantage point of the 1990s, as she looked back on her career, culminating in responsibilities as a senior scholar-university administrator, Dawson understood the historical significance of her personal achievement in earning her doctorate. She recalled, "In August 1956, I returned to Richmond as Dr. Dawson, a first for a Black female in the Richmond public school system."[26] Dawson now saw the realities of segregated Richmond she had known as a child and early career teacher through the lens of her graduate studies and interest in helping to create change through education. The Brown decision did not erase the years of institutionalized racism in Richmond schools that had prompted the Eatons to choose Catholic school for their daughter. In fact, by mid-1955, as historian Robert A. Pratt described vividly, "The seeds of bitter defiance had already begun to germinate, and roost Virginia politicians were now steadfastly committed to maintaining segregated schools throughout the state, even if it meant a direct confrontation with the federal courts."[27] A belief that the post-Brown era called for rethinking classroom culture and preparing more socially aware teachers became the springboard of the next chapter in Dawson's career, taking her from the classroom to the professoriate.

INNOVATION AT HAMPTON: A NON-GRADED APPROACH TO ELEMENTARY EDUCATION IN THE POST-BROWN ERA

From her supervisory role in Richmond public schools, Dawson was recruited to an associate professorship in teacher education at Hampton Institute (known today as Hampton University). One of the country's leading HBCUs, Hampton's roots date back to 1868. The Institute, founded to educate freedmen after the Civil War and well known for training Black teachers, stood not far from where the *White Lion*, carrying enslaved people to Virginia, arrived in 1619.[28] By the 1930s, Hampton began to offer bachelor degrees in education. The campus's George P. Phenix School provided Hampton educators with a laboratory environment for teaching and learning, but in 1944 the Institute established an experimental program to send Hampton's preservice students off campus for internships.[29] Hampton's longstanding commitment to teacher education appealed to Dawson.

Dawson's hire came in anticipation of noted educator Dr. Eva C. Mitchell's planned retirement. Mitchell, a 1921 alumna of Hampton, had completed her graduate studies at Columbia University (master's degree 1920; PhD 1942) and spent her career building education studies at Hampton. In 1959, Dawson became chair of Hampton's department of elementary education.[30] Over the next eleven years, she solidified Hampton's standing as a hub of innovative preservice education for Black teachers and earned a reputation as an outstanding teacher educator. She advised various student groups, worked with state teacher associations and the American Association of University Women

(AAUW), assumed leadership roles in national curriculum circles, and was tapped as a consultant and evaluator for Title IV programs.

Most important, under Dawson's leadership Hampton's elementary education program raised the institute's profile as a leader in the post-Brown era's push to achieve equitable desegregated schooling. Dawson's founding of an acclaimed nongraded school laboratory on Hampton's campus dovetailed well with Hampton's legacy of teacher training and the equity reform mindset that also prompted the institute not to renew the city's lease of the Phenix School building, an all-Black high school on campus. In 1963, Dawson's projects related nongraded schooling (an alternative to the lockstep of year-by-year classrooms) attracted funding from the Lilly Endowment and earned her promotion to full professor in 1964.[31]

Dawson's work at Hampton developed in dialogue with a national nongraded school movement that brought together educators who for a variety of reasons were critical of the rigid, bureaucratic structure of the graded, "egg crate" school.[32] By the late 1950s, the concept of the nongraded classroom, which put the child's individual needs and the goal of continual growth and development front and center, was gaining momentum on the national scene—with John Goodlad, director of the Laboratory School at UCLA, as its most prominent advocate.[33] Dawson centered her work at Hampton on connecting the reform of nongraded schooling to education debates about "the culture of poverty" and the "urban crisis" (to use the terminology of the period).[34] Under Dawson's leadership, the Hampton program forged strong connections to educators in the region and achieved growing visibility in national discussions of nongraded education in relation to social policy and the learning needs of the youngest, most vulnerable children.[35]

DAWSON AS PROGRAM DESIGNER AND DIRECTOR

Whereas her early classroom experiences and doctoral studies were set against the backdrop of the 1954 Brown decision and its immediate aftermath, Dawson's years at Hampton bore the imprint of the 1960s—a period when education was significantly influenced by landmark legislation concerning social, economic, and racial disparities (the Civil Rights Act, the Economic Opportunity Act, and the Elementary and Secondary Education Act).

In the mid-1960s, Hampton Institute received a contract from the Office of Educational Opportunity, US Department of Health, Education, and Welfare (HEW), funding a five-week workshop on the nongraded approach to improve education in desegregated classrooms. Dawson served as director of the project, working with Helen Holston, head teacher at the Hampton Institute Nongraded Laboratory School. Workshop attendees engaged with invited speakers and discussed readings on leadership in the transition to nongraded schools and individualizing instruction for students many contemporary observers described as "underachievers" or "disadvantaged" children. Dawson and her colleagues designed the workshop to give particular attention to reading and social studies methods and to foster collaboration in an interracial class setting.[36]

Another high-profile activity Dawson led at Hampton was a summer program known as Operation Step-Up. Thirty educators (teams of administrators and teachers, among them twenty-four Black educators and six white educators from twelve school districts) and one hundred boys and girls (approximately one-third of applicants) were selected competitively. Students received instruction—an "educational booster"—and attending educators learned from teaching and observing in a nongraded desegregated classroom.[37] Such activities raised Dawson's profile in the field of teacher education because she ran well-received workshops and skillfully translated these hands-on experiences into scholarly publications and materials for school districts. By the end of the 1960s, Dawson had gained considerable recognition for her work at Hampton and its service to districts and teachers in the region. But how might the ideas and strategies she leveraged effectively in the South translate into reform work with teacher educators and schools in the North? This question would help bring her back to Indiana University.

THE INDIANA UNIVERSITY YEARS: CULTIVATING MULTICULTURAL APPROACHES IN TEACHER EDUCATION AT A PREDOMINANTLY WHITE MIDWESTERN UNIVERSITY

IU's offer of a full professorship in 1970 presented Dawson with a timely career opportunity: having spent over a decade at Hampton, she found herself both able to relocate and intellectually eager to accept a new professional challenge. On the personal level, Dawson had divorced after twenty-five years of marriage. Her youngest daughter, born when the couple's two older children were already in college, could move to Bloomington with her. On the professional level, Dawson was an established scholar whose Hampton years were a solid foundation for the work she envisioned at IU. The IU position would be an opportunity to design an entirely new program and held the challenge of bringing the multicultural curricular ideas she had written about and implemented in her teacher education work at Hampton to a predominantly white university setting in a northern state.

Together, Herman C. Hudson, head of IU's newly created Office of Afro-American Affairs and a pioneer in Black studies, and David L. Clark, dean of IU's School of Education, recruited Dawson. Her appointment as professor of education with tenure made her the first Black female scholar to hold that rank at IU.[38] Her addition to IU's newly formed Department of Urban Education came as student demands and federal affirmative action guidelines brought growing pressure for IU to diversify its faculty ranks. Moreover, faculty and administrators at the School of Education were searching for better ways to prepare teachers for Indiana's increasingly diverse classrooms.[39] From an institutional perspective, Dawson's hire meant the return of an accomplished alumna who had remained connected to her IU mentors and alma mater over the years. Her identity as a senior Black woman educator and expertise in multicultural education held the potential to help transform IU's approach to teacher education and significantly bolster the School of Education's and university-wide efforts to address gender and racial diversity. [40]

In her shift from Hampton to IU, Dawson left the environment of a southern HBCU with a predominantly Black faculty and joined a 150-year-old northern university with a sparse Black enrollment that had appointed its first Black scholar only two decades earlier, after WWII. Richard Davis Johnson, a New Jersey native and returning veteran, earned his bachelor of music from IU in 1950, studied briefly in Paris, and then became an instructor of percussion in 1951. News of his appointment drew violence from the Ku Klux Klan, which lit a cross ablaze on the front lawn of his residence.

Johnson was promoted to associate professor in 1958 and remained IU's lone Black faculty member until the 1960s, when Benjamin Peery was recruited to an assistant professorship in astronomy.[41] Over the next ten years, amid the political shift in the nation from the Civil Rights to the Black Power era, further changes came to IU's campus, though progress was too slow for those denied equitable opportunities. Black enrollment increased to approximately six hundred but still was not aligned with state demographics and remained only 2 percent of IUB's total student population.[42] Incremental efforts to diversify the IU faculty were evident in the mid-1960s. In 1966, Orlando Taylor, a recent University of Michigan PhD, returned to IU. As a master's student at IU, he had participated in NAACP sit-ins against Bloomington's "whites-only" barbershops. Taylor's appointment to the Department of Speech and Theater made him one of only three Black faculty members then at the university.[43]

The significance of Dawson's 1970 hire to spearhead a multicultural teacher education program at IU must be viewed in light of this early history of the dearth of Black representation on the IU faculty. It also can be seen as part of the university's response to student protest against racial inequality and bias unleashed by two major events of 1968—one national (the assassination of Martin Luther King Jr.) and one local (the bombing of Bloomington's Black market). IU's student protesters called for a number of actions: the hiring of more Black faculty, a more relevant and inclusive curriculum, an end to discriminatory practices in student life (controversy swirled around racial and cultural biases inherent in the Homecoming Queen contest and racial exclusions by fraternities and sororities), and steps to increase minority student enrollment and improve the status and opportunities of Black students. One tangible outcome of student demands was the creation of the Office of Afro-American Affairs in the spring of 1968. Herman Hudson, an alumnus of the University of Michigan, joined IU in 1968 as an associate professor after time spent at Florida A&M University, the University of Puerto Rico, and Kabul University in Afghanistan. He was appointed IU's vice chancellor of the Office of Afro-American Affairs the next year.

According to data on Black faculty compiled by Herman Hudson, in 1970 there were five tenured associate professors and two full professors. By 1985 there were twenty-one Black faculty.[44] In addition, the Bloomington campus saw Black scholars and artists spearhead a number of culturally diverse initiatives such as the Soul Revue (directed by Portia Maultsby), the Choral Ensemble, and the African-American Dance Company (directed by Iris Rosa). The Groups Program worked to bolster the recruitment and support of Black and first-generation students, and administrator (and alumnus) Jimmy Ross, in IU's Office of Scholarship and Financial Aid from 1973 to 1988, found ways to help more students of modest financial means study at IU.[45]

As Dawson's work in urban education at IU took root, interests in faculty diversity and aligning the School of Education's scholarly profile and course offerings to the policy concerns of the day began to shape junior faculty appointments. Three early career scholars of color would join the School of Education faculty in the early 1970s: child development specialist Sadie Grimmett (who had earned her PhD in 1969 studying with Head Start pioneer Susan Gray at the George Peabody College for Teachers [Vanderbilt]); counseling specialist Dorris Jeffries; and historian of education James D. Anderson (both recent graduates of the University of Illinois).

DESIGNING A TEACHER EDUCATION PROGRAM
TO TRANSLATE SOCIAL IDEAS ABOUT EQUITY
AND DIVERSITY INTO PRACTICE

Reflecting her lived realities as a Black woman from the Jim Crow South, Dawson saw multiculturalism as intimately connected to US history. Multicultural education was concerned with history in the curriculum but also a product of history, a movement emerging from and shaped by the progression of ideas in the ongoing, evolving pursuit of equity: it called for an examination of issues of race, class, gender, age, and ability. She observed goals and frameworks in reform change over time. "During the sixties, desegregation—not multicultural education—was the major goal of politicians and educators committed to equal justice. Their objective was a forerunner of multicultural education."[46] Whereas earlier generations of intercultural or intergroup educators had tended to focus on cultivating tolerance, educators in the 1960s and early 1970s shifted the discussion to an analysis of culture and theorizing of the oppressive or exclusionary structures in society.[47] Dawson was among a generation of young Black academics and school-based educators whose influence came from the rising ethnic studies movements and from new, growing federal interest in schooling as a lever of social policy to address the needs of poor children.[48] Such reform work stood in stark contrast to a resurgent genetics-based explanation for differences in educational achievement.[49]

In the early 1970s, IU's School of Education could look back on its record of graduating Black leaders and having enrolled more Black students than most units of the university, but its history was not unblemished. Local racial norms and attitudes had still circumscribed opportunities for Black students. For example, in the 1940s, Black IU teacher candidates were not permitted to do their required field placement in the university's campus laboratory classrooms or Bloomington's local schools. They instead had to travel to Indianapolis (expenses paid by the university) so they could complete their student teaching requirement at all-Black Crispus Attucks high school.[50]

By the time Dawson returned to IU in 1970, the politics of public schooling in Indianapolis was taking on a new dimension. The Justice Department had lodged a civil rights case (related to segregation in public schools) against the city of Indianapolis. With issues of race in education in the headlines, reform-minded faculty in the School of Education embarked on finding ways to bring a more diverse cohort into its teacher preparation program and to achieve a cohesive focus on urban education within the School of Education curriculum. The new program would replace what until then had been scattered courses on the "inner city" or "ghetto" or guest lectures on topics related to urban education offered by graduate student consultants.

The rationale and design for the program emerged from what IU educators like Dawson saw as the dramatic gap between the most urgent needs of underserved school populations and the cultural and racial homogeneity of the existing teaching corps and most teacher preparation offerings. Regardless of where they would be hired, teachers needed to be empathetic, culturally aware, and more cognizant of their values and biases in order to be effective teachers of students whose background differed from their own. "Often through naivete the classroom teacher makes minority group pupils feel like unwelcome guests," Dawson noted in a 1973 essay.[51] Many teacher educators and theorists among Dawson's contemporaries experimented with ways to make the curriculum more inclusive but also to rethink the training of teachers, structures of schooling, and connections between universities and communities in times of rising dropout rates and glaring racial and economic disparities.[52] "We should not have to retrain the current graduates!" Dawson asserted in her comments to Bloomington's *Herald Times* reporters in 1971.[53] The IU program cast its net wide: all promotional materials emphasized the program as interdisciplinary and designed to reach the various populations living in urban or rural poverty in Indiana—poor whites in the Southern region, Blacks in the capital city of Indianapolis and industrial Gary, and Latinos in East Chicago.[54] "Teachers working with children who live in the midst of poverty need to become highly skilled in human engineering as well as have deep insight into the cultural heritage and the scars of poverty which these youngsters bring to school."[55]

At a time when some reformers pushed for alternate models of schooling (based on Britain's Summerhill), free school, or even de-schooling, efforts by Dawson and her IU colleagues were community-based, interdisciplinary, experiential, and designed to shift the orientation among teacher educators from compensatory measures to multicultural curriculum and teaching.[56] Dawson developed a five-year program that required students to build upon coursework by completing a field experience component interning at a social agency or nonprofit, such as the Black social settlement Flanner House in Indianapolis, to learn about the community environment (second semester of fourth year and first semester of fifth). In Dawson's view, this experimental, community-based complement to coursework introduced students "involved with real people in the real world—away from the university."[57] The weekly sixty-mile road trip from IU's Bloomington campus to school sites in Indianapolis created a bridge from the university to the real world of schools. But for the Black professor and her students, the drive carried extra meaning; it meant traveling through small towns linked to the contemporary accounts and memories of racial intolerance the enterprise of multicultural education confronted.[58]

Dawson fully recognized that civil rights legislation and educational reform had not achieved a truly more democratic society. Others in education who had worked hard for change had reached a similar appraisal. As Michael E. Manley-Casimir and Ian Housego observed of the 1970s, many reform-minded educators looked back and felt the promise of the 1964 Civil Rights Act and the Coleman Report had yet to be fulfilled. Progress had stalled because equality of educational opportunity was still conceptualized as "desegregation and not integration, and . . . awareness of race, sex, and individual differences but not acceptance or affirmation." [59] Dawson had felt a sense of otherness firsthand growing up in the segregated South and, later, as a Black woman scholar in a predominantly white (and male-dominated) academy. She also understood the distance classrooms still needed to travel in order to be truly inclusive. In a 1974 commentary for the Association for Childhood Education International, she asked teachers to reflect on how the United States's racial context has made Black children "unwelcome guests" in the public school classroom: "The Visible Minority in a multicultural school the Afro-American child comes with two burdens. He is perhaps the most visible minority because of color and number. He has been the most aggressive in forcing the masses to provide liberty and justice for all. His fight has caused national resentment. Legislation has put the Black child into particular classrooms. Other things have made him truly an unwelcome guest."[60]

Dawson also understood that the influences of race and gender made it more difficult for Black women in the academy and, further, that building a more diverse and inclusive university was not merely a matter of numbers but of changing attitudes and levels of awareness. It was important to her that her intellectual contribution as a faculty colleague be recognized. As she wrote in her 1997 autobiographical essay, "I had demonstrated that a Black female could not only develop a viable teacher model but could also attract interdisciplinary faculty members and predominantly white students."[61]

At IU she made it a point to take ownership of her own professional development. She served on key committees in her home unit but also purposefully engaged in university affairs beyond the School of Education, such as serving on the university-wide Promotion and Tenure Committee. To her mind, academic citizenship was both a lever for promoting ideas and values one embraced and a mode of self-development and strategy for professional advancement. Her own experiences anchored her advice to women who wished to "climb the academic ladder":

> There is limited room at the top. If she is not offered the position, she must vow to make a difference where she is.... Success and mobility are based on diverse networking. One cannot expect to move into and assume leadership in the broad arena of society or a university when her contacts have been confined to a limited sphere of the larger world...One must develop a track record that attracts the attention of others. .... An administrator must give the same attention to her current appointment as she would give to the presidency or vice presidency if such became available.[62]

FULL CIRCLE: RETURNING TO VIRGINIA
STATE UNIVERSITY AND TO HAMPTON

Dawson's track record at IU positioned her well for a senior appointment in university administration. By the mid-1970s, some progress, but not equity, was achieved as a number of Black women rose to high-level administrative positions at predominantly white institutions and HBCUs.[63] To name a few, Mabel Parker MacLean headed her alma mater Barber-Scotia from 1974 to 1988 (and later 1994–96); Lorraine A. Williams served as Howard University's vice president for Washington, academic affairs; Mary Frances Berry was appointed provost of the Park Behavioral and College Park, Maryland Social Sciences Division then chancellor of the University of Colorado at Boulder from 1976 to 1977 and served as assistant secretary for education in the US Department of Health, Education, and Welfare from 1977 to 1980. In 1978 Gwendolyn Baker was named by the Carter administration to head minorities' and women's programs for the National Institute of Education. Baker's own career trajectory—public school teaching, attendance at a predominantly white university (University of Michigan), and a scholarly focus on multiculturalism in teacher training—was similar to Dawson's.

It was not surprising, then, that Dawson had attractive administrative opportunities before her. But one was especially compelling. In 1977, Dawson left IU to become dean of the School of Education at her undergraduate alma mater, Virginia State. She directed her energies to faculty development, the institution's reaccreditation and transition into university status, and a Teacher Corps grant that funded a linkage program with rural Surrey County Schools.

Her time at Virginia State was far shorter than she had anticipated. She left the deanship there to return to Hampton, where years earlier she had begun her academic career, to now serve as vice president—academic affairs/provost in 1978. Dawson was ready for the challenge: she had been a productive faculty member, an engaged academic citizen, and an accomplished administrator.

Even while taking on new administrative duties, Dawson was able to continue her work promoting multicultural education and in fact chaired the Commission on Multicultural Education of the American Association of Colleges for Teacher Education (AACTE).[64] Dawson pointed to successes but resistances. Despite state requirements and the National Council on Accreditation of Teacher Education (NCATE) multicultural standard for colleges and universities, too little had changed in teacher preparation programs.[65]

Family and faith, books and art, and engagement in a range of academic pursuits but also owning a small fashion business were important parts of Dawson's life. She left her mark on the field of education as a mentor to students, as a scholar who could translate ideas into programs, and as an administrator with a broad perspective on various levels of education, from the elementary school classroom through the university lecture hall. In wider professional circles, she was active in a number of associations related to her expertise in reading and teacher education. And, she served as a vice president of the American Association of University Women and belonged to Catholic Daughters of America.

She retired as from Hampton as vice-president of academic affairs emerita in 1991 and in a final gesture of service to the university accepted President William Harvey's invitation to write an institutional history, *Hampton University: A National Treasure* (published in 1994).Dawson's narrative highlighted Hampton's increased enrollments, improved fundraising, and rise to university status and the consequences of the increased competition HBCUs faced for Black students. In 1993, Dawson, though retired, answered the call to service yet again and took on her last full-time professional role, returning to her undergraduate alma mater as Virginia State College's provost and vice president for academic affairs.[66] She retired from VSC as provost emerita in 1998 but stayed engaged in academic life as a member of Hampton's campus community.[67]

Scholars like Dawson, whose contributions have been largely as teacher educators and administrators, have figured less prominently in the historical narrative of multicultural education than the male-dominated story of theorists and national advocates. Stories of innovation at HBCUs, such as Hampton's work on the nongraded classroom, and midwestern state universities, such as IU's push to multicultural education in the 1970s, have figured less prominently than stories of elite, private institutions and laboratory schools. More research on figures like Dawson—women who contributed to the world of ideas in teacher education and who successfully navigated the path from teacher, to teacher educator, to administrator; who navigated racism and sexism and crafted careers against the backdrop of post–WWII civil rights and women's rights movements, merit further study.

As she penned her 1997 autobiographical essay, "Climbing the Academic Ladder," Dawson could look back across a forty-year academic career that included a number of firsts, but the essence of her career, even as she "climbed ladders," was continuity. "I do not feel that my leaving will sever my relationship with the university but will move it to another dimension," she assured IU administrators when she left IU in 1977 to assume the deanship of the School of Education at her undergraduate alma mater, Virginia State University.[68] Dawson did in fact remain connected to IU. After leaving the Bloomington faculty, she continued to confer with IU administrators on shared interests, was honored with a Distinguished Alumni Service Award in 1980, and returned to campus as a member of the Board of Visitors for the School of Education. From Dawson's perspective, her many ties to IU, Virginia, and Hampton were both satisfying and helped extend her circle of influence as an educator. When she passed away in 2015, each of the institutions with which she had long been associated felt the loss of a trusted friend and colleague.[69]

NOTES

1. Details of Dawson's entire career—from classroom teaching before entering the academy to her retirement—are found in Martha E. Dawson, "Climbing the Administrative Ladder in the Academy: An Experiential Case History," in *Black Faculty Women in the Academy: History, Status, and Future,* ed. Lois Benjamin (Gainesville: University Press of Florida, 1997), 189–200. When she passed away in 2015, Dr. Dawson had marked forty-plus years in academic life and more than sixty years since she had completed her teacher training at Virginia State. Context for understanding Dawson's scholarly career may be found in Sheila T. Gregory, "Black Women in the Academy: Challenges and Opportunities," *Journal of Negro Education* 70, no. 3 (Summer 2001): 124; American Association of Colleges for Teacher Education Commission on Multiculturalism, "No One Model American," Washington, DC, 1972; Donna M. Gollnick, "Multicultural Education: Policies and Practices in Teacher Education," in *Research In Multicultural Education: From the Margins to the Mainstream,* ed. Carl A. Grant (London: Falmer, 1992), 215–38; William B. Harvey, ed., *Grassroots and Glass Ceilings: African American Administrators in Predominantly White Colleges and Universities* (Albany: SUNY Press, 1987). The author wishes to thank Stephanie T. X. Nguyen, IU professor emerita Enid Zimmerman, and the Dawson family.

2. Kathleen F. Slevin and Ray C. Wingrove, *From Stumbling Blocks to Stepping Stones: The Life Experiences of Fifty Professional African American Women* (New York: New York University Press, 1998).

3. See Dawson's comments on her childhood and youth during an interview marking her Lifetime Achievement Award, Jill Keech, *Daily Press*, March 6, 1991, http://articles.dailypress.com/1991-03-06/features/9103070245_1_dawson-s -mother-hampton- university-dawson-s-three-children. For general biographical details, see "Obituary for Martha E. Dawson," *Daily Press* (Newport News, Virginia), July 22, 2015, A9.

4. Dawson, "Climbing the Administrative Ladder," 192.

5. Dawson, 192.

6. Margaret Meagher, *History of Education in Richmond* (Richmond: University of Virginia, 1939); Louis Brenner, "Negro Education in the City of Richmond" (honors thesis, University of Richmond, 1943); Michael Eric Taylor, "The African-American Community of Richmond, Virginia: 1950–1956," (master's thesis, University of Richmond, 1994). Robert P. Winthrop, "Architects of Richmond: Charles M. Robinson," *Architecture Richmond*, January 27, 2015, http://architecture richmond.com/2015/01/27/architects-of-richmond-charles-m-robinson.

7. For a recollection of seeing Dawson display her tuition receipt, see Sharon Smith, "Private Schools for Blacks in Early Twentieth Century Richmond, Virginia" (master's thesis, College of William and Mary, 2016), 1–2.

8. Dawson, "Climbing the Administrative Ladder," 189.

9. Stephanie Shaw coined this phrase in her study of eighty-five African American women born between 1853 and 1935. See *What a Woman Ought to Be and Do: Black Professional Women Workers during the Jim Crow Era* (Chicago: University of Chicago Press, 1995), 2; and Nancy E. Bertaux and M. Christine Anderson, "An Emerging Tradition of Educational Achievement: African American Women in College and the Professions, 1920–1950," *Equity & Excellence in Education* 34, no. 2 (Summer 2001): 16–21; Linda M. Perkins, "Bound to Them by a Common Sorrow: African American Women, Higher Education, and Collective Advancement," *Journal of African American History* 100, no. 4 (fall 2015): 721–47; Stephanie Evans, *Black Women in the Ivory Tower, 1850–1954: An Intellectual History* (Gainesville: University of Florida Press, 2008).

10. Jeanne L. Noble, *The Negro Woman's College Education* (New York: Teachers College, Columbia University, 1956).

11. Peter Wallenstein, "Segregation, Desegregation, and Higher Education in Virginia," paper delivered at Policy History Conference, Charlottesville, Virginia, June 3, 2006. See also https://explore.lib.virginia.edu/exhibits/show/uvawomen /breakingtradition (accessed October 25, 2021).

12. Cally L. Waite and Margaret Smith Crocco, "Fighting Injustice through Education," *History of Education* 33, no. 5 (September 2004): 581; Vernell Danae

Larkin, "Dreams Denied: The Anderson Mayer State Aid Act, 1936–1950," (PhD diss., University of Kentucky, 2001).

13. Edgar A. Toppin, *Opening Day Centennial: A Century of Service at Virginia State University, 1883 to 1983* (CPS Systems, Virginia State University, 1983).

14. Vanessa Siddle Walker, *Their Highest Potential: An African American School Community in the Segregated South* (Chapel Hill: University of North Carolina Press, 1996).

15. Dawson, "Climbing the Administrative Ladder," 191.

16. There is no family connection between IU professor Merrill Eaton and Martha Eaton Dawson.

17. In the 1950s, IU did not consistently keep the total number of Black students. This enrollment number came from correspondence in presidential papers. See CE Harrell to Herman B Wells, September 12, 1951, RE_Number of Negros Enrolled during Summer Session, C213 (Indiana University President's Office records, 1937–62), Box 414, Folder "Negro 1951–52." Emma Lou Thornbrough, *Indiana Blacks in the Twentieth Century* (Bloomington: Indiana University Press, 2000), 48–49. Maureen Reynolds, "The Challenge of Racial Equality," in *Hoosier Schools: Past and Present*, ed. William H. Reese (Bloomington: Indiana University Press, 1998), 174–77, 179.

18. Margaret Smith Crocco and Cally L. Waite, "Education and Marginality: Race and Gender in Higher Education, 1940–1955," *History of Education Quarterly* 47, no. 1 (Spring 2007): 69–91. Bettye Collier-Thomas, "The Impact of Black Women in Education: An Historical Overview," *Journal of Negro Education* 51, no. 3 (Summer 1982): 173–80; Donna J. Jordan-Taylor, "'I'm Not Autherine Lucy:' The Circular Migration of Southern Black Professionals Who Completed Graduate School in the North during Jim Crow, 1945–1970" (PhD diss., University of Illinois, 2011). See finding aid for Jane Ellen McAllister papers, http://collections.msdiglib. org/digital/collection/jsu/id/286/ (accessed October 14, 2020).

19. Jordan-Taylor, "'I'm Not Autherine Lucy,'" 89–145; Tilman C. Cochran, "The Attitude of Negro Students Toward Indiana University" (master's thesis, Indiana University, 1942).

20. See Larkin, "Dreams Denied," and Jordan-Taylor, "'I'm Not Autherine Lucy,'" 162, 163.

21. Cochran, "Attitudes." For Comer, see *Beyond Black and White*, 35, *Washington Post*, August 10, 1986, sec. K, 1. Comer was recognized by IU with a College of Arts and Sciences Distinguished Alumni Award (1989), an honorary degree from IU (1991), and a Distinguished Alumni Service Award (1992).

22. Scott received an honorary degree from IU in 1977 and the Distinguished Alumni Award in 1992 (see https://honorsandawards.iu.edu/about/history.html).

23. Cora Smith Breckenridge, oral history interview with Barbara Truesdall, June 19, 2009, https://iu.aviaryplatform.com/collections/123/collection_resources /10111?embed=true.

24. Martha Eaton Dawson, "A Study of Vocabulary Size of Third Grade Pupils in Relation to Home-Environmental Factors" (EdD diss., Indiana University, 1956); Jeanne L. Noble, "Negro Women Today and Their Education," *Journal of Negro Education* 26, no. 1 (winter 1957): 15–21.

25. For Bond's data, see Crocco and Waite, "Education and Marginality," 74–75; Tony Badger, "Southerners Who Refused to Sign the Southern Manifesto," *The Historical Journal* 42, no. 2 (June 1999): 517–34; James P. Kaetz, "Autherine Lucy," *Encyclopedia of Alabama*, last modified May 9, 2019, http://www.encyclopediaof alabama.org/article/h-2489.

26. Dawson, "Climbing the Ladder," 190.

27. Richard A. Pratt, *The Color of Their Skin: Education and Race in Richmond, Virginia 1954–89* (Charlottesville: University Press of Virginia, 1992), 13.

28. Gail Cash, "Women at Hampton, 1930–1959," (PhD diss., Marquette University, 1994); Charles E. Cunningham and D. Keith Osborn, "A Historical Examination of Blacks in Early Childhood Education," *Young Children* 34, no. 3 (March 1979): 20–29. Hampton Institute was renamed Hampton University in 1984.

29. Cash, "Women at Hampton," 66. Sharon Pierson, "A 'Laboratory of Learning': A Case Study of Alabama State College Laboratory High School in Historical Context, 1920–1960," (PhD diss., Teachers College Columbia University, 2012).

30. Rockefeller Brothers Fund, *The Pursuit of Excellence* (New York: Doubleday and Co. 1958); John W. Gardner, *Excellence: Can We Be Equal and Excellent Too?* (New York: Harper, 1961). *Michael Harrington, The Other America: Poverty in the United States* (New York: Macmillan Publishing Company, 1962).

31. Barbara Beatty, "The Debate over the Young 'Disadvantaged Child': Preschool Intervention, Developmental Psychology, and Compensatory Education in the 1960s and Early 1970s," *Teachers College Record* 114, no. 6 (2012): 1–36.

32. David B. Tyack, *The One Best System: A History of Urban Education* (Cambridge: Harvard University Press, 1974), 44.

33. Alice V. Keliher, "A Critical Study of Homogenous Grouping," *Contributions to Education, No. 452* (New York: Bureau of Publications, Columbia University, 1936). Robert H. Anderson, "The Nongraded Elementary School: Lessons from History," paper presented at the Annual Meeting of the American Educational Research Association (San Francisco, CA, April 20–24, 1992). Stuart Ernest Dean, *Nongraded Schools* (US Department of Health, Education, and Welfare, Office of Education, Division of Elementary and Secondary Education, Instructional Programs Branch, 1964). See John I. Goodlad and Robert H. Anderson, *The Nongraded Elementary School* (New York: Harcourt, Brace and Company, 1959); Roberto Gutiérrez and Robert E. Slavin, "Achievement Effects of the Nongraded Elementary School: A Best Evidence Synthesis," *Review of Educational Research* 62, no. 4 (winter, 1992): 333–76.

34. For intellectual backdrop, see Beatty, "The Debate over the Young 'Disadvantaged Child.'" See Michael Harrington, *The Other America: Poverty in the*

United States (New York: Macmillan, 1962); John W. Gardner, *Excellence: Can We Be Equal and Excellent Too?* (New York: Harper, 1961); and Rheable M. Edwards, "Race and Class in Early Childhood Education," *Young Children* 30, no. 6 (September 1975): 401–11.

35. Valora Washington, "Historical and Contemporary Linkages between Black Child Development and Social Policy," in *Black Children and Poverty: A Developmental Perspective*, ed. D. T. Slaughter, New Directions for Child and Adolescent Development 1988, no. 42 (winter 1988): 93–105.

36. Martha E. Dawson and Helen H. Holston, *The Nongraded Approach to Curriculum for Administrators and Teachers of the Disadvantaged*, Interim Report for Office of Education (Washington, DC: Distributed by ERIC Clearinghouse, 1966).

37. Dawson and Holston, *The Nongraded Approach*, 3.

38. Leo Fay, Dawson's former IU faculty advisor, had nominated Dawson for IU's coveted Distinguished Alumni Award as early as 1968, two years before Dawson returned as a faculty member. See Leo Fay to Philip Peak, March 11, 1968, IU Archives Reference File (Martha E. Dawson). The new department was proposed by the Human Relations Commission of the School of Education and established in January 1970. John F. Brown, of the Indianapolis Urban League, was appointed director of the new program.

39. Claire Mangers, "Education School Adds Department for Inner City Problems," *Indiana Daily Student*, December 12, 1969, 12; Press release, November 23, 1970, "Infant Department Growing Up Quickly"; "Urban Education Department OK'd 29 January 1970"; "Noted Educator to Join Faculty," *Bloomington Herald Telephone* June 11, 1970.

40. Memo from the Office of Afro-American Affairs to the Faculty Council discussing a consolidation of Afro-American Programs includes no women scholar in its list of possible planning conference attendees or candidates to direct a proposed Institute.

41. Johnson remained on the faculty until his death. See Memorial Resolution Professor Richard Davis Johnson (December 29, 1921–August 29, 1983), *Bloomington Faculty Council Minutes*, Circular B42-1985, http://webapp1.dlib.indiana.edu /bfc/view?docId=B42-1985 (February 19, 1985). For Peery's discussion of the positive personal and professional experiences of his seventeen years at IU and his deep respect for Herman Wells, see https://www.aip.org/history-programs/niels -bohr-library/oral-histories/33698.

42. Black enrollment at IU minimally grew between 1950 and 1980. Unfortunately, IU did not keep consistent Black student enrollment before 1975. In 1964–65, IU had 395 Black students—or 1.9 percent—of the 20,953 total enrollment on the Bloomington campus. By 1968–69, IU enrolled an estimate of 600 Black students—or about 2.1 percent—out of 29,006 total student enrollment. By 1980, Black enrollment at IUB accounted for 1,569—or 4.9 percent—of the total enroll-

ment of 31,877. See Donald W. Adams, "An Analysis of the Black Undergraduate Student at Indiana University," (PhD diss., Indiana University, 1969), 9, in Reference Files, Folder "African-Americans—Enrollment," IU Libraries University Archives, Bloomington, Indiana; University Budget Office, "Total Student Headcount Enrollment by Campus, Ethnic Group and Sex: Fall Semester, 1980–81," *Indiana University Factbook 1980–81*, November 1, 1980, Reference Files, Folder "Fact Books 1980–1982," IU Libraries University Archives, Bloomington, Indiana, 26.

43. For a brief interview with Orlando Taylor, see The History Makers (June 14, 2004), https://www.thehistorymakers.org/biography/orlando-l-taylor-38.

44. Herman C. Hudson, "The Black Faculty at Indiana University, Bloomington 1970–1993," n.d., Reference Files, Indiana University Archives. In 1976 the founding meeting of the Black Studies Council was hosted on IU's campus. Joseph J. Russell, who earned his master's degree from IU in 1968 and his doctorate in education three years later, served as chairman of IU's Department of Afro-American Affairs and executive director, and Hudson served as the national advisory chairperson. See Charles P. Henry, *Black Studies and the Democratization of American Higher Education* (New York: Palgrave, 2017), 101; Herman Hudson, "The Black Studies Program: Strategy and Structure," *Journal of Negro Education* 41, no. 4 (Autumn 1972), 294–98.

45. Ross had firsthand experience as a student at both an HBCU (earning his bachelor's from University of Arkansas at Pine Bluff in 1965) and two large midwestern predominantly white institutions (master's, University of Illinois, 1966) and Indiana University (doctorate, 1976).

46. Martha E. Dawson, "A Matter of Linkage: Multicultural Education and Educational Equity," *Educational Equity: The Integration of Educational Equity into Preservice Teacher Preparation Programs* (Washington, DC: Teacher Clearinghouse, 1981), 1–15; quote at 1. One of the pioneering usages of the term *multicultural education* appears in Jack Forbes, *The Education of the Culturally Different: A Multicultural Approach* (Berkeley: Far West Laboratory for Educational Research and Development, 1969). See also Gwendolyn C. Baker, "The Effects of Training in Multi-ethnic Education on Preservice Teachers' Perceptions of Ethnic Groups," (PhD diss., University of Michigan, 1972).

47. Maxine Schwartz Seller, "Politics, Pedagogy, and Pluralism—Multicultural Education in American Public Schools in the Twentieth Century," *Revue Française d'Études Américaines* Année 1997 no 74 (October 1997): 11–23; Zoe Burkholder, *Color in the Classroom: How American Schools Taught Race, 1900–1954* (New York: Oxford University Press, 2011); Raymond H. Giles and Donna M. Gollnick, "Ethnic/Cultural Diversity as Reflected in Federal and State Educational Legislation and Policies," in *Pluralism and the American Teacher: Issues and Case Studies*, ed. Frank H. Klassen and Donna M. Gollnick (Washington, DC: American Association for Colleges of Teacher Education, 1977), 115–16.

48. American Association of Colleges for Teachers Education Commission on Multicultural Education, "No One Model American: A Statement on Multicultural Education," *Journal of Teacher Education* 24, no. 4 (December 1973): 264–65.

49. Jensen's controversial work concluded that genetics were the most salient factor in IQ differences between Black and white students. Arthur R. Jensen, "How Much Can We Boost IQ and Scholastic Achievement?" *Harvard Educational Review* 39, no. 1 (February 1969): 1–123.

50. Taylor-Jordan, "I'm Not Autherine Lucy," 114.

51. Martha E. Dawson, "Am I Ready, Willing, or Able to Teach in a Multicultural Setting?" 52–54, in Part III, "Are There Unwelcome Guests in Your Classroom?" in *Children and Intercultural Education: Some Minorities Speak Out; Overview and Research; Are There Unwanted Guests in Your Classroom?*, ed. Martha E. Dawson (Washington, DC: Association for Childhood Education International, 1973).

52. For example, James Bank, then a newly minted PhD from Michigan State University, joined the faculty at the University of Washington in 1969. See Quinn Russell Brown, "Thanks, Professor Banks: 'The Father of Multicultural Education' Is Retiring after 50 Years at UW," *Columns: The University of Washington Alumni Magazine*, December 2018, https://magazine.washington.edu/feature/james-banks-uw-retires-multicultural-education.

53. "New Program Started at IU," *Herald Times*, November 3, 1971.

54. Dawson, "Climbing the Academic Leader," 195.

55. "What's New in Educational Programs," *Chalkboard*, October 1972, 2.

56. John Fancher, "Future Teachers: Produce or Else!," *Herald-Telephone*, November 24, 1970; John Fancher, "Many People Trained as Teachers Can't Teach Inner-City Children," *Herald-Telephone*, November 18, 1969. Martha E. Dawson, "From Compensatory to Multicultural Education: The Challenge of Designing Multicultural Education Programs," *Journal of Research and Development in Education* 11, no. 1 (fall 1977): 84–101.

57. "New Program Started at IU," *Herald Telephone*, November 3, 1971; Leonard O. Andrews, "Experiential Programs of Laboratory Experiences in Teacher Education," *Journal of Teacher Education* 1, no. 4 (December 1, 1950): 259–67; Evelyn R. Hodgdon and Robert W. Saunders, "Using the Community in Teacher Education," *Journal of Teacher Education* 2, no. 3 (September 1, 1951): 216–18.

58. Enid Zimmerman, interview.

59. M. E. Manley-Casimir and Ian Housego, "Equality of Educational Opportunity as Social Policy," quoted in Carl A. Grant, "Education That Is Multicultural as a Change Agent: Organizing for Effectiveness," *Journal of Negro Education* 48, no. 3 (Summer 1979): 431–46; quote at 436.

60. Martha E. Dawson, guest editor, "Are there Unwelcome Guests in Your Classroom?" Part III of *Children and Intercultural Education: Some Minorities Speak Out; Overview and Research; Are There Unwanted Guests in Your Classroom?* (Washington, DC: Association for Childhood Education International, 1974): 36–39.

61. Constance M. Carroll, "Three's a Crowd: The Dilemma of the Black Woman in Higher Education," in *Academic Women on the Move*, ed. Alice J. Rossi and Ann Calderwood (New York: Russell Sage, 1973), 173–86.

62. Dawson, "Climbing the Ladder," 199.

63. Brunetta Reid Wolfman, "'Light as from a Beacon:' African American Women Administrators in the Academy," in *Black Women in the Academy: Promises and Perils*, ed. Lois Benjamin (Gainesville: University of Florida Press, 1997), 158–67.

64. Dawson, "A Matter of Linkage," 1.

65. American Association of Colleges for Teacher Education Commission on Multiculturalism, "No One Model American," Washington, DC, 1972; Donna M. Gollnick, "Multicultural Education: Policies and Practices in Teacher Education," in *Research In Multicultural Education: From The Margins To The Mainstream*, edited by Carl A. Grant (London: Falmer Press, 1992), 215–35.

66. "Outgoing VSU Administrator Named Provost Emerita," *The Virginia Statesman*, September 25, 1998, 7. Thank you to archivist Francine B. Archer at VSU for providing me with this newspaper clipping. Martha E. Dawson, *Hampton University: A National Treasure* (Silver Spring, MD: Beckham House, 1994).

67. Thank you to Andreese A. Scott, at Hampton University Archives, for bringing Dr. Dawson's obituary in local newspapers to my attention. See "Obituary for Martha E. Dawson," *Daily Press* [Newport News, Virginia], July 22, 2015, A9.

68. Martha Dawson letter of resignation, to Dean Robert Gousha, November 7, 1977, Box C176 Martha E Dawson, Indiana Libraries University Archives, Bloomington, Indiana.

69. On October 1, 2021, Indiana University unveiled a portrait of Martha Dawson, to recognize her pioneering contributions to the fields of elementary and multicultural education and her distinguished career as a professor and administrator. The portrait was commissioned as part of the IU Bicentennial's Bridging the Visibility Gap Initiative, which "identifies women and underrepresented minorities in IU's history and adds them to the historical narrative and the built environment." "Martha Dawson Portrait Dedicated," Indiana University, Honors and Awards, accessed October 30, 2021, https://honorsandawards.iu.edu/about/stories/20211021-01.html.

THIRTEEN

—ɯ—

ELINOR OSTROM

On Interdisciplinary Living, 1933–2012

SARA CLARK

Sara Clark furthers the discussion of IU women and the knowledge enterprise with an essay on Elinor "Lin" Ostrom, who received the Nobel Prize in Economics in 2009. Rather than focusing on the well-known litany of Ostrom's publications, honors, and awards, Clark offers an intimate portrait of Ostrom's storied career. Her essay draws on her recent dissertation. Using a mix of published interviews, original oral histories, and archival records, Clark emphasizes the many intellectual and social ties that guided Ostrom to adopt an interdisciplinary approach to her scholarship and personal life.

RECOGNITION BY THE ECONOMIC SCIENCES Nobel Committee in 2009 finally gave Elinor Ostrom—whom colleagues, students, and friends referred to by the nickname Lin— a bit of peace with her interdisciplinary practice: "As a person who does interdisciplinary work, I didn't fit in anywhere. I was relieved that, after all these years of struggle, someone really thought it did add up."[1] Some will remember Ostrom for her contributions as a field researcher, others for her part in developing collaborative research networks, others for her use of laboratory methods, others as a collector of local arts and crafts (particularly Native American ones), others as a teacher, others as a philanthropist, and others as an administrator and entrepreneur. Those at Indiana University most remember her as the cofounder of the Workshop in Political Theory and Policy Analysis, which has its home on the IU campus in Bloomington.

Ostrom integrated knowledge and brought together diverse thinkers; this was her interdisciplinary practice, to combine formerly separate knowledge production processes, to cross-communicate, delivering results not previously possible by recognizing the benefits and facilitating cross-pollination of disciplinary advances and methodological innovations. Ostrom did not claim expertise in multiple fields—though she continued to acquire disciplinary skills, like learning mathematical economics, outside of her original graduate training throughout her professional career.[2] In her resolve never to be done learning, she found her greatest weapon. Ostrom's scholarship brought together disciplinary experts to understand problems—often involving questions about how humans interact with limited resources—that necessarily benefitted from forging intricate interconnections among disciplines, especially integrating methods.

To produce these results, Ostrom made choices that structured her life in ways that challenged boundaries between personal and professional. As I will demonstrate in this chapter, her interdisciplinary approach can be characterized helpfully by examining her tireless work ethic; her commitments to artisanship, contestation, and collaboration; and her openness to multiple solutions to complex problems. The blurred boundaries between Ostrom's personal and professional lives should not be classified as a symptom of what ailed her but instead as an emblem of a methodology she developed and applied throughout her life. Ostrom's contributions are significant not only because of the ways in which she challenged the conceptual borders of economic analysis but also because her methodology for living provides an alternate interdisciplinary model for organizing knowledge. Through biography, this analysis ultimately seeks to answer: how did Ostrom develop and understand interdisciplinarity as a methodology for living?

Indiana University leaders recognized Ostrom's scholarly contributions only after she received national and international academic prizes late in her career. Early on she struggled to find an academic home in IU's Political Science Department, so she and her husband and intellectual partner, Vincent, co-founded Indiana University's Workshop in Political Theory and Policy Analysis in 1973 (later renamed the Ostrom Workshop in their honor). The Workshop received approval from their department and limited funding but otherwise operated independently.[3] The reach of Lin and Vincent's impact can also be measured financially; together their lifetime giving to the IU Foundation via the Tocqueville Endowment—which funded student and professional research efforts through the workshop—totaled more than $2 million (not including interest from the endowment).[4] Only ten years after Ostrom completed her PhD at UCLA and began her career at IU, she took entrepreneurial action with Vincent to found the workshop and to create the Tocqueville Endowment, allowing them to develop a place within the university that fostered an interdisciplinary academic community that did not require extensive oversight by the university. They applied the tenets of self-governance they studied in their research to develop their own institution at IU. Their intellectual home geographically expanded in 1999 when Elinor founded a sister research center, the Center for Behavior, Institutions and the Environment, at Arizona State University (ASU).[5]

While the scope of Elinor's scholarly impact is not limited to IU, the reputation of IU continues to benefit from distinctive elements of Ostrom's career there—the creation of an interdisciplinary structure, the Ostroms' intellectual legacies, and the global scholarly network founded at the Ostrom Workshop. The workshop brought together diverse scholars to develop the Bloomington School of Political Economy, geographically based in Bloomington, Indiana. Recognized in 1988 as a school of thought led by the Ostroms, the Bloomington School signified that work by Indiana University scholars should be compared to work by those at the Rochester School of Political Science led by William Riker and the Virginia School of Political Economy led by James Buchanan and Gordon Tullock.[6]

Ostrom's relationship with her husband, Vincent, represents the ways in which she integrated personal and professional. Because they were partnered intellectually and through marriage, categorizing aspects of their relationship as only personal or only professional is limiting. When they authored scholarly publications together, were they not also loving life partners?[7] As intellectual counterparts and lovers, they disagreed and supported one another about matters of career and of heart. When Vincent requested in 1964 that his new office at IU have enough space for a desk for his wife—"for some of the work we shall be doing together"— he shared their personal relationship while also publicly advocating for her career as a female academic in a male-dominated field.[8] Through their shared hobby of building furniture, they learned ideas about craft and artistry that they then incorporated into their scholarship and design of the workshop; to them, academics should be craftspeople. Workshopper Jimmy Walker laughed recalling, "As Ostrom said in making the furniture, she was the sander."[9] Vincent's impact on Elinor, and vice versa, is most accurately represented as simultaneously important for each partner on multiple fronts.

Though the Bloomington School received its name more than twenty years prior, Elinor's Nobel sparked interest among the Ostroms' Workshop colleagues and students to begin documenting the school's history and impact. These researchers share the goal to explore the value of Elinor's broad-reaching contributions (and, in many cases, the cross-pollination of her academic work with Vincent's); however, review of their various perspectives shows few attempts to identify connections among research, teaching, relationships, hobbies, and other aspects of life. Though as this essay is being written, Barb Allen has released only clips of her forthcoming documentary film about Elinor and Vincent, the film promises to foreground the couple's relationship as central to their impact and seems most similar to this chapter's approach: "I think of Lin and Vincent's work and lives as a love story that became a global gift. Over their half-century relationship, they built an enduring, loving marriage; an influential intellectual partnership; and a wide-ranging movement of people dedicated—as the Ostroms were—to addressing the enormous problems that plague human societies."[10]

No single scholar may be as uniquely qualified to document Ostrom's interdisciplinary research as she was to conduct it. Her extended network included academicians, students, and friends who now share the endeavor to create a collective account across multiple publications of her intellectual legacy.[11] Uniquely, Vlad Tarko framed his recent contribution as an intellectual biography.[12] Still others within the Ostroms' network jointly authored texts to extend their mentors' approaches to help answer the next generation's questions.[13] Elinor and Vincent continue to inspire new research, as evidenced by citations of their publications, the impact of their students, and the continued strength of the workshop.

ACADEMIC ACCOLADES

Ostrom remains most widely recognized for her mixed-methods research examining common pool resources—resources with porous boundaries making it difficult to exclude users like fisheries, forests, and water. However, Ostrom's research also included the study of public goods and services like policing and, later in her career, the interactions between humans and their ecosystems involving natural resource problems like climate change. In a 1997 grant progress report to the National Science Foundation written by Ostrom and her collaborator Emilio Moran, they characterized her research broadly: "Since 1965, she has pursued an active research program linking institutional arrangements at a local, regional, and national level to the actions of individuals and their outcomes."[14] The notion that "'governance' has a much broader scope than the activities of governments" influenced Ostrom throughout her career.[15]

Ostrom's academic efforts earned recognition and research grants from some of the most prestigious US institutions: Numerous universities awarded her honorary doctoral degrees and more than 30 research grants, most from the Ford Foundation, MacArthur Foundation, National Science Foundation, Andrew W. Mellon Foundation, US AID, and US Department of Justice. Ostrom authored sixteen books and edited seventeen collaborative volumes; she published most frequently with collaborators; as with other aspects of her life, this record is indicative of her preference for working in teams. She served as president of the Public Choice Society (1982–84), the Midwest Political Science Association (1984–85), the International Association for the Study of Common Property (1990–91), and the American Political Science Association (1996–97). As her prominence rose with the publication of *Governing the Commons* in 1990—her first independently authored book—the American Academy of Arts and Sciences recognized Ostrom as a fellow in 1991. Other honors followed: she was recognized as a member of the National Academy of Sciences in 2001, as a member of the American Philosophical Society in 2006, and as a fellow of the American Academy of Political and Social Science in 2009. Ostrom continued to grow in prominence by receiving the Johan Skytte Prize in Political Science in 1999 and, less than a decade later, by receiving the William H. Riker Prize in Political Science from the University of Rochester in 2008. In 2009, the Nobel Committee named Ostrom the co-recipient, with Oliver Williamson, of the Sveriges Riksbank Prize in Economic Sciences in Memory of Alfred Nobel.

An outsider to political science and economics examining her scholarly record might perceive these awards and prizes as a pipeline leading to inevitable recognition by the Committee for the Prize in Economic Sciences in Memory of Alfred Nobel; this was not the case. Her accolades were well known by her peers long before the general public noticed her achievements.[16] She worked closely with other Nobelist economists like Vernon Smith and Reinhard Selton, but Ostrom's Nobel surprised many because of her perceived identity as a political scientist. After all, Ostrom trained as a political scientist and not as an economist during graduate school—the secondary and higher education system limited Ostrom's access to the math courses required for acceptance into graduate economics education. UCLA's Department of Economics denied Ostrom entrance as a graduate student because she had not completed advanced math courses; though Ostrom graduated college with a degree in political science, faculty members first told her "girls who received good grades in college" in the 1950s would find careers only as teachers.[17]

With women facing a narrow path for graduate education in math and science fields, Ostrom and her female counterparts were unlikely to earn influential positions in economics. Between 1947–48 and 1960–61, a total of 3,079 graduates of US universities earned doctorate degrees in economics. Of these degree earners, just 154—or 5 percent—were women. Instead, Ostrom graduated with a PhD in political science from UCLA in 1965 and became a visiting assistant professor in IU's Department of Government the next academic year.[18] Though Ostrom's cohort at UCLA included a few other women, very few women possessed the advanced training in economics or political science needed to serve as mentors to upcoming female colleagues. In the years from 1956 to 1958, only 20 women (4.78 percent of the subfield) in the United States worked full-time in the "social sciences (esp. economics)," though female graduate students might have looked to women working in research associate positions for mentorship. In other words, women social scientists routinely occupied supporting roles, despite equal qualification. By 1970, the number of women economists increased to 812, but their overall footprint only made up 6.07 percent of all economists.[19]

COMPOSING AN INTERDISCIPLINARY LIFE[20]

Ostrom did not set out to become a world-class political economist, and she did not identify as a champion for interdisciplinarity; the problems she studied and her genuine enthusiasm for inquiry drove her. Commitment to the hard work needed to facilitate interdisciplinary research verified through artisanship, contestation, and collaboration propelled Ostrom's approach. Further, her openness to multiple solutions to complex problems solidified her methodology. Together these commitments suggest four tenets for interdisciplinary living and in turn illustrate the approach Ostrom developed over a lifetime. These tenets are overlapping, personal, and non-exhaustive. However, they attempt to give shape to a methodology that has defied adequate definition because of its boundary-breaking, dynamic nature. As elucidated by Ostrom's life, interdisciplinarity can flow between personal and professional.

I. Hard Work

Expressions like *never take work home* and *leave the office at the office* broadcasted the Western notion of separation between personal and professional lives that took root in the second half of the twentieth century. For Ostrom, finding balance between these divisions did not resonate. Her colleagues remember her exuberance and tireless pursuit of answers to complex, everyday problems. Mansee Bal, a friend and student, captured Ostrom's delight for living: "I guess if somebody asks in the middle of the night, 'Let's do this, let's go and count the trees,' she would just be ready to go. That's how I feel: That's how she reflects, that she's just ready to work."[21] This is not to say there were no negative consequences to her lack of work-life boundaries. Ostrom woke up very early in the morning, often sending emails at all hours. To manage her fatigue, she took catnaps in her office on campus.[22] Hard work is not unique to interdisciplinary practice, but it is essential. Many types of academic research might be characterized by strenuous labor. What make Ostrom's hard work distinctively linked to her interdisciplinary practice are the extra steps she willingly navigated to facilitate interdisciplinarity. Ostrom honed an exhaustive work ethic during her childhood and early adulthood and ultimately aimed these skills toward communicating with clear definitions of terms across knowledge borders.

Traces of how Ostrom organized her life in adulthood—around the pursuit of ideas through exhaustive efforts—can be found in her childhood. Ostrom was born during the Great Depression in 1933 and grew up on the edge of affluent Beverly Hills, California. Her parents, Leah and Adrian Awan—neither of whom had more than a high school education—divorced, but both remained active in their daughter's life. Ostrom watched (and acted in) Los Angeles area theater productions with her father, a producer and set designer, but lived primarily with her mother, who taught her to grow her own food in their home garden: "Now I must confess that the long, hot August days that I spent canning peaches and apricots are not my favorite memories of my childhood, but I certainly learned a lot about the household economics of a poor family—long before I studied these problems in developing economies."[23] Ostrom further developed her communication skills by participating in high school debate and continued to garden throughout her life. While these skills and experiences shaped her personality and helped her to develop mental toughness, exposure to college-bound teens at Beverly Hills High School—who regularly exercised social and cultural capital along with economic wealth toward entering higher education—allowed Ostrom to normalize college attendance.[24] Even though her parents did not see the need for Ostrom to complete college or provide financial support, Ostrom described her choice to attend UCLA as just wanting to "keep up" with her high school friends.[25]

Ostrom worked thirty to forty hours a week to pay tuition at UCLA, where she graduated with a degree in political science in 1954.[26] As a professor years later, Ostrom reflected on working her way through college in a recommendation she made on behalf of Edna Bryan-Cummins, then a secretary at the workshop applying to IU's law school: "As a person who put herself through college by typing, I can testify that it is not always easy to read for understanding while typing."[27] Ostrom worked hard and expected the same from her team; having experienced all levels of employment—from typist to leading academician—and rejection by UCLA economics faculty during her own graduate admissions process, Ostrom endured.[28] In adulthood, Ostrom's patience and persistence characterized her resistance; she played the long game, recognizing her incremental efforts would add up.

Genuine curiosity and an unbroken commitment to identifying the method (and, in most cases, combinations of methods) that pointed toward understanding of complex real-world problems and their possible solutions motivated Ostrom. Her studies of metropolitan police performance conducted in the 1970s and 1980s were an early symbol of her ability to integrate multiple methods for decades to come. Ostrom and her students carefully crafted questionnaires to guide thousands of interviews gauging attitudes toward police in multiple cities, conducted detailed observations by riding alongside on-duty police officers, and mailed thousands of surveys, producing a stream of qualitative and quantitative data to analyze and synthesize.[29] Hard work for Ostrom meant commitment to large-scale, longitudinal studies over many years and willingness to mediate cross-expertise communication difficulties that could have derailed projects. It also meant finding the strength within to lead: "I must confess that I was a little nervous myself the first day we went out," Ostrom divulged in a letter to her mother in 1970 just after she and her students began conducting interviews with citizens about police services in downtown Indianapolis.[30] Ostrom sometimes felt overwhelmed: "I have four separate research projects going on and at times I could scream with the frustration of having too much to do."[31] However, her hands were never idle; she also crocheted, sewed, gardened, hiked, and completed other home projects with Vincent.[32]

II. Artisanship and Contestation

Over four decades, Elinor and Vincent shaped the workshop around a structure of citizen as artisan and used contestation to further their intellectual mission to "understand patterns of organization in multiple environments using the tools of comparative institutional analysis and development."[33] Elinor and Vincent saw themselves as co-artisans in their direction of the workshop, an enterprise they viewed as the craft they skillfully fashioned with the help of their peers, students, and workshop staff. These shared identities were tied to how they viewed knowledge production: "The term 'workshop' was chosen on a presumption that scholarship is a form of artisanship that is best pursued in a circumstance that involves collaboration where individuals of varied experiences contribute to and learn from one another."[34] Elinor and Vincent also exercised their commitment to artisanship outside of the workshop through a shared interest in making furniture; they collaborated with a local Indiana master cabinetmaker and built a primitive cabin on Manitoulin Island, Canada, where they worked during the summers for more than thirty years. They supported other artisans financially by collecting nearly three hundred works of art and artifacts, many created by Ojibwe artists local to Manitoulin.[35]

Ostrom characterized her marriage with Vincent more than four decades later as "enriching and strengthening." His IU colleagues, however, recognized Vincent for his gruffness and unrestrained debate style. "Vince is a tough son of a gun," commented Ostrom. "I think that this is a hard thing to learn in marriage, to fight back and not take it personally," she continued.[36] In Vincent, Ostrom found an intellectual partner she admired and someone with whom she could verbally spar. In 1990, Ostrom dedicated what would become her most widely recognized publication, *Governing the Commons*, "To Vincent: For his love and contestation."[37] For those in the Ostroms' close network of peers, students, visiting scholars, friends, and staff around their workshop, contestation became a shared method for intellectual discovery early on. "And by contestation they meant intense engagement in discussion but actually in a respectful way and actually listening to what the other was saying. And so it's really engagement," explained the Ostroms' friend and colleague Michael McGinnis.[38] Like athletes who committed to regular exercise regimens, Elinor and Vincent committed to stretching their minds, pushing through any pain as essential to their intellectual growth.

About their dynamic, Vincent said, "Without Lin's complimentary interests my work would have ground to a halt many years ago."[39] While Vincent was known for his interest in theory, Elinor complemented his work through her application of public choice theory to studying situations when humans had limited resources. She conducted field studies using interview and survey methods to understand human interactions, used game theory to predict human behavior, and considered how global communities developed arrangements to govern limited resources and how these arrangements are shaped by culture and environment. Through their exchanges—each having distinct yet well-matched academic strengths—they learned and modeled disagreement as a means for identifying innovative solutions to problems.

The interdisciplinary approach Ostrom developed with Vincent through their workshop depended on contestation. David Swindell, an alumnus of the Ostrom Workshop, recalled the intellectual and personal model he observed in the Ostroms' partnership: "there were tender moments that were really interesting to see and understand that you could have great disagreements, really intense disagreements and that does not define the relationship at all. In fact, it can strengthen the relationship."[40] Workshoppers participating as students, staff, peers, or visitors practiced contestation as a way of doing business, a key process of knowledge production at the Bloomington School.

Though Ostrom eventually received broad financial backing to study police performance in major United States cities, her initial findings based on Indianapolis research were harshly received by skeptical establishment scholars unwilling to trust citizen survey data over traditional quantitative metrics: "we received considerable criticism when we presented papers at professional meetings about our reliance on survey data, rather than official crime data, as measure of performance." Practicing contestation in the workshop prepared Ostrom for the challenge of gaining the trust of her peers. In response to "skepticism about citizen capacity to measure performance," Ostrom and a team of scholars associated with the workshop developed the Measurement Project. In order to establish the credibility of their citizen respondents, the team developed a method for measuring street brightness using a light meter and, similarly, one for measuring road roughness, a "roughometer." This device could be dragged behind a vehicle, producing a graph of the roughness of neighborhood streets, including measuring the depth of potholes. Comparing citizen observations with those of the light meter and roughometer gave support to the notion that "citizens could give [them] reasonable evaluations of public services." Her patience and persistence were supported by contestation with Vincent and other workshoppers. Ostrom sought active engagement with ideas and with people. Through contestation Ostrom created community and collaboration.[41]

III. Collaboration

Collaboration to Ostrom meant, most importantly, to give full consideration to others, to assemble teams of globally and disciplinarily diverse thinkers, and to create structures that facilitated teamwork. In all of these efforts, Ostrom also communed with others by developing personal connections, offering trust, and sharing her personality. The workshop has been called an institution and a network; it is a physical location and a set of ideas that work to assemble a global community of scholars.[42] In the year after she received the Nobel, Ostrom remarked on the importance of the unique organizational structure of the Workshop to her success, saying, "We have a different style of organizing. It is an interdisciplinary center—we have graduate students, visiting scholars, and faculty working together. I never would have won the Nobel but for being part of that enterprise."[43] The boundaries of the workshop research were fluid, flowing between the physical walls of the workshop building and the Ostroms' home in Bloomington, and carried with those who identified as workshoppers.

On a typical occasion for those associated with workshop research, dinner at the Ostroms' rural Bloomington home brought the community together: "This next weekend I will have the entire crew of people who went to St. Louis here to the house for a hike and [an] early supper."[44] Other structures for scholarly exchange and community for workshoppers included regular colloquia presentations by local and visiting scholars, opportunities for long- or short-term visiting scholar positions, internal publications support, and financial backing for small- and large-scale research programs for junior and senior scholars. Beginning in 1994, workshoppers gathered at Indiana University every five years for WOW, a Workshop on the Ostrom Workshop. Like a family reunion, the conference creates physical stability for this otherwise geographically disparate group.

Two residencies at Bielefeld University's Center for Interdisciplinary Research helped to shape the development of the approach to interdisciplinary collaboration that Ostrom cultivated with Vincent at their workshop. Studying at the center—locally known as ZiF (Zentrum für interdisziplinäre Forschung)—at Bielefeld University in Germany gave Ostrom awareness of a successful institutional arrangement that could help to facilitate interdisciplinarity. In 1981, she joined Vincent to participate in a research group on "Guidance, Control, and Performance Evaluation in the Public Sector," and she returned again on her own in in 1988 to join one of her mentors Reinhard Selton to study "Game Theory and the Behavior Sciences." "This was an important event in both of our intellectual journeys," Ostrom said of these experiences decades later.[45] As part of a group of elite scholars from across the social sciences living and working together in Bielefeld, the Ostroms recognized the potential for facilitating interdisciplinary research through environmental arrangements. The structure provided by the research group and regular presentations allowed for intersections across disciplines to emerge.[46] More important than learning German during her stays at ZiF, Ostrom participated in interdisciplinary communication by identifying and defining terms relevant to their research group's inquiry. Their skills in contestation allowed Elinor and Vincent to bridge the biggest obstacle of understanding "the way colleagues from different disciplines *think*—their assumptions; concepts; categories; methods of discerning, evaluating, and reporting 'truth'; and styles of arguing—their disciplinary cultures and habits of mind."[47] Elinor and Vincent put these tools into action as they planned their workshop, including refocusing globally to prioritize a comparative research program.[48]

As a team member and leader, Ostrom brought people together but also relished in the details of group exchange. Ostrom recognized the importance of trust to the success of her collaborations. "In small to medium-sized groups, it's really important. In the lab, the face-to-face communication builds trust, agreements, coordination. Without it, you don't go anywhere," she stated in an interview in 2010.[49] In a memo typical of the way she synthesized research developments and communication through detailed written reflection, Ostrom wrote, "David's comments reverberated in my head all day Sunday as Vincent and I madly tried to get started with some of our packing and planning for our trip to Poland. I thought I would try to write out some of my reflections this morning while they were still fresh." The Saturday prior in April 1986, Ostrom had met with colleagues David Feeny, Hartmut Picht, Peter Bogason, and Susan Wynne to discuss forms for coding pool resources. Those around her took note: "She always focuses on content, is generous in providing feedback and collaboration, and is constantly innovative and explores new approaches."[50]

Ostrom practiced collaboration as an instructor in traditional classroom settings as well as by involving students in long-term research projects. Her teaching philosophy centered on learning as a co-productive process. "She expected you to be a co-producer of knowledge. This concept of coproduction is important. . . . In order for something to be produced the consumer of that product or service has to participate in the production process," stated former student Paul Dragos Aligica, now a senior research fellow at the F. A. Hayek Program for Advanced Study in Philosophy, Politics, and Economics at the Mercatus Center at George Mason University. "You can't generate education and learning with people that don't want to participate in the process of learning and being educated, right?" he continued.[51]

IV. Openness to Multiple Solutions

Ostrom's willingness to pursue divergent methods, to contemplate diverse ways of thinking, and to consider multiple solutions to complex problems connected her life in and out of the classroom. The two most important theoretical foundations for her work were the theory of polycentricity, developed by Vincent with Charlie Tiebout and Robert Warren, and the theory of bounded rationality, developed by 1978 recipient of the Nobel Prize in Economics, Herbert Simon.[52] Polycentricity, "literally meaning 'having more than one center,' was adopted by the Ostroms to describe situations in which authority and decision making are shared among a number of people or organizations" and remains the most relevant to Elinor's interdisciplinary practice.[53] Her willingness to consider options beyond the market or a hierarchical approach to governance made her exceptional; through the findings of field research early in her career, Ostrom could see these were not the only possible solutions. "Basically, I believe that solving problems related to the long-term sustainability of common-pool resources and the efficient provision of public goods is difficult but not impossible," Ostrom summarized.[54] For Ostrom, there were "all sorts of ways of organizing at multiple scales, not only big or only small"—a polycentric approach.[55]

Interdisciplinarity is easy to comprehend once polycentric governance is understood. The decentralized approach to governance that Ostrom often studied echoed the institutional arrangements she developed with the workshop and later at ASU through the Center for the Study of Institutional Analysis (renamed the Center for the Study of Institutional Diversity), established in 2006. Like the systems she and Vincent studied outside the university, both enterprises offered polycentric structures by providing an alternate center for organizing outside of the discipline-based department system. Governance within the university might come from one's "home" department, the university president, or any number of workshops.

As awareness increased of Ostrom's response to Garrett Hardin's "tragedy of the commons" thesis—that individuals will act in their own self-interest leading to shared resource depletion—confusion also arose.[56] Ostrom argued there were alternate solutions to the commons dilemma. In studying Ostrom's findings, one must inevitably conclude that situational details are important; "some individuals organize themselves to govern and manage [common pool resources] and others do not."[57] A motto Ostrom's students knew well suggested there are "no panaceas" or single solutions to complex problems. "Policy analysts who would recommend a single prescription for commons problems have paid little attention to how diverse institutional arrangements operate in practice," wrote Ostrom in her introduction to *Governing*.[58] However, Ostrom's ability to see and prove multiple solutions for commons resource management where others had seen only a single option caused controversy. In an academic conversation focused on centralization and privatization, Ostrom's multiple solutions pushed a new paradigm: "People say I disproved him, and I come back and say 'No, that's not right. I've not disproved him. I've shown that his assertion that common property will always be degraded is wrong.' ... It's just that he went too far. He said people could never manage the commons well," Ostrom continued.[59]

One outgrowth of Ostrom's research program—supported by her entrepreneurial instincts—included her ability to create collaborative research networks that aligned interdisciplinary research scholars. Ostrom fostered an interdisciplinary practice in her work and the work of others that facilitated cross-disciplinary communication through standardized data collection protocols like the International Forestry Resources and Institutions (IFRI) program established in 1992. By 2010, IFRI protocols could be found in use in Uganda, Kenya, Tanzania, Guatemala, Mexico, Bolivia, Colombia, Nepal, India, Thailand, Ethiopia, and China. Like her other collaborative efforts, its success depended on not only assembling diverse disciplinary perspectives but also capitalizing on the diverse methodological expertise the represented disciplines offered. IFRI, for example, included "doing careful research on both the social and ecological aspects of how governance affects forests."[60] Her Social Ecological (SES) Framework was a hallmark interdisciplinary result, an integration of concepts allowing for broader analysis across the interactions of humans and their physical environments.[61] Ultimately products of these research efforts offered ways to manage the complexity of human behavior and to document our diverse institutional arrangements so that human behavior might more accurately be understood, rather than by applying oversimplified metaphors.

CONCLUSION

When asked about the challenge of finding a place to do the kind of interdisciplinary research she wanted to do, Ostrom replied simply, "Yes, it's always been difficult."[62] Elinor, with Vincent, created places to practice interdisciplinarity across a global intellectual community in all of their partnerships and especially through their workshop. "Finding a home for cross-disciplinary work is never easy in the highly compartmentalized and narrowly turf-conscious environment of the contemporary American university," observed their dear friend and colleague Mike McGinnis.[63] McGinnis and many others found a home for this unique practice at the workshop and in the networked community that extended beyond its walls.

NOTES

1. The quote appears in an interview with Elinor Ostrom appearing in Fran Korten, "Elinor Ostrom Wins Nobel for Common(s) Sense," *Yes!* 53 (Spring 2010), https://www.yesmagazine.org/issues/america-the-remix/elinor-ostrom-wins -nobel-for-common-s-sense. This chapter draws on Sara Clark, "Elinor Ostrom: A Biography of Interdisciplinary Life" (PhD diss., Indiana University, 2019). A copy of Ostrom's CV is posted at https://ostromworkshop.indiana.edu/about /bibliographies/elinor.html.

2. Elinor Ostrom to Leah Awan, April 21, 1982, Box 174, Folder: EO-Correspondence Awan, Leah 1977–1982, Elinor Ostrom Papers, The Lilly Library, Indiana University, Bloomington, Indiana.

3. Pamela Jagger, Jacqui Bauer, and James Walker, "Thirty-Five Years of Scholarship at the Workshop in Political Theory and Policy Analysis," *Indiana University, Bloomington,* 2009, https://ostromworkshop.indiana.edu/pdf/ArtisansOf PoliticalTheory_Jagger.pdf.

4. "Elinor Ostrom: Nobel Laureate," *The College: Indiana University's Commitment to Arts and Sciences* 32, no. 2 (2009): 7.

5. The ASU center was originally named the Center for the Study of Institutional Diversity and is now directed by Marco Janssen.

6. William C. Mitchell, "Virginia, Rochester, and Bloomington: Twenty-Five Years of Public Choice and Political Science," *Public Choice* 56, no. 2 (February 1988): 101.

7. See, for example, Vincent Ostrom and Elinor Ostrom, "Public Choice: A Different Approach to the Study of Public Administration," *Public Administration Review* 31, no. 2 (March–April 1971): 203–16; Elinor Ostrom and Vincent Ostrom, "A Theory for Institutional Analysis of Common Pool Problems," in *Managing the Commons,* ed. Garrett Hardin and John Baden (New York: W. H. Freeman and Company, 1977), 157–72; Vincent Ostrom and Elinor Ostrom, *Public Goods and Public Choices* (Bloomington: Indiana University, Workshop in Political Theory and Policy Analysis, 1978), 157–72; Elinor Ostrom and Vincent Ostrom, "The Quest for Meaning in Public Choice," *American Journal of Economics and Sociology* 63, no. 1 (February 2004): 105–47.

8. Vincent Ostrom to Walter H. C. Laves, July 31, 1964, Box 281, Folder "Personnel Files Indiana University Dept. of Government Position," Elinor Ostrom Papers, The Lilly Library, Indiana University, Bloomington, Indiana.

9. James Walker, interview by Sara Clark, June 11, 2014, transcript, "Coming Together" (in author's possession)/

10. Barbara Allen, "Actual World Possible Future: A Documentary about the Lives and Work of Elinor and Vincent Ostrom," accessed September 3, 2018, https://ostromsthemovie.tumblr.com/about.

11. Peter Boettke, Liya Palagashvili, and Jayme Lemke, "Riding in Cars with Boys: Elinor Ostrom's Adventures with the Police," *Journal of Institutional Economics* 9, no. 4 (December 2013): 407–25, https://doi.org/10.1017/S1744137413000118; Juan Camilo Cardenas and Rajiv Sethi, "Elinor Ostrom: Fighting the Tragedy of the Commons," *Books and Ideas,* last modified September 12, 2016, http://www .booksandideas.net/Elinor-Ostrom-Fighting-the-Tragedy-of-the-Commons.html; Ben Ramalingam, "Conversations on Complexity: A Tribute to Elinor Ostrom," *Aid on the Edge of Chaos,* accessed October 14, 2020, https://aidontheedge

.wordpress.com/2012/08/16/conversations-on-complexity-a-tribute-to-elinor
-ostrom.

12. Vlad Tarko, *Elinor Ostrom: An Intellectual Biography* (Lanham, MD: Rowman & Littlefield, 2017).

13. Vincent Ostrom et al., *Elinor Ostrom and the Bloomington School of Political Economy: Policy Applications and Extensions*, ed. Daniel H. Cole and Michael D. McGinnis (Lanham, MD: Lexington Books, 2018); Filippo Sabetti and Dario Castiglione, *Institutional Diversity in Self-Governing Societies: The Bloomington School and Beyond* (Lanham, MD: Lexington Books, 2017); Daniel H. Cole and Michael McGinnis, eds., *Elinor Ostrom and the Bloomington School of Political Economy: Polycentricity in Public Administration and Political Science* (Lanham, MD: Lexington Books, 2014); Jayme Lemke and Vlad Tarko, eds., *Elinor Ostrom and the Bloomington School: Building a New Approach to Policy and the Social Sciences* (Montreal: McGill-Queen's University Press, 2020).

14. Emilio Moran and Elinor Ostrom, "Progress Report to the National Science Foundation," report, February 1, 1997, box 84, folder "Annual Reports," Elinor Ostrom Papers, The Lilly Library, Indiana University, Bloomington, Indiana.

15. Michael McGinnis, "Elinor Ostrom: A Career in Institutional Analysis," *PS: Political Science & Politics* 29, no. 1 (December 1996): 737.

16. "The World's 100 Most Influential People: 2012," *Time*, April 18, 2012. See also Sydney Murray, "Prime Time: IU Professor Elinor Ostrom Follow Up Nobel Prize on Time Magazine's Top 100," *Indiana Daily Student*, April 25, 2012, newspaper clipping, Box 179, Folder "Writings-EO-Writings about EO 2012," Elinor Ostrom Papers, The Lilly Library, Indiana University, Bloomington, Indiana.

17. Elinor Ostrom, "Learning from the Field," in *Elinor Ostrom and the Bloomington School of Political Economy: A Framework for Policy Analysis*, eds. Daniel H. Cole and Michael D. McGinnis, vol. 3 (Lanham, MD: Lexington Books, 2017), 390.

18. The Department of Government was later renamed the Department of Political Science.

19. Margaret W. Rossiter, *Women Scientists in America: Before Affirmative Action, 1940–1972* (Baltimore: Johns Hopkins University Press, 1998), 84, 101–3.

20. Mary Catherine Bateson, *Composing a Life* (New York: Grove Press, 1989).

21. Mansee Bal, interview by Sara Clark, June 21, 2014, transcript, "Coming Together."

22. Catherine Tucker, interview by Catherine Guerro, July 9, 2014, transcript, "Coming Together" (in author's possession).

23. Ostrom, "Learning from the Field," 389.

24. "Elinor Ostrom—Biographical," The Nobel Prize, accessed October 31, 2013, http://www.nobelprize.org/nobel_prizes/economic-sciences/laureates/2009/ostrom-bio.html.

25. Ostrom, "Learning from the Field," 389.

26. Elinor Ostrom, interview by Kristen Monroe, ca. 2000, transcript, Box 178, Folder "Publicity-Interviews Given Transcript Nov. 6, 2000," Elinor Ostrom Papers, The Lilly Library, Indiana University, Bloomington, Indiana.

27. Elinor Ostrom to Admissions Committee, June 2, 1975, Box 267, Folder "EO—General Correspondence Material Related to Job Openings & Recommendations," Elinor Ostrom Papers, The Lilly Library, Indiana University, Bloomington, Indiana.

28. Elinor Ostrom, "A Long Polycentric Journey," *Annual Review of Political Science* 13, no. 1 (June 2010): 3, https://doi.org/10.1146/annurev.polisci.090808.123259.

29. Elinor Ostrom to Leah Awan, April 17, 1970, Box 174, Folder "EO-Correspondence Awan, Leah 1968–1976," Elinor Ostrom Papers; Elinor Ostrom to Leah Awan, 9 February 1972, box 174, folder "EO-Correspondence Awan, Leah 1968–1976," Elinor Ostrom Papers, The Lilly Library, Indiana University, Bloomington, Indiana.

30. Elinor Ostrom to Leah Awan, April 17, 1970, The Lilly Library, Indiana University, Bloomington, Indiana.

31. Elinor Ostrom and Vincent Ostrom to Leah Awan, December 5, 1971, Box 174, Folder "EO-Correspondence Awan, Leah 1968–1976," Elinor Ostrom Papers, The Lilly Library, Indiana University, Bloomington, Indiana.

32. Elinor Ostrom and Vincent Ostrom to Leah Awan, March 5, 1973, Box 174, Folder "EO-Correspondence Awan, Leah 1968–1976," Elinor Ostrom Papers. Courtesy, The Lilly Library, Indiana University, Bloomington, Indiana.

33. Pamela Jagger, Jacqui Bauer, and James Walker, *Artisans of Political Theory and Empirical Inquiry: Thirty-Five Years of Scholarship at the Workshop in Political Theory and Policy Analysis* (Bloomington: Workshop in Political Theory and Policy Analysis, 2009), 1.

34. Elinor Ostrom and Vincent Ostrom, "General Introduction [to the Workshop," ca. 1985, Box 372, Folder "Workshop Enterprise," Elinor Ostrom Papers, The Lilly Library, Indiana University, Bloomington, Indiana; see also Vincent Ostrom, "Artisanship and Artifact," *Public Administration Review* 40, no. 4 (July–August 1980): 309–10.

35. See Indiana University Mathers Museum of World Cultures Elinor and Vincent Ostrom Collection, Bloomington, Indiana.

36. Elinor Ostrom, interview by Kristen Monroe, ca. 2000, transcript, Box 178, Folder "Publicity-Interviews Given Transcript Nov. 6, 2000," Elinor Ostrom Papers, The Lilly Library, Indiana University, Bloomington, Indiana.

37. Elinor Ostrom, *Governing the Commons: The Evolution of Institutions for Collective Action* (New York: Cambridge University Press, 1990).

38. Michael McGinnis, interview by Sara Clark, June 10, 2014, transcript, "Coming Together."

39. Minoti Chakravarty, "Vincent and Elinor Ostrom: Intellectual Entre-prenueurs in the Political Sciences," *Polycentric Circles* 6, no. 1 (December 1999), Box 380, Folder "Workshop-Miscellaneous Polycentric Circles, 1998–2004," Elinor Ostrom Papers, The Lilly Library, Indiana University, Bloomington, Indiana.

40. David Swindell, interview by Joseph Stahlman, June 21, 2014, transcript, "Coming Together" (in author's possession).

41. Ostrom, "Learning from the Field," 397–98.

42. Paul Dragos Aligica, interview by Joseph Stahlman, June 18, 2014, transcript, "Coming Together" (in author's possession).

43. Fran Korten, "Elinor Ostrom Wins Nobel for Common(s) Sense," para. 9.

44. Elinor Ostrom to Leah Awan, April 10, 1972, Box 174, Folder "EO-Corre-spondence Awan, Leah 1968–1976," Elinor Ostrom Papers; Elinor Ostrom to Leah Awan, October 23, 1972, Box 174, Folder "EO-Correspondence Awan, Leah 1968–1976," Elinor Ostrom Papers, The Lilly Library, Indiana University, Bloomington, Indiana.

45. Elinor Ostrom, "A Long Polycentric Journey," 11.

46. Sabine Maasen, "Introducing Interdisciplinarity: Irresistible Infliction? The Example of a Research Group at the Center for Interdisciplinary Research (ZiF), Bielefeld, Germany," in *Practising Interdisciplinarity*, ed. Peter Weingart and Nico Stehr (Toronto: University of Toronto Press, 2000), 176.

47. Myra Strober, *Interdisciplinary Conversations: Challenging Habits of Thought* (Stanford: Stanford University Press, 2011), 4.

48. Vincent Ostrom and Elinor Ostrom to John Lombardi and Morton Lowen-grub, "Ten-Year Prospectus for the Workshop in Political Theory and Policy Analysis," ca. January 1, 1986, Box 383, Folder "Addl. Acc.-Jan. 2014-Writings-VO-Notes-1989; VO on the Workshop," Elinor Ostrom Papers, The Lilly Library, Indiana University, Bloomington, Indiana.

49. "Working Together: A Q&A with Elinor Ostrom," *IU Research & Creative Activity* 32, no. 2: 6–9.

50. Sarah Auffret, "Collective Action, Singular Accomplishment: ASU Maga-zine Interviews 2009 Nobel Laureate Elinor Ostrom," Box 115, Folder "Writings-EO-Publicity-Writings about EO 2010," Elinor Ostrom Papers, The Lilly Library, Indiana University, Bloomington, Indiana.

51. Paul Dragos Aligica, interview by Joseph Stahlman, June 18, 2014, transcript, "Coming Together."

52. Vincent Ostrom, Charles M. Tiebout, and Robert Warren, "The Organiza-tion of Government in Metropolitan Areas: A Theoretical Inquiry," *American Political Science Review* 55, no. 4 (December 1961): 831–42; V. Ostrom, "Polycentricity (Part 1)," in *Polycentricity and Local Public Economies*, ed. Michael McGinnis (Ann Arbor: University of Michigan Press, 1999), 52–74; Vincent Ostrom, "Polycentric-ity (Part 2)," in *Polycentricity and Local Public Economies*, ed. Michael McGinnis

(Ann Arbor: University of Michigan Press, 1999), 119–38; Herbert A. Simon, *Models of Man, Social and Rational* (New York: Wiley, 1957).

53. Barbara Allen, "The Story of Vincent and Elinor Ostrom," interview by Jay Wallijasper, *On the Commons*, January 10, 2014, para. 16, http://www.onthe commons.org/magazine/story-vincent-and-elinor-ostrom.

54. Ostrom, "Learning from the Field," 407.

55. "Working Together: A Q&A with Elinor Ostrom," 6–9.

56. Garrett Hardin, "The Tragedy of the Commons," *Science* 162, no. 3859 (December 13, 1968): 1244, https://www.science.org/doi/10.1126/science.162.3859.1243.

57. Ostrom, *Governing the Commons*, 27.

58. Ostrom, 21–22.

59. Korten, "Elinor Ostrom Wins Nobel for Common(s) Sense," para. 16.

60. "Working Together: A Q&A with Elinor Ostrom," 6–9.

61. For background on the SES Framework, see Harini Nagendra and Elinor Ostrom, "Applying the Social-Ecological System Framework to the Diagnosis of Urban Lake Commons in Bangalore, India," *Ecology and Society* 19, no. 2 (2014); Michael D. McGinnis and Elinor Ostrom, "Social-Ecological System Framework: Initial Changes and Continuing Challenges," *Ecology and Society* 19, no. 2 (2014); John M. Anderies, Marco A. Janssen, and Elinor Ostrom, "A Framework to Analyze the Robustness of Social-Ecological Systems from an Institutional Perspective," *Ecology and Society* 9, no. 1 (2004).

62. Sarah Auffret, "Collective Action, Singular Accomplishment: ASU Magazine Interviews 2009 Nobel Laureate Elinor Ostrom," Box 115, Folder "Writings-EO-Publicity-Writings about EO 2010," Elinor Ostrom Papers, The Lilly Library, Indiana University, Bloomington, Indiana.

63. Michael McGinnis, "Elinor Ostrom: A Career in Institutional Analysis," *PS: Political Science & Politics* 29, no. 1 (December 1996): 738.

FOURTEEN

—ɯ—

"WE CHANGED MINDS"

A History of the Women's Studies Program at IUPUI

CATHERINE A. DOBRIS, RACHEL JEAN TURNER,
AND LORÉE B. WILCOX

Catherine A. Dobris, Rachel Jean Turner, and Lorée B. Wilcox present a forty-year retrospective of the Women's Studies Program (WOST) on the Indiana University–Purdue University Indianapolis (IUPUI) campus. Drawing on oral histories and reminiscences shared by former affiliated students, faculty, staff, and administrators, the essay captures the perspective of participants on the distinct challenges and achievements as the WOST program developed. The interviewees speak to the dynamics of the IUPUI campus context on the WOST program's trajectory and to the influence of the rise of women's studies within the academy more generally.

FOR A YOUNG URBAN COMMUTER CAMPUS in a very red state, the establishment of a women's studies program at Indiana University–Purdue University Indianapolis in the 1970s seemed unlikely. Yet, as Professor Emerita Linda Haas suggests, "we changed minds" about women's studies through creative strategies that brought the emerging discipline to the attention of colleagues.[1] For example, she recalls celebrating the birthdays of well-known women in the early days of the program by inviting "all faculty to pitch-in lunches.... We put up posters for the famous woman whose birthday we were celebrating, offered a small lecture on her, and made the point that most people didn't know about her accomplishments because it was not an avenue of study at IUPUI. This worked wonderfully."[2]

Some forty years later, the Women's Studies Program at IUPUI remains an integral part of the School of Liberal Arts on our campus. For example, on April 24, 2018, IUPUI's Women's Studies Program (WOST) welcomed a standing-room-only gathering of more than thirty students, professors, and staff to its

annual Women's Studies Awards and Reception. Kimberlé Crenshaw's pro-
vocative work on intersectionality and feminism—exploring the connections
among race, ethnicity, sexuality, class, and gender—set the tone for the evening
and was reflected throughout the presentations. Specifically, from Crenshaw's
perspective, feminists recognize the interconnected nature of social categories
as they apply to given individuals or groups, and the ways in which they create overlapping and interdependent systems of discrimination, disadvantage,
and privilege.[3] This theme of intersectionality was front and center as students
presented brief excerpts of research, including studies of feminist movements
in the Middle East, identity creation, and the marginalization of Latinas in Hol-
lywood. The awards reception made evident that the Women's Studies Program
at IUPUI, just shy of its fortieth birthday, continued to fulfill the promise of the
January 30, 1979 curriculum committee's vote to create a program and minor.

This essay explores forty years of Women's Studies at IUPUI. Given the
dearth of archival holdings related to the rise of women's studies at IUPUI, we
turned to oral history to tell the story. The recollections and insights of individuals involved in WOST over the years provide the backbone of this essay
and offer a vivid sense of the program's significance both in individual lives
and on the IUPUI campus. Taken together, their stories capture early efforts
to establish women's studies at IUPUI, chronicling the evolving aims of the
program as well as its more recent history, including the 2017 decision to adopt
the new name Women's, Gender, and Sexuality Studies (WGSS).[4] The WOST
Program claimed its space during an era that featured the emergence of the
discipline itself and has been an important feature of liberal arts programs on
the Indianapolis campus for four decades.

Professor Emerita of History Miriam Langsam, a founding mother of WOST
and former associate dean of student affairs, in describing early women's studies at IUPUI, points to the difficulties inherent in the institutional setting.
She explains that in IUPUI's earliest years, it was difficult "to create traditions
and institutional connections," and it took nearly fifteen years to establish a
place for the liberal arts to flourish alongside the already vital medical center
on the campus. The deep division between the young university's "health and
non-health elements" was made visible in the contrast between medical center
staff coming to meetings "dressed in white coats" while liberal arts faculty
"came looking like 1970s hippies."[5] Understanding how to create meaningful
interactions among the various schools, Langsam and other faculty council
committee members worked toward developing collaboration in both teaching
and research. Their approach to collaboration led to the eventual breakdown
of differences that helped foster what IUPUI historian Ralph Gray called the

development of "mutual understanding and respect" among colleagues. Specifically, Gray noted that "special interest groups such as medical history and women's studies" had "adherents from most schools on the campus."[6] These collaborations helped to strengthen the development of WOST as a permanent program in the School of Liberal Arts (SLA).

The character and trajectory of women's studies at IUPUI have reflected the possibilities and constraints of the campus context as scholars initially sought ways to infuse the study of women's perspectives and experiences into and later to consider gender within the existing curriculum by working to develop courses, a minor, and eventually a program. A young, teaching-focused urban campus that primarily served commuting students in the late 1960s and early 1970s, IUPUI had limited resources to direct to any program not deemed essential by those in a position to enact policy. In their efforts to establish women's studies at IUPUI, however, early advocates of WOST were in step with national trends in the evolution of similar programs. The IUPUI women's studies website conveys that the effort to understand the history of the program is a process of examining the development of IUPUI itself. The late 1960s was a time when most aspects of contemporary culture were questioned and reassessed, and institutions of higher education were often central to this quest. Ideas outside the academy—about democracy, freedom, and equity—provide the basis for critiquing a conventional university structure and the development of curricula whose manifest claim to create social change was both a part of tradition and a challenge to it.

Participants who shaped the contours of early women's studies and later historians have similarly pointed to the field's deep rootedness in currents of women's history and US history more generally. According to feminist scholar Florence Howe, the first "political" women's studies course in the United States emerged from the student movement and was taught at the Free University of Seattle in 1965.[7] Marilyn J. Boxer notes that Women's Studies courses were initially developed in the late 1960s "when women faculty in higher education, stronger in number than ever before, began to create new courses that would facilitate more reflection on female experience and feminist aspiration."[8] In *The Evolution of American Women's Studies: Reflections on Triumphs, Controversies, and Change*, Alice E. Ginsberg underscores the forces challenging the traditional curriculum that ushered in curricular change as new courses were created in response to cultural conditions including the Civil Rights Movement, anti-Vietnam War protests, gay and lesbian protests, and, of course, the rise of the Women's Liberation Movement.[9] Ginsberg explains how "every aspect of the field has been questioned and debated," including the interdisciplinary nature of women's studies, the scope of its nomenclature (e.g., what it should be called *and* what should be studied), the role of men in women's studies, or the notion of gender overall, the lack of intersectionality, and the connections (or lack thereof) to other interdisciplinary studies such as "American, African American, Jewish Studies, and the like."[10] According to Ginsberg, the goal of Women's Studies programs "was to transform the university so that knowledge about women was no longer invisible, marginalized or made 'other.'" [11] Certainly, an aspect of women's studies that sets it apart from other ostensibly "objective" disciplines is the manifest claim to create change within the structure of higher education as well as outside the walls of academe.

The first women's studies program in the country was created at San Diego State University in 1970, shortly after IUPUI was established in 1969 as a merger between the Indianapolis programs of Indiana University and Purdue University. IUPUI held its first graduation in 1970, granting degrees to 1,535 students.[12] Consonant with nationwide trends, specific courses in women's studies were first offered on the new IUPUI campus within a decade. As Boxer notes, "Students deserted fields of study long favored by women such as history and literature for newer pastures, and universities eliminated graduation requirements that formerly sustained enrollments in the social sciences," thereby reducing demand for those fields and ultimately boosting support for disciplines such as women's studies.[13] Although no "coherent program had yet been established" at IUPUI, that situation changed in 1977 with the creation of a subcommittee on women's studies.[14] At a time when programs and departments were being inaugurated throughout the country, the IUPUI subcommittee "was tasked with debating the relevance of, need for, and creation of a Women's Studies program on the campus."[15] The committee was comprised of faculty who later assumed administrative roles in the School of Liberal Arts, including John Barlow (German), Linda Haas (sociology), Barbara Jackson (anthropology), Kathy Klein (English), and Miriam Langsam (history). Barlow recalls that Klein initiated the first meeting. While initially the dean indicated that funding could not be provided, eventually the dean's office offered release time for faculty to teach courses for WOST.

Langsam also recalls that early WOST faculty members developed creative strategies for publicizing the work of the newly established program by, for example, throwing birthday parties for famous women. The tradition apparently evolved at a "surprise birthday party" for Langsam, after it was suggested that they celebrate famous women's birthdays to educate the academic community about women's contributions to history and culture. This was the inauguration of what became a regular event in the program, as faculty members showed off their culinary skills and provided a way for WOST faculty to learn about women in other disciplines and "to consider thinking more positively about WOST."[16] Clearly, from its inception, WOST was more than a curricular enterprise; it sought to involve the entire academic community.

Professor Emeritus John Barlow (later dean of SLA) remembers that initially there was not great enthusiasm for the program primarily, in his view, because of limited funding as well as a lack of administrative understanding of what the program might entail. Creative thinking was needed in order to offer the first women's studies course within tight budget constraints, suggests Barlow: "Consequently, we decided that some of us would volunteer to teach a segment of a full semester's course. The segments would reflect the ways different disciplines deal with women, calling each segment something like 'Women and Society,' 'Women and History,' 'Women and Literature,' etc."[17] However, Barlow and others apparently found this collaboration "cumbersome," and thus the course evolved over time into team-taught courses with "two professors . . . one from the humanities, the other from the social sciences" working together. [18] The strategy eventually proved beneficial, according to Barlow, when instructors finally received some release time for offering collaborative courses.

Barlow's recollections appear in line with national trend Ginsberg notes in observing the development of other programs. She suggests that during this period, "many women's studies courses and events were advertised through flyers, mimeographed newsletters, and by word of mouth. . . . Feminism in the U.S. academy was not so much an organized entry as a group of courses, many of them listed on bulletin boards and/or taught for free."[19] Early efforts at IUPUI, as elsewhere, were cobbled together by dedicated faculty who saw a cultural, sociological, and academic need, which was consistent with their own academic interests and which they worked to bring to fruition.

Reflecting on the program's beginnings, as the only male faculty member to participate in the formation of WOST, Barlow considers his motivations in light of contemporary sociopolitical conditions. Addressing why he was drawn to assist in the development of WOST, he asks and answers, "Why did I sign up to join the Program? Because of the sort of thing we, as a society, are still dealing with right now: the subtle and overt misogyny that is so pervasive in American culture. As with racism, there seems to be no end to this kind of malady. The importance of Women's Studies and Gender Studies can't be emphasized enough."[20]

One of the WOST program's founding mothers, Haas recalls her years in the various stages of the program. As director from 1987 to 1990, she developed and taught many of the most significant courses, including Introduction to

Women's Studies, Gender and Society, and Gender and Work, in addition to offering colloquia and overseeing internship opportunities. She notes that she "was part of the group that initiated all the WOST numbered courses; I don't remember any problems once we had permission for a program. . . . Indeed I was hired originally in 1977 to develop a course on 'sex roles.'"[21] Haas observes that "the original group of founders of Women's Studies" were all eventually tenured, which is significant given the resistance to women's studies scholarship often experienced by academics elsewhere.[22] But while tenure is in many ways a benchmark for academic respectability, Haas suggests that a crucial opportunity for WOST was overlooked at IUPUI: "At that point, it would have [been] great if some of us had been offered split positions in Women's Studies as a way to institutionalize the Program, as IU-B[loomington] did. Without additional resources and split appointments, I believe the Program continued to serve students adequately but did not serve WOST faculty as well. Once the curriculum was set and institutional support could be taken for granted (albeit at a low level), there was no reason for annual planning retreats, frequent meetings, or special projects to grow the Program and keep up our profile."[23] Obioma Nnaemeka, at her initial appointment in 1992, requested and was granted a joint appointment (WOST and the French Department—now subsumed under the Department of World Languages and Cultures). The joint appointment was a condition for accepting the job offer.

In 2002, Peg Brand was granted a joint appointment in WOST and the Department of Philosophy. These two joint appointments were the exception rather than the rule. No other faculty were appointed directly to WOST. Thus, adjunct professors and lecturers provide all teaching and service to the program in exchange for minimal direct compensation, such as course releases predicated on the goodwill of chairs and deans. By the time of Haas's retirement in 2014, the SLA was once again operating under significant financial constraints, including a hiring freeze that did not allow a replacement, causing some of Haas's courses to be eliminated entirely.

As Langsam, Barlow, and Haas describe, although the late 1970s ushered in a new era for the study of women at IUPUI, there were continual struggles for financial and administrative support, reflecting similar trends in other universities across the nation. It was during this time of development that proponents of many WOST programs at various institutions encountered resistance from their own academic communities. For example, in Florence Howe's *The Politics of Women's Studies: Testimonies from Thirty Founding Mothers* (2000), Electa Arenal, an early women's studies advocate at Richmond College, describes problematic interactions with administrators who inquired, "*What* women writers?" when she proposed a course on women writers of Spain and Latin

America. Their dismissive response indicated doubt as to whether such writers existed.[24] Arenal shares her experiences with course development and her fear of segregation, much like those described by feminist literary critic Annette Kolodny, who was criticized by administrators for being overly zealous in her efforts while jumping through countless hoops to establish a women's studies program at University of British Columbia, Vancouver.[25]

Similarly, founding director of women's studies at University of Arizona Myra Dinnerstein notes receiving minimal financial support from her institution in the 1970s.[26] Historical evidence points consistently to a reluctance in providing funding and support for women's studies programs to flourish. However, despite these significant impediments, programs began to be established nationwide with increasing success.

At IUPUI, in January 1979, a proposal to inaugurate a program was presented to the Faculty Assembly of the School of Liberal Arts, and "Kathy Klein was unanimously voted to be the first coordinator (the position would later be renamed 'Director') of the Women's Studies Program."[27] At the end of the month, "on January 30, 1979, the [SLA] curriculum committee voted in favor of creating a women's studies minor and program." Soon after the vote, "the program . . . received five formal applications for the minor," and in May, "Toni Wise-Hackett . . . was conferred the first Women's Studies minor" while "the second conferred minor followed in August 1979."[28] In the four decades since, the Women's Studies Program has successfully continued its mission of "offer[ing] . . . students a new way of looking at the world and themselves with the introduction of the forgotten and neglected material which influences and encompasses the female experience."[29]

LEADERSHIP

Over the course of developing the program, different styles of leadership were implemented in the position of director. In general, various faculty members volunteered to serve in the position for relatively brief terms. But in some years, stewardship was especially hard to come by due to lack of resources and incentives for undertaking significant service in the program. There was no additional salary provided for directors of programs at IUPUI, and course releases were scant.

Throughout the years, directors served for one to three years and included (the late) Anne Donchin (philosophy), Rebecca Van Voorhis (School of Social Work), and Linda Haas (sociology) in the 1980s; and Susan Shepherd (English), Amanda Porterfield (religious studies, Robert White (sociology), Miriam Langsam (history), Missy Dehn Kubitschek (English), and Marianne Wokeck (history) in the mid- to late 1990s. By the late 1990s and early 2000s, there was a fair amount of turmoil in the leadership of the program when it became difficult to find faculty willing to serve as director until finally Richard Turner (English) and Obioma Nnaemeka (WOST and world languages) served for several years, first as acting and later as co-directors. In October 1998, under the auspices of WOST, IUPUI hosted an international women's conference, Women in Africa and the African Diaspora (WAAD), addressing health and human rights. The conference attracted hundreds of participants from forty-eight countries on four continents. WOST faculty and numerous members of the IUPUI family showed strong support for the conference. In 2011, Nnaemeka delivered the keynote lecture at the Women World-Wide Women's Studies/Gender Studies Undergraduate Student Conference at IUPUI.

Then, in 2005, Associate Professor Nancy Marie Robertson (history) assumed leadership and remained as director until Associate Professor Catherine Dobris (communication studies), who covered for Robertson during her 2009–10 sabbatical, took over in 2012. Both brought welcome continuity to the leadership of the WOST program. It is ironic that in the early 2000s, as administrators and faculty increasingly emphasized IUPUI's research mission, it was primarily women who were asked to sacrifice research time for unrewarded service obligations, which took time away from more highly venerated scholarly ventures. This issue was hardly unique to IUPUI, as work in women's studies was often "unrecognized and unrewarded" in universities as the rule.[30]

In addition to lack of salary or course release time as incentives, space was often an issue throughout the first decade of the program's development. Some thirty years ago, Professor of Philosophy Anne Donchin posed the question, "How far can we push our guest status?" in an article titled, "The Woman Who Came to Dinner: The Women's Studies Administrator in the House of Academe."[31] Underscoring the value of gaining "permanent residency," she elaborates on the necessity for physical occupancy that programs require to prosper and meet the needs of research, teaching, and service for faculty and students. Donchin described finally obtaining "a room of their own" for the program: "a suite of Women's Studies offices adequate to bring all of our resources together for the first time. Our reading room, secretary, files and my own office are now housed in a single location ... [and] the Dean has promised us increased secretarial support, so we will have a full-time secretary committed to the work of our academic programs."[32]

Starting in 1989, program directors received some assistance with the establishment of the Friends of Women's Studies Executive Committee. Initially, the Friends of Women's Studies was developed primarily as a fundraising mechanism. It sought to promote connections between people on the campus and in the community who were "committed to the advancement of women in society," thus aiding in developing the necessary resources "to advance scholarly research and teaching, as well as academic conferences, community programs, and scholarships in an effort to support such endeavors in Women's Studies."[33] In 1991, there were twenty members of the committee, including professors such as Donchin but also community members, including Rabbi Sandy Sasso and community activist Norma Bradway. The committee eventually established the Friends of Women's Studies Scholarship, which still thrives and awards approximately $1,000 a year to an outstanding IUPUI student.

Another former director, Professor Emerita Marianne Wokeck, tells of joining the program in 1991 when she became an assistant professor in the History Department. During Wokeck's tenure at IUPUI, WOST "went through different phases of development."[34] Wokeck suggests that the predilections of different program directors, as well as disagreement on prioritization in a school whose mission was teaching but which aspired to emphasize research, along with "the little weight that engagement in WOST carried in the promotion and tenure process," influenced perceptions of the program throughout the university. Ultimately, Wokeck posits that some may have viewed WOST as "a separate and even separating Program."[35]

Wokeck also notes how WOST faculty were pulled in many directions simultaneously, including a heavy burden of advising, especially mentoring, particularly in areas that were not typically rewarded by administration, "such as the Office for Women, the Office of Equal Opportunity, Intergroup Dialogue, and mentoring initiatives." Some of the discussions Wokeck recalls involved disagreements over a name change, which "reflected a larger debate about the focus, theories, and methods of Women's and Gender Studies." Wokeck also suggests that collaboration in and outside of the program was mostly idiosyncratic and somewhat difficult to sustain and "tended to be very much dependent on the contacts and energies of individuals, and sustainability of the efforts could rarely be achieved." Outside of IUPUI, Wokeck notes, "There was cooperation with colleagues at Butler and with the Indiana Women's History Association." Those collaborations have ebbed and flowed over time, as Wokeck suggests, but continue to enrich the program periodically.[36]

As other former WOST faculty members also suggested, Wokeck recalls opposition to the development of WOST from "colleagues and administrators who did/do not support WOST or feminist courses" for any number of reasons.[37] Certainly, money has always been an issue in the School of Liberal Arts from its inception, and supporting some endeavors necessarily meant not supporting others. Moreover, according to some early faculty members, resistance might also have stemmed from the perceived lack of practicality for women's studies as a scholarly pursuit. At the same time, however, Wokeck suggests that there has been "generally articulated support, especially when it is useful to emphasize the role of women such as the number of female faculty, especially in medicine, IT, [and] science," but, unfortunately, support has been "rarely backed up with funds such as faculty lines, space, and administrative support."[38]

Associate Professor Emerita of English Susan Shepherd also served as director in the middle years of the program and remembers her time as co-director, serving with Wokeck and Missy Kubitschek. Shepherd shared a "suite" in the basement of the Cavanaugh Hall building with Obioma Nnameka and Assistant Director of the Continuing Education Center for Women Pat Boer. Two administrative assistants were also housed in this area, and there was a small adjacent room that served as the "start of the WOST Reading Room," where "faculty members, staff, and students often gathered informally for lunch."[39]

Shortly after Wokeck and Shepherd led the program, Amanda Porterfield became director and remembers this period as a particularly difficult one for WOST: "When I came on board, it was at a low point—near extinction I would say. There was no one willing to take it on, and so to enable it to survive, even though I didn't feel like I was the most qualified person, I feel like it was a good thing to do. I received some resistance from [the Religious Studies] Department personally, in terms of taking this time . . . and I think as part of that resistance, there was a negative view of WOST."[40] Porterfield suggests that the program had lost "momentum" in particular because of the strain between service and scholarship, as IUPUI continued to bill itself as a research institution. Porterfield recalls that there were conflicts in WOST as to its role in promoting research versus providing a support system for women students and faculty. But she also notes that several positive developments occurred during her tenure as director, including attention from leadership in both Bloomington and IUPUI.[41] Following Porterfield's departure from IUPUI, former dean Robert White recalls his time in WOST in the late 1990s, as acting co-director with Langsam: "Miriam sort of volunteered the two of us to do it. I think we both considered it a very valuable part of the curriculum. . . . Unfortunately, there were a lot of things unsettled. . . . I think there was a sense that the Dean's office didn't support the Program enough in a sense of compensation."[42] Eventually, White recalls, "It would have been the appointment of Nancy Robertson as Director, that things became much more settled. Throughout, though, I would

say that it was a valuable part of the curriculum and the campus. . . . There were
people in key positions of leadership who clearly saw a need and saw the benefits
of having the Program. . . . Nancy . . . did a great job. [She] was very organized,
conscientious, and really positive for the Program and the same holds for Catherine Dobris in keeping it visible, etc."[43] White also suggests that there were
and are "people on campus who grossly undervalue what the Program does.
And are resistant to it, in one form or another."[44] He recalls, "I do know of at
least one faulty member who I remember describing that the Program wasn't
important or valued . . . and then things happened, and I have a feeling her
opinion changed as soon as she had been treated very poorly . . . because she
was a woman. . . . [Not everyone] realizes what's going on until sometimes it
affects them at which point people can change. [They] become more aware and
then suddenly 'oh' you know? And that's why it's good to have an intellectual
home that is aware of these things."[45] Expanding on some of White's observations, Richard Turner, now professor emeritus, recalls the fragility of this
point in the program's history when he served as director from 2000 to 2002
and co-director with Obioma Nnaemeka in 2002–03: "Dean Saatkamp asked
me to direct the Program until the members of WOST could find someone to
lead it. He said that unless he could find someone, he would close it down or
ship it off to another school. . . . I said I would do what he needed to keep the
Program running."[46] Eventually, Turner agreed to co-direct the program with
Nnaemeka, taking over the management details while Nnaemeka focused on
the development of the academic side, focusing on energizing current adjunct
faculty and investigating growth for the graduate program. Nnaemeka recalls
"the very vibrant intellectual community of seasoned feminist scholars" that
she met when she was hired earlier in 1992.[47] According to Nnaemeka, along
with colleagues well-versed in feminist scholarship—including Anne Donchin,
Barbara Jackson, Linda Haas, Missy Kubitschek, and Amanda Porterfield—
they "created an enabling environment for growth on many levels—scholarship, pedagogy, community engagement."[48] As a result, Nnaemeka explains,
the program began attracting faculty from departments outside of the School
of Liberal Arts in the active building of the institution. Graduate-level courses
in feminist theory were also developed and taught by Nnaemeka and colleagues
such as Peg Brand, focusing on disciplines in the humanities and social sciences
and taken by graduate students from the IU School of Nursing. Additionally,
Nnaemeka recalls that the Friends of Women's Studies was quite active and
"truly invested in the Program," and there were many community women who
"were committed collaborators" to women's studies endeavors.[49]

According to Turner, "In its early days, WOST spent a lot of time and energy in explaining and demonstrating the intellectual coherence and the authority of the work it did," and he recalls that the program was "met with the same hostility that most WOST programs found when [they] began." Still, Turner adds, the program was notable because "its work made distinctive progress in a relatively short time of making and supporting its claims as a discipline rather than just a study area such as American Studies or Urban Studies." During this time, he notes, the Office for Women was created, "and that created an ongoing conversation about the roles of the two areas [WOST and the Office for Women]." Turner recalls that in the early 2000s there were some discussions "about changing the name of WOST to 'Women's and Gender Studies,' but there wasn't much traction for any change" at the time, although, of course, IU Bloomington had changed its name to the Department of Gender Studies in 1997. There were also issues raised about the nature of the discipline itself as "gender identification became a more and more complicated and contested discourse."[50] Feminist scholar Nellie Y. McKay discusses similar complexities surrounding the debate of understanding gender awareness as a necessary avenue of heightening consciousness.[51] Turner notes, "Peg Brand worked pretty hard to create strength for Women's Studies by setting up initiatives for all IU WOST programs to collaborate on projects and share their work and the work of their students."[52]

Former WOST director Nancy Robertson recalls that Brand was a major supporter of the Women's Studies Undergraduate Conference, initiated when Pat McNeal of IU South Bend (IUSB) called a meeting at IU Kokomo (IUK) to discuss a statewide conference. According to Robertson, over fifty students attended the first conference in 1989 from IUK, IUB, IU East [IUE], IUSB, IU Northwest [IUN], and IUPUI. Over the years, students and faculty members attended from IU campuses across the state, as different campuses took turns hosting. "Because of its central location," explains Robertson, "and faculty who were active at the time, IUK was one of the most frequent hosts; that stopped when there was a change in faculty (and priorities) there."[53] Originally it was called the Women's Studies Undergraduate Conference, and Robertson recalls further that "by 2008—the twentieth anniversary—the conference began to use 'Women's Studies/Gender Studies Undergraduate Student Conference'; sometimes research is specified, sometimes not. Students have presented both creative work and research projects. In succeeding years, sometimes 'women's and gender studies' was used. Because it's organized by different campuses (and different groups over the years), there is not consistency."[54] Themes have included "Gender Inequalities and Empowerment: Linking the Local and the Global" (IUK, 1999); "Women, Bodies, Expressions" (IUB, 2003); "The Global Community of Women" (IU Fort Wayne, 2007); "Talking Gender: Conversations about Culture, Sexuality, and Power" (IU Southeast, 2010); and "Women World Wide" (IUPUI, 2011). During Robertson's time as director, she prioritized bringing the conference to the IUPUI campus, hosting over sixty students from around the state as well as thirty to forty local students and more than twenty faculty members. In more recent years, adjunct faculty, including Janice Bankert-Countryman and Rachel Turner, have helped support students by attending, mentoring, and chairing panels. IUPU–Columbus hosted "Art as Resistance: Imaging Radical Feminist Spaces" in 2018, and Director Aimee Zoeller notes the "incredible campus collaboration" required for a successful conference.[55] In 2019, IUN hosted "Women & Power: Policing Gender in Public Spaces." Robertson adds that these are the longest continuously running conferences for undergraduates in the IU system.

While the collaborations across the IU system to produce the undergraduate conference are significant, at home on IUPUI's campus resistance to the development of the program has always been a feature of its existence. Turner recalls, "there was a general hostility and dismissal among the male (and some female) members of the faculty. There were certainly few resources devoted to the Program and so it was built on the dedication and commitment of its members." Throughout its evolution, suggests Turner, "WOST has been a crucial part of IUPUI's emergence as an important and powerful university."[56]

Over the years and through changes in administration and enormous growth on the IUPUI campus, WOST directors encouraged various measures for creating interest and support for the program, as noted earlier by Haas and Langsam. For example, former assistant dean for development and external affairs Gail Plater recalls the "women's biography series, headed by IUPUI community advocate Jean Bepko, [was developed] to raise funds for WOST." Working with directors including Rebecca Van Voorhis and Amanda Porterfield, Plater explains, two events "focusing on women's biographies" were planned each year, in which authors or editors were asked to discuss their work at a luncheon and discussion.[57] Participants were provided with the works in advance and had the opportunity to engage with the authors, editors, and faculty members.

Genevieve Shaker, associate professor of philanthropic studies, adjunct professor of liberal arts and women's studies, who succeeded Plater as associate dean of development and external affairs, also recalls the biography series."[58]

She remembers, "Jean [Bepko] was . . . a driving force behind the Friends of Women's Studies board as well. She brought various community members into the group."[59]

Plater recalls that the intent of these events was to bring community members into contact with WOST and raise awareness and support for the program as well as raise money for scholarships. In fact, Plater explains, the biography series raised interest within the community and resulted in important financial support that had not existed previously.

English Professor Jane Schultz recalls attending "the annual WOST retreats hosted by alumna Barbara Lieber at her beautiful 'cottage' on Lake Maxinkuckee."[60] She reminisces, "We always had a big crowd and enjoyed talking about gender research, program issues, cooking together, and going out on the lake with Barbara. I have photos somewhere of one of the retreats in autumn 1992 when my daughter Miranda was only six or seven months old. Everyone was wanting to hold Miranda. . . . Miriam and her partner Jean [who taught adjunct courses in women and the law] always came to the retreat as well—and, of course, Linda Haas."[61] Co-director Susan Shepherd elaborates on the "sense of community" at the Maxinkuckee retreats: "As I remember, twelve to fifteen of us attended each time over a weekend. We brought food to cook and also had a meal delivered by a local restaurant. The house had enough bedrooms for us all (with a big dormitory-style room and a sleeping porch). We would select readings for discussion in advance and at least once had an invited guest to lead discussion."[62] On other occasions, Shepherd remembers, "There were book groups and work-in-progress presentations. We met once or twice a semester over a period of several years, sometimes at the homes of faculty members."[63]

Serving from 2005 to 2012, Nancy Robertson became the first director to steward the program for longer than three years in over a decade. Pausing only for a sabbatical, Robertson's continuity in the directorship served to provide a strong presence in the School of Liberal Arts, strengthen relations among faculty, advertise course offerings to students, and build the minor. She brought the IU Undergraduate Conference back to IUPUI in 2011. Also in 2011, she nominated director of the Office for Women Kathleen Grove (attorney and adjunct lecturer in WOST) for the National Women's Studies Outstanding Achievement Award. Grove became one of two recipients of the prestigious national honor.

Finally, Dobris, lead author of this chapter, became director in 2012. On the advice of Robertson, she created the WOST Advisory Board and sent out invitations to adjunct faculty in 2014. The first board members included Janice Bankert-Countryman, Obioma Nnaemeka, Nancy Robertson, and Aimee

Zoeller. Dobris also proposed and secured a name change for the almost forty-year-old program, revisiting a debate from decades earlier on whether to expand the purview of Women's Studies to include "Gender" and "Sexuality."

ADMINISTRATIVE ASSISTANTS

Although records of administrative assistants are not complete, the names of Barbara Mondary, Lena Jones, Nicole Collins, Penny Saltsman, and Rachel Turner are recalled anecdotally by previous directors and adjunct faculty. Some were hired as staff, and most were IUPUI alumni who later advanced to higher positions at IUPUI and/or went on to take coursework toward further degrees. All were integral to the maintenance and success of the program. For example, Shepherd recalls, "Barbara Mondary was the administrative assistant when I was Director, and she contributed a lot to the Program, including putting out a monthly newsletter, assembling huge amounts of scholarship info for students (not only WOST-related) which drew in a lot of students, and helped to make the area what may have been the first openly LGBTQ-friendly space on campus."[64] Later in the evolution of the program, Jones, Collins, and Saltsman were instrumental in providing support for faculty and students, in addition to working as support staff for other similarly underfunded programs. All three went on to advance their careers at IUPUI. After Saltsman's departure, a hiring freeze prevented the program from replacing her, so in fall 2016 communication studies graduate student Rachel Turner, second author on this project, was offered a part-time position to assist the director. Although working only fifteen hours per week, she provided full-time support during her two-year stint until completing her Master of Arts degree in 2018, when the position was reduced further to a work-study appointment. WOST then hired an advanced undergraduate, Gina Suarez, to provide ten hours of service per week. A reduction in the level of support and hours per week has taken its toll on some of the Program's development, but overall the quality of support via expedient hires was maintained. Beginning in 2017, the SLA moved to a centralized administrative support system, which is still evolving, making the future of administrative assistance for the program unclear.

MOVING THROUGH THE TWENTY-FIRST CENTURY

For the past four decades, students have completed minors in the program by accumulating sixteen credit hours, including an Introduction to Women's Studies course, four cross-listed courses across a range of disciplines, and a one-credit capstone, allowing students to develop a special project with an adjunct WOST professor in the program. In addition, one or two students a year choose to pursue an individualized major plan (IMP) with a focus on women's and gender studies.

IUPU–COLUMBUS (IUPUC)

A significant addition to the program occurred in 2012 when IUPU–Columbus developed its own program as an offshoot of IUPUI's. Professor Aimee Zoeller established the program in collaboration with Nancy Robertson and became its first coordinator. Then, in 2012, Zoeller established a unique space for the WOST program at IUPUC, which was developed "with a 20-thousand-dollar grant from IUPUI." Zoeller explains that obtaining the space "was a really notable point of collaboration between faculty at IUPUC and the administration at IUPUI" —a space that houses the Columbus campus's Feminist, Spectrum, and LBGTQ clubs.[65]

Consistent with other comments from administrators, Zoeller explains that while administration is generally supportive, the program is not backed up with adequate financial assistance: "In Columbus, there really hasn't been resistance, but when we approached administration about adding this minor, they said 'OK, that's fine, but we're not going to add any kind of administrative support, there won't be a salary increase, there won't be a course release,' so, kind of like saying if you want to do it that's fine, but we can't support it."[66] Lack of support is usually excused on the basis of ever decreasing budgets, and finances may also dictate if, how, and when new courses are added to a minor. For example, Zoeller notes that innovation in curriculum is not, in her view, always fully endorsed by administrators. Specifically, when offering a course on Black Feminism, Zoeller recalls, "The first time we put Black Feminism on the books it didn't have very high enrollment. So, it was 'maybe we should go ahead and cancel this and maybe we shouldn't even try it again because it's not going to get high enrollment,' so that [lack of backing] kind of feels like resistance."[67]

At IUPUC, as elsewhere in the IU system, both budgetary and enrollment constraints frequently outweigh pedagogical concerns, as might be true in any other academic setting, which is dependent on the former to support the latter. Zoeller believes that the Program overall "has been a valuable part of IUPUI," which she has experienced from the perspective of a graduate student, under Linda Haas, and as faculty.[68] Overall, Zoeller is confident that administrators at IUPUC are supportive of WOST. She concludes, "I think that it's been really beautiful to be at the birth of the program at IUPUC. You can see that the students who typically feel marginalized feel like they have a home. [Sometimes] these are students who have barely survived high school because of their perspectives or their identity . . . and they get to college and you see this burden relieved, like, 'Oh, there are other people that are like me or see the world like I do.'"[69]

THE PRESENT AND FUTURE

Triota: A Women's and Gender Honor Society

In 2016, WOST undergraduate minor Matt Preston proposed that the program sponsor a chapter of Iota (Triota), the National Honor Society for Women's Studies. A returning adult learner, Preston chose a minor in WOST to complement his two majors and three minors, and advanced a proposal for a Women's and Gender Studies Honor Society, explaining, "I think that there are too many stigmas about what Women's, Gender, and Sexuality Studies [WGSS] entail. . . . [In classes] the most important thing I learned, while seemingly intuitive, is that women do not necessarily have the same position on any given issue. The program at IUPUI taught me to identify these kinds of similarities and differences. The WGSS faculty at IUPUI—Amanda Friesen [political science], Shana Stump [history], Janice Bankert-Countryman, and Catherine Dobris—taught me to empathize with others in a way I never had before."[70] Preston, who went on to the University of Michigan law school after graduation, elaborates:

> After my deployment to Afghanistan while in the Army, I found my own definition of liberty and freedom: that each person should be able to identify themselves as they see fit. When I joined the WGSS program at IUPUI, I learned that although I defended that freedom abroad, the opportunity for everyone to exercise it did not exist equally at home. This is why I founded the IUPUI chapter of Triota. I wanted others . . . to be able to show their pride in this educational program which seeks to teach people that, despite our differences, we all deserve the same opportunity.[71]

The first group of six students was inducted in spring 2017, and its first president, Maryann O'Connor, was selected from the new membership.

Changing Our Name: Women's, Gender, and Sexuality Studies

In the fall of 2016, the Women's Studies Program began to explore the prospect of changing its name, a possibility that had been debated previously at various points throughout the years. As one of the authors, Dobris, recalls, "When I first arrived at IUPUI in 1993, I remember an animated discussion at a WOST faculty meeting on the topic of a Program name change. Although I was a new faculty member and largely silent in this discussion, I was relieved that the overriding sentiment was to retain the original phrasing. It took more than two decades of teaching and scholarship at IUPUI to change my mind."[72] Thus, in 2016, a study was undertaken by the program, under Dobris's direction, to examine the most common name choices of other institutions both in the Midwest and nationwide. While there was great variability, in many cases the "women's studies" moniker had been replaced years earlier with titles that were both more inclusive but also less centered on women's issues. After input was sought from all stakeholders—including faculty, students, and administrators—in March 2017 a proposal was created to officially change the name of the program. While many possibilities were considered, the director, along with the Women's Studies Advisory Board, ultimately proposed the new title Women's, Gender, and Sexuality Studies. The general sentiment was to keep *women* first and foremost in the title, followed by *gender* as a more inclusive noun, especially in a sociopolitical landscape that was acknowledging gender beyond a binary construct. Including *sexuality* as the final descriptor spurred some discussion about the offerings, or lack thereof, in the current program. Most were won over by the two-pronged argument that first, sexuality was a central issue in many, if not most, of our course offerings; and second, this final term could be seen, in former director Robertson's words, as "aspirational," providing a broader umbrella as we expand course offerings in years to come.[73]

Our Students

In the final analysis, the ultimate worth of any academic program can best be judged by the impression it leaves on its students. So, it is fitting to end this history with a reflection on that influence. Currently an instructor in the School of Social Work at IUPUI, 2009 graduate Myranda Warden recalls, "Being a student in the Women's Studies Program was transformative, allowing me to see myself for the first time: in my history, in the present and future co-construction of this world, and in the mirror."[74]

Currently a PhD student in human development and family studies at Michigan State, 2015 graduate Finneran Muzzey notes, "Women's, Gender, and Sexuality Studies gave me an educational home when I wasn't sure I fit in any other educational discipline. . . . I found an intellectual space where I could apply my own life experiences, hear from others' life experiences, and develop a theoretical foundation that still informs my current research. My time in the Program introduced me to lifelong mentors that supported me personally and professionally and continue to support me now as I pursue my PhD."[75] Another recent graduate Sarah Bahr, winner of numerous WOST and SLA awards and scholarships, now a graduate student at IUPUI and a freelance journalist for the *Indianapolis Star* and *Indianapolis Monthly*, reflects, "The IUPUI Women's Studies Program allowed me to explore an eclectic range of interests, from the persecution of 'witches' during the Salem witch trials to a capstone project investigating the status of female journalists in sports media. Every class I took in the Program, whether a Spanish Women's Literature course or a survey of US Women's History, was taught by a passionate, prepared professor whose love for the subject was contagious."[76] For her part, admissions counselor and graduate student Liz Forster recalls, "[The Program] . . . has been essential in the development of not only my education but also my world view. I have met so many incredible people, faculty and students, who are changing the world as we speak."[77]

Utilizing IUPUI's Individualized Major Program (IMP) option to focus on women's and gender studies, 2017 graduate Aspen Christian wrote an ethnological analysis on "Access to Reproductive Health Care in Mapleton-Fall Creek." After graduation, she entered a master's degree program in women's and gender studies at the Graduate Center, City College of New York (CUNY), later moving on to pursue a PhD while holding a full-time position as marketing and communications coordinator at SAGE, Advocacy and Services for LGBT Elders. According to Christian, her focus on gender and activism in the program "helped develop my academic interests and taught me how to set realistic, attainable goals. Receiving a degree from the WGSS Program provided me with the analytical and personal skills to thrive in both graduate school and nonprofit work."[78]

The Future

The history of the Women's Studies Program at IUPUI has been one of both struggle and triumph, and the immediate future of the WGSS appears to augur likewise for the coming years. The program has a new name, which promises more diversity and inclusion, but in the 2018–19 school year enrollment numbers in the SLA continue to decline, as incoming students amass substantial credit hours in high school advanced placement courses and choose to pursue less expensive curricular options at community colleges in lieu of costlier options for 100- and 200-level courses at IUPUI. Consequently, enrollment in entry-level courses, such as Introduction to Women's Studies (W105), suffers. While in 2019 the program boasted a more than respectable thirty-five minors and graduated eight to ten of them, plus one to two individualized majors a year, the future is still uncertain. Like other departments and programs in the school, WGSS is working on ways to bolster enrollment and help students meet the challenges of the twenty-first century in the classroom, the political and corporate arenas, and interpersonal and global realms, but all within the landscape of ever-diminishing resources. And in an era marked by issues that include concerted political efforts to constrict the civil rights of women as well as feminist movements to uncover and defeat sexual exploitation such as #MeToo, WGSS has a crucial role to play for all stakeholders. Moreover, the twenty-first century has brought increasing scrutiny of the relative value of many aspects of a liberal arts education in comparison to STEM careers and jobs training. Thus, as the future of academic programs in general seems somewhat uncertain, so, too, does the future of the newly named WGSS program. Historical reflection shows us that despite bouts of occasional apathy and even antipathy, lack of funding, occasionally nominal respect from colleagues, and overall inconsistent administrative support, we are still standing. And in so doing, our forty-year retrospective points the way to a hopeful future.

Most feminists of a "certain age" can recall being warned by well-meaning and less well-meaning colleagues to avoid a career in connection to the fledgling field of women's studies. We were told that women's studies was at best "trendy" and at worst "dangerous," marking our careers and attendant vitae with a potentially unemployable stamp as "radical feminists." Likewise, according to this oft-cited view, women already had equality, and even if they did not, they soon would—rendering the field and our careers irrelevant. Decades later, women's studies has established credibility in most major US universities, boasts a roster of rigorous peer-reviewed journals, has expanded into gender and sexuality studies, and seems in no danger of going away any time soon. In a world in which public and private figures challenge everything from the gender binary to the insidiousness of sexual harassment and the perpetuation of rape culture, our evolving field has never been more relevant. But in attaining legitimacy on campuses throughout the country, professors, staff, and students have worked hard to assume our places as WOST and WGSS scholars and students in academe; and at IUPUI, we are no exception. The Women's Studies Program at IUPUI, now renamed as Women's, Gender, and Sexuality Studies, has survived and even thrived despite the odds. Our founding mothers and a few fathers, as well as many of their second-generation offspring, have since moved on or retired, and some have passed away. But the program continues to change minds through the interdisciplinary scholarship of its faculty and the development of its curriculum and anticipates a future of meaningful struggle as we work to highlight what Angela Barron McBride, PhD, RN, distinguished professor, and IU School of Nursing dean emerita, describes as "the importance of women's experience and interdisciplinary scholarship" across the IUPUI campus.[79]

NOTES

1. Linda Haas, one of the founders of the Women's Studies Program at IUPUI, email message to authors, September 24, 2018. We are immensely grateful to the twenty faculty, staff, and students who responded to our surveys and consented to interviews, as well as to those who contributed peer reviews (in particular, Gail Plater, Nancy Robertson, and Jane Schultz) to help us create a cohesive picture of the history of WOST at IUPUI. Copies of all email communications and interviews used in this study are in the authors' possession.

2. Haas, email message to authors, September 24, 2018.

3. Kimberlé Crenshaw, *On Intersectionality: Essential Writings of Kimberlé Crenshaw* (New York: The New Press, 2017).

4. Women's, Gender, and Sexuality Studies, IUPUI, accessed November 3, 2020, https://liberalarts.iupui.edu/wost.

5. Miriam Langsam, email message to authors, October 19, 2018.

6. Ralph D. Gray, *IUPUI—The Making of an Urban University* (Bloomington: Indiana University Press, 2003), 240–41, quotes at 241.

7. Florence Howe, "Feminism and Women's Studies: Survival in the Seventies" in *Report on the West Coast Women's Studies Conference*, ed. Florence G. Howe (Pittsburgh, PA: Know, 1974), 19–20.

8. Marilyn J. Boxer, "For and about Women: The Theory and Practice of Women's Studies in the United States," *Signs: Journal of Women in Culture and Society* 7, no. 3 (July 1982): 663.

9. Alice E. Ginsberg, *The Evolution of American Women's Studies: Reflections on Triumphs, Controversies, and Change* (New York: Palgrave Macmillan, 2008).

10. Ginsberg, *The Evolution of American Women's Studies*, 2.

11. Ginsberg, 10.

12. "A Visionary University with Humble Beginnings," IUPUI History, accessed December 2, 2018, https://www.iupui.edu/about/history.html.

13. Boxer, Marilyn J. "Women's Studies as Women's History," *Women's Studies Quarterly* 30, no. 3/4 (2002): 42–51.

14. "IUPUI Women's Studies Changes Its Name to Women, Gender, and Sexuality Studies," IUPUI, accessed November 3, 2020, https://liberalarts.iupui.edu /wost/pages/history/index.php, para 1.

15. "IUPUI Women's Studies Changes Its Name to Women, Gender, and Sexuality Studies," para 1.

16. Miriam Langsam, email message to authors.

17. John Barlow, email message to authors, October 4, 2018.

18. Barlow, email message to authors.

19. Ginsberg, *The Evolution of American Women's Studies*, 11.

20. Barlow, email message to authors.

21. Linda Haas, email message to authors, September 30, 2018.

22. Haas, email message to authors.

23. Haas.

24. Electa Arenal, "What Women Writers? Plotting Women's Studies in New York," in *Politics of Women's Studies: Testimony from Thirty Founding Mothers*, ed. Florence Howe, the Women's Studies History Series (New York: Feminist Press, 2000), 191.

25. Annette Kolodny, "A Sense of Discovery, Mixed with a Sense of Justice," in *The Politics of Women's Studies: Testimony from Thirty Founding Mothers*, ed. Florence Howe (New York: Feminist Press, 2000), 54–64.

26. Myra Dinnerstein, "Has It Really Been Thirty Years?" in Howe, *The Politics of Women's Studies*, 230–46.

27. "IUPUI Women's Studies Changes Its Name to Women, Gender, and Sexuality Studies," para 4.

28. "IUPUI Women's Studies Program Celebrates Thirty-Fifth Anniversary."

29. "Proposal for Minor in Women's Studies," Indianapolis December 12, 1978 (copy in authors' possession).

30. Marilyn J. Boxer, "Women's Studies as Women's History," *Women's Studies Quarterly* 30, no. 3/4 (winter 2002): 47.

31. Anne Donchin, "The Woman Who Came to Dinner: The Women's Studies Administrator in the House of Academe," *Women's Studies International Forum* 9, no. 2 (1986): 190.

32. Donchin, "The Woman Who Came to Dinner."

33. *IUPUI Friends of Women's Studies*, Indianapolis, IN: IUPUI, 1989 (booklet, in authors' possession).

34. Marianne Wokeck, email message to authors, October 2, 2018.

35. Wokeck, email message to authors.

36. Wokeck.

37. Wokeck.

38. Wokeck.

39. Susan Shepherd, email message to authors, November 1, 2018.

40. Amanda Porterfield, phone interview by Lorée B. Wilcox, October 25, 2018. Porterfield left IUPUI in 1998 and is currently at Florida State University.

41. Porterfield, phone interview.

42. Robert White, personal interview by Lorée B. Wilcox, October 4, 2018.

43. Robert White, personal interview.

44. White, personal interview.

45. White.

46. Richard Turner, email message to authors, October 4, 2018.

47. Obioma Nnaemeka, email message to authors, January 1, 2019.

48. Nnaemeka, email message to authors.

49. Nnaemeka.

50. Turner, email message to authors.

51. Nelly Y. McKay, "Charting a Personal Journey: A Road to Women's Studies" in *The Politics of Women's Studies: Testimony from Thirty Founding Mothers*, The Women's Studies History Series, ed. Florence Howe (New York: Feminist Press, 2000), 206.

52. Turner, email message to authors.

53. Nancy Robertson, email message to authors, November 2, 2018.

54. Robertson, email message to authors.

55. Aimee Zoeller, phone interview by Lorée B. Wilcox, October 2, 2018 (transcript in authors' possession).

56. Turner, email message to authors.

57. Gail Plater, email message to authors, September 24, 2018.

58. Genevieve Shaker, email message to authors, September 27, 2018.

59. Shaker, email message to authors.

60. Jane Schultz, email message to authors, November 1, 2018.

61. Schultz, email message to authors.

62. Schultz.

63. Susan Shepherd, email message to authors.

64. Shepherd, email message to authors.

65. Aimee Zoeller, phone interview by Lorée B. Wilcox.

66. Zoeller, phone interview.

67. Zoeller.

68. Zoeller.

69. Zoeller.

70. Matt Preston, email message to authors, October 23, 2018.

71. Preston, email message to authors.

72. Catherine Dobris, personal interview by Lorée B. Wilcox, November 1, 2018.

73. Robertson, email message to authors.

74. Myranda Warden, email message to authors, November 1, 2018.

75. Finneran Muzzey, email message to authors, November 1, 2018.

76. Sarah Bahr, email message to authors, October 23, 2018.

77. Liz Forster, email message to authors, October 23, 2018.

78. Aspen Christian, email message to authors, October 23, 2018.

79. Angela Barron McBride, email to authors.

BUILDING THE "OPERA FACTORY"

Elsie Irwin Sweeney's Philanthropic Leadership in Funding the Indiana University Music Arts Center

JACOB HARDESTY

Jacob Hardesty tells the story of benefactor Elsie Sweeney's engagement in the project to build Indiana University's Music Arts Center, known as the MAC. The state-of-the-art building helped to solidify IU's School of Music reputation as a national leader. The essay focuses on the interactions between Sweeney, a patron with considerable knowledge of the arts, and university leaders, especially President Herman Wells. Such profiles of women's philanthropy at work capture an important but understudied dimension of the story of women at IU.

EVEN BEFORE THEIR ADMISSION to IU in 1867, women participated in a legacy of educational philanthropy that connected them as donors and friends to the young state university in Bloomington and helped to support Indiana University's growth and distinction. Notably, women joined efforts to aid the college after the fire of 1854. Later, in 1883, women were among the Monroe County residents who helped to raise $50,000 toward rebuilding IU after another fire destroyed buildings at Seminary Square. By then, the university was open not only to the sons of local families but also to their daughters. In the early decades of the twentieth century, IU women and their community supporters helped fund construction projects to provide recreational and, eventually, residential space for women on the new Dunn Woods Campus. Perhaps most prominently, women advocated for and spearheaded the fundraising drive for the new Student Building (1906) and, later, after World War I, volunteered time and donated funds to ensure the success of the campaign to build Memorial Hall (1925).[1] Examples of women's volunteerism and financial support to IU's regional campuses would follow in the decades ahead.

As we look anew at IU's history, with a sharper eye to women's history, women's philanthropic support to Indiana University over the decades merits closer exploration. Such study provides the opportunity to recognize the level of women's generosity at work but also to consider the creativity, imagination, and humanistic approach many brought to the donor-university relationship.

In notable instances, women's motivations to support IU drew on family traditions. For example, Ruth Lilly (1915–2002) followed in her great-grandfather Eli Lilly's legacy of educational philanthropy by bequeathing approximately $10.7 million to IUPUI's Center on Philanthropy and the Herron School of Art and Design. Many women also joined a spouse or relative in endowing a scholarship fund or in supporting a favored university initiative or academic unit at a pivotal time. Such was the case, for example, when, in 1912, Dr. Robert W. Long and Mrs. Clara Long donated the parcel of land for the construction of a teaching hospital for Indiana University's School of Medicine in Indianapolis.

IU's women faculty, as has been true of their male counterparts, have also donated financially and given back in various other ways to the academic institution where they taught and developed their careers. Professor Elizabeth Sage's 1937 donation of clothing and textiles she used for instruction in the Department of Home Economics became the core of the university's historic costume collection. Social scientists Elinor and Vincent Ostrom's gift of their Ojibwe art collection to the Mathers Museum of World Cultures stemmed from the inspiration these interdisciplinary researchers drew from handicrafts and artisanal creativity. And the generosity of women benefactors has enhanced the aesthetics of public spaces on campus with the display of artwork and sculpture. The iconic fountain of the goddess Venus fronting the IU Auditorium was a gift given by alumna and IU Foundation director Grace Showalter in honor of her husband's memory. The fountain, along with the Lilly Library, the auditorium, and the art museum, defines IU's arts square.

As even this brief list suggests, women's philanthropic support of the university—through gifts, bequests, and volunteer hours—has, alongside public means, been influential in forging connections between IU and the state of Indiana and in shaping IU's distinctive strengths and character as a public midwestern university. Perhaps one of the most salient examples of this powerful phenomenon, though, and one that is especially striking given the university's midwestern location, is the role private generosity has played in nurturing IU's rise to preeminence in the field of music. In 2005, Barbara Jacobs, an alumna (class of 1948) and longtime IU supporter alongside her husband, David, left what has been a transformative gift of $40.6 million in her estate to support IU's School of Music (which has since been renamed in their honor as the Jacobs School of Music).[2] The Jacobs gift, then the single largest ever received from an IU alumna, exemplifies a tradition of philanthropic giving, including the giving of women, that has been integral to achieving IU's world-class excellence in music, both performance and education.

This essay looks back to an earlier snapshot in the history of women's giving to the arts at IU. Focusing on donor-university ties, it tells the story of Hoosier philanthropist Elsie Irwin Sweeney (1888–1972), widely admired as Indiana's "First Lady of the Arts," and her engagement in the building of Indiana University's Musical Arts Center. This architectural project, noteworthy for its attention to both performance and education, helped further solidify IU's School of Music's distinction as a world-class institution and became a landmark on the Bloomington campus and in the university's wider cultural landscape.[3]

Sweeney was born in 1888 into a prominent Columbus, Indiana, family that provided financial backing and, together with family chauffeur and inventor Clessie Cummins, founded the Cummins Engine Company. Started in 1919, the company was an early producer of diesel engines, particularly for trains. Cummins engines became increasingly more widely used in cars following the post–WWII road construction boom and the business significantly expanded, resulting in considerable wealth for the already prosperous related-by-marriage Miller, Irwin, and Sweeney families.[4] Founded in 1952, the Irwin-Sweeney-Miller Foundation (ISMF), a private multigenerational family foundation shaped by Sweeney and other relatives, drove the families' philanthropic endeavors. The ISMF's largesse was directed to supporting religious life and faith-based activities (particularly efforts of the Disciples of Christ) and to enriching civic and cultural life.[5]

Elsie Sweeney filled her life with her two loves: music and architecture. She designed her magnificent Columbus home, Castalia, as a "modern day castle." Featuring an eclectic mix of Persian rugs, Venetian Gates, and two replicas of the Louvre's Venus de Milo, Castalia was "built to house music."[6] Her living room doubled as a music room, and acoustical adjustments could be made for performances or receptions. Her philanthropy reflected similar passions and interests. Most notably, in the 1950s she led a US-based fundraising effort to restore the famous Bayreuth Opera House in Germany.[7] In 1956, the Federal Republic of Germany awarded her the Officer's Cross, Order of Merit, for her efforts. But it was her ongoing relationship with Indiana University's School of Music, one that extended beyond financial contributions, that had the greatest lasting impact to shape the region she so adored. This chapter outlines her leadership in helping create the IU's Music Arts Center, the so-called "Met of the Midwest."[8] In heeding the call from university leaders to support the nascent MAC project, Sweeney recognized the opportunity to bring exceptional large-scale opera and orchestra performances, those she had witnessed during her travels in Europe, to her beloved Indiana.

EXPANDING THE "CULTURAL HERITAGE" OF MIDDLE AMERICA

Sweeney's philanthropy to the arts, like her support of religious work, reflected her extended family's deep and longstanding connections to improving, serving, and building community in their local town and state. While reflecting a cosmopolitan worldview, her philanthropy was also grounded in her pride as a native Hoosier, seeing Indiana University as an ideal vehicle to elevate the arts in midwestern life. A 1910 graduate of Smith College with a degree in music performance, Sweeney's collegiate education was reminiscent of the nineteenth-century approach, one that treated "music as a subject of artistic value, not merely one representing social accomplishment."[9] In the years between Sweeney's graduation from Smith and her donation to the MAC, enrollment in higher education spiked, from under two million to over eight million by 1970.[10] In addition to a midcentury enrollment boom, many universities, including IU, came to offer a growing variety of professional and liberal arts programs, becoming what historians, adopting Clark Kerr's term, would later describe as "multiversities."[11]

Sweeney watched as, beginning in the 1920s, the School of Music began a concerted effort to expand its musical offerings, particularly opera performances. Administrators sought to increase enrollment and, subsequently, the number of concerts offered each year.[12] Indeed, Sweeney's multiple philanthropic gifts to the School of Music were all designed with the purpose of contributing to this process, reflecting positively on the cultural potential of the region she treasured. She wrote, "When I was a young girl, Columbus was the center of population of the United States. The center has not gone much further west since that time. . . . The new Musical Arts Center . . . [provides] a proper setting to help foster the observance and growth of our cultural heritage and I am happy to be able to contribute to its being."[13]

Sweeney's dedication to and involvement at IU were not rooted in any sense of affinity for an alma mater, strictly defined. Instead, Sweeney saw the School of Music in general, and the Musical Arts Center (commonly known as the

MAC) in particular, as necessary spaces where the cultural contributions of a potentially overlooked region could be realized. Speaking after the public recognition of her MAC contribution about the role of the arts in American life, Sweeney said, "I feel that, since we live in the heart of America, we have a role of leadership to play."[14] This affinity for the School of Music's potential was also realized in her views of its students; she often referred to them as "my children."[15] Sweeney visited the school often, taking private piano lessons and attending concerts, even earning the unofficial title "special student" in the 1960s.[16] In 1963 she gave a lecture-recital, "Music from Three Centuries," a rare honor extended to a donor. Four years later, she received an honorary doctorate—one of five women so honored on Founder's Day 1967 (recognizing the centennial of coeducation at IU).

Sweeney also contributed financially to various projects and programs at the School of Music. Her first gift was a $49.40 check to cover a lecture on her favorite opera, Wagner's *Parsifal*. A list of her donations to the School of Music between 1950 and 1968 suggests a willingness to support a range of institutional needs: $500 for bringing in a "foreign conductor"; $250 "to help defray expense of University Signers Orchestra Tour"; and $500 for "quality instruments."[17] Between 1960 and 1968, Sweeney also provided just over $58,000 to the IU Foundation specifically for various scholarship funds—among them the Ernest Hoffzimer Scholarship funds and the Friends of Music Scholarship.

Sweeney's largesse came at a time of significant institutional development for the School of Music. Beginning with the deanship of Winfred Merrill, one that began a generation earlier in 1919, the School of Music experienced a period of unprecedented and sustained growth. Deans Merrill, Robert Sanders, and Charles Bain (who reigned for twenty-six years) developed the School of Music into America's leading school of music. As incoming dean in 1947, Bain articulated his high expectations to students. When they came for any school ensemble rehearsals, he expected students to prepare on the level of professional musicians employed in renowned orchestras and choirs. Bain reasoned, sensibly, that the majority of performance graduates would not find careers as solo performers but could have sustained and fulfilling careers as ensemble performers. To fulfill this vision, Bain, whose twenty-six-year tenure as dean remains the longest in the institution's history, pushed for greater programming of opera and symphonic works, as opposed to smaller scale performances such string quartets.[18] This strategy not only allowed for greater student participation in those larger ensembles but also drew in larger crowds to the Bloomington campus, as music fans were more likely to attend a well-known opera than a faculty trombone recital. That strategy, coupled with Bain's ability to recruit prominent faculty like Janos Starker and Menahem Pressler, pedagogues who already had extensive performing careers, helped the school grow in status and stature. According to Starker, Bain "went on recruiting, recruiting, recruiting. Wells gave him blank[et] support for whatever he wanted." Pressler tells a similar story of Bain's stubbornness to bring in the faculty he deemed best for the School of Music. Pressler had told Bain "no" three times before Bain apparently recruited Willi Masselos and Sidney Folster, School of Music faculty and personal friends with Pressler, who succeeded in bringing Pressler to campus for what was supposed to be a one-semester residency—and turned into an over-sixty-year professorship.[19] By 1973, IU's school was largely viewed as the best in the country, besting two frequent rivals, both in the Northeast—Julliard and the Eastman School of Music.[20] As George M. Logan points out in his institutional history, by that point the School of Music was "a major world cultural institution . . . amid the cornfields of southern Indiana."[21]

As School of Music dean, Bain routinely compared his institution with some of its primary competitors. Much of his analysis was structural, focusing on developing new programs of study and strengthening existing ones. Bain focused much of his attention on the Eastman School of Music, which, like IU, had evolved as a core component of a larger "multiversity." Writing in one annual report about music composition study, Bain noted, "In this category, Indiana University in no way compared with a school such as the Eastman School of Music, where literally hundreds of young student composers have received instruction."[22] In another report, Bain recounted how the University of Southern California, Northwestern University, and Florida State University, along with IU, had secured approval by their states to grant doctoral programs, though Eastman had not.[23] Apparently, Eastman's rejection was rooted in some confusion about whether the doctoral degree would also continue to be offered as an honorary degree or not. Bain seemingly included the anecdote in his report as a cautionary tale about good campus governance, an unnecessary roadblock the School of Music should avoid as it grew its programs, faculty, and enrollment.

Sweeney looked on at the School of Music's growth with delight, seeing it as an opportunity to bring musical offerings she had experienced in Europe to her native Indiana. But it was Sweeney's involvement in the efforts to build the MAC where she could best draw on her formal collegiate education in music and subsequent recognition of the cultural capital that accompanies a sustained space for opera performances. In contrast to her other financial contributions, those that typically supported the necessary logistics to develop an increasingly internationally recognized music school, Sweeney's interest in the MAC and potential for the region extended beyond sharing her financial resources.

Her reputation for opera fundraising (she spearheaded necessary renovation funding for one of the world's most famous opera houses, Bayreuth), combined with her identity as a Hoosier, provided her the experiences not only to engage university officials financial terms but also to provide input regarding the necessary repertoire and opera programming that would help the MAC continue to draw in audiences, especially after the initial enthusiasm for the new building began to dissipate.

Widely considered one of the more spectacular buildings on the Bloomington campus, the Musical Arts Center has been a cornerstone of IU's music landscape since 1972. A 1984 *Opera News* article heaped praise on the building, mentioning its nickname, "Met of the Midwest," and describing it as one of best performing spaces for acoustics in the country. Indiana-based author Nancy Kriplen went on to describe it as "the opera factory," a reference to the number of productions put on yearly.[24] The building seats just under 1,500, and the stage measures ninety feet by sixty feet—one of the largest among American universities. There is ample space for instrument storage lockers, classrooms, and rehearsal halls.[25] Indeed, the MAC was designed with both the public audience and music student in mind—a creative vision Sweeney, the former music student turned arts patron, applauded. It was Sweeney's early recognition of the value such a permanent performance venue could bring that garnered her the most appreciation from IU leaders. As then-chancellor Herman B Wells wrote in a letter after Sweeney committed to funding the MAC, "This is the first cash to be received toward this great new facility in the Arts. We shall ever be grateful to you."[26]

OPERA BEFORE THE MAC

Sweeney's interest in supporting the MAC was born out of the school's institutional need and circumstances. At the mid-twentieth century, the need for a new performing arts space at IU became evident. Since the first IU-sponsored performance in 1947, student operas were held in a variety of ill-equipped venues for their size and scope—the likes of North Central High School in Indianapolis, the Indiana University Auditorium, and, most often, the Bloomington campus's East Hall. Such makeshift venues were far from ideal. The East Hall stage was too small for most opera performances, the facility lacked adequate space for the orchestra, and the hall's mechanics (switchboard, lighting, etc.) were dated. In *The Indiana University School of Music: A History*, George M. Logan includes a picture of the barren-looking building, clearly inadequate for staging large-scale opera productions, sarcastically adding "East Hall in its glory (1950)."[27]

Music school dean Wilfred Bain repeatedly reminded the IU administration through the early and mid-1960s that using the East Hall for opera performance "greatly hampered development" of the school's reputation.[28] Bain worried that potential students, in both opera and other areas of musical education, would be dissuaded from attending because of the combination of inadequate funding and poor performance venues. Apparently, Bain's concerns convinced the upper university administration to lobby for state assistance to improve facilities. IU president Elvis Stahr underscored the inadequacy of the school's faculties in a letter to Governor Branigin in 1966, writing, "It is ironic . . . that what is quite probably the best opera school in the nation is quite definitely saddled with the worst physical facilities."[29]

In spite of the limitations of the East Hall as an opera performance space, the opera program continued to develop, albeit slowly, due largely to a patchwork of funding initiatives and faculty hires. In one of the first performances that brought the School of Music opera program national recognition, Bain's predecessor, Robert Sanders, scored a competitive coup with other universities when the famous Metropolitan Opera Company staged their first ever performance at a university at IU in 1942. By the middle 1950s, the school was regularly employing professional painters, carpenters, and clothing designers alongside students in set and costume construction. In 1961, the opera program, under the leadership of Mario Christini, began its first televised performances. Christini proved to be a particularly creative guide for the often conservative world of opera. In 1963 he successfully spearheaded an effort to hold the opera *Aida* in the school's football stadium.[30] The maestro balanced out that innovation by also scheduling performances on a repertoire basis, regularly presenting the most popular and significant operas the same year—an effort that would have likely appealed to major patrons such as Sweeney.[31] The numbers of operas performed continued to increase modestly, from twenty in 1950–51 to twenty-seven in 1970–71.[32]

These innovations helped bolster the music school's overall reputation and prestige. This increase in prestige furthered and benefitted from increasing enrollment. In 1950, the total enrollment for IU's School of Music stood at 402, which doubled to 810 just over a decade later. Two years later, in 1962, enrollment topped 1,000 for the first time.[33] The enrollment increases inevitably put rehearsal and performance space at a premium. As a result, beginning in the early 1960s, rehearsals and classes had to be scheduled at night and on the weekends because rooms and halls quickly booked during the weekdays. Such conditions were not ideal for the institution as it sought to maintain its reputation as one of the best music schools in the country.

Although it was generally agreed the East Hall was a poor option for opera performance, the space served the university admirably in that role for twenty years. And then, overnight, it was gone, further increasing the urgency for a space for the continued growth of the school. In 1966, East Hall burned to the ground. Driving back from Indianapolis, university chancellor Herman B Wells noticed the smoke rising from the Bloomington campus, saying to himself, "Bain gets his building."[34] Since the East Hall was completely destroyed, a variety of campus locations, from the roughly fifty-person Frangipani Room in the Indiana Memorial Union to the IU Auditorium, served as opera performance locations until the MAC was completed in 1972. This transition period also featured more performances away from IU Bloomington, on the IU South Bend and Kokomo campuses and at Purdue University.[35]

Yet while there was a clear institutional need for a new performing space, securing the estimated $11 million construction cost was no small task. Indiana University officials looked to a combination of public and private resources to raise the capital. The university received approximately $322,000 in insurance payments for the loss of the East Hall. This amount was coupled with just under $2.5 million in federal dollars to support the project awarded by the Office of Education under the 1963 Higher Education Facilities Act. In addition, W. George Pinnell, Indiana University treasurer, oversaw the $5 million bond issue, to be repaid primarily through student fees, with public bids opened and read on October 24, 1972.[36] Indiana University officials also solicited support from an existing circle of benefactors. Bloomington-born and IU- educated, Hoagy Carmichael (bachelor of law, 1926), the composer of "Stardust" and other jazz standards, as well as "Chimes of Indiana," contributed $100,000 to the MAC. To honor the composer's contribution, the grand foyer in the MAC was named after him. Carmichael's donation was both financially enabling as well as symbolic, bringing a sense of Indiana identity to the opera house designed to rival the best in Europe. This would be an opera house, but it would also be a uniquely Hoosier opera house. Ads in the football program and news bureau releases also pointed to the benefits the new performance hall would bring to "Hoosierland."[37]

As the School of Music dean, Bain spoke to the importance of the planned building and provided an expert explanation on the necessity of a multipurpose facility to donors; he was also often called upon to explain precisely why such a building was necessary. In particular, Bain acted as the primary contact with the IU Foundation.[38] As part of his appeal for financial support, he did not hesitate to articulate the importance of opera for a school of music's general development and contribution to the university. In an interview for an IU Foundation publication Bain said, "Opera is the perfect vehicle for the complete musical experience for the student, for the faculty, and for the audience. Opera fulfills the total need of the student. Opera, an involved experience, is training for excellent [sic] under optimum conditions. Opera is the crossroads where the audience, the artist, the set designer the costumer, the dramatist, the vocalist, the soloist and a host of others meet for an experience unique in the performing arts. Opera sets a cultural goal for an entire region."[39]

ELSIE SWEENEY AND THE "CULTURAL POTENTIAL OF INDIANA AND MID-AMERICA"

Elsie Sweeney's involvement with the MAC project began in the early 1960s. Dean Bain presented the early fundraising and building plans to her, George Newlin (head of the Columbus investment firm Irwin Management Company), and Randall Tucker (secretary of the Cummins Engine Foundation) in 1962. The group warmly received Bain and voiced support for the planned building. And though Sweeney, Newlin, and Tucker did not make any pledges at that time, they did leave the door open to future capital contributions. They also challenged Bain to be prepared for the difficulty of the upcoming fundraising campaign. Strategizing with Bain, they suggested he establish a personal relationship with each donor and, particular to the validity of the MAC, be able to convey the message that opera should be seen as more than a "frill."[40]

Wells kept Sweeney updated with the developments of the planned building. In early 1966, he sent her a photograph of the early building model and a copy of a memo about the project by architect Evans Woollen. Wells noted aspects of the auditorium he felt they would find important, particularly the sense of intimacy it would bring. Sweeney responded with some skepticism. She responded to Wells's initial shared plans that, while she initially liked the connection with the audience a shallow and wide hall can provide, it could also limit the performers' abilities to project sound. To support her argument, she provided Wells with a January 22 article from *Opera News* on the problems the Pittsburgh Opera had with their performing hall. According to that publication, opera-goers in that city were complaining that the wide stage there limited the ability of people sitting on the sides to hear and see adequately. Sweeney was concerned, given the model and Wells's description, that a similar fate may befall Indiana's opera hall.[41]

This exchange lends some clues to the nature of the relationship between Sweeney and her primary university contact, Chancellor Wells. Clearly, Wells wanted Sweeney to be an involved and a knowledgeable participant in the project. This meant voluntarily providing her with current information, such as the architect's rendering. Wells likely reasoned that keeping Sweeney abreast of developments for the MAC could increase the likelihood of future philanthropic giving. Of course, such arrangements come with some potential critical responses. As her correspondence demonstrates, Sweeney felt comfortable enough in her relationship with Wells to suggest alternative ideas for the design of the MAC, if not to push back on particular points when she felt necessary. If she felt there could be any possible retribution for doing so, that she would be excluded from later updates, she did not show it, likely recognizing the natural back-and-forth between philanthropist and recipient.

Like Wells, Sweeney understood the dual-nature purpose of the building. Perhaps attributable to her time as a music student, Sweeney felt strongly that the MAC should be a place for both learning and performing. She stressed to Wells that the funding campaign should reflect these simultaneous uses and not focus on performance alone. In doing so, Sweeney cautioned Wells not to appeal only to the gratification attendees would receive from performances in a state-of-the art concert hall. Instead, her interest in the building—and, she thought, the interests of other donors—rested in how that performing space would affect opera for future generations. In particular, she encouraged Wells to focus on the advantages such a building would have for "youth." Sweeney's wish to cultivate the arts particularly in Indiana was evident. She wrote, "There can be no future for the performers unless an audience is available, and that, at present, rather negligible in Indiana."[42] While young performers could learn their craft there, young audience members would also be developing a taste for the genre as well.

Meanwhile, Chancellor Wells and Indiana University President Stahr kept in contact with the Cummins Engine Foundation and its president, E. Don Tull. It was Wells who made the formal request for a meeting to discuss any "financial support" Cummins could offer. In doing so, he again emphasized the dual nature of the building, as performance and teaching space. But, perhaps attempting to appeal to Tull's business sense, he also noted the economic development such a hall could bring the region. Wells's argument was straightforward. When people traveled to Bloomington to see performances, they would be financially supporting the Bloomington area and southern Indiana as a whole. They would eat at local restaurants, stay at local hotels, and fill up at local gas stations. Wells's communication with Tull was particularly influenced by Sweeney, as she had suggested the funding rationale Wells and Stahr should communicate to Cummins. Sweeney offered the chancellor suggestions on dealing with the Cummins board, with whom she had frequent dealings. Specifically, she told Wells to "amplify" his original letter to the foundation. Indeed, it is possible mentioning the regional economic development came at her suggestion. Regardless, her willingness to help Wells craft his message demonstrates her willingness to engage the project beyond solely financial donations. And Wells's willingness to incorporate her suggestions speaks to the value he placed on her feedback.[43]

Both Wells and Stahr made presentations before the Cummins board, though on different occasions. Wells made the first presentation at a lunch meeting on March 26, 1966, and Stahr, along with architect Woollen, met with the same group exactly two months later. In his presentation, Wells emphasized he did so as "President Stahr's agent." Wells shared with the board an overview of the MAC funding and construction plans, documents prepared and signed by Stahr. Wells was more of the pitchman for the project, yet his relationship with Sweeney, certainly a Cummins insider, likely only helped the cause. Still, it was only after the May meeting with Stahr that the board responded with a $250,000 pledge, which they made the day after Stahr visited. Such a quick turnaround may indicate that the board had given the matter substantive discussion through April and May; the Stahr meeting may well have been something of a formality, the decision to donate having already been made.[44]

Sweeney's own gift came just before the Cummins pledge. By April 1966, Sweeney had made the decision to donate to the MAC fundraising project. News of Sweeney's intended contribution absolutely thrilled Wells. Hers was the first pledge for the project, and the size of her donation, $500,000, heartened Wells that the campaign to build the MAC was off to a strong start. After receiving the first payment installment he wrote to her, "Again, you are first! This is the first cash to be received toward this great new facility in the Arts. We shall ever be grateful to you."[45] Characteristically, Wells saw Sweeney's donation as not the end of her involvement but instead just the opposite. He promised to keep her involved in the developments of the building, promising to keep in "close contact" as building plans were realized. In pledging her support, Sweeney echoed the university's vision for the hall as both a teaching facility and performance hall. Clearly, she understood the current and future value in such a dual-use building.[46]

Sweeney's donation would come to the university in two equal parts that would arrive at different times. The first $250,000 contribution would come from a yet-to-be-determined combination of her personal finances and the

Irwin-Sweeney-Miller Foundation. The initial installment of the MAC payments came in early January 1968 as a discounted stock sale. The university would purchase shares of stock from her at a discounted rate and, upon selling them on the market, would keep the difference. The second half would come as a bequest paid by the executor of her estate. By this arrangement, the university would quickly begin to receive payments for the project but not receive the full contribution until she passed away.[47]

Wells included and informed Sweeney on the various MAC developments for the years following her donation. In an October 1967 letter to Sweeney, Wells wrote about how an appropriations delay in Washington, DC, had pushed back the date the university planned to open its public bids. Three months later, Wells sent Sweeney a telegram that the university had been given a "great Christmas gift": permission to advertise for bids.[48] Wells's willingness to update Sweeney on financial developments unrelated to her contributions suggests how much he valued Sweeney's abilities to help navigate the world of large-scale fundraising for the arts. He wrote her again in January of the next year, telling her bids would be opened on April 4. Wells also provided Sweeney with updates on and photographs of the site and later the construction of the building itself, which she enthusiastically accepted, though she also expressed frustration that the building would not be completed by the university's sesquicentennial.[49]

Still, from Sweeney's perspective, her most significant involvement with the university during this period likely came from a piece of paper of a different sort. The spring 1967 commencement marked the one-hundredth anniversary of women's admission to the university. During the ceremony Sweeney received an honorary degree, a doctor of music. The importance of the centennial of co-education at IU was not lost on Sweeney. Writing to President Stahr to accept, Sweeney noted the "deep appreciation" "to celebrate the 100th anniversary of the admission of women to the University" as a "representative of my sex."[50] This declaration marked the most singularly explicit time Sweeney attached any significance to her gender in her correspondence with Wells. Perhaps the magnitude of the public honor prompted Sweeney to reflect on her individual actions and impact on Indiana University as a benefactor in larger, gendered terms. It is difficult to discern, though, how Sweeney thought about gender given the lack of personal sources and her reticence on the topic.

PRIVATE GIVING TO "TRIGGER" A PUBLIC GOOD

Despite the publicity that came with Sweeney's honorary doctoral degree and reputation as Indiana's "First Lady of the Arts," likely furthest from her mind was any public acknowledgment of her donation to the MAC.[51] Much to her surprise, Wells's assistant Dottie Collins called Sweeney on December 23, 1969, to set a firm date and discuss arrangements for the public announcement of her gift. Sweeney believed the news of her donation had already been made public, telling Collins, "I thought it had already been announced."[52] But contrary to Sweeney's understanding, no announcement had been made public. The two women, Collins and Sweeney, agreed on the date of January 17, to coincide with the Friends of Music meeting during the day and opera *La Pietra del Paragone* (*Love on Trial*). When questioned about guests for the public announcement, Sweeney requested music school dean Bain attend. Sweeney also felt it appropriate to include others who had given to the school. Friends of Music president Ross M. Robertson pushed other members, including Wells, to attend their January 17 meeting to thank "substantial contributors."[53]

Less than a week before the formal announcement, university officials were still unsure how much Sweeney planned to give. The IU Foundation knew they would receive $750,000 total toward the project.[54] The question was what portion of the $750,000 would be coming from Sweeney, the Irwin-Sweeney-Miller Foundation (ISMF), or some other family member. This was a frequent point of confusion for university officials. A 1970 memo from Paul K. Klinge at the IU Foundation reads, "We need a list of all gifts for the last few years from Cummins Engine, Irwin-Sweeney-Miller or various contributors thereof."[55] At the heart of this misunderstanding, university officials were not sure where Cummins Foundation or ISMF money ended and Sweeney's began, which, given her association with the foundations, seems sensible. Indeed, early drafts of Wells's announcement speech simply left the amount blank, to be filled in later.[56] It apparently fell to Dottie Collins to clarify to him the breakdown of the contributions. In a note to him, she wrote:

$250,000	Miss Sweeney
$250,000	Irwin, Sweeney, Miller
$250,000	Cummins Engine Foundation.[57]

Sweeney had concerns about public recognition, even to the point of inquiring whether a public announcement of her donations was needed at all. Or, as she wrote to Dottie Collins, "I questioned its necessity." Collins may have suspected Sweeney's hesitation when the two talked and later read Sweeney a copy of Wells's speech for her approval. Sweeney's nephew, J. Irwin Miller, the prominent Indiana philanthropist—as well as president and board chair at Cummins—also discussed the symbolic importance of such an event. He persuaded her that such announcements might act as a catalyst for more funds from other potential donors. That is, other donors could be persuaded to give if Sweeney, a widely recognized philanthropic figure, supported the project. As she wrote Collins, she would allow such a public announcement "if it will be helpful to your drive for more funds."[58]

Such an argument appealed to Sweeney's desire to improve the status of classical music throughout the Midwest, which the MAC would certainly do. Though she still believed the need for such a public announcement was "unfortunate," Sweeney agreed to take part in the January 17 news conference and photo opportunity in front the MAC site with Herman Wells, newly installed President Sutton, Friends of Music President Robertson, and 150th Birthday Fund President General Butcher. To broadcast the announcement as quickly and as far as possible, the Indiana University Foundation arranged for couriers to drive pictures and short "movies" to Louisville and Indianapolis that evening.[59] In 1967, over a year after Sweeney's donation, Wells looked back appreciatively on how her "magnificent gift" had "'triggered' the chain of events that have now culminated in our magnificent new facility."[60] Certainly, in those early stages of the fund drive, acquiring gifts the size of Sweeney's must have left officials optimistic about the prospects of fully funding the MAC. Such optimism aside, as funds slowed and funding prospects soured, the possibility of "triggering" more financial gifts would have seemed appealing.[61]

Why the public announcement? The primary reason may well have been financial. Donations to the MAC were not as forthcoming as officials had originally hoped. Though the university had authorized up to $6.9 million indebtedness through the bond issues, officials hoped to avoid that maximum amount. The announcement of a gift similar in size to Sweeney's also noted that the 150th Birthday Fund (which went to other campus projects besides the MAC) was only 60 percent full.[62] Accounting for the other 40 percent in less than a year must have seemed a daunting task, and university officials would have likely been looking for means to bring in more funds. Indeed, when the building was finally completed and dedicated in 1972, the fund had declined to just over $1.5 million due to the project.[63]

The donation announcement was likely one of the few times Sweeney saw any part of the MAC. She died on May 2, 1972, just weeks after the opening series of dedicatory concerts. The university would honor her memory in two ways. First, after consulting with her family, the School of Music established the Elsie I. Sweeney Memorial Scholarship in 1980. This selective scholarship, the most prestigious in the School of Music, was initially funded in part by Sweeney's niece, Clementine Miller Tangeman. Public donations to the scholarship, managed through the IU Foundation were, and continue to be, accepted. Second, at Dottie Collins's suggestion to Wells, the university established a plaque honoring Sweeney near the campus rock garden (near the IU Auditorium), which she had had a hand in funding.

Planning for the plaque began in 1975, and the dedication—which also marked the completion of the $100,000 Elsie I. Sweeney Memorial Scholarship—took place in December 1980. A picture in the *Herald-Telephone* shows Wells and Tangeman next to the plaque—an important addition to the IU campus as one of the few public recognitions on the university's part of the contributions of a female donor.[64]

Ultimately, Elsie Sweeney's vision of philanthropic leadership encapsulated in the story of her engagement with the MAC project was inseparable from the pride she felt as a native Hoosier. Her conceptualization of the creativity and leadership one must bring to donor-recipient ties extended beyond financial contributions to also include helping President Wells hone his fundraising message to the Cummins board, agreeing to the public news conference, and a series of repertory and performance logistic suggestions.

As a donor, Sweeney generally preferred to give quietly. She was inclined to shy away from publicity surrounding her financial support to a cause or institutions, having faith the recipient would carefully allocate her funds. But if ever there were a time to agree to a public announcement, late 1969 to early 1970—a time when donations had slowed and nearing the original date for the building to be completed—was it. An initially reluctant Sweeney agreed. In his remarks delivered at the public announcement of Sweeney's gift, Wells shared his recollection of an early conversation that crystallized for him Elsie Sweeney's sensibilities as a donor and her engagement with IU's state of the art MAC project in particular. No doubt Wells himself resonated with Sweeney's sentiment. In tribute to her at her passing, not long after the MAC's opening, he focused not on the dollar amount of her gift to the School of Music but on her philanthropic vision and leadership. What later admirers dubbed the "opera factory" in the heartland wedded university need and donor vision. As Wells observed of Sweeney, "She believed in the cultural potential of Indiana and Mid-America. She believed in the talent of Hoosier youth and did much to encourage and develop it."[65]

NOTES

1. Elijah Cody Howe, "Visions of the Greater Good: A History of Student Philanthropy at Indiana University" (PhD diss., Indiana University, 2017).

2. David Jacobs Jr., Barbara and David Henry Jacobs's son, was a member of the IU Foundation Board of Directors for sixteen years and received the Thomas Hart Benton Mural Medallion in 1988 and an honorary degree in 2000.

3. Sweeney Speech Draft 3, ca. December 1969, Indiana University Chancellor Records of Herman B Wells, 1939–94, Administrative Record Series C145, Box 22, IU Libraries University Archives, Bloomington, Indiana.

4. Jeffrey L. Cruikshank and David B. Sicilia, *The Engine That Could: Seventy-Five Years of Value-Driven Change at Cummins Engine Company* (Boston, MA: Harvard Business School Press, 1997).

5. Andrea Walton, "'To Bind the University to Nothing': The Giving of Clementine Miller Tangeman as a Case Study in Donor Motivation," *CASE International Journal of Educational Advancement* 2, no. 4 (fall 2001): 126–46.

6. Susan Clarke, "A Woman's Castle Is Her Inspiration," *The Courier-Journal Magazine*, June 14, 1964, 18–21, Indiana University Chancellor Records of Herman B Wells, 1939–94, Administrative Record Series, IU Libraries University Archives.

7. "Miss Elsie Sweeney, Music Patron, Dead," *New York Times*, May 3, 1972; No author, "Miss Sweeney Gives Time, Talent, Energy to Benefit Concert for Beyreuth Theatre," *The Republic*, December 1, 1955.

8. Nancy Kriplen, "The Opera Factory," *Opera News*, November 1984, 16–18, 20, Indiana University Chancellor Records of Herman B Wells, 1939–94, Administrative Record Series, IU Libraries University Archives.

9. Jewel A. Smith, *Transforming Women's Education: Liberal Arts and Music in Female Seminaries* (Urbana: University of Illinois Press, 2019), 3.

10. John Rury, *Education and Social Change: Contours in the History of American Schooling*, 4th ed. (New York: Routledge, 2012), 208.

11. Clark Kerr, *The Uses of the University* (Cambridge and London: Harvard University Press, 1963); G. George Fallis, *Multiversities, Ideas and Democracy. Toronto, Buffalo, and London* (Toronto: University of Toronto Press, 2007); Julie Reuben, *The Making of the Modern University: Intellectual Transformation and the Marginalization of Morality* (Chicago: University of Chicago Press, 1996).

12. George M. Logan, *The Indiana University School of Music: A History* (Bloomington: Indiana University Press, 2000), 63.

13. Sweeney Speech Draft 4, ca. December 1969, Indiana University Chancellor Records of Herman B Wells, 1939–94, Administrative Record Series C145, Box 22, IU Libraries University Archives, Bloomington, Indiana.

14. "Elsie Sweeney Dies at 83," *Indiana Daily Student*, May 3, 1972, 8.

15. Hugh Hazelrigg, Indiana University News Bureau, Press Release on Death of Elsie Sweeney, May 2, 1972, Indiana University Chancellor Records of Herman B Wells, 1939–94, Administrative Record Series C145, Box 22, IU Libraries University Archives, Bloomington, Indiana.

16. "Elsie Sweeney Dies at 83," 8.

17. Undated List of Contributions for Miss Elsie Sweeney, Indiana University Chancellor Records of Herman B Wells, 1939–94, Administrative Record Series C145, Box 22, IU Libraries University Archives, Bloomington, Indiana.

18. Logan, *Indiana University School of Music*, 136–37.

19. Julieta M. Alvarado, "Dean of Deans: Wilfred Bain and the Rise of the Indiana School of Music" (PhD diss., Capella University, 2013), 94–96.

20. Peter M. Blau and Rebecca Zames Margulies, "The Reputation of American Professional Schools," *Change* 6, no. 10 (winter 1974): 42–47, Indiana University Chancellor Records of Herman B Wells, 1939–94, Administrative Record Series C145, Box 22, IU Libraries University Archives, Bloomington, Indiana. George Logan argues that, not incidentally, this improved status came at a cost, particularly the immense pressure and stress put on students. Logan cites an increase in mental health and substance abuse issues as consequences for students that came from increasing performance demands. See Logan, *Indiana University School of Music*, 142–44.

21. Logan, *Indiana University School of Music*, 5.

22. Wilfred C. Bain, *The Bain Regime*, 1947–73, vol. 1 and 2 (unpublished manuscript, n.d.), 93–94, Indiana University Libraries Archives. Bain also briefly referenced Yale and the University of Chicago as institutions with more robust composition programs.

23. Bain, *The Bain Regime*, 327–28.

24. Kriplen, "The Opera Factory," 16–18, 20.

25. Bain, *School of Music Annual Report 1962–1963*, Indiana University President's Office Records, 1937–62 C213, Box 115, IU Libraries University Archives, Bloomington, Indiana; Indiana University Enrollment in the School of Music by Class Standing, Bloomington Campus, 1940 to 1967, Enrollment Statistics Reference Files, IU Libraries University Archives, Bloomington, Indiana.

26. Wells's relationship with Sweeney dates back to his tenure as president and continued when he moved to the newly created position of chancellor in 1962. Herman B Wells, Letter to Elsie Sweeney, April 27, 1966, Indiana University Chancellor Records of Herman B Wells, 1939–94, Administrative Record Series C145, Box 22, IU Libraries University Archives, Bloomington, Indiana.

27. Logan, *Indiana University School of Music*, 69; Wilfred Bain, *School of Music Annual Report 1963–1964*, Indiana University President's Office Records, 1937–62 C213, Box 115, IU Libraries University Archives, Bloomington, Indiana.

28. Bain, *School of Music Annual Report 1963–1964*.

29. Elvis J. Stahr, Letter to Governor Branigin, August 15, 1966, Indiana University President's Office Records, 1962–68 C304, Box 27, IU Libraries University Archives, Bloomington, Indiana.

30. Logan, *Indiana University School of Music*, 66, 78.

31. Wilfred Bain, *School of Music Annual Report 1961–1962*, Indiana University President's Office Records, 1937–62 C213, Box 115, IU Libraries University Archives, Bloomington, Indiana

32. Marianne Williams Tobias, *Opera for All Seasons* (Bloomington: Indiana University Press, 2010), 312; Wilfred Bain, *School of Music Annual Report, 1966–1967*, Indiana University President's Office Records, 1937–62 C213, Box 115, IU Libraries University Archives, Bloomington, Indiana.

33. Indiana University Enrollment in the School of Music by Class Standing, Bloomington Campus, 1940 to 1967, Enrollment Statistics Reference Files, IU Libraries University Archives, Bloomington, Indiana.

34. Logan, *Indiana University School of Music*, 219.

35. Bain, *School of Music Annual Report 1967–1968*, Indiana University President's Office Records, 1937–62 C213, Box 115, IU Libraries University Archives, Bloomington, Indiana; Tobias, *Opera for All Seasons*, Appendix I, 334–36.

36. It is worth noting the dedication of the MAC took place in spring of 1972. Thus, the financial arrangements of paying for the building were not resolved before performances had begun.

37. See W. G. Pinnell, Interdepartmental Memo to Donald H. Clark, January 6, 1972, Buildings-Bloomington Campus-MAC; W. George Pinnell, *Official Notice of Sale, $5,000,000, Indiana University Musical Arts Center First Mortgage Bonds*, Buildings-Bloomington Campus-MAC; Williams Adams Littell, Memo to General Butcher, January 31, 1969; Indiana University News Bureau, "Still Time to 'Endow-A-Chair'-in IUMAC Auditorium," December 7, 1971, IUB Buildings and Grounds, Musical Arts Center, Indiana University Archives Reference File, IU Libraries University Archives, Bloomington, Indiana; Indiana University News Bureau, "For Use in Football Program-Musical Arts Center," August 1970, all in IUB Buildings and Grounds, Musical Arts Center, Indiana University Archives Reference File, IU Libraries University Archives, Bloomington, Indiana.

38. Bain's responsibilities were more focused on managing the design and logistics for the building. In 1962, he and his wife, Mary, toured European opera houses for a month and met with architectural firms in New York. He also hired Mario Christini, a former stage manager at La Scala and the Met, to head the opera program and rehired Ted Jones, who had managed touring repertory theater in the United States and Germany. Not only did each man help with running the opera company, but he also had a say in the design of the new building. Logan, *Indiana University School of Music: A History*, 223–24.

39. Indiana University Foundation, *150th Birthday Fund*, Indiana University Chancellor Records of Herman B Wells, 1939–94, Administrative Record Series C145, Box 22, IU Libraries University Archives, Bloomington, Indiana.

40. Randall Tucker, Letter to Winfred C. Bain, February 2, 1962, Indiana University Chancellor Records of Herman B Wells, 1939–94, Administrative Record Series C145, Box 22, IU Libraries University Archives, Bloomington, Indiana.

41. Herman B Wells, Letter to Elsie Sweeney, February 7, 1966, Indiana University Chancellor Records of Herman B Wells, 1939–94, Administrative Record

Series C145, Box 22, IU Libraries University Archives, Bloomington, Indiana;
Elsie I. Sweeney, Letter to Herman B Wells, February 14, 1966, Indiana University
Chancellor Records of Herman B Wells, 1939–94, Administrative Record Series
C145, Box 22, IU Libraries University Archives, Bloomington, Indiana.

42. Elsie I. Sweeney, Letter to Herman B Wells, February 14, 1966, Indiana University Chancellor Records of Herman B Wells, 1939–94, Administrative Record Series C145, Box 22, IU Libraries University Archives, Bloomington, Indiana.

43. Herman B Wells, Handwritten Draft Letter to E. Don Tull, ca. February 1966, Indiana University Chancellor Records of Herman B Wells, 1939–94, Administrative Record Series C145, Box 22, IU Libraries University Archives, Bloomington, Indiana; E. Don Tull, Letter to Dr. Herman B Wells, February 14, 1966, Indiana University Chancellor Records of Herman B Wells, 1939–94, Administrative Record Series C145, Box 22, IU Libraries University Archives, Bloomington, Indiana.

44. The first payment installment of the $250,000 did not arrive at the university until 1971, five years after the Cummins pledge. Wells, Handwritten Draft Letter to E. Don Tull, ca. February 1966; Herman B Wells, Letter to E. Don Tull, ca. March 26, 1966, Indiana University Chancellor Records of Herman B Wells, 1939–94, Administrative Record Series C145, Box 22, IU Libraries University Archives, Bloomington, Indiana; E. D. Tull, Letter to Dr. Elvis Stahr, May 26, 1966, Indiana University President's Office Records, 1937–62 C304, Box 152, IU Libraries University Archives, Bloomington, Indiana; Bonnie [no last name provided], Memo to Dr. Wells, August 3, 1971, Indiana University Chancellor Records of Herman B Wells, 1939–94, Administrative Record Series C145, Box 22, IU Libraries University Archives, Bloomington, Indiana.

45. Herman B Wells, Letter to Elsie Sweeney, April 27, 1966, Indiana University Chancellor Records of Herman B Wells, 1939–94, Administrative Record Series C145, Box 22, IU Libraries University Archives, Bloomington, Indiana.

46. Elsie Sweeney, Letter to Herman B Wells, April 28, 1966, Indiana University Chancellor Records of Herman B Wells, 1939–94, Administrative Record Series C145, Box 22, IU Libraries University Archives, Bloomington, Indiana; Herman B Wells, Letter to Elsie Sweeney, December 26, 1967, Indiana University Chancellor Records of Herman B Wells, 1939–94, Administrative Record Series C145, Box 22, IU Libraries University Archives, Bloomington, Indiana.

47. H. B. Higgins, Letter to Herman B Wells, December 22, 1967, Indiana University Chancellor Records of Herman B Wells, 1939–94, Administrative Record Series C145, Box 22, IU Libraries University Archives, Bloomington, Indiana; R. E. Hickman, Letter to Herman B Wells, January 5, 1968, Indiana University Chancellor Records of Herman B Wells, 1939–94, Administrative Record Series C145, Box 22, IU Libraries University Archives, Bloomington, Indiana; Herman B Wells, Letter to Elsie Sweeney, January 6, 1968, Indiana University Chancellor

Records of Herman B Wells, 1939–94, Administrative Record Series C145, Box 22, IU Libraries University Archives, Bloomington, Indiana; Invoice Voucher, Indiana University Foundation, January 5, 1968, Indiana University Chancellor Records of Herman B Wells, 1939–94, Administrative Record Series C145, Box 22, IU Libraries University Archives, Bloomington, Indiana.

48. Herman B Wells, Telegram to Elsie Sweeney, December 18, 1967, Indiana University Chancellor Records of Herman B Wells, 1939–94, Administrative Record Series C145, Box 22, IU Libraries University Archives, Bloomington, Indiana.

49. Herman B Wells, Letter to Elsie Sweeney, October 25, 1967, Indiana University Chancellor Records of Herman B Wells, 1939–94, Administrative Record Series C145, Box 22, IU Libraries University Archives, Bloomington, Indiana; Herman B Wells, Letter to Elsie Sweeney, January 31, 1968, Indiana University Chancellor Records of Herman B Wells, 1939–94, Administrative Record Series C145, Box 22, IU Libraries University Archives, Bloomington, Indiana; Elsie Sweeney, Letter to Herman B Wells, June 11, 1968, Indiana University Chancellor Records of Herman B Wells, 1939–94, Administrative Record Series C145, Box 22, IU Libraries University Archives, Bloomington, Indiana.

50. Elsie Sweeney, Letter to Elvis J. Stahr, March 13, 1967, Indiana University President's Office Records, 1937–62 C304, Box 154, IU Libraries University Archives, Bloomington, Indiana.

51. "Elsie Sweeney Dies at 83," 8.

52. Dorothy Collins, notes for "HBW," December 23, 1969, Indiana University Chancellor Records of Herman B Wells, 1939–94, Administrative Record Series C145, Box 22, IU Libraries University Archives, Bloomington, Indiana.

53. Ross M. Robertson, Letter to Herman B Wells, December 10, 1969, Indiana University Chancellor Records of Herman B Wells, 1939–94, Administrative Record Series C145, Box 22, IU Libraries University Archives, Bloomington, Indiana.

54. Dorothy Collins, Letter to Miss Elsie Sweeney, January 12, 1970, Indiana University Chancellor Records of Herman B Wells, 1939–94, Administrative Record Series C145, Box 22, IU Libraries University Archives, Bloomington, Indiana.

55. Paul K. Klinge, Interdepartmental Communication to Ray Martin and Martin Knudson, May 26, 1970, Indiana University Chancellor Records of Herman B Wells, 1939–94, Administrative Record Series C145, Box 22, IU Libraries University Archives, Bloomington, Indiana.

56. Sweeney Speech Draft 3.

57. Dottie Collins, note for Herman B Wells, 1969, Indiana University Chancellor Records of Herman B Wells, 1939–94, Administrative Record Series C145, Box 22, IU Libraries University Archives, Bloomington, Indiana.

58. Elsie I. Sweeney, Letter to Mrs. Dorothy Collins, January 5, 1970, Indiana University Chancellor Records of Herman B Wells, 1939–94, Administrative Record Series C145, Box 22, IU Libraries University Archives, Bloomington, Indiana.

59. Dottie Collins (marked "DC"), note for "HBW," ca. December 27, 1969, Indiana University Chancellor Records of Herman B Wells, 1939–94, Administrative Record Series C145, Box 22, IU Libraries University Archives, Bloomington, Indiana; Indiana University Foundation, untitled press release draft, January 1970 [?], IUB Buildings and Grounds, Musical Arts Center, Indiana University Archives Reference Files.

60. Herman B Wells, Letter to Elsie Sweeney, December 26, 1967, Indiana University Chancellor Records of Herman B Wells, 1939–94, Administrative Record Series C145, Box 22, IU Libraries University Archives, Bloomington, Indiana

61. This enthusiasm for the new building was not limited to the university; even Governor Branigan called Sweeney to discuss how the new hall would benefit the state. J. Irwin Miller, Letter to Herman B Wells, July 11, 1967, Indiana University Chancellor Records of Herman B Wells, 1939–94, Administrative Record Series C145, Box 22, IU Libraries University Archives, Bloomington, Indiana.

62. Indeed, when the building was finally completed and dedicated in 1972, the fund still owed just over $1.5 million to the project. Donald H. Clark, Interdepartmental Communication to W. G. Pinnell, Indiana University Chancellor Records of Herman B Wells, 1939–1994, Administrative Record Series C145, Box 22, IU Libraries University Archives, Bloomington, Indiana.

63. Donald H. Clark, Interdepartmental Communication to W. G. Pinnell, January 6, 1972, Indiana University Chancellor Records of Herman B Wells, 1939–1994, Administrative Record Series C145, Box 22, IU Libraries University Archives, Bloomington, Indiana.

64. "A Firm Foundation," *Herald Telephone*, December 12, 1980; Dottie Collins, Note to Dr. Wells, July 28, 1975, Indiana University Chancellor Records of Herman B Wells, 1939–94, Administrative Record Series C145, Box 22, IU Libraries University Archives, Bloomington, Indiana; Indiana University Foundation, Pamphlet "The Elsie I. Sweeney Scholarship," ca. 1979, Elsie Sweeney Clippings, Indiana University Archives Reference Files, IU Libraries University Archives, Bloomington, Indiana: Letter, Clementine Tangeman to Herman B Wells, October 23, 1978, Box 22, Indiana University Chancellor's Records, 1939–94, Indiana University Chancellor Records of Herman B Wells, 1939–94, Administrative Record Series C145, Box 22, IU Libraries University Archives, Bloomington, Indiana; Clementine M. Tangeman, Cashier's Check to Indiana University Foundation, October 31, 1978, Indiana University Chancellor Records of Herman B Wells, 1939–94, Administrative Record Series C145, Box 22, IU Libraries University Archives, Bloomington, Indiana; J. T. Clapacs, Interdepartmental Communication to J. D. Mulholland, September 28, 1979, Elsie Sweeney Clippings, Indiana University Archives Reference Files, IU Libraries University Archives, Bloomington, Indiana.

65. "Elsie Sweeney Dies at 83," 8.

SIXTEEN

MAKING THE INVISIBLE VISIBLE

Women and Philanthropy at Indiana University

LAURIE BURNS McROBBIE

Laurie Burns McRobbie looks at IU's past and toward the future, reflecting on the broader theme of the volume—IU's effort to recover lost voices and the stories of underrepresented individuals in the university's history. Using the lens of philanthropy and highlighting the tradition of recognition in higher education (the practice of naming buildings, schools, scholarships, and endowed chairs in honor of individuals), McRobbie outlines the "quiet history" of women's contributions as donors and the significant new trends in women's giving to IU during the past four decades. McRobbie concludes with a description of two history-related projects involving women's philanthropy and recognition at IU. The first, the Bloomington Colloquium for Women, started in 1995 as an annual alumnae relations event that developed into a major women's philanthropy program at IU. The second, "Bridging the Visibility Gap," launched in 2016, highlighted women's contributions to IU as part of the IU Bicentennial observance and will continue in perpetuity, sustained by an endowed fund.

But to whatever source woman's recognition in the past may be attributed, in the future higher education will form the "open sesame" for our women to all honors, all distinctions, all happiness, all opportunities, that are in any way desirable in after-life.

—Tamar Althouse, first woman graduate of the IU Law School, 1892

INTRODUCTION

When Sarah Parke Morrison stepped into her first class at Indiana University in the fall of 1867, she set in motion a transformation that changed the entire institution. She broke through decades of resistance, not to the idea of women's education, but to the idea that young women could be educated together with young men. Women's education had been firmly established in Bloomington, Indiana, for decades. Shortly after Indiana Seminary was founded in 1820, the wives of IU's first faculty members initiated efforts to ensure that young women in Bloomington would have their own school, efforts that culminated in 1833 with the establishment of the Monroe County Female Seminary. For the next thirty years, scores of young women received an education there and, in the decade or so just before the Civil War, at a second female seminary run by the Methodist Church. Collectively, the seminaries provided an education that was considered to be equivalent to what young men received; some even considered it to be superior.[1] Legislative action by the state of Indiana in the early 1850s included instructions to the board of trustees to organize a "normal department" in which both men and women were to be admitted free of cost as long as they sought to qualify as teachers in Indiana's burgeoning public school system. But neither parents nor legislators were prepared for Hoosier sons and daughters to be in the classroom together, and financial pressures prevented the construction of separate facilities.[2] Even at that, fifteen years later IU was among the first public institutions in the country to admit women.

Sarah Parke Morrison's entry into the IU student body was followed in 1873 by her entrance into the professoriate as an instructor in English. She broke another barrier in 1883 when she became the university's first publicly acknowledged female donor.[3] She contributed $5 (over $100 today) to help re-stock the library destroyed in the devastating Seminary Square fire that nearly wiped out the small university and led to its reconstruction at its present-day location. And Sarah is notable in one other way—she has a building named for her. Morrison Hall was built in 1940 as part of Wells Quad, the university's first residence hall complex for women students, and was originally named Beech Hall. Wells Quad itself is named for Agnes Wells, IU's longest serving dean of women, and another building in the quad carries the name of one of her predecessors, Louise Goodbody.

Those who have worked and studied on the Bloomington campus of Indiana University over the years may be forgiven for not connecting any of these build-ings with women. Until recently, there had been little to mark the origins of the names, and the larger campus context would lead a visitor or new student to believe that there must have been a Mr. Morrison, or that Wells Quad honors legendary IU president Herman Wells. Fewer than a quarter of the buildings and structures across IU's seven campuses are named for or by women. At IU and elsewhere, long-held traditions in institutional recognition, formed as the modern university developed, still influence the way in which distinguished contributors to the character and spirit of an institution are memorialized. These traditions in turn permeate contemporary conceptions of who counts as an important figure in institutional history, define whose stories get told, and find expression in philanthropic practices.

The discussion that follows describes the quiet history of women's giving at Indiana University, a history that is now being recognized and has resulted in a more complete look at the contributions of women and others who have been unsung pioneers in their disciplines and careers, who have quietly transformed the lives of countless students, or who have achieved national and international recognition for their work but have not been as heralded at their home institution. Through archival research, personal interviews, and investigations beyond IU, thousands of women whose stories need to be told are being discovered so they can be honored and, alongside their fellow alumni, held up as exemplars of the Hoosier spirit. "Bridging the Visibility Gap," a project of the IU Bicentennial, has widened the institutional lens and changed its ideas about legacy as IU enters its third century.

PHILANTHROPY AND RECOGNITION IN AMERICAN HIGHER EDUCATION

Indiana University's practices for recognizing distinguished individuals throughout its history are not unusual. Several forces influenced the situation today where many of the contributions of women to the university, from their scholarship to their philanthropy, remain largely hidden from view. Major gifts and wealthy male alumni have long drawn the attention of institutional boards as well as the public. Scholarship on the history of educational philanthropy focuses primarily on large gifts from foundations and male donors, which is also an accurate reflection of how American colleges and universities evolved.[4] This large-scale philanthropy, rather than legislation or public pressure, benefitted women's colleges too; indeed, it is safe to argue that without the philanthropic efforts of many who saw the advantages of women's education for society as well as issues of equity and fairness, women's access to education equal to that for men would have been much longer in coming. Women themselves were involved and leading these developments from the earliest days. The first endowed scholarship in the history of US higher education, a gift of a hundred pounds to Harvard College, came from Anne Radcliffe, Lady Mowlson, in 1643.[5] Despite this, it took over two hundred years for her contribution to be memorialized in the naming of Radcliffe College in 1884.[6] Emma Willard, who founded the Troy Female Seminary in New York in 1820, and Mary Lyon, who founded Mt. Holyoke in western Massachusetts in 1837, were pioneers in women's education. Other philanthropists, socially conscious and interested in putting their money into progressive causes, found it easier to create new colleges than to persuade existing institutional boards to admit women or to adopt coeducation. One such philanthropist was the brewer Matthew Vassar. It was his niece who first brought the issue of women's education to his attention. In proposing his Vassar Female College in early 1861, Matthew Vassar declared "that woman, having received from her Creator the same intellectual constitution as man, has the same right as man to intellectual culture and development."[7] Smith and Wellesley Colleges were also entirely the products of philanthropy, in Smith's case by a reluctant heiress who nonetheless understood the importance of higher education for women.[8] Wealthy women such as Mary Garrett used their philanthropy to influence university boards, making gifts with conditions for the enrollment of women.[9] Female philanthropists like Elsie Clews Parsons went beyond the founding of institutions to building up the resources and programs that would attract and retain them, by supporting new disciplines that drew women students, some of whom continued into the professoriate.[10] Philanthropy, their own as well as that of their male relatives and allies, fueled women's access to academia as students and as scholars.

But large gifts, despite their impact and notoriety, do not tell the entire story. American higher education is also the product of hundreds of thousands of smaller gifts, like Sarah Parke Morrison's $5, that sustained institutions particularly during difficult financial times. John Gardner referred to "the Mississippi River of small gifts" that came from citizens at all levels of financial capacity in building educational institutions.[11] In his doctoral dissertation in 1922, Jesse Brundage Sears offered a similar observation when he wrote, "One is impressed at every point with the very large number of small gifts . . . (that apply) to the entire history of American college building."[12] Many of these came from women, and from local communities that saw the advantages of having a college or university driving population growth and economic development in the area (as the city of Bloomington did in 1857). But as important as these smaller gifts were to the development of American colleges and universities (as they continue to be today), they began to disappear from the historical record, particularly as the economy recovered from the Civil War. It was not only these small financial gifts that became invisible to the historian's eye, but also women's gifts of time that were excluded from the "male-centered 'high' history of educational philanthropy," creating a narrower definition of what it meant to be a philanthropist.[13] This "high history" continued into more recent times. Curti and Nash's 1965 history of educational philanthropy includes a reference to the Women's Building at Indiana University, but only as a major gift of John D. Rockefeller. They make no mention of the woman who spearheaded the building campaign and secured that contribution along with those of many others.[14]

There are other reasons behind why public recognition through the naming of buildings, scholarships, professorships, and other institutional mechanisms remain heavily skewed towards men. Beyond the fact that until the latter decades of the twentieth century, men made up the majority of the faculty, the student body, and the administration of academic institutions and were overwhelmingly the ones earning the wealth from which philanthropic gifts came, social norms and customs also reinforced conventions for naming, and shaped how women themselves sought recognition or anonymity. Margaret Olivia Sage is a case in point. The widow of the railroad financier Russell Sage, she came into a fortune, even by today's standards, when he died in 1906. He was far from being a philanthropist in his lifetime—contemporary accounts refer to him as "miserly"—but his wife was. When he died, her benevolence was released, and she showered money on a variety of causes and organizations, most of them involving women, such as suffrage and women's education. Her greatest legacy, however, is the foundation she established with the bulk of her husband's estate. Despite his lack of philanthropic spirit and despite being urged to call it the "Sage Foundation" as a means of recognizing her role in its very existence, she insisted on adding "Russell" to the name, determined that it be a memorial to him alone. With the exception of a teacher's college at Syracuse University, Mrs. Sage never permitted a building for which she provided the money to bear her name.[15]

It is perhaps easy to understand why a widow would use her inheritance to honor the man who generated it, whether out of love, loyalty, or a sense of duty. But it is also the case that women do not enjoy the same reputational benefits from having their names on display as do men. Even a century after Margaret Olivia Sage memorialized her husband, women are moved to make gifts for many other reasons ahead of the opportunity to name something. Current research also shows that many women, particularly older women, prefer to give anonymously, due to modesty or to concerns over being targeted for further large gifts if they are seen to be capable of one or two. This research also reflects the preference women of all generations show for spreading their largesse over multiple organizations and causes, rather than making fewer and larger gifts that would come with naming rights.[16] Women are also drawn to joining giving circles more than men are, which amplify their individual gifts but therefore also dilute their individual impact.[17] These trends are not static, however, and as women's education and incomes continue to rise, women are increasingly willing to step into the limelight, as well as to be highly strategic and risk-comfortable, in their giving.[18]

WOMEN'S GIVING EMERGES

In the last quarter of the nineteenth century, a veritable explosion of women's clubs and associations across the United States led many Progressive Era men to think of their historical moment as "the woman's century."[19] One could claim our current era as another "woman's century," given the emergence of women's philanthropy as a major force in American life and in the US. economy. Women have been earning college degrees at a greater rate than men for several decades (women comprised more than half the student body at IU in the 1977–78 academic year[20]), and today are the majority of the country's wealth holders by some accounts.[21] These societal trends spurred an increasing body of research on gender differences in giving, as foundations and nonprofits began to awaken to a new reality in the world of philanthropy. Research on gender differences in giving had been underway since the mid-1990s, most notably at the Women's Philanthropy Institute (WPI) founded at the University of Wisconsin. It operated as a free-standing institute until 2004, when the IU Center on Philanthropy, now the Lilly Family School of Philanthropy, gave the WPI a new academic home at Indiana University. The WPI ramped up its research and practitioner education programs through a series of publications and symposia. In 2010, the "Women Give" series was launched, an annual publication that explores different facets of how women of different ages, incomes, ethnicities, and socio-economic categories engage in philanthropy and volunteerism.[22]

Women's giving at Indiana University echoes the trends seen elsewhere. While it is difficult to gather a detailed statistical picture of women's philanthropy over time (for much of the early decades of the IU Foundation's existence, gifts from couples, even when the wife was the alumna, were recorded as *his* gift, a common practice in fundraising), the available historical data reflect small, consistent contributions over a long period rather than a number of multi-million-dollar gifts. In the early 1980s, this began to change. Women's philanthropy was starting to increase in all sectors, consistent with the entry of women into the workforce and the professions in historic numbers. By the 1990s, scores of million-dollar gifts to Indiana University from both single women—alumnae and non-alumnae—and alumnae married to non-IU alumni were being recorded. In 2005, the single largest gift ever received from an alumna, $40.6 million to name the School of Music, was made by Barbara Jacob in honor of her late husband, David. Her gift joined several other multi-million-dollar donations in the 2000s, including one from Indianapolis philanthropists Gene and Marilyn Glick, who openly stated that it was her passion and her gift, regardless of it being in both their names.

In 2014, philanthropist and IU alumna Cindy Simon-Skjodt gave $40 million to name IU's legendary basketball arena, Assembly Hall, belying the stereotype that only men are interested in athletics. Cindy was not the only one; in 2016, IU Athletics Director Fred Glass announced that 74 percent of the leadership gifts to the IU Athletics campaign, or $54.5 million, had come from women.[23] Cindy herself exemplifies women's attitudes towards naming. She explained that it was not her first choice to have her name on Assembly Hall, but that she did it to serve as an inspiration to others, particularly to young women. It is for precisely this reason that visibility matters—names have stories attached to them, and Cindy's is etched in stone, there for future generations to see and learn about.

WOMEN'S PHILANTHROPY AT IU TODAY

The IU Foundation had been working to increase its outreach to alumnae and women friends of IU since the 1990s, most notably with the launch of the Bloomington Colloquium for Women. Begun in 1995, the Colloquium quickly became the university's flagship program in alumnae relations. The Colloquium was developed as an educational and cultivation tool to respond to women who were looking for something deeper and more relevant to their interests in IU's outreach activities. The Colloquium draws 100 to 125 women to Bloomington for a weekend in the fall to hear a keynote speaker of international renown—the late Pakistan Prime Minister Benazir Bhutto in 2004, Nobel Peace Prize laureate Wengari Maathai in 2006, and in 2010, Academy Award winning actress Meryl Streep—along with presentations from IU faculty, students, and staff. The program and the speakers naturally are major draws, but the attendees also come to be with one another and nurture valued friendships. The Colloquium has engaged more than 400 individual women over the last twenty years, and attendees have been inspired to support programs that reflect their passions.

The greatest philanthropic success historically for the Colloquium is the scholarship fund for the Women's Little 500, the annual bicycle race in Bloomington immortalized in the movie *Breaking Away*. Since 2002, groups of donors, friends, and community leaders have joined together and raised over $138,000 for scholarships to support female student riders. The Bloomington Colloquium has also been the model for outreach efforts on IU's other campuses, particularly in Indianapolis, Ft. Wayne, Kokomo, and South Bend. These programs, and others that followed, built on the passion that women have for Indiana University by providing a stimulating array of intellectual content and plenty of opportunities for networking. In this the organizers were also reflecting a characteristic of women's philanthropy, that of wanting deep and meaningful connections to the organizations and causes they care about, and to engage directly in understanding the impact of their gifts of time, talent, and treasure as part of their philanthropic decisions. Engagement often comes first.[24]

The origins of the Colloquium reflect another aspect of women's giving and its evolution in the past two decades at IU. In 1995, its leaders were hesitant to explicitly attach the idea of "philanthropy" to the Colloquium's purpose. The inaugural Colloquium Steering Committee was direct: there would be no "cup at the door" nor an expectation of a monetary contribution to IU in exchange for a Colloquium invitation. The practical effect of this was to constrain discussion of more comprehensive philanthropic activities beyond the identification of potential spin-off programs and a series of fundraising efforts with relatively modest goals. However, the Colloquium's approach did not constrain individual gifts—one of which was for $1 million from alumna Dale Stark Leff to endow the Peg Brand Chair in Gender Studies—that were in many cases directly linked to involvement in the Colloquium. These gifts provided an answer at points when the value of the Colloquium was questioned, but in general terms it remained difficult to claim a clear, statistically based, bottom-line effect from the Colloquium's existence. The Colloquium continues to be a self-supporting and valuable cultivation experience for alumnae, but women's philanthropy at IU entered the twenty-first century with much of its potential unrealized.

In 2008, that began to change. The Colloquium had become a biennial program, and the Steering Committee was voicing increasingly strong support for something during the off year, as well as more opportunities in general to engage with new developments at IU. The existence of the WPI as part of IU made the next step obvious. A number of Colloquium Steering Committee members attended the WPI's 2008 Symposium, and lightbulbs went off. In addition to learning how powerful women's giving was at that point and was projected to be, the attendees heard from philanthropists, researchers, and nonprofit leaders in all sectors about how they were giving, and why. It validated their own experiences and lent their subsequent efforts the force of data.

In 2010, the WPI's research led to the founding of the Women's Philanthropy program at the IU Foundation, a signal initiative embedded in the university's advancement enterprise aimed at engaging alumnae and women donors in more scalable and meaningful ways. A forty-five-member Women's Philanthropy Leadership Council (WPLC) was formed to provide strategic direction to the program, which conducts grant-making across the university and holds numerous educational programs across the country to engage women more deeply with their alma mater. Thousands of women, as well as men who share the program's goals, have connected with IU, many making gifts for the first time through these engagements. In addition to its advisory role, the WPLC functions as a giving circle, with half of each member's dues going into a fund under the Council's control. Since 2012, the first year that funds were allocated, the WPLC has granted over $1.35 million to 136 projects and initiatives, many of which have gone on to become permanent programs with sustainable funding from other sources. Collectively, since 2010 the 105 individuals who have been or are active members of the WPLC have given just under $228 million in new gifts to IU, of which nearly $6 million is directly attributable to the existence of the Council and the Women's Philanthropy program.

The university's bicentennial in 2020 offered an unparalleled opportunity to further amplify women's contributions to the excellence of IU. A variety of efforts to recognize distinguished women and minority individuals were already active and received additional attention as bicentennial planning got underway. A major step was taken in 2014 with the introduction of the Women's Portrait Gallery in the East Lounge of the IMU in Bloomington. IU's extensive art collection contains multiple portraits of women and by women artists, from First Lady Charlotte Lowe Bryan to Frances Marshall to Elinor Ostrom. The relocation of the portraits of IU's presidents from the IMU to the newly renovated Franklin Hall created the opening for a permanent women's portrait exhibit with rotating items, highlighting the women who have contributed to IU's excellence. Since the exhibit opened, several new portraits have been commissioned and dedicated, including the first appointed female Trustee of IU, Harriet Inskeep (BA '48, MA '55, LHD '96), federal district court judge Sarah Evans Barker (BS '65, LLD '99), and retired IU General Counsel Dottie Frapwell (JD '73). As chronicled in chapter 3, the unveiling of the portrait of Carrie Parker Taylor in 2016 was a signature demonstration of the power of such images. Portraits tell stories, providing windows into the history of the institution as well as of the women themselves. The unveilings have become community events as much as they are events for the families of the women depicted, as Mrs. Taylor's was.

BRIDGING THE VISIBILITY GAP

A cornerstone of plans for the Bicentennial was a $3.5 billion-dollar fundraising campaign, the largest in school history and one of the largest for a public university in the United States. With the advent of the campaign, the WPLC saw an opportunity to accelerate its mission by creating its own campaign with three goals: to double its grant-making, to dramatically increase the number the alumnae reconnecting to the university and helping to support their areas of interest, and to create permanently funded mechanisms to recognize women and minority individuals who have contributed to the spirit and character of Indiana University. "Bridging the Visibility Gap," a project to highlight these unsung pioneers, was launched in September of 2016 with the naming of the Frances Morgan Swain Student Building. The rationale for this naming is well documented in chapter 1, and the renaming itself drew alumnae and current women students alike to celebrate Mrs. Swain's achievement and to imagine a campus enriched by the visible imprint of many others.

The Visibility project was supported by the Office of the Bicentennial in the form of a sequence of student interns equipped to conduct, synthesize, and present archival research. The first of these interns produced a database of 1,700 names, gleaned from records of achievements, letters, testimonials, and other artifacts that signaled the impact of individual women. Out of this trove, a committee led by Provost Lauren Robel selected an initial cohort of six women who were under-recognized in visible and material ways relative to their achievements. All six were associated with the Bloomington campus, which is not surprising given Bloomington's status as IU's oldest campus and therefore one with the biggest deficit in recognizing women. As work continued to deepen the information on these women and to prepare proposals for the next set, unit and IU Foundation development staff worked to identify appropriate recognition mechanisms. These include named professorships, named scholarships, and/or portraits, along with markers or plaques. The first six to be recognized are the following:

- Tamar Althouse, author of the quote that opens this chapter and the first female graduate of the Maurer School of Law in

1892. After graduation, she was the first woman to practice law in Vanderburgh County. She went on to work for the Indiana Speaker of the House and to found a network of women's rotary clubs across the state in the decades before women could even vote. While her history is known to many Law School students and faculty, nothing in the school bears her name. Fundraising is planned for a named scholarship to honor her.

- Alice McDonald Nelson, Director of Residence Life from 1920 to 1965, who is credited with creating the university's residence hall program and resident scholarships for students who, as she put it, were "long on brains but short on cash," which became a model for other universities in the Big Ten and beyond. Ironically, Alice Nelson has a building named for her, but it has been known primarily by its street address—801 North Jordan—and for a time, the sign outside her building de-emphasized her name. The sign has been redesigned with her name prominently shown, and there are plans to raise funds for a scholarship in her name.

- Ingeborg Schmidt, a German immigrant after World War II who was on the faculty of IU's School of Optometry from 1954–1970 and who discovered the "Schmidt sign," a genetic marker for color-blindness that earned her international renown as "the first lady of vision science." Aside from a few photographs of graduating classes, there is nothing in today's School of Optometry to recognize her, and the only photo in IU's possession came from the Smithsonian's collection of photographs of women scientists. Plans for a commissioned portrait are underway.

- Martha Dawson, the multicultural education pioneer and first African American woman to become a tenured full professor at IU. Martha is well known to her School of Education colleagues, but her impact went far beyond her own discipline. A portrait has been completed and as of this writing is awaiting installation in accordance with her family's wishes. Dawson's career is explored in chapter 12.

- Camilla Williams, a voice professor at the Jacobs School of Music from 1971 to 1997. She broke the color barrier on several opera stages and sang the national anthem on the steps of the Lincoln Memorial moments before Martin Luther King Jr.

stepped to the podium to deliver his "I Have a Dream" speech in 1963. Fundraising is underway for a professorship in voice named for her, which is expected to help increase faculty diversity in the Jacobs School of Music as well. A full-length portrait of her now hangs in the IMU, commissioned by the Visibility Gap project.

- Elinor Ostrom, the first woman to win the Nobel Prize in Economics. Lin's work is captured in Sara Clark's essay, "Elinor Ostrom: On Interdisciplinary Living, 1933–2012" (chapter 13). Lin and her husband and collaborator Vincent are memorialized in the name of the Ostrom Workshop in Political Theory and Policy Analysis, which is how Lin wanted it, despite the fact that it was she alone who earned the Nobel. Several years after her death, her colleagues and friends chose to respectfully give Lin the recognition she deserves in her own right by commissioning a statue. In November of 2020, the statue was installed in an outdoor area named the Ostrom Commons, outside of Woodburn Hall, home of the Political Science department. At its installation, it became the first statue of a woman on the Bloomington campus in IU's two-hundred-year history.

The database of prominent women contains hundreds more stories like this, women who invented, discovered, created, influenced, led, and advocated within and beyond their fields of endeavor. As work goes forward to find ways of recognizing them, current students and alumnae alike are finding inspiration in their achievements and in understanding more about how they accomplished what they did in their own time. The renaming of the Frances Morgan Swain Student Building alone sent a powerful message about the importance of women's contributions to the identity of Indiana University. This message resonated deeply with the Women's Philanthropy Leadership Council when it voted to establish the Visibility Endowment Fund, a project corresponding to the third goal of its bicentennial campaign. The Fund was launched in early 2018 with a goal of $500,000 and got a jumpstart with a $250,000 gift from alumna Julie Christopher (BA '94). In June of 2019, it reached its goal, and has contributed to several projects since then, including the portrait of Camilla Williams and a historical marker adjacent to the statue of Eleanor Ostrom. The Fund will continue to grow through investment income as well as continued contributions, providing a steady stream of support for portraits, plaques, plantings, and other small-scale recognition mechanisms in perpetuity.

EXPANDING OUR VISION

Collegiate institutions are many things—places of discovery and learning, of exploration and innovation, of the preservation and cultivation of knowledge, and of economic acceleration and training for the future work force. But first and foremost, they are collections of people, and the spirit and character of a university is reflected in the individuals who have studied, researched, worked, led, and reconnected with it over time. As IU Chancellor Emeritus Ken Gros Louis said in his Remembrance Day remarks in 2011, "the campus lives through the lives of those who contributed so much to it."[25] When we don't see the full picture of those contributions, we don't see the full history of the institution.

In a seminal speech to the Organization of American Historians in 1984, historian Anne Firor Scott laid out a fundamental question about the fact that historians and non-historians alike do not see all that is there to examine about the past, and thus do not see the present accurately either. She argues that visibility is a cultural artifact, born of a kind of selective blindness that relegates certain groups and individuals to the margins in the collective memory. She asks, "What must happen to bring some hitherto unseen part of past reality into visibility?"[26]

By expanding our vision and intentionally bringing names, faces, and stories into what we experience around us every day, we make the invisible visible. As we memorialize the contributions of unseen exemplars of IU's character and spirit, we indelibly weave their legacies into the traditions and heritage of the university, thus ensuring a richer and more complete story of Indiana University for generations to come.

NOTES

The epigraph is from Tamar Althouse, "A Question," *Indiana Student*, November 1, 1892.

1. "Girls Weren't Allowed at IU, So Female College Was Started," *Daily Herald Telephone*, September 4, 1968.

2. Thomas D. Clark, *Indiana University: Midwestern Pioneer*, vol. I (Bloomington: Indiana University Press, 1970), 83–84.

3. Minutes of the IU Board of Trustees meeting on July 24, 1883, Indiana University Archives and Indiana University Libraries Digital Collection Service (https://purl.dlib.indiana.edu/iudl/archives/iubot/1883-07-24). It is possible that one or more women had made gifts to the university before 1883, particularly when the citizens of Bloomington collectively raised money to help defray debts associ-

ated with rebuilding after an earlier fire at Seminary Square, but there are no extant records of who those individuals were (see Minutes of the IU Board of Trustees, June 2, 1857, https://purl.dlib.indiana.edu/iudl/archives/iubot/1857-06-02).

4. Merle Curti and Roderick Nash, *Philanthropy in the Shaping of American Higher Education* (New Brunswick, NJ: Rutgers University Press, 1965); John R. Thelin, *A History of American Higher Education* (Baltimore: Johns Hopkins University Press, 2004).

5. See Radcliffe College Library Collection relating to Ann Radcliffe, 1984-1977, Harvard Library, Harvard University (https://hollisarchives.lib.harvard.edu/repositories/8/resources/5595) and "Lady Mowlson Bequeaths the First Undergraduate Scholarship," History of Financial Aid website, Harvard College, accessed July 27, 2020 (https://financialaid.hcf.harvard.edu/lady-mowlson).

6. As notable as this is, Radcliffe was created to allow Harvard College to remain male only, which it did for more than another one hundred years. In 1999, Radcliffe was fully absorbed into Harvard College. Today, the Radcliffe Institute for Advanced Studies is the remaining acknowledgment of Anne Radcliffe Mowlson's generosity.

7. Curti and Nash, *Philanthropy in the Shaping of American Higher Education*, 92.

8. Barbara Miller Solomon, *In the Company of Educated Women: A History of Women and Higher Education in America* (New Haven: Yale University Press, 1985).

9. Curti and Nash, *Philanthropy in the Shaping of American Higher Education*, 104; Kathleen Waters Sander, *Mary Elizabeth Garrett: Society and Philanthropy in the Gilded Age* (Baltimore: Johns Hopkins University Press, 2008).

10. Andrea Walton, "Rethinking Boundaries: The History of Women, Philanthropy, and Higher Education," *History of Higher Education Annual* vol. 20 (2000), 29–57; Andrea Walton, ed., *Women and Philanthropy in Education* (Bloomington: Indiana University Press, 2005), especially "Introduction: Women and Philanthropy in Education—A Problem of Conceptions," 1–36; Mary Ann Dzuback, "Creative Financing in Social Science: Women Scholars and Early Research," in Walton, ed., *Women and Philanthropy*, 105–26.

11. Gardner as cited in Walton, *Women and Philanthropy in Education*, 4.

12. Jesse Brundage Sears, *Philanthropy in the History of American Higher Education*, with a new introduction by Roger L. Geiger (New Brunswick, NJ: Transaction Publishing, 1990), 105.

13. Walton, *Women and Philanthropy in Education*, 3.

14. Curti and Nash, *Philanthropy in the Shaping of American Higher Education*.

15. Ruth Crocker, *Mrs. Russell Sage: Women's Activism and Philanthropy in Gilded Age and Progressive Era America* (Bloomington: Indiana University Press, 2006).

16. Debra J. Mesch, "Women Give 2010: New Research About Women and Giving." Indianapolis, IN, Women's Philanthropy Institute, Indiana University Lilly Family School of Philanthropy (2010), report available at https://philanthropy .iupui.edu/files/file/women_give_2010_report.pdf (accessed October 12, 2020).

17. Julia L. Carboni and Angela Eikenberry, "Giving Circle Membership: How Collective Giving Impacts Donors," Collective Giving Research Group, Indianapolis: Women's Philanthropy Institute, Indiana University Lilly Family School of Philanthropy (2018), report available at https://scholarworks.iupui.edu/bitstream /handle/1805/17743/giving-circle-membership18.pdf (accessed October 12, 2020).

18. Debra J. Mesch, et al., "Giving by and for Women: Understanding High-Net-Worth Donors' Support for Women and Girls." Indianapolis: Women's Philanthropy Institute, Indiana University Lilly Family School of Philanthropy (2018), report available at https://scholarworks.iupui.edu/bitstream/handle/1805/15117 /giving-by-and-for-women-update180131.pdf (accessed October 12, 2020).

19. Anne Firor Scott, *Natural Allies: Women's Associations in American History* (Urbana: University of Illinois Press 1992), 3.

20. *IU Fact Book*, 1977–78. The total IU student population was 78,009.

21. The Quantum Group, "Financial Facts for Women's History Month", March 13, 2017, https://thequantum.com/financial-facts-for-womens-history-month/.

22. See Women's Philanthropy Institute, https://philanthropy.iupui.edu /institutes/womens-philanthropy-institute/index.html. The WPI, currently through a grant from the Bill and Melinda Gates Foundation, produces multiple studies a year on different facets of gender differences in giving in addition to the Women Give series.

23. IU Hoosiers.com, "IU Women's Philanthropy Makes Major Impact in Success of IU Athletics Capital Campaign," October 12, 2016, https://iuhoosiers.com /story.aspx?filename=general-iu-womens-philanthropy-makes-major-impact-in -success-of-iu-athletics-capital-campaign&file_date=10/12/2016.

24. This conclusion is based on experience in the women's philanthropy program over the past decade, and is supported by research findings that examine gender differences in prosocial motivation, measures of empathy and altruism, sensitivity to social norms, and rates of volunteering which are significantly higher for women than men in the US (see "How and Why Women Give: Current and Future Directions for Research on Women's Philanthropy," Women's Philanthropy Institute, IU Lilly Family School of Philanthropy, 2015).

25. Kenneth R. R. Gros Louis, Remembrance Day remarks, delivered March 27, 2011, Kenneth R. R. Gros Louis speeches, Collection C220, IU Libraries University Archives, Bloomington.

26. Anne Firor Scott, "On Seeing and Not Seeing: A Case of Historical Invisibility," *Journal of American History*, 51, no. 1 (June 1984): 8.

CONTRIBUTORS

KATHERINE BADERTSCHER is Director of Graduate Programs at the IU Lilly Family School of Philanthropy. She teaches BA, MA, and doctoral classes on the ethics and history of philanthropy and has published articles in the *Indiana Magazine of History*.

NANCY VAN NOTE CHISM is Professor Emerita of Higher Education and Student Affairs at Indiana University. She served as Associate Vice Chancellor for Academic Affairs at IUPUI. Her publications focus on professional and organizational development in higher education.

SARA CLARK is a 2019 graduate of the Indiana University School of Education History, Philosophy, and Policy doctoral program with a History of Education specialization.

CATHERINE A. DOBRIS is Associate Professor in the Department of Communication Studies at Indiana University–Purdue University Indianapolis. She is Director of the Women's, Gender, and Sexuality Studies program (formerly the Women's Studies program).

MARY GIORGIO has a Master of Arts in Public History from IUPUI. She worked with the IUPUI Office for Women on the history of women on campus for about ten years.

KATHLEEN SURINA GROVE has directed the Office for Women at Indiana University–Purdue University Indianapolis since 2004. Her career includes work in the fields of law, business, mental health counseling, and higher education. She has published on the topics of women and leadership and multicultural teaching.

JACOB HARDESTY is Dean of the College of Social Science, Commerce, and Education as well as Associate Professor of Education at Rockford University, where he teaches courses in the foundations of education. He is a 2013 graduate of the Indiana University School of Education's History, Philosophy, and Policy doctoral program with a specialization in History of Education.

EBELIA HERNÁNDEZ is Associate Professor in the Graduate School of Education at Rutgers University. Her research centers on the Latina/o/x college student experience and critical qualitative methodologies. She is particularly interested in how student engagement may influence holistic development. This work has led to publications and presentations at national conferences in the areas of Latina/o/x college student activism, the history of Latinxs in higher education, spirituality, self-authorship, and engagement.

DINA M. KELLAMS is Director of the IU Libraries University Archives. A native Hoosier, she holds BA degrees in English and History and a Master of Library Science, all from Indiana University Bloomington. Recent writing projects include contributions to *200: The Bicentennial Magazine* and to Indiana University Press's inaugural Bicentennial book, *Indiana University Bloomington: America's Legacy Campus*.

LAURIE BURNS McROBBIE is eighteenth First Lady of Indiana University. She founded the Women's Philanthropy Leadership Council and the Women's Philanthropy program at the IU Foundation. She earned a BA in History (1978) from the University of Michigan and an MA in Philanthropic Studies (2016) from Indiana University. She holds adjunct faculty positions in the IU Lilly Family School of Philanthropy and the IU Luddy School of Informatics, Computing and Engineering.

ANGEL CASSANDRA NATHAN obtained a PhD in Higher Education and Student Affairs with minors in Nonprofit Management and Inquiry Methodology and a certificate in Institutional Research. Currently, Nathan serves as a Project Manager for the IUPUI School of Education's Cultural Competency:

Leading Radical Change Program, a partnership with the Lumina Foundation to deliver technical assistance to local education agencies within Indiana through on-site and web-based professional learning experiences.

STEPHANIE THANH XUAN NGUYEN is a PhD student in the Higher Education program at Indiana University Bloomington. She earned a BS in Business (2009) from the University of Notre Dame and a MS Ed in Higher Education and Student Affairs (2014) from Indiana University Bloomington. Her upcoming dissertation focuses on the history of Asian American Studies at research universities in the Midwest.

ANGELA BOWEN POTTER is a doctoral candidate in History at Purdue University focusing on the history of mental illness and public health. She is also a graduate student in Medical Humanities and Health Studies at IUPUI with a focus on the history of medicine and medical education.

SARAH J. REYNOLDS is Assistant Professor of Physics and Earth-Space Science at the University of Indianapolis and a PhD candidate in History and Philosophy of Science at Indiana University. Her research focuses on the history and philosophy of science education.

MERYLOU RODRIGUEZ is a PhD candidate in the Higher Education program at Rutgers Graduate School of Education, New Brunswick. Her research focuses on the recovery, re-centering, and reclaiming of Puerto Ricans' histories and stories in the United States. In addition to pursuing her doctorate, she is also an administrator.

KELLY C. SARTORIUS is a higher education consultant in the areas of advancement and external relations. A higher education historian, she recently received a Smith College Special Collections Research Fellowship, and her dissertation won NASPA's Ruth Strang Research Award. In 2014 she published *Deans of Women and the Feminist Movement: Emily Taylor's Activism*. She has directed advancement and taught at both the University of Kansas Honors Program and the University of Arkansas. She was an alumni relations and development director at both Washington University in St. Louis and Kansas State University.

TANNER N. TERRELL is a PhD candidate in the Higher Education program at Indiana University with a minor in the History of Education. Born and raised a

Hoosier, he holds both baccalaureate and master's degrees from Indiana University. His other research interests relate to race and (dis)ability in higher education.

RACHEL JEAN TURNER is Adjunct Instructor at IUPUI. Rachel completed her MA thesis titled *The Rhetoric of Rape-Revenge Films: Analyzing Violent Female Portrayals in Media from a Narrative Perspective of Standpoint Feminism*.

ANDREA WALTON is a historian of education. She is Associate Professor in the Department of Educational Leadership and Policy Studies, Indiana University. Her research focuses on the history of women in education, higher education, philanthropy, and educational policy.

LORÉE B. WILCOX completed her undergraduate work in American Studies at University of Maryland, College Park. She is currently a master's student in the Department of Communication Studies at IUPUI, studying intercultural organizational communication.

INDEX

Page locators in italics refer to figures and tables

www.ingramcontent.com/pod-product-compliance
Lightning Source LLC
Chambersburg PA
CBHW030913050726
47498CB00003BA/715